JUPITER 6

JUPITER 6

John E Gross

iUniverse, Inc.

New York Lincoln Shanghai

Jupiter 6

iUniverse books may be ordered through booksellers or by contacting:

iUniverse
2021 Pine Lake Road, Suite 100
Lincoln, NE 68512
www.iuniverse.com
1-800-Authors (1-800-288-4677)

ISBN-13: 978-0-595-35132-9 (pbk)
ISBN-13: 978-0-595-79834-6 (ebk)
ISBN-10: 0-595-35132-8 (pbk)
ISBN-10: 0-595-79834-9 (ebk)

Printed in the United States of America

For Katie,

My inspiration and encouragement.

ACKNOWLEDGEMENTS

The history of the U.S. Army Ranger began during the French and Indian War and continued through the Revolution, the Civil War, and on through World War II and Korea. Ranger units were disbanded at the end of the Korean War and did not exist again until the early 1970s, near the end of the Vietnam War. During the intervening years, the mission of the Ranger Department of the U.S. Army Infantry School was to train individual Rangers as expert small-unit leaders who had the task of returning to their divisions to raise the level of training and tactical expertise. Little has been written about the Rangers during those years. I wish to acknowledge the contributions of thousands of individual Rangers during the difficult and challenging era of the '50s and '60s. They made our army better and no doubt saved the lives of countless numbers of soldiers by making them more proficient in tactics, fieldcraft and leadership.

Although I served in the 82nd Airborne Division and in the 9th Division in Vietnam as did the protagonist in this book, one should not assume I am Captain Jason Spencer. He was a better soldier and commander than was I. Some of the things that happened to him, happened to me. I did fight the battle on Hill 108 and my company counter-attacked the Viet Cong as they tried to take over the city of Bien Hoa during Tet, 1968. Other events in the book also came from my experiences.

Many of the fictional episodes in the book were inspired by true stories told to me by my friends. When I returned from Vietnam, I was assigned as an instructor in the swamp phase of Ranger school at Eglin Air Force Base in Florida. All of the instructors, whether officer or NCO, were recent returnees from Vietnam. All of us had had the same experience upon coming home. We had been ripped from the jungles, put on a plane, and deposited back in a country far removed in distance and understanding from Vietnam. Many of us were still suffering the effects of close combat when we returned to our loved ones, who had no concept of what was going on in our minds.

In Florida, we had the mission of teaching young leaders how to survive and how to keep their soldiers alive in Vietnam. That mission became a salve to our souls as we shared our experiences with young soldiers during endless patrols. Our classrooms were the coastal pine forests and marshes of the Florida panhandle. Teaching Ranger students became a sort of swamp therapy, as we talked the war out of our systems. Also, over C-ration meals under the trees, or as we waited for parachute jumps, or during breaks in instruction, we opened our hearts and nightmares to our buddies and were able to "come down" slowly. We leaned on each other as we returned to normalcy.

Most of us never realized the extent to which our assignment at the Florida Ranger Camp helped us. But because of the uniqueness of time and circumstance, we became closer than most veterans groups. In my 22 years in the Army, I served with many fine soldiers, most of whom I have lost contact with. But I know where my Ranger buddies are, and we stay in touch on a regular basis. After nearly 40 years, we're still close. I am telling this for a purpose, and that is to acknowledge the contributions of these Rangers to this book. Many of their stories, told to me under the pines, became the experiences of Jace Spencer. For example, I never killed with a knife, but one of my fellow instructors did. I never saw anyone blinded by a booby trap, but Captain Mike Burton, one of my closest friends, lost his eyes when he tripped a mortar shell tied to a tree during his second Vietnam tour.

I want to acknowledge the service, the friendship, and the unknowing contributions to this book by Lieutenant Colonel Jim Tucker, the finest commander any soldier could ever have, and Clark Welch, Frank Duncan, Mike Burton, Jim Cantrell, Tom Cruise, Jessie L. Stevens, Jr., Harold Bradshaw, Bill Nuckols, Hank Kilgrove—and many others too.

I want to thank John Steele, professor and life-long friend, who introduced me to a friend of his named Lewis Green. Lewis had just published a novel entitled *Spirit Bells* about the Korean War, and was scheduled to be interviewed on WETS, the local public radio station in Johnson City, Tennessee. John called me to ask if I would participate in the program. He said that since I was the only person he knew who knew the names of the four Japanese aircraft carriers sunk at Midway, I surely knew enough about military history to discuss the Korean War on the radio with Lewis.

I found Lewis Green to be one of the most interesting people I ever met. He fought with the Army in Korea, and later served a hitch with the Marines. He is a novelist, poet, newspaperman, teacher, lecturer, publisher, part-time lawman and a sharp knife to those on the receiving end of his investigative reporting in Western North Carolina.

When we met to discuss his book, I told Lewis that I had written some poems about Vietnam. Not only did he publish them, he told me that hidden between the poems was a novel, and that I needed to get started on it. Without his encouragement and inspiration, I would never have written this book. Not only did he push me to write it, he edited it and even loaned me the K-Bar knife I photographed for the cover. Lewis is a friend, mentor, and trans-generational, combat-veteran soul brother.

The characters in the book are fictional, but some were inspired by real soldiers. During my tour in Vietnam, I had the honor of serving under two great battalion commanders, Lieutenant Colonels Arthur Moreland and John Tower. Both of these officers merged to be the inspiration for Lieutenant Colonel McKenzie. Lieutenant Colonel Price is a composite of many self-centered asses I crossed paths with later in my career. The models for First Sergeant Hector Baez were First Sergeant Richard Robles, my top-kick in Vietnam, and my friend and Florida Ranger buddy Command Sergeant Major Henry Caro, one of the finest NCOs who ever lived. Henry was killed in a parachute jump in the 1970s.

When I starting writing this book, I was afraid that there might be little interest left among the reading public about the Vietnam War. I have since come to realize that Vietnam was such a trauma in America's consciousness that generations will probably come and go before the events in the late '60s and early '70s are forgotten. Vietnam still haunts us. Almost every foreign policy decision our leaders make today must still pass through the filter of our Vietnam experience. During every use of American military power in the '70s, 80's, and 90s, and indeed, during the current war in Iraq, comparisons have been made to Vietnam. The "quagmire" word was even used while we defeated Iraq's army in 100 hours during Desert Storm.

We who served honorably in Vietnam still deserve to have our stories told. Most of us feel that ours was a noble cause, even if it went awry.

5-39 Battalion Organization

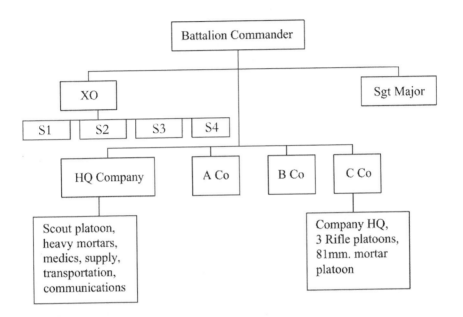

The battalion staff consists of the: S-1: Personnel Officer
S-2: Intelligence Officer
S-3: Operations Officer
S-4: Supply Officer

Each Rifle company has a company headquarters consisting of communications personnel, drivers, cooks, medics, and clerks.

Each rifle company has a weapons or mortar platoon consisting of three 81mm mortars plus a fire direction center.

Each rifle platoon consists of three squads of eleven men each, plus a weapons squad with machine guns and anti-tank weapons.

CALL SIGNS

Battalion commander:	Cougar 6
Executive officer (XO)	Cougar 5

S-1 (Personnel Officer)	Cougar 1
S-2 (Intelligence Officer)	Cougar 2
S-3 (Operations Officer)	Cougar 3
S-4 (Logistics Officer)	Cougar 4
S-5 (Civil Affairs Officer)	Cougar 5

Company commanders:

HQ company commander	Cougar Hotel 6
A company commander:	Cougar Alpha 6
B company commander:	Cougar Bravo 6
C company commander:	Cougar Charlie 6
C company executive officer:	Cougar Charlie 5
C company first sergeant:	Cougar Charlie 7

Platoon leaders: (Listed are Charlie company platoon leaders, A and B company platoons would be Alpha or Bravo 16, 26, etc)

1st Platoon leader:	Cougar Charlie 16
2nd Platoon leader:	Cougar Charlie 26
3rd Platoon leader:	Cougar Charlie 36
Weapons platoon leader	Cougar Charlie 46

Battalion scout (recon) platoon (part of Headquarters company): Cougar Romeo 6
Battalion heavy mortar platoon (part of Headquarters company): Cougar Mike 6

Suffixes:
Alpha: Radio telephone operator, headquarters, or base station (Cougar Charlie 6 Alpha is Charlie company commander's radio telephone operator)
India: Assistant (Cougar Charlie 5 India is the assistant Charlie company executive officer)

For most routine radio transmissions, Cougar was omitted, and only the company and platoon designations were used (a sample transmission would be: Charlie 16, this is Charlie 6, Over.)

PROLOGUE

▼

31 January, present year

"Honey, are you sure you don't want me to go with you?" she asked.

"No, but thank you, Babe. This is something I need to do alone. I've been needing to come here for a long time."

"But you look so—I don't know—sad? Melancholy? I just worry about you."

"Thanks, Sweetie, but I'm fine. Look, just drop me off and make a couple of circles, I'll be right back here in about 20 minutes."

"OK, if you say so," she said as she pulled to the curb along Constitution Avenue. Her husband smiled at her and quickly got out. As his wife drove off, he stood for a moment then started off at a quick pace along the walkway that descended toward the black polished wall of the Vietnam Veterans Memorial.

He was surprised by the number of people paying their respects on this cold late-autumn day. There were men in business suits, veterans in camouflage, grandparents, women with children, and others like him—lone, nondescript visitors with personal, private agendas.

He had been warned about the effect the monument was likely to have on him. As prepared as he thought he was, his emotions surprised him. His breath caught in his throat as he was first made out the names on the wall. He moved slowly along the walkway, scanning the panels and wondering how the men who belonged to the names had been killed. He wondered how many of them had died by accident. He wondered which names belonged to truck drivers killed by mines along lonely roads, to helicopter pilots mangled in twisted wreckage, or tank crewmen burned beyond recognition. He selected a name and reached out to touch it. Was this one a clerk killed at his desk by a random mortar round? Was he a medic who was shot down while trying to save a buddy? Or did this name belong to one of them? One of the ones in tattered, sweat-ringed fatigues and holed jungle boots. One of the ones with insect repellent, cigarettes, or weapon-cleaning brushes stuck behind the camouflage bands of their helmets. One of the ones with strips of cloth or army-green towels draped around their necks to sponge away the ever-present sweat. One of the ones who, no matter how they lightened them, found that their rucksacks still weighed fifty pounds. One of the ones with leech sores, mosquito welts, jungle rot, immersion foot or scores of other minor ailments. One of the ones who had no talents in demand in the headquarters, offices, motor pools, or communications shops. One of the ones who were too unskilled and uneducated to do anything but walk—and kill. He wondered if this name belong to an Infantryman?

From his jacket pocket, he removed a folded sheet of notebook paper. Finding a national park ranger, he offered his list and asked how he could find the names. The ranger showed him how to locate the panels on which his names were inscribed. It took a while, but eventually, he scribbled the location of each.

He was totally unprepared for the sob that shook him when he found his first name. Through a blur of tears, he reached up to touch the letters. As he did so, the image of a face almost came back. Events, places, conversations, postures and mannerisms all returned, but the face would not quite solidify in his memory.

Avoiding a group of camouflaged veterans, he moved on to the next name on his list. Lingering there, he regained control of his emotions, then went on to the next. Suddenly, like a black-and white photo, faded and yellowed in an old album, a face materialized. He shut his eyes and tried to focus it. The features were fuzzy, but the gaunt shape, the cocky grin, and the tilt of the head slowly took form in his memory. With his fingers touching the letters, he stood immobile for a long moment, reaching back through the years.

After he had found and touched all of his names, he stepped back, letting the aura of the place descend on him. As he stood motionless, he became aware of slight movement at his feet. Small bits of paper, faded flowers, photographs, notes and letters fluttered in the breeze at the base of the wall. Bending, he scanned a letter from a mother written on her son's birthday. With misspelled words and poor grammar, she had written how much she loved and missed her son. He regretted intruding.

He stood for another long moment, allowing his memories and the names of the dead to envelope him. He swiped at his eyes with his sleeve, looked about to see who might be watching, then took a few steps to an empty space among the offerings to the dead. In one swift movement, he pulled his gift from his jacket pocket, bent, and placed it at the base of the wall. Then turning, he walked away without looking back.

CHAPTER 1

$$\blacktriangledown$$

5 March 67

The boom operator watched as the last of the F-105D Thunderchiefs nosed into position behind his KC-135 tanker. Using his joy-stick to fly the boom, he coordinated the movement of the nozzle with the bouncing of the big fighter bomber until he felt the fueling probe lock into place. Getting a thumbs up from the visored aviator looking up at him from a few feet away, he heard the boom-lock confirmation in his earphones, checked his panel light to make sure all was as it should be, then turned on the flow, pumping fuel into the sleek bomber. Like mating insects, the two linked aircraft sailed through a clear, brutally cold patch of northern-Laotian sky known by the pilots as "Green Anchor". Here, tankers met combat aircraft as they went back and forth from Thailand to North Vietnam.

Fifteen other Thunderchiefs, already topped off by this and other tankers, cruised in loose formation behind their strike commander. The nozzle shot a fine mist of fuel over the fuselage of the jet as it broke contact. The pilot gave a perfunctory wave as the operator pulled the boom up and away.

Each of the F-105Ds on this mission carried eight 750-pound general-purpose bombs. Half of these had delays set into their fuses so they would detonate a fraction of a second after they hit the ground, causing deep explosions to ferret out anything hidden below ground.

The raid had been carefully planned to destroy a suspected supply dump at the entrance to the Ho Chi Minh trail in North Vietnam. Instead of multiple raids, the U.S. Air Force would attempt to destroy this target in one mission. It was a sizable effort. Besides the full squadron of 16 strike aircraft, there were eight tankers, four for the trip in and four for the trip out. There was a command-and-control EC-121D that would remain over Laos, a search and rescue team consisting of two CH-54 rescue helicopters and four propeller-driven A-1 Skyraiders for their protection, an electronic-warfare EB-66, four F-4C chaff bombers to confuse enemy radar, a flight of F-105G Wild Weasels to take out enemy missile sites, and four rocket-firing F-100s to shoot up enemy anti-aircraft guns. Eight F-4C fighters to protect the bombers from enemy fighters and a photo-reconnaissance F-101 Voodoo rounded out the strike package.

During the pre-mission brief the pilots had been warned of the anti-aircraft threat, which consisted of eight SAM-2 missile batteries and several 23, 37, and 85-millimeter radar-controlled anti-aircraft guns. These primarily protected the coastal city of Vinh, but also provided regional coverage of the central portion of North Vietnam.

Poor visibility had forced many previous missions to be canceled, but the weather on this day looked promising. The forecast in the target area was for high, scattered clouds, an unlimited ceiling and visibility of twenty miles—well within planning parameters.

As the Thunderchiefs crossed into North Vietnam, the mission commander in the control aircraft notified the strike leader that they were on time and on profile.

"Arrow this is Crazy Horse, Wigwam, over." This code word was permission to proceed to the next phase of the mission.

"Arrow One, Rog."

"OK, Arrow, clean 'em, green 'em and turn on the jukebox! We have a GO."

As the bombers bounced along in the clear-air turbulence, their pilots stowed their maps and charts, checked their panels for green lights indicating armed weapons, and turned on their radar-jamming pods. Arriving over their initial point, the flights banked onto their strike heading, stringing out in echelon formation as they went. A constant chatter on the internal net kept all of the pilots current on aircraft status, weather, navigation changes, and the threat from missiles, guns and Migs.

"Junebug! Junebug!" came the call from the electronic-counter-measures aircraft.

"Talk to me, somebody!" called the strike commander.

"Tomahawk One's got a launch light!"

"Anyone see it?"

"Tomahawk 4, Tally Ho. It's on you, One! Break right!"

Static, then, "One. Where's it at?"

"Ah, low, at your eight, and gaining. Break back left!"

"OK, Tomahawk, lighting up," said the technician in the ECM bird. Confused by chaff dropped from the F-4s and the jamming by the bombers' on-board pods and the ECM bomber, the Soviet-built surface-to-air missile swished past the formation and exploded harmlessly well above the aircraft.

"All right, knock off the chatter. Tomahawk check." called the flight leader.

"Two."

"Three."

"Four."

"One, Rog. OK, tighten it up, we're getting close."

"Warhawk has guns at twelve!" another flight reported.

"Look like 85s—got black bursts at one o'clock, high."

Squelch static, then, "Rog—they don't look like a threat"

The strike leader cut in with, "OK, stand by for pitch-up Good luck guys!"

Nearing their targets, the Thunderchiefs climbed steeply to 20,000 feet to throw off the anti-aircraft gunners trying to find the correct altitude settings for their airbursts. As the pilots identified their target, they nosed over into 45-degree dives, their speed increasing as they fell toward the earth. In a long staggered file, the diving Thunderchiefs released their bombs one by one as they passed through 5,000 feet. Free of their loads, the pilots deployed dive breaks and strained in their G-suits as they pulled out. Compressed humidity streaked from the wings of their aircraft as they lit their after-burners and began jinking to evade enemy fire. Green tracer bullets and angry black and gray blossoms of exploding flak chased them as they streaked back into the clouds.

As the big jets climbed to safety, their bombs, in a rippling cacophony of violence, tore into the small village. The buildings, along with most of their inhabitants, were obliterated by the 128 bombs that arrived within 90 seconds. The effect was catastrophic. When the dust and smoke cleared, the place was nothing but a cluster of craters and debris swirling in the wind.

Cao Dinh Chi awakened early. There was more traffic than usual on Highway 15 that ran through the town of Long Thanh. The Americans were on the move again. Armored personnel carriers, fuel tankers, flat-beds carrying dozers, jeeps, and trucks of all kinds blew exhaust smoke into the rainy dawn as they rolled past her door. Chi poured water for tea in a battered old pot-metal pan and set it on the edge of the charcoal fire, then poured rice from a burlap bag into a black iron kettle. When it looked like the correct amount, she shook the kettle to level the white grain, covered it with water, then added the depth of two knuckles on her index finger more. Swirling the pot to make sure everything was just right, she placed it on a hanger close over the coals.

Enjoying the morning mists, she decided to allow her son Huong and her two sisters sleep a little while longer. There was still plenty of time before the truck would come to carry them to work at the American base, where she worked behind the counter, sewed patches, and shined boots at the PX laundry. Huong worked on a labor gang that filled the sand bags the Americans used to build bunkers and fortify seemingly everything standing above ground.

When the water was hot, she added a sizable pinch of her treasured Jasmine tea. Before they had gone to work at Bear Cat, her family had had no money for tea, or anything else other than rice, and little of that. Chi was the widow of a successful local merchant who had died of cancer ten years before. She and sixteen-year-old Huong, the younger of her two sons, lived in her husband's family home along with her two younger sisters, also widowed, their children and assorted orphaned cousins, nieces and nephews. Duc, her older son, had recently married and moved to his own home nearby.

Chi and her kin lived well. With their husbands dead, the future of the three sisters and their extended family had been bleak until the U.S. Army had arrived. Now the three women and their children who were mature-looking enough to get away with lying about their ages, all worked in some capacity or another for the Americans. It seemed the foreigners wanted local labor for everything and they were willing to pay. In two months, they had built the base they called Bear Cat, a huge city of wood, sheet metal and sandbags. The Long Thanh airfield had been completed in weeks, and a nearby Special Forces camp had been thrown up in no time. The Vietnamese were amazed at the ferocity of the pace at which the Americans worked.

Chi had lived through Japanese occupation and the war that had thrown the rude French out of her country. Now foreigners had once again established themselves at Long Thanh and were apparently digging in for a protracted stay. Chi had not taken sides in any of the wars. Like most Vietnamese civilians, she was more concerned about eking out a survival living than who sat in power in Saigon or Hanoi. The only loyalty she had to the Americans came from the fact that they paid well and on time. Her job at the laundry also gave her the opportunity to bring home detergent, needles and thread, and food from the snack bar.

She squatted in the open doorway, watching the traffic and sipping her tea. When the rice pot began to boil, she covered it with a mismatched lid and moved it the exact distance from the fire where it would simmer properly. She would know by experience when it was time to remove it from the heat. Chi never made a mistake with her rice.

"Huong, wake up! Wake your aunts. It is time for work."

Her son rubbed the sleep out of his eyes, shook his aunts awake, then headed for the outhouse. Chi brewed more tea for her sisters, sipped another cup, then shared a bowl of rice with her family, talking little. Her sisters washed the breakfast dishes while she rolled large balls of rice in brown paper for their noon meals. As Huong finished his morning chores, Chi dressed in black pajama pants, a short, gray, long-sleeved tunic, and conical straw hat. Huong put on an old sport shirt and khaki shorts as his mother checked the fire.

"I almost have enough money," said the boy.

"Huong, I am very concerned about the possibility of your flying in and out of the huge American machines on a motor bike. It all seems so dangerous to me."

"Mother, I am almost fully grown." said Huong as if he had heard nothing his mother had said. "I work and make my own money. I can afford to buy the motorbike without placing a burden on you at all."

"As I have told you many times, it is not the money. It is your safety. The highway is extremely dangerous with all this war-time traffic. You could be killed."

"And I have told you as many times, Mother, that I will be careful."

"You are being impertinent! You never talked to me like this until you began begging for a motorbike."

"I am sorry, Mother. All I am trying to say is that I will not take risks."

"Simply going to Saigon to buy the machine will be a huge risk if you ask me. We will talk of it later. Now we must go to work."

"Yes, Mother," smiled Huong, happy for the moment that he had not been overruled.

Chi and her sisters looked around the house once more as women all over the world do before leaving for the day, slipped on sandals, and stepped into the drizzle. As Huong strode jauntily ahead, the women were in no hurry as they walked out to the highway to join the throng waiting for the five-ton trucks that would take them to work on the American base.

"What is Imperialism?" asked Colonel Ngyuen Van Lau, Commissar for Inter-party Committee of Military, Number Two.

A young soldier eagerly raised his hand.

"Yes, comrade." nodded Colonel Lau.

"Comrade Colonel, Imperialism is the process by which dictatorial capitalists attempt to occupy and subjugate our smaller, poorer nation. The richer and stronger nation uses its military might and industrial superiority to enslave the masses of our country and turn our nation into a colony. These reactionary imperialists, first the French, then the Japanese, and now the Americans, attempt to take over our country for their own purposes."

"Very good, comrade private. What is your name?"

"Comrade Colonel, my name is Le Van Hiet."

"What is your position?"

"Comrade Colonel, I am an anti-aircraft gunner. My weapon is the ZSU 23 millimeter, four-barreled gun."

"Have you had any success as a gunner?" asked Colonel Lau.

"Yes Comrade, Last month my crew shot down a fighter known as the Crusader, F-8. It is a Navy type that flies from ships sailing illegally in our waters."

No one other than the private and the colonel knew this part of the rally had been carefully rehearsed and staged to make the other soldiers feel guilty that they weren't as successful or knowledgeable as young Hiet. Manipulation was a subtle technique Colonel Lau had learned during his own training sessions in the ruins of the city of Vinh. There, the chief commissar of The Inter-provincial Party Military Affairs Committee had taught Lau and his colleagues the fine art of political indoctrination.

Lau finished his political rally, then conducted the required inspection of the collective farm near the anti-aircraft battalion he was visiting. There he presented a letter from Ho Chi Minh himself designating a young boy a "Flower of the Nation" for helping capture a downed American flyer. Lau then walked the paddies, carefully examining the preparations for planting the next crop. Afterwards, he held another carefully-staged, but seemingly impromptu lecture for the farmers, telling them that their contributions were as important as those of the nearby anti-aircraft battalion.

Anxious to get home, Lau finished the rally a little early. Bowing and waving to the farmers and soldiers respectfully lining the road, he mounted his motor bike for the hour-long ride to the village where he had lived since birth. As he cruised along the road that linked Vinh with the Laotian border, he was in a surprisingly good mood. Time at home was rare. Having four days before his next scheduled rally, he thought about things he needed to get done.

As Lau neared his village, he was shocked to see an ugly pyre of black smoke rising above the jungle. As he rounded the last turn and the village came into view, he slid his bike to a stop, and in shock, fell with it to the ground. The houses, huts and small shops that had been Ha Tan were nothing but a cluster of ugly holes in the ground. Here and there, a fire consumed what was left of someone's home while piles of smoking embers were all that marked other dwellings. Like Lau, most of the people who stood gaping at the destruction had not been at home when the bombs fell. As they returned, the women squatted and wailed in misery and the men tugged frantically at the shattered remnants of their homes, searching beyond hope for a voice or a movement.

Lau was momentarily disoriented. He rushed to the place he thought his home had been, but he simply couldn't identify anything. His house had been in the area that was hardest hit. Nothing remained but deep clay-orange craters that had begun to fill with water.

"Colonel Lau, Colonel Lau!" came the frantic cry from a neighbor. "Please help me. I think I hear a voice down here! I think it is my wife!"

Lau shook away the shock long enough to see his friend clawing at some smoldering thatching at the edge of a twenty-foot-deep crater. "It's no use, my friend," he said. "They're all gone."

Still reeling from the trauma of losing his home and family, Lau moved in with his only surviving relatives, a cousin and his family, in a nearby jungle hut made of bamboo and palm thatching. The modest home was adjacent to a series of cooperative rice paddies a safe distance from any possible American target. Lau asked no permission, nor was any invitation offered. He simply showed up at his cousin's door with the comfortable certainty that he would be allowed to live there. His cousin welcomed him with polite inquiries about his health, formal bows, ritual sympathies for the loss of loved ones, and offers of food and tea.

"You are the guest," offered his cousin, aware of Lau's rank and status. "You may have our bed."

"No," replied Lau, as politeness required. "You are too kind. I am humbly at your service. An out-of-the-way corner will suffice."

Before his present assignment, Lau had been the political officer of the 372nd Division of the People's Army of the Democratic Republic of Vietnam. His main function had been to conduct political education and reorientation meetings, which were a combination of lectures on communist dogma and political pep rallies. The 372nd Division was made up of misplaced southerners who had been caught on the wrong side of the line at the partitioning of Vietnam in 1954. For over a year, Lau had promised they would have the chance to return to the land of their birth for the purpose of overthrowing the puppet lackeys of the foreign invaders and driving the hated Americans from their country.

Their chance had come, and they had gone off down what the Americans called the Ho Chi Minh trail. For some reason, however, Lau had been ordered to remain behind. He had been told by the chief commissar of his region that orders for him would be forthcoming. In the meantime he had become commissar of Inter-Party Committee of Military, District Number Two, southwest of Vinh.

Lau had not minded being left in the North. Serving as political officer for the few home guard and anti-aircraft units left in his sector after his division had gone south had its benefits. Living quietly at his home, he had had more time to spend with his family—a luxury in war-torn North Vietnam. As he had waited for orders, he had routinely made the rounds to his remaining units to hold his political rallies. He had secretly begun to hope the Central Committee had forgotten him.

Then had come the day when he had returned home to find his village simply gone. Ha Tan had sat astride one of the roads in North Vietnam that formed the beginnings of the Ho Chi Minh trail. Although the small village had held nothing of military significance, its mere location had sealed its fate. On the target list for the American bombing campaign know as Operation Rolling Thunder, the village had been listed as a "staging area".

When he had sufficiently recovered from the shock of his loss, Lau went to see his chief commissar in Vinh to plead for a new assignment.

"My entire family is in the spirit world." he told his superior. "I cannot bear to stay behind and do so little when so much is needed in the south. Please allow me to go where I may be of greater service. The village where I spent my whole life is no more. I have nothing here to hold me back. The fight is in the south—and I know I can serve our cause better there."

As he spoke, his expression burned with such intensity that his superior had to avert his eyes. Quietly moved, the senior commissar said, "Look, Comrade Lau, you know these things take time and there are reasons for everything. You can be sure I will do my best to grant your request. I will seek instructions."

Stoically awaiting his orders, Lau strengthened his muscles and maintained his sanity by rigorous work in the rice paddies. Stooping hours on end over the rice shoots, carrying heavy loads of human excrement used for fertilizer in buckets balanced on a bamboo pole, and repairing dikes and flood gates in preparation for the season's planting made him strong and made him hurt. By refusing to turn his head away or to cover his nose, he used the stench of the fertilizer to strengthen his resolve. He practiced overcoming the gag reflex that rose in his throat and watered his eyes. He even disciplined himself to ignore the flies that swarmed around him, knowing there might be a time when he might have to remain motionless for long periods, flies or no flies.

He used the pain in his back caused by endless hours of stooping and pulling to replace the pain in his soul caused by the loss of his loved ones. He used the physical exercise of digging and hauling to strengthen his body for the task he hoped would be given him. He forced himself to eat and drink sparingly. A small portion of rice, some wild onions, maybe a paddy shrimp or two was all he allowed himself each day. At night he slept on a thatched mat on the floor.

He spoke little around his cousin's hearth. His relatives, knowing of his pain and his request to go south, politely kept their distance. The only respite he enjoyed was occasionally making his rounds to conduct the required political rallies. When possible, he walked to the meetings to further toughen himself for his coming pilgrimage. His only happiness came when playing with his cousin's children, whose laughter warmed his heart and became his only link with the sanity of his previous life.

Lau knew when he was ready. Hard work and an austere and sacrificial life style had strengthened his body and his spirit. His weight was down to 105 pounds. His muscles were tight and stringy; his spirit dedicated to his crusade. Every day heightened his hatred for the Americans. He sensed what was happening within him and fostered, welcomed, even enjoyed the malice growing in his bosom. Opening his whole being to the hatred, his soul soared with the exquisite agony of his loss. He looked forward to the day when the loathing he was consciously sciously nurturing would serve him well.

As he worked the paddies he thought continuously of his family while he watched the vapor trails high in the sky. From time to time an American jet screamed by at tree-top level, scattering the workers. He wondered what manner of men could drop death on innocent children. He looked forward to meeting one or many of them face to face.

Lau prayed daily at a small temple near his cousin's home, promising the spirits of his family and his ancestors that he would do his best in the quest he sought. He promised revenge and atonement. He promised sacrifice and endurance. He promised he would never give up until the foreign imperialists were driven from his country for good.

At long last, his superior officer came to visit. His cousin and his family made themselves scarce after polite welcomes and required small talk. As the two commissars sipped tea, the superior handed Lau a letter order.

"Your wish has been granted. You will make your way to the Central Office for South Vietnam," said his superior.

"I'm afraid I'm not familiar with that office," said Lau.

"Well, it is not exactly an office," smiled his boss. "It is actually a huge headquarters complex in the Cambodian jungles north-east of Saigon. It has control of all of our political and military activities in the south."

"I see," nodded Lau. "I suppose I will receive further orders from there?"

"I suppose," said his superior as he handed him a thick envelope.

The orders were very short, giving him the names of guides and where he was to meet them. There was also a packet of maps and travel instructions, a wad of South Vietnamese piasters, fake identity cards, leave papers, and even letters from a fictitious family in Vinh Long. The maps outlined the route south and showed details of trails, roads, bridges, villages, way-stations, mess halls, hospitals, and fueling points. He was to travel six hundred fifty miles down the system of jungle trails, rivers and roads known as the Ho Chi Minh Trail.

He would have to traverse the provinces of Khammouane, Savannakhet, Vapikham Thong, Sedone, and Champassak in Laos, where he could not speak the language. He would then cross into Cambodia in the province of Stun Treng. There he was instructed to meet a boat for the long trip down the Tonle Kong River to the Mekong. There he would transfer to another, faster sampan for the journey down the great river to a point close to the South Vietnamese border. His guides would then take him overland to The Central Office for South Vietnam.

After his superior had left, Lau packed his meager equipment in a small knapsack. For the trip, his cousin gave him one of his most treasured belongings—a round metal canteen covered by green canvas.

As his departure approached, Lau slept fitfully, nervous anticipation of the journey ahead robbing him of rest. In his dreams he faced the huge, foreign enemy, daring them to fight him. When the day finally came, goodbyes were formal and short. His cousin's wife gave Lau four rice balls wrapped in jackfruit leaves to use as food for the first few days of his trip. The children hugged his legs and waist; his cousin and his wife bowed deeply and waved as he walked away. They did not expect to see him again.

Lau tied his belongings onto his small motorbike, waved once more, then, instead of heading toward the Laotian border, he rode northeast, toward Ha Tan. When he arrived at his former home, he parked his motor bike and walked to the edge of the craters that had been his home village. After the air raid, identification of the dead had been impossible. Rescue workers had respectfully placed what few remains and body parts they were able to find in a mass grave. Communist officials had come for rousing political speeches at the site. Later, wary of official religious persecution in communist North Vietnam, Catholic priests and Buddhist monks had stolen back for secret services with survivors over the graves of their loved ones.

He stood for a long moment, breathing in the death and sadness of the place. Then he burned incense and invoked the spirits of his family. He promised he would return to live out his life in their presence if he survived his task. Fighting back tears, he returned to his bike, checked the cord holding his knapsack and canteen on the luggage rack, adjusted his sun helmet, started the machine, and turned southwest toward Laos.

Over his toes, the captain watched the cargo plane flying away from him with bodies falling from both sides. He felt the harness dig into his crotch as the opening canopy swung him to the vertical. The next C-130 in line swooped over in a roar just feet above him, as paratroopers, some in tight, correct body positions, and others with legs flailing, tumbled out to join him in the sky. He pulled apart the risers that were twisted behind his neck and gaped upward to check his chute. Satisfied with the canopy that billowed above, he began to bicycle-pump his legs causing him to spin like a kid in a swing as the straps began to untwist.

Once his parachute was riding right, he took a second to look around. Off to his right, behind the bleachers full of dignitaries, he saw brown army busses lined up like so many loaves of whole-wheat bread. Below him, in a cloud of white smoke, army pathfinders and members of the air force combat-control team stood near their radio jeeps they used to guide the jump aircraft to the drop zone. Off to his left he could see the assembly area—trucks, jeeps, tents and antennas scattered among the scrub-oak trees on the edge of the white-sand drop zone. To his front, fading into the distance, were the jump aircraft, with smudges trailing their engine exhausts and parachute deployment bags spinning from their doors.

In the bleachers sat over a hundred NATO, allied and U.S. admirals and generals, as well as members of congress, local big-wigs, and, of course, the press. The jumpers were part of a huge demonstration designed to show the VIPs how an airborne battalion arrived at a modern battlefield. As the paratroopers hit the ground, they left their parachutes where they landed, then ran off toward the assembly area hidden on the far side of the drop zone. On their way, the jumpers ran through another battalion, also hidden from the audience by a slight rise in the middle of the landing area, and arrayed in perfect assault formation. As the jumpers hurried to their assembly area, the attack battalion was to move out. To the dignitaries sitting in the bleachers, it would appear that the parachuting battalion had hit the ground, then suddenly and dramatically appeared, approaching the bleachers in a text-book attack. The fact that it took a trained airborne battalion at least an hour to assemble and begin an attack under normal circumstances was lost to most of the audience. The VIPs who knew that two separate battalions were involved smiled and exchanged knowing glances.

The captain watched as the ground rose toward him. An experienced jumper, he pointed his toes, flexed his knees slightly and waited for the impact. Instead of looking at the horizon as he had been taught in jump school, he searched the ground and picked his spot. He plowed into the sand, rolled easily, and came up in a sprint to chase down the parachute which was riding on the slight breeze. With practiced ease, he ran around the billowing nylon, grabbed the skirt and collapsed the canopy.

Knowing the scenario called for the jumpers to get off the drop zone quickly, he slapped the harness quick release, shrugged clear of the webbing, gathered his equipment, and began to jog toward the assembly area. On the way, he ran through the troops of the attack battalion that had been placed as precisely as chess pieces on a board.

Grinning as he ran past a fellow company commander, he yelled "Be careful now! Don't trip and bust your ass in front of all the nice generals!" He got a grin and a raised middle finger in reply.

Arriving at the assembly area, he found his first sergeant who had begun to round up B company's troopers.

"Sir, the colonel wants to see you", said the top sergeant.

"What about, do you know?" the captain asked. He did not normally receive good news when summoned by the battalion commander.

"No, sir," answered the first sergeant. "He just said when you came in to come and see him. The only thing I can tell you is that he had a packet of paperwork the S-1 just brought him from the rear."

"OK, thanks, Top. As the troops get here, make sure they get their names checked off before they head to chow. Did you see which way the colonel went?" asked the captain. "The last time I saw him he was walking down toward the mess tent."

Since this was a demonstration and not a war game, the assembly area was administrative instead of tactical. Out of site from the bleachers, a full field kitchen was prepared to feed the jumpers a hot meal after they landed. As he walked toward the mess tent, Captain Jason Spencer, Jace as he was known by his friends, tried to anticipate what the battalion commander might want. Hearing explosions, he looked over his shoulder to see the attack battalion moving over the rise toward the bleachers, artillery simulators banging and smoke grenades forming a dramatic mist on the mock battlefield. In the distance he could see dots in the sky that were the C-130s bringing the heavy-drop loads to the show. As the attack battalion cleared the drop zone, nine plane loads of jeeps, trucks, howitzers, and supply pallets were to be parachuted onto the sandy stage.

Jace stooped to enter the mess tent, squinted in the relative darkness, found the battalion commander, and reported with the 82nd Airborne Division's time-honored greeting, "All the way, sir!"

The lieutenant colonel looked up, grinned and answered,

"Airborne! Well, Bravo Six! How was your jump?"

Jace smiled back and answered, "Good, sir. Smooth as silk. My first sergeant said you wanted to see me."

The battalion commander's face became serious as he pulled a sheet of pink paper from a folder. "Jace, I'm afraid I've got some bad news for you." he said. "You'd better sit down."

Jace had a fleeting fear that something might have happened to his father or his sister. A look of concern shot across his face as he took the paper with faint gray typing forming a short paragraph. He recognized that it was an electronically transmitted message known in the military as a "twix".

"Officer's command tour broken due to priority assignment to the 9th Infantry Division, Republic of Vietnam." read the document. Jace sat down heavily.

"Damn," he said softly. "Sir, I knew all along that I would be going to Vietnam like everyone else," he said. "I just thought I would get to command B company for more than four months—and what's this 9th Division? I thought for sure I'd get the 101st or 173rd. A leg division? A damned leg division!"

"When do you go?" asked the lieutenant colonel, "I didn't notice the date."

"Report date of 28 June," answered Jace. "I'd better start clearing post tomorrow if I'm going to get any leave at all."

"Look, don't get discouraged." offered the battalion commander. "When you get in-country, you can probably finagle your way to an airborne outfit. These orders will just get you to Vietnam. I'll admit, I haven't seen a request for orders mention a particular division before, but you'll see, everything in that place is flexible. Just be persistent. I'm like you—I'd be scared to death in a leg unit. Those bastards'll get you killed."

On his right shoulder, the lieutenant colonel wore the combat patch of the 101st Airborne Division, the Screaming Eagles.

"Yes, sir—persistent," mumbled Jace as he stood to leave. "I need to see to my troops. Is that all, sir?"

"Yes, Jace, that's it—except for telling you that you've done a great job and that I hate to lose you."

"Thank you, sir. I appreciate that—All the way, sir." Jace saluted as he turned to leave.

He walked the short distance to where his men had assembled. He moved easily among them, listening to and enjoying their youthful banter. He was relaxed and comfortable with his men. He cared for his them and they respected and liked him.

Jace was tall, lanky, physically tough, and hot-tempered. His men knew by experience that he could run most of them into the ground. He could be hell on earth, too, if one of them ended up in front of his desk for punishment.

They also knew that he knew his stuff. Even the combat veterans and experienced non-coms could tell by the way he did the little things and was able to see situations and circumstances others couldn't see, that he knew what he was doing. He had a grasp for the ground, a nose for weather, a feel for vegetation, and was unquestionable with a map and compass. He understood tactics, and not just the book version either. He could lay a proper tactical deployment on a piece of ground so it looked as pleasing to a senior commander as a quilt on a feather bed. He could walk a defensive line and sense, rather than see, any dead spaces or gaps. His intuition allowed him to speed up or slow down marches so the company would arrive at exactly the right place at the right time. And he listened. He combined the practical lessons he learned daily from his veteran non-coms with the formal knowledge he had gained at the infantry school and during the grinding rigors of the ranger course. To all of this experience he added what he called cold Tennessee logic. The Vietnam veterans and NCOs felt he would do fine in combat—if he lived long enough.

The troops also saw that he honestly cared for them. He seemed to have radar that honed in on problems. He could see who was hurting because of a woman, worried because of lack of money, or scared of a parachute jump. He dealt with problems before they became problems. The troops knew this instinctively and returned the peculiar brand of affection known only between a good commander and his soldiers.

The savvy among his men eyed the pink twix in his hand and exchanged glances, knowing they would soon have to break in a new company commander.

"Hey, sir, whatcha got thar?" asked a young sergeant. "Sho looks like somethin' official!"

"Yes," said Jace, "I've got orders—and not to Hawaii either!"

Colonel Lau rode his motorbike along the cratered road linking Ha Tan with the Laotian border. It was impossible for him to tell when he actually crossed into Laos—American bombs had long ago obliterated any highway signs along with the rain forest. The trunks of once-lush trees stood like bare ship masts, their foliage blasted away by concussion and bomb fragments, or wilted away by Agent Orange. Climbing into the Laotian hills, Lau couldn't believe his eyes. The Americans apparently had enough wealth and military might to simply blast miles of jungle away from the little road so their bombers could more easily get at the ammunition trucks heading south.

As he passed, he waved to the labor crews who worked with crude farm tools to fill in the bomb craters in the road. He passed other, better equipped crews working at rebuilding the bridges destroyed by American explosives. Here and there, sweating operators wearing khakis and pith helmets drove Russian-built dozers to repair seriously damaged sections of the trail.

After riding for two days, Colonel Lau came to the place where he was to rendezvous with a truck and his guides for the trip south. He found them near the designated stream crossing, hidden from the air by the beginnings of the unbombed and unmolested Laotian jungle. At the shady ford, three guides who would double as body guards introduced themselves.

While waiting for some other travelers, it occurred to Lau that he had no further use for his motor bike. On impulse, he approached a regimental commander marching south with his men.

"Comrade Colonel, it looks as though I will not need my motorbike. I will be riding on that truck. Could you use the machine?

"Why thank you, comrade. It will help me move up and down my column as they march. I hope the trail will not be too rough to ride on. Where do I get fuel?"

"I have been siphoning it from vehicles I met along the way. Make sure you use gasoline instead of diesel fuel! Come and I will help you get some fuel from our truck."

After refueling the bike, and wishing the grateful officer luck, Lau climbed aboard the canvas-covered Russian truck that awaited him. There was no doubt in his mind that he was ending one life and beginning a new one. He was sad, elated and frightened at the same time.

The last week had been chaotic for Jace. His most demanding task had been to complete a one-hundred-percent inventory of over a million dollars worth of government equipment with the captain who was replacing him in B company. He had listened to all the required briefings, had all his pre-deployment shots, and had cleared up a hundred administrative problems. When the last small, but important task had been completed, he had cleaned and turned in his field gear, cleared out of his BOQ room, moved into transient quarters, and rushed all over Fort Bragg having his clearance papers stamped by one agency after another.

As he dumped the contents of his desk drawers into a cardboard box to be gone through later, he looked around the office he had occupied for such a short time. At noon, he walked outside to pass the company's guideon in a brief change-of-command ceremony. That night, he was roasted at a farewell party thrown at the officers' club for him and seven other officers from his brigade—all of whom were headed to the 173rd Airborne Brigade Vietnam. After having senior parachutist wings pinned on him by the battalion commander, he received his going-away gift, a small bronze statuette of a paratrooper. He choked out a short speech, then shook hands with his lieutenants.

"Jace, are you going to be all right?" It was the colonel's wife.

"Oh, Uh—Yeah, I'm fine."

"Honey, you look so tired. You go straight home and get some sleep."

"Thanks, but I think I just decided to head on to Tennessee tonight."

"Oh, Jace, do be careful. Is there anything we can do for you? Anything you need?"

"Thank you, no," he said, giving her a hug. "Just take care of the colonel and be as good to my replacement as you have been to me."

Before he knew it, he was standing in the parking lot, confused, lonely, and a little afraid. Then, shaking his head clear, he unlocked his car, drove to his room, and began packing. When he had carried everything to his car, he drove to division headquarters, signed out, and headed west. As he drove his 1959 Corvette into the early-morning chill of the North Carolina mountains, he thought briefly about the fact that at 25 years of age he could still fit almost all his worldly belongings into the trunk and on the luggage rack of his aging sports car. He knew that someday he would probably get married and have children, but for now, the army was his life and he didn't need material things to make him happy. For the last two years, simply getting out of bed each morning and going to work in what he considered to be the best division in the army had been more than fulfilling.

As it began to rain, he pulled onto the shoulder to check the vinyl poncho he had wrapped around the cheap suitcases and duffel bags strapped atop his trunk. He relieved himself, did a few pushups and took several deep breaths to clear his head, poured black coffee from his thermos, and slumped into the bucket seat once more. He turned up the volume on the radio to keep himself awake. He had four more hours to drive.

As the Corvette hugged the mountain curves, its headlights punched a tunnel of light through the darkness. Nothing was going as he had planned or imagined it. He had thought he had it all figured: a year of company command in the 82nd, command of a company in Vietnam—in an airborne unit of course—the advanced course at the infantry school, and then, if the war lasted long enough, a tour as an advisor to a Vietnamese ranger battalion or as an operations officer in an airborne outfit.

He thought he had a right to expect things to go his way—after all, hadn't they always? He had been branched infantry as he wanted. His initial assignment had been the 82nd Airborne, the unit he had requested. He had volunteered for ranger school and had immediately gotten the orders. He had been a rifle platoon leader, weapons platoon leader, company executive officer, assistant battalion operations officer and had finally had been assigned as B company commander. He had done everything the army had asked him to do. He knew the army wouldn't, couldn't let him down.

He thought of a buddy who had been a classmate at the infantry officers' basic course. His friend had gone to be a training officer at Fort Jackson. Basic training, for God's sake. Jace had thought it a fate worse than death. Now, it seemed he was in the same boat. In his mind, a leg unit in Vietnam was as bad as being in a basic training outfit in the states.

In the pre-dawn of the brisk spring morning, Jace crossed into Tennessee and drove through the small community of Watauga where he had worked his way through school. Finishing near the top of his military class in the ROTC program at Watauga State College, he had known from the start what he wanted. He had grown up a country boy in the foothills of the Great Smoky Mountains where his dad's small farm adjoined the Cherokee National Forrest. Running the ridges with a rifle or shotgun came as easily to him as breathing. He could never visualize being in the army without being in the infantry.

His mentor, the Professor of Military Science at Watauga State had been a platoon leader and company commander in the 101st Airborne in World War II. He had jumped into Normandy, had fought for the bridges around Eindhoven in

Holland, and had been one of the "Battered Bastards of Bastogne". Jace had thought he was the finest man that had ever lived.

When the movie *The Longest Day* was released in 1964, Jace had become obsessed with the history of the Second World War. He had already changed his major to history and as he had neared graduation, he had begun to read everything he could get his hands on concerning the great battles of the war. His reading had verified his decision. When it came time to submit his "dream sheet", he had not hesitated. He had put infantry as his first choice and volunteered for airborne and ranger school.

It was curious that he did not want to be a marine as his father had been. Walton Spencer had served in the Pacific in WWII and had made the landing at Guadalcanal. He had been wounded, and after a short hospitalization, had spent the rest of the war in supply. His father had never talked about his war experiences, except for the funny episodes about garrison life. Jace had thought his father's combat experience short and uneventful except for a million-dollar wound. He had never seen anything glamorous or exciting in his father's stories. The marines had not beckoned him.

As the Corvette purred into the Tennessee darkness, a fog of resignation settled over Jace Spencer. Overcome with the feeling that he had no power to influence even the smallest aspect of his army career, he pulled off onto a dirt road, locked the doors and drifted off to sleep. When he awoke, stiff and groggy, it was daylight. He was forty miles from home.

After stopping at the Blue Circle drive-in in Elizabethton for bacon, eggs, and especially, coffee, he drove to the post office where his father worked. He walked into the lobby in the rumpled jeans, sneakers and T-shirt he had changed into after last night's party. He looked about the familiar building for his father, finally finding him bent over a mail bin.

"Hey!" said Jace. His father looked up disapprovingly.

"You didn't drive all night, did you?" asked Walton Spencer. "Good way to get your dern self killed."

Jace grinned and hugged his father.

"Sleep deprivation is a way of life in the airborne." he said.

Spending a month with his father would be hard. Jace loved and respected his father and, looking back, had enjoyed what he considered to be a happy childhood. In retrospect, however, he knew that he had never been especially close to his dad, who could be moody and uncommunicative. His mother had often been the go-between, acting as mediator when Jace and his father were at odds. But, faced with the danger and enormity of his next undertaking, Jace vowed he'd do his best to get along with Walton Spencer. Often, he tried to talk to his father, but when he asked questions or made comments, all he would get for an answer was a grunt or and expletive

During the first week of his leave, Jace awakened each morning at his usual five a.m., dressed in shorts and sneakers and went for a run. He had breakfast waiting for his dad when he got up at 6:30. Gradually he eased into his time off, sleeping a few minutes longer each day. He spent his time visiting his sister and her family, old high school teachers, and the ROTC department at Watauga State. He tried a couple of dates with an old girl friend who was still single, but found she was still locked into small town routines and habits he could no longer relate to. Also, in the back of his mind lay the possibility he might never return to Watauga County, Tennessee. Reluctantly, he stifled his natural urges and shunned anything more serious than dinner and a movie.

On Monday of his second week of leave, Jace drove to Knoxville to pay respects to retired Colonel Richard Foster, who had been the Professor of Military Science at Watauga State when he had graduated.

"Well, young man, so you're on your way to war."

"Yes, sir. I thought I'd come down and get your blessing before I ship out."

"Well I'm glad you did. It's good to see you, son. You were commanding a company at Bragg, right?"

"Yes, sir. And I thought I'd get to stay in command longer than four months."

"Well, I guess these are trying times for the Army, figuring out how to keep all the units manned while keeping Vietnam going. How bout a beer?"

"Yes, Sir, that would be great."

"On the phone, you said you were being assigned to the 9th Infantry Division. Is that right?"

"Yes, sir. I thought for sure I'd get an airborne assignment."

"Well, the 9th was a fine division during the big war. General Westmoreland was chief of staff of the 9th, did you know that?"

"No, sir. I'm sure it's a fine outfit, I just took for granted that since I was in the 82nd, I'd get to go to the 101st or the 173rd."

"What made you think that?"

"Well, I'm an airborne-ranger infantry officer and a company commander in the 82nd. I just assumed that would qualify me to serve in combat with an airborne unit."

"Jace, I recon you're still idealistic. You probably won't get cynical till much later in your career. You have got to come to the understanding that the army doesn't have the same affection for you that you have for it. The army doesn't care what you want."

"But I thought—"

"Listen, you remember when you filled out your dream sheet, don't you? Remember the term 'needs of the service'?"

"Yes, sir."

"Well, what that means is an assignment officer in Washington with a stack of requirements and a list of names to pick from. The 9th Infantry Division obviously needs an infantry captain—any infantry captain—right now."

"But what about my command tour at Bragg?"

"That assignment officer does not care. He's simply filling slots from his list of names."

"But all my buddies at Bragg got the 173rd. Why them and not me?"

"Who knows? Random chance? They might be brothers-in-law of the assignment officer—or more than likely members of the WPPA."

"Yeah, I guess the West Point Protective Association is more than just a rumor or a myth."

"But, who knows? The important thing is to get the job done where you find yourself. You can't always pick and choose your assignments. Every job in the army is an important one. The way you've got to look at it is that if the job weren't important, it wouldn't be given to you. Don't fight the system. Excel wherever you end up."

"I've heard that the leadership in leg units is just not what it is in the airborne."

"You seem to've developed an elite mentality. Are you sure that's healthy?"

Jace did not answer. He thought silently for a moment.

"What do you think of trying to get my orders changed when I get in country?"

"Give it a shot if you think it's worth it. But I wouldn't get my hopes up. Can you stay for dinner? Jane is whipping up some of her fine lasagna."

"Yes, sir. That would be great."

Later in the week, Jace tried fishing with his father, but the silence in the boat was uncomfortable. He and his father were keeping them apart.

For years, Walton Spencer had maintained a small farm as well as his job as postal clerk. Now, he ran a couple of cows and grew a large garden each summer. Without his wife, who had died four years earlier, to help with the canning, he had bought a freezer, but found the vegetables going bad before he got around to eating them. The garden was now just a habit now, a throwback to younger, happier, more energetic times. These days he gave away most of his crop to the neighbors.

A week before he was to leave, Jace helped his dad with the weeding. The tension between them had grown to the point that it was tangible. They both felt it as a heavy, wet blanket that had descended over them. Neither knew how to pull it away. Their silence had almost conquered them; they both knew that now was not the time to grow further apart. Years of guilt and regret might result from words not spoken in the next week.

Walton mopped his brow with a bandanna. Father and son stood in rows of waist-high corn in the heat of the June afternoon. Jace wore running shorts and sneakers, his dad bib overalls, their attire accentuating the gulf between them. They stood, staring in different directions, the same hopeless expression on both their faces.

Jupiter, the old family cat, sat motionless next to the fence, patiently listening to something moving in the weeds.

"That's the secret, you know." said Walton.

"The secret?" echoed Jace.

"Yeah, the secret." his dad said distantly.

After a long pause, Jace said, "The secret to what, Dad?"

"The jungle." answered Walton.

Again, silence, then, "Dad, I'm not following you."

"Watch old Jupiter. Whatever he's after is moving in the weeds, but he's stark still. That's the secret of jungle fighting. The one who moves is dead. The one who sits and watches lives."

Jace thought about this silently.

Walton suddenly turned to his son. "What do you think this will be all about?"

Flustered, Jace answered, "What, Vietnam?"

"You know damn well that's what I mean," said Walton. "Do you have any idea what you're getting yourself into? On the news they talk about operation this or operation that and the number of our boys killed in the past 24 hours. In the Pacific, we went days without casualties, then they would attack and we would kill them by the hundreds and they would kill a bunch of us. In that damn place you're going to, our boys die every day, hundreds a week. I can't understand what's going on, except they must not know how to fight in the jungle. Evidently they don't know when to just sit and listen."

"Dad, it's a different war, different rules. We're trained different—"

"I don't give a damn how you're trained." growled Walton. "I've heard you bitchin' about going to a straight-leg division. I can tell you that being a paratrooper ain't worth a hoot in hell once you get in the bush. It's what you feel, what you smell, what you sense, like that damn old cat yonder. Don't go over there thinking about stuff like which outfit is better or what will help your career, think about where they are, and what they're up to and learn to listen for 'em. You'll learn to smell 'em. I guess it's the dampness in the jungle that holds the smells close to the ground. You'll learn that they smell different from us—not bad, I'm sayin', just different."

Jace was stunned. After years of near silence about his war experiences, his father's venomous outburst had shocked him. He suddenly felt like the little boy he once was, playing around his father's feet. No longer the confident, hard-charging paratroop captain, he was a child in the presence of an experienced and angry parent. The transition in how he viewed his father came so swiftly that it left him breathless.

Now Jace was able to understand his father's silent times, his dark moods, and his scathing denunciations of everything Japanese. He recalled the hateful things his father had said about America's deepening involvement in Southeast Asia. He now put his father's reluctance to bless his military career into a different perspective. He even remembered his dad's emotional and sometimes angry reactions as he had watched news broadcasts from Vietnam, old war movies, or *Victory at Sea* reruns on TV. More than anything else, he now knew why his dad had never mentioned the fighting, only the stories about his time in supply.

"You saw a lot, didn't you, Dad?"

They were both silent for a time.

"They—there were so many of them—" Walton struggled for words. "They just kept comin'. We was dug in around the air strip. At night, the two navies battled. It looked like a nighttime thunderstorm in the mountains. We knew if our navy lost, we were stranded, cut off—doomed. During the day their bombers came. You could see 'em high in the sunlight, but you couldn't hear 'em. The bombs, even the ones that missed ruined everybody's hearing. A lot of boys died from concussion. And I'll tell you something else, too. A bomb didn't care if a boy was a marine or a dog face. It killed him just the same. Hell, we was all deaf. Then at night—At night they would come screaming. At first it scared hell out of us until we learned we were the ones waiting, like old Jupiter there. We were the ones safe in our fox holes in the dark. They were the ones running towards us. We waited till they were right on top of us—then we opened up. They came at us out of the dark like screaming wild men and we cut them down in piles. The only times I got really scared was out on patrol. Then we was moving and they was waitin' in the dark. Watchin'. There's no way you can be quiet in the jungle. They can always hear you comin'.".

Walton Spencer turned and grabbed his son by the shoulders.

"I won't ask you why you're doing this. I couldn't tell anyone why I had to join the marines. I didn't wait for the draft, I had to join. Had to. But I couldn't just join the air corps or the navy. No, I had to be a marine just like you have to be a paratrooper and a ranger. I know if I asked you, you couldn't tell me anything that makes sense. Just remember this, an enemy bullet don't give a damn if you're a paratrooper or a straight-leg—it'll cut you down just the same. It don't matter which patch you wear on your shoulder. The only thing that matters is what you do!"

Walton paused, the strain of the moment heavy still on him.

"Son, I want you to do something for me."

"Sure, Dad, anything." Jace answered quietly.

"No matter what them colonels tell you, no matter what the tactics books say, I want you to be still. Make your men be still. Watch and listen. Squirrel-hunt them. Squirrel-hunt the bastards."

Another pause.

"Remember when we used to sit under a hickory tree for hours with a .22 up on Walnut Ridge? We'd sit and watch and listen for the squirrels? Sit and wait. Watch and listen like old Jupiter there. I know there'll be times when you have to move, but even when you're moving, stop from time to time and watch and listen—no matter what anybody says. If you need to stop and listen, just do it. Don't pay no attention to the colonels and generals. They got a plan they're looking at. They move arrows around on maps. You'll be moving live human beings in the bush. Do what will keep your men alive. Plans and maps be damned!"

Spent, Walton let go of his son.

"I don't reckon I ever told you, but I'm proud of you. I know I couldn't help you much in college, but I'm proud of you graduating. I'm proud of what you've done in the army. In a way I'm even proud you're going to war for the country. Most ways, though, it just scares me to death. I just can't figure out what we're tryin' to do in them jungles ten thousand miles from here and what difference any of it makes to anybody."

They weeded in silence for a time, then put the tools in the shed and started back toward the house. As he went, Jace scooped up old Jupiter who was still staring into the weeds. As he walked down the bank to the back door, he cuddled the scraggly old cat to his chest.

Bombs had fallen nearby during the night, a hair-raising, nerve-shattering experience. As Colonel Lau and his comrades bounced along the war-torn track in their ancient vehicle with no shock absorbers and worn-out springs, they were already battered and exhausted. But, as bad as he and his party had it, Lau saw that his designation of "special traveler" made their trip through Laos much easier than it could have been. Every day, the old truck lurched past thousands of soldiers and workers plodding miserably along in the mud.

At night they stayed in sprawling rest stops hidden in the jungle. These way-stations had sleeping quarters, mess halls, fresh water and fuel points. Some had vegetable gardens and pens holding live chickens and pigs. At one station, they even watched a movie, an old French film staring Maurice Chavalier. At each way station, Lau and his companions were given a detailed briefing on the weather, the road conditions ahead, enemy bombing activity, and the location of the next rest stop. Still, the trip was exhausting.

When he and his three guides entered Cambodia, the extent of the planning for his journey again became obvious.

"Greetings, Comrade Colonel," said the boatman.

"I hope you know where we are going, because I surely do not," smiled Lau.

"We will depart the normal trails for the remainder of your trip," Comrade Colonel, "we will simply go down the Tonle Kong River to the Mekong. The only time we will leave the river is to walk around the Khone and Trapeung rapids. That will be a walk of about fifty kilometers, which will take three or four days. Another boat will be waiting on the other side of the rough waters."

"After riding in that damnable truck, walking will be a pleasure," laughed Lau.

Compared to the truck trip through Laos, the boat trip through Cambodia was heaven on earth. They made good progress, they were comfortable, and they even managed to augment their diet with fresh fish, killed by dropping grenades in the water. As they neared the Mekong, however, American planes were overhead constantly. Under the triple-canopy jungle of Laos, Lau had not been able to see the sky, let alone airplanes, but the roar of jets, the drone of turboprops, and the chatter of rotor blades had been constant company. While they were on the river, American planes streaked over in plain view, keeping the travelers in a constant state of fear. Although the small boat hugged the shore staying under the overhanging trees as much as possible, they were still harassed by the planes. Twice, bombs struck so near that Lau and his companions were knocked flat by the concussion. In constant fear of being attacked by American aircraft, his guides recommended they try traveling at night. They slept in the heat of the day, their sampan tied to shady banks.

Once Colonel Lau and his guides arrived at the Mekong, and transferred to a larger, motorized sampan, the trip became less frightening.

"Why are the airplanes not bombing us?" Lau asked the boatman.

"I suppose the Americans have trouble deciding on a target with so many boats available to choose from." the man answered. "Or they might have trouble explaining why they are bombing civilian watercraft in "neutral" Cambodia."

Lau didn't care; he was just thankful for the respite. As the travelers passed Phnom Penh, they began to feel that their journey was nearing its end, though they still had many miles to travel. They had been ordered to avoid the sprawling Cambodian capitol. Criminals, spies, diplomats and thousands of people who would sell them out for a song, not to mention a large number of Americans, filled the huge city with danger. But getting lost in the profusion of watercraft plying the muddy waters adjacent to the stinking slums made them feel safer than they had during their entire journey.

After another day on the river, Lau's guides thanked the boatman, and walked into a small village. Here, after some lengthy and often heated conversations with several people, they found the driver of the old Citroen that would take them from the Mekong down Highway 1 toward the South Vietnamese border. Since it was still early in the day, they left immediately, wanting to make Svey Rieng by dark.

It was dusk when the travelers bounced into the last city they would encounter before entering South Vietnam. They rented rooms, ate in a fairly decent noodle shop, and enjoyed three days of relaxation before pushing on to their destination. They knew the war would be waiting for them when they arrived in South Vietnam. After being bombed, bounced, rained on, and insect-bitten, they figured they owed the three days to themselves. Lau slept almost continuously, dreaming about his family and his home in North Vietnam.

After a much-needed rest, the companions reluctantly loaded their baggage into the beat-up old car, piled in, and headed east, toward the South-Vietnamese border. As the highway snaked between vertical walls of jungle, Lau dozed in the heat and drizzle. At the end of a long day on the road, the driver slid to a halt at a seemingly innocuous mile post.

"We are here, Comrade Colonel, said a guide. "We must hurry. If we tarry too long on the road, we might give away the entrance to the trail."

They grabbed their bags and hurried away from the car and into the jungle, where a well-hidden foot path led them from the road. It took Lau several minutes to walk the kinks from his joints after the long car ride. His companions, seemingly anxious to distance themselves from the highway, plunged into the jungle at a blistering pace. Soon Lau was awake and aware of how the truck and boat rides had eroded his physical condition.

They had hiked for almost three hours without a break when an armed soldier stepped into the trail and challenged them. After Lau's traveling companions showed identification and answered with the appropriate password, the guard led them to a small jungle hut hidden off the trail. They sat quietly until another guard came up a trail from another direction. He motioned for the party to follow him.

Without warning, Lau saw he was finally at his destination. Hidden under the hundred-foot trees of the rain forest was a camouflaged city. Called the Central Office for South Vietnam, COSVN, or simply Headquarters "R", the command facility was a maze of huts, living quarters, hospitals, offices, briefing areas, planning bays, classrooms, mess halls and under-ground supply areas. Beautifully and naturally camouflaged under the triple-canopy jungle, the complex was totally invisible from the air, and practically invisible from the ground, unless one knew what to look for.

"Come, I will show you to sleeping quarters and where to get something to eat," said the soldier who had guided them in. "You must not build fires without permission. American planes often bomb smoke emerging from the jungle."

"When will we be given our orders?" asked Lau.

"I do not know, Comrade Colonel. All I know is that someone will come for you in the morning. Sleep well.

The three five-ton trucks loaded with Vietnamese workers pulled off the road just inside the main gate of Bear Cat. The workers jumped to the ground and lined up as they did every morning. Two MPs searched their tote bags and lunch containers. They frisked several of the males selected at random. The searches were cursory, since the workers' scanty clothing left no room to hide anything. After the searches, the workers split up, leaving with different supervisors.

Chi watched as her son and about ten other men followed an engineer sergeant toward the day's work site, then climbed back on the truck for the trip to the snack bar. The drivers always dropped off Chi and the women who worked at the snack bar, then went in for coffee. One of the drivers helped her down from the bed of the truck, swinging her small frame as though she were a child. As was her custom, she followed the cooks into the snack bar, chatting with the them for a while to ease into the work day.

An obese staff sergeant that everyone called Buddha was the proprietor of the snack bar.

As Chi walked in with the others, Buddha yelled at her in his good-natured pigeon English, "Mamasan, you numba ten—late, late, all time late. No work, You bookoo lazy ass. You numba ten."

Enjoying the banter from the enormous funny-looking American, she shot back, "Mamasan numba one! Buddha numba ten. Buddha beaucoup fat. No work. Beaucoup lazy!"

Buddha made an exaggerated show of chasing her into the laundry to begin the day.

She was happy working here. The laundry shack had an electric fan, she could help herself to food and ice water from the snack bar, and Buddha, despite his loud accusations and threats, was good to the Vietnamese workers. She also made good money. In addition to her salary, she did sewing for the soldiers, charging what she thought they would pay. She got a cut from embroidered specialty items sold in the laundry. She even got tips from some of the more generous troops.

This day went as every other day normally went. Chi had busy times and times when she sat in front of the fan and watched the rain. She had brought some of her favorite golden-green tea to drink with her lunch. Her friends from the snack bar heated water for her, and joined her to eat. She offered them tea, but they preferred cola.

The afternoon was oppressively hot and humid. Chi tried to stay busy, but she dozed during slow periods, sitting in a comfortable folding chair. At first she was afraid that someone might fire her if they caught her sleeping, but now she realized that no one seemed to care.

At five p.m. the truck came to pick up the workers. The giant drivers made a show of lifting the small women into the bed of the truck, paying a great deal of attention to the younger ones. Chi sat on the board seat as the driver ground through the gears. She smiled at the thought of this huge machine hauling only four small women.

Jace's leave had flown by. In the evenings, he and his father had watched news reports from another war—this one in the middle-east desert. Although it was over in less than a week, it had dominated the TV news, allowing for only scant coverage of Vietnam, usually just the daily casualty figures. Any other time, Jace would have been fascinated by the news specials about the Arabs and Israelis shooting it out, but he had been preoccupied by what he had learned about his father, and by his impending journey half way around the world.

He spent his last full day in Tennessee preparing for his trip. He shined his jungle boots and decided on the few civilian clothes he would take. He packed his faded ranger patrol cap, a small camera, a transistor radio, and his army-green towels, underwear, and socks. He decided to take one extra set of khakis, selected the toilet articles he would need, and packed the five new sets of jungle fatigues he had bought at Fort Bragg before he left. Finally, he cleaned out his wallet, keeping only money and his military identification card.

In the afternoon, he went to the bank in town where he converted his last pay check to travelers' checks and took out a safe-deposit box for his important papers he could not take with him. He had the oil changed in the corvette, got a fresh crew-cut, then drove to his sister's house. After a short but emotional visit, she drove him back to their father's house. She would keep the corvette during the year he would be gone.

When Walton Spencer came home from work, Jace was shining his brass for the uniform he would wear on the trip. His dad said nothing, he just squeezed his son's arm as he passed. As Jace was pinning his parachute wings on the khaki shirt, his dad approached him from behind.

"Take this. It might bring you luck—but I hope you never get in a situation where you have to use it."

Jace turned as his dad handed him a corroded scabbard holding an old fighting knife which Jace recognized at once. It was a K-Bar, the knife issued to combat marines during World War II. Still being manufactured, it was the knife of choice of infantrymen in Vietnam, army and marine alike. He remembered that several of his friends at Fort Bragg carried them on their field gear. Jace had never seen this knife. In fact he had no idea his dad even owned it.

"It ain't regulation in the army. I don't know if they'll let you take it on the plane. I carried it on Guadalcanal and I wish you'd take it—for me."

Jace removed the blade from the scabbard. Although the case and the handle were scratched and scarred, the blade was razor sharp. As he turned the old knife over in his hands, he wondered how all the dents and scrapes had gotten there.

"I'll pack it in my duffle bag. Besides, I doubt if there is anybody big enough to keep me from taking it with me."

He and his father looked at each other for a moment. Then Walton said, "Come on, let's have a beer."

Jace's dad took him to the Tri-cities airport the next day. His sister and her kids were there, and to his surprise, his old girlfriend showed up. Jace was in khakis, bloused and spit-shined jump boots, and garrison cap with paraglide patch. He wouldn't do away with the airborne accouterments until he had to. From the trunk, his dad removed the duffel bag into which Jace had packed everything he would use for the next year. The old K-Bar was wrapped in a shoe-shine cloth and tucked into one of his jungle boots.

The goodbyes were quick and mercifully tearless. Jace hugged his sister and the kids, received a surprisingly passionate kiss from his girlfriend, who obviously did not consider herself in the "old" category anymore, then turned to his father.

"I'll never forget what you told me, Dad," he said.

His father grinned self-consciously, then embraced his son.

"You come back in one piece," whispered Walton Spencer." After losing your mom, I don't think I could stand it if I lost you."

It was uncomfortable for Jace to hear his father speaking so sensitively.

"You got it, Dad," sounded ridiculous, but it was all he could come up with. On impulse, he embraced his girlfriend once more before turning and walking to the plane.

Distracted by the reality of the change in his relationship with his father, the sudden understanding that the young woman he had been dating cared much more for him than he had thought, and the magnitude of going off to war, he was on the ground in Nashville before he realized he had really left. In an emotional fog, he changed planes for Dallas, where he had a brief layover before flying on to San Francisco. After a scenic ride across the bay to the Oakland Army Terminal, he checked into a BOQ room, showered and took a nap. As the sun sank in the Pacific, he sat on the edge of the bed trying to shake himself out of the mood he was in. Deciding he needed a change of scenery, he changed clothes and caught a shuttle bus that took him back across the bay bridge into San Francisco. From the bus station, he caught a taxi to Fisherman's Wharf. He had always heard about the seafood restaurants along the waterfront, and he thought he would give one a try. First, he thought he would have a drink.

As he walked into an exclusive bar overlooking San Francisco's fishing fleet, Jace heard an exuberant "Airborne!" erupt from a chorus of male voices. Turning, he saw his seven buddies from the farewell party at Fort Bragg. Glancing at the bartender, who had a resigned look on his face, Jace knew it would be a long night.

CHAPTER 2

▼

28 June 1967

Lau and his guides stood in the shade near a road junction just outside the village of Hoc Mon, 15 kilometers northwest of Saigon. He was nearing the end of his long and perilous journey, and was becoming more fearful of making a mistake the deeper he got into South Vietnam. Since he and his companions dared not go into town, which was guarded by soldiers and national police, they were waiting for a bus on the outskirts of the village. Although the travelers wore civilian clothes and carried identification cards of government soldiers, they were still nervous. Lau walked with a cane, pretending to be a sergeant on convalescent leave from his unit. Even though his papers were in order, he feared he might be confronted by an ARVN soldier who might know the area around his false home-town. He knew he could not stand up to detailed questioning about a place he had never seen. Suddenly, the people squatting around him began to stand and chatter, as they saw the bus approaching. As it grew nearer, he said goodbye to his senior guide.

"How can I ever repay you for your kindness and your service?" he asked his bodyguard.

"Comrade Colonel, just kill Americans. That will be payment enough."

Lau wished he could properly thank them all, but knew that speaking openly to them in public might put them in danger, so he simply nodded at them as they turned away, and hoped they could feel his indebtedness.

As the ancient vehicle squealed to a stop, a noisy confrontation erupted between the driver and the crowd of would-be travelers. Lau stood in the background and watched and listened carefully. He could see that the bus was already packed full of passengers. What was being negotiated was the price of a place among the luggage on top of the vehicle. The driver listened as an impromptu auction began, the price of transit being bid higher and higher. Some of the crowd drifted away as the cost surpassed their meager funds. The driver accepted money from some and harangued others. Finally Lau managed to work his way to within shouting distance of the driver.

"How much for a wounded soldier?" he shouted.

"For you, the price doubles," the driver scowled. "I know you soldiers are well paid."

Lau was shocked. In the north, soldiers, particularly wounded ones, were revered. Here, this capitalist pig was taking advantage of someone he thought was defending his country. It was outrageous. Lau reached into his knapsack and retrieved the required amount from the cheap plastic wallet that held the pictures of his fake family. As soon as the driver saw the bills, he snatched the piasters from Lau's hand and shot an angry thumb toward the ladder on the back of the bus. Lau climbed past the urine-streaked windows. Roof riders, both men and women often let fly while the bus was in motion. Lau found a place between two enormous bags of what, he did not know. One, at least offered a soft backrest.

The bus was heading to Saigon, and after a short stop there, would continue through Binh Hoa on to Xuan Loc. As he prayed he would not encounter questioning soldiers or police, his fatigue took over and soon he was dozing in the humid mists, rocked to sleep by the movement of the vehicle.

The stop in Saigon was noisy, but eventless. As the bus lumbered down the tree-lined streets, Lau was amazed at the difference between the war-torn north and the capitol of South Vietnam. The streets were clogged with people going about their normal business. Sidewalk restaurants were doing a booming trade, and markets were heaped high with produce and merchandise. Here, there was no evidence a war was going on at all. As they left the city and entered the countryside once more, Lau dozed again.

Passing Binh Hoa, the road paralleled the massive U.S. Army Long Binh compound, where bumps from a series of potholes roused Lau from his nap. The sight of the sprawling base shocked him out of his grogginess. He had no idea the Americans had established themselves here in such magnitude. The size and complexity of the huge base overwhelmed him. Antennas, vehicles, helipads, motor parks, ammunition dumps, hospitals, and barracks buildings went on forever. The bus seemed to drive for several kilometers before finally leaving the hundreds of foreign-looking tin-roofed wooden buildings that were constructed better than those in the adjacent villages. He began to believe the task before him might be more difficult than he had imagined.

Lau no longer carried his packet of maps and orders. Memorized long ago, it had been burned in the Cambodian jungle. In his perch atop the bus, he took a sip of water from his canteen and began to go over the dangerous link-up at Xuan Loc in his mind. His instructions were to be at the central marketplace at noon on the last day of June. Since he didn't know the town, he intended to arrive a day early so he could do a thorough reconnaissance. Where he would sleep, he did not know, and this aspect of the plan worried him. He still had plenty of piasters for food, since he had spent practically nothing during the entire trip down the Ho Chi Minh trail. He guessed that an ARVN sergeant would probably not have enough money to rent a room, even if a hotel existed in Xuan Loc. He did not have a reason to be on leave in Xuan Loc, since his make-believe family was supposed to be in Vinh Long, in the Mekong delta. He would have to come up with a reasonable-sounding story to explain what he was doing so far from home. The only part of the plan he was sure of was that he was to stand in the market place at noon with an ARVN sergeant's fatigue cap atop his walking cane. He would be contacted by a woman who would lead him to the headquarters of the Second Regiment, 5th Viet Cong Division, where he would become senior commissar.

About eight kilometers west of Xuan Loc, the old Mercedes bus slid to a muddy stop at a Regional Forces/Popular Forces outpost where Highway 20 turned northeast to Da Lat. As two men in ragged government uniforms pushed their way out of the interior of the bus, Lau, on an impulse, rushed toward the ladder at the back of the vehicle. He was half way down from the roof when the bus lurched forward. He threw his stick and jumped. His landing made the limp he had affected look a little more authentic. Ignoring the laughter of the RF/PF soldiers, he hobbled off toward town.

Lau spent the afternoon looking for a place to spend the night. He saw nothing that remotely resembled a hotel, so he searched for a sign indicating a room for rent. After a while, it became obvious that without asking someone, he would not be able to find a place to stay. As he familiarized himself with the market place and slurped a bowl of noodles at a street stand, he decided that inquiring about a room would probably be too dangerous. Not wanting to be seen hanging around too long at the place of the link up, and having no other plan, he began walking south down Highway 1.

As the sun sank lower over the jungles, he found himself confused and alone. Not knowing what else to do, and seeing no one on the road for a stretch, he simply walked off into the jungle. He moved about fifty meters away from the highway through the tangled vegetation, then stopped and looked around. After a minute or two, he found a thicket so dense that no one could possibly walk through it. Deciding to make himself a hideout, he took his time working his way into the tangled vegetation. Ignoring scratches and cuts, stooping, crawling and closing the vines and brush behind him as he went, he pushed his way deeper and deeper into the thicket. When he was close to the center of the briar patch, he began to work his way toward the ground. In a squat, He began to break off the smaller limbs and branches, pushing them to the side. Most of the saplings and vines were easy to pull out of the rain-soaked jungle floor.

In a few minutes, Lau had succeeded in clearing a space large enough for him to hang his hammock. From his knapsack, he took a tattered piece of plastic sheeting and the worn mosquito net, which had protected him throughout his journey. He carefully hung his hammock inside the mosquito net, and then tied the plastic inches above it all for a crude shelter. He had no food, but he had water. He hoped he was close enough to the road to avoid random artillery and mortars fired nightly by the Americans and the Army of the Republic of Vietnam, known to the Americans as ARVN. He also hoped that no ground troops would patrol this close to a major town. Having no way of knowing anything for sure, he just had a feeling he was safer here in the jungle than in the capitol of Long Khanh province. As evening approached, rain began to pound hard on the thicket. While he relieved himself, Lau watched the ground leeches inch-worming their way toward him. Depressed, lonely and afraid, he climbed into his makeshift shelter where he would spend the next two nights.

Jace was awakened by the captain speaking over the intercom.

"We have begun our descent into Bien Hoa. We'll be on the ground in approximately forty minutes, provided they have fixed the holes in the runway— just a joke, guys. The local time is 1820 on the 28th of June—remember the International Date Line. The weather in the Bien Hoa area is fair to partly rainy and 92 degrees."

Jace put the airline pillow aside and slid up the window shade. He couldn't see anything yet. There was nothing below but a solid white covering of clouds. Above, the sun burned in the thin, blue air. Jace made his way back to the lavatory where he dry-shaved, toweled off his face, and ran his hands through his crew cut. Then he went over his belt buckle with a blitz cloth and his boots with toilet tissue and did his best to straighten up his uniform. He didn't like to be seen looking like a bum.

He returned to his seat and tried to read another chapter in the paperback he had brought. It got darker in the 707 when it nosed into the clouds, and with nothing but gray outside to look at, Jace tried his book again. A sudden thud of turbulence made him look out the window as the airliner dropped out of the cloud cover somewhere over the northern corner of the Mekong delta.

It was the harshest view Jace had ever seen from an aircraft. The angry lid of dark clouds was broken only by a yellowish slash across the horizon to the west. Rain streaked the window as he pressed his face to the scratched Plexiglas for a better view. The terrain below was gray-green and pockmarked by water-filled orange craters, some in lines, some in clusters, but most strewn randomly across the endless flats. Dark tendrils of vegetation and muddy canals crisscrossed the rice paddies, which mirrored the gray-brown clouds. In the distance an air strike was working over one of the olive-colored treelines. It was too far away for him to identify the aircraft, but they were swarming around a smoky swath of ground like angry hornets. Twice he saw yellow flashes of bombs or napalm rip the treeline the jets were pounding. The lower, slower dot circling the conflagration would be the forward air controller, Jace knew.

Sampans went about their business on the rivers and canals below, oblivious of the battle raging a few miles away. Small military craft plied to and fro between junks and sampans. Helicopters slid noiselessly beneath the airliner as they went about their chores, no doubt carrying supplies, troops, staff officers or generals about the battlefield.

As the 707 settled lower, the rice paddies became less pock-marked. Roads bustled with pedestrians and vehicles of every type. Villages of yellow stucco-walled houses with tin, thatched or red-tiled roofs lined both sides of every main road. Off to the right was the enormous dirty smudge that was Saigon. In the adjacent river, freighters and tankers rode at anchor near busy docks.

The airliner made an easy bank to the right, crossing a wide brown river as the flaps and gear were lowered with whines and bumps. Jace watched, fascinated, as the huge silver wings sailed over a sea of people in round hats who were walking, riding motor bikes, and pedaling bicycles of every size and description. Dirty-white cathedrals with square churchyards were islands in the maze of back alleys, shacks and businesses that made up the city of Bien Hoa. All at once the shanties were gone, replaced by grass, lights, beacons and gray, striped concrete. The 707 touched down.

The captain came on again: "Welcome to Bien Hoa Air Base in the Republic of Vietnam. It has been a pleasure and a privilege to serve you. On behalf of the entire crew, I'd like to wish you success and above all health and safety. We hope we are the crew to fly you home one year from today. God Speed."

As the plane turned off the runway and taxied to a parking ramp adjacent to the cluster of tin-roofed sheds that served as a terminal, a gun-jeep rolled along beside them. Jace noticed that a live belt hung from the M-60. As they braked to a stop, he turned his attention to the nearest shed. Perhaps two hundred soldiers clutching carry-on bags and boarding passes were cheering wildly. It warmed his heart to think these soldiers were cheering for their replacements. Jace was a believer in team spirit.

The door was opened and the line of troops ahead of him in the aisle began to shuffle forward. Jace thanked the stewardess and turned toward the open door. As he stepped onto the mobile stairs, he was met by a stench that took the air out of him. Carried on the hot, steamy breeze, the combined aromas of open sewers, rotting plants, putrid mud, and thousands of other scents wafting from humans packed into crowded, urban slums assaulted him. He gagged.

The debarking troops were led without ceremony toward a line of army busses. As they passed the shed where the veterans awaited permission to board their 707, they were met by a hoarse chorus of male voices. Jace realized that the cheering he had thought was for the incoming soldiers was actually for the plane—the plane that would take these veterans home. And what he had thought were cheers were vile jeers and catcalls.

"So long, suckers! Tell Charlie I said bye! I'll tell your mamma I saw you the day before you died! War may be hell, but you gonna find out actual combat is a real mother, fool!"

These insults, accompanied by obscene gestures, pelted the newcomers as they streamed toward the busses. Most of the arrivees were so tired they didn't care, but some part of Jace took the jeers to heart.

A hell of a welcome, he thought. He remembered how at Bragg, units of the 82nd were in constant competition. But there was also a professional courtesy and respect that resulted from working daily to accomplish the same mission. Sure, paratroopers, whether officer or enlisted, ragged each other with ribald insults born from unit rivalries, but nothing he had ever heard on Ardennes Street equaled the vitriolic diatribe that was now being hurled at the newcomers.

Without thinking, Jace searched the unruly crowd of departees for the airborne soldiers. He identified them by their bloused boots and paraglide patches on their garrison caps. They were as surly as the others. As Jace turned back to join the throng of arrivees, he was aware of a subtle change. The bond he had always treasured with other airborne soldiers seemed to have been broken. The paratroopers in the rowdy crowd waiting to board the plane did not seem to care that there were jumpers in the planeload of replacements. To Jace their shouts were affirming a new truth—they were veterans and survivors, a cut above the poor bastards who had just landed. Just as the day Jace had arrived at Fort Bragg, he was a novice, a cherry once more. Here he would have to prove himself all over again. The silver jump wings on his chest and the yellow-and-black ranger tab on his left shoulder meant nothing. He was not even sure his captain's bars meant anything here.

The travel-worn troops piled onto the waiting busses. Windows were covered by wire mesh, which Jace supposed was to keep grenades out. He worried that in an emergency, the chicken wire might keep those inside from getting out as well. A military policeman stood in the front of the bus with an M-14. Jace saw only one magazine for the rifle, the one in the weapon. After their baggage was piled on a pair of 2 ½-ton trucks, the busses rolled out through the narrow streets for the short drive to the sprawling Long Binh complex that bordered Bien Hoa.

As the convoy turned off the highway, through the gates of Long Binh and the 90th Replacement Company, the new reality that had hit Jace at the air base continued to tug at his confidence. The welcome the newcomers got was hollow and scripted. Bags were thrown off the trucks into the rain as a master sergeant, at the top of his lungs, told the officers to find their belongings and follow a lieutenant to their briefing area. By the time Jace had found his bag, he was wet to the bone and it was getting dark.

The briefing bay was a concrete pad with a sheet-metal roof. Bags were piled in the back and the officers found seats on folding chairs. An Adjutant General lieutenant, who looked to be about seventeen years old, began the briefing. The officers were assigned buildings and bunks and told where the mess hall and the officers' club were located. The lieutenant told the new officers not to wander around too much because the ARVN soldiers who guarded the perimeter were not too trustworthy—sometimes there was random shooting from their bunkers. Also, he said he had heard there were minefields out there somewhere. After the briefing, the lieutenant asked if there were any questions. Jace raised his hand.

"Who do I talk to about changing my assignment?" he asked.

The lieutenant switched to another mode of speech, like a tape recorder that had played the same tape so many times it was nearly worn out.

"If your orders assign you to the 90th Replacement Company, your in-country assignment will be placed on the bulletin board within 72 hours. No requests for changes can be made until the orders are posted. You can make your request through the orderly room clerk, but I can warn you that you should not expect your orders to be changed. If your orders assign you to a specific unit in country, no changes can be made here. You must make your request for reassignment through your G-1 once you arrive at your unit. Any other questions?"

The answer plunged Jace further into depression. It looked more and more like his fate was sealed. He sat motionless as other questions were asked. When the briefing was over, he shouldered his bag and slogged up the hill toward the clapboard barracks building were he had been assigned a bunk. He did not even try to find out about sheets and pillows. He pulled his poncho liner out of his bag, stripped to his shorts and piled into bed, using his rolled-up civilian clothes for a pillow.

Jace did not know how long he had been asleep when a huge boom shook him awake. It was dark and for a moment he did not know where he was. Still groggy, he looked out the large screened area that served as the upper half of the barracks wall. The only sign of activity was a pair of parachute flares hanging low on the distant horizon. Again, a huge boom rocked the building. Jace realized where he was—in Vietnam! He had enough experience with mortars and artillery in training to know the sharp crump made by exploding shells. By the third boom, he had figured out that the sounds were made by out-going artillery from a nearby battery. No one in the company area seemed to notice or be concerned by the sound, so he lay down and tried to get back to sleep.

He slept fitfully the rest of the night and awakened at dawn. Despite the fact that he had a full night's sleep, he felt exhausted, no doubt the result of jet lag. He found his shower clogs and a towel and looked for the shower, which turned out to be a huge tank of cold water above a long screened-in stall. After shaving and showering, He dressed in his new jungle fatigues and boots and set off in search of a cup of coffee.

Sitting on the bench of a picnic table in the ubiquitous clapboard, tin-roofed, concrete-floored building—this one used as a mess hall—Jace tumbled further into depression. Not only was he bound for a straight-leg division in Vietnam, his confidence had been shaken by his father, he understood that he was a novice here, and he was absolutely alone. He sipped his coffee, not feeling like eating.

The screen door slammed and Jace looked up. Walking into the mess hall was an infantry captain, clad in worn-out jungle fatigues and scuffed jungle boots, and carrying his helmet with its faded camouflage cover under his left arm. His load-bearing equipment hung easily from his shoulders, unbuckled. On his left shoulder, beneath his ranger tab, was the winged bayonet patch of the Sky Soldiers, the 173rd Airborne Brigade. With a shout Jace jumped to his feet. He recognized Rusty Doyle, a West Pointer and one of his ranger classmates. He was the grandest sight Jace had seen in a long time.

"Well I'll be!" Doyle said as he pumped Jace's hand. "Haven't seen you since ranger graduation—when was that? November of '64?"

"I guess so," said Jace. "Damn, it's good to see a familiar face."

"When did you get here?" Doyle asked.

"Sometime yesterday. My body clock is all screwed up"

"Yeah, it'll take you a week or so to get your days and nights straightened out." Jace went for a refill and Rusty Doyle poured himself a cup.

"What's your job in the 173rd?" asked Jace.

"I got a company in the second batt."

"Then you made the jump during Operation Junction City in February?" asked Jace.

"Yeah, they called it a combat jump, but it was really just an experiment to see if we could get a battalion on the ground as quickly by parachute as by helicopter. As far as I could tell it was a tie. Anyway, I got a combat-jump star on my wings." explained Doyle.

"How long have you had the company?" Jace asked.

"Three months. I'll try to hang in there for at least two more, then go to the 'three shop. There'll be a battle for the S-3 air slot. Three of the five company commanders turn over at the same time. Seems like you no sooner learn your job and you're gone—but I guess everyone has to have his chance to excel. Most guys only have four or five months to make a name for themselves on the line. Getting a combat company command efficiency report is getting mighty hard. Where you being assigned?" asked Doyle, leaning to see the patch on Jace's left sleeve.

"Ninth high-speed, long-range straight-leg division," answered Jace with an attempt at humor he did not feel.

"Ninth? Listen, that's no damn good. Do you know what they do? They operate off of boats in the delta like jar-heads. I hear their feet get so bad from wading in the swamps and paddies they have to dry out a week for every three days they're in the bush. Can you imagine creeping down those narrow canals in second-world-war landing craft? Just inviting an ambush. No, you need to try to get the hell out of there. The delta ain't where it's happening, anyway. We make more contact with Charlie in a week up north than leg units around Saigon do in a month. All the big battles are in the highlands. Don't you read the papers?"

"What do you think my chances would be if I tried to get to the 173rd?" Jace asked hopefully.

"Somewhere between poor and none." said Doyle, sipping his coffee. "The entire West Point class of '66 is in the herd. Every platoon leader is a West Pointer. We have so many officers that some platoons even have a lieutenant as an assistant platoon leader. Captains are stacked three deep. Officers' calls look like a West Point founder's-day dinner. You probably know every officer in the brigade. Most of them came from the 82nd."

"Why are you all so fat in officers?" asked Jace.

"What unit did you want when you got orders?"

"The 173rd, the One-O-One, First Cav, of course."

"Well, so did everyone else—except they've got sponsors."

"Sponsors?"

"Yeah—Don't you know someone who'll make a phone call or write a letter for you—a general or a congressman?" Doyle was studying Jace's face.

"No, I don't reckon I do." answered Jace, "and I'm not sure I'd ask them to if I did."

"Why the hell not? Everyone else does. You need to be aware of how the politics of assignments works. I've always heard you need a brother-in-law who is an assignment officer at branch. I guess I found out here that you need an uncle that is a three-star."

"Did you have a sponsor to get you here?" Jace asked.

"No, I just got orders. I guess I was lucky."

"Changing the subject, what are you doing here at the 90th Replacement Company?" Jace asked.

"Oh, I had to bring a prisoner down to the Long Binh Jail—the LBJ. It has a nice ring to it, huh? A sergeant from my company was court-martialed for throwing a grenade in a whorehouse when he didn't like the service he got. Killed two whores. We're standing down and I thought I'd get out of Dodge for a day or so. S-1 asked if I'd stop by the 90th repple depple to see if we had any replacements I could bring straight back. We get 'em quicker that way—and God knows we need 'em. Casualties have been high."

"How long are you gonna be here?" asked Jace. "Maybe we could get together for a beer tonight. There're plenty of empty bunks in my barracks building."

"Wish I could," said Doyle getting up for a refill. "A C-130 is leaving at 1130 going up-country. It's a local milk run. Have to make two stops before we get to Pleiku. I just stopped in for a cup of coffee. I was lucky to get to see you. I've got just enough time to get over to the orderly room and round up our replacements."

Doyle thought for a moment.

"Listen, you remember Joey Sorrell from ranger school? His dad is the XO of the airborne brigade in the first cav. He's the only one I know that smacks in any way like a horse you could hitch your wagon to. You might call him or write him a letter. Let him know you're a friend of Joey's and you'd love to serve in the First Cav. Might be worth a try. The Hundred and First is as crowded with captains as the herd is. The third brigade of the Cav is the only airborne unit I know of that might have a slot open. Give Colonel Sorrell a call. He might help you. The First Cavalry is a fine division. Look I gotta go. Drop me a line. Let me jot down the address. Stay in touch—we'll have that beer yet."

Doyle wrote down his address on a napkin, dumped his coffee dregs and slid the empty cup to the Vietnamese woman washing dishes.

Jace said, "I'll walk over to the orderly room with you. Maybe you can show me how to call the cav."

"Sure," said Doyle. "It may look complicated, but once you get the hang of it, you'll be calling all over country."

In the orderly room, Doyle scanned the list for 173rd replacements. He saw there were fourteen and sent a runner to round them up. Then Doyle showed Jace how to place the call to the First Cavalry Division at An Khe. The call had to be routed through Long Bien, Xuan Loc, Phan Thiet, Cam Ranh Bay, Nha Trang, Tuy Hoa, Qui Nhon, An Khe, and finally to the division switch board. Each city had an army switch board manned by a Vietnamese operator trained by American signal corps advisors. They were taught to ask, "Have you finished, have you finished?" before disconnecting a call. Having learned the form, but not the substance of the technique, they didn't seem to understand that they had to listen for a second before breaking the connection.

As he picked up the phone and waited for the Long Binh operator to answer, Jace shook hands with Doyle and waved goodbye.

"Working! Working! Don't cut me off!" he screamed. Once, he was put all the way through to Qui Nhon before the operator there didn't hear him yelling and pulled the plug.

Jace started all over again.

"Long Bien, this is 90th Replacement, give me Xuan Loc. Hello Xuan Loc, give me Phan Thiet. Phan Thiet, give me—"

"Damn, cut off again."

The company clerk, a specialist with a surly attitude, said, "Sir, you can't tie up my phone all morning. I've got incoming calls I'm expecting."

Jace banged down the receiver. He was beginning to feel like the call to Joey Sorrell's dad had about the same chance of success as a snowball here in Long

Binh. His depression now took on an edge. He slammed the screen door of the orderly room as he left. Thoroughly disgusted, he walked over to the bulletin board, almost a building itself. Built from a piece of 4'X 8' plywood, it had its own roof to keep the papers tacked on it out of the monsoon rains.

There always seemed to be a crowd around the structure. Stuck to the bulletin board by government-issue thumb tacks, fate, whether cruel or serendipitous, awaited each arrivee. The luck of the draw, a position on an alphabetized list, or a call from a "sponsor" placed names on orders to places where, in a day, a week, or a month a bullet waited—or didn't wait. Who knew? Who wanted to know? The whole assignment process seemed to Jace like choosing a parachute from the back of a truck. Was this one packed right? How about this one? Had he put back a good one in favor of one that would fail to open? That's why Jace always took the first one he put his hand on. It had as good a chance of being packed right and opening properly as all the others. It was impossible, and probably bad luck, to try to pick and choose. He suddenly got the feeling that orders were the same way. Why try to get to the cav where a bullet might be waiting for him the first week? The same fate might await him—or might not—in the 9th division.

As he scanned the board, the loud-speaker on the corner of the orderly room blared: "Anyone needing transportation to the 9th Infantry Division at Bear Cat, report to the orderly room at this time."

Jace hurried back to the screen door he had just slammed in the clerk's face. Standing outside was a young sergeant wearing a helmet and web gear and holding a clipboard. He wore a 9th-division patch on his shoulder.

Jace said, "I'm going to the 9th. Do I have to sign out of the 90th Replacement?"

"May I see your orders, please sir?" asked the sergeant. He glanced at the rumpled paper Jace produced and said, "No sir, your orders assign you straight to the division. All you have to do is get your bag."

To Jace's surprise, the troops bound for Bear Cat, the base camp of the 9th division, were all piled on the backs of four two-and-a-half-ton trucks, each with an armed guard riding shotgun. An MP gun jeep led them out of the 90th Replacement Company's gate. As on the bus ride from the air base, Jace thought the small convoy didn't have much protection. Just as he had begun to think Bear Cat might be a part of the sprawling Long Binh base, the trucks headed out of a gate manned by ARVN guards. The gray skies of the rainy season still made everything look gloomy, but the countryside here looked and smelled cleaner. As they got farther and farther from the slums of Bien Hoa, the air lost the pervasive, offensive odors. Jace realized he had gotten used to the smell that had nearly knocked him down at first.

The road opened into rice paddies surrounded by small jungled hills. Here and there, red-tiled villas, probably rich farmers' homes, sat in groves of palm trees. The rice plants were a vivid green, almost chartreuse, the jungle beyond, an exotic darker shade. The only signs of war on Highway 15 were the Regional Forces/Popular Forces, known as Ruff-Puffs by G.I.s, who guarded all of the bridges they crossed. Soon, Jace began to relax and enjoy the scenery. There didn't seem to be any reason to worry. If more security were needed, they would no doubt have had it. Unarmed except for his father's K-Bar fighting knife in his duffel bag, there was nothing he could if they were shot at anyway.

As the trucks turned left onto a wide dirt road, the MPs in the gun jeep waved and continued south on Highway 15. After a mile or so, Bear Cat came into view. A six-foot-high dirt berm, accented every few yards by bunkers covered by sand bags, stretched off into the distance on each side of the road. The base was much larger than he had anticipated. Behind the berm, unpainted wooden build-ings were a dark yellow-blond color, streaked by red mud. There was no grass anywhere, only red-orange laterite clay. Rising over the entire camp were col-umns of black smoke, which made the low, gray clouds even more threatening. The trucks were waved through the main gate under a plywood arch that read: **THE OLD RELIABLES—FROM KANSAS.**

As the trucks pulled up in front of a series of the now-familiar wooden build-ings, Jace wondered where all the smoke was coming from and if perhaps there had been a mortar attack. A large sign reading **9th Division Replacement Detachment** stood among sand-bagged trenches and bunkers adjacent to the road. After everyone had jumped from the trucks, a guide came and took the enlisted men away. Then the sergeant with the clipboard led Jace, the only officer, to G-1 in-processing. After turning over his 201 file, he was led to finance where he arranged to keep a hundred dollars a month, sending the rest of his pay check to his sister to put in the bank for him. Then he was then taken to the G-1 for his assignment.

Jace waited patiently, while the sergeant with the clipboard brought him a cup of coffee.

"What's all the smoke from?" Jace asked.

"Burning shit," the sergeant answered. "Ain't no sewer system here, so we pull the barrels out from under the outhouses and dump gasoline mixed with diesel fuel into them and burn it. Not a pleasant duty—but I guess it's the only sanitary way of getting rid of it."

Jace grinned. Some mortar attack, he thought as he sat and sipped his coffee. Presently, a lieutenant colonel came out of an office and offered his hand.

"Welcome to the Old Reliables," said the colonel. "Airborne, huh? We don't get many of your kind here—and a ranger to boot. Well, well. Some battalion commander will sure as hell be glad to get you."

"Thank you, sir. I was wondering—"

"Let me tell you a little about the division. Sit down. Take a load off. We came from Fort Riley, Kansas. We landed in Vung Tau, south of here on the coast last December. We've been here about six months. That's why you're here. You're the first of a bunch of officer replacements that will be running the division when all of us go home this December."

"This is the division base camp, but you'll find the majority of the combat units are down at Dong Tam in the delta, or out on the ships that form the MRF—the Mobile Riverine Force. It's a new concept. Army troops aboard navy ships. Looks like a marine mission to me. Why we're down here and the marines are doing a traditional army mission up north is a mystery."

"Sir," Jace interrupted, "May I—"

"A lot of this division was formed by national guard troops who volunteered for active duty. The majority of the soldiers are draftees. You'll find the NCO's are not what you might expect. Where did you come from?"

"Fort Bragg, sir. I commanded a company in the 82nd."

"Damn. The battalions will be fighting over you! What did you want to ask?"

Here it was—Jace's last chance to request a transfer. He thought of pulling a parachute off of the truck. Was it the right one? Would the battalion where he would be assigned be the right one? He thought of what Rusty Doyle had said—you only have a short time to make a name for yourself. Was that what was important? No, the troops were what was important. He thought of the advice his dad had given him, and the admonition to come home to him. Survival had to be more important than making a professional reputation, didn't it? Hell yes! It had to be. If that's the case, then it came down to taking the first parachute that you put your hand on. One infantry battalion was probably like another. In his prejudiced mind, paratroop volunteers were better soldiers than draftees. But there wasn't a thing he could do to influence any of that now. No, he would not try to change his fate. He would take the parachute that was offered.

"Sir, I was just going to ask which battalion would offer me a better chance to command a company right away."

"Let's look at the manning board," said the G-1.

They both studied the chart silently for a moment—the G-1 looking for empty slots, Jace looking for names he knew. None were familiar.

"Looks like the fifth of the 39th Mech."

"Mech?"

"Yeah, when we came over, each brigade had a mechanized battalion, but when the second brigade went on the boats in the delta, their mech battalion, the fifth of the 39th, stayed at Bear Cat. Now it's in the first brigade. The fifth of the 60th is in the third brigade down at Tan An, and the second of the 47th is division reserve. Right now, they're also here at Bear Cat."

Jace had not considered the possibility of mechanized infantry. He had not been near an M-113 armored personnel carrier since the combined arms exercise in the basic course at Fort Benning. He didn't know squat about the steel and aluminum monsters. Suddenly he was overwhelmed by the same feeling he had had driving through the Carolina mountains—that he was no longer in control of his fate.

As he continued his in-processing and as the afternoon wore on, Jace remembered he had eaten nothing all day. The sergeant with the clipboard was nowhere to be found so an Adjutant General captain who was an assistant G-1 drove him down to the jungle operations school, where he would spend the next week learning how things were done in the 9th division. He took a bunk, stowed his bag and went to chow with the AG captain. The food was different—mostly dehydrated B-ration meat, called MOUO (meat of unknown origin) by the troops, canned vegetables, white bread and kool-aid. It was not great, but it filled him up.

After saying thanks to the assistant G-1, Jace was on his own again. Still jet lagged and dead tired, he decided to go to the officers' club for a beer. Walking down the road, it came to him that except for tactical operations in the field, he had never had to walk anywhere before. His corvette had served him well while he was off duty and his jeep with driver had always been standing by at the company area at Bragg. As he neared the division officers' club, his mood was still dark.

The club was empty except for a large table surrounded by loud, mostly drunk captains and lieutenants. Jace went to the bar and ordered a beer. He sat and listened. After a moment, he surmised the young officers were replacements like him. When they mentioned the week-long course at the jungle operations school, Jace decided it was time he joined them. He looked them over first. There were four lieutenants and three captains, all infantrymen and one captain of artillery. There was not a ranger tab or pair of jump wings among them. Jace walked over.

"I take it y'all are FNG's too." said Jace.

"Unfortunately, sir, that seems to be the case." said a lieutenant.

"Hell yeah we're new!" shouted a drunk captain. "Sit down, by all means, sit DOWN! We're in the midst of deciding which is the safest, easiest and quietest way to spend a year in this lovely place."

They introduced themselves all around. A teen-aged lieutenant asked Jace where he was coming from. Jace was proud and pleased at their reaction when he told them he had been at Bragg. Jace learned that the majority of the new officers were going to the second brigade, the Mobile Riverine Force, in the delta. The artillery captain was to be assigned as liaison officer with the 2-47 Mech at Bear Cat. They all would begin the jungle operations course two days hence. There seemed to be nothing to do until then. Jace decided he'd try to make some friends. God knows he needed them.

Lau crawled carefully from his hideout. He had awakened after the sun was up, and carefully packed his knapsack. He had left the sleeping mat and the plastic sheet where they were, not wanting to be caught with them in his pack. Once he was clear of the dense thicket, he stood, stretched and checked himself carefully. It took several moments to pull the last of the leeches from his waist and ankles. His mosquito net had kept out the flying insects. Unfortunately, he had learned that the thicket in which he had hidden was infested with huge, red ants. As a result, his head, neck and arms were covered with ugly welts. As the insects had attacked, he had thought of moving, but had considered it too dangerous. Instead he suffered and endured. He guessed at what he must look like. Perhaps spending two nights and days in the jungle might have been a mistake. He did not want his appearance to call attention to him in Xuan Loc.

He crawled to the edge of the road, looked up and down, and when finding a gap in the traffic, stepped out and headed toward town. When the highway crossed a small stream, Lau went down to wash his shirt and his tortured body. It didn't matter that he couldn't dry himself, since during the rainy season, everything stayed soaking wet anyway.

Jace awoke at 0800, feeling as if he were in an oven. The sheet-metal roof above him buckled and popped in the heat as sunlight streamed through the cracks in the board building. He arose, showered and shaved, then headed to the mess hall. His companions from the previous evening were all there, all of them crumpled and a couple unshaven, drinking coffee. Jace joined them, saying noth-ing, but not approving of the way they looked. It was all right to raise hell, he thought. But come morning, an officer had to look like an officer.

The same line of conversation began over breakfast that had been beaten to death the night before—survival statistics, the safest jobs, how to avoid getting killed etc. Jace listened for about ten minutes, then headed out. He wanted to find the headquarters of the Fifth Battalion, 39th Infantry.

Stopping by G-1 for directions, Jace walked toward his new battalion head-quarters. He had already been told that the battalion was in the field, out near Xuan Loc, wherever the hell that was, and that no one was likely to be at the rear headquarters but some clerks and bottle-washers. But Jace didn't care, he just needed to do something—to get started. It was a half-mile walk down to the bat-talion area. The sunlight was gone again, replaced once more by dark skies, rain, heat and humidity. The miserable weather seemed to fit his mood perfectly.

The Fifth Battalion, 39th Infantry, when it was in the base camp, resided in a cluster of buildings that, for the most part, looked like all the rest Jace had seen since he arrived. The company streets, however, were formed by GP medium tents stretched over wooden frames. The structures had wooden floors, screened-in sides, and screen doors. Sand bags were piled waist-high to protect sleepers inside from fragments in the event of a nighttime mortar attack. Wooden shipping pallets formed walkways in the mud. Metal piss-tubes, designed to keep soldiers from urinating anywhere and everywhere, extended from the ground near the latrines.

Jace found the headquarters building and walked in. It was mostly deserted. An NCO, a clerk and a couple of walking wounded were the only people he saw. He was about to approach the sergeant when a tall, beefy major walked out of an office. He looked at Jace for a long moment.

"May I help you?" he asked.

"Sir, I am Captain Spencer, newly assigned to this battalion."

"Man, am I ever glad to see you!" said the major.

Happily, Jace saw master parachutist's wings on his fatigues.

"I'm the S-3, Colin Churchwell. My friends all call me C.C. You can call me sir." grinned the major as he offered Jace his hand.

"Sir, my name is Jason. My friends all call me Jace."

"When the battalion commander sees your qualifications, he may call you sir! When did you get here? Where did you come from? When do we get our hands on you?"

"Day before yesterday, Fort Bragg, and as soon as I finish something called the jungle operations school at division." answered Jace, already liking Major Churchwell.

"Well, you're lucky you caught me. I came in for the division briefing last night, and I'm on my way back to the field. I catch a chopper at noon. Get on in here. Raines, get us some coffee!"

Once he had made himself as presentable as he could, Lau had walked along the highway back to Xuan Loc. At a street vendor's stall, he ate a bowl of noodles, a bowl of rice and two cups of tea, his first food in two days. Since he didn't have a watch, he would have to guess at when noon was. After his meal, he walked around the market, pretending to look for something to buy.

Lau was fascinated by the market and the amount of food for sale here in the south. Northern markets stayed empty most of the time, a result, he supposed, of the American bombing. But here, rice, vegetables, fish, charcoal, and cooking oil, as well as ducks, chickens and pigs—both alive and dead—were offered for sale by noisy vendors. Merchants squatted behind wooden slabs that served as counters built only inches off the ground. Raw and prepared foods of all types were heaped high on the low counters. Everything that could not be sold fresh each day was simply scraped off into huge compost heaps at each end of the counters to rot. Fresh produce was brought out beside the rancid piles each day.

The market was covered by corrugated roofing held up by poles. The rain dripped through holes in the roof continuously so the vendors held umbrellas over themselves as they squatted, chatted and sipped tea. Clouds of flies swarmed over the refuse heaps and the produce. Around the square surrounding the market, food booths and bars selling Beer 33, the local brew, abounded. Behind these booths, in the buildings that lined the market, a thriving black market sold Japanese radios and tape recorders, gasoline, American cigarettes, beer, whiskey, and canned foods. G.I. C-rations, insect repellant, flashlights, batteries and all sorts of other goods were stacked high, the asking prices exorbitant. Lau thought how good a beer would taste—it had been over a year since he had drunk one. He had drunk only a little rice wine in Svey Reing, the last city he had stopped at in Cambodia. In the back of one of the shops he saw a clock showing that it was only ten thirty in the morning. He decided to have that beer.

As he sat down at a stool in the street facing the makeshift bar, he realized he had a perfect vantage point. He would not have to walk around, calling attention to himself. He ordered his beer, paid, and glanced about. In the north everything had a purpose. Every movement, every activity, every bicycle trip, everything had a reason for happening. There were only two reasons for doing anything—personal survival and to serve the state. One didn't just take a Sunday afternoon off and go to the park. In North Vietnam, American war planes and the war effort had made leisure time a thing of the past. People in the north moved with a purpose.

Here, where the war was supposedly raging, people went about their daily lives as if nothing at all were unusual. They came and went, shopped, ate, drank and talked. ARVN soldiers ambled in twos and threes about the shops, smoking and laughing. Watching the easy pace of the town, Lau began to ask himself if his worries about being stopped and questioned were overblown. Sipping his warm beer slowly and enjoying it immensely, he observed that everyone was ignoring him. He watched the crowds, even said hello to an old man, and felt more relaxed than he had in months. This was supposed to be the critical stage of his journey, but nothing felt threatening at all. Feeling more at ease, he opened his knapsack, took out the sergeant's fatigue cap, and placed it on his cane.

At 11:45, he scanned the streets, starting to look for his contact. Draining the bottle and feeling the beer, he started at the unexpected tap on his shoulder. He turned, expecting to see the woman that was supposed to meet him, but instead looked into the faces of two national policemen. Immediately he knew that his expression had betrayed him, now he fought to regain composure.

"Good day, sir," said the shorter of the two policemen. We are checking for deserters. I can see you are a serviceman. Are you on furlough?

"Yes, sir," said Lau. "I am on convalescent leave from my unit. I am here to visit a cousin and his family since my medical treatment brought me near Xuan Loc." Lau repeated the cover story he had decided on and gone over in his mind so many times.

"What is your unit, please?" asked the taller one.

"I am assigned to the 21st division near Can Tho."

Whoever had planned his cover had cleverly picked a unit too far from Xuan Loc to be easily queried about the authenticity of his papers.

"How did you come to travel so far from your unit?" the shorter one asked.

"I have been in the hospital in Saigon. When I was released I caught a bus to Xuan Loc to visit my relatives. I have two weeks remaining on my leave."

"May we see your identification and furlough papers, please?"

"Of course, sir." Lau reached into his knapsack and withdrew his wallet and his papers, which were wrapped in a scrap piece of plastic. He handed them to the shorter policeman.

The taller policeman had been eyeing him carefully.

"Sir, if you do not mind my asking, how did you get all of those scratches and insect bites on your body?

Lau opened his mouth to answer. This question had caught him off guard. His heart was in his throat. He had no idea what he was going to say. "I was—"

"So there you are!"

Lau and the two policemen turned as a striking young woman wearing a conical hat smiled at them. She wore sandals and the *ao dai*, traditional black pajama pants worn under a long, white tunic, which was split up the sides to the waist. Her long, jet-black hair fell over her shoulders. Her unusually large eyes sparkled with confidence. Lau, badly shaken, said nothing.

"Did you find what you were looking for?" she asked, opening the recognition procedure.

"No, I could not find a camera in all the market that I could afford," said Lau, regaining enough composure to answer her with the correct countersign.

"Good day, gentlemen," she bowed to the policemen. "My cousin is allergic to mosquito bites. It takes only a small insect to inflict great pain on him." She looked back at Lau.

"Come with me, then, I know a shop where we can look."—the next part of the recognition code.

Lau looked at the policemen who were now leering at the woman. He quickly blurted the last part of the code: "I hope I have enough money left if we find one."

"If you gentlemen have finished with my cousin, we must hurry. He does not have much leave time left and we want to take some pictures he can take back to his family in Vinh Long."

The policemen handed the identification card and leave papers back to Lau. They returned their attention to the woman who was smiling demurely. They bowed and said, "Good day", and walked on. The policeman who had asked about his condition looked over his shoulder and said something to his companion, who laughed. Lau didn't know whether they were talking about him or the woman. He just wanted to get out of here as quickly as possible.

"Where do we go?" Lau asked under his breath.

"To buy a camera, of course," answered the young woman.

During the next two hours, Jace learned about Major Churchwell, the battalion, and some of the operations it had been on. Jace told the major about commanding in the 82nd, and that he wanted a command as soon as possible. The major became expansive and excited, telling Jace about the capabilities of the M-113 armored personnel carrier.

As they talked, Jace learned that Churchwell was married and had two daughters, was a graduate of Ohio State, had been in the army for ten years and was a graduate of officer candidate school. He had been a company commander in the 101st Airborne at Fort Campbell. After the advanced course at the infantry school at Benning, Churchwell had spent a year in Vietnam with MACV as an advisor to a battalion. He had just finished the Command and General Staff College at Fort Leavenworth, Kansas before coming back to Vietnam for his present tour. Jace also learned that Churchwell loved to read military history. For the first time since he got orders to the 9th Division, Jace had found someone he felt he could talk to.

"Damn, look at the time." Churchwell said. "I've got a chopper to catch. Come on—ride down to the airfield with me. I'd take you out to meet the old man, but he'd kill me bringing you out there before you finish jungle school. Look, I'll do what I can to grease the skids for your company command. No slots are open now, but you never know. One thing for sure, when you get out to the field, we'll find you a job worthy of your qualifications. We'll definitely put your ass to work!"

Jace rode with Churchwell to the airfield, shook hands and saluted, then watched as he took off. When the duty driver dropped him off back at the jungle school, the disheveled crew of new officers was going to lunch. Joining them, Jace ate quietly, feeling enormously better about his situation. The new officers continued to bitch and groan about their assignments, about their survival chances and about what they would do after their tours of duty were up. As they were leaving, Jace acted on impulse.

"You four lieutenants, let me have a word with you, please."

The three captains ambled into the rain. The lieutenants stood beside the screen door, nervously holding their caps.

"Look," said Jace, "I am not your boss and I'm not chewing you out—I want to make that clear. Where did you guys get your commissions?" One was ROTC, three came out of OCS.

"If we had a mirror, which we don't, what would you guys see if you looked in it?"

None of the lieutenants answered.

"Let me tell you." Jace continued. "You wouldn't see anything to make your OCS or ROTC instructors proud. I'll bet not a single one of you got a haircut before you got on the plane, did you?"

A couple of them shook their heads, two were guiltily silent.

"One of you didn't even shave this morning! Now those captains out there can do anything they want. It's you guys I care about. We are about to enter something called the jungle school. I don't know what it will be about, but I can tell you this: you don't want to start this assignment off on the wrong foot. I know conditions are rough here, but there are showers, you have razors, and there is a laundry and barbershop down by the PX—I went by them this morning. Oh yes, and the PX sells shoe polish. Again, I am not chewing you out. This is friendly advice. Get squared away, OK?"

All four lieutenants blurted, "Yes, Sir!" in unison, and hurried from his presence. Jace felt like an officer again for the first time since his last parachute jump.

After walking brazenly around the Xuan Loc market for over an hour, the young woman turned to Lau and asked cheerfully, "Are you ready to go home now?"

Following the brush with the two policemen, Lau was ready to go anywhere. The woman had bought a camera, a used and no doubt stolen Nikon, from a small shop that sold nearly everything.

"What should I call you?" Lau asked the woman.

"By my name, of course." she laughed.

"Well, would you mind telling me what it is?"

"Ngyuen Thi Phun," she answered, smiling.

Despite the danger and the encounter with the police, Lau found himself feeling somewhat light-hearted around the pretty young woman. Thirty-four years old, Lau had never been much of a lady's man. In fact, except for his wife, he had never been around women much at all except for members of his family. Phun's impish smiles intrigued him and her recklessness and seeming disregard for danger worried him somewhat, but at the same time somehow excited him. He willingly followed her. What other choice did he have, anyway, he kept thinking. He refused to admit to himself that he would have enjoyed following her around the market even if he hadn't had to.

Phun grasped his hand and led him down a side street away from the market. After a series of turns, they entered a dead-end alley, a small path actually. Phun discretely looked around the alley, then removed a large board that was part of a shabbily-built two-story structure.

"Go!" she hissed at Lau, who quickly slid into the dark space behind the board. Phun stepped in behind him, and replaced the board in a smooth, practiced motion. Goose flesh formed on Lau's arms as she placed her hands on his shoulders and brushed against him as she slid past. She took one of his hands and placed it on a ladder.

"Follow me, quickly," she said as she scampered upward.

Opening a trap door at the top, she crawled out into a small, narrow room which was built in an unused part of the rambling structure. It had no windows. Only a small space near the ceiling, hidden under the eaves of the building, offered ventilation. A small pallet for a bed, a low table, and some pillows for sitting on the floor were the only furnishings. No one could look at the building and guess the room was there.

Phun opened a small tin box that sat on the table. Four neat rice balls were inside. A large plastic bottle of water also stood on the table.

"There is a toilet-hole behind the bottom of the ladder, she whispered. You must be very quiet. The people on the other side of the wall do not know this room is here. I will come tomorrow or the next day to take you to our comrades. I suggest you rest. I will come back at sundown to bring you some salve for your sores. You must tell me how you got them when we can talk. It must be quite a story. I must go now," she smiled.

"One thing," whispered Lau as he handed her some piasters. "When you return, will you bring me some beer?"

Phun took the money and smiled brightly.

"Of course—now get some rest."

She disappeared down the ladder.

It didn't take Lau long to learn what the building housed. He had been asleep for about an hour when giggling and laughing awakened him. He lay quietly, listening. An ARVN soldier was telling the whore they must hurry because he didn't have much time. The price had already been paid downstairs, but the girl said for fifty more piasters, she would give him a time he would never forget. He said he did not have that much, and offered twenty. They quickly agreed on thirty. She apparently took the money and got quickly to her work. They were quiet for a while, then the soldier moaned a little, and the bed began banging against the wall. Lau smiled, thinking that the filthy little stooge of the capitalist barbarian American pigs at least had some stamina.

Phun came back at dusk as she said she would. She didn't have to worry about banging the trap door. The couple on the other side of the wall were providing all the covering noise she might need. Feeling embarrassment well up in him, Lau averted his eyes, looking for something to comment on. As Phun giggled quietly and squeezed his arm, a thrill shot through him. She opened one of the beers she had brought, and as he sipped, she removed his shirt and patiently applied ointment from a small jar. As the dark room got darker, Lau sat quietly on a cushion, enjoying her touch, listening to the amorous noises next door, and feeling better than he had felt in a long time.

He hadn't realized he was as tired as he was and how his long journey had sapped him. As he ate, drank and rested, he felt his strength returning. Also, the salve seemed to do wonders for the welts on his skin.

When Phun returned the next afternoon, his sores were markedly better. She brought more rice, two more beers and some more of the salve. To his great disappointment, she gave him instructions on how to apply it—but did not offer to help. She told him to stay in hiding and rest. She said she was going to meet someone tomorrow to find out when they would travel.

On the morning he was to start jungle school, Jace turned off his alarm at five a.m. He sat on his cot for a moment, rubbing the sleep from his eyes, then arose and put on the jungle fatigue pants he had worn since his arrival, an olive-drab T-shirt, and his sneakers. As the sun came up, he was running his gloomy mood and his still-lingering jet lag out of his system. He ran the entire perimeter road inside Bear Cat. He guessed that the base camp was a mile long and a half mile wide, measurements that his normal time for running three miles seemed to confirm. Back at the barracks, he did situps and pushups and went to the shower greatly refreshed.

As he headed to breakfast, he met his fellow replacement officers. The lieutenants gleamed with their fresh haircuts, clean fatigues, shined boots and new attitudes. The three captains skulked toward the mess hall as the lieutenants fell in beside Jace. Conversation over powdered eggs and black coffee was up-beat as his new wards seemed to be ready to take on the world.

As Jace and the other replacements filed into the building used as a classroom, they eyed the two men standing at the raised platform at the front. One was a tall, slim, evil-looking staff sergeant, the other a stocky, old-looking lieutenant colonel.

"I want to welcome you to the jungle operations school," said the colonel, who wore a Combat Infantryman's Badge with a star over it. Jace guessed the two awards were from World War II and Korea.

"I am Lieutenant Colonel Wayne W. Brock, the commandant. What we will do in the next week might just keep you alive during your tour here. All of my instructors are combat veterans—listen to what they say, and you will learn something that just might keep your fat out of the fire."

With that, the lights went out as a film was projected onto the screen at the front of the classroom. In the movie, John Wayne, of all people, was standing in the middle of a Vietnamese village giving a lecture on the importance of what the U.S. was trying to accomplish in Vietnam. Standing beside villagers in their traditional dress, he used sympathy and patriotism, accompanied by stirring music, to encourage the audience to go forth and fight communism. When the film blinked to an end and the lights came back on, the colonel was gone and Staff Sergeant Jeeter was alone on the platform. John Wayne, for God's sake. What did he have to do with this war?

Sergeant Jeeter spent the morning explaining the nature of the war and the terrain on which the 9th Division fought. Jace thought his explanations a bit trite, but he listened intently anyway.

As they broke for lunch, the colonel stepped out of his office and said, "You three captains, in here!" The officers sheepishly followed him into his office, the door slammed and an ass chewing, the likes of which Jace had never heard, ensued. There were no secrets behind un-insulated walls as Brock ripped the captains over their appearance. No doubt the colonel knew his lesson was being heard by the other soldiers outside, who scampered out of harm's way as quickly as possible. Grinning to themselves, Jace and his covey of lieutenants walked toward the mess hall. Nothing needed to be said. At lunch, the young officers, now thankfully in his presence, hung on every word he said.

To Lau's great regret, Phun didn't return for three days. He was out of rice and water, and was beginning to dehydrate in the violently hot, windowless room. He was starting to consider going out to get something to drink when he heard the board at the bottom of the latter move. As he listened to the soft footsteps on the ladder, he raised the trap door and looked down into Phun's smiling face.

"I'm sorry I could not come back here during the last few days. I had to go into the jungle to arrange for the next part of your journey," she whispered as she unwrapped a bundle she had brought.

Lau couldn't believe his eyes. Phun began to lay out egg rolls, roasted chicken, fried vegetables, rice and *nuoc mam* to flavor it all. She also brought three beers and two large bottles of water. She opened one of the beers for him and inspected his insect bites, which had all but healed.

"We travel three days from now. I hope this food will do until we depart. I'm not sure I can get back here before we leave. Have you seen or heard anything suspicious?" she asked.

"Nothing except the activity on the other side of the wall," he said, blushing.

She laughed prettily.

"You will find the puppet army and police are extremely lax here. They care about nothing except their own comfort and safety when they are in town. Although I believe you have nothing at all to worry about here, we must still be extremely careful." Phun said. Then, smiling, she added, "Eat, drink, and sleep. Enjoy your time of rest. There is much we must do and we will be in the jungle for a long time. There will be many times when you will wish you could be back in this small room, so enjoy it now. Here, I brought you something to read." She handed him a small propaganda book published by the government in Saigon. "This will help you learn about the puppet government and the lackeys of the Americans. Their lies must be understood if we are to defeat them. I was instructed to have you read this." She paused and smiled into his eyes. "I must go now. I will return three days from now. You must be ready to travel then."

I wish to thank you for this feast," said Lau. "I have not eaten anything this good in a long time. How can I repay you?"

When she placed her tiny hand on his arm, electricity shot through him. "This meal is to show our appreciation for your long and dangerous journey and your volunteering to come and fight with us. We have all heard about the loss of your family. We share your sorrow because we have all suffered and lost. I am afraid there will be more suffering before we finally prevail. We are in your debt."

Without another word, she was down the ladder and gone. Lau missed her already.

The fifth day of classes covered relations with the Vietnamese civilians. The G-5, the division staff officer responsible for civil affairs, gave an hour-long lecture on the division's policies for dealing with non-combatants. He stressed over and over the importance of "winning hearts and minds". When he finished and left, a tall African-American sergeant-first-class named Jenkins took the stage and began to tell the class his opinion of what dealing with civilians was really like.

"Don't trust them," he said. "You can't tell who is V.C. and who is not. The best policy is to treat every one of them like they are the enemy. They like nothing better than to get a crowd around a street stand, then pull a wire connected to a bomb that will blow you all to hell. They will put ground glass in your beer, battery acid in your coke, and they will spit in your soup. If you go to a local restaurant and order a steak, you may think it's juicy as hell. What you'll be eating is a hunk of water buffalo some little gal has chewed on for an hour before it's cooked to make it good and tender."

"Every village has weapons hidden in it, you just don't know where. Check the water cisterns, the roofs of the hootches, and the manure piles—or better still, make the village chief check the manure piles. (He got a laugh at this.) Don't trust 'em—any of 'em. Oh, yes, if any of you feel like provin' your manhood—listen to this. A guy in the 4-47, down in the delta, got himself a girl off to herself. Just as he slid it in, he learned the hard way she was a V.C. She had stuck a razor blade in a chunk of bamboo shoot and shoved it up herself. Damn near sliced the dude's pecker off. Also, they got V.D. here that eats rubber and will kick the shit out of penicillin."

When the laughter died, one of Jace's lieutenants raised his hand. "What about winning hearts and minds like the G-5 said. How can you do that if you treat all civilians like V.C.?"

"Look, lieutenant. That colonel has his job, and you'll have yours. He drops leaflets and flies around with loudspeakers yelling 'Chieu Hoi'. You'll be out on the ground where you and your troops will live or die by the instant decisions you make. I don't care what the G-5 says, I say grab 'em by the balls and their hearts and minds will follow!"

The next morning, Jace sat quietly and listened as basic tactics such as the ambush and the defensive perimeter were explained by the instructors. Tactically, there was nothing new at the jungle school. Jace had learned it all before, had taught it to his troops at Bragg, and practiced it all countless times in training. At the end of the sixth day, Sergeant Jeeter was teaching pre-mission coordination.

"Let's say you just got alerted that you are going out on a mission," said Jeeter. "What's the first thing you should do?"

Since no one else volunteered an answer, Jace raised his hand.

"Yes, sir." Jeeter nodded.

"Issue a warning order to the troops." Jace answered.

"Naw, you don't have time for any of that infantry-school bullshit," said Jeter, "This is Vietnam—all you gots time to do is to coordinate your artillery fires and arrange for transportation, whether it be by chopper or truck."

Jace raised his hand again. "Sergeant, it takes only a few minutes to get your subordinate leaders together and tell them what the mission is, what time you are leaving and any special equipment they may need. While you're doing the coordination, they could be getting their stuff squared away. Why wouldn't you want to issue a warning order?"

The sergeant stared at him and began more slowly, "Look, sir, I'm telling you that you won't have time. You normally have to move on a moment's notice and you ain't got time to waste on silly crap like a warning order."

Jace wouldn't let go. It was becoming a point of honor.

"Sarge, your original question was that you had just been alerted for a mission and what was the first thing we should do. I can't believe that every mission is received at the last minute. The army spent a great deal of time and money training officers and NCO's in proper planning and troop-leading steps. I don't believe these techniques should be junked just because we are in Vietnam."

Jeeter, now clearly agitated, shot back, "This ain't ranger school and this ain't some stateside exercise. I'm telling you that when you receive an order, get the important stuff done right away because you ain't got time to do nothin' else!"

Jace replied calmly, "Sarge, I am not arguing with you. If you are time-constrained, of course you must cut corners. All I'm saying is that if time exists, proper troop-leading and coordination steps should be followed. I learned at Bragg that often-times the troops don't even know where they are going if the commander doesn't make a conscious effort to inform them. Uninformed troops can quickly get a case of bad morale—that's all I'm saying."

The entire class had turned and was now looking at Jace. He couldn't see, but the class was also looking at Lieutenant Colonel Brock, who had come out of his office when the disagreement started. He was standing at the back of the classroom and he did not look happy.

Jeeter, angry and feeling challenged stood his ground.

"Sir, have you ever been in combat?"

"No, but that doesn't have a thing to do with what we're talking about."

"Well, sir, until you get some time leading soldiers in the Mekong Delta, you might do well to listen to those of us who have."

"We are talking about proper pre-mission planning and coordination," said Jace. "I may not have been shot at, but I have done one hell of a lot of pre-mission coordination at Bragg. All I am saying is that you shouldn't take short cuts if you don't have to."

"Captain!" The word exploded from the back of the room.

"You get your ass in my office right now!"

Jace was stunned. He stood up automatically and walked toward the office. As he went, something began to boil up in him. He had been polite but candid, he believed in the training and experience he had acquired, and he didn't believe he had done anything wrong.

The door slammed and the red-faced colonel slammed his hand on his desk and pointed his finger in Jace's face.

"I told you when the class started to listen and you might learn something that might save your life," Brock shouted. "Now here you are talking back to one of my instructors in front of the class and destroying his credibility. Nobody here gives a damn what you did at Fort Bragg. You're being insubordinate and I won't have it."

"Excuse me, sir but how can a captain be insubordinate to a sergeant?"

"And I'll tell you this, If you start talking back to me, I'll take you to the commanding general.

"And what?" shot Jace. "Tell him that one of his officers expressed an opinion in class? That one of his officers disagreed with a staff sergeant? That one of his officers was actually thinking? That one of his officers was actually using the training the army spent a lot of money giving him? I'll tell you what, sir, I wasn't out of line. I was the only one to answer his question. I do have some experience in the area we were discussing. Also, I am not being insubordinate to you now, sir, I'm just telling you what I thin—."

"Let me tell you, captain, I've seen young punks like you come and go—I won't tolerate being challenged by the likes of you!"

"Sir, I do not change a single thing I have said. I stand on my right—if you will, my responsibility to say what I think! I mean no disrespect to you, sir, but I will not be called a punk. I think it is time we did go see the commanding general."

"You bet your ass we will, you bet your sweet ass I'll see him right now!"

Brock stormed past Jace, put on his cap and flew out the door. Jace returned to his seat and looked at Sergeant Jeeter without expression.

During the break for lunch, Jace, ever mindful of following the chain of command, went to the office of the G-3, the staff officer who, besides planning combat operations for the division, supervised the jungle school. Jace had now had it with all legs, the 9th Infantry Division and Vietnam in general. He vowed he'd do anything to get out of this crazy place. Unfortunately, he learned from an assistant operations officer that the G-3 was not at Bear Cat. He was at Dong Tam with the commanding general, over-flying an airmobile operation.

"What's this all about?" asked the major.

"A disagreement," said Jace "I'm a student at jungle operations school. I would like an appointment with the G-3 as soon as possible. I should be easy to find. I'll be in class."

When Jace walked back to the classroom, the afternoon session had already started. Jeeter was holding forth, unchallenged now. He half smiled, half sneered at Jace as he entered. Brock was nowhere to be seen. Jace took his seat and kept his mouth shut. He was never called to see the G-3.

The last twenty four hours of the jungle school consisted of a live patrol, with Sgt Jeeter acting as patrol leader. Although he had more than enough time to go through doctrinally correct troop-leading steps, Jeeter insisted on doing it his way. No warning order was given, no patrol order was issued, and only partial coordination was accomplished. No emergency signals were covered, no reaction drills were rehearsed, and no contingency plans were discussed. Jace shook his head in amazement. As they spent the afternoon doing what Jeeter called planning, Brock was noticeably absent.

That evening at dusk, the patrol, made up of mechanics, cooks, infantrymen, cannoneers, and officers, was issued live ammunition, a scary enough proposition on its own. After a cursory inspection, the patrol mounted trucks and started to retrace the route that had brought Jace to Bear Cat. About five miles up the road toward Long Binh, the trucks stopped and the patrol dismounted.

Ignoring the fact that they were in a combat zone, Sgt Jeeter gathered the class around him for a pep talk before moving out. "This is Indian country," he said dramatically. "This ain't some stateside cake walk, this is real! Keep your heads out of your ass and listen to me and you'll be all right."

Jace, who had more time walking patrols than the entire class put together, probably including Jeeter, was paired with another captain. The only difference now, he realized, was that his extensive tactical experience had been in training, and that this patrol was real—in Vietnam. As the patrol crossed the rice paddy, Jace got a bad feeling walking out in the open. He thought that a Viet Cong ambush in the treeline could have killed them all since Jeeter did not have the point team check for danger before they entered the jungle. The patrol moved in single file over a small hill to a trail, where Jeeter noisily went about setting up the ambush. He walked back and forth on the trail that would be the kill zone while loudly giving instructions. He set out live Claymore mines and put each buddy team in place. Since he hadn't given any type of patrol order, he had no plan and therefore had to improvise the whole thing on the spot.

As the ambush settled down for the night, Jace's captain buddy whispered, "You go ahead and sleep. I'll take the first watch."

Jace nodded, lay down, pulled the beat-up patrol cap that he had worn through ranger school down over his eyes, and was soon sound asleep. He awakened sometime during the night to find that the rain had stopped and the moon was out. Mosquitoes droned, but G.I. insect repellent kept them at bay. His captain buddy sat clutching his M-16, his eyes wide open.

"You want me to take it for a while?" asked Jace.

"Nah, there's no way I can sleep." answered his buddy.

Jace shrugged, turned over, and was soon sleeping soundly again. When he awoke, totally rested, it was daylight. His buddy still sat wide awake, not having moved. Before they headed to the trucks, Jeeter showed them how to set off a live Claymore mine. They returned to the road by the same route they used on the way out—a violation of basic patrolling technique and common sense. Enemy soldiers seeing them go in could be waiting for them on the way out. Jace shook his head.

Back at the jungle school, the class cleaned their weapons and listened to a general critique given by Jeeter. As he talked, Jace added to the several pages of notes he had made on violations of basic tactical techniques he had observed during the planning and while on patrol. After Jeeter's critique, the students showered and ate breakfast, then reassembled in the classroom. Brock was there.

During the closing remarks, Brock acted as if nothing had happened between him and Jace. The instructors handed out after-action report forms and encouraged the students to write their impressions of the training. They laughed as they hinted that favorable write-ups would be appreciated. The instructors gave the students only a few minutes to jot down their opinions before they took up the forms. Before the class was dismissed, the student officers were told they could have the rest of the day off, but they should report the next morning to G-1 for transportation to their units. Then the enlisted troops were marched away by a sergeant and the officers were dismissed. No one noticed that Jace had slipped his after-action-report form inside his shirt.

Phun returned early the next morning wearing a fresh *ao dia*, sandals and conical straw hat. Not appearing to be in a hurry, she watched as Lau packed his belongings.

"Bring your cane—for now you must maintain your sergeant's identity—at least until we get into the jungle."

After he was packed and ready, they slid down the ladder. At the bottom, Phun looked through a peep hole to see if anyone was about.

"When I move the board, you must move quickly," she whispered. She watched for a long moment, then deftly removed the board and slid outside. Lau followed. Within five seconds she had replaced the board and had begun to walk away. She led him through a maze of turns, mostly keeping to the back alleys. Finally they came to the edge of the town which was bordered by Highway 1. Across the road and two hundred meters of rice paddy lay the edge of the jungle. She quickly looked about to insure there was no sign of soldiers or police.

"Listen, Comrade Lau," she began, "There is no plan now. We must simply cross the highway and walk across that paddy dike to the edge of the jungle. At the end of that dike is a hidden trail which is very narrow and hard to see. We will simply walk slowly. If we are challenged, or if we are fired at, you must run as fast as you can to the jungle. Someone is waiting for us there. If I do not make it, you must continue. Do not stop for me if I am shot. Do you have any questions?"

Lau was taken aback. Throughout his entire journey there had always been a plan. To hear her say there was no plan now scared him. He glanced about nervously. Farmers working the rice were the only people in sight. Without any further word, Phun crossed the highway, which was about as wide as the average American two-lane country road, and started toward the dike. Lau followed, feeling exposed—more exposed than he had at any time in his journey.

When they were half way across the paddies, Lau heard the popping of rotor blades, and, looking to his right, saw the angry silhouette of an American gunship bearing directly down on them. He had the sudden urge to bolt and run.

"Keep walking," said Phun. "Keep your head down, don't look up."

Lau forced himself to keep a steady pace as the whup-whup of the rotor blades got louder and louder.

"Almost there—whatever you do, don't run or look up!" shouted Phun above the increasing noise.

As the gunship thundered overhead, Lau couldn't resist a glance upward. The squat craft had angry eyes painted on the nose making it look like a hungry tiger. The pilots wore brightly-painted helmets with huge sunglasses that covered most of their faces. A variety of weapons hung from the sides of the aircraft. A gunner, staring down from his perch on the side of the helicopter trained his machine gun at them. Feeling as if he had looked a monster right in the face, Lau again had the feeling that his pilgrimage here in the South might be more difficult than he had imagined.

A small man with an old Chinese-made SKS rifle waited in the bushes at the end of the paddy dike. He wore a faded green plaid shirt that blended with the jungle, khaki shorts and sandals. He nodded to Phun and without a word moved off noiselessly into the jungle. Lau followed, noticing they were walking on a well-worn trail, not a foot wide, but beaten an inch in the moist jungle floor. The trail wound snake-like through the forest. There were practically no straight stretches, but no sharp turns, either. Looking at the dense foliage ahead and behind, Lau could see no evidence of this much-used route. Its serpentine turns and incredibly narrow width made it practically invisible, yet Lau imagined it possible for a person to run noiselessly at full speed over the trail's packed mud.

After they had moved a few hundred meters, Phun raised her hand, signaling a stop. She reached into the small bag she was carrying and pulled out a rolled-up pair of black pajamas. Handing them to Lau, she motioned for him to change. Then, without ceremony, she unbuttoned the white bodice of the *ao dai* and removed it. Lau had seen women without clothes countless times since nakedness was taken for granted in the Vietnamese society. But Phun was something else again. He couldn't take his eyes off of her as she took a black silk shirt out of her straw bag and slipped it on. As soon as they were dressed, she nodded and they moved on.

They marched southeast, away from Xuan Loc and crowded Highway 1, moving deeper and deeper into the jungle. From time to time, when the trail branched, their guide did not hesitate for a second. He knew exactly where he was and where he was going.

After walking for several hours on the system of narrow, beaten footpaths, they descended into a stream bed. The guide, cautious now, slowed the pace. At a bend in the stream, he stopped, squatted and motioned for Lau and Phun to do the same. They stayed motionless for several minutes. Suddenly, a figure emerged from behind the stream bank and stood in the water. He wore the traditional black pants and shirt, and held a Kalishnakov assault rifle. He waved for them to follow, then waded noiselessly upstream.

When they came to a high bank, the sentinel parted some foliage, revealing the entrance to a man-made tunnel about a meter in diameter. The guide bent and disappeared. Lau looked questioningly at the sentinel, who nodded imperceptibly. Lau bent over and plunged into the tunnel, followed by Phun. The tunnel was shored by bamboo stakes and poles. Bamboo strips formed a rough floor and long bamboo poles laid side by side formed the ceiling. Lau did not know how far they had gone when suddenly the tunnel opened into a large, subterranean room.

The room had a low ceiling and was shored and braced everywhere by lashed-together bamboo. Tunnels entered the room at every side. A bamboo ladder stood in the center of the room, linking the floor with a tunnel exit in the ceiling. Bamboo had been fashioned into chairs and tables and a thatched mat covered the floor. The chamber reeked of fresh dirt, soy sauce and nuoc mam, a fermented fish sauce eaten with rice. Faint smoke wafting from several candles rose toward ventilation shafts in the ceiling. From somewhere, he couldn't tell exactly where, came the noise of a homemade bellows blowing fresh air into the underground vault.

A staff officer told Lau that this was the headquarters of the Second Regiment, 5th Viet Cong Division.

The next morning, after his run, shower, and breakfast, Jace said goodbye to his classmates and walked down to the headquarters of the 5-39. He approached the NCO who recognized him from his visit with Major Churchwell.

"Hi. Remember me? I'm Captain Spencer. I'm being assigned to this battalion. If you don't mind, I need a desk and a typewriter to do a little staff work."

"Sure thing, sir," said the sergeant. He led Jace to the S-1's office and told him that the adjutant went back and forth to the field and was not due back until dark, so his office was available all day. Jace sat down and took out the after-action report form and his notes.

He started his report by reviewing the charter of the ranger course at Fort Benning: to graduate highly-trained junior leaders who would return to their units and raise the level of tactical proficiency through strong leadership and the application of tough, realistic training. He explained that only two percent of the army was ranger qualified and that he took the ranger charter extremely seriously. In his next paragraph he attacked the classes which he claimed were nothing more than war stories with no instructional value. He pointed out that the jungle school instructors taught students information which directly conflicted with the policies described by division staff officers. Specifically, he used the example of the G-5 and the divisional goals of winning the hearts and minds of the Vietnamese people. He went on to criticize the poor instructional techniques, lack of professionalism and military courtesy and the instructors' ignorance of basic infantry tactics.

In his final section, Jace took apart the training ambush patrol piece by piece. He started with the poor planning, improper troop-leading steps, and the fact that the instructor gave no warning order or patrol order. He went on to describe the failure of the instructors to inspect the patrol members prior to departure, the atrocious fire-support coordination, errors in route selection, security, movement techniques, noise and light discipline and communications procedures. He described how Jeeter had gathered the patrol together in a tight group for a pep talk in the middle of the road in a war zone, and how this invited disaster. Finally he pointed out the fact that the patrol had retraced its route when traveling back to the truck pick-up point. At no time did Jace mention the conflict with Brock.

When he was finished, he proofread the six-page document, making sure he used a professional tone and proper language. He wanted to make sure it didn't sound like sour grapes or revenge.

The S-1 sergeant stuck his head in the door and said, "Sir, if you have something that needs to be typed, Specialist Raines is a whiz. He can knock it out for you in no time flat. Right now he doesn't have anything to do."

Jace thought a second. The document would be more effective if it looked professional. "Sure," he said, "if you don't mind."

He handed the pages to the sergeant.

"How long do you think it will take him?" Jace asked.

"Be back here right after noon chow and it'll be done." said the sergeant.

"Thanks." said Jace. "What do I do to in-process into the battalion?"

"We can do it all this afternoon," said the NCO.

Jace borrowed the duty driver and jeep, retrieved his bag from the jungle school barracks and went to the division headquarters mess hall for lunch. Lieutenant Colonel Brock walked in, ignored him completely, and joined a group of colonels at a corner table. Jace finished eating, then drove back to battalion, chatting easily with the driver. He picked up his document, proofread and signed it, and thanked Sp4 Raines. Then the duty driver took him to G-3 where he dropped his report off with same major he had talked to after the confrontation with Brock. Having no idea what a bomb he had just dropped, he went back to battalion to in-process.

That afternoon, Jace went to central issue were he signed for a steel helmet, liner and camouflaged cover, harness, pistol belt, ammo pouches, two canteens, first aid pouch, rucksack, poncho, duffel bag, and air mattress.

"Where's the laundry?" he asked the duty driver. I've got some stuff that's standing in the corner by itself."

"Down next to the snack bar," said the driver. "If you want, we can drop it off on the way."

"That would be great," said Jace retrieving his dirty laundry bag.

The laundry looked like an after-thought addition onto the building that housed the combination snack bar and amusement center. Jace was met there by a tiny Vietnamese woman wearing a gray tunic and black silk pants. Her streaked gray hair was pulled back from a wrinkled face that seemed to wear a perpetual smile. Jace realized that she was the first Vietnamese he had come in close contact with. She stood just short of five feet tall, and Jace would have bet a month's pay she didn't weigh more than 85 pounds. She was delicate and fragile looking, but Jace sensed a strength in her. He tried not to stare, but he was fascinated. At six-two, he towered over her.

"Good afternoon." Jace said with a slight bow. He had learned no Vietnamese as of yet.

She said something that sounded like, "Chow die wee" and returned his bow.

As Jace handed her the laundry, she smiled and said, "You come bok maybe tree day."

"OK. Three days. Thank you very much."

Jace returned to the jeep and made arrangements for the duty driver to retrieve his laundry and get it to the field.

"Sir, would you mind if we stopped for a coke?" asked the driver.

"No, I wanted to check out the snack bar myself." he answered.

Country music blared from a jukebox as they pushed open the screen door of the standard wooden building with the sheet-metal roof. The driver hailed the manager, an obese sergeant he called "Buddha". As a few soldiers ate burgers at board picnic tables, a tall black private shook and rattled a pinball machine. Three young Vietnamese women worked the grill, the deep fryer, and the drink cooler.

"Hey, Cap'n," said Buddha. "You new?"

"Yeah, just over a week."

"Well, ever you get hungry, come on down. We fix a mean breakfast if you can't get to the mess hall. You sound like you from the south. We got grits, too."

"Thanks, just give us two cokes for now."

"Well, that's it." said the driver as they walked back to the jeep. "It ain't much, but it'll give you a break from the mess hall every now and then."

"If you've seen one army snack bar, you've seen 'em all." said Jace as they drove back to the battalion area.

He left his records and orders with the S-1 sergeant, then went to the armorer to sign for a .45 caliber pistol, the standard arm for a staff officer. Jace asked about a CAR-15 assault rifle, but the armorer said he would have to wait until he got to a rifle company to get one.

Jace lugged all the new equipment to the headquarters building where he assembled his harness, put together his helmet, and hooked his .45 holster to his pistol belt. He tried on his web gear, adjusting it several times. When he was happy with the feel of it, he taped the scabbard of his father's K-Bar knife upside-down on the left side of his harness. Finally satisfied with the fit of his gear, he found the S-1 sergeant and asked how he could get to the field.

CHAPTER 3

▼

14 July 1967

The beat-up Huey helicopter rattled and shook as it settled onto final approach to Fire Base Cougar, home of Headquarters, Fifth Battalion, 39th Infantry. The tactical operations center, better known as the TOC, was guarded by A company. The rest of the battalion was scattered up and down Highway 1. Jace sat on the floor of the utility bird. The doors and seats had been removed to facilitate the different loads that were thrown aboard the aircraft daily—everything from ice, beer, sodas, ammunition, food, and combat troops to dead bodies.

From the air, Jace observed the soggy perimeter, covered by a greasy-slick sheen from the rain. Mud-covered M-113 armored personnel carriers, called APCs or "tracks" by the troops, were spaced at equal intervals around the circle. Beside each track was a bunker with a rain-soaked roof of olive-green sandbags for protection from enemy mortar fire. Concertina wire stacked three coils high ringed the firebase outside the bunker line. Trip flares on metal stakes and claymore mines at the end of long electrical cords were scattered in the puddles under the wire. Inside the circle were various tents and structures built of mud-spattered ammo boxes and sandbags.

In the exact center of the circle, six 155-millimeter self-propelled howitzers squatted in their muddy, sandbagged pits. Off to the side, the snouts of the battalion's 4.2-inch mortars poked out of their tracked carriers. Barber-pole aiming stakes stood among garbage pits, burn piles, and canvas-screened two-hole latrines. Stacks of rations and a water trailer next to a GP medium tent marked the mess area. Wreckers, recovery vehicles and broken trucks and jeeps made up the maintenance stand on the far side of the circle. The aid station with ambulance tracks painted with red crosses stood near the TOC. Ammunition and ration boxes lay everywhere. Everything was splattered and streaked with red, sticky clay. Some patches of dingy, trampled grass survived here and there forming small islands in the sea of mud. Deep tire tracks full of water criss-crossed the perimeter, converged on a gap in the wire between two bunkers, then opened onto a muddy lane leading to the main highway. The soldiers lounging on the tracks and bunkers and walking about the perimeter were miserable-looking in their wet jungle fatigues, which were uniformly muddy from the knees down.

The chopper flared and bounced onto an "H" made of staked-down engineer tape. Litter blew across the perimeter while troops turned their backs and held their helmets in the blast of the rotor wash. The helipad stood next to the TOC, which consisted of two of the top-heavy M-577 headquarters tracks standing back-to-back, connected by poles and covered by canvas forming a tent between them. Jace grabbed his bags and ran at a crouch from under the whirling rotors.

Leaning against the sandbagged wall around the TOC was a short man with a round face, small potbelly, and thinning hair. Thick G.I.-issue glasses made his eyes look too large. Despite his slightly chunky appearance, he gave the illusion of being thinner now than he ever had been. As Jace neared, he saw the black oak-leaf insignia on his collar. It was Lieutenant Colonel Arthur McKensie, the battalion commander of the 5-39. Jace dropped his bags, squared himself, saluted, and automatically blurted out, "All the Way, Sir!" the salute greeting of the 82nd Airborne Division.

"All the way where?" smiled McKensie. Jace was surprised when the colonel didn't return his salute. Jace noticed he was holding a can of Falstaff beer.

"Here, I guess, sir—sorry, that's habit, I guess."

"Well, well, you must be—"

"Jace!" His name being shouted from inside the TOC surprised him. Major C.C. Churchwell ran in front of the colonel and embraced Jace like and old friend.

"Boy, are we glad you're finally here. The famous Jace Spencer who single-handedly shot up the jungle operations school."

"What?" asked Jace.

"Yeah. Didn't you know?"

"Know what?"

"Your after-action report hit G-3 like a seven-fifty high-drag bomb. Colonel Brock got called in and had your report read to him like the riot act. He wanted to bring charges on you for insubordination, but the G-3 ordered an investigation, which took all of about twenty minutes. One of the G-3 majors interviewed your officer classmates, and all of them told the same story, that you'd not done or said anything wrong. They backed up what you had written, too. The chief of staff ordered G-3 to do a top-to-bottom review of everything the jungle school does. A major from G-3 will sit through the entire next class. Damn, boy, you're a hero."

"Field-grade officers don't have to go through the jungle school," explained Colonel McKensie, "Just enlisted soldiers, captains and lieutenants. Evidently, Brock got away with intimidating them into silence. Every officer assigned to us said the same thing—that the jungle school is bullshit, and Brock is a tyrant. Looks like Colonel Brock is on his way out and the jungle school will be re-worked. Not bad for a week's work, young captain."

"Wonder why they didn't want to talk to me?" asked Jace.

"Well they did want to. They called G-1 and battalion rear, just missing you. By the time they called us out here they had decided they didn't need to talk to you since you had submitted a written report which was substantiated by a whole bunch of credible witnesses." C.C. explained.

"Oh, well," sighed Jace. "What a hell of a way to make an entrance to a new assignment!" They all laughed, instantly at ease with each other.

"Had chow?" the battalion commander asked.

"No, sir." Jace answered.

"C.C. take him to get a plate, then join me in the briefing tent."

When Jace returned, the colonel handed him a beer. Jace must have hesitated a half second, so the colonel explained: "It's three-point-two beer. Each man gets two cans a day to drink with his meals. There's no way you can get drunk on two cans of watered-down Falstaff a day—and it's a morale booster."

Jace took the can and opened it with the church-key McKensie handed him.

"Be sure to wipe off the top of the can real well," offered C.C. "The ice we get sometimes may be contaminated. We don't need anyone getting sick from a beer can."

Over meat-of-unknown-origin, canned peas, instant mashed potatoes and sliced bread, McKensie began to fill Jace in. Sitting at the table, he pointed at a map on the wall of the tent with a collapsible pointer. "This is our present area of operations. We call it AO Forsythe. It encompasses all of the southern slope of Gia Rai mountain to the southern border of the province. Xuan Loc, the provincial capital is a raggedy little town on Highway 1. Two Field Force maintains a signal site on the top of Gia Rai. We rotate platoons up to guard it. It ends up being a week-long break for the troops. They rest and pitch horseshoes up there."

The colonel took a bite, chewed, swallowed, and continued. "V.C. activity in Long Kahn province has been negligible, mostly sniping and a few mortar rounds lobbed at us. We believe there is only one unit, the 274th V.C. battalion in our area. Also there are a few local force guerrillas around here."

As the battalion commander conducted his extemporaneous briefing, Jace was impressed by his relaxed professionalism. He had had two different battalion commanders at Bragg, both seemingly cut from the same cloth. They were both tall, fit, lean, crew-cut, no-nonsense types. Jace had respected them, but had kept his distance. Ruling with iron hands, they had been unforgiving for even the smallest mistake. To be called into their presence was enough to cause an excess of acid in the strongest stomach.

McKensie was totally different. He seemed to lead by hint, sarcasm and humor. He acted as if everyone wanted to do his bidding, so he had no need to yell. He spoke in normal, friendly tones to everyone, even the enlisted men. If he asked something, they scrambled to get it done. His grasp of the enemy situation and his area of operations were impressive. Most important to Jace, McKensie had made him feel like a critical part of the battalion from the moment he landed.

"Now let's talk about our troops. We are thirty-eight percent Negro, eleven percent Mexican or Puerto Rican, and three percent Asian, including the Hawaiians. Every soldier that could turn a wrench or type has been pulled out of the pipeline at division or brigade to be clerks and mechanics and what have you. The troops that make it to battalion are for the most part poor, uneducated and unskilled draftees. Only eighteen percent of the enlisted soldiers below the rank of sergeant are RA volunteers. Only sixty-two percent of the troops below the rank of sergeant graduated from high school."

"You'll find the NCO's you were used to in the 82nd, the Korean War veterans and the sergeants with previous tours in Vietnam, all seem to be in the airborne units up north. Mostly, we have national guard NCO's who've volunteered for active duty, ex-drill sergeants, or NCO's we have promoted ourselves—too quickly for their own good, sometimes."

"Mid-level leadership, whether junior officer or NCO is hurting across the division." added C.C.

Jace said, "I ran into a buddy of mine who commands a company in the 173rd. He said officers up there are stacked three-deep. Why doesn't some one just thin them out and send some of them down here?"

The colonel said, "That might be possible if we could get general officers and congressmen out of the officer assignment business—but so far it hasn't happened. That brings us to our officers. Most are OCS. Some are good; most are average. Some lieutenants are still in their teens. Hell, some don't even shave yet. Some are only high school graduates. The company commanders are pretty good, but some won't, can't or don't know how to get their lieutenants and sergeants to do their jobs. A couple of our C.O.'s try to do everything themselves—and get burned out in a hurry."

"That brings me to you, Captain Spencer. I don't have a company commander's job open right now. What I need is a trainer. I can't wait to read your after-action report on the jungle school. Sp4 Raines said it was a beaut. You are a ranger—the only one we have in the battalion—and I am aware of the ranger school charter. Your ranger tab, plus your experience as a commander in the airborne makes you the perfect choice for what I have in mind. I am going to make you the assistant S-3, working for Major Churchwell. Besides learning the AO, the way we operate, and getting acclimated, you will design a training program for the battalion. We will train between combat operations and we will make combat operations training vehicles themselves. I think you'll find things are pretty sad here. I want you to help us fix the 5-39. What do you say to that?"

"I say Airborne, sir! When do I start?"

"Tonight," said McKensie. "I want you to go out on an ambush patrol with Alpha company."

"Yes, sir." said Jace. "Just one request. Please explain to the company commander what my mission is. If he thinks I am a spy who'll rat on him, I won't get to first base."

"Exactly what I had in mind," said Colonel McKensie. "Welcome aboard." Jace felt at home.

At the command and staff meeting that afternoon, Jace was introduced and the company commanders were told of his mission. He also met the rest of the battalion staff and the executive officer, a sour-looking old major, who didn't say much. As Jace had anticipated, the company commanders were concerned that he might be a spy from battalion headquarters, that he might undermine their authority, and that he was too new in country to judge their operations. Also, they had all heard about his report on the jungle school. Whether he liked it or not, Jace now had the reputation of being a hatchet man. The company commanders, particularly Captain Wilson, who commanded Charlie company, didn't hesitate to let their feelings be known.

After listening patiently to their gripes, Colonel McKensie asked, "How many of you are satisfied with the training your troops arrived in country with?"

No one raised his hand.

"How many of you, if you were me, knowing that the state of training is sub-standard, would do nothing about it?"

Silence.

"Look, guys, I don't care if you like Captain Spencer or if you hate his guts. The fact is that he is the only ranger-qualified officer in the battalion, in the brigade, maybe even in the division. For us to have him and not use him would be nuts—or criminal. As I said, you don't have to like him, all I'm asking you to do is cooperate with him and help him do what I've asked him to do."

After the meeting, the three line company commanders and the scout platoon leader shook Jace's hand and somewhat reluctantly welcomed him to the battalion. Understandably, they were resentful of him, his qualifications, and his mission. There was something else that went unsaid—they all knew if one of them screwed up, Jace would be his replacement. He was in a bad situation and he knew it.

After the meeting, Jace sat with C.C. over coffee.

"OK, so you're in a tough spot," said the major. "The old man wouldn't have given you this mission if he didn't think you could handle it. Look, don't worry about those guys. A couple of them are not worth the powder it would take to blow them away. It's no secret, I've told the old man the same thing. You'll have a company before long—then you can have your head. Right now you can help us heal a sick unit. The colonel knows it's sick and he wants to heal it. Those are my words, don't repeat them. Understand? That's just between you and me.

"Now, let's get down to business. Look here—" he pointed at the map on the wall of the tent, "We're here. The brigade S-2 sent word that a reliable agent reported there would be a V.C. unit crossing this saddle, about three clicks south of us—right here—some time tonight. We're going to send a platoon-sized ambush from A company down there. Their mission will be to find out if there is a trail coming through there—as you can see there is none on the map—and set up an ambush. You're going with them."

"Have you given them the word yet?" Jace asked.

"No, as you heard in the meeting, the S-2 just briefed the agent report. They suspect someone will get the mission, but they don't know who yet."

"Let me know the exact time you alert them," said Jace, "I want to run a time line on their decision process and planning procedures. What they do or don't do may be the result of planning."

"OK, you're the expert. We'll just decide right now. What time is it?—I've got 1422. We'll alert them by land line at 1430."

"Well, it looks like I've got work to do," said Jace, rising.

"Jace?"

"Yes, sir."

"I've only known you a couple of days, right?"

"Yes, sir."

"So far, I trust your judgment. You'll be walking a tightrope. Do your job, but, if you can get it done without creating chaos in the battalion, it'll be better for all of us."

"I know that, sir. If I get in a bind, I'll bounce the problem and my thoughts off of you before I say anything to anyone officially."

"That's not what I'm saying. I—"

"I know that, sir—I've only known you a couple of days also. But, maybe I trust your judgment too—so far." They both laughed.

Jace walked across the perimeter to the Alpha command post. He entered the tent, was introduced around, then sat and listened. At exactly 2:30 p.m. the field phone buzzed. The radio-telephone operator jotted down the information, then replaced the phone in its carrier.

"Sir," Jace said to Captain Leon Cole, the A company commander, "We've got a mission."

"Well, what is it?" asked Cole, feeling he was in some kind of stateside training evaluation.

"Ambush, sir, platoon-sized ambush."

"Where?" asked Cole.

"The RTO relayed the coordinates.

Cole plotted the point on his map, then called for the first platoon leader. A few minutes later, a teen-aged lieutenant showed up, cleared his weapon outside the tent and sheepishly walked in. Behind him was a grizzled staff sergeant with a handlebar mustache.

"Captain Spencer, this is Lieutenant Dubois and Sergeant Adams, his platoon sergeant. Guys, Captain Spencer will accompany you on your mission tonight. He is evaluating the training status within the battalion. He will not interfere with you in any way." Captain Cole shot Jace a threatening glance. "The colonel just wants him to see where we might improve our training."

Jace shook hands with the two leaders, then stepped into the background as the company commander briefed them. Jace followed as they went the few yards back to their tracks. There, the lieutenant called the squad leaders together and told them about the mission.

"Well, well, maybe they do give warning orders in this division," thought Jace. He turned out to be wrong. The short warning was all the troops ever got. No planning was done, no patrol order was given, the squads were not told the order of march, or where they would be placed in the ambush. Jace went along when Sergeant Adams went to coordinate fires with the artillery. No fires were coordinated with the battalion's 4.2 mortars or with the company's own 81's.

The lieutenant took a nap while the troops went on with their routine, which consisted of listening to Armed Forces Radio on their transistors, playing cards, and bitching about the rain. The .50 caliber gunners on the APCs were the only security in the platoon. Jace watched as these soldiers dozed occasionally as they sat behind the guns under their ponchos.

After supper, which consisted of MOUO, dehydrated potatoes and canned green beans, the platoon sergeant got the squad leaders together for a short meeting.

"Ah, finally," thought Jace.

The platoon sergeant and the squad leaders discussed who should not go on the patrol and why. They decided who would man the guns and which NCO would supervise while the platoon was away. They settled on eight soldiers they thought should not go out for various reasons. Then they adjourned to their tracks.

The lieutenant woke up, ate chow and called for Sergeant Adams.

"What time do we leave?" asked Adams.

"We need to leave as soon as possible," said Lieutenant Dubois. "Otherwise, we'll be traveling in the dark."

Adams gathered up the platoon. The men had packed anything they wished, since no one had told them what to carry or checked anything. As they milled around ready to depart, a soldier armed with an M-79 grenade launcher slung the weapon on his shoulder, muzzle up, and without thinking, hooked his thumb on the trigger.

"Thack" went the launcher as a forty-millimeter grenade went straight up in the air. The troops all looked at each other for a second, then scattered, yelling "IN COMING!" About thirty seconds later, a loud crump echoed across the perimeter as the grenade landed safely a few yards outside the wire.

"Sonuvabitch!" yelled the platoon sergeant. "How many times have I told you shit-birds to keep your weapons clear inside this perimeter. Who shot that round? Williams? I ought to get you an Article Fifteen. You know I ought to! I will too, if you do somethin' like that again. Now listen, all of you, clear your weapons and don't lock and load till I tell you. You could have killed somebody!"

Without further orders, the platoon sergeant said, "Let's go, and the platoon walked across the perimeter to the exit at the access road. They walked in a mob through the gap in the wire, then halted. The lieutenant got out his compass and tried to figure the route. Sergeant Adams said, "Sir, I make it 190 degrees at 2,800 meters. The lieutenant agreed and told the platoon sergeant to move the troops out. They spread out in a long, single file and headed back around the perimeter, just outside the wire. No coordination had been done with the other platoons guarding the perimeter. Jace figured they would not be shot at since it was daylight and the patrol was clearly American G.I. It was coming back in that worried him.

No order of movement had been given, so the troops just found themselves a place in the file. The platoon seemed to have a regular point man, who automatically moved to the front. The lieutenant fell in fourth in line; the platoon sergeant took up the tail-end position. Jace joined the file about in the middle.

"Lock and load." ordered Adams. Weapons clicked and clacked.

As the platoon snaked through the jungle, Jace could hear hacking from the front. The jungle was thick, but not so thick that someone would have to use a machete, yet the hacking continued. No one checked to see who was doing it. The noise as they moved was loud and continuous. As troops became snarled in the briars that rangers called "wait-a-minute vines", they yelled for their buddies up front to hold up. Sergeant Adams, from the drag position kept yelling, "Keep the damned noise down!"

Troops in the file kept breaking contact with each other. Often one half of the platoon would have to go looking for the other half. When Jace checked his compass, he found the patrol was weaving all over the jungle. Once, a soldier screamed in exasperation as he got tangled in the vines, prompting more shouts from leaders to be quiet. Keeping a rough pace count to measure the distance, Jace figured the patrol had gone about eight hundred meters in the first hour. At this rate, it would take them three and a half hours to travel about two miles.

Just when he thought things couldn't get any worse, it got dark and the platoon simply fell apart. When the breaks in the file became continuous, Jace began to move back and forth, quietly pulling the formation back together. He had told himself he would not get involved, but there was a danger that a man might get lost. Besides, in the dark, no one knew he was helping.

Suddenly, there was another loud thack, followed by a scream, the sound of running, fatigues being ripped by briars, shouts of alarm and a scuffle.

"What NOW?" came the shout from the platoon sergeant in the rear. "What the hell was that?"

"Over here, Sarge!" someone yelled. "Williams shot another M-79 round!"

"What? Where?"

"Williams got hung up in the vines and accidentally shot a round inta th' ground in front of him. He's scared shitless. Damn near ran over the rest of us gettin' out of there. We had to tackle him."

A flashlight went on in the back of the file. Sergeant Adams came storming up the line.

"Williams! You've had it this time, shit-for-brains!" shouted Adams as he shined his flashlight in the young black's face. He was in a state of wide-eyed shock.

"Gimme that damn thump gun before you blow somebody's damn head off with it."

"Sarge—the round didn't go off—it was a dud." someone said.

"Of course it was a dud. It didn't spin enough times to arm itself. You guys are lucky."

Red-lensed flashlights were winking on all up and down the line as troops talked excitedly in normal tones, not attempting to whisper at all. During the entire chaotic episode, the lieutenant never said a word. It took about thirty minutes to sort everything out. Finally, flashlights were extinguished and the patrol started forward again. They continued their jerking, accordion-like movement with constant breaks in contact for two more hours. Jace had a pretty good idea where they were, but he was sure that no one else in the patrol did. No one had kept the pace count to measure distance and they had been weaving all about their compass heading. Since they had not yet begun climb, Jace knew they were nowhere near their objective, which was in a saddle between two hills. Now, finally the lieutenant spoke.

"This looks like the place," he said. "There's no trail here, so we'll just form a perimeter."

Jace figured they were about eight hundred meters short and a good bit off to the west of where they were supposed to be. The lieutenant called in to the company CP that the platoon was in position. Thoroughly disgusted, but glad they were all safe, Jace pulled the radio-telephone operator aside and reported their actual location to battalion. Since they were not where they were supposed to be, he didn't want any random artillery or mortar rounds, called harassing and interdicting or H&I fire, to hit them. This done, he wrapped up in his poncho and went to sleep. At 1:45 a shot rang out.

"What the hell is going on now?" screamed the platoon sergeant.

"I saw something over there!" a young and frightened voice answered.

"You ain't seen nothing—its too damned dark! Now everybody just be still and be quiet!" growled Sergeant Adams.

Having decided he had better not go back to sleep, Jace was the only one awake when daylight came. He simply watched and waited until, one by one, the troops stretched, stood up, relieved themselves, then began opening C-rations and talking in quiet tones to each other. They didn't seem to be concerned. It had been just another night—another mark on their short-timer's calendar—another night they were still alive. Finally the leaders woke up and the platoon began to come to life.

The movement back was about the same as it had been the night before. The patrol missed the perimeter entirely and came out of the jungle on Highway 1. The troops milled around in the road for a few moments, then Jace violated his self-imposed silence.

"It's that way," he said, pointing westward down the road.

Without any further word, the platoon formed into a column of twos and marched off down the highway, turning left when they came to the access road to the battalion perimeter.

Jace went straight to see Major Churchwell.

"Well, how was it?" asked C.C.

"Sir, I don't know where to begin. There was no planning, no orders, no coordination, except with the artillery, no route selection, no leadership, and to cap it all off, they didn't accomplish their mission. They never got to their objective. Movement was atrocious, there was no light and noise discipline, they got lost, they all went to sleep at what they thought was the ambush site, and there were three accidental or unauthorized discharges of weapons. Other than that, how'd you like the play, Mrs. Lincoln?"

"That bad, huh?"

"I didn't cover the half of it—those are just the high points."

"Well, what do we tell the old man? Do you think any leaders need to be fired?"

"Let me tell you something, sir—if you fire a company commander, a platoon leader or a platoon sergeant because of my going out on one patrol with them, I might as well leave the battalion right now. I will be totally ineffective here. The distrust would be enormous!"

"Well, we've got to do something quick!" Major Churchwell said. "Someone could end up getting killed."

"Sir, If it's as bad in the whole battalion as I think it is, it's systemic. I don't think what I saw was an aberration. I don't think firing one officer or two will solve anything. They will just be replaced by the likes of what I saw at the jungle school. If the problem is as deep as I believe it is, we need a training stand-down.

We need to see if the old man can get us a week or two back at Bear Cat. Take the operational pressure off and let's turn this thing around. First, let me check out B and C companies and the scout platoon. I don't mean just patrolling, I mean map reading, fire support coordination, troop leading skills, the whole gamut. Just do this for me. Try to keep anybody from going in harm's way for three days. Give B and C companies some short, harmless patrols that I can check, but don't get anybody in a fight. I'll make a report to the colonel in three days. Until then let's try to keep a lid on this thing. Sir, that's my recommendation."

The S-3 rubbed his chin and thought for several minutes.

"OK—that's what we'll do. I'll talk to the old man."

"Today I'm going to check weapons, the mortar platoons, headspace and timing on the .50 cals, and marksmanship," Jace continued. "You don't mind if I have some troops do some firing, do you?"

C.C. absently shook his head.

"Listen, if what you're saying is true, the old man's head might be in a noose, too. We've got to be careful," said C.C.

"Listen, sir. The old man has a right to expect his officers and troops to arrive in his combat battalion trained and ready to do their jobs. I don't know what is going on in basic training, AIT, OCS or the infantry school right now, but it doesn't appear that they are getting people ready to fight in a war. By the time they learn they could be dead. That's not the old man's fault."

"Jace, do you believe we can fix it?"

"We've got to try, don't we?"

That afternoon, Jace walked the perimeter, talking to the troops. He was warm and friendly with them and they were candid in return. He began by asking where they were from, what their jobs were and finally he felt them out as to what they knew. He was surprised when he found that they were fairly knowledgeable about their jobs. Their individual weapons were clean and functional, but when he asked them to fire at targets at various ranges, he found that few could hit what they were shooting at.

"Have you ever zeroed this weapon?" Jace asked one young soldier.

"No, sir. They told us since we would be fighting in the jungle where you can't see more'n ten feet that we didn't need to zero. When we make contact, we just put it on full-auto and hose away."

When he took an M-60 machine gun team to the edge of the perimeter to fire, Jace learned another important lesson. The gunner and assistant gunner had ammo belts wrapped around themselves like the bandits of the old west. When they went into the prone position to fire, the belts of ammo were pushed into the ground where they picked up dirt, mud, leaves and foreign matter of all kinds. The dirty belts were fed into the gun, which often jammed. Jace made his notes.

He found the mortar platoons competent, but they were rarely called on to support a firefight. The leaders normally went straight to the heavy artillery and never requested support from their own organic weapons. As a result the mortars mostly fired harassing and interdicting fire, nothing more than random shots fired to keep the V.C. off guard. When he gave the fire direction center a practice mission, he found they plotted the data about as fast as his mortar platoon did back at Bragg.

Jace wrote a map test, which he gave to seven lieutenants and seven sergeants. Three flunked outright, none made more than eighty percent. He then checked out communications procedures, maintenance, and field sanitation, all of which he found lacking. The scout platoon was the only bright spot. They seemed to know what they were doing. After going out with squad-sized patrols from B and C companies, neither of which was any better than A company's ambush, he was ready to report to the battalion commander. Jace stayed up all night writing a detailed report about his findings. He did not mention names and he did not accuse anyone. He simply reported the state of training as he had found it.

The next morning, Jace, who had not slept in 72 hours, met with Colonel McKensie, He handed the battalion commander his written report and followed it up with an hour-long description of the training status of the battalion.

He ended his report by hypothesizing: "It seems to me that everyone thinks that Vietnam is not a war—not a proper war anyway. They seem to think that this is something different, like when everyone called Korea a "police action" or a "conflict". Since the powers-that-be call this thing a "counter-insurgency" or "counter-guerrilla war", the troops seem to think that the lessons they learned in training don't apply here. They think that field manuals are useless and that everyone should improvise as they go.

"Sir, I believe that the troops are OK. What has happened is a breakdown in leadership. The fundamentals seem to have fallen by the wayside. The emphasis has been solely on getting the job done.

If a patrol went out and came back in one piece, it was a successful mission. If a small contact was made with the enemy and no one was hurt and we happened to kill a Charlie, it was a great operation. No one noticed when proper procedures and fundamentals started to slip—then one day they were gone. Sir, this might sound like I am criticizing you. I don't mean to point fingers at anyone. You gave me a mission and I must report what I have found. I believe if you looked, you would find that this problem exists to some degree or another in every unit in this country—it sure did at the jungle school. The rules do not apply because we are in a different kind of war. Sir, I recommend we stand this battalion down for as long as we can get away with and retrain from top to bottom, stressing fundamentals."

A long pause followed.

"Captain Spencer, do you know what the Thirty-Ninth Infantry Regiment's motto is?" Colonel McKensie asked.

"Yes, Sir—it's AAA-O."

"Do you know what it means?"

"Yes, sir. I read some history when I got my orders to the 9th Division. It stands for 'Anything, Any time, Any place, Bar None'."

"I'm impressed. What you are now saying is that this unit can't live up to its motto?"

"That's what I'm saying, sir."

"Thank you, Jace. Get some rest. S-3, get brigade on the horn."

It took some doing, but the battalion commander managed to get a month-long break from routine operations. It was not a total reprieve. The 5-39 replaced the 2-47 as division reserve and reaction force, and took over the mission of securing and patrolling the village of Long Thanh and the Binh Son rubber plantation which sprawled to the south of Bear Cat.

McKensie gave Jace the mission of writing the battalion's training plan for the month. For two days he hid away with field manuals, technical manuals, training schedules, and his trusty Ranger Handbook. He kept Sp4 Raines busy typing nonstop. When he finished, he briefed Major Churchwell and the battalion commander.

"OK, sir, here it is." said Jace, handing a thick sheaf of papers to the Colonel and a copy to the S-3. I recommend we split the training into four stations and rotate the companies and the scout platoon through them one week at a time. The stations are patrolling, weapons and defensive perimeter, offensive operations, and leadership. I recommend we find the best NCO's we have for the weapons training. Major, I believe you should teach the defensive perimeter. I recommend you also cover offensive operations to include formations, assault techniques, airmobile operations, cordon and search, and search and destroy. These could be map exercises for the leaders and practical exercises on the ground for the troops. I volunteer to teach patrolling to include search and destroy and the ambush."

"Major Churchwell, sir, you have been to Command and General Staff College. I recommend you have some evening officers' calls where you could cover staff planning, coordination, and troop-leading steps. The Sergeant Major could do the same for the NCO's. The battalion XO could teach maintenance operations, and the medics, first aid. All of this is in the schedule in front of you."

"Also, I recommend a series of tests for the troops, the NCO's and the officers. The troops should demonstrate they can hit what they are shooting at, and that they can maintain their weapons and vehicles. The officers and NCO's should take tests on map reading, planning, coordination, troop-leading steps, tactics, communications, first aid and maintenance. We can form a team of experts to write, administer and grade the tests. We could even give some incentives for the top scores."

"Finally, the patrols in the rubber plantation can be the graduation exercises. I'll take out every rifle squad in the battalion one night at a time. I'll act the same way ranger instructors do in ranger school. I'll let the patrol leaders lead, and I'll jump in only when things are not going right. I'll give them a good critique when they come in. By the way, that way we'll cover our tactical responsibilities and train at the same time. Notice, also, that there is some free time built into the schedule. I hear that nobody but the rear-echelon troops ever get to use the clubs, the swimming pool, the library, and the snack bars. If we plan for every troop in the battalion to have two days completely off during this month so they can take advantages of the goodies, I believe morale will improve."

Lieutenant Colonel McKensie spoke first. "Captain, your plan is approved. The only change I will make is that I will be the one to do the officers' calls. I think I still remember how to do staff planning and coordination. I think getting the officers together is a great idea. We will continue officers' calls every chance we get, even in the field."

Major Churchwell asked, "What do we do with an officer or NCO who flunks one of the tests?"

"Recycle them until they pass." said Jace. "I believe it'll take only one flunking and the rest will get the word real quick."

While the battalion waited to return to Bear Cat. Jace adjusted to the routine of being assistant S-3. He sold C.C. on practice of sending formal operations orders to the companies for combat operations instead of calling on the radio or field phone. He kept the battalion log, conducted aerial reconnaissance and coordinated the battalion's activities with adjacent American and Vietnamese units. He went along on company-sized search-and-destroy operations, keeping his mouth shut in the field, but keeping C.C. informed of everything he saw. He walked the perimeter at night, observing the laxity and slothful habits of the line companies. In his journal, he wrote over twenty pages of notes that he hoped would stand him in good stead when he finally got to command a company.

Lau was anxious to visit the three battalions he was responsible for. He had been in the underground regimental headquarters for three weeks, being briefed on all aspects of their area, their operations, and their mission. The regiment had been ordered to conduct a massive resupply effort. Something big was to happen soon, and division wanted to make sure each unit had everything it needed.

After his long and dangerous journey, Lau had needed rest. Now his old hatred for the Americans and his grim determination to come face to face with one or all of them burned anew in his breast. Although the size of the American base at Long Binh and the brush with the gunship had unsettled him, Lau was ready to tackle his assignment. What he had been ordered to do was extremely different from anything he had ever done or imagined. He intended to succeed at the regiment's new commissar. His comrades expected him to be strong, he owed his dead family, and for some reason he wanted to prove himself to Phun. It was time to go to work. He would visit the 274th battalion first, since it was the closest.

Lau, Phun, a guide and two bodyguards lowered their heads one by one and started out of the tunnel leading to the stream. A bodyguard emerged first to watch and listen. He waded upstream for a short distance, then climbed the bank into the thick jungle. Again, he squatted and observed for a moment, then rose and scouted the entrance to the narrow beaten path they would take. Satisfied, he went back down to the stream to motion to the others.

The guide led the way, moving about thirty meters ahead. One of the bodyguards took up the second place in the file, Lau and Phun came next, and the other guard brought up the rear. Carrying nothing but assault rifles and small packs, they made excellent time. On the narrow trail, the jungle did not hamper their movements at all. Lau found himself beginning to relax as the small party wound through the steaming jungle.

The scout platoon was the only unit Jace had not been out on patrol with. On the day before the battalion was to begin moving to Bear Cat, he finally had the opportunity to accompany the scouts on a sweep of the jungle near the battalion perimeter. Jace respected the scout platoon leader, who was confident, audacious and cocky. He was one of the few officers in the battalion who seemed to know what he was doing. He cared for his troops and they liked and respected him.

The patrol had been moving for about 45 minutes when the lieutenant signaled a break. As the troops knelt quietly for a breather, Jace studied the jungle. Looking down, he observed what looked like one of the game trails he had seen so often in the Tennessee mountains. No more than a foot wide, worn smooth and beaten an inch into the moist jungle floor, the trail disappeared in a gentle turn yards from where he was resting. Looking around, Jace saw that none of the scout platoon soldiers had noticed the trail.

As he studied the small beaten trace, a figure suddenly appeared out of nowhere. Moving silently along the footpath only yards to his left was a small Vietnamese man wearing faded gray shirt and pants. He wore heavy sandals and carried an AK-47. Jace saw the guerrilla at the same time the guerrilla saw him. Armed only with a .45 pistol, which was in its holster on his hip, Jace had no chance. He dived to the right front and rolled, tugging at his holster, and as he did so, yelled "Contact Left!" The guerrilla had stopped dead still and was raising his assault rifle.

In horror Jace watched the assault rifle begin flashing as the muzzle rose toward him. He had his pistol in his hand now only to remember it had no round in the chamber. The vegetation around him began to fall as if it were being hacked by hedge clippers. In the close, damp air near the jungle floor, the communist assault rifle sounded like a rapid-fire cannon. Like the popping of a large bull whip, the supersonic bullets cracked loudly as they passed inches from his head. Terrified, he felt the shock, the wind and the vibrations as the bullets cut the jungle to pieces around him. In seeming slow motion, he chambered a round into his pistol and began firing in mad confusion. As the enemy soldier emptied his magazine and turned to flee, Jace continued to pull his trigger as fast as the adrenaline surging through him could make him pull it. All he saw was the impact of his bullets in the jungle foliage. The enemy soldier was gone.

As the Viet Cong guerrilla disappeared and Jace fired his last shot, the scout platoon exploded with wild automatic firing in all directions. In a few seconds, they had emptied their magazines and begun to reload. Shaken, Jace took stock. He lay in a shattered circle where thirty 7.62 millimeter bullets had hacked the jungle around him. Leaves, twigs and bits of vine covered him head to foot from the shredding the jungle had taken. He had a neat hole in the side of his jungle fatigue shirt and a nick on the soul of his left jungle boot. A bullet had pierced the canteen he wore on his right hip.

Shaking all over, Jace felt chills in the heat of the jungle. He felt and looked himself over. He could find no wounds, but he felt as if he were going into shock. He took several deep breaths, then sat with his head between his knees, feeling his control returning. He stood up and was changing magazines as the scout platoon leader came running up.

"Sir, are you all right?" asked the lieutenant.

"Yes," Jace answered. "I suggest we get some artillery and mortar blocking fires off in that direction. Charlie might run under it as he escapes."

"Yes, sir!" said the platoon leader as he reached for the radio handset and his map. Jace listened as the young officer radioed in the fire mission, then eased off a few yards in the jungle and vomited.

Lau had been lulled into complacency by the march in the hot, humid air. A sudden yell that he couldn't understand, the explosion of automatic rifle fire and the popping of pistol shots had shocked him so badly that he had jumped into the air and come down on his back. He had momentarily lost his grip on his rifle, and had groped to find it. As he had picked it up and turned to see if Phun was all right, the guide who was on point had come charging back toward them, his Kalishnakov still smoking. A firestorm of automatic fire had then erupted as the small party got to their feet and turned to flee back down the trail. Lau had taken only three steps when the bodyguard behind him had slammed into his back. Lau had gone down hard—the body of the guard on top of him, most of his head gone.

"Quickly—get his rifle," screamed Phun above the din.

The guide and the remaining bodyguard picked up the body of the dead guerrilla, then, running at a crouch, sped back the way they had come. When they were safely in a fold of terrain that shielded them from the American fire, they stopped.

"We must hurry on. They will begin firing artillery next. We will mark the place and leave the body hidden in the jungle. Someone will return to bury him. Keep his rife. We must go quickly now." the remaining bodyguard ordered.

"Well if it ain't ole quick-draw!" yelled C.C. as Jace entered the TOC.

Jace, still shaken, grinned as best as he could.

"Did you get him, partner?"

"I don't know."

"Well, you probably did. Recon Six found a blood trail."

"I don't know about that," replied Jace, "but I sure as hell learned two things."

"Well, what might they be?" hooted C.C., still affecting his western drawl.

"First, they travel on what look like animal trails, no wider than a foot, beaten in the mud. Second, we made contact while we were sitting quiet and listening."

The 5-39 made a convoy five miles long as it crept its way back to Bear Cat at twenty miles per hour. Jace rode in C.C.'s jeep since he and the battalion commander were flying non-stop up and down the column in an H-23 bubble-nosed chopper. As the convoy made the turn from the main highway, Jace saw the now-familiar columns of black shit-smoke. The main road through the base camp went past the jungle school where Lieutenant Colonel Brock was standing by the classroom door. When Jace saw him, he saluted smartly.

That night there was one hell of a party. The battalion was not scheduled to take over the reserve mission from the 2-47 until the next day, so the night was free. After the troops cleaned their weapons, showered and changed out of their nasty fatigues, they broke out the beer and split up in ethnic groups for the party.

After chow, the officers gathered in a back room of the battalion mess hall that doubled as an officer's club. Jace entered feeling awkward and out-of-place, and looked around to size up the situation. He did not feel accepted by these men and did not want to intrude on their conversations. A loud group of lieutenants was whooping it up in the center of the room while the company commanders and captain staff officers talked quietly in a corner.

"Well, if it's not Moses," said Captain Wilson, the C company commander as Jace approached. "Here to deliver us from the wilderness of poor training."

"And sloppy combat operations," added Leon Cole of A company."

"Hey, don't pay any attention to them," grinned Captain John Thomaston, the B company commander. "They're just mad 'cause they command route-step outfits. Notice Bravo doesn't mind what you're doing. Come and join us. What are you drinking?"

"Beer's fine."

"We were just talking about your shoot-out. I guess you're kind of famous."

"Ha!, it's hard to see how firing a whole magazine without hitting anything and nearly shittin' my pants makes me famous."

"Oh, come now—Jace is it?—let's not be so modest," spat Wilson. "You're all we've heard about since your arrival."

"Look, guys, this ain't so easy for me either. I'm just trying to get my feet on the ground and do the job the old man told me to do," said Jace.

"Well, Mr. Airborne Ranger," continued Wilson. "Let me give you a piece of advice. While you're busy telling the colonel how screwed up we are, just don't get involved in my company's business."

"Being a little tough, aren't you Charlie Six?" said Thomaston.

"I don't think so," snapped Wilson. "We've been beating these damned jungles for six months and this FNG comes in here and tries to tell us we don't know what we're doing. I don't think I'm being tough at all."

Not knowing what to say, Jace took a pull from his beer and looked expressionless at Wilson. Just then, Lieutenant Colonel McKensie and Major Churchwell swept into the club to a loud welcome by the group.

"Just remember what I told you," said Wilson as he turned led the other captains toward the battalion commander.

"Look, Jace, we're not all assholes," said Thomaston, turning back. "I know you're in a spot. Don't worry about it. They'll come around. They resent your experience, they resent the fact the old man trusts you, and they resent the fact that you and the S-3 hit it off right away. I guess they also resent your elite background—and the fact you're new to combat."

Thomaston threw his arm around Jace's shoulder as they joined the other officers thronged around McKensie and Churchwell. Later that evening, in an impromptu ceremony, the battalion commander pinned the Combat Infantryman's Badge on Jace's jungle fatigues. Jace had coveted the decoration, but he never expected he would earn it while he was a staff officer.

The training got off to a rocky start, but smoothed out quickly. Jace stayed busy ironing out the few wrinkles in his schedule. C.C. enjoyed his role of senior tactics instructor, teaching the defensive perimeter and offensive operations. The battalion sergeant major, freed from his normal routine, began to hold rap sessions with the young NCO's, cramming them full of all kinds of hints and pearls of wisdom. He taught the differences between officers' and sergeants' duties, and how to be proud of being a sergeant. Soon, he had the junior NCO's enthusiastically trying to do their jobs. The tactics training went so well that C.C. handed the responsibility for teaching offensive operations off to Captain Thomaston, of B company, who had done well when his company had taken its turn. Soon, the Bravo commander prided himself in being the local tactics expert. The training had now taken on a life of its own.

A platoon sergeant in A company rose to be the battalion weapons authority. Crew drill competitions developed between the mortar platoons, which came up with a rotating trophy in the form of an inert mortar round. The best marksmen were formed into an informal sniper squad that didn't snipe at enemy soldiers, but helped every soldier in the battalion adjust their sights. Once their rifles were zeroed, most troops could routinely hit man-sized targets at three hundred meters. Grenadiers thumped away and troops threw hand grenades, fired off Claymore anti-personnel mines, and shot recoilless rifles.

Jace spent all afternoon of each day teaching hand-and-arm signals and control measures. He taught the soldiers how to send up the count to make sure all patrol members were accounted for, and what to do when they broke contact in the dark. He taught them how to issue warning orders and detailed patrol orders. He took each squad along as he coordinated artillery and mortar fires. He showed them techniques for leaving and entering a friendly position in the dark. He taught contingency plans such as using rally points in case the patrol got scattered in the night. Most importantly, he taught squad leaders to drive their formation through the jungle without saying a word, day or night. Remembering his father's admonition, he taught them to sit patiently and wait.

Each night during the month of August, Jace took a different squad into the jungle for a live ambush. If they didn't do well, he took them back out the next night. He brought them in through the friendly lines at about 4:00 a.m., slept for about five or six hours, then started the whole process over again. Jace was becoming exhausted, but he saw the progress the battalion was making and was very pleased.

Perhaps most positive part of the refresher training was the battalion commander's evening officer's calls. Over beers the lieutenants and captains critiqued the day's training and recommended changes. The colonel taught correct planning and troop-leading steps—some from the book, some from his experiences and common sense. Together the officers put together a book of standing operating procedures. Several times, the Sergeant Major brought in the NCO's for an open give-and-take between officers and sergeants. The colonel controlled it all, not letting things get out of hand.

A close bond seemed to be developing between the leaders of the battalion. Several of the officers, led by Captain Wilson, still seemed to resent Jace, but most now accepted him as a spirit of cooperation spread out over the 5-39. Lieutenant Colonel McKensie played his battalion like a violin, squashing problems as they arose. He seemed to be everywhere at once, encouraging, counseling, patting backs, even firing his own pistol at the make-shift range. He attended the maintenance classes given by the motor sergeant. He acted as a wounded soldier in a first aid class, allowing privates to bandage him. He even practiced driving his own APC.

One afternoon, as Jace was giving the operations order for the nightly ambush, Colonel McKensie showed up in full battle attire. He never said a word, but did everything the squad did in preparation for the patrol. As they departed the base camp, McKensie took his place in the file. The only difference between him and one of the squad members was that the colonel took along his own radio operator—after all, he still commanded the battalion. The next morning when the patrol came in, McKensie listened to Jace critique the squad. His only comment was a thumbs-up sign as he went off to bed.

After a week of traveling, Lau had returned to regimental headquarters near Xuan Loc. It had taken almost a day of walking the jungle trails to get to the underground headquarters of the 274th battalion, which was nearest to regiment. Because of the distance, he and his bodyguards had emerged from the jungle to take busses to Long Thanh and Phuc Le. From the towns, they had vanished into the jungles, taking the small winding trails to travel to the C-240 and C-80 battalion hideouts. He now had visited all of his battalion headquarters and two supply caches. One of the caches he had visited surpassed anything he had ever imagined. Twenty levels deep, it held thousands of rifles, machine guns, RPGs, recoilless rifles, mines, grenades, millions of rounds of ammunition, medical supplies, and tons of rice.

He had been greatly impressed by the zeal and commitment of the guerrilla fighters he had met. He now planned to make the rounds to the various companies and subordinate units to conduct his political rallies. He would also venture into the towns of Long Thanh and Phouc Le to recruit fighters and supporters for the front. It would be a huge job. The area inside the triangle formed by Bien Hoa, Xuan Loc and Phouc Le, known to the National Liberation Front as Base Area 302, consisted of 1500 square miles of jungle. Besides the headquarters of the 274th, the C-240, and the C-80 battalions, there were 18 company and platoon hideouts, tunnel systems and weapons caches. Visiting all these units and sites would be exhausting and nerve wracking since the Americans patrolled the vast jungles of Base Area 302 on a daily basis.

As Lau arrived at the underground headquarters, he was excited to see that Phun had returned. She had been gone for ten days. Knowing there was no doubt an important reason for her absence, he had swallowed his concern about her being away and walking the dangerous jungle trails. It had taken a great deal of discipline not to ask when she might return.

But now Phun was here and she had come back with a mission. Lau, the senior commissar of the second regiment, along with his military counterpart, the regimental commander, were to proceed to a meeting during which the commander of the 5th Division of the National Liberation Front would instruct them concerning events that would have earth-shaking consequences. The meeting would be held on 18 August. The participants would travel openly on civilian transportation, again disguised as ARVN soldiers on leave. The meeting would be held in a secret room in back of a restaurant in Cholon, the Chinese section of Saigon. Lau was pleased to hear that Phun would guide them. Having already gone to Saigon to scout the restaurant and the surrounding area, she knew the location of two safe houses they could use in the event of trouble. They would leave in two days.

At the end of the work day, Chi and Huong lined up with the other workers for pay. Huong was extremely excited. Except for helping his mother buy food, he had saved almost every piaster he had made for the motorbike he hoped to buy, and this pay check would put him over the top.

Chi had spent her entire life in and around Long Thanh. She had never even been to Saigon, less than fifty kilometers away. She found the prospect of her son going into the capital city alone to buy a motorbike very frightening. Since she did not have the experience of traveling and the excitement of seeing new places and things, she couldn't understand why Houng couldn't he be happy with living a quiet life in Long Thanh as the rest of the family did. Why did he have to venture out on the dangerous highways during this time of war?

Chi bowed as she accepted her stack of piaster notes, then tucked them away in her straw bag. When he received his pay, Huong turned toward her with such excitement she knew she could not say no to his trip.

"Will you do this one thing for me?" she asked Huong. "Will you ask your brother Duc to go with you to Saigon. Duc is older and more experienced and he has been to Saigon. You don't even know how to ride a motorbike, but I know he can, and he can keep you out of trouble until you get home safely."

"Yes, mother." Huong replied. "I will take Duc. If necessary, he can drive the cycle back home. I can learn to ride here in Long Thanh where there is not so much traffic. You worry too much. I can ride a bicycle, can't I? How much harder can a motorbike be?"

"When will you go?" Chi asked, accepting the inevitable.

"I must ask the sergeant who oversees my work gang if I may be excused from work one day. Duc works for himself cutting wood; he can go any time he pleases."

At the road junction near their home, Huong helped his mother down from the truck, then excitedly asked permission to go and speak to Duc to arrange for their trip into Saigon. Chi smiled and told him to go on, secretly chastising herself for giving in and spoiling her younger son. She said a prayer to the Virgin Mary, asking that her leniency not contribute to something bad happening to her boy. She could not visualize a trip so far and so dangerous.

Duc had his own small home where he lived his new wife. He made his living cutting wood from the jungles, preparing it in exact lengths, then selling it to the charcoal makers. It was hard work, and it was often dangerous. To cut the wood, he had to venture into the jungles where he could be mistaken for a Viet Cong by American patrols. He always carried an identification card and a permit written in Vietnamese and English, signed by both the mayor of Long Thanh and the district chief, giving him permission to go into the jungle. Duc always followed the rules. He only went out during daylight and he only went into areas approved by the Vietnamese and American authorities.

Duc was excited by the prospect of taking his younger brother into Saigon. There were some things he needed to buy that were not available in Long Thanh. He needed a new saw blade and a large whetstone for sharpening his tools. Also, if there was time, he thought he might see a film at one of the movie houses. Duc loved the old provincial capital with its tree-lined streets and beautiful architecture. He had only been there twice. He saw the trip as a vacation, a chance to get away from the boring routine of cutting wood.

Two days later Huong got his day off. Early in the morning, as Chi climbed aboard the truck to go to work, Duc and Huong, dressed in their best clothes, waited for the bus to Saigon. As the truck pulled out, headed for Bear Cat, Chi knew it would be a long day waiting for her sons to return.

All day long, Chi could do nothing but worry about her boys. After work, she squatted in the doorway of her house, trying to fight off the sense of foreboding that was sweeping over her. As darkness approached, Huong and Duc were still not home. All sorts of images sprang into her imagination—accidents, murder, kidnapping. Wartime Vietnam was not a safe place in which to travel. Outwardly calm, she chewed her betelnut, but inside, she was almost frantic with worry.

As panic nearly burst from Chi, almost anticlimactically, her sons were home. Duc rode the small Honda into the yard with Huong sitting behind him, beaming. Chi suppressed the tears filling her eyes and walked out to greet them. The only show of emotion she allowed herself was squeezing her son's arm.

"Good evening." bowed Duc, greeting his mother formally.

"I am happy you two are home safe," said Chi.

"What do you think of the motorbike?" asked Huong excitedly. Before she could answer, he said, "I have already learned how to ride it. Let me show you!"

Without waiting for her to answer, Huong jumped on the bike, started it, and raced around the yard. They all laughed as he squealed like a child. Duc joined his mother for tea as the boy raced off down Highway 15. In spite of the war, life was good.

Jace was out with one of the last of the squads to go through his ambush training. They had quietly crept a thousand meters into the Binh Son rubber plantation at dusk. Jace let the squad leader run the patrol as much as possible, but at the objective rally point, he took charge.

When they were about fifty meters from the intended ambush site, Jace put the squad into a small perimeter, as they had rehearsed. Then, carrying a Starlight scope, he took the squad leader and the radio-telephone operator and went forward for a leader's reconnaissance. He searched for the main trail through the plantation that was on the map, but after a thorough examination, concluded that all the lanes between the trees looked exactly the same.

Then he noticed a suspicious-looking narrow trail snaking through the rubber trees. Like the trail in the jungle where he had been in his shoot-out, it was no more than a foot wide. Meandering through the rubber it did not follow the rows. Since he couldn't find the main trail, and since this footpath looked promising, he changed the pre-planned ambush site. His instinct told him to set up on the small, but apparently well used trail. After sneaking back to the patrol, he briefed them on the change, then led them forward.

At the new ambush site, Jace placed each two-man team quietly, exactly as he had specified in his patrol order. Being careful to stay out of the kill zone, he placed two-man buddy teams well to the right and left of the main ambush line to give early warning. He tied telephone wire to their legs and told them if they saw the enemy coming, to tug on the wire twice. He tied the other ends of the wires to the legs of the troops on each end of the main ambush line. He set claymore mines where their deadly pellets would sweep the kill zone without endangering his patrol members. He placed his M-60 machine gun on the right side of the line, so it could fire diagonally across the entire front. Jace then assigned each buddy team a sector of fire, making minor adjustments from the patrol order where terrain and trees dictated. Finally, he placed a trip flare on the trail near the center of the line. He ran the wire from the flare and the clacker-triggers for the claymores to his position, then sat down and called in the coordinates for the new ambush site and changed one of the pre-planned mortar targets.

Jace had adjusted to his routine of taking patrols out nightly. Since he had timed his body clock to the schedule, he was now getting plenty of sleep. Taking his responsibility for the soldiers in his charge seriously, he stayed awake and alert the entire night while out on his ambush patrols. He didn't intend to get any one of them hurt or killed because he was asleep.

The patrol had lain quietly for about two hours when a youngster on the left side of the line began to snore. Jace moved quickly and quietly to awaken him. As he got back to his position, the soldier on the right of the line felt two tugs from the wire tied to his leg. He sent the alert down the line to Jace.

Jace saw sparkles of light dance in front of his eyes and felt his breathing rate increase as adrenaline surged through his system. Quietly and deliberately, he picked up the Starlight scope and peered down the trail. Appearing grainy gray-green in the night vision device were four shadowy figures creeping quietly through the rubber trees. Jace watched, fascinated and frightened, praying that the Viet Cong he saw in the scope were not the point team for a larger formation. Slowly, he put down the Starlight scope and carefully picked up the clackers for the claymores. As the enemy soldiers walked into the middle of the kill zone, one of Jace's soldiers moved imperceptibly, probably to get into a better firing position, while another clicked the safety of his M-16.

Hearing the noises, one of the Viet Cong froze, while the other three turned to run. They had only taken two steps when Jace squeezed the claymore triggers. Two shattering explosions accompanied by blinding flashes propelled hundreds of BB-sized pellets into the kill zone and through the rubber trees in every direction except where the patrol lay. After pulling the wire which popped the trip flare, Jace saw that all four guerrillas were down, one twitching wildly. The squad lay in shock for a half second, then all hell broke loose as they emptied their M-16's into the kill zone. When the M-60 joined the din a second later, tree limbs flew, leaves fell like green snow flakes, and puffs of muddy-bloody mist kicked into the air as bullets smashed into wet soil and the guerrillas' bodies. The tracer bullets from the machine gun streaked into the inert forms lying in the trail, then ricocheted off in obtuse angles. Bullets from M-16s and the M-60 tore long, jagged scars into the nearby rubber trees. Liquid rubber sap began oozing over the blood spattered onto the trees from the claymore blasts.

"Cease Fire, Cease Fire!" Jace screamed during the lull in the din when the troops' magazines emptied at the same time. The M-60 still blasted away, turning the bodies in the trail into mush.

"Cease Fire, dammit!" yelled Jace again. "Reload, put your weapons on safe. Security teams, be alert, more of them may come down the trail. Check for wounded. Search team—Check them out."

Two scared soldiers darted into the trail and stared at the bodies, not wanting to touch them.

"Kick their weapons away." Jace ordered.

The two young troops complied, but immobilized by the sight of the mutilated bodies on the ground, made no move to search them. Jace jumped up and ran into the light-circle made by the trip flare. Already the radio was squawking, the battalion RTO demanding to know what was going on. The ambush site was close enough to the base camp for the explosions and firing to be heard there.

"Sir, battalion wants you on the horn." said the radio operator. "Tell them to wait," said Jace, turning over one of the guerrillas.

Jace was shocked as well. He had never seen a dead body except in a funeral parlor. The Viet Cong he was searching had first been blasted by the claymore pellets, then torn apart by the panicked firing of the squad and the machine gun. His abdomen was ripped open. Intestines, chopped apart by bullets, spilled onto the ground. The smell was overpowering and blood was everywhere. Jace patted the shirt pockets, feeling nothing but warm, wet mush beneath.

Choking back a gag, he yelled, "Quick, you two, search the others. Is everybody all right?"

A couple of weak "Yes, sirs" came from the line.

The two men of the search team reluctantly bent to the task. As they turned over the fourth body a canvass satchel rolled into view. One of the search team picked it up. "Sir, look here."

"Lemme have it—you all grab those weapons!"

The search team scooped up three enemy assault rifles and tossed the satchel to Jace just as the trip flare began to sputter out.

"Now listen, all of you. We've got to get the hell out of here now! This might be the point team for a company or battalion. Get up and form your file. We're moving in thirty seconds. Compass man, take up a due-north azimuth. MOVE!"

The battalion duty officer was now on the radio, frantically calling over and over. The security teams stood up and tried to walk, but tripped on the wires still tied around their legs. Cursing and thrashing, they blinked and fumbled at freeing themselves, their night vision shot because of the trip flare. Initially silenced by the violence, the squad now began to babble in the dark. One of them gagged. One just said "Jesus Christ" over and over—more of a prayer than a curse.

"Quiet, all of you—and we may just get out of this alive."

Grabbing the radio handset, Jace said "Cougar Three India, this is Three Alpha."

The radio rushed back: "This is Three India, sitrep, over."

"This is Three Alpha, ambush popped, four enemy KIA, three weapons and a satchel captured, no friendly casualties. We're moving. Call Mike Six and tell him to fire target alpha-bravo-one-zero-zero-one on my command. I can't change freqs on the move, so you'll have to relay."

"Listen, everybody. I am calling a four-deuce mortar concentration on the ambush site in case more charlies are comin' up the trail. This is the last word I want spoken. Grab hold of the man in front of you. We can't lose anybody now. Last man, send up the count. Now MOVE!"

The patrol snaked out between the rubber tree rows, crouched and walking fast, not worrying about noise. After they had gone about a hundred and fifty meters, Jace reached for the radio handset.

"Cougar Three India, tell Mike Six to fire. They had gone only a short distance further when they heard the banging of the heavy mortars from Bear Cat. They moved faster still.

"Hold on to the man in front of you," yelled Jace. "and keep driving."

The patrol charged on, heads down and pushing through the darkness blanketing the neat rows of rubber trees. The count came up to Jace—everyone was accounted for. The first mortar round crumped close, but far enough behind them that Jace knew they were clear. In rapid succession, more rounds fell, blasting the ambush site and masking the noise of the escaping patrol. He drove them relentlessly on for ten more minutes, then called a halt.

Jace eased along the file of kneeling soldiers, wide-eyed and breathing hard in the dark. He patted each one of them on the shoulder, telling them they had done fine and were going to be all right. In turn he told each man that from here on they would be moving quietly. Sensing they were calming, he signaled for them to stand, then, like a wagon master in a western movie, motioned them forward. When they came to the boundary between the rubber plantation and jungle, Jace changed the compass reading, shooting for the point in the bunker line where he intended to enter Bear Cat.

When the patrol halted at the edge of the area that had been cleared of vegetation around the base camp, Jace radioed battalion to alert the bunker guards they were coming in. When the word was out, he fired a green star cluster from a hand-held flare. After the same signal was fired from the berm, the squad headed toward home.

"Halt, who goes there?" came the challenge.

The patrol froze, then Jace answered "Ambush patrol from fifth of the 39th."

"Advance one to be recognized."

Jace crept forward.

"Halt!—Yellow!" came the challenge.

"Baboon." Jace responded with the password.

"Come on in—What in hell did you guys get into?" asked a soldier with a New England accent.

"Some real shit." said Jace as his troops entered the base.

McKensie, Churchwell, the XO and the Sergeant Major were all standing next to the radio when Jace walked into the battalion headquarters building. They all turned and gaped. Other than a squint caused by the bright electric lights, Jace's camouflaged face was expressionless. His right hand gripped the slings of three AK-47s; his left clutched the satchel. Blood covered his jungle fatigues.

"Son, are you all right?" asked the colonel.

"Yes, sir." Jace answered, quietly.

"Were all your boys OK too?"

"Yes, I checked them every one. Some were scared half to death, but they are all in one piece. I just took them to their company area."

The S-2, who had been quietly listening to everything interrupted, "Excuse me, Jace. I'll take those weapons if you want—and I'd like to see what's in the satchel."

"Oh—sure—go ahead," replied Jace, handing the items to the intelligence officer.

C.C. said, "Jace, I want you to take a day off. Get some sleep. It won't hurt to back the schedule up one day. If you want to let someone else take the rest of the patrols out, it's OK."

"No, sir. I only have two squads left to take out. This was my idea—I started it and I would like to see it through. If you don't mind, I'd like to drive on and finish the last two squads. Then, if it's OK, I'll take that day off."

"Well, it's early. You're normally not back in until zero five hundred or so. Get cleaned up and I'll debrief you over a drink," said McKensie. "You know, you've personally had more enemy contact in the last month than the rest of the battalion put together."

"Hey, Sir, look at this!" It was the S-2, the intelligence officer, who was holding two fists full of South Vietnamese money. "I believe Jace whacked a pay team.

The satchel is full of money and a list of names that looks like a finance document."

"Well, I'll be damned," said McKensie. "Look, S-2. Count it in another officer's presence. Make a memo for record as to the amount, then turn it in to brigade. We don't want anyone accusing us of anything."

"Yes, sir," said the S-2. "Just one thing more. The V.C. have always gathered taxes from the locals to pay their troops. Now, here comes a highly professional, probably North Vietnamese pay team. This is a marked departure from they way they've always worked. I believe this is significant. I believe something's up."

"O.K. S-2," said Churchwell. Write it up and send it along with the money to brigade. Good work."

Pleased with himself, the S-2 captain left.

"One more thing," said Jace.

"What's that?"

"All patrols need to carry two radios. One on command freq and one on the fire support net. A patrol leader can't change freqs in the dark when shootin's going on. Also, it's good to have a backup."

"Son, forget that right now," said McKensie. "Clean up and then we'll talk."

"Yes, sir."

That night Jace wrote his dad. He ended his letter with: "I just thought you'd like to know. Squirrel hunting works! Pet old Jupiter for me. Love, Jace"

Jace finally took his day off. He slept half the day, then cleaned up and went to visit the squad that had been with him on the ambush. They looked different in the daylight—so young and innocent. He asked each one of them their names. There was Rodriguez, Sutter, Jarvis, Johnson, Villalobos, Otis, Kodbrebski, Paige, and Sergeant Kirkland, the squad leader. One, in youthful bravado, gave only his nickname—Super Private. He was a scrawny southerner with tobacco-stained teeth and deep-set, intelligent eyes. Despite the fact that this group had recently killed four fellow human beings, they acted like members of a high school football team.

"I just wanted to look you in the eye and tell you how proud I am of you fellas. Have any of you been in contact before?"

Five raised their hands.

"Have any of you had a confirmed kill before?"

"No, sir," they answered in unison."

"Well, I'm not here to glorify killing. I know that's our job here—but if you're like me, you're not exactly crazy about it when it happens. You guys did exactly what you were supposed to do—exactly as we trained and rehearsed."

"Thank you, sir," they answered.

"Well, I'll let you get back to your training. I just wanted to stop by and tell you all that I'd be proud to lead you anywhere—or for that matter, just go with you."

They chuckled, then Super Private asked, "Sir, when you gonna come down here and take command of this rag-tag piece-of-shit company—we could sure as hell use you!"

The others nodded agreement. Jace didn't know what to say.

That night, Jace and C.C., solid friends now, went to the division officers' club. The usual assortment of rear-echelon types were busy trying to hustle three tired-looking nurses from the evac hospital. Lieutenant Colonel Brock sat in the corner, thoroughly drunk.

C.C. looked at Brock for a long moment, then said, "I finally read your after-action report on the jungle school—it was good. It hit the nail right on the head."

Jace nodded, also looking at Brock.

"You know what?" continued C.C. "In your report, you hinted at something that has concerned me since my first tour."

"What was that? Jace asked.

"You know, when you pointed out that in the jungle warfare course the instructors were telling every soldier that entered the division not to trust the Vietnamese."

"Oh, yeah, when that Sergeant Jenkins said he didn't care what the G-5 said about winning hearts and minds, if you trust them, they'll end up killing you."

"Yeah—reminded me of a paper I wrote in C&GS."

"What was it about?" asked Jace, sipping his beer.

"Well, I was in MAC-V my first tour. I was the senior advisor for an ARVN infantry battalion up at Phu Loi. I ate, slept, bathed, laughed, cried, and fought with those little guys. Time after time they would pull me down in a firefight to protect me. They would literally jump in front of me if they thought I was in danger. They gave me the best cuts of the chicken when we had one—by the way, that's normally the beak and the feet. They made sure I had twice as much rice as they had, because I'm big. They were kind and generous to a fault. Their commander was as brave as any officer I have ever known, certainly braver than those REMF weenies trying to pick up those nurses. I will never forget those people—you know, they had their wives and children there in their base camp with them, sharing the danger. Well, anyway, when I went to the advisor course at Bragg, they told me if I wanted to be successful in the job that I had to practically become Vietnamese—to learn the language, eat the food, appreciate their culture and their customs. I tried my best to do it too. I lost thirty pounds in the process. At any rate, when I got in country, I heard the U.S. units were telling their people to stay away from the locals, that they were probably all V.C—like they told you at our jungle school here."

"Getting back to my paper, I wrote that we were violating a principle of war with our split command in Vietnam. General Westmoreland commands the MAC-V advisors who live with the Vietnamese troops and try to win their hearts and minds. He also commands USARV, the American divisions who are told not to trust the Vietnamese. The two halves of Westmoreland's command are working at cross-purposes, violating the principles of unity of command and unity of effort. The damnedest thing you ever heard of, teaching the principles of war at Leavenworth, then violating them on the battlefield—at the same damned time."

"You know why I think that is?" asked Jace.

"Why?"

"The same thing I told the old man—the same reason the training at the jungle warfare course and our battalion stunk. Everyone thinks this is a new kind of war—a guerrilla war, a counter-insurgency—and our established techniques and rules no longer apply. We don't have to do things right. We can take shortcuts. We can make up our own ways of doing things. This is different—this is Vietnam."

Brock got up and staggered toward the door. As he passed them, he looked at Jace and said, "Go to hell, punk!"

C.C. looked at Jace and grinned. "I heard he was going back to the states to retire."

"Too bad," said Jace, "too bad."

"You know, in a way, it really is," replied C.C.

"What do you mean?"

"Actually, he's kind of pitiful, isn't he?"

"I don't know what you mean," answered Jace. "To me he's just an evil old fart that has no business in the army!"

"Did you see his CIB?" asked C.C. "A star over it. Two awards. One from World War II and the other from Korea. I bet he came here thinking that with his combat experience, he would be king shit. Instead, he found the war being run by young Turks, speaking a new language."

"A new language?" repeated Jace.

"Sure. You said it yourself. This is a different kind of war. New rules. The tried and true techniques don't work here, remember? Brock is probably very proficient in standard infantry tactics. You know, attack, defense, movement to contact, retrograde—that sort of thing. I hear he landed at Normandy and was a platoon leader in the Hurtgen forest. I don't know what he did in Korea, but if he survived there, he sure learned some lessons. Then he got here thinking he was a proficient soldier only to find colonels and majors with much less combat experience talking about search and destroy, jitterbugging, piling on, cordon and search, eagle flights—the list goes on. My guess is, when he couldn't relate, he found himself on the scrap heap—ironically in charge of a school with the mission of teaching the very things he didn't understand. I guess he got bitter."

"What about the generals?" asked Jace. "Didn't they come up from World War II and Korea? Why aren't they on the scrap heap like Brock?"

C.C. sipped his beer and continued, "Oh, I suppose they were the ones who were smart enough to adapt. Most of them, like Westmoreland, are part of the airborne mafia."

"What the hell is the airborne mafia?" laughed Jace. "I guess you and I are members too, then, aren't we?"

C.C. explained. "Nah, we're too young. Look at the number of generals who came out of the 82nd or the 101st in the war. Remember, after World War II, the airborne divisions had the mission of testing the airmobile concept. A lot of the generals in command in Vietnam were in on the ground floor when the helicopter came of age. I guess counter-insurgency fit right in with the airmobile tactics they helped develop."

Jace sat rubbing his chin. "Do you think that will happen to us one day?"

"What's that?"

"Will we end up on the scrap heap because all we know is counter-guerrilla warfare?"

After the training stand-down was over, the 5-39 received a new mission. They were to keep the battalion headquarters and one company at Bear Cat as reserve and reaction force. One company was to secure the village of Binh Son, on the southern edge of the rubber plantation, and occupy the old French villa that had been the plantation owner's home. From there, they would patrol the rubber. The third company would occupy Fire Base Cougar, on Highway 1 near Xuan Loc, where Jace had joined the unit. Their mission would be to patrol the vast jungle area northeast of Bear Cat. Lieutenant Colonel McKensie decided Charlie company would stay at Bear Cat, Bravo would go to the rubber plantation, and Alpha would patrol the jungles south of Highway 1.

Jace began to settle into the routine of being assistant operations officer. He wrote orders, kept the battalion duty log, pulled night radio watch, and did everything else around the headquarters that C.C. wanted done. The days were long, hot and humid, but living at Bear Cat was plush—showers, cot, and hot meals. On his own, Jace kept his eye on the status of training in the companies. The battalion had come too far to let it slip again.

In mid August, McKensie decided to rotate the companies. He would send Charlie to Binh Son, Bravo to Fire Base Cougar, and Alpha to Bear Cat.

On the morning of the sixteenth, the twenty APC's and several wheeled vehicles of C company rolled out of Bear Cat, headed to Binh Son. By early afternoon, they were nearing the French villa. Jace was working on the duty log when the screams came over the radio. A track had hit a mine. Several soldiers were wounded and the situation was very confused. A frantic voice came on the radio calling for a dust-off. The Charlie company commander came on the air saying he was moving forward to access the situation. More screaming, confusion, and cursing came over the radio. No matter what question Jace asked, he couldn't get a coherent answer. The battalion commander and C.C. quickly joined Jace, taking over the radio. Finally, one of the platoon leaders came up on the net saying that four soldiers were wounded and the driver of the track that had hit the mine was dead. He said that an enemy RPG had just been fired at Charlie Six's track and they were trying to sort out that situation. After more confusion and cursing, the lieutenant reported that the rocket-propelled grenade had hit the C company commander in the face and that they couldn't find the top half of his body.

The battalion commander sat by the radio, his head in his hands. When he sat up, there were tears in his eyes.

"C.C., call the airfield and tell them to warm up a Huey. Jace, go pack your bag. You're going down there to pull those boys together. I'll go with you."

"Yes, sir," was all Jace could say. He had wanted a company, but not like this.

CHAPTER 4

▼

16 August 1967

The helicopter with Lieutenant Colonel McKensie and Jace aboard banked and flared for landing at the Binh Son plantation house. As they touched down, Jace quickly glanced around—seeing nothing outwardly unusual.

"The soldier that was killed was in the first platoon," said McKensie. "Before we go to the CP, let's drop by there and pay our respects."

They asked directions, then walked the short distance to the section of the perimeter guarded by first platoon. The troops manning the tracks and bunkers were going about their business as usual, but as Jace and the colonel approached, they stood and were cordial, but distant. To Jace, an obvious disquiet in the soldiers was so real he felt he could touch it. The platoon leader, Lieutenant Green, shook hands with Jace and welcomed him to the company. Although he was polite, there was no sincerity in his actions. McKensie and Jace walked from bunker to bunker, track to track, Jace shaking hands and introducing himself, the colonel offering the troops his condolences for the loss of their friend Jacobs. Though nothing seemed out of order, Jace continued to sense something ominous in the demeanor of the men. As he and the battalion commander left first platoon and walked toward the plantation house, Jace's discomfort grew. He couldn't name what he felt, but it ate at him as it grew larger in his chest. Anger, pain, frustration, guilt, mourning—something was emanating from the soldiers of C company. Maybe it was because of the trauma of the two deaths. But no, it seemed to be more than that. He could almost taste the antipathy in their demeanor.

As Jace and the colonel entered the command post inside the once-elegant villa, someone called attention. McKensie quickly put everyone at ease.

"Captain Spencer, this is specialist Vincent Manning. Everyone calls him by his call sign, Five India. I may not know all of my troops as well as I should, but I do know this one—you can trust him. Ask him anything and he will be honest with you."

As Jace shook his hand, Manning modestly said, "Thank you, sir. Welcome aboard, Captain, I've talked to you on the radio."

The colonel and the new company commander listened as Manning filled them in on the incident that had killed the driver and the captain, and wounded four soldiers. Manning was direct, thorough and to the point. He left nothing out.

"Sir, do you have any questions?"

"No, thank you," said McKensie.

"Probably a thousand, but only one right now." answered Jace.

"What should I call you?"

"Just call me Five India, sir, everyone else does."

Jace smiled and thought for a moment.

"As we landed, I sensed something extremely bothersome in the body language of the troops I saw. Is it a result of this incident, or is it this way after every time a unit has a man killed?"

Five India paused, studying his boots, then, looking up, answered, "Sir, you're very perceptive. I've been in this company since it was formed at Fort Riley, and I can tell you I've never seen anything like the mood they're in right now. We've had guys killed before—several. Most of the time there is grief—maybe even a feeling like: I'm glad it wasn't me—but I've never seen them act the way they're acting now."

McKensie listened intently. He had not felt or observed anything different in the mood of the troops he had seen outside, yet it was obvious that Manning and Jace were agreeing on something that was apparent to them. Five India walked over and closed the door. He looked at the colonel, then at Jace.

"This puts me in a very difficult position, you understand," he said. "I've always considered myself loyal to my boss, my unit and to the guys I serve with. If I tell you what I'm thinking right now, I could sound disloyal."

Five India had McKensie's undivided attention now.

"I believe what you are sensing from the troops is a mixture of sadness over the loss of Spec Four Jacobs—and a feeling of justice—hell maybe even happiness—over the death of Captain Wilson."

"Explain." said McKensie.

"Sir, to say the captain was not liked would be the understatement of the year. I feel like I am violating something religious by telling you this—you know, like a man ought not to say anything bad about the dead—but you asked—and I owe you loyalty too."

Five India paused and shook his head slightly. "Jacobs was a good man. He was well liked by the guys. I know they are grieving for him. The captain, on the other hand was not that well liked—no, dammit—he was hated."

Jace listened quietly. He had never expected this amount of insight and candor from a radio operator. He had never expected to have anyone be this brutally honest about something as emotionally charged as the death of a commander. He also appreciated the fact that he was being afforded a unique chance to learn about the heart and soul of his new company, a chance he might not have again.

McKensie listened with a mixture of disbelief and dismay. He trusted Five India, but he had not been aware of any serious turmoil in C company and he hated to admit it to himself. On two occasions he had been worried about C company's morale, but other than talking with Captain Wilson, had done nothing about it. He had always thought of himself as a problem identifier and solver, but this one had ambushed him.

"Sir, Captain Wilson never did anything exactly dishonest—notice I said exactly! He never did anything that you could even really put your finger on. He had a way of manipulating everyone. He had a way of making you feel like shit, no matter what happened. He pissed everyone off, no matter how well we did. He could turn a situation that was nobody's fault into a big deal that had to be blamed on someone, or everyone. Everything that happened had to be somebody's fault—somebody other than him. When he was caught short, even in little things, he had a way of passing the buck. He had no friends or favorites; he treated everyone the same. He either hated you, disliked you, acted as if you were not even there, or were not important. If you asked me to name an incident, I probably couldn't. You just had to be there to witness it. If he sounded concerned about something, it was because he thought he ought to be concerned. He would make a show of caring when you knew he didn't really give a shit. He would ask you how you were and you would know in your gut he didn't care. He would take credit for every little thing that went well—no matter who did it. If he did something as trivial as tripping over a tent rope, he would blame it on somebody—usually some poor unsuspecting troop. All I can tell you is that during the five months he commanded C company, he did it to all of us, one at a time or collectively.

"The funny thing was that he was able to project a good image upward, to the S-3, the XO, the sergeant major, and to you, too, Sir. He put a snow job on you, Colonel. He seemed to know what you were interested in, and he would make sure you saw him doing it, even if the company was dead on its ass in that area. During the training cycle we just finished, when all the other units were coming together, he made everyone outside the company believe he was a team player too. All of us in the company knew he resented hell out of what was going on—probably because he couldn't figure a way to take credit for it."

Five India paused thoughtfully for a moment.

"This company is a hollow shell," he continued. "He drained the guts from it—from all of us. When he died, it's like the guys all said at the same time, 'Pay-back is a mother, captain!' I think what they are feeling is some kind of release, like justice has been done, and maybe a little guilt for feeling it."

"Why didn't someone let me know?" asked McKensie.

"Let you know what, sir? Like I said, there was never a reportable incident. It was all subtle. You couldn't put a finger on it. If one of us had come to you, it would have been with a fist full of fog."

Jace and the colonel sat silently in folding chairs. Five India stood with his arms crossed, leaning against the wall. All had been said.

Lieutenant Colonel McKensie finally spoke. "You know we will have a memorial service."

"Yes, sir, and if I were you, I'd make it short and sweet." Five India replied.

Jace studied Five India. "Specialist, you are extremely rare. You are a radio/telephone operator, an RTO. But you just handled an issue more explosive than anything I've come up against without flinching. You told us the truth as you see it. My question now is: Where are the officers and NCOs? Where is the first sergeant? I know they saw us land. Where is the XO? He ought to be in here reporting to the colonel."

Manning replied, "Sir, I told you—I believe this company has lost its heart. I believe they are hanging back, waiting to see what happens next. The platoon leaders are outside, no doubt doing busy work. The NCOs probably are in name-tag defilade. The first sergeant is back at Bear Cat. He has a month before he retires. He will never come back to the field, even if you court-martial him. Captain Wilson drained him, ruined him, ground him to a nub. He was once a damned good man.

"I believe they're waiting to see what you'll do—how you'll come in to take over. They're letting me brief you because they know I'm only an E-5. They know I don't give a shit and that I'll tell you what I think. I think they're afraid another ass hole will come in here. Most of them have never had another company commander. Hell, they probably think all captains are alike—all officers, for that matter. I think they are scared and I think they have a feeling of being trapped—doomed if you will—in a hard-luck unit in a combat zone."

"Let me ask you this," asked McKensie, "What do you think this company needs most right now? How do you think Captain Spencer should come in to take over Charlie company?"

"Yes, for God's sake give me a hint—you know these guys and I sure as hell don't," Jace added.

Again, Manning thought for a moment, then said, "They need their guts, their heart back. Captain—just be careful."

Outside, Jace and the battalion commander walked the entire perimeter. The troops were hesitant and vague when asked questions. As Jace shook the hand of each man, most looked away.

He made a mental note of the ones who looked him in the eye. He smiled as he came to the surly little guy with the nickname. What had he called himself? Super Private—that was it.

Before he left, Lieutenant Colonel McKensie scheduled a time for the memorial service, then he gathered the officers and the NCOs for a pep talk. He said he was sorry for their loss and to please give the new company commander their support. Then he called Jace aside.

"Jace, remember the rules of engagement here. You can't fire any mortars or artillery in the rubber plantation unless you are in enemy contact. Also, you cannot shoot into the village of Binh Son, even if you receive fire from there. This place has special political protection. The Vietnamese economy drastically needs the revenue from the rubber plantations. We can't hurt these precious trees."

Jace answered, "Yes, sir. Well, the ambush we popped sure hurt some of the trees."

"Yes, I know," replied Colonel McKensie. "And I guarantee the U.S. Army will pay full price for every tree with a bullet hole in it."

"You're kidding!" gasped Jace.

"No, I wish I were. We are involved in nation building as well as war fighting. We will no doubt prop up every economic endeavor those weenies in the Saigon government can dream up."

"Sir, this house bothers me. Do we have to keep the company fire base around this place?"

"Yes—you must. Again, this place has special political importance. Protecting the plantation house and the village are part of the orders that come from division—in fact, probably from General Westmoreland himself."

"Jace, son, I don't envy you. You seem to have a tiger by the tail down here. Watch yourself. This thing could blow wide open. I can tell you this: you can trust Five India. You were right, he is rare." McKensie was silent for a minute, then added, "As I walked the perimeter, I tried to think of something profound to say as I leave you today. Guess what? I can't think of a damned thing. But I'll say this—your intuition will serve you well. Don't be afraid to use it. If there is anything I can do for you, don't be afraid to ask."

Jace stood nervously, rocking from one foot to the other. "Sir, the only thing I will tell you is that I will do my best—and that I will be asking for help. Some of my requests may sound a little strange."

He then came to attention and saluted. "All the way, Sir!"

McKensie grinned as he returned the salute. "This time, I believe you mean it."

"I do." said Jace. "I do."

Staff Sergeant Ezell Munn, from Otter Banks, South Carolina, watched from the back ramp of his second-platoon APC. Sergeant Smith, one of his squad leaders, a rotten-toothed loud mouth that the troops called Sergeant Breath, stood beside him. They watched as the battalion commander's Huey lifted off.

"Mark my words, there's trouble." said Munn.

Sergeant Breath picked his teeth with a twig. "Why's that?"

"You watch. Wilson's dead. Whenever they's a change in command, the new cap'n comes in like Jesus Christ cleansin' the damn temple," answered Munn. "He'll thank we's all screwed up. He'll drive us crazy for a month till this damned place starts to grind him down."

"Maybe he 'on't be so bad. He seemed straight to me."

Munn turned and looked at the man. "You thank so, huh? I tell you what—if he starts to listen to ever two-dollar nigger in the comp'ny, he'll have us all doin' the Alabama high-step."

"Well, we got one thang goin' for us. He's from the south, you can tell by the way he talks. I hear tell he's from Tennessee. Maybe he be OK. We just got to play it cool an' git him on our side, that's all."

"And you thank you smart enough to do that, do ye?" laughed Munn.

"I ain't sayin' that. I just mean—"

"I know what you mean. Just don't go brown-nosin' the new C.O. Let's just see what shakes out. We'll keep a low profile. Let the LT deal with the cap'n.

We'll just keep doin' what we been doin'. Keep an eye on the niggers. If one of 'em wants to talk to the C.O., let me know. You just he'p me keep a lid on thangs till everythang settles down." Munn said as he watched the captain walk the colonel to his helicopter.

Private Peoples, a young African-American soldier sitting behind the .50 caliber on top of the track heard the entire conversation—particularly the word "nigger". Frowning, he pulled his poncho around his shoulders to ward off the drizzle. Once, he turned his head to look at the new captain and wondered what changes he would bring. He hoped things would get better. He didn't see how they could get much worse.

This time Jace remembered the prohibition against saluting in the field and simply waved to the battalion commander as his chopper nosed over and climbed out. McKensie returned a thumbs-up. Jace knew the colonel had other fires to put out—this one belonged to Captain Jason Spencer. He turned and walked back toward the villa, feeling totally alone. He thought about getting the officers together, then thought better of it. He needed time to think. He needed to decide how he could get the soldiers on his side. He needed to figure out his entrance strategy. Should he be tough? Should he be gentle with them? Was he putting too much stock in what Five India had said? Should he take time and gather more information? Should he make changes immediately? Should he wait? He just didn't know.

Back at the plantation house, he looked in on Five India, who was busy doing the hourly radio checks. Jace decided he would not bother him but would look around the villa instead. He found a large kitchen, but was amazed that the mess tent was set up outside in the mud. There were four small bedrooms. The radios were set up in the corner one; it appeared the officers had set up cots in the others. There was a large parlor, which was not being used, and the master bedroom, where the dead company commander had lived. His personal belongings had been removed, but a cot with mosquito net, a small table, and a foot locker were still there. There was no other furniture, electricity, or water, but the building was luxurious by Vietnam standards.

Jace walked to the window to look out on the troops. They huddled under ponchos in the drizzle. The mud was ankle deep in the places where there was no grass. Jace tried to see where the troops slept. He imagined they crashed on air mattresses in the damp bunkers or inside the muddy APCs.

He stood and thought for a long time—then on impulse, headed for third platoon. Jace found Super Private heating a can of spiced beef over a can of dirt soaked with gasoline. He was trying to keep the rain out of his supper by holding his helmet over the can. Jace stood watching until the private looked up.

"Damn, sir, you scared hell out of me," he said.

"Don't let me bother you, I was just poking around, trying to get my bearings."

"The only bearings around here is rusted to a road wheel."

"Where do you sleep?" asked Jace.

"Where ever I can find a dry place—bunker, track, poncho hootch."

Jace stood and watched as the spiced beef began to steam.

"Look, I'll just tell you the truth. You impressed me after the ambush as a guy who'll say what he thinks. I thought I'd ask you what you think."

Super Private looked up at Jace and squinted one eye, a smirk on his face. "Think about what?" he asked.

Jace knelt beside the private.

"About the shape this company is in." replied Jace.

"Damn, sir! What you tryin' to do to me? I got a reputation to uphold here. The dudes see me talkin' to you and they won't trust me with nothin' again."

"I'm sorry," said Jace, standing. "I remember when I came to see you guys after our ambush, you asked when I was going to come and take over this 'piece-of-shit company'. Well I'm here. I need to know where to start. I need some information and I don't know any of you. I thought you would be honest with me. Sorry to bother you—enjoy your chow."

At dusk, Jace finally got the officers together. He introduced himself even though he had met these officers when he had taught patrolling at Bear Cat. He told them about his background, then asked about theirs. There was First Lieutenant Wallace Driscol, the executive officer, an OCS graduate from Kansas. Second Lieutenant Kevin Green of first platoon was an OCS officer from the mountains of western North Carolina, near Jace's home. Second Lieutenant Richard Nevin of second platoon was an ROTC graduate from the University of Georgia. Second Lieutenant Joe Cappaccelli of third platoon, whose nickname was Little Caesar, hailed from New Jersey and was also an OCS officer. First Lieutenant Justin Otis, the weapons platoon leader was a soft-spoken cowboy from Idaho. He was ROTC. Jace thought of the West Pointers stacked three deep in the 173rd.

"I have nothing for you tonight," Jace said in his mildest tone of voice. "See to the security. I'd like one of us walking the perimeter all night. You all decide shifts. I'll take the one that's left over. That's all, unless you have any questions."

No one said anything. They stood, looked uncertain, nodded, then left.

Jace went outside and looked around. He was unsettled, feeling out of his element. In the 82nd he had jumping out of airplanes and physical training every morning in common with his troops. Here, he had shared a successful ambush with one squad—that was all. He had never had difficulty communicating with soldiers. But there was a wall here, twenty feet high, and very, very thick.

As he turned back toward the house, a voice came from the darkness.

"Cap'n!"

"Yeah, who is it?"

Super Private stepped from the shadows.

"I swear, if you tell anybody I talked to you, I'll deny it."

"What're you afraid of?" asked Jace.

"I ain't 'fraid of shit."

"Then why the secrecy?"

"They's bad blood here. Bad blood between the officers and the men. The NCOs are the same way—they're done with officers!"

"What do I need to know?" Jace asked warily.

"Just that—the guys don't trust nobody. There's been too much shit. I tell you what—don't believe me, just watch—if you're as hip as I think you might be, you'll see."

Jace looked at the small man. He was wearing only jungle fatigue pants and shower clogs. His ribs looked like an accordion; his head seemed to balance on his adam's apple. He looked like he hadn't shaved for days. Rheumy eyes darted to and fro under the bill of his G.I. cap. Jace had the feeling those eyes didn't miss much, if anything.

"You're not telling me anything. O.K., so there's bad blood. What kind? Who? Who do I need to watch? Who's been treated unfairly?

Super Private scuffed his feet in the mud. He took off his greasy cap, smeared his matted hair back, replaced the cap and pulled the bill back over his eyes. Cocking his head, he seemed to weigh several possibilities or outcomes.

"I can tell you this. When we popped that ambush, it almost drove the captain crazy. He tried every way in the world to take credit for it. He claimed it was the training he give us. He claimed he told you where to take us to find Charlie. He even tried to claim you were asleep when the 'bush popped. All the guys just laughed at 'im—and that drove him crazy. He turned on our squad. It was like we couldn't do nothin' right.

"Let me get this straight. He punished you for being successful?" asked Jace.

"It was like we done somethin' against him for killin' those dinks under your control rather than his. The fact that he couldn't figure out how to claim credit made him mad as hell at us. Two of the guys got Article 15's for stuff they didn't do. He never said nothin' but we all knew he was out to get us."

"Let me look into the Article 15s. If I can prove they're bogus, I'll make them go away." What else can I do to make it right?" asked Jace, quietly.

"Right now, nothin'. The guys have been ragged out so bad that they don't trust nobody with bars. The lieutenant is O.K., but they even watch him like a hawk. If I wuz you, I'd just be myself and be honest with us. They'll come around. If you try some grandstand play, they'll know it for what it is. It'll take time."

Jace stared off into the darkness. They were both quiet for a moment.

"Is there anything else I need to know?" Jace asked.

"You can trust Five India. He's smart, but he's one of us. He ain't never crossed us, even though he's in the position to. He's a real guy."

"I got that feeling, too," replied Jace. "Is there anything else?"

"Just one thing more. Watch Sergeant Munn! He's a snake. He hates the coloreds. He's cool about it, but if he gets the chance, he'll screw one of 'em just for fun. Some of the bad blood, particularly in second platoon comes from him. Cap'n Wilson knew what was going on, but he never did anything about it. Keep an eye on him. If he keeps it up, he might get shot out in the jungle one day. I've heard talk."

Jace drew a deep breath. "Is that all?" he asked.

"For now." answered the private.

"Look, I don't know what I'm going to do. I won't know what's the right thing 'till I see it. But I can tell you one thing. What you've told me might just save us all. I can't thank you enough."

Super Private reached out an oil-stained, nail-chewed hand. Jace took it and the two men stood momentarily looking at each other. Then the private was gone.

Jace walked back into the villa. Five India saw him coming.

"Oh, sir, Cougar Three just called. Said to call him when you got back in."

"OK, look, set me up a prick-25 on the battalion alternate freq."

Five India nodded; Jace picked up the hand set.

"Cougar Three, this is Charlie Six."

"This is Cougar Three, I just wondered how you were doing."

"This is Charlie Six. Can you meet me on the alternate freq?"

"Roger, wait." said C.C.

Jace picked up the back pack radio and walked out on the veranda.

"Cougar Three, are you there?"

"Roger," shot back C.C., "What's up?"

"Need some advice."

"Go," said C.C., the concern evident in his voice.

"Talk to Cougar Six, he'll fill you in. I've got a real can of worms down here. I just don't know how to proceed. I wish you could get down here, I really need to talk."

"No can do. Big time busy here. Cougar Six filled me in. We can't talk about this on the radio."

"Roger. In the morning I've got to hit the ground running. I'm just praying nothing happens tonight."

"This is Cougar Three. The only advice I can give you is don't hold back. If everything Six told me is true, you can't waste time. Don't be afraid to wade in. Make changes if they need to be made, and make them now. Be yourself. That's what will carry you."

"This is Charlie Six. Roger. That helped. Tomorrow is likely to be a long day."

"Hang tough, I'll get down there as soon as I can."

"Thanks, over."

"This is Cougar Three, Out!"

Jace went back inside.

"All straight, sir?" asked Five India.

"All straight. Why do they call you Five India? Five is the exec's call sign. Five India would mean assistant—what?—assistant XO?"

"Yes, sir. It seems they didn't know what to do with me. I know more and can do more than a radio operator, but I'm not an officer, I'm not really an NCO either. If the truth were known, though, many times I've found myself running things. Assistant company executive officer or whatever—take your pick. Look, I don't mean to brag on myself, sir", Five India added quickly, "It's just the way things shook themselves out."

"Makes sense in some distorted way," said Jace. "I've just never seen a set-up quite like this one. Tell me more about the first sergeant, I think I met him at Bear Cat. Tall skinny fella if I remember right. Do you think I should try to get him out here?"

"No, sir. If I were you I'd leave him be. He retires in a month and he's been caught in the middle of such an unbelievable bunch of crap between Captain Wilson and the troops that his nerves are shot. Plus, he's lost face. The troops don't trust him any more and the officers think he's a shithead, even though none of it was his fault. I'd let him stay at Bear Cat and do the morning reports and handle the admin. He does a good job with that stuff. Then, I'd just let him retire with dignity. He's a casualty of this war the same as if he were wounded."

"Did he ever do anything wrong, you know bad?" asked Jace.

"No, sir. He always tried. Then one day he just caved in."

"You know how to write awards recommendations?"

"Yes, sir."

"Write him a bronze star for his retirement." ordered Jace. "We'll let him keep his dignity."

"Who is the field first, the senior NCO?" asked Jace.

"Well, I don't know who the senior NCO is, but I guess I've been acting as field first."

"I don't mean you any disrespect, but you are only a specialist fifth class—like you said, you're not even a real NCO. Why doesn't one of the platoon sergeants act as field first?"

Lowering his voice, Five India said, "None of them wanted to be anywhere near Captain Wilson. They said they needed to be with their troops, and I told the captain I thought I could handle anything that came up in the headquarters, and it just worked itself out like it is."

Jace sat down on a folding chair, shaking his head.

"What do you think I should do tomorrow?" Jace asked slowly.

"Sir, if I knew that, I would be in command, not you."

"You know what? I'd bet a dollar against a stale donut you could handle it."

Five India grinned, asked, "You want a beer?"

"What the hell could it hurt?" answered Jace, grinning back.

Jace put his folding chair against the wall, pulled the lantern nearer, and opened his notebook. He thumbed through the notes he had made during the training cycle. All the pages he had written were about tactics and training, not a clue about a leadership crisis. He sat listening to Five India answering the radio checks, the hissing of the lantern and the rushing of radio squelch the only other sound. Jace stared at the ceiling. Five India felt his mood, his dilemma, and his anxiety and left him alone. From time to time a soldier would come in for some reason, probably to get a look at Jace or just to get some comfort from being in a lighted building for a minute or two.

Jace sat, stared and thought as the evening wore on. All of a sudden, just after midnight, he picked up his steel pot, slung on his web gear and walked out on the verandah. He stood quietly, letting his eyes adjust to the dark. On the horizon hung the ubiquitous parachute flare. He listened to the night sounds of insects, coughing, random clanks of metal, and snoring. Just as he was getting used to the rhythm of the night, a starter whinnied and a track roared to life. Another on the other side of the perimeter answered. Soon, several tracks were idling, charging the batteries run down by the radios, which were kept in constant operation. There would be no chance to listen for danger in the constant rumble of track engines.

When he got his night vision, Jace started around the perimeter. He had no idea what the challenge and password might be, so he stopped at the first platoon leader's track, where he and the battalion commander had visited that afternoon. No one saw him or challenged him. A soldier was slumped behind the .50 caliber machine gun on the top of the vehicle. Hearing snores inside, Jace crept silently by and headed to the three other armored personnel carriers of first platoon. At each track, he found one soldier, supposedly on guard, and the rest asleep, the leaders included. Continuing around the perimeter, he checked the other platoons and found the same thing. He went to the mortar platoon, situated behind the house toward the center of the perimeter, and saw that they too were all asleep. Anxious and thoroughly disgusted, he stood for a moment, then walked quietly back inside the house. After checking the radio watch—a different soldier was on now, reading a paperback in the lantern light—Jace went from room to room in the darkened villa. All the officers were snoring under their mosquito nets. When no one had come to tell him what shift he had, he had thought they were deferring to him because he was the new company commander. Now he knew the truth. None of the officers cared enough to stay awake to supervise their soldiers.

"Five India, wake up." Jace said in a rough whisper as he shook Manning.

"Yes, sir." said Five India, instantly awake.

"There are perhaps ten soldiers in this 150-man rifle company awake right now," whispered Jace. There is no leadership on the line. I just walked the entire perimeter. We're in a dangerous spot."

"What do you want me to do?" asked Five India.

"Do you have any red paint?"

Jace and Five India stayed awake all night going from track to track keeping the guards alert. As badly as Jace wanted to wake everyone up and rip into the leadership for endangering the whole company, he remembered his temper and the certainty that if he made a mistake now, he might never be able to correct it. He told Five India not to chew anyone out, but to simply make the rounds talking to the guards, keeping them alert. Jace, on the other hand, became a one-man patrol. Armed with pistol and a Starlight scope, he watched the ground outside the perimeter for movement. Between visits to the guards, he stood on top of the bunkers, and walked to the edge of the wire, scanning for danger. During the night, he saw that very few of the guards were relieved and there did not appear to be any pattern in the shift changes. If a soldier was too timid to wake someone up to relieve him, he was left to his own devices behind the .50-caliber all night long.

As the sun came up, the soldiers of C company rolled out, stretched and went to relieve themselves. As they stood urinating or scratching, they were jolted wide-awake. Large red Xs were painted on most of their armored personnel carriers. The sand bags of almost all of the bunkers were smeared bright red. Some soldiers even had red splotches dabbed on their fatigues.

Jace sat in the radio room of the villa, sipping coffee. They had made it through the night alive; now he waited for his officers to awaken. One by one, they crawled out of their net-draped cots and headed toward the latrine or coffee pot. Only one of them said good morning to Jace as he went past.

Jace shaved, checked the radio log, cleaned his .45, then went to the mess tent, still waiting for a reaction. There was hot coffee, but only C-rations for breakfast. He chose a B-1 unit, hoping the fruit would be peaches, which went great with the can of pound cake he had squirreled away. He went back to the radio room, ate breakfast, and continued to wait. When the battalion commander called, asking how things were going, Jace was vague, telling McKensie he would brief him later. At 0830, the company executive officer, First Lieutenant Driscol walked in.

"Sir, I don't understand what's going on." he began. "It seems that our vehicles have been painted red."

"What?" asked Jace.

"Red, sir."

"I don't understand," said Jace, "Is someone playing a joke?"

"Sir, I don't know, but I'll tell you I don't like it one little bit."

"What don't you like?" asked Jace calmly.

"Sir, If this is your idea of something funny—"

"What makes you think I had anything to do with this?" asked Jace.

"The troops said you were up and around last night. In light of all that has happened to this company in the past couple of days, I think this whole thing is inappropriate, definitely not funny, and maybe a little weird."

"Well, at least you're not afraid to speak your mind," said Jace. "Assemble the officers on the front porch. Have them standing there in the position of attention exactly five minutes from now."

Jace gave them the allotted five minutes, then went outside.

"Gentlemen, it was I who painted your tracks and bunkers. It could have been Viet Cong sappers with satchel charges, but it was only me with a paint brush. My orders to you last night were for you to walk the perimeter in shifts. I told you to tell me what shift I had. You failed to carry out those orders. You slept all night, and so did the troops. Five India and I and about twenty soldiers guarded this whole company all through the night. I did the painting rather than wake anybody up—the point being that someone could have blown up the vehicles instead of painting them. Notice not all of the tracks have paint on them. The ones with guards who were alert I left alone. The lesson is that all the tracks and bunkers that are painted red could have been blown to hell."

"Sir, I—" gulped the XO.

"You are at attention, lieutenant. Not only did you officers sleep through the night, so did your NCOs. Not a single leader was checking the line. The entire mortar platoon was asleep, too. I suppose you thought that shooting would wake you if someone needed a mortar round fired."

No one spoke. They stood rigidly at attention with hate-looks on their faces.

"Here are my orders," continued Jace. "If any one of you doesn't like what I'm about to say, I want you out of my company area by noon."

"Sir, I believe—" the XO started again.

"If you interrupt me again, you may be departing sooner than noon. As I was saying, my orders are—first, all of you will move out of this damned house and will sleep with your troops. Second, you and your platoon sergeants will split the night walking your section of the line. When I walk the perimeter, which I will do often until I am satisfied you are doing your jobs, I had better find one of you supervising, outside in the rain, not in the track. Third, I will issue a challenge and password that will change each day, which hopefully will keep someone from accidentally getting shot. Fourth, the troops who were asleep will paint the tracks green again, not the ones who were on guard. Fifth, from now on there will be a hot breakfast and a hot supper fed to the troops each day. The only C-ration meal will be at noon. Sixth, the radio watch will move out of this house into the command track. The only company personnel I want in this house are the cooks who may use the kitchen. At night I don't want a single light on inside his building. Last, I will conduct an inventory and inspection of your troops, weapons, and vehicles at 1400 today. You should not have any trouble getting ready, since you all are well rested. You are dismissed."

That afternoon, Jace found what he had suspected. Despite all the effort put forth during the training cycle, things had begun to slip. Individual weapons were fairly clean, but the crew-served weapons were in bad shape. The spare barrels for the .50s and M-60s were rusty, maintenance on the vehicles was poor, logbooks entries had stopped the day the battalion refresher training had ended, and explosives were stored in very unsafe conditions. The troops seemed to know their jobs, but when Jace made some of them take off their boots, the medics found twelve cases of immersion foot.

One thing that he found that he did not understand was that the company had nearly twice the machine guns and radios it was authorized. Five India explained that each time they made enemy contact or a track was destroyed, they would report a few radios and machine guns missing or destroyed and order replacements, even if there were none lost. Charlie company, it seemed, had plenty of fire power and communications.

On the morning of Jace's second day in command, Lieutenant Colonel McKensie, C.C., the battalion sergeant major and the battalion chaplain flew in for a memorial service. Jace had seen to it that two M-16s with bayonets were stuck in the ground, muzzle down, between the toes of two pairs of jungle boots. Helmets were placed on the butts of the rifles, the standard arrangement for a combat memorial service. Each set of equipment represented a dead soldier. The chaplain read scripture and led a prayer, and Lieutenant Colonel McKensie said a few words. As Five India had recommended, it was short and sweet.

Over coffee, Jace told the battalion commander that what he had observed since taking command verified what Five India had told them. He told McKensie that the officers had lived like kings, having almost no contact with the troops. The dead company commander had ruled with an iron hand, treating sergeants like privates, and privates like dirt. The officers, following his example had done the same thing, causing a gulf of resentment and mistrust between the ranks. The NCOs had stopped trying, since they were not listened to or respected. The ones who had suffered most in this arrangement were the troops.

"The amazing thing is how this company got through the training cycle without any of us seeing that anything was wrong," said Jace.

"That doesn't matter now," said McKensie. "We have now seen that something is definitely wrong. What can I do to help fix it?" Jace sensed Colonel McKenzie's loss of face. C company was in sorry shape and as battalion commander, he had not realized it. It took a hell of a man to swallow that fact and continue soldiering instead of lashing out and blaming someone. Jace felt sorry for him and respected him at the same time. It was not his fault. His chain of command had let him down.

"Sir, I need a couple of chess sets, four or five checker boards, some playing cards, a four-by-eight piece of plywood, two saw horses, some ping-pong paddles and balls, and ten cots."

"Sergeant Major, you got that?" asked the colonel. "By the way, I hear you've done some painting on your vehicles. I know you got permission from the motor officer before you did it, didn't you?"

"Oh, yes, sir," grinned Jace, "It was all on the up and up."

After the battalion commander and his party had left, Jace called the officers together. He acted as if the chewing-out he had given them on the verandah had never happened.

"Gentlemen, one thing that concerns me when I walk the line at night is the constant idling of the vehicles to keep the batteries charged. During my inventory, I found that we have an abundance of PRC-25 radios. From now on, the company headquarters, the squads, and platoons will communicate solely on PRC-25s. XO, make sure we order more prick-25 batteries. I want the tracks totally shut down at night. Since we won't be operating the vehicle-mounted radios, there will be no reason to run them to charge batteries. When it gets dark, I want the perimeter totally quiet. Not a sound. All conversations will be in whispers. I want us to be able to listen to the night sounds. One day we might hear something that could save a life. Are there any questions?"

When no one spoke, Jace dismissed them.

"Sir?" Lieutenant Driscol said as the other officers left.

"Whatcha got, XO?"

"I guess this is yours now," said the lieutenant as he held out the CAR-15. It's the company commander's assigned weapon. Captain Wilson never used it—gave it to me to carry."

Jace took the short assault rifle, turned it over in his hands and looked it over carefully.

"Never carried it, huh?"

"No, sir. I can't remember him ever going out on any kind of operation where he might have to use it. He stayed with the tracks all the time."

"Well, thanks." said Jace. "I'll sure carry it when I'm out in the bush."

"The stuff you ordered is coming down on the mail chopper," said the XO.

"OK, here's what I want," said Jace. "I believe that house is dangerous." I don't want anyone in it at night—but during the day, the cooks can use the kitchen and the big rooms are going to become an R&R center." explained Jace.

"Sir?"

"I want ten cots set up in the master bedroom. I want a ping-pong table made of the plywood and the sawhorses out on the porch. The parlor will become a game room. Every day, I want the squad that is coming in off the night ambush patrol pulled off the line and allowed to stand down for twenty-four hours. They can sleep all day if they want to, and dry out their feet. They will have a double beer ration. They can play cards, games, or ping-pong."

"Yes, sir.—Uh—May I explain something, sir?"

"Sure, shoot."

"The other night when all the officers were asleep—it was my fault." said Lieutenant Driscol.

"Oh?" said Jace, studying Driscol's face.

"Yes, sir. Joe Cappaccelli was walking the perimeter before my shift. He came and woke me up, then he went to bed. I remember sitting up, but the next thing I knew, it was daylight, and I was still in my cot. Also, it was me that made the decision not to bother you with a shift. I don't want you to blame the others. It was my fault."

"You know what? Your stock just went up a hundred percent in my book. We were lucky that we didn't get hit—we got away clean. Your being honest and taking responsibility just made my whole day." said Jace, reaching to shake his XO's hand.

"Sir, there's something else you need to know." said the executive officer. "Yesterday, Sergeant Neeley came back from R&R. He said in Saigon everyone was talking about what happened in the 25th Division."

"What's that? What happened?" asked Jace.

"Over near Tay Ninh, a mech company in the 25th Division was attacked by the Viet Cong. The troops had apparently come in late from a search-and-destroy operation. They were tired and didn't dig in. They left one guard on each track, and everybody went to sleep. The guards were tired, and they zonked out too. Evidently, no leaders were out supervising the perimeter. Charlie sneaked in, wired the doors shut on the tracks, then threw explosive charges under each one. Fifteen tracks were destroyed. Neeley said over thirty troops were killed and nearly 100 wounded. He said the V.C. took the .50-cals guns off the tracks and were shooting at helicopters and the flare ships with them. When it was over, Charlie disappeared without a trace. God, that is scary."

Jace nodded, but didn't say anything.

"Sir, that word spread like wildfire around the company. We all know that could have happened to us. I guess what I'm saying is that your stock is up with all of us, too."

That night, the V.C. fired a B-40 rocket into the side of the plantation house. Deadly shell and brick fragments ricocheted around inside. None of Jace's troops were hurt since there was no one inside. The hole in the wall was quickly patched so the South Vietnamese government and Headquarters, MACV would not be upset that a prized national asset had been damaged.

Jace soon found the Binh Son mission boring. One squad, on a rotational basis patrolled the village and stayed at the market place at night. In addition, a squad-sized ambush patrol went nightly into the rubber plantation. From time to time battalion ordered a platoon-sized sweep of a part of the plantation. He felt things were getting better, but they still had light years to go.

As he sat on the verandah watching two soldiers playing table tennis, Lieutenant Colonel McKensie called on the command net. Jace was instantly on edge, since the battalion commander rarely called personally.

"I'm sending my chopper down to get you. You have an appointment. I'll explain when you get here."

Jace picked up on something in McKensie's voice and was unnerved. "What's this about? Can you tell me over the air?"

"I said I'd explain when you get here. Out!" McKensie terminated the conversation abruptly, further disquieting Jace.

Thirty minutes later, the H-23 arrived. Jace briefed Five India and Lieutenant Driscol, then took off for Bear Cat. When he landed, he went straight to battalion headquarters. The colonel and C.C. were out visiting A company, so Jace had to wait. With nothing to do, he dozed in C.C.'s office.

He was awakened by someone kicking his feet. It was the battalion commander. Jace jumped to his feet.

"What's this all about, sir?" asked Jace, instantly awake.

"Well, maybe bad news for us—maybe good news for you."

"What do you mean?" asked Jace.

"You have to go to Two Field Force G-1 for an interview. It seems that every ranger-qualified officer in the southern part of this country is being pulled together to form some new units. Two Field Force is going to set up several Long-Range Recon Patrol outfits. You're probably familiar with the concept. They operate in six-man teams deep in enemy territory. Classic ranger missions. They'll do recon patrols, prisoner snatches, call in air strikes and set up mechanical ambushes. They'll all be on jump status, too. Jace, it goes without saying we'll hate to lose you, but we may not have any say about it."

Jace was stunned. All he had thought of earlier in his tour was getting to an airborne unit. Now, as he realized he was practically being drafted for one, a thrill shot through him. To be back with real soldiers—Airborne Rangers! He couldn't believe it was happening to him.

During the short flight up to Long Binh, Jace was so beside himself with excitement that he remembered nothing about the flight. His imagination was aflame with all sorts of possibilities. A ranger unit, jump status, special operations, long-range patrols! He might even get the opportunity to make a combat jump. He could have a gold star on his jump wings, just like the troops in the second battalion of the 173rd. He would be working with the best soldiers and NCOs in the army. His dream had come true.

He had expected to be interviewed with other ranger officers, but he found himself alone in the G-1's outer office. The G-1 colonel must have been busy, because Jace had to wait for half an hour. As he waited, he thought of the unit he would be leaving. Thoughts of Five India, Super Private, and the honesty of Lieutenant Driscol crept into his mind. He thought of his friend C.C., of the down-to-earth decency, caring, and competence of Lieutenant Colonel McKensie, and of the training cycle he had made happen. A flood of conflicting emotions washed over him as he waited.

His last thought before he was summoned was of the silhouette of a wet, tired teenager slumped behind a .50-caliber on top of an armored personnel carrier in a dark night in the Binh Son rubber plantation. Jace walked in, saluted, and told the Two Field Force G-1 that he wanted to stay with Company C, Fifth Battalion, 39th Infantry, of the 9th Infantry Division, and that he would fight to do so.

Jace had little else to do, so he walked the perimeter non-stop, getting to know his soldiers. He made corrections as he found they were needed, but didn't raise his voice or chew anyone out. Mainly, he wanted to get to know his men and let them see that he was interested in them. He approached the troops with the attitude that he believed that they were responsible and that they wanted to do things right. As he made his rounds, he patted backs for things he found being done correctly, and only made notes of the things he needed to address later. Slowly the men seemed to warm to his leadership. By forcing the officers out of the villa and by giving the NCOs their jobs back, Jace began to pump some life back into Charlie company. At least everyone was adhering to the letter of his orders. He felt as if he were making progress, but the spirit was still not in them.

There were 182 troops on Charlie company's morning report. Several were wounded, sick, on emergency leave, on R&R, or had come up with any number of reasons not to be in the bush. Jace made a concerted effort to learn the names of all 153 of his troops that were present for duty in the field. As he made his way around the third platoon section of the line, he came upon a medic working on the feet of a soldier. He had seen the medic several times before, but didn't know his name. As he watched the man gently working on the swollen and cracked foot of a young soldier, Jace noticed that he wore the stubble of a beard. He stopped and looked over the medic's shoulder at the man's feet.

"What's the trouble, Doc?"

"Immersion foot. The cracks in the skin caused by his feet staying wet all the time are gettin' infected."

"Doc—I'm sorry, I haven't learned your name yet—what can we do to get the troops' feet out of the mud?"

The medic stood, faced Jace and offered his hand.

"Sir, I'm Spec Four Daniel Roberts, your company senior medic."

Jace shook his hand and studied his face. Roberts was a sturdy, well-built man of medium height. His face radiated kindness, confidence and intelligence. He watched as Jace's eyes cut to the growth on his face.

"In case you're wondering about the beard, I have a shaving profile. Folliculitis—in-grown hairs. Believe me, I'd rather shave." said Roberts. "To answer your question, pallets. If we had couple of truckloads of wooden shipping pallets we could make walkways on the well-traveled paths around the tracks. That would keep the guys' feet out of the water a good portion of the time. Several units at Bear Cat use them in their company areas. They work."

Jace answered, "I admit I wondered about the beard. Thanks. I'm glad to meet you. I've watched you work and I'm impressed with the job you do and your bedside manner."

Roberts grinned. "Thank you, sir. We're not used to hearing many compliments around here."

"Saigon docks!"

Jace turned. He hadn't seen Super Private eavesdropping.

"You can get all the pallets you want at the Saigon docks."

"How do you know?" asked Jace.

Super Private grinned and ignored the question.

"I tell you what, Cap'n, you give me a truck and somebody to help me and I'll get you all the pallets you want." answered Super Private excitedly.

"How do you know all this?" asked Jace again.

"Sir, there are some things you just don't want to know. You just get me the truck."

"All right, but you don't go by yourself. I'll send a platoon of tracks to escort you out to Highway 15. You wait there and attach yourself to a convoy. Take a radio. Coming back, go to battalion headquarters at Bear Cat. We'll figure out how to get you back from there. If I catch you running the roads alone, you've had it." ordered Jace.

The next morning, PFC Tucker, Jace's driver, with Super Private riding shotgun, pulled out of the company perimeter in the company's supply truck wedged between the four armored personnel carriers of third platoon. When the tracks came back in an hour, Lieutenant Cappaccelli reported the truck safely in a convoy headed north.

Jace worried about the two soldiers all day as he walked the perimeter and issued the patrol orders for the night's ambushes. At dusk, he received a radio call from C.C.

Jace ran to his command track and grabbed the radio hand set.

"This is Charlie Six, Go."

"This is Cougar Three. I've got a couple of your yard birds up here in a truck loaded with all kinds of crap. What do you want me to do with them?" radioed C.C.

"This is Charlie Six. Keep them there overnight. In the morning let them go out to the main road and latch on to a convoy. I'll send a platoon out to the main road to meet them."

"Wheelin' and dealin' already I see. You just be careful."

"This is Charlie Six. I just wanted some pallets to get the troops' feet out of the mud."

"This is Cougar Three. You just got took. There are all the pallets you want at Bear Cat. Just ask G-4 and they'll deliver. Besides, pallets are about half the load on your truck. Looks like your guys just went shopping."

"Thanks for the info—when are you coming down?"

"In a day or so—How're things on your end?

"Boring." answered Jace.

"Keep up the good work—see you soon."

"This is Charlie six, looking forward to seeing you."

"This is Cougar Three, out."

After supper, Jace felt uneasy about the squad in Binh Son.

"Five India, crank up the jeep. Let's go down and check the village."

In a moment, Five India slid the jeep to a stop as he fumbled behind the seats turning on the command radios. Jace thought about bringing along a bodyguard, but thought better of it. He didn't know what his troops would think.

Only 500 meters from the company perimeter, Binh Son was a cluster of thatched-roofed huts that lined two parallel dirt streets. Both streets opened onto a kind of town square—a town clearing would be more accurate. Around the clearing were the village chief's house, the school, a small temple, and the market. All of the buildings, as well as the square, were shaded by tall palm trees. Shorter nippa palms with fan-like leaves grew in groves that marked the village boundary. A few rice paddies and a large vegetable garden surrounded the village on three sides. The ominously straight wall of the rubber plantation stood silently beyond the cultivated fields.

As they had each time they had come to the village, Jace and Five India drove first to the village chief's house. Jace reached under the back seat of the jeep and pulled out two ice-cold Carling Black Label beers. The village chief, who could speak no English, came out immediately, bowing and clapping his hands softly. Jace climbed out of the jeep, bowed, and offered a beer to the chief. Pleased and embarrassed, the small man accepted the can and in sign language, invited Jace to sit down. The tall American and the small Vietnamese sat, smiled and drank together. After what he thought was a suitable length of time, Jace rose, bowed, and left to go to the market.

The squad that supposedly guarded the market lounged in the shade, their equipment scattered about them. When the squad leader saw Jace, he jumped to his feet self-consciously. Jace started to rip into him, but thought better of it, not wanting to embarrass the troops in front of the villagers. When he got back to the company, he would speak to the platoon leader and let him straighten the squad out. For now, the mere presence of the company commander seemed to be enough to make the troops stand up, button up and spread out.

As he prepared to leave, Jace looked about the market. Fruits and vegetables were on display on fly-covered cloths on the ground. At one stand, ceramic figurines were offered for sale. Jace scanned the wares, glanced away, then did a double take. His eyes fell on the black-glazed clay figurine of a cat sitting in the same alert posture affected by old Jupiter on the day he and his dad had talked and weeded the garden. He turned to the small woman with the black-stained teeth and blood-red gums of a betel-nut chewer.

"How much?" he asked in English?

The small woman tilted her head with an embarrassed smile.

Jace picked up the figurine of the cat. He withdrew his wallet and extended it to the woman.

"How much?" he said again, smiling.

The woman reached gently with her tiny hand. Without taking the wallet from his hand, she deftly removed a ten-piaster bill and held it aloft for him to see. She turned to her purse, withdrew some change, and handed it to Jace. She bowed, smiling, knowing she had just charged three times what the figurine was worth.

"Thank you very much!" bowed Jace, thinking he would have paid many times as much to get the ceramic cat.

As he climbed into his jeep, Jace cradled the glazed cat and smiled to the villagers. They seemed pleased at the attention—or by the fact that the woman had taken the American in the purchase. He didn't know why they were smiling. They didn't know why he wanted the cat figurine.

Back at the company, Jace placed the ceramic cat next to the radios in the command track, saying nothing. When his troops asked—if they asked, he would tell them.

After receiving instructions to spend the night in Bear Cat, Super Private and Tucker decided to skip the evening meal at the mess hall. Parking the supply truck in the dirt road in front of the snack bar, Tucker secured the chain that was welded to the floorboard around the steering wheel with a padlock. Vehicle theft was a common problem at Bear Cat. Every unit liked to have a spare jeep or truck they could keep at the base camp to run errands and scrounge with.

The snack bar wasn't much, but after the Binh Son perimeter and the rubber plantation patrols, it was relative heaven. The two privates swaggered in like two prospectors back from the Klondike. They ordered two each of the biggest burgers Buddha had on the menu and beer to wash them down with. While they waited their food, the two men ambled into the laundry to look at the nick-nacks on sale there.

Super Private's eyes immediately went to the jacket hanging on the wall. It was black nylon and had a huge yellow and red dragon, and, "When I die I'll go to heaven, because I've spent my time in hell—Vietnam 1967" embroidered on the back.

"Damn, Tucker, look at that! It's beautiful. Ask me how I'd look back on the block wearing that. Hey Mamasan, how much for that jacket?"

"Fifteen dollah, no hollah. Mamasan make. Numba one. You buy?"

"Try on, Mamasan, I need try it on." said Super Private.

"OK, OK, you try. You buy. Fifteen dollah numbah one."

Super Private slipped the jacket on. It was much too large. Chi laughed at the comical site of the large jacket swallowing the small man.

"Number ten. Too big." said Super Private disappointedly.

"OK. OK, you! Mamasan make. You size. No sweat! Mamasan make you numbah one jack'. Maybe ten day. You come bok maybe ten day!"

Pulling a tape measure out of the back of the counter, Chi walked around to where the pair of soldiers stood.

"Burgers up." Yelled Buddha from the snack bar. Tucker headed through the door to get his.

"OK, look-see." Chi quickly measured Super Private's arms, neck, chest and waist, jotting the measurements on a note pad.

"OK, maybe one week, maybe ten day. You come back. OK numba one. Fifteen dollah!"

"Yeah, Mamasan, I'll be back in a week."

Then, an idea struck Super Private.

"Mamasan, do you sew anything—I mean everything?" he asked.

Chi tilted her head, not understanding.

"You sew?"

"I sew numbah one! What? What?"

"Hey Soop, your burger's are gettin' cold," yelled Tucker from the snack bar.

"Yeah, hold on." Super Private yelled back.

Looking around to make sure no one was about to enter, Super Private took the pencil and the note pad. He drew a rectangle with a star in it. He colored the top half of the rectangle.

"You sew?"

Shocked, Chi recognized the drawing of the Viet Cong battle flag. She shook her hand back and forth in front of her face.

"No good, numbah ten. Beaucoup bad. Beaucoup bad. No good! No good!" she blurted.

Speaking rapidly in Vietnamese, Chi tore the drawing from the pad, wadded it up and threw it in the cardboard box she used as a waste can.

"Mamasan, it's OK. Souvenir. You bic? Souvenir. You souvenir me, I souvenir you five dollars. OK?"

Chi stopped to think, quickly weighing the odds. She could not sew the flag at home because she couldn't be caught bringing a Viet Cong flag through the front gate of the American base. She could sew it here during slack times, but if she were caught, there would be big trouble. Still, five dollars for one flag. Her share of the intricate dragon jackets, which took days, was only seven dollars each. She looked at the counter, the space behind, and the board wall. The loose board! The loose board that had aggravated her when it fell out, banging her leg. She could hide the flag behind the loose board if anyone came in. If she worked on it behind the counter, no one could see. Five dollars!

"OK, you write, you write souvenir." she said, handing the pad and pencil to Super Private.

"OK, fair enough. When will it be done?" he asked.

"Same same jack'." Chi replied.

"OK, same same jacket." said Super Private as he handed her the note saying he wanted the flag as a souvenir. As an afterthought, he wrote "Super Private" on another sheet of the note pad and showed it to Chi.

"Name for jacket front."

"Huh?" asked Chi, not understanding.

Super Private took the jacket down off the hangar and pointed where he wanted his nickname.

"OK, OK, maybe two dollah."

"OK, Mamasan, two dollars for the name."

She would have gladly taken fifty cents.

"Soop, your burger's are gittin' icy!"

"OK, here I come. Thanks Mamasan. Week or ten days."

Grinning, Super Private sat down and munched his burger.

Jace was pacing when the platoon of tracks escorted the supply truck back to the perimeter. It was loaded with all kinds of things. There were some pallets, but there was also plywood, lumber, carpenter's tools, nails, wooden packing crates and three sheets of pierced steel planking.

Super Private proudly jumped from the cab. Tucker sheepishly hung in the background.

"Mission accomplished, sir! Look at all this shit. We can build a super highway with all this. I saw all kinds of stuff we can get next trip." beamed Super Private.

"Well, there probably won't be a next trip," said Jace. "You forgot to tell me that we could get pallets at Bear Cat."

Super Private was not taken aback in the least.

"Hell, sir, I didn't know that. A buddy of mine in the engineers at Bear Cat went to Saigon all the time. Took stuff there to trade with the navy. Came back with cases of steak and lobster. He said if you had the right trading material, you could get anything you want."

"What kind of trading material?" asked Jace, suddenly intrigued.

"Anything captured. Weapons are the best. AK-47s are good. SKS's are better, because they're not automatic and you can ship them home. A Chinese nine-millimeter pistol will get you anything you ask for. I know a dude at Bear Cat that got six cases of frozen sirloins for a captured V.C. flag."

"Well, for now we're going to order the pallets we need through supply channels. I'm glad you guys are back safe. You're sure you didn't know we could get pallets at Bear Cat?"

Super Private got serious. "Sir, I won't bullshit you. If I wanted to go tradin' in Saigon, I'd tell you. If I'd a known there was pallets at Bear Cat, I'd a told you that too."

Jace looked hard at the scruffy private. He had a feeling that what you saw with this man is what you got.

"OK. Do what you can to build a walkway from each platoon to the chow tent out of this stuff. I'm going to order more pallets from G-4. Thanks, guys. You did your best." said Jace.

"Sir!" said Super Private.

"Yes?" answered Jace.

"After chow, I'll whip your ass in ping-pong."

"You're on!" Jace replied.

After the ambush patrol called in that it was in position, Jace listened as Five India made a radio check with the squad in the village. He did not have as much to do since he had backed off of his aggressive perimeter checking. The platoon leaders and platoon sergeants now supervised their portions of the line just fine. Five India reported "negative sit-rep", meaning nothing was happening, to battalion. Jace was finishing a letter to his sister when the call came in. When He recognized Lieutenant Colonel McKensie's voice on the radio, he was instantly alert.

"Charlie Six, this is Cougar Six, over."

"This is Charlie Six, over."

"We've got a real ticklish situation here. An ambush patrol from the unit you wrote the after action report on seems to have disappeared. They haven't made a radio check in four hours, and they won't answer our calls. We've got to find them. Cougar three will give you the location. What I want to tell you is that this is as hard an egg to crack as I've ever seen. You have to see if you can find an ambush patrol without being ambushed yourself—I know I don't need to tell you to be careful. I want you to take a whole platoon with you. Take the tracks. The ambush will be less likely to shoot you up if you are mounted. Be sure of your targets before you open fire, they might be the good guys. Leave Charlie five in charge of your perimeter and be sure to tell him to adjust the positions after you leave. I want you to move ASAP. Any questions? Over."

"This is Charlie Six, I've got it. All I need is the location. Also I request permission to pull my ambush patrol back in. I don't want too many chickens away from the nest at one time."

"This is Cougar Six. No can do. The ambush missions come down from on high. I know you'll be split up, but we have no choice. If you get in trouble, we'll get you some help quick from this location. Good luck, Out."

Then C.C. came on the net with the location. It was in the northern part of the Binh Son plantation, a good kilometer and a half from the plantation house. Jace wondered why McKensie didn't give this job to A company who was pulling reserve duty at Bear Cat. He thought of asking C.C., but thought better of it. The colonel had no doubt taken everything into consideration before giving C company this mission.

Jace thought through the situation quickly. The ambush patrol was from second platoon, and the third had the village squad. That left the first as the only intact line platoon. He hated to look over the platoon leader's shoulder, but the colonel had told him to lead the mission. He called the leaders together.

"OK, guys, here's what's happening. First platoon, you're on this one. Second and third, I know your lines are thin with your squads gone. XO, when first platoon rolls out, I want you to adjust the perimeter. Put the maintenance section and the cooks on the line and spread the remaining tracks out as best you can. I trust you to do it right. Five India, you'll run the company net. XO I want you up and supervising all night long. Wess, I was directed by the colonel to go with the rescue mission. I hope you don't mind my looking over your shoulder. I want Doc Roberts with us. No telling what we'll find. Any questions?"

No one had any.

"Hey, sir, don't you worry one little bit about looking over my shoulder on this one—I'm glad as hell to have you along. This looks like it could get dicey. I'll go get the guys ready. When do we leave?" asked Lieutenant Green.

"Now." said Jace.

After a quick briefing, first platoon's four armored personnel carriers rolled through the gap in the wire with headlights blazing. Jace and Lieutenant Green had carefully planned the route they would take. The rubber trees were planted in neat rows running north and south, east and west. Jace figured that once they entered the right lane between the trees, the row should take them directly to the site of the lost ambush. Keeping track of the distance in the rubber would be difficult, so he planned to use the odometer of the track he was riding on to judge how far a kilometer was.

The four tracks roared down the road to the village, and turned right onto the dirt track that ran around the perimeter of the rubber plantation. Since the perimeter road was not straight, Jace realized that estimating the distance to the spot they should enter the rubber was going to be difficult. Standing inside the track, Jace radioed the platoon leader.

"One-six! Hold up! With this winding road, I don't know how far to go before we turn into the rubber."

"This is One-six. Why don't we measure the distance between trees," offered the lieutenant. "We can count the rows from the edge of the village, multiply by the distance between trees, and we can figure the distance exactly."

"You a math major?" Jace asked with a grin.

"Negative, phys-ed, over."

"That's pretty good thinking," said Jace over the radio. As the troops looked on, he jumped down and quickly paced the distance between two rubber trees.

"I make it seven meters between trees." Jace yelled above the idling engines. "We have to go 700 meters down this trace—so we count 100 rows from the edge of the village. Take a track back there and start counting the ones we missed. We'll pick up the count here."

When the track came back with the number of rows from the village, they moved out, pointing and counting as they went. After counting 100 trees, Jace signalled another halt.

"Here's where we enter. The coordinates Cougar 3 gave me are exactly one kilometer north of here. Have your driver stop after six-tenths of a mile." Jace radioed the lieutenant. "Now Go!"

The tracks leaped forward and turned left into the row Jace pointed out. He decided to leave the head lights on, risking ambush so the lost soldiers could see them coming. As far as he knew, the V.C. didn't drive APC's.

As soon as they made the turn, the rubber plantation swallowed them. In a matter of seconds, all they could see in any direction were the endless rows of trees stretching off to their front, their sides and diagonally. Yellow and black garden spiders with leg spans of eight inches hung upside down in webs suspended from the trees. The troops on top of the tracks pulled the webs aside and slapped at the huge spiders as they crept through a surreal tunnel; green foliage above, grass below, gray-brown rubber-tree trunks to every side.

After a seeming eternity, the lead track lurched to a stop. The driver reported six tenths of a mile—one kilometer.

"This should be the place." said Jace. "Turn off the engines."

All was suddenly deathly quiet. The headlights illuminated the trees stretching endlessly into darkness.

"Jungle school ambush—Hello!" Jace yelled into the silence.

Nothing.

He called again. Again, nothing.

"Have all four tracks blow their horns." ordered Jace.

Again, nothing.

"OK, here's what we do. We start from here, making ever-widening boxes until we find something. Be careful if someone steps into the trail, it might be a good guy."

They were all soaked with sweat from the tension and the humidity. Jace could tell from the looks on the soldiers' faces that they didn't like this one little bit.

"There!" someone yelled.

The tracks slammed to a halt.

"Look there, what is that?"

They all strained to see.

"It's only a stump." said Jace gently, trying to relax the tension.

All night they made their boxes, yelled, blew their horns, slapped at spiders and mosquitoes, then sat quietly and listened. As the sun came up, the fear and the anxiety relaxed somewhat, but they all knew the dangers in the Binh Son.

Then, "Charlie Six, this is Cougar Six, over."

"This is Cougar Six. You can head in. They're back in. Seems they just went to sleep. They woke up at dawn and walked in."

"This is Charlie Six. I don't know what to say! You can tell them I said—Well, I know you'll know what to say to them."

"This is Cougar Six, be careful on the way back. Out."

Jace sat shaking his head.

"You know something, Cap'n?" asked a soldier sitting next to Jace on top of the track.

"What's that?" replied Jace.

"We've just spent another normal night in 'Nam."

CHAPTER 5

▼

16 September 1967

The still and violently hot morning inched toward noon as Jace leaned back in his folding chair on the verandah, watched his soldiers going about their routines and reflected on his first month in command. From where he sat, he could see that Charlie company had made the Binh Son fire base livable, if not comfortable. Wooden pallets now criss-crossed the perimeter, keeping the troops' feet out of the mud. During the day, the plantation house hummed with activity as cooks banged and clattered in the kitchen and dog-tired troops dried out, rested and played. Soldiers were more alert and active as lieutenants and sergeants now supervised the perimeter.

Between his other duties, he had visited the village often, checking on his soldiers, walking around with the village chief and playing with the children. Acting more as a ranger instructor than a commander, he had gone on some of the platoon-sized search-and-destroy sweeps through the rubber, teaching as he went. His troops had made no contact with the enemy, but one soldier had been slightly wounded by a booby trap in the edge of the plantation.

His first month in command had been a busy one. Besides accomplishing all the tactical missions he was assigned, he had shown his soldiers that he was serious about winning the hearts and minds of the people of Binh Son. During his first visit to the village Jace had been shown the school, which was an empty hut with chairs and tables, but no books. That night he had written his ROTC unit describing the situation and suggesting they sponsor the school. The teacher had been ecstatic when paper, pens, pencils and books of every description began coming in the mail. Charlie company soldiers were now involved in all types of civic-action projects. They had thrown a party for the children of the village for which the cooks had whipped up an oriental stew and rice that they served with ice-cold cans of soda. After the party, Doc Roberts had held a medical clinic for the villagers. Although he was only a medic, he had treated every ailment he had found, even suturing a cut on a young man's leg.

A breathless radio call shook Jace from his reflections. He listened intently while Five India wrote furiously in the radio log. While on a routine sweep south of the plantation, second platoon had stopped for a break. As they stood to move on, one of the soldiers had accidentally stepped into a small hole in the ground. The Platoon leader had called for the platoon tunnel rat, a small soldier with a flashlight and a pistol. He had disappeared into the hole for a long moment, then emerged saying he had found a small underground room with tunnels running from it in all directions. When his soldiers found the first weapons, Jace notified battalion and went to the site as soon as he could get there.

Starting that afternoon, Charlie company got all the help it needed and then some. Almost the entire brigade and division staff landed on a hacked-out helipad to examine the find and take souvenirs from the booty. The next day, a 200-man combat engineer company, along with an explosive ordnance disposal team, arrived to help excavate the site. Before the searchers were through, 3,000 rifles, 150 machine guns, 200 RPG launchers, and over a million rounds of ammunition were hauled off—and that was after everyone kept a rifle or pistol for himself. Documents, clothing, medical supplies and tons of rice were also removed from the massive underground complex. When General Westmoreland came to visit Charlie company and to look over the display of captured weapons set up especially for VIP visitors, the proud tunnel rat told him that the complex was over twenty levels deep. Intelligence officers eagerly hauled off huge piles of hand-written papers found in the underground chambers to be interpreted and studied. When they reported that some of the documents stated the weapons were to be used to capture the city of Binh Hoa, everyone laughed.

Lau, Phun, the regimental commander and two guards carefully emerged from the tunnel leading from the headquarters. After the moist coolness of the underground vault, the air outside was humid and oppressive. Following his encounter with the American patrol, Lau traveled the jungle trails with trepidation. Only his hatred and his desire for revenge drove him to overcome his fear of being ambushed. He had found that the Americans were easy to hear when they were moving through the jungle. Twice, while walking quietly on moist beaten paths, Lau had heard enemy patrols crashing through the undergrowth nearby. It was when they were sitting quietly, coiled like an angry snake, that the enemy was most dangerous.

The small party took a trail that brought them out at a point on the road west of Xuan Loc. The guards stayed in the jungle as Lau, the commander, and Phun stepped into the open. As before, they had to cross rice paddies, but this time they saw no one. With audacity Lau didn't feel, they walked directly to a bus stop. As they waited, Lau checked his packet of papers for the tenth time. As before, he was masquerading as a convalescing ARVN sergeant. The regimental commander's papers identified him as a low-level government official. Only Phun had no papers.

The same ancient Mercedes bus that had brought Lau to Xuan Loc lumbered toward them from the town. As usual, there were no empty seats, so they found room on top of the foul-smelling vehicle. As they rolled toward Saigon, the three Viet Cong ignored each other.

Lau was amazed with the ease with which they were able to travel in the capital city. Security around Saigon was extremely lax. Everywhere they looked, civilians by the thousands walked, rode bicycles or hailed lambrettas or pedal-cabs. With thousands of people going about their daily business, blending in was no problem for the three travelers. Taking a variety of means of transport, and following a meandering route, they made their way to the safe house Phun had already visited. The only policemen they saw during the entire trip were directing traffic.

The two men ordered tea at a sidewalk restaurant as Phun went to the small dwelling in an alley a short distance from the crowded street. There a moon-faced matron with a black-toothed smile welcomed her. After surveying the premises, Phun waited for a few moments, then went back into the street. She walked past Lau and the commander, nodded imperceptibly, then went on to a corner shop to buy a gift for their hostess. As soon as she had walked past, the two men arose, paid their bill, and walked leisurely to the safe house. They didn't have to knock; their hostess opened the door as they approached.

That night the trio was treated to a feast of shark's fin soup, steamed dumplings, spring rolls, roast duck, prawns in oyster sauce, rice wine and beer. Lau ate more than he had in years. Used to the silence of the jungle, he slept fitfully in the noise of the city.

The next morning, during a breakfast of rice and green tea, the three guerrillas were briefed on the security and escape arrangements for the meeting by their round-faced hostess. They then bowed their thanks, and made their way to the meeting.

The gathering was to be held in a rambling wooden, bamboo, brick and stucco structure that covered an entire city block. Roofed by a mosaic of different materials, the building had not been planned, it had simply grown over the years as new additions were tacked on. Besides the restaurant, it housed several shops, apartments of the proprietors and several interior rooms with secret entrances and no windows or exits to the outside. Most of these hideouts were used by spies, smugglers, drug dealers, or rich merchants for their mistresses. One secret room was the meeting place for the commanders and the staff of the 5th Division of the National Front for the Liberation of South Vietnam.

Lau, Phun and the regimental commander, entered the small restaurant, open today only to a special party, which in reality, was a group of elite security guards. After they were identified, Lau's party was led to the small living quarters, then through a curtain at the back of a closet that opened into a surprisingly large room.

Seated on cushions on the floor, were perhaps twenty men and five women. The members of the group met each other as old friends. The senior security guard reminded the assemblage of the emergency procedures. Then without cere- mony, the commander of the 5th Division, a youthful man dressed in khaki pants and a loose white shirt, entered the room and welcomed each person in turn.

When he came to Lau, he smiled and bowed deeply.

"Comrade, we have all heard of your journey, your loss, and your bravery under fire. We welcome you to our cause."

Phun smiled proudly as the general bowed deeply to Lau. Lau wondered if it was from Phun that they had heard of his exploits.

"The news I bring to you today is of an event that takes place only once in every thousand years. Our revered Uncle Ho, in conjunction with the politburo and the central committee in Hanoi has ordered a general offensive."

The division commander paused and let his opening statement take effect. Some of the audience glanced at each other, but most stared straight ahead, afraid that any emotion might be misread.

"The decision for the offensive was made in July, after careful study of the political and military situations in both America and South Vietnam. As you know, the sham elections held in September placed in office two of the most notorious criminals in the camp of the American puppets. We have it on good authority that their new so-called president, Nguyen Van Thieu is one of the most notorious thugs in the puppet government. And Ky tries to impress the Americans by being a cowboy from one of their movies."

The guerrilla commanders laughed at this characterization of the flamboyant pilot who had been elected vice president. The division commander continued. "The people know the reputations of Thieu and Ky and will refuse to follow them. In fact, we know that these two criminals are widely hated.

"This is perhaps the most vulnerable the American government has been since the beginning of this phase of our struggle. Next year will be an election year in the United States and the war is becoming increasingly unpopular. A decisive stroke now will cause the American people to understand they cannot win. They will turn out the murderous Johnson and will elect a peace candidate who will end the American military involvement in our country.

"Finally, we must have a decisive victory now to end the migration of farmers to the cities. Many people, fleeing the war, have come to Saigon. This trend is causing a dwindling of our tax base and is hurting our ability to obtain rice to feed our freedom fighters. We must win this war now to allow the people to return to the fields.

"This general offensive will decide the future of the country and will bring an end to our decades-long struggle. To bring about the victory, the general offensive will be in conjunction with a general uprising of the people to throw off the tyrannical yoke of the puppet government and their puppet-masters. When the offensive starts, the people, the puppet army, government officials and intellectuals will throw their support to the National Liberation Front. They will either fight on our side or will refuse to support the Americans and their lackeys. The people will throng to the streets in the cities to hamper the movement of enemy troops while we seize radio and television stations to spread the word of our victory. The combined general offensive and general uprising of the people will be simultaneous, devastating, and completely successful.

"To prepare for our offensive, we must accomplish the following tasks. First, the people must be told that when we are successful, they will be given complete freedom of speech, religion, association, correspondence, residence and employment. Without giving away the date, time or method of our offensive, we must let the people know that those who support us will have their deeds recorded for future rewards. Those who oppose us will be remembered for their cowardice when our victory is complete. They must know that even if they have worked for the Americans or their puppets, they will be rewarded if they join the uprising.

"To ensure the general uprising is complete and effective, we will now concentrate our political efforts in the cities, towns, and villages. We must all be ever vigilant to recruit those who have been wronged or hurt by the Americans and their stooges. Recruiting and proselytizing will be the main focus of the efforts of our commissars between now and the offensive.

"Now, as for the timing of the attack. As you know, our comrades on the politburo in the north have offered the Americans and their puppets a cease-fire during the Tet holiday every year since 1965. We understand the purpose of these cease-fires has been to lull the enemy into believing that the new-year's celebrations are safe for them each year. They have been led to believe that nothing of significance ever happens during Tet. This year they will find out how wrong they have been. In November, the National Liberation Front will proclaim cease-fires of three days each for Christmas and the occidental new-year's. Also there will be a seven-day cease-fire for Tet.

"We will use the cease-fire period for the build-up and staging of our forces. We will move our fighters into their attack positions disguised as holiday travelers. The offensive will be spearheaded, not by the regular forces of the People's Army, but by the local and main-force battalions of the National Liberation Front. The people will know these local fighters and will flock to the sides of their neighbors for the great battle.

"With that fact in mind, replacements will no longer come from the local units to fill out the main-force battalions and regiments. The flow will be reversed. Freedom fighters from the Peoples' Army and the main force battalions will replace losses in the local units. It is imperative that the people see that their local freedom-fighting units are leading the effort to crush the enemy.

"Special cachets of weapons, medical supplies and food are being established to supply the offensive. A new effort to bring weapons from the north is already underway. The main priority for supply during the next two months will be to replace the weapons and equipment lost to the Americans in the second regiment's sector near Binh Son.

"Now, I know each of you are burning to know what your assignments for the great battle will be. First regiment, to you will go the main prize. You will have the honor of seizing the U.S. embassy in Saigon. You will also seize enemy's airfield at Tan Son Nyut. Second Regiment, you will seize the headquarters the Americans call II Field Force and destroy the ammunition dump at the enemy's Long Binh base. You will also seize the puppet army's 3rd Division headquarters in Bien Hoa city. Third regiment, you will take the American aerodrome at Bien Hoa.

"Comrades, always remember our main tactic is to seize the enemy by the belt and strike him in the face. In other words, get in so close to the enemy that they cannot bring their overwhelming firepower against us without hitting themselves. This tactic is a brutal one. It requires bravery and sacrifice—but, believe me—if we allow the enemy to stand away from us, he will pound us with artillery, helicopters, and air strikes. Get in close. Open fire when we are but meters apart. Then lunge in for the kill. The general offensive will succeed only if we are brutally brave.

"Finally, comrades, the date of the general offensive. We will attack on the 31st of January—the first day of the Year of the Monkey."

The H-23 flared onto the lawn of the plantation house. Holding his helmet on his head, C.C. ran from beneath the rotors.

"Well, well, I've been trying to get you down here for weeks. Why now all of a sudden?" asked Jace, shaking C.C.'s hand.

"Business and pleasure. The business is to tell you that the battalion has a new mission. We keep the Binh Son protection mission. B Company relieves you tomorrow. The rest of the battalion goes back to Fire Base Cougar. We picked up a chunk of War Zone D north of the river. The pleasure is that I want to sit on the porch and take a break."

Good, thought Jace. Bravo company would come to Binh Son and they could have it. Although Charlie company had suffered no deaths and but a few wounded since Jace had been in command, and life at Binh Son had improved greatly, there was still something irregular and unsettling about a combat fire base with a mansion in the middle of it. Also, he hated the rubber plantation. The trees placed in perfect rows made for natural fields of fire and ambush lanes. He felt relatively safe in the confines of the jungle, but the endless rows of rubber trees always left him feeling uneasy. Also, the ridiculous rules of engagement were more than a nuisance. They seemed to be a symptom of this whole screwed-up war.

Jace and C.C. sat at a field table on the verandah sipping coffee. There was news galore from battalion headquarters. Jace soaked it in, relishing the change in routine and the time spent with a friend.

"Your first sergeant is leaving next week. He appreciated the Bronze Star and the kind words you wrote—especially since you hardly knew him." said C.C.

"I'll try to stop by and see him off," said Jace. "I am his company commander and he is my first sergeant. Like Five India said, he is a casualty of this war the same as if he had been shot."

They both sat silently for several moments.

"There's something creepy about this place," said Jace.

"I don't see what you're complaining about. From here, you can sit in comfort and survey your entire kingdom."

"That may be, but for the troops, perimeter guard and patrolling the rubber is as nasty as it is anywhere. There's just something not right here. The house gives you a false feeling of security. You feel safe because there's a roof over your head and you're out of the mud. Somehow, this set up seduces you into thinking comfortable thoughts and that's when it gets dangerous. I don't know why we're ordered to protect this house anyway. Who owns it? Does anyone know?"

"Well, I sure don't." answered C.C.

Jace continued, "The village is friendly enough, but every time I go down there, I get the feeling something or someone is watching or something bad is about to happen. I feel like lightening is going to strike this place. I'm glad to be leaving here." explained Jace.

"Well, if it does strike you, it'll have to strike tonight, 'cause you'll be headed toward Xuan Loc tomorrow at noon. If it were me, I'd rather be here than in the jungles out there."

"Listen," said Jace nervously, "I know the ambush requirements come down from division or brigade, but I'd like to keep everyone in the perimeter tonight. Can you give me permission to do that?"

"Nope, I'm sorry, but the ambush patrol is orders. You gotta send it out."

"Well, how about the squad in the village? Can I bring them in to the perimeter?"

C.C. rubbed his chin and thought.

"I don't know. That may be negotiable. Unless I call you back, plan on bringing that squad in. I'll see if I can give you an ambush site that is close in. You really feel something, huh?"

"Yes, I do." answered Jace. "Something bad is going to happen here. Is there any chance you can get the rules of engagement changed? Not being able to return fire if we're shot at really stinks."

"No, I'm afraid not. This place, along with the other rubber plantations, is politically protected. The national government needs the tax revenue from the overseas sale of the rubber. They feel that they must show the world that production from the rubber plantations can be counted on, I guess."

"You know what? I can whip Mohammed Ali. They might have stripped him of his title, but to me, he's still the champ. And I'm telling you that I can whip the best heavyweight in the world—and I'm not even a boxer."

"What the hell are you talking about?" asked C.C.

"I can." said Jace. "I can whip hell out of him."

"OK, go ahead. This ought to be good."

"Yeah," Jace grinned. "All I have to do is get him to agree to the rules we have to follow in this war."

C.C. leaned back, grinned, locked his fingers behind his head and said, "I'm listening."

Jace began carefully. "Let's say you are Ali and I am the challenger. That is to say you are the U.S. and I am the Viet Cong. You must agree to the following rules. First, you can't come out of your corner, but I can go anywhere I want. I can sit in my corner, go home and eat supper, sleep, or go on vacation, but you can't come out of your corner—the same way we are locked in South Vietnam. We can't chase Charlie into Cambodia, Laos or North Vietnam. He has the run of Southeast Asia and we lock ourselves in this country."

"Second, the fight will last ten years—or longer. I don't care. Fighting on my terms, I can make the fight last as long as I want it to. I can come and go when I want to. I can sneak up in the middle of the night and knock hell out of you when you are asleep, then run back to my corner and you can't touch me. We fight when I want to—and I will hit you when you least expect it."

"Go on." said C.C., intrigued.

"Third, You're restricted in the punches you can throw. You can't use your heavy stuff. You can only jab at my nose and try a left hook now and then. You cannot use an overhand right, an upper cut, or anything else. Since I know what to watch for, I'm not afraid of the punches you can't use."

"You know what I'd say to rules like that if I were the champ?" asked C.C.?

"You'd say to hell with it, its not worth it. You'd say 'I quit!' and you'd go home." answered Jace quietly.

"Are you saying that's what we're going to do?"

"If we don't change the rules so we can fight like the champs we are, I don't know—I just don't know."

Duc arose early. He planned a long workday. He had carefully thought out his route and his work schedule. Today he would go into the jungle west of Long Thanh, where good wood of the right type and thickness was easily found. First, he would cut the trees down, then saw them into the half-meter logs demanded by the charcoal makers. Today he would do the cutting and piling. Tomorrow he would make several trips with his hand-cart to bring the wood to his yard in Long Thanh for drying.

Duc selected a bow saw with the new blade he had bought in Saigon and a small, sharp ax. He finished his second cup of tea and placed a large rice ball and a bottle of water into a small knapsack. Waving to his wife, he walked out of the clean-swept yard in front of the modest shack that was their home.

He walked south on Highway 15 for several hundred meters, then turned right onto a dike that took him across the rice paddy to the jungle's edge. A wide trail took him into the dense foliage. When he was a boy, he had traveled this trail to the Dong Nai river often with his father and other villagers to fish for carp.

This UH-1, like almost all helicopters in Vietnam, flew too many hours on too little maintenance. It vibrated and shook as it flapped southward along the Dong Nai River. The mottled brown paint was chipped and scratched. Several bullet holes in the tail boom had been patched and spot painted, further adding to the ragged appearance of the aircraft. A twenty-year-old warrant officer was at the controls with his co-pilot, another warrant officer who was a year younger. The crew wore standard army flight suits, but their helmets were decorated with brightly painted lightening bolts and nicknames. Both door gunners sported huge mustaches and sunglasses.

The vibrations from the rotors made the pilot's voice a husky vibrato as he joked with the co-pilot. They had left Di An, the base camp of the 1st Infantry Division and were headed for Vung Tau, a resort area on the coast south of Saigon used by the Americans as an in-country rest and relaxation resort. There they were to pick up six soldiers and return them to Di An. To avoid the heavy air traffic around both the Bien Hoa Air Base and the Long Thanh army airfield, they were flying at treetop level southward paralleling the river.

As they flashed over a wide trail in the jungle, one of the door gunners yelled into the intercom. "There's a gook on the trail!"

Without thinking, the pilot put the helicopter into a steep bank to the left as he asked the gunner, "Was he armed?"

"I couldn't tell for sure. He was carryin' a bunch of stuff. Could have been a weapon."

"OK, be careful. I'm going to put the trail on the right side. If you can, see if he's armed. If he points anything at us, waste him."

The Huey strained in the tight bank, the door gunners leaning out as far as their seat belts would allow. The pilot leveled the ship as he found the trail and slipped off to the side to give the right gunner a better view.

"There he is!" yelled the gunner.

"What's he doing?" the pilot rasped in the intercom.

"He's just lookin' at us. He's got a bunch of stuff in his arms. Hey—that looks like a weapon."

"Lost him, we're comin' around again, be ready!"

"Wonder why he ain't runnin' or hiding?" asked the co-pilot.

"Cause he's probably goin' to try to take a shot at us!"

"OK, there's the trail. See him?"

"No not yet, the little bastard probably took off."

"There! There he is!"

Duc was walking along, watching the circling helicopter. The skies around the Long Thanh airfield swarmed with the machines day and night. He was so used to the sight and sound of the aircraft that he was no longer afraid of them. He wondered what this helicopter was up to. He hadn't done anything wrong, and he was in an area approved by the government and the Americans for wood-cutting.

Duc was carrying his ax in his right hand, which he raised shade his eyes.

"He's pointing something at us!" screamed the door gunner.

"Waste him!" ordered the pilot.

As Duc blinked up at the circling helicopter, the ground around him erupted under a hail of bullets. He was so surprised he didn't have a chance to run.

Jace did not sleep at all during the night before C company was to leave Binh Son. He brought the squad back from the village and was given permission to keep his ambush patrol close in. Despite the fact that there had been negligible enemy contact, Jace could not shake the overpowering feeling that something bad was going to happen. He walked the perimeter, made radio checks with the ambush patrol, and visited each platoon leader several times during the night. He was sure he was making a nuisance of himself, but he couldn't help it—the feeling that something horrible was going to happen was just too strong.

At daybreak, the company began to pack up. As Jace watched the company's preparations, a young black soldier ran up to him.

"Cap'n can I talk to you?"

"Yes, by all means." Jace was instantly aware that something was very wrong. "What's the trouble, son?"

"Sergeant Munn punched me!" screamed the young man.

"All right, just sit down here. I'll get to the bottom of this." said Jace.

He didn't have to look far for Sergeant Munn, who was hot on the heels of the sobbing soldier.

"Jackson, I tol' you if you wonted to see the C.O. you had to go through the chain of command! Now git yore sorry ass back to the platoon area!"

Turning to Jace, Munn said, "Sir, this don't concern you. Hit's platoon business. We'll handle it."

"Sergeant Munn, did you strike this man?" asked Jace looking Munn straight in the eye.

"No, sir. I wuz jus' tryin' to git him to do his job. Dumb bastard won't do nothin' he's tol'."

"Jackson, go on back to your platoon area." said Jace. "We'll sort this out."

Jace turned to Munn. "Go get Jackson's squad leader and your platoon leader. Bring them here."

Munn, steaming mad now, left and shortly returned with Lieutenant Nevin and Sergeant Smith. Munn started to say something, but Jace raised his hand for silence.

"I'm not accusing anyone of anything. I will check to see if there are any witnesses, but I will not get into a who-shot-John argument about whether you struck that soldier or not. I will tell you this. Hitting the troops—even calling them names—will not be allowed in this company. If Jackson was not doing what he was supposed to be doing, there are many leadership techniques you can use to make sure he does. You are a senior NCO. You ought to know how to lead without violence."

"Sergeant Smith, you let your platoon sergeant down by not making sure Jackson was doing his job. The platoon sergeant should not have even been involved in whether or not Jackson was doing what he was supposed to do. That was your job and it appears you weren't doing it. I want all of you to know that striking soldiers is a court martial offense and I will not condone that practice in my company. If you did not strike him, as you contend, then you have nothing to worry about. If you did, and you are lying, you possibly have a lot to worry ab—."

"Sir, I told you I didn't punch him. Who're you going to believe—a senior NCO or that—that—" interrupted Munn.

"And I told you that if you didn't strike him, you needn't worry. If you did, you have committed a court martial offense. And don't interrupt me again. You NCOs are dismissed. Lieutenant Nevin, we need to talk!" said Jace, in his most official tone.

When the NCOs had left, Jace said to the lieutenant, "I don't believe that soldier would have come to me unless Munn punched him. Check to see if there are any witnesses—but my guess is that you won't find any. There's probably no proof one way or the other, but I want you to watch those two. I don't like Munn's attitude and I don't like to hear my soldiers called names. Keep me informed."

"Yes, sir." answered the Lieutenant.

Jace made a mental note to check on Munn and Jackson later.

Since Binh Son was a politically protected area, it could never be left unprotected. Hence, B company had to arrive before C company would be allowed to pull out. Jace was tremendously relieved when the APCs of B company came around the curve out of the jungle and rolled up to the plantation house.

"Well, if it ain't Bravo Six," Jace laughed as John Thomaston jumped from his track. "Welcome to Binh Son, garden spot of South East Asia."

"Looks great to me—beats the hell out of the jungles," said Thomaston as he shook Jace's hand.

"Don't let the appearance fool you. There's something spooky about this place. I recommend you don't occupy the house at night. We took a B-40 round one night but no one was hurt 'cause we were all outside."

"Anything else?" asked Thomaston.

"Yeah. You know about the rules of engagement, don't you."

"Oh Yeah," answered Thomaston. "The old man was very clear on that."

"Well, we're ready to roll," said Jace. "Look, one more thing—I never thanked you for being so thoughtful at the club the other night. I just wanted to say I appreciated what you said."

"Thanks," said Thomaston. "I feel bad about calling Wilson an asshole, now. No one deserves what happened to him."

"I agree. Just don't let it happen to you. Keep your head down."

"You too, buddy."

It was noon, and time to go. Satisfied that he had done everything he needed to do for the relieving company, Jace yelled "Saddle Up!" and swung himself up to the driver's hatch of the command track where he would ride during the trip to Fire Base Cougar. He checked his head set, did a communications check and watched his soldiers clamor onto the tracks. Once they were mounted, he waved to Thomaston, then ordered C company to roll. He was glad to be free of Binh Son.

Twenty APCs, along with jeeps, trucks, a tracked wrecker and an ambulance, made a tactical column a mile long. The company could only go as fast as the slowest vehicle, in this case, the second squad track of second platoon. Named the "V.C. Stomper", it had been submerged in a flash flood and had not run right since. Now, it crept along at fifteen miles per hour.

As the column neared Long Thanh, Jace looked at his watch for the ump-teenth time. The plan called for C company to make Fire Base Cougar by dark. Nearly fifty road miles separated the Binh Son plantation from the firebase. He was sure now they could not make it there by dark. The prospects of a thrown track or a broken down vehicle on the dark, lonely stretches of Highway 1 made up his mind. Over the radio, he asked battalion for permission to remain over night at Long Thanh air field. The battalion commander radioed permission to stop. But instead of the airfield, he routed the company to a large open meadow on the west side of Highway 15, south of the village.

It was 3:00 p.m. by the time Jace got C company circled into a perimeter. He ordered his troops to dig in and put out wire, claymores and trip flares. The troops grumbled and groaned, but remembering the story about the attack on the mech company in the 25th Division, they quickly finished their foxholes before opening their C-rations for supper.

Jace was heating a can of ham and lima beans when Super Private approached.

"Hey, sir, hows about lettin' me take your jeep into Bear Cat. There's some-thing I need to pick up at the laundry."

"And what might that be?" asked Jace.

"OK, sir, I'll be honest with you. I'm having a V.C. flag sewed up. I figure I can take it to Saigon and trade it to the navy for enough steaks to feed the whole company. Fire Base Cougar is on Highway 1, so there'll be plenty of convoys to tag onto to get into Saigon. What do you say—for the good of the whole com-pany?"

Jace thought for a minute.

"OK, I ought to have my head examined, but go ahead. Just be careful."

"Yes, sir. You don't mind if I take my man Tucker with me do you?"

"OK, just be off with you!" laughed Jace. "If you get me in trouble, I swear, I'll skin you!"

In a few minutes the jeep nearly left the ground as it bounced across the field toward Bear Cat, the two privates whooping at their buddies as they left.

"I've got to be out of my mind." muttered Jace. He was not as worried about the enemy as he was about the two soldiers killing themselves in the jeep. Return-ing to business, Jace called Lieutenant Cappaccelli to the C.P.

"Little Caesar, it's your turn in the barrel. I want you to send a squad-sized patrol on a sweep north of us." Jace traced the route on his map. "After their sweep, have them set up an ambush on this trail—right here. Be sure you give them a complete order and make them plan their mortar fires."

Cappaccelli made sure he was clear on everything, then hurried off to brief his troops. Jace finished his C-ration instant coffee, then started a turn around the perimeter. He stopped and listened to the squad preparing for the patrol.

"Not bad planning, for a bunch of rookies." Jace said to the squad leader. "Not bad at all."

Later, he stood on top of his track and watched the patrol move away from the perimeter. In the open field, they were properly dispersed. Still a safe distance from the jungle, they stopped and allowed the point man time to check out the tree line. "Not bad at all." repeated Jace to himself.

The sun was a red ball over Saigon when Super Private and Tucker returned from Bear Cat. Jace and the two privates admired the flag and Super Private's new jacket.

"I've got Mamasan working on five more flags," said Super Private. If what my buddy in the engineers says is true, I can get anything I want for this. I've got three AK's from the tunnel at Binh Son, too. The next trip to Saigon will be profitable as hell."

"Kind of warm for the coat, ain't it?" joked Jace.

"Wait till the guys back on the block—"

"Charlie Six this is Three Six, over."

Jace ran to grab the hand set.

"This is Charlie Six."

"Three Six. My alpha pappa just found a body on the trail. Said he looked like a wood-cutter. Had documents and an I.D. card. They said he looked like he'd been hosed by a gun ship. No weapons, just a saw and an ax, over."

"Roger, have them bring the tools and the papers back. Good work, continue the mission."

Jace reported the incident to battalion, then returned to his C-rations. For some reason, he still had a very uneasy feeling.

Chi awoke at her usual time. Having no alarm clock, she timed her rising by the morning light and the soft stirring of the village. As she shook off sleep, she began the routine she had kept since she was a girl—first, going to the toilet, then stoking the fire, making the tea, and finally, boiling the rice.

As she poured handfuls of white grain into the pot, she heard a scream—a wail so primordially frantic and sad that it provoked panic in her. Duc's wife was at the door, her young face streaked with tear-soaked hair and the slits that were her eyes nothing but red wounds. Chi's sisters and Huong appeared, instantly jolted from their beds by the screams.

"He never came home! He never came home!" wailed the young woman. "He went yesterday morning to cut wood. He never came home."

"Please, please—here, here." crooned Chi as she pushed the girl to a cushion on the floor. "He was probably caught by the curfew. Watch, he'll be here this morning soon after the curfew lifts."

"But, he's never done this. He's never even been late for the evening meal. He's always here. He never leaves me alone."

"These are troubled times," said one of Chi's sisters. "Sometimes things happen that are beyond our control. He will be here."

"I will ride to the police station and make inquiry about Duc," said Huong, acting more authoritative than he felt.

Huong worshiped his older brother who had lived with the others in Chi's home until he had married. Huong had missed him terribly when he had first left, but since Duc had moved less than a hundred meters away, he had recovered quickly. In time the short distance between the two homes seemed to disappear as Duc's young wife was accepted into the family and life continued.

At the mention of the police, the young woman cried louder still. The women of the family closed around the anxious wife, comforting, patting, consoling. Huong kept his distance, acting older and wiser than his years. Duc's absence worried him, too. Silently, they waited for the first passing bicycle or scooter to signal the end of the night's curfew. Then the morning's traffic loosed as if a dam had broken. As Long Thanh came to life, Huong rolled out his motor bike.

"I'll see what I can find out," he said importantly. He started the bike and sped away toward the police station. With Huong gone, the women tightened their circle, hoping for the best, but fearing the worst.

Third platoon's patrol came in about an hour after daylight, bringing with them the tools and the documents, which they took to Jace straightway. He looked them over, but being unable to interpret the papers, he decided to get them to the S-2 at battalion as soon as possible. He radioed the battalion commander, who was not available, then asked the battalion S-2 what he should do with the documents and tools.

"There's no one here that can interpret them. Can you drop them off at our higher at Bravo Charlie?"

Jace answered, "Roger, will do. Thanks, out." Jace called his XO to the command track.

"Look, I'm going to drop this stuff off at brigade. It's the only chance I'll have to say goodbye to the first sergeant. You start the company moving. I'll catch you before you get to Long Binh."

Jace called for Tucker, jumped into the jeep and bounced across the field toward Long Thanh and the south entrance to Bear Cat. He swung by the brigade headquarters, where he left the tools and documents, then went to battalion rear to say goodbye to his first sergeant. His uneasy feeling would not go away.

The brigade intelligence shop had an interpreter attached. When Jace dropped the documents off, the S-2 asked the man to read Duc's identification papers.

"This man was a civilian who lived in Long Thanh," said the interpreter. "He had permission from the province chief to cut wood in the jungles near the river. I suggest you take these papers to the national police in Long Thanh so they can notify the family."

"How about the tools?" asked the S-2.

"They should also be taken to the police. They will take them back to the family," answered the interpreter, who at times visited another headquarters—the 5th Division of the National Liberation Front.

That night, the interpreter/spy added Duc's name to the list he was preparing to give the chief commissar of the 5th Division of On the list were the names of people who had been killed by accident or by mistake by the Americans or by government soldiers. Soon, political officers would visit the relatives of those on the list. They would attempt to turn them to the side of the Viet Cong.

The two policemen walked sternly into Chi's yard, followed by Huong. Startled but hopeful, Chi, her sisters and Duc's wife sprang to their feet. Then they saw what the men were carrying—Duc's tools.

"*Chao Ba*." bowed the senior policemen to the women. "I regret that I must bring bad news."

Duc's wife, who had spent the day in sobbing silence, erupted anew into screams. Chi embraced the young woman as the policemen waited for her to regain enough composure for them to finish their unpleasant task.

"I regret to inform you that Cao Tho Duc has been accidentally killed." said the senior policeman with practiced formality.

None of the women could speak. Finally, One of Chi's sisters asked how it happened.

Huong answered before the policemen could speak.

"I have been at the police station all day. I know the whole story. I will relieve these men of the burden of retelling the story. I will tell you all that is known."

Despite her grief, Chi was astounded by the maturity of her son in this difficult situation. The policemen stepped forward, bowed, and handed Duc's belongings to Chi. The young wife dropped into a swoon.

"These are sad times for our people. I regret this terrible thing has happened. Our condolences to your family," said the senior policemen, who bowed once more, then gratefully turned and left the yard with his partner.

"He was killed by an American helicopter." announced Huong, with the towering indignation of youth. "Our entire family works for the foreigners. We build their structures, we wash their clothes, and we dig their ditches. They repay us for our labor and our loyalty with murder!"

"But the policeman said it was an accident." said an aunt.

"How could it have been an accident?" screamed Huong. "He had his permit. He had his identification. He was cutting in an approved place. An American flying machine came by and shot him down—Why?"

"Where is his body?" asked Chi, as if she had heard nothing Huong said.

"On the river trail." said Huong. "I will go there with some of the local soldiers to bring him back. We will go early in the morning, as soon as the curfew lifts."

Startled back to reality, Chi said, "If they shot Duc, they could shoot you also! You cannot go!"

"I am going with the local forces. His body must be brought home. If a helicopter flies over, we will hide in the jungle. They cannot shoot what they cannot see." answered Huong.

"Huong, let the soldiers bring him back—please do not do this!" cried Chi.

No longer the little boy, or even a teenager, Huong answered, "He is family. I am his brother. No one else will bring him back."

"What about work. You cannot go with the soldiers and be home in time to catch the truck for work." said Chi, hopefully finding a reason he couldn't go.

"I no longer work for the Americans!" said Huong.

CHAPTER 6

▼

9 October 1967

As Charlie company snaked its way along Highway 1, Jace sent Lieutenant Dricsol and Five India ahead in the jeep. He felt that the lone vehicle would be safe enough if it joined one of the many convoys that traveled the highways. This advanced party would go to battalion headquarters to find out what section of the perimeter the company would occupy and get any special instructions Jace would need as he brought the company in.

Fire Base Cougar had initially been set up for one rifle company, the scout platoon, and the battalion headquarters company. With the new mission the firebase would more than double in size. Besides the 5-39, minus Bravo company which would stay at Binh Son, an artillery battalion headquarters and one firing battery, and an engineer company now clogged the base. For the past week, the engineers had been blowing down trees and pushing back the jungle with dozers to expand the clearing.

Five India stuck his head into the TOC and waved at the battalion commander.

"Well, well, Chargin' Charlie company is finally here. What took you guys so long?" McKensie asked as he shook hands with Five India, whom he gave the respect normally given to commissioned officers.

"Beat up old tracks won't go more than a snail's pace." answered the specialist.

"You're the advanced party, I suspect. Come on and I'll show you where I want you." said McKensie.

He walked Five India over Charlie company's sector of the perimeter while the battalion XO showed Lieutenant Driscol the mortar platoon position, mess area and maintenance stand. McKensie told Five India that telephone lines would be used inside the fire base so the battalion could minimize radio transmissions.

Once he had all the information the company commander would need, Five India thanked the colonel and walked to the access road to wait for the company. As he stood by the gap in the wire, he scanned the jungle. Everything felt different here. Perhaps he was just accustomed to Binh Son. Perhaps it was the fact that the rainy season was ending and the days were now bright and hot. On the warm breeze he could hear the high-pitched whine of APC engines and the clatter of treads as the lead tracks of Charlie company pulled off Highway 1 and headed toward the fire base. Shielding his eyes from the sun, he stared up the access road and saw something he had not seen for months—dust.

Five India directed the lead platoon to a parking area, then waved at Jace as the command track lurched to a halt.

"A totally groovy place." grinned Five India.

"Where do we go?" asked Jace.

"The XO is right over there. He'll show you where your track and the mortars go. Our section—"

"I tell you what," interrupted Jace. "You put in the CP, the mortars, the mess tent and the maintenance section. I'll place the platoons on the line. You just show me where our flanks are."

"I've put up stakes with engineer tape at our right and left tie-ins. You'll see 'em." said the specialist. "The scout platoon had a few tracks holding our line till we got here. They're moving out of the way now."

After the platoons were in their approximate positions, Jace walked to the company's left limit, then started down the line, pointing out where he wanted each bunker and track. That done, he ordered the company to dig in. Foxholes would be all they could finish tonight. Building bunkers with sandbag roofs for protection from enemy mortar fire would be the priority for tomorrow. Once the troops began to dig, Jace headed off toward the battalion TOC.

Expecting a hearty welcome, he was surprised by the silence and tension inside the command center. Quietly alert, Jace walked to where Lieutenant Colonel McKensie and Major Churchwell were standing. He started to ask what was going on, but was stopped by the colonel's hand signaling silence.

"They're dead!" sobbed a young voice on the radio.

"Now listen, son," said McKensie quietly into the hand set. "You don't know that. We'll get a medic down there as quick as we can. Go find Bravo Six. Tell him to get to the village. Tell him to take your whole unit, and be careful, it may be a trap. Tell him to call me ASAP."

The young soldier on the other end of the radio call was calming, but was still agitated.

"Roger, we're looking for him now."

McKensie turned toward C.C. "That's all I can do till I can talk to the company commander." Then to Jace, "The first platoon leader and a driver were heading down to the village to check on the squad at the market. The jeep was ambushed. The lieutenant and the driver are down, not moving. Judging from what they're saying, they might be—"

He paused. "It happened within site of the market. The squad leader called the company. Bravo Six is outside checking things. That was his RTO. Poor kid's about to go to pieces. The ambush might have been part of a trap to draw more troops in. I told—"

"Cougar Six, this is Bravo six."

It had taken only a moment for Thomaston to get to the radio, but it seemed an eternity.

"Cougar Six, go."

"Bravo Six—I just heard what happened. Understand you want me to take my whole unit to investigate."

"That's affirm'. Sweep the whole area. Look—keep the element at the market where it is. If they move around they might get hit also."

"It's too late, they just went to the site. They reported both people in the jeep are KIA. I'm moving, I'll call you when I get there." radioed Bravo Six.

They were all quiet.

"This is what I hate most about this job," said the battalion commander. "I've got troops in trouble and they are so far away the only way I can talk to them is by radio relay. It's up to the company commander now. I have to trust him. If he's smart, he'll do OK. If not—Oh well, this is a captain's war—Colonels seem to be irrelevant."

That was all the reflection McKensie allowed himself.

"C.C. get the bubble bird warmed up. Call brigade and request they alert the reaction force. Let's get down there!"

Jace moved out of the way, not part of this crisis, but knowing deep inside that it could have been him. He and his platoon leaders had driven the same trail many times. The same trail. The only way in, the only way out of the village. He had hated Binh Son. He had known something like this was coming. He just didn't know when. It could have been him.

In many ways, the routine at Fire Base Cougar was similar to what went on at Binh Son—platoon sweeps during the day, squad-sized ambushes at night. Occasionally, Charlie company was called on for a convoy-escort mission or a road-runner. Probably the insane invention of some staff officer, road-runners were designed for heavily-armed mounted patrols to keep the highways open. Actually, all the platoons did as they drove up and down the highway, often out of radio and artillery range, was to expose themselves to ambushes, snipers, and mines.

Since no artillery was allowed at Binh Son, Jace and his soldiers had gotten used to quiet nights. In the center of Fire Base Cougar, however, stood six 155-millimeter self-propelled howitzers. Besides firing for the 5-39, they had the mission of shooting harassing and interdicting fires all night. To feed the hungry guns, ammunition trucks rolled in off the highway non-stop. During the day, the cannoneers, stripped to the waist, worked at unpacking the shells, fitting fuses, and stacking the projectiles next to the cannons. At night, the noise of the guns made it impossible for anyone to sleep. To reach north of the Dong Nai River, the artillerymen had to fire maximum charge. At this range, the additional powder bags caused the projectiles to break the sound barrier as they left the tubes. The sonic booms, together with the muzzle blasts of the howitzers, were nerve-wracking and ear-splitting. At least there was plenty of wood from the ammo boxes for building things.

Just after dawn, Jace was awakened by the sound of a Huey landing on the pad. Just before daylight, there had been a lull in the artillery's firing and he had slept soundly for two hours. Now as the chattering aircraft shook him from his sleep, he knew he needed to check the perimeter. The troops were as tired as he was and unless someone checked them, there was a danger that they might be asleep at their posts. He poured himself a cup of coffee from the thermos jug, pulled on his jungle boots, grabbed his pistol belt and helmet, and ducked out of the tent. He walked slowly around the perimeter, making this more of a social visit than an inspection. He knew by their haggard looks that his troops were dangerously fatigued. What they needed most right now, besides sleep, was encouragement.

As Jace returned to his command track, the field phone rang.

"Charlie." he barked into the phone.

"Hello, may I speak to the company commander?" said the polite, soft voice.

"You've got him," said Jace tiredly.

"Sir, this is your new first sergeant. I just came in on the chopper. I just met the battalion commander and the sergeant major. I need directions to your C.P."

"Just stay there. I'll send someone to get you," said Jace.

He hung up the phone, suddenly taken aback. He had not even considered the fact that a new first sergeant would replace the one that had just left. Although the company had received several enlisted replacements, no NCOs or officers had arrived since he had been in command of Charlie company. With his old first sergeant permanently dug in at Bear Cat, he had gotten used to running the company without a top-kick. No, that was not right either—he had used Five India, who handled all of the company's administration and solved nearly every little problem, as a first sergeant. Now here was some new guy they would all have to adjust to—and the guy sounded like a wimp on the phone. The last first sergeant had been an old national guard soldier who had been brow-beaten into submission by the previous company commander. What would this one be like? At Fort Bragg, Jace had relied heavily on his first shirt. Here, things were different. He had never served with someone like Five India, who had no rank to speak of, but who had intelligence, intuition, common sense, and the respect of the company. Jace had gotten comfortable with his people and this odd set up and didn't want the situation to change. But, now it would change whether he wanted it to or not.

"Five India, go to the TOC. It seems that we have a new first sergeant. Go pick him up and bring him back."

There was silence in the Charlie company command post.

"Oh, shit, just when things were starting to go good," said Five India.

Tucker, who sat barefooted and shirtless, felt his chin.

"I'd best get a shave." he said, then disappeared.

Jace looked at Five India, knowing that he must feel threatened.

"Maybe it won't be so bad. Maybe he'll fit in just fine."

"If he doesn't, what'll become of me? I have no slot here. You're not authorized a spec five assistant anything in your company headquarters—and I don't want to go to battalion or brigade. I fit in here, and I like what I do. If a war starts between me and the first sergeant, you know I'll be the one to lose."

"You're forgetting one thing," said Jace. "Me—I won't let that happen. I don't give a damn about who or what I'm authorized. You're too good—too valuable to let go. We'll work this out. Let's don't borrow trouble before it gets here. Now go get the first sergeant."

Jace had been unsettled by his short conversation on the phone with the new first sergeant. Not only did he have a soft speaking voice, but he talked in a laid-back, easy-going accent from where? Jace guessed California.

After Five India left, Jace looked about the C.P. tent, which was a mess. He realized he had let his normally high standards slip. He remembered how appalled he had been at the conditions in the company when he had first arrived. What would the new first sergeant think when he saw this mess? Suddenly insecure, Jace began to straighten up the tent, picking up the empty C-ration, coke and beer cans. He then attacked the command track, the interior of which was a mess. He crammed papers, empty C-ration boxes, and discarded cigarette packages into a trash bag. Looking around, he decided that was the best he could make it look. As he straightened up the poncho liner on his cot, the tent flap flew back.

A giant of a man stepped inside. First Sergeant Hector Baez's huge hand swallowed Jace's as they shook. His torso swept in a V from huge shoulders to a trim waist. His brown face beamed confidence, friendliness and humor. Jace glanced at the first sergeant's chest, taking in the master parachute wings, pathfinder badge, and Combat Infantryman's Badge patches sewn on his shirt. On his left shoulder, above the division patch was a ranger tab. On his right shoulder, indicating he had served in combat with that unit, was the patch of the 173rd Airborne Brigade. Baez grinned beneath his huge mustache.

"Sir," he said with his deceptively quiet voice, "Glad to meet you. Just tell me what you need and where I start."

"Well," said Jace glancing at Five India, who shrugged as he turned away, "I need a first sergeant, and it looks to me like you probably know how to be one. Welcome to Charlie company."

Jace and Baez spent the next hour swapping stories about the 82nd Airborne Division. Baez had been in a different brigade, but he and Jace knew many of the same people.

"Let me ask you something." said Jace carefully. "What are you doing here. Don't get me wrong—I'm glad as hell to have someone with your experience. But, I was wondering why you aren't in an airborne unit."

"Sir, this is my second tour. I was a platoon sergeant in the 173rd. I came in country with them. Beat the bush for a year, then went back to Bragg. For some reason, the army in all its wisdom wanted me here instead of the 173rd. I guess the herd was full of senior NCOs."

"Yeah, tell me about it. I found the same thing on the officer side when I got here." replied Jace.

"I've got a feeling the troops in this company need me as much as any company in the herd," said Baez. "But I'll miss the jump pay!"

"I like your attitude, Top." grinned Jace.

Five India rolled his eyes.

"My last first sergeant did his admin work from the rear. How do you see yourself operating?" asked Jace.

"Sir, if the troops are out here, this is where I belong. There are many things I can do to take pressure off of you. I'll go where ever you want me, but I think I need to be with the troops."

Jace nodded, smiling. "They're a ragged-looking lot, but they're good troops. Come on and I'll show you around."

Jace still felt uneasy, even a little ashamed at how far he had let his standards slip. As he hoped Baez would not think badly of him or his troops, he made a resolution to tighten things back up.

As they walked the line, Baez shook hands with each of the soldiers. He was relaxed and friendly, but business-like at the same time. He seemed to assume the troops would do what he asked, so he had no need to be disapproving. There would be time later to inflict his will. Now he just wanted to meet the soldiers and get a feel for them.

When Jace and Baez came to the third platoon, they were met by Lieutenant Cappaccelli. The first sergeant was polite and gave no indication he intended to get into the platoon leader's business. He carefully scrutinized the platoon sergeant as they were introduced. His eye narrowed in a humorous squint as if to say, "We'll get to know each other real well, real soon."

As the first sergeant was introduced around, Super Private suddenly appeared from behind his track. He wore beltless jungle fatigue pants that were a size too big for him, shower clogs, and an unauthorized floppy camouflaged hat that he called his go-to-hell cap. He wore no shirt and three day's growth of beard, and held Falstaff beer in his hand. When he saw the first sergeant, he went into a tirade.

"Oh, shit! Here this new first sergeant gonna dig in my shit! I've had it now. I might as well plan on being a private for the rest of my natural life! Things were gettin' groovy around here. I knew it was too good to be true. And look at this guy. Airborne-Ranger! That's all we need—two of 'em—the C.O. and the first sergeant!"

The platoon laughed as the small private walked in circles, continuing his soliloquy. As they laughed, they watched the new first sergeant, who knew he was on trial. Baez folded his massive arms across his chest and grinned as he watched Super Private enjoying center stage, stomping and fuming about his misfortune. Suddenly, the private stopped and became serious. He walked up to Baez, cocked his head and grinned.

"Welcome to Charlie company, Top." he said as he held out the Falstaff.

First Sergeant Baez looked down at the scruffy soldier as the laughter subsided and the soldiers of third platoon as one leaned forward to see what would happen next. Slowly, Baez reached for the proffered warm beer. He took it, studied the can, looked around the platoon, then held the beer high in a toast.

"I'm glad to be your first sergeant—I'm here to make sure this is the best damned company in Vietnam!"

He drained the can in three rapid gulps, crushed it in his huge hand, and threw it to the ground. Then he went from man to man, shaking hands and introducing himself to the soldiers. As he and Jace turned to continue the tour of the line, the first sergeant looked back over his shoulder at Super Private.

"The next time I come around, that can had better not be on the ground!" he grinned.

"Oh, yes, Top! No problem, Top! What ever you say, Top!" bowed Super Private in mock subservience. Third platoon howled in laughter. Five India watched and frowned from the door of the C.P. tent.

Lau and Phun stepped out of the jungle onto Highway 1, beginning what would be a long series of recruiting trips into the local towns and villages. Today they would go to Long Thanh, a dangerous trip since the village lay so close to the huge American base.

Lau had memorized the list of names given to him by the regimental commander. Provided by a trusted spy, the list contained names of people who had lost loved ones accidentally or mistakenly to the Americans and were considered to be prime candidates for recruiting into the NLF. There were four families in Xuan Loc, seven in Bien Hoa, and one in Long Thanh. Taking Phun along had been Lau's idea. In the Vietnamese society where sexual roles were clearly defined, Phun would be able to communicate with the women in ways Lau could not. Besides, he liked having her with him.

Lau was once again disguised as an ARVN soldier—a different one now that he had shown his identification to the police in Xuan Loc. Phun posed as Lau's wife, who, like almost every woman in the country, carried no identification papers. Their story was that Lau was on leave and they were on their way to visit family members.

Walking along the dusty shoulder of Highway 1, the narrow road that ran the length of Vietnam, they sought transportation. Having no idea when a bus might run, Lau watched as heavy traffic of motor bikes and bicycles streamed past.

Every now and then, Lau tried waving down a lambretta, a small three-wheeled truck built on the back of a motor scooter. But as each rolled by, packed with passengers, the drivers ignored him.

After walking for over an hour, Lau waved down a man riding a motor bike.

"Excuse me, sir. My wife and I are seeking transportation to the village of Long Thanh. Could you possibly give us a ride? We will be glad to pay." explained Lau.

The man thought for a second, then said, "I am going to Saigon. Long Thanh is out of my way, but I will take you as far as Long Binh. I must buy petrol there to continue my trip. If you would buy the gasoline, I will give you a ride."

"We would be glad to pay. Thank you for your kindness." said Lau.

Three people on a motor bike was a common sight on Vietnamese highways. Lau had often seen families of as many as five on one bike. Phun straddled the bike behind the driver, and Lau balanced himself behind her. Having nothing to hold onto, he squeezed her with his legs to stay on the bike. He tried to ignore the fact that her small body felt extremely good to him. He had not been this close to a woman since his wife had died and he prayed he would not become excited. Since this was not the time or place, and since it would be difficult to hide, an erection would be very embarrassing to him and would cause him to lose face with Phun—something he could not stand to think about.

Bouncing along the pitted highway into Long Binh, Lau again was amazed by the size and complexity of the American base. As they pulled into a dilapidated Texaco station, a huge convoy of tanks and armored personnel carriers thundered past, blowing hot air and black smoke from their exhausts. Lau paid the man for the gasoline, then he and Phun walked to the edge of the road, watching the powerful machines rumble past. American soldiers riding on the personnel carriers were monstrous looking in their helmets and flak jackets, and were bristling with weapons of every sort. Many of the solders had stern, evil looks on their faces, but some laughed and joked. Most of the Americans ignored them, but one small, very young-looking boy smiled and waved at the couple. As they waved in return, Lau wondered where this huge convoy was heading and what it would do when it got to its destination. As they watched, he remembered his long-felt desire to face the Americans—not like this, as an observer, but as a warrior. Now he could watch. Some day he would face them in battle. Watching the armor rumble past, he wondered how anyone could fight such power.

The couple rolled into Long Thanh in the back of a lambretta that they had been lucky to find that was not too crowded. After paying the driver, who had been friendly and had not charged them an exorbitant rate, Lau and Phun stood by the roadside and again went over their plan. They would ask around the village, pretending to be distant relatives come to pay respects to the family of the man who had unfortunately been killed by the Americans. They would be alert to people making angry remarks about Duc's death or about the Americans. They would return and talk to them later, but first they would speak to Duc's family.

As they asked directions, Lau and Phun discovered that the people of Long Thanh were tight-lipped and wary of strangers. Many ignored them altogether, but most gave hurried, incomplete information about Duc's kin. None of the villagers said anything at all about the Americans.

Finally Lau and Phun were directed to Duc's home, which was empty. A neighbor pointed them toward Chi's house, telling them that Duc's wife was living there now. As they walked the short distance to their recruiting targets' house, Lau felt a wave of fear sweep over him. In the north, he had conducted carefully staged and rehearsed political rallies where he had always known the outcome. He had simply spouted the party line with the full knowledge that everyone would enthusiastically respond to his every word. This was different. He was entering a home that was less than three kilometers from a huge American base— a home full of people who were not communists and who worked for the enemy. Lau could not predict what would happen. At best, he hoped to sway one or two family members away from the influence of the Americans. At worse, he and Phun could be turned in to the police and apprehended. They would have to be very careful.

As they entered the yard, Lau and Phun bowed to the children in the doorway.

"Are your parents home?" asked Lau.

"My mother and aunts are working," said a young girl shyly. "My cousin Huong and the wife of my cousin, now dead are here," she added.

"That is the reason we are here," said Lau, gently. "To offer condolences and to see if the family needs help with anything."

Huong appeared at the door, staring, but saying nothing.

Lau and Phun bowed deeply.

"We regret your recent loss. We represent a committee that assists the widows and orphans of war dead. We understand that Cao Tho Duc has been killed in an unfortunate incident."

"You may call it an unfortunate incident if you wish," answered Huong with a glare. "I call it murder!"

Lau and Phun glanced at each other.

"May I speak to the widow?" asked Phun.

"She is inside. Please come in." offered Huong.

Lau and Phun entered the house, taking stock. By northern standards, this was a home of wealth. The house had four large rooms, a wooden floor, furniture, decorations on the walls, and doors that could be closed and locked. The kitchen was well stocked with food and a radio blared tinny Vietnamese music. A motor bike stood in the back yard.

Phun introduced herself to the young widow and soon they were brewing tea. Phun kept up a singsong reverie of condolences and sympathy. Duc's widow said little as Lau turned to Huong.

"How did it happen?" he asked.

"He went on the river trail to cut wood. He made his living cutting and selling wood to the charcoal makers. He received permission to cut in that section of the jungle and was walking along the trail when an American helicopter flew over and murdered him. I went with the police and popular-force soldiers to bring his body home," answered Huong bitterly.

"Did the Americans think he was an enemy?" asked Lau, hiding his excitement over the fact that Huong was practically recruited already.

"How could they? He had only an ax and a saw. He had no weapon. He was a civilian with permission from the government to cut wood. He had proper identification and was doing nothing wrong."

This was Lau's first attempt at recruiting. He was desperately afraid that he would spoil the effort somehow. Despite Huong's obvious hatred of the Americans, Lau was not sure how to proceed.

"Please tell me if there is anything we can do for the family." he offered.

"Please tell me again what organization you represent." said Huong with an authority that belied his young age.

Lau decided to risk everything.

"We represent an organization that is dedicated to removing all foreigners from our country. First the French subjugated us, then the Japanese came, then after the war the French returned, and now the Americans are here. All we want is Vietnam for the Vietnamese. We have enormous sympathy for those who have lost loved ones to the foreigners. We are simply here to offer our help and condolences."

"The organization you represent—does it fight the Americans?"

"Our organization does not fight. We only offer help where we can. There are organizations that we know of that do fight." answered Lau.

"You are from the National Liberation Front." Huong's voice was level and cool. His eyes locked on Lau's.

Lau hesitated for a second, then said yes.

"You must leave before my mother comes home. She works for the Americans. Although I do not believe she owes them any particular loyalty, our living depends on the pay our family gets from them. She might not be happy about your being here." said Huong.

"Then let's not tell her whom we represent right now. We would like to meet her and to see if there is any way our organization can assist your family," said Lau.

"All right. But I want nothing to upset my mother and my aunts. They have suffered a great loss and are in mourning. Please respect their feelings.

"You can be sure of that," said Lau.

"I wish to join your organization," said Huong, simply. "Can you help me?"

"Of course. First I would like to meet the rest of your family. We will proceed carefully. I do not wish to offend anyone," said Lau.

Phun and Duc's widow were squatting by the fire, their heads together, talking lowly. Duc's wife had said almost nothing since the death of her husband. Now, she was pouring out her soul to this stranger. Phun cooed and clucked sympathetically as she stroked the young woman's hair. As Lau and Huong sipped tea and made small talk, a huge truck squealed to a halt at the road junction. The people on the back scrambled down and scattered toward their homes. As Lau watched Chi and her sisters approach the house, He was again filled with apprehension.

"Who is the stranger?" Chi asked her sisters. "Does either of you know him?"

"No, I do not know him," replied the younger of Chi's sisters. "But whoever he is and whatever he wants—you know it cannot be anything good."

The stranger, dressed neatly in white shirt, black pants and sandals bowed deeply. Huong looked disconcerted.

"*Chao Ba.*" said the stranger.

"Welcome to our humble home." said Chi, also bowing. "What may this poor family do for you?"

"It is not for you to ask." answered Lau. "It is we who come to ask if there is any assistance you need after the death of your son."

"We? Is someone else here?" asked Chi, worriedly looking about.

"My wife is with the young widow. We humbly offer our condolences."

"Whom do you represent?" asked Duc's mother.

"We represent those who deplore innocent death. Ours is an altruistic organization with the mission of helping those in need. We are simply here to offer assistance if you need it."

"What is the name of your organization?" asked the older of Chi's sisters, who was feeling uneasy with the strangers' presence.

"Don't worry, Aunt. They are polite, considerate visitors, who bring or mean no harm." offered Huong in response.

Chi noticed that the question went unanswered.

"Have you had tea?" asked Chi. As the matriarch, hospitality was her responsibility.

"Yes, thank you," bowed Lau. "These young people have been most polite."

"Would you dine with us? All we have to offer is a simple meal, but you are most welcome to join us." offered Chi, more out of social necessity than any heart-felt wish for company. She too was unsettled by the presence of the strangers.

"A bowl of rice would be more than generous. We will of course pay for our meal. Actually we are in Long Than for the first time. We have no place to stay and curfew is not far off. Do you know of lodging we could use?"

"Duc's home near here is empty. Please feel free to sleep there," answered Huong.

"Thank you, younger brother. We would be honored, if it is acceptable to the young widow—and again we insist on paying for the lodging as well as the meal."

Duc's widow only shrugged.

As they dined on rice, green onions, boiled squash and cabbage, there was little talk.

As Phun helped clear the dishes, she asked, "Have the Americans offered assistance to you? After all they were responsible for your son's death."

"No, I'm afraid not. The people we work for did not even seem to be aware of Duc's death," answered Chi.

"I find it odd. They pay you to do their dirty work, then they kill your family member. Can money ever pay for what you have lost?"

Chi and her sisters squirmed uneasily on their cushions and glanced at each other, seeming to know what was coming next.

"Their soldiers drink beer and loaf while our labor gangs fill sand bags to fortify their camp. They are lazy and some even taunt us as we work. They seem to enjoy exploiting and subjugating us," said Huong haughtily.

"Our organization believes that foreigners should leave our county entirely. They have no business here." offered Phun.

"You have not told us the name of your organization," said Chi.

Lau fought his rising anxiety. If he did not handle this right, some member of the family could go to the police. Getting out of Long Thanh might prove to be impossible. If he blew his first attempt at recruiting, he might lose the respect of his regimental commander and the other political officers, not to mention Phun. Everyone was silent. It had been Lau who suggested that they not tell Chi whom they represented. If he violated his word, Huong would be offended. If they admitted they were Viet Cong, they might be reported. Lau looked at Huong helplessly.

"They are from the National Liberation Front," blurted Huong. "They are not fighters. They are from a different wing of the front that only wishes to help us against those who killed Duc. I intend to join them."

"What? What do you mean? You would become a guerrilla? A fighter?" screamed Chi.

"I don't know what they will ask me to do. I am still young and inexperienced and I don't know how to fight. But I know I could be of use in some way. All I know is that I hate the Americans for killing Duc—and anything I can do to hasten their departure from our country, I am willing to do," said Huong, proudly.

"I will not allow it. We work for the Americans. They are good to us and pay us well. The rice you are eating came from the money we make at their base. How could you invite these people into our peaceful home?" sobbed Chi, trying to calm herself.

Then turning to Lau, she said, "Will you send guerrillas to kill us because we work for the Americans? I have heard stories of the Viet Cong killing those civilians who will not follow their orders. Are we in danger?"

"Absolutely not, honored lady. As I said, it is only our wish to help you in your hour of need," replied Lau.

"I know you are earnest in your beliefs. But Huong is the only child I have left. I cannot allow him to become Viet Cong. He is too young. When he is older, he may make his own decisions—but for now, I cannot allow it."

"We are not here to recruit." lied Lau. "As we have said, this is a benevolent mission we are on. There are others we must visit. All we ask is that you honor our beliefs and our commitment by not informing those who killed your son that we were here."

"We will not divulge that you have been here. But you put us in danger with your presence. The police could arrest us simply because you visited us. Please, let us return to our lives. Let us recover from the death of my son in our own time and in our own way."

Lau, remembering the party doctrine for dealing with civilians, said, "We will go now. Please accept our pay for the meal and for tonight's lodging. We will place you in no danger. I promise you this. Tomorrow morning, as soon as curfew lifts, we will be gone."

He paused, then added, "We have one request. There may come a time when the whole country will rise up and throw out the foreigners—and that time may come sooner than later. When it happens, our party will remember who was with us and who was against us. When the day of the great uprising comes, all we ask is that you do not help the Americans or their puppets. If you wish to fight at that time, your courage will be rewarded. If you cannot fight, then any small thing you do to help our cause will be remembered. Something as simple as offering lodging to a fighter as you do for us this night could be of earth-moving importance. Even the smallest act of support for our cause will be noticed, remembered and rewarded."

The significance of what the man was saying was not lost on Chi. By offering food and lodging to a known enemy of the state, she had already crossed the line. She was already committed whether she wanted to be or not.

"Again, please accept our heart-felt condolences at the loss of your family member. Of course we will respect your wishes concerning your son. He is young. Perhaps when he becomes older—. Again, thank you and good evening."

Lau and Phun bowed their way from Chi's home. Huong volunteered to take them to Duc's house. When they arrived at the hut, he turned to Lau.

"I am ready to go. How do I join your organization?"

"We do not wish to go against your mother," said Phun. "What you must do is work diligently to turn your family to our point of view. For now, we ask that you go back to work on the base. Any and all information that you gather is potentially useful. One of our agents will be in touch with you. He will tell you what information is needed. You can be more useful than you know."

"I will make a good spy!" said Huong proudly.

"Is your mother or your aunts likely to turn us in tonight?" asked Phun, slightly worried.

"No." answered Huong. "I will tell them that I am with you and if they turn you in, they turn me in also."

"Good! Now run home like a good son. Don't talk openly to anyone about your anger over your brother's death. That might draw attention to you. Be patient and be strong in the knowledge that the information you provide us from the base will be used to avenge your brother's death." said Lau.

In youthful exuberance, Huong bowed, then saluted before turning to run home. As they watched him leave, Phun leaned against Lau who responded with an arm around her waist. For the first time since they met, they would be alone tonight.

In the gray light of dawn, Lau lay cuddled to Phun's back. Last night, he had been worried about Chi or one of her sisters turning them in. Now, in the cool, quiet of the morning, that threat seemed distant. Sexual satisfaction seemed to change his outlook on everything. As he awakened slowly, enjoying the feel of Phun's body, the war seemed a thousand miles away. Feeling her breathing gently beside him, he marveled at how his life had changed since he had left the north.

When he had lost his family, he had decided that happiness was a thing of the past for him, and had imagined his journey south to be one of austere sacrifice and misery. Although he had faced danger and fear, he had felt more alive here than he ever had in the north. He had a hard time reconciling the stark dangers of the jungle trails with the insane freedom of openly traveling the highways. Instead of enduring hardship and pain, he had enjoyed beer and wine, good food, and companionship. Even in the jungle camps there was more rice to eat than was ever available in the north. He thought he had even gained weight here.

Lau pushed the memories of his son and his daughter out of his mind. He simply could not yet bear to think of them; the pain could still overwhelm him if he let it. His thoughts drifted to his wife, who, at thirty-five when she died, had looked fifty, long years of hard work in the paddies having bent and aged her. His marriage had been arranged. Instead of love, the union had been built on mutual respect, hard work, sacrifice, duty, and responsibility. The idea of loving her had simply never entered his mind. Now he realized that when he thought of his dead wife, he remembered only a kind of contented familiarity. The embrace of the entire family unit, rather than a strong love between husband and wife had been his comfort in the north.

He had never felt the thrills and excitement with his wife that he now felt with Phun, whose intelligence, bravery, and audacity in the face of danger, made her the perfect soldier-spy. But her child-like beauty, her impish flirtatiousness, and her sense of humor—not to mention her strong sexuality—all combined to drive Lau crazy with desire for her.

He had never thought of his wife as a friend. She had been a kind of subordinate business partner in the family structure. In fact, he had never thought of a woman as an equal—until now. Phun was the only friend he had made in the south. In fact, he now felt that she was the best friend he had ever had. When he was with her, he felt a wild, reckless freedom surge through him.

In one cruel stroke, he had been severed from his past life, and had come south fully expecting to die avenging his family. He still wanted to come face to face with the hated Americans who had killed his children, but now he knew he wanted to live. He knew he was hopelessly in love with Phun.

A soft shuffling in the yard jolted the couple into full alert as Huong's face appeared in the door.

"You must hurry. Policemen are going door to door, looking for something. They are only two houses away from here. Curfew will lift any minute. Come, I will hide you!" hissed Huong in a loud whisper.

Lau and Phun scrambled to dress and gather their belongings. Tucking in his shirt, Lau pulled Phun out the door and after Huong. They ran along a dirt path between the thatched huts of Long Thanh. As they hurried onto a side street, they came face to face with the policemen. Several people were out of their houses now, doing morning chores. With a slight gesture, Lau signaled Huong and Phun to slow down and mingle with the villagers. As the policemen turned to enter another house, the trio walked within feet of them. Once they were safely away from the house being searched, they turned right and dashed along a perimeter path that separated the village from the adjoining rice paddy. Huong pulled up at a dike, bending over out of breath.

"Here, the paddies are at their narrowest. Come!" whispered Huong. Lau and Phun followed blindly as they dashed across the paddy dike toward the jungle. As the two Viet Cong and their young friend disappeared into the safety of the jungle, the pair of white-shirted national policemen knocked on the door of Duc's shack. After knocking again, one of the policemen stepped inside and looked around. Seeing nothing suspicious, he was turning to leave when he spotted the wallet on the dirt floor. Opening it, the policeman saw the identification card of an ARVN sergeant, and a fairly large sum of money. Looking quickly to see if his superior was watching, he removed the money and stuffed it into his pocket.

"Sergeant Lam, look what I found." said the policeman.

The supervisor took the wallet, examined the identification card, then said, "We'll take it back and trace it. It is odd to find such a thing in an empty house."

Although he didn't say so, the junior policeman found it odd that a sergeant could have so much money in his wallet. Oh well, at least they would try to get the card back to the rightful owner, if it didn't turn out to be too much trouble. As they continued their search for the deserter who had escaped from the regional forces compound brig, the junior policeman inwardly beamed at his windfall of cash.

At the edge of the jungle, Huong told Lau and Phun to stay where they were until he came back for them. He would try to find out what the police were looking for and would bring them some food. Even at this time of danger, Lau remembered his training. "I will be more than happy to pay for our breakfast," he said, opening his knapsack.

"That won't be necessary." said Huong. "My mother always prepares more than enough rice. I'll bring you—."

"Wait!" cried Lau. My wallet. I cannot find my wallet."

Phun looked at him, horrified.

"I must have dropped it as we left the house. Quick, go back and look. If I have lost the wallet, we are in danger. I am far from my home base without iden- tification. Please hurry."

Without a word, Huong darted back onto the dike and ran toward the village, searching the ground as he retraced their route. Once he was sure the police had moved on, he searched Duc's house high and low. Not finding the wallet, he squatted in the doorway and tried to think. If Lau lost his wallet here in the house, there was a good chance the police had found it. He had seen them search before—they were very thorough. Lau and Phun were in the jungle, safe for the time being. But with no identification, Lau, and Phun were extremely vulnerable. If the police checked the I.D. card and found it was fake, they would want to know what it was doing in Duc's house. Huong did not know what to do about the wallet, but he did know he had to get his new friends out of Long Thanh.

As he ran to his mother's house, Huong wondered what he should tell her. He had never been successful at lying to his mother—she always seemed to be able to see right into his heart. Desperate with anxiety, he decided to tell her the truth.

Chi was squatting next to the fire, sipping her morning tea. Watching the rice that had come to a rolling boil, she was placing the lid on the pot and removing it from the coals as Huong burst in.

"Where have you been so early in the morning?" she asked, knowing the answer.

"Mother, our visitors from last night are in trouble. The police were searching the village—"

"I know! They stopped here. They were looking for a deserter."

Huong continued, "I went to warn them the police were coming. They are now hiding in the jungle. As they ran from Duc's house, Mr. Lau dropped his wallet. I searched, but I could not find it. If the police have found it, they will want to know what it was doing in Duc's house. But that is the least of their trou- bles—they are stranded in Long Thanh without identification—and I must help them."

"Help them do what?" screamed Chi. "They are not our responsibility. Do not get involved in this. This is a bad dream! I warn you—only trouble can result from this."

"Mother, we are involved. We fed them and we gave them lodging for the night. If the police find the identification is false, they will be here asking questions. They will want to know what the wallet was doing in Duc's house. I must go now. I need some money."

"What do you need money for?" cried Chi.

"Gasoline." answered Huong. "And please let me take them some breakfast."

"There are rice and vegetables left over from last night in the pan. Take that if you must, but please—do not get involved."

"I must, Mother. The Americans killed Duc. These people fight the Americans. I must help them. I will help them!"

Huong scooped up the leftovers and wrapped them in a cloth. As he placed the food in his knapsack, he also threw in his identification card and the few piasters his mother had given him. Shouldering his pack, he ran out the back door.

"Please do not worry, Mother." he said. As he pushed his motorbike out of the back yard and into the highway, Huong tried to ignore his mother's wailing sobs. Curfew having lifted, the traffic suddenly flowed as if it had never stopped for the night. Huong kicked the small motor into life and sped off northward. Seeing the policemen emerge from a neighbor's yard, he turned the pros and cons of asking them if they had found a wallet over in his mind. If they had found the wallet, they would probably ask questions—questions he had rather not try to answer. He decided to wait until they had left the village, then to get Lau and Phun as far away from Long Thanh as possible.

The policemen didn't seem to be in any hurry going from house to house. Huong hung back and watched them, not wanting to be seen. Finally, after what seemed an eternity, the pair of lawmen worked their way to the northern edge of the village, then turned to walk back to their station on the south end of town.

Huong fought the impulse to go as fast as the bike would travel to his two friends. He forced himself to ride slowly along the highway, then turn into the trail to the paddy dike. After stopping to look around, he rode across the dike toward the jungle. As Huong pulled up at the end of the dike, Lau, who had been watching his approach, grabbed the boy's arm and jerked him into the jungle, then pulled the motor bike under the foliage.

"You are acting very suspiciously. You must not stop and look around like that. If someone is watching you, they must be led to assume you are going about routine business. If you hesitate, if you act in a suspicious manner, you could find yourself in trouble," said Lau forcefully.

"Remember the old saying: Naked is the best disguise!" added Phun. "If you are caught naked, or in the open, acting as if nothing is wrong is the best thing to do. No one will suspect you then."

Huong lowered his head, embarrassed. Having acted boldly, he had thought he was in total control. Now he was being lectured and rebuked by his new heros.

"I brought you some food," he said, trying to change the subject. "I thought that I could carry you north to Bien Hoa, safely out of this area.

"No," said Lau. "That is too far. We would have to go through too many areas controlled by the enemy. Besides, what would I do in Bien Hoa without money or identification? If we could get to Xuan Loc, we would be safe, but that is nearly 160 kilometers from here—too far to go on a small motorbike. No—we must go south—to the village of Binh Son. There are contacts there and a Liberation Front base nearby. It is within range of your motor bike. Also you can be home by dark so your mother will not be worried."

"I must buy some gasoline. The station is north of here. I do not think you should go with me there. The police may still be in the area. You must wait here. I will get gasoline and come back as quickly as I can," said Huong, his voice made high-pitched by fear.

"You have come here twice—a third time might establish a dangerous pattern." said Phun. "Is there somewhere else we can meet you?"

Huong thought hard as he looked about. "Come to the market. There will be crowds there, so you won't be noticed. As you said, naked is the best disguise."

Phun smiled. He was learning.

"We will meet you at the market place in one hour."

Without another word, Huong mounted his bike and sped off across the paddy dike toward the village.

Lau was horrified at the thought of entering the village marketplace without his identification card. Still, if Huong returned to them along the same trails and dikes, someone could notice the pattern of his movements. The police had finished their search and were gone. Phun agreed that it was best to go to the market.

They had no choice but to cross the dry rice paddy to get back to the village. There was little to be done in the fields during the dry season, so this side of the village was deserted. Most people, going to work at Bear Cat or to the market, were out on the highway. Lau made sure there was no one in sight before they left the jungle.

Deciding to alter their route as much as possible, they crossed the dry rice field to enter the village closer to the market. When they got to the perimeter path, they turned left and continued northward for two hundred meters then ducked down a side street which took them directly to the market.

"What should we do while we wait?" asked Lau, deferring to Phun's knowledge of southern villages.

"Well, how long has it been since you had a beer?" smiled Phun.

"It's still early in the morning." said Lau. "Tea would taste better."

"Then tea it will be. We'll find a tea stand that is out of the way. Since you do not have any identification, it will be better if we stay together. You don't mind do you?" asked Phun, with a coy smile.

"Staying together with you will not be hard to do," answered Lau, embarrassed at her forwardness.

"Why comrade Lau, your face is hot!"

Lau, totally flustered, grabbed Phun's hand and pulled her toward a street stand. They ordered tea, then sat on a wooden bench under the shade of tall palm trees. As they sipped, Lau was amazed at how light-hearted he felt, even though he and Phun were vulnerable and exposed—and probably in a great deal of danger. Phun seemed to make everything a game. Her boldness in the face of danger frightened and thrilled him at the same time.

"When the war is over, what will you do? Will you go back to the North?" asked Phun, suddenly serious.

"I have nothing to return to there," answered Lau.

Watching the people swarming through the market, Phun was quiet for a time.

"It would be very nice to have a home in a small village like this one. Life could be very good," she said quietly.

"If one lived in that home with the right person." answered Lau. "I was thinking—"

"Look—here comes Huong."

The boy had learned his lesson. He ignored the couple entirely as he rode to the edge of the market. Dismounting, he pushed the bike past Lau and Phun to where a side street dead-ended into the market. There, he pretended to inspect the tightness of the chain. Lau and Phun waited a moment, casually looking around for signs of danger, then stood and walked toward Huong.

Phun spoke to Huong as an older sister would casually greet a younger brother.

"Well, young hero, are you ready to go?" she asked sweetly.

"Yes," answered Huong nervously.

"You did quite well this time," said Phun under her breath. "You acted in such a way as not to attract curiosity."

"Thank you, older sister," said Huong, enormously proud of the compliment.

Without another word they all mounted the motorbike and rode away from the market at normal speed. Huong turned from the side street onto Highway 15. All signs of danger had disappeared as they headed south toward the turn-off that would take them to Binh Son. At mid-morning, the dry-season sun beat down on the black pavement and the heat became oppressive.

As they rode past the U.S. Army's Long Thanh airfield, Huong watched the helicopters landing and taking off, and thought of Duc's senseless death at the hands of the Americans. Safely out of Long Thanh, Huong's anxiety subsided and the hatred he felt for the Americans took over again. He was proud to be doing something to fight the imperialists, even if it was an act as small as helping two National Liberation Front fighters to safety.

As the highway plunged into the jungle, the trio ran up behind an American convoy. Huge dump trucks followed flat-beds carrying dozers with slanting, knife-like blades. Helmeted troops with armored vests stood in the back of the dump trucks, their rifles pointed outward, toward the jungle. Armored personnel carriers bristling with big machine guns escorted the engineer unit.

At first, Huong was overcome by fright. Phun, who sat behind him, holding him tightly around his chest, reminded him, "Remember—act normally. Naked is the best disguise."

Huong took three deep breaths, then charged around the APC that brought up the rear of the convoy. As they sailed past the Americans, Phun held her conical straw hat on her head with one hand and waved with the other. The Americans responded to the pretty young woman with waves and catcalls. On-coming traffic forced Huong to slip between two dump trucks in the convoy. When the way was clear, He zipped out to pass again. Phun resumed smiling and waving. None of the Americans seemed to care who they were or where they were going.

Suddenly, they came out of the jungle into a huge clearing, several kilometers square. A platoon-sized unit of rag-tag troops, probably mercenaries, together with six tall Americans wearing green berets and several jeeps and trucks, stood a hundred or so meters off the road. Lau guessed they were from the special forces camp near Bear Cat. Whatever they were doing did not appear to be warlike, so Lau assumed that this must be some sort of a training exercise. A teardrop-shaped balloon with tail fins rode at the end of a cable a thousand feet up in the clear, blue sky. As they passed the field, a huge cargo plane with a V-shaped attachment on its nose crossed the highway and slammed into the balloon cable. The balloon broke free as the cable trailed out behind the airplane. Then the trio saw something truly incredible. At the end of the cable, flying straight up out of the group of mercenaries was the figure of a man. As the airplane flew out of sight, it was reeling in the soldier on the end of the cable.

Lau made mental notes. He knew the intelligence officer at regiment would be very interested in this information. This was obviously a method of retrieving someone from the ground. Downed pilots, spies or prisoners might be jerked out of the jungle using this technique. Lau was amazed that the Americans made no attempt to hide anything they did. Their arrogance was astounding. Soon they would learn an important lesson, he thought.

As Huong leaned the motor bike into a steep curve, Lau punched him hard on the back. Ahead was a road block and checkpoint. A platoon of regional/popular-force soldiers and two white-shirted national policemen stood in the road next to several military trucks and jeeps that were parked along the shoulder. A soldier standing behind the ring-mount on a truck trained a machine gun at the approaching traffic. There was not much traffic on the highway at this time of day, so only a few vehicles waited to be searched.

"What do I do?" yelled Huong over his shoulder.

"There is nothing we can do now but go through the checkpoint. We are already too close. If we turn and run, they will shoot us down. At least you have an identification card. That may be enough to get us all through, so we must hope for the best. Huong, remember! Let us do the talking!" ordered Lau.

As Huong pulled the bike up behind an old truck that was being searched, Phun whispered to him, "Remember, act confidently. You have done nothing wrong." To Lau she said, "What name will you use?"

"What name are you more comfortable with?" Lau asked in return.

"Ngyuen Thi Phun, my real name. Any other might confuse me in rough questioning. Remember, I have never been stopped, so they do not know me."

"Then I too will use my real name," whispered Lau in a quiet, confident voice. "That way we will both have the same family name. Remember, I am your husband."

"I wish you really were," she said as she smiled nervously over her shoulder.

As the truck was waved through the checkpoint, the soldiers motioned for Huong to come forward. Stopping in front of the policemen, Huong removed his knapsack to get at his identification card. As he did so, two soldiers leveled their carbines at him.

"Stop! Do not open that bag. Hand it here!" yelled a policeman.

Huong obeyed. Phun and Lau offered their bags as well.

"Step off of the motor bike." ordered a soldier.

The policemen searched the bags as Huong held the handlebars of the bike. Lau and Phun stood nervously but calmly beside him. Then the policeman scrutinized Huong's papers and asked, "Why do you have an identification card?—you are only sixteen."

"I work for the Americans at their base. They require me to have a card."

"You, sir—you have no identification?" asked the policeman.

"I'm sorry. I have lost my wallet. I am a sergeant on leave from my unit. This woman is my wife."

"What is your unit?" asked the other policeman.

"The 21st Division. I am from Vinh Long." answered Lau, politely.

"You are a long way from the Mekong River. What are you doing here?"

"I was injured and spent time in the Saigon army hospital. My wife joined me there. I had a few day's convalescent leave, and since we were this close, we wanted to visit relatives in Binh Son."

"I see no signs of wounds, where were you wounded?"

"Sir, I did not say I was wounded. I was injured. I hurt my back lifting sandbags. I could not walk for nearly a month."

"The names of the relatives, please."

"They are my aunt and uncle. My uncle is the village chief," blurted Phun before Lau had a chance to answer.

"What about you? You are from Long Thanh?" the policeman asked Huong.

"Yes. I am Mr. Lau's nephew. When he was injured, I traveled to Saigon to visit him in the hospital. My mother allowed me to bring him and his wife to Binh Son on my bike." said Huong coolly, surprising himself with his confidence.

"All right. You, boy, and you, madam, may continue. You, sir, will stay with us until your story can be verified or your identification found. Please come with us."

Lau immediately stepped toward the policemen as a signal to Huong and Phun that they must do as they were told.

Phun said to Lau's back, "I will bring your identification card back as soon as I find it."

Huong and Phun mounted the bike and were waved through the checkpoint. Looking back, Phun saw the policemen leading Lau to an army truck. She tried not to panic. What was Lau trying to tell her when he said he would use his real name? Was there an identification card somewhere with that name on it? Where might it be? Did the comrades at regimental headquarters have it? If so, it would take days of walking the dangerous jungle trails to find it and get it back here. Why had they made no plans? What must they do now? Each contingency that came to mind was immediately canceled out by practical realities. One thing was clear. She could do nothing until Huong returned through the roadblock. After he was safely on his way, she would decide what course of action to take. As Huong turned off the highway onto the dirt road that led to Binh Son, Phun finally allowed the tears to flow. She had no idea what to do next. She had been to Binh Son before and knew where to find the contact who would help her get to the nearby C-240 battalion headquarters. But no matter what plan came into her mind, it always ended the same way: Lau was in custody without any identification and she had no way to remedy his situation. The policemen who were searching Long Thanh had no doubt found his wallet. She had no idea where or how to find him another identification card—in fact she didn't even know if another card existed. Even if she were able to locate such a card, how would she know where they had taken him? If the police had found his wallet, checked his identity, and confirmed that it was false, taking another false identification card to him in an enemy jail would be madness anyway. Why had they not planned better?

Huong was confused and frightened.

"What do we do now, Older Sister?" he yelled over his shoulder.

"I do not know for sure," she answered. "I must go into the jungle to report what has happened and you must go home to your mother. Without training, you cannot go into the jungles with me. When you go to Long Thanh, see if you can find out where they took Lau—but be careful. Just listen and ask no one anything. If the police suspect him or prove his story to be false, you might be in danger. If they remember you were with him and that you live in Long Thanh, they might come looking for you."

They were both lost in silent thought as the road suddenly came out of the jungle. On the hill in the distance they could see the plantation house surrounded by American armored vehicles. Beyond, the rubber plantation stood in stark contrast to the tangle of the jungle that had surrounded them since they had left the highway. As they rode into the village of Binh Son, Phun guided Huong to the market.

"Remember, act normally. There are no police in this village, but you saw the Americans at the plantation. They keep ten soldiers at the market at all times. The foreigners do not know one of us from another, but they might become curious if you act suspiciously." lectured Phun.

"My big sister, you have no need to worry about me. I have learned my lesson. Where do we go?"

"Our contact has a stall where she sells ceramics. She will notify her son who will lead me to the C-240 battalion. If you ever need to get in touch with me, leave a message with her. I will introduce you."

Huong parked his motorbike a safe distance from the ceramic stand, then walked to a food stall and ordered noodles. As he ate, Phun pretended to shop. With Huong watching from the corner of his eye, she made her way slowly to the ceramics stand. Slurping the last of his noodles, Huong paid his bill and walked deliberately, but not too quickly, to intercept Phun. He caught up with her as she admired the ceramic figurines on the table.

"This is my young friend, Huong," said Phun under her breath without looking up. "There may be a time when he needs to contact me. Remember him. If he needs help, please get word to me."

Huong looked up briefly at the small woman who was contentedly chewing betel nut. The woman smiled and nodded imperceptibly.

"Now, young hero of the people, go home and await word. We will contact you soon," said Phun.

As Huong was bowing goodby to the woman at the ceramics stand, a tremendous explosion of small arms fire erupted from the direction of the road they had ridden in on. As they might in a bad thunderstorm, the people nearby stirred anxiously, not knowing whether to try to make it home or to remain here in the market. Some merchants huddled behind their wares while some of the more adventurous among them strained on tiptoes to try to see what was happening. Stray bullets cracking through the thatched roofs ended all curiosity. People scattered in all directions as the sound of whining engines and clattering treads came from the plantation house on the hill. Ten armored personnel carriers roared past the village in a cloud of red dust and disappeared into the jungle. Moments later, their heavy machine-gun fire joined the din of the battle.

"Huong, you cannot leave now," shouted Phun. "You must go with me. This woman will keep your motor bike safe. Come, we must find our guide."

Two ARVN soldiers led Lau to the back of a two-and-a-half ton truck.

"We will take you to the police station in Long Thanh where we will attempt to verify your identification. If your story is true, you will be on your way tomorrow morning. If you are lying—"

"My unit in the delta will confirm my identity. I am due back there in three days. You must let me go. If I do not report on time, I will be in considerable trouble."

"Then you should have been more careful with your wallet. You might be in considerable trouble here." smirked the soldier.

Lau was not shackled or confined in any way on the back of the truck. As the vehicle growled northward, he took stock of his situation, which did not look good at all. Various possibilities branched through his mind, each spreading in several directions as option layered on option, and contingency stacked on contingency. What if the policemen who had found his wallet awaited his arrival at the Long Thanh police station? What if the police had already contacted the 21st Division at Vinh Long? What would he say when they did not confirm his identity? What if the truck stopped and he made a run for it? What if—? What would happen when—? He shook his head to clear his thoughts as the two guards sitting at the rear of the truck stared at him intently.

The ride back to Long Thanh did not take long at all. As the truck pulled up in front of the small police box, the soldiers motioned for Lau to follow them. Inside sat the same two policemen who had searched the village and found his wallet. The arrival of the soldiers escorting the man in civilian clothes did not seem to be important enough to cause a reaction on the part of either one of them.

"*Chao Ong.*" said the senior policeman, hardly looking up. "Who have we here?"

"Good day, sir. This man was riding south on a motor bike with a woman and a youth. He says he is a sergeant in the army stationed at Vinh Long. He says he has lost his identification."

A thought shot through Lau's brain like a high-voltage electrical shock. He had given the soldiers his real name, but the identification card in his wallet was in another name. Not anticipating being brought back to where his wallet had been lost, he had used his real name to help Phun in case she was too scared to remember the false one. How stupid could he possibly be, he asked himself. Not only had he been irresponsible in losing the wallet, he had given his real name to the soldiers instead of the one on the fake papers.

He had one hope. Nearly half of the people of South Vietnam shared the surname of Nguyen—in fact, he shared that name with Phun. Both of the names he used, his own and the one on the identification card, began with the surname Nguyen. There was a chance the soldiers would not remember the name he had given them. This pair did not look all that interested in what they were doing—

in fact, they did not look all that bright. Lau did his best to recover his composure.

"Your name, sir?" asked the policeman.

"Ngyuen Dinh Thang, sir. I am a staff sergeant assigned to the 21st division near Can Tho," said Lau with all the confidence he could muster. He dared not look at the two soldiers who had escorted him to the police station. He would know soon enough if they realized the difference in the names. As of now, they had said nothing.

"Well, you might be in luck," said the senior policeman as he tossed the billfold onto the small table. "We found this wallet this morning while we were searching for a deserter. We have placed a call to Vinh Long to verify the papers, but as of yet they have not called back."

One of the soldiers opened the wallet and retrieved the identification card and the fake furlough papers. As he did so, Lau caught a glimpse of the inside of the billfold and made an instant decision.

"Where is my money?" he shouted. I had several months back pay! I am glad to have my papers back, but where is my money?"

The junior policeman was instantly on the defensive. "There was no money in the wallet when we found it. Where did you lose it?" He shot a quick glance at his superior, who was eyeing him closely.

"It must have fallen from my pocket on the road. Where did you find it?"

"In an empty house." The junior policeman saw an out. "Whoever found it must have taken your money and thrown the wallet there."

Enormously relieved, Lau guessed that the policemen had taken the money. He also knew they would not admit it and they would probably rather be done with him quickly, so he continued to rail about his lost money.

"Where can I go without money? My wife and nephew have gone on to Binh Son without me. Where can I stay? What will I do? How will I get back to my unit? Can you help me find the thief who stole my money?"

The senior sergeant laughed. "You are the one who lost your wallet. Be glad we found your identification at least. You know we could never find the person who took the money. Be reasonable."

Lau was now in control. "Well, can you take me to Binh Son to find my wife?"

"We cannot. There are only two of us and we must remain on duty here. Perhaps these soldiers can drive you there."

"What? Drive a single truck through the jungle and through the rubber trees over a dangerous road? No, I am afraid not," answered the incredulous soldier.

"Well, may I go, then?" There are Americans at Binh Son. Perhaps I can catch a ride with a truck going there."

"Feel free. Good luck." said the junior policeman nervously.

Lau stood up, placed the wallet in his pocket, and thanked the policemen. Nodding to the soldiers, he turned toward the door as the phone rang. The senior policeman answered and listened intently as he watched Lau walk away.

"Stop that man!" he yelled. "There is no staff sergeant named Nguyen Dinh Thang in the 21st division!"

CHAPTER 7

▼

24 October 1967

A shadow fell across the door of Jace's command post tent.

"Anybody home?" called C.C.

"Well, hello stranger." said Jace, glad to see his friend.

"You've been noticeably absent lately. Haven't seen you in three days."

"Been busy as hell. Old man keeps me moving nonstop."

Jace opened a beer and handed it to C.C., then offered him a seat on a folding chair. Jace opened himself one and sat down on his cot.

"How's the new first sergeant?" asked C.C.

"Totally different from the last guy. He's a ball of fire. Doesn't seem to step on anybody's toes, but he has sure as hell tightened up things around here." answered Jace.

Five India, sitting at the radios in the command track attached to the tent, shifted his weight and cleared his throat.

"Not that they were all that bad, though." Jace added.

"Look. Big meeting tonight at 1800 hours. Come to chow with the colonel. I'll give you a warning order now—you're going to get orders to airmobile into War Zone D, north of the Dong Nai River. Charlie has been shooting 122-milli-meter rockets at Binh Hoa airbase from up there. You will take your whole company, minus track drivers and .50 gunners. Let's look at the map—you'll go in here, in this old rice paddy. You will have this entire area to search. We suspect the rocket launchers are hidden somewhere in this patch of jungle—right here.

You know War Zone D is a free-fire zone. No civilians. Anything you see, you shoot."

"Where do we lift out of? How many choppers do we have? What's the aircraft load? What about—?"

"You'll get all that at the meeting tonight. I can tell you that you'll go in at about 1300 tomorrow afternoon. That should give you plenty of planning time. As far as choppers, you can count on an entire lift company plus gunships."

"Should I plan on taking my mortars?" asked Jace.

"I would if I were you. I'd have the weapons platoon walk with you. We'll lift the tubes and ammo in to you each night on the supply bird. You can fire up what ammo you have left at H&I targets before you move out each day. We'll lift the tubes out when we pick up the night kit each morning. Plan on covering about ten clicks a day."

"You know, I've been in command over two months and this will be the first time I will take the whole company into the bush dismounted." said Jace.

"I know. If anyone can get this done, I know you can. Be careful up there—that's Indian country. There's been some good people killed in that AO. That's where my battalion operated my first tour. Look, got to run. See you tonight."

C.C. drained his beer, plopped his helmet on his head and ducked out of the tent.

Jace knew all he would know until the meeting after chow. He took a few minutes to think through what his troops would need, then called his leaders together.

One by one, the officers of C company cleared their weapons and stepped inside the C.P. tent. Jace offered them seats on his and the first sergeant's cots. Cappaccelli and Driscol sat on their steel pots. Jace had trained them well—as they sat down, they all took out notebooks and pens. Jace stood at the edge of the circle formed by his company leaders. A map taped on a cardboard C-ration case rested against the back of a folding chair.

Jace looked at his officers. He could not help compare them with the West Pointers he had had in his company at Fort Bragg. These guys were not water-walkers, but they were getting the job done. As he looked from face to face, he felt a sense of pride.

"Well, guys, it looks like for the first time we'll be going into the bush as a company. I want you all to know that I'm proud of the way the company has improved and come together. This is going to be a test—we'll get to see what we're really made of."

The officers cut glances toward one another as they unconsciously leaned forward for the news. Jace adjusted his tactical map on the folding chair and got right to the point.

"You may consider this a formal warning order. The enemy situation is that Charlie has been shooting 122 rockets at Binh Hoa airbase from this patch of jungle in War Zone D. The friendly situation: 5-39 will continue to operate with Bravo company at Bien Son and Alpha company and the rest of the battalion plus attachments here at Fire Base Cougar.

"Mission: Charlie company, minus track drivers, .50-caliber gunners, and the admin overhead will airmobile into a landing zone—here—and conduct search and destroy operations in assigned A.O.—here.

"Special instructions. Weapons platoon will walk with us. Tubes and ammo will be lifted out to us each night. XO: Make a plan for a night kit. I want shovels, wire, claymores, starlight scopes, trip flares, sandbags, hot chow, C-rations, water, mortar tubes and ammo brought out by chopper each night. If lift is available, I want you to send a cook with a burner unit, bacon, eggs, coffee bread and butter with the hot chow. He can spend the night, cook a hot breakfast each morning, and fly out with the night kit. Make sure he brings weapon and gear. If something happens, he may have to walk with us. I want you to have an emergency resupply of all types of ammunition, medical supplies, C-rations and water piled at the helipad, ready to go in a second if we need it.

"First Sergeant, you will supervise the drivers, gunners, the maintenance section, and all other stay-behinds. Besides doing your daily admin stuff, you will supervise the perimeter here at the firebase, assist the XO with supply, and make sure we get our mail out there. Five India, you will go with me as supervisor of the field C.P. and my battalion-net RTO. Tucker will carry the company radio. Weapons and equipment: Each man will carry at least ten loaded magazines, four frag grenades, two canteens, entrenching tool, poncho, air mattress, extra set of fatigues, at least three extra pairs of socks, personal hygiene items, and three C-ration meals with heat tabs. Don't forget water purification tablets. I want each man to carry a 100-round box of ammo for the M-60s. I don't want this ammo wrapped around bodies like Poncho Villa. Carry it in the rucksacks. If we get in a fight, toss the boxes down the line to the guns. That way, the ammo won't get dirty and we'll have plenty of firepower. Platoon leaders, I want each platoon to carry two radios, each with five extra batteries, eight claymores, five smoke grenades, five trip flares, C-4 and blasting caps, a machete, a signal mirror and spare barrels for the M-60s. Make sure you carry all the M-79 grenades you can haul.

Doc Roberts, take full medical kit, including plasma, but no stretcher. We'll improvise if we have to.

"I want every man to know what we are going to do and where we are going to go. I will give a detailed operations order at 0600 in the morning. That will give us all night to plan. Any questions?"

Lieutenant Cappaccelli asked, "Who do we pick to stay back as .50 gunners?"

"Good question." answered Jace. "Anyone with a medical problem, anyone who might have trouble keeping up, or anyone with a severe enough emotional or personal problem that might cause him to fold on us in the bush. The final call is yours. One thing more. I want to reiterate my policy about relations with the Vietnamese. I doubt if we will come in contact with any civilians in War Zone D, but if we do, I want everyone to know how seriously I take the issue of winning hearts and minds. We will not harass, mistreat, or inconvenience any civilian at any time while I command this company. We will treat them with respect and courtesy. I want every man to know this policy. Any questions?"

No one spoke.

Jace paused and took a deep breath. Without another word, he bent to the right and picked up something from the ground behind his cot. He placed the ceramic figurine of the cat on the ground in the center of the circle. He was not sure what to say, but he wanted desperately to get an idea across to them.

"Gentlemen, this is Jupiter." He paused and the reactions of his leaders, who shifted in their seats and cut glances at each other. Baez nervously cleared his throat.

"After I received my orders to Vietnam, I took some leave at home with my father. My father is a good man. I didn't know until last June that he is a great man who fought the Japanese in the jungles of Guadalcanal in World War II. One day while I was on leave, I helped my father do some weeding in our corn patch. Our old family cat, Jupiter, was sitting at the edge of the garden, listening to something moving in the hedgerow. My father told me that was the secret of jungle fighting—to sit still and listen."

Jace paused. His leaders were staring intently at the figurine now. Feeling that he had their attention, he continued, "Many of you have more combat experience than I do. Some of you have been in big firefights. I suspect, though, that most of the combat many of you have seen has been on the receiving end of action initiated by the enemy. In other words, he surprised you—you didn't surprise him. My combat experience is limited to two contacts—but I will tell you this: In both of my firefights, the unit I was with was sitting still—listening. I believe in my father. I believe what he told me about jungle fighting. And my own experience has proven him right."

First Sergeant Baez was nodding now, a slight smile on his face. Joe Cappaccelli was looking Jace in the eye. The others still stared at the cat figurine.

"I'm not making any changes. I'm not directing you to worship this craven image."

Laughter broke the tension.

"What I want is for this figurine of old Jupiter to become our company mascot. In fact, on our company net, my call sign from now on will be Jupiter Six. I want a cat, no larger than six inches high, painted on the front of all the tracks. Let the troops use their initiative and creativity to come up with the cat of their choice. But under each cat, I want the name 'Jupiter' painted."

Jace paused again.

"Now for the important part. I want us all to learn to operate like old Jupiter. I want us to move like cats through the jungle—no hacking with machetes, no talking, no rattling equipment. Leaders, check your troops for rattles. In ranger school, they made us jump up and down in our equipment to see if it would rattle when we moved. Do the same for your soldiers. Tape dog tags so they won't clink. Tie down anything loose.

"When we move, we'll move slowly and quietly. We will stop often to listen. At night, in our perimeter, I want absolute silence—no transistor radios and no talking above a whisper. We'll put out listening posts to give us advanced warning."

Jace looked around. He knew he had them now.

"Gentlemen, I'm a graduate of ranger school. I know all about the ranger jokes, about how our knuckles drag the ground. But this ranger tab means something else to me. I believe in the army. The army sent me to ranger school to learn to be a better leader—to learn tactics and techniques designed to make the unit I command more effective. I take that role very seriously. I will not compromise the things I learned in the ranger course simply because we're in Vietnam and things are different here. I will teach you all everything I know. But I'll tell you another thing. My father and old Jupiter taught me more in five minutes in a garden in Tennessee than I learned in all of ranger school. I was lucky in my first fire fight. A squad from third platoon was successful in my second contact. I take no credit for that. I give credit to an old Guadalcanal marine and a raggedy old tom cat."

Again, a pause.

"We'll spend all the time we need to this afternoon working out hand-and-arm signals we'll all use so we can operate silently in the jungle. I want these signals standardized throughout the company. You can use old Jupiter in your explanations to your troops if you want to. I don't care how you do it—it's up to you. But, when we move out, I want every soldier in this company to know that it is our SOP to move like a cat and to be quiet and listen from now on. It may sound childish, but I honestly believe that it will save our lives. Are there any questions?

There were none.

"Guys, as I said, this will be our first company-sized operation. We're going into a dangerous area, so plan carefully. Begin packing up this afternoon. Inspect your troops. Make sure they carry what they need, but watch extra stuff. The weight will slow us down. I'll feed you more info as I get it. Now get busy."

Charlie company stood in groups of six, spaced fifty meters apart along a dry rice paddy adjacent to Highway 1. Jace waited with Five India, Tucker, his artillery forward observer, and two men from weapons platoon. They would all be on a helicopter that would fly in the middle of the formation and would put them down in the center of the landing zone. First platoon would be first in line, third would bring up the rear. Second and weapons would be in the middle.

The company had been carried to the pick-up zone on their tracks, which were lined up on Highway 1. The drivers and gunners, wanting to wait and watch the lift-off, sat atop their vehicles, laughing and joking. Like the dismounted troops, they scanned the skies for the lift birds. The first sergeant stood with his hands on his hips atop an APC, a king surveying his kingdom.

Soldiers in their faded gray-green jungle fatigues, weighted down by their rucksacks, suddenly sensed the approaching choppers. Off in the distance, the formation of Hueys flailed at the air, causing visceral drumbeats the troops felt in their chests before they could hear the rotor blades. As the thrumming grew louder, the company came to life. Leaders began tucking their maps inside their shirts as men who had been adjusting their gear swung their loads onto their backs. Others picked up steel helmets from the ground while sergeants gave last-minute instructions. High in the sky above them Jace saw the command-and-control ship carrying Lieutenant Colonel McKensie and Major Churchwell and the Cessna Bird Dog carrying the forward air controller.

Troops began pointing as the distant dots took on shape and the drumming became more intense. The helicopters flew past the troops, turned in a wide arc, then lined up on the rice paddy for landing, their blades popping in the hot air. As the choppers swept over Charlie company, hovering down beside the groups of waiting passengers, the troops leaned into the rotor blast, their pant legs and shirt tails flapping in the machine-made storm.

Jace stood apart, watching his heavily-laden troops struggle aboard the aircraft. When the last troop had boarded, Jace gave a thumbs-up to his pilot and jumped on. Gunships whistled past, their noise swallowed by the lift company's thundering rotors.

One by one, the Hueys lifted inches off the ground as the birds in the front of the line nosed over and slowly started forward. In swirling dust clouds, the rest of the formation followed suit. Lost in the dust, one ship darted straight up, out of the red cloud to avoid a collision. Gaining his bearings, the pilot moved back into his place in line. As they climbed out, the grit and blowing dust was replaced by clean air that became progressively cooler as the altitude increased. When they emerged from the red dust cloud, the thatched huts and nippa palm rows that stood beside the dry paddies slid by beneath them. Off to the right, the drivers and gunners waved from the tracks. In the distance, Binh Hoa was a mosaic of colored roofs.

The formation of Hueys reformed into a column of twos with gunship out-riders as they turned north and swept across the Dong Nai at two thousand feet. Troops sat on the floor of the birds, legs dangling in space. Forgetting their destination for a moment, the soldiers of Charlie company shut their eyes and drank in the cool air. Boatmen sculling sampans on the river looked up at the armada chattering overhead. Troops waved at the boats as empty cigarette packs flew from gaping doors into the breeze. No one said anything—noise from engines, blades and wind made talk impossible. Anyway, nothing needed to be said. Instructions at this stage of the operation would be meaningless. The plan had taken over and the die was cast. Nothing would stop them now.

Knowing Lieutenant Colonel McKensie to be a skilled professional, Jace had enormous respect for his battalion commander. But he had not known how competent McKensie was—until now. Since Jace was just a passenger during this phase of the operation, all he could do was watch. He knew that once Charlie company was on the ground, he would be the man, but while they were in the air, Cougar Six ruled. Keeping the handset of the radio set on the battalion frequency glued to his ear, Jace listened as McKensie orchestrated Charlie's insertion. Still several miles out, Jace watched through the Huey's wind screen as eight F-4 Phantoms plastered the edges of the landing zone with cannon fire and napalm. As the jets pulled off, the artillery began. He could see the angry gray-brown puffs as they walked across the woodlines adjacent to where his company would land.

Jace figured the formation was less than a mile from the LZ when the last artillery round, a white phosphorous shell, blossomed in the jungle next to the clearing. The white smoke was the signal for the gunships to dart forward and begin their suppressive fire on the LZ. Although he knew it was coming, Jace was startled as rockets blasted away from the cobra flying a few yards away from his bird. The gunships' miniguns ripped the jungle's edge as the lift ships set up their approach for landing. When the Hueys reached treetop level, the gunships peeled away and the door gunners opened up on the treeline.

The grass under the choppers blew flat. Before the Hueys even touched down, troops began leaping to the ground and running for the treeline. Jace stood on the skid, holding the door jamb of his bird as it flared for landing. While it was still five feet from the ground, he stepped off and landed hard.

The lift birds, having been emptied in seconds, began to nose over and pick up speed as if they couldn't get away quickly enough. Jace cleared his ears from the altitude by holding his nose and blowing, as he had done on parachute jumps. Even though the lift ships still beat the air as they climbed out, it was quieter on the ground than it had been in the air. Jace could hear his platoon leaders yelling instructions as they pushed their troops into the woodline.

"Cougar Six, this is Charlie Six, Over"

McKensie came back, "This is Cougar Six, Go."

"This is Charlie Six. LZ is cold. I'll let you know when it's secure. By the way, if you don't mind my saying so, that was nicely done."

"This is Cougar Six. Brown-nosing will get you nowhere. I'm going to keep the gunships on station as long as they have fuel in case you need them."

"Roger, Over"

"Cougar Six, Out."

Jace stood in the edge of the treeline watching white phosphorus from the last artillery round smoldering on the ground. Trunks of trees were shredded by cannon and machinegun fire, huge sections of jungle were burned to a crisp by napalm, and the smell of cordite hung thick in the air. It was sure no secret that Charlie company had arrived. Even though he wanted the company away from the LZ as quickly as possible, He had Tucker call the platoon leaders to his position for a quick meeting.

"Well, the whole world knows we're here," said Jace. "We need to put as much distance between us and this place as we can before dark. You know the order of march. Take up a 285-degree azimuth and let's move."

He took a long pull from his canteen. He knew the platoons would need a few minutes to form up for the move. As he stood in the edge of the jungle watching the platoon leaders placing their men in march order, he fingered the hilt of his father's K-Bar knife strapped upside-down on the left side of his harness. He wondered how many other jungles this knife had been carried through.

"Charlie Six, I mean Jupiter Six, this is One Six, ready to move, over."

"This is Jupiter Six, roger. What about you two six?"

"Ready, over."

"Three Six?"

"Ready to move."

"Four Six, are you ready?"

"That's affirm, over."

"This is Jupiter Six, move out."

The point man checked his compass and pushed into the dense jungle. The compass man allowed him to get well ahead, then looked around at the platoon leader who motioned him forward. The file began to move.Charlie company snaked its way through the heavily jungled, rolling hills of War Zone D. It had been months since Charlie had moved dismounted together as a company—long before Jace had assumed command. Accustomed to small ambush patrols and platoon-sized search and destroy missions, the company moved in fits and starts. As Jace had witnessed when he had accompanied the Alpha company patrol, jungle movement in large formations was difficult to say the least. As they moved through the dense undergrowth, there were constant halts, breaks in contact, and too much noise.

Trying to live up to the example set by its new mascot, Charlie company picked its way through the vines, brush, and foliage on the jungle floor. Reluctantly, Jace realized that without using a machete to clear a path through the jungle that movement was going to be painfully slow. Deciding to check progress, he worked his way forward, tapping each soldier on the shoulder and edging past on his way to the front. Stopping just behind the compass man, who was second in order of march, he could see the point man, sweating and frustrated, pushing vines from his path with one hand and using his rifle to parry branches from his face. The constant bending, stooping and pushing had totally exhausted the young soldier. Jace turned to the platoon leader.

"Do you have anyone else to put on point? That kid is beat!"

"Yes, sir. I can put almost anyone out there for a while—but there are some that are not cut out for it," answered Lieutenant Nevin.

"We'll have to rotate the point. If your guys wear out, let me know and I'll move another platoon to the front for a while."

"Yes, sir." answered Nevin. Give me a minute to get another man up there."

Jace turned his palm down and pushed toward the ground in a signal that meant to kneel for a break. The troops alternated facing right and left as they had been trained, then sank to their knees. All along the line, the sound of canteen covers unsnapping and helmets hitting the ground could be heard. Although there was a murmur as the troops whispered to each other, there was no loud talking.

From inside his shirt Jace pulled his map, which was protected by a transparent plastic bag in which radio batteries were shipped. To his right, the ground seemed to slope upward. To his left, under the dense foliage, he could see the trickle of an intermittent stream. He knew it would be useless to ask the pace man how far they had traveled. It would have been impossible to count steps at the snail's pace at which the company was traveling. Jace compared the terrain to the contour lines on the map. They were still traveling upward through a shallow valley which would end at a saddle between two small hills. He estimated the company had traveled eight hundred meters in the last hour. At this pace, two hours per mile, they would only get half way to the phase line they were supposed to reach by dark. Something had to change.

"Cougar Six, this is Charlie Six, over." Jace said into the radio hand set.

"This is Cougar Three, over."

Jace brightened as he recognized C.C.'s voice on the radio.

"What will happen if we don't reach phase line blue by dark?" asked Jace.

"Well, the world won't end, I guess." answered C.C.

"The going's tough—pace is slow. I suspect we'll get to—let me see—from Buick, left 1.4, down 2.1." said Jace, using a pre-arranged map code.

"You're kidding. Look, you've got to get further than that. We'll never get the area searched if you don't get a move on."

"This is Charlie Six. I can move faster, but I'll have to throw caution and security to the wind. We might blunder into something if we charge too hard. The kids are exhausted."

"This is Cougar Three. Roger. I know that area from my first tour. I'll brief Six. In the mean time, do the best you can. If there is any way you can speed up, make it happen."

"This is Charlie Six, Roger, one more thing—from now on, my call sign is Jupiter Six. I'll explain later. The only thing I can say is that it's important. over." said Jace.

"This is Cougar Three. I don't know how Cougar Six will react to that, but it's OK by me."

"This is Jupiter Six. When I got this job, Cougar Six told me to ask if I need anything—I'm asking."

"This is Cougar Six," interrupted the battalion commander. "I'm monitoring—I don't know what it's all about, but I know you've got something up your sleeve."

"This is Jupiter Six," radioed Jace, "I'll explain later. I feel it's very important."

"Roger. Approved. Speed up if you can. Out." Lieutenant Colonel McKensie signed off.

"Cougar Three, did you have anything else for me?" asked Jace.

"Negative. Keep pushing. See you soon. Cougar Three, Out."

"Sir, we're ready to move." reported Lieutenant Nevin.

Jace turned palm up and pushed toward the sky in a hand signal that meant "stand up". The long file of sweat-drenched troops struggled to their feet like new-born calves. When they were standing, Jace waved his arm forward like a wagon master pushing his train toward California. The front of the ragged file took a step, then another. They were moving again.

As Charlie company reached the small saddle, they were making better progress. Although they had picked up the pace somewhat, Jace knew they would be well short of the clearing at the blue line on the map where the night resupply was to come in. As he signaled a short halt, Jace heard the radio break squelch.

"Jupiter Six, this is Cougar Three, over."

"This is Jupiter Six, go."

"Sit rep, over." C.C. was asking for a situation report.

"This is Jupiter Six. we're moving better, but we'll still be short of phase line blue by dark. I need an alternate position to bring in the night kit. Can you get a bird up to recon a clearing?"

"Roger. Cougar Six is headed to the pad right now. He should be over you in about one five. He's not happy with your progress, over."

"This is Jupiter Six. If I could do any better, I assure you I would."

"Roger that. Six will be over you in a bit. Got to go. Be careful!"

"This is Jupiter Six, roger, over."

"Three, out."

Jace handed the hand set back to Five India and turned around. A skinny soldier with a crop of dirty blond hair faced him. Jace remembered that this was a replacement that had joined the company the day before they flew out.

"Sir, you need me on point." said the soldier.

"Is that right? Why you?" asked Jace, intrigued.

"These punks don't know what they're doing. This is my second tour. I extended. My first tour was in the 4th Division in the highlands. I spent nine months on point up there. It drives me crazy watching these guys screwing up like this."

"What can you do better?" asked Jace.

"What these guys do is worry about themselves. They make a hole for them to climb through, then they let it close up behind them so the next man and the next have to do the same thing. Give me a good man to work with me. I'll mash the vines down and push the limbs out of the way. A good pair of wire cutters will snip the vines without making noise. The man behind me can make the opening bigger. That way the guys behind don't have to bust the bush, they just walk through the tunnel in the jungle that me and my back-up will make."

Jace was amazed. Even in ranger school he had never heard of a technique like this.

"And you've done this before?" asked Jace.

"For nine months in the Ah Shau valley. I got wounded and spent two months in Japan in the hospital. Then I extended and came here. Sir—you got to let me on point. These dudes are going to get somebody killed."

"What's your name?" asked Jace. "I met you when you joined us, but I have 150 names to remember," said Jace.

"Johnson, sir. Friends call me Stony."

"Where're you from in the world?"

"West By-God Virginia, sir."

"Well, Johnson—Stony, have at it. Is there anyone special you want up there with you?"

"Yes, sir. I've got a buddy in the second platoon. I just met him, but he seems straight. His name is Ramos—Puerto Rican dude. Just give us a try."

"Well, go get Ramos and move to the front. We'll give you a crack at it."

"Thanks, sir. I'll tell you I feel better up there myself than trusting any rookie that happens to be up front."

There was only slight rustling and swishing of foliage as Johnson made his way back to second platoon to get Ramos. While he was gone, Jace explained the change to the platoon leaders.

"I hope he's not a hot dog." said Lieutenant Cappaccelli.

"He's only been with us for two days, but he sure seems to know what he's doing." said Lieutenant Green.

Johnson and Ramos walked past the officers on the way toward the front of the file. Jace noticed that Johnson slinked along like a cat, making hardly any noise at all. He also noticed that his rucksack was half the size of the other troops. Jace was amazed at how quickly and quietly the pair moved through the jungle.

"I've got to see this," he said as he positioned himself, Five India and Tucker just behind the compass man. He raised his hand and watched as his troops groaned under their loads, struggling to their feet. Once everyone was standing, He turned toward Johnson and Ramos. He didn't use a hand signal this time; he simply nodded. The point team silently disappeared. Behind them, the vines were pushed out of the way and branches were bent aside, making the way clear for those behind them. By the time Lieutenant Colonel McKensie's H-23 chattered overhead, Charlie company had doubled its pace while moving more quietly.

"Charlie Six—correction—Jupiter Six, this is Cougar Six, over."

"This is Jupiter Six."

"Cougar Six. Pop smoke so I can get a fix on you."

"Wilco." answered Jace. He turned and jerked a yellow smoke grenade off of Five India's harness, pulled the pin and tossed the canister into the jungle. As the grenade spewed, a foul-smelling yellow haze surrounded the weary soldiers. Jace waited until the yellow cloud broke through the jungle ceiling.

"Smoke's out." he radioed.

"I see yellow." answered McKensie.

"That's affirm, over."

"You guys are creeping. Is there no way you can move faster?" asked McKensie.

"We've made some changes on point and we're picking up the pace, but we'll still have a hard time making phase line blue." replied Jace.

"O.K. do the best you can. I'll take the heat from higher headquarters."

"I didn't know they cared." joked Jace.

"Oh, they care more than you think—and they're probably listening on this freq now, so be nice."

"Roger." said Jace, serious again. "I need an alternate site to bring in the night kit."

"O.K. I see two possibilities. There is a large clearing about a click to your north. I would like to see you get further than that before tonight. There is a smaller clearing about three clicks from you on an azimuth of about 320 from where you are.

That will put you less than two clicks from phase line blue. I'd like to see you make it there."

"We're moving better. I think we can do that, over."

"All right, get cracking. I'll be back to guide you to the clearing if you need me."

"Thank you, over."

"This is Cougar Six, out."

Jace was extremely happy with the way the company was moving now. From time to time, Ramos would wait until the rest of the file caught up to see if Jace had any instructions. If there were none, he slipped back into the greenery to catch up with Johnson. After a while, Jace realized that Johnson and Ramos had pulled another man up with them, forming a three-man point team. The compass man, who was the first man in the main file, was supposed to keep the company on the right course as it picked its way through the jungle. But Stony Johnson, now firmly in charge of the front of the company, was following the compass heading as well as pulling frontal security. The compass man was no longer needed. Johnson now further recommended that they place a man between the point team and the main body to relay hand signals and allow the point to operate even further ahead. He said this arrangement would keep Ramos from having to move back and forth to watch for instructions. Jace approved the suggestion immediately and soon the company's movement became even smoother.

In the late afternoon, the battalion commander flew out to guide them to the clearing. After the night kit was delivered by two Hueys, Jace decided to set the company up around the clearing. Although Viet Cong mortar gunners might have the clearing targeted, there were advantages to being in the open. The mortar platoon would be able to fire from the center of the clearing, leaders could move about freely to check the troops at night, and they would not have to carry the heavy night-kit gear through the jungle.

First, Jace ordered the troops to stand in pairs where their foxholes would be. By checking and approving the positions before the troops started to dig, he eliminated the possibility of a pair of soldiers having to move a half-dug foxhole if the location wasn't right. After walking around the circle making adjustments, he ordered the company to dig in. When the holes were dug, his soldiers strung concertina wire outside the line, placed their claymore mines and trip flares and began to clean their weapons. Only then did Jace allow the cook to set up the chow line. Meat, potatoes, vegetables, bread and one cold beer per man was served to the exhausted troops from the insulated containers brought in on the choppers.

When all was done, the company settled down for the night. Jace ordered each platoon to send out a two-man listening post. As they lay in the jungle about fifty meters outside the perimeter, these LPs would hopefully alert the company if the enemy tried to approach in the dark.

As the sun went down, Jace called a meeting of the officers to give instructions for the night and the next day. As they sat in a circle on their steel helmets, Jace smiled, reached into his rucksack and withdrew the ceramic cat. Sitting silently in the center of the circle, old Jupiter seemed to watch and listen as the leaders discussed the day's movement and the next day's operations. After doing everything he could think of that needed done, Jace stood alone in the clearing with a cold Pabst Blue Ribbon beer, rubbing the back of his neck, and looking up at the stars. He had never seen the sky this clear or the stars this vivid. As he touched the hilt of the old K-Bar knife on his harness, he wondered if his dad had stood in a jungle clearing on Guadalcanal and stared at the stars. Allowing his mind to relax after this trying day, he rode his imagination back twenty-odd years to a different jungle, a different time, a different enemy, a different war. Jace thought that if his soldiers were whisked backward in time to the Solomon Islands, as in the plot of some science fiction movie, the only way the marines would have been able to tell that Charlie company had come from the future would have been that the rifles and radios would have been different. Otherwise, Jace was sure, his troops would have melted un-noticed into the perimeter around Henderson Field on Guadalcanal in 1942. The Japanese were different from the enemy his troops faced, he knew. They were more aggressive, but were they craftier than the Vietnamese? He doubted if they were. The Japanese were quite willing to die for their emperor, but what motivated the Viet Cong? They had no emperor to worship or die for. Was uniting their country under communism worth what they were enduring in these jungles? He tried to imagine what went on in the minds of his enemies.

Jace's thoughts then wandered to his family in Tennessee. He wondered how his father was doing and vowed to write him more often. He remembered that he had received letters from his sister that he hadn't answered and vowed to do better at writing. He knew they all would be worried. Draining his beer, Jace took the first of the several turns he would make around the perimeter this night. Five India and Tucker had split the radio watch while the platoon leaders and platoon sergeants took turns supervising their sections of the line. The night went smoothly.

An hour before daylight, Jace placed the whole company on alert while the cook lit the stove unit and heated water for coffee. The mortar crew fired up the night-kit ammunition so the choppers wouldn't have to haul it back to the firebase. The sky grew lighter as the troops filed by the open-air kitchen a few at a time to fill their canteen cups with hot, violently strong coffee. As they deflated air mattresses and packed their rucksacks, they could smell bacon frying. By 0730, breakfast had been eaten and the night kit piled in the center of the perimeter. At eight o'clock, the popping of rotor blades signaled the arrival of the Hueys, right on time.

As Charlie company prepared for another day in the jungle, Jace stretched his knotted muscles, returned the ceramic cat to his rucksack, then tightened the straps on his gear. The soldiers tossed their trash into their foxholes before filling them in—they would leave no holes for the enemy to use. They chased aspirin tablets and anti-malaria pills with coffee dregs, lit their last cigarettes for a while, and topped off their canteens. As they waited to move out, they smeared their faces and arms with insect repellent, and used matches or cigarettes to burn away the ground leeches that had wormed their way under their jungle fatigues during the night. While they smoked and made small talk, the troops checked their rifles, changed radio batteries, and made last-minute trips to relieve their nervous bladders. When they had emptied the last water can, they threw the night kit aboard the choppers. They were as ready for what the day might bring as any troops anywhere.

As the two Hueys lifted above the jungle and nosed over to gain speed, Jace signaled for the company to form into march order. The new point team stood at the jungle's edge, watching for the company commander's signal. When he was satisfied, Jace turned to Johnson and Ramos and waved them forward. Without a word, they turned and disappeared into the dense foliage.

As the company entered the jungle, Jace radioed battalion.

"Cougar Three Alpha, this is Jupiter Six—we're moving."

Charlie company spent the second night of their search-and-destroy mission in an abandoned rice paddy just across Phase Line Blue, a line that was imaginary on the ground, but very real on commanders' maps. Jace was acutely aware that they were already a day behind schedule as he walked the perimeter to check the placement of the night's foxholes. The night kit was choppered in, holes dug, wire strung, artillery concentrations registered, food eaten, ambush patrols and listening posts sent out, mail read, meetings held, corrections made, injuries treated, and the night endured.

Jace's orders were to continue moving west, deeper into the area of operations from which communist gunners had been firing Soviet-built Katusha rockets at Bien Hoa air base. As his soldiers finished their preparations for the day, Jace studied the map and the terrain. He was worried about moving into the woodline which was a kilometer away, across the matted grass of the abandoned rice field. At dawn, he had sent a squad-sized patrol to sweep the woodline, to make sure no ambush awaited them as they approached the jungle across the open field. The patrol had found nothing and the company was ready to move.

The two Hueys that came to carry away the night kit blasted another layer of dust onto the already filthy troops who had turned their backs, shut their eyes and held their helmets against the rotor wash. Jace waved to the cook sitting amidst the tangle of wire, food containers, water cans and mail bags on the second chopper. The young African-American grinned and waved back, no doubt glad to be returning to the relative safety of Fire Base Cougar. The choppers climbed into the wind, banked to the left and swept over the company as the soldiers fanned out line-abreast to approach the distant woodline. It was 0830 and already murderously hot.

Five hundred meters from the jungle's edge, Jace halted the company and sent the point team ahead to check the spot where they would enter the tangled greenery. Fifteen minutes later, he got a thumbs-up from Johnson and he motioned for the company to stand. He windmilled his arm in a signal that meant for the company to move from line formation into the single file they would have to use in the jungle. In their morning meeting, Jace had warned the platoon leaders to keep their troops from bunching up in the open as they entered the treeline. Now he moved back and forth among the soldiers to keep them spread out.

The order of march today was third platoon, company headquarters, second platoon, weapons platoon, and finally, first platoon. As the last soldier from the third platoon entered the jungle, Jace sent Five India and Tucker ahead, then turned to Lieutenant Nevin and motioned for second platoon to move into a file and follow. Nevin stepped off to the side to give his troops room to converge on the point of entry into the green wall of jungle. Everything was going smoothly as second platoon changed formation without a word being said. Nevin stood watching, pleased with how his soldiers were performing this simple-looking, but complicated maneuver.

As Lieutenant Nevin turned to enter the jungle, he felt a tug on his ankle. Looking down, he saw a thin wire against his jungle boot. Following the wire, his eyes fell on a mortar shell tied upright against a tree. It was the last thing he would ever see.

The explosion was loud, close and hateful. Dirty gray smoke, tree bark, shredded leaves and slivers of metal flew in all directions. A large piece of the shell's casing smashed into Nevin's rifle, bending it double. Hundreds of hot metal shards punctured his skin and tore at his vitals. A dime-sized piece of shell casing tore into his right eye, exiting from his temple. His left eye was turned to pulp by hundreds of pin-head fragments of dust, bark and metal. There was no part of him not pierced.

Two other soldiers from second platoon were also down, one with a piece of metal in his thigh, another hit in the chest by a fragment. Confusion erupted around the explosion as soldiers threw themselves to the ground, some firing wildly. Officers yelled for the troops to cease fire while others yelled for a medic. Jace ran to Lieutenant Nevin, who was conscious but going into shock. Doc Roberts, who was still in the open paddies when the explosion went off, was on the scene before the debris settled.

"We got to get a dust-off quick!" screamed Roberts as he ripped his field dressing out of its pouch. As he applied pressure on Nevin's face, he directed another medic to cut the fatigues off of the lieutenant's body.

"You guys—get your field dressings out. I'll show you where to apply pressure. Captain! Get a dust-off here—now!"

Jace's voice sounded high-pitched and shaky as he called battalion and demanded a medical evacuation helicopter. To save time, he skipped the map coordinates, telling C.C. to route the chopper to where the company had spent the night. He knew C.C. would translate the location into map coordinates for the pilot.

Knowing there was nothing else he could do to get the dust-off to come quicker, he turned his attention to his company, which was in complete chaos, and grabbed his company net radio handset.

"Three six, this is Jupiter Six. Get back to the clearing. Be careful of booby traps—that's what the explosion was."

Cappaccelli acknowledged.

Jace raced to the two soldiers who were down. With Nevin's horrible wounds, no one had helped them yet. The young Puerto Rican with a hole in his thigh seemed all right. Jace then turned to the young black who had been hit in the chest. Ripping the shirt off the soldier, Jace examined the wound. There was no gurgling to indicate a punctured lung. In fact, it looked as if a rib had deflected the metal sliver. The youngster showed slight signs of shock, but he appeared to be in no immediate danger. Jace took the combat dressing out of the carrying case on the soldier's harness, tore it open, and pressed the sterile side to the wound.

"Lie down. Prop your feet up on your helmet. Hold this," said Jace as he placed the man's hand on the outside of the bandage. "A dust-off bird is on the way. You're going to be fine."

He patted the young man's cheek as he moved away to check on Lieutenant Nevin. Doc Roberts had an IV sack hung on a rifle with a bayonet stuck in the ground. Two junior medics and three soldiers were applying pressure to the shattered body of the young officer. Jace stood apart, knowing there was nothing he could do. As he watched, Sergeant Munn walked up.

"Bloody damn mess!" he said, almost disinterestedly.

Jace realized he had been in some kind of dream-like state and immediately shook himself back to reality. In doing so, he sounded a bit overly formal.

"Sergeant Munn, you are now second platoon leader. Go get together with your squad leaders and get reorganized. We have no time. As soon as the dust-off gets here, we'll be moving. If there is anything I can do to help you in your transition, let me know."

"Yes, sir," said Munn as he looked at Lieutenant Nevin again, then yelled for the second platoon squad leaders to come to him.

After a seeming eternity, but actually only twelve minutes later, the chatter of the approaching medical helicopter caused the entire company to look up and listen. Third platoon was emerging from the jungle. They walked into the clearing, alternating staring at Lieutenant Nevin and the efforts to save him and searching the sky for the med-evac chopper. Lieutenant Cappaccelli began to yell at them, partially to break the shock of what they had seen, and partially to put his platoon quickly into a security shield around the chaotic first-aid efforts.

Jace was on the radio. "That's affirm, the LZ is secure. Booby trap—no enemy contact. Three WIA, one critical, two slight. Smoke's out."

The Huey with the red crosses painted on white squares blasted purple smoke into swirls as it bounced onto the dry paddy. As carefully and quickly as possible, Doc Roberts and his assistants moved Nevin to the aircraft. The two other wounded soldiers hobbled to the bird on the arms of their buddies. The medics on the helicopter began working feverishly on Nevin as soon as he was aboard. Stunned teenagers watched silently as the dust-off swooped over the rice paddy, turning south toward Long Binh.

Standing in silence, the soldiers of Charlie company looked about uncertainly. Most had had the feeling that nothing like this would ever happen to them. But watching this horrible event unfold so suddenly, so senselessly and indiscriminately, left them all knowing that death was close now, and could strike anytime. Many had been innocent boys only twenty minutes earlier. They were older and wiser now. Jace could sense the change in them.

Five India had tears in his eyes. Doc Roberts kicked at the discarded bloody bandages. Super Private cursed from the edge of the third platoon. Sergeant

Munn had finished his meeting with his squad leaders and was walking toward the jungle's edge. As he passed a black soldier adjusting his gear, he said quietly, "You bastards have had it now."

CHAPTER 8

▼

25 October 1967

Nearly insane with grief, fear, and worry, Chi stared out the open door of the laundry at Bear Cat. Since Duc's death, nothing had had meaning for her. She seemed to be going through the motions, living in a dream world. Not only had she lost her first-born son, she had allowed known communists to eat in her home and sleep in Duc's empty house—and one of them had lost his wallet there. Police had been to her home twice. And now—now, her only remaining son had gone who knows where with the Viet Cong couple.

As she sat staring and chewing betel nut, Buddha entered the laundry from the snack bar.

"What's a matter you? You sick?" he asked, concerned.

Chi only looked up at him forlornly. She couldn't talk.

"Mamasan look number ten. Buddha think Mamasan sick."

Chi's only response was to bury her face in her hands.

"You no eat, you no talk—you so sad."

Chi's shoulders shook as she began to sob. Buddha had no idea what was wrong or what to do. He genuinely liked this little woman. He liked their daily banter and her sense of humor. He was greatly disturbed by her sadness and crying.

Buddha moved closer and massaged Chi's shoulder as she cried.

"Buddha numba one friend. Buddha always—"

A jeep with two MPs slid to a stop in the dust outside. A tall lanky MP sergeant with crisply starched fatigues and spit-shined boots strode toward the laundry followed by the driver who sported a huge mustache. As they walked up the steps, another jeep carrying an officer and his driver pulled up beside the MP vehicle.

"Hi fellers." said Buddha. "Mamasan don't feel so good. You need your laundry, I'll get it.

"Don't need any laundry. We're here on another matter."

A captain wearing military intelligence insignia got out of the other jeep and walked toward the laundry. He did not look happy. Buddha realized something was amiss, and feeling threatened, began to back toward the door of the snack bar.

"You stay right here, Sarge," said the MP sergeant.

"What's going on here?" asked Buddha.

Chi knew what was going on—they were here to tell her something bad about her son. They were here to ask why the Viet Cong had been in her home. They were here to ask why the wallet of someone who had been identified as a communist was inside her dead son's house.

"We've got a report that someone in this laundry has been making Viet Cong flags." said the captain.

"What?" cried Buddha. "There ain't nobody doin' no such thing."

Chi only understood about a forth of what was being said. Although the Americans spoke too fast and were using words she didn't understand, she did catch two words: Viet Cong. She buried her face in her hands and began to sob anew.

"We are going to search this place," said the MP. "Sarge, get all the Vietnamese workers in the snack bar to sit down and tell them not to move. Wilson, you go guard 'em."

The MP enlisted man entered the snack bar and motioned for the cooks to sit down. The MP sergeant grabbed Chi by the arm and pushed her through the door leading to the snack bar. He motioned her toward a chair into which Chi slumped and resumed wailing. She knew the world was about to end.

The MP's searched the racks of hanging laundry, the folded fatigues stacked in the corner, then the display case. They even tore the cover off the ironing board. The flags Chi was sewing for Super Private were hidden behind the loose board in back of the counter and were not found.

Buddha went into the snack bar, spoke softly to his workers as they sat down, patted Chi on the back, then turned to the MPs.

"Look, these women just cook. They don't go near the laundry. Mamasan here just washes and irons. The only sewing I've ever seen her do is on patches and nametapes. She ain't done nothing wrong."

"Maybe not, but they will all have to be questioned. A witness saw a woman in this laundry hide a Viet Cong flag when he came in to get his laundry. He'll swear to it. An interpreter is coming to help us get to the bottom of this."

"What is this all about?" asked one of the cooks.

"I do not know," sobbed Chi. "I have done nothing wrong. I heard them say something about the Viet Cong. I have never—"

"Tell them nothing. We all know you have done nothing wrong. We will back you. Tell them noth—"

"Quiet, you two!" yelled the MP. "Spread out. You move over here so you can't talk to each other. You sit here! Here!"

Through the open door, Chi could see the MPs and the captain searching the laundry. What were they up to? She had been so frantic about Huong she had forgotten about something—the flags.

A new wave of panic swept over her.

Chi sat on a folding chair inside the division headquarters G-2 interrogation section. A major, a captain and a sergeant, all Americans, stood around the room. A Vietnamese intelligence officer, a slick dandy of a captain, acted as interpreter.

"So, tell us why you were making communist flags," said the American captain. The interpreter asked the same question in Vietnamese, even though Chi had understood most of the English.

"As I have told you, sir, an American soldier came into the laundry and asked me to sew them. He wanted them as souvenirs and said he would pay me well. I am a poor widow woman who knows nothing of the war or politics. It was a chance to make money. He gave me a letter from him saying that he asked me to make the flags. If you had given me the chance, I could have found the letter and given it to you. It is in the cabinet at the laundry."

"Tell us where the letter is and we will have someone retrieve it," said the major.

"Tell them it is on the left side, on the lower shelf of the counter, in the back," Chi told the interpreter, who gave the directions in English. The sergeant left after quick instructions from the major.

"What did this soldier look like?"

"All Americans look alike to me," answered Chi. But this one was small.

"What unit was he from? Where is he now?" The questions continued. Chi patiently and politely answered each one: she did not know.

The sergeant came back in a few minutes carrying Super Private's note, which the major scanned quickly and handed to the captain.

"Get over to G-1 and find out where this man is assigned. Then get to G-3 and see if you can find out where his unit is located."

Then to Chi he said, "How do we know this letter is authentic? How do we know it is not a forgery?"

Chi's fear kept her tone polite although she was becoming more and more agitated and frustrated. "Sir, I have no reason to lie. I am not a communist sympathizer. I simply have a job washing and sewing—a job that I do not wish to lose. I wash what I am asked to wash and sew what I am asked to sew."

"Don't you know that doing anything connected with the communists is extremely dangerous?" asked the interpreter on his own. "You are in a great deal of trouble here."

"What did you say?" asked the major.

"Sir, I told this woman that she should answer your questions more honestly," said the interpreter with a smirk, which he turned on Chi.

"Where are the flags? Do you have any of them finished? Are you working on more of them now?" asked the major.

The translation came out differently. "If you have any flags you had better give them to us now," threatened the interpreter. Chi understood enough English to know the difference in what was being said. Her anger now began to overcome her fear. Her anxiety over Huong, her grief over Duc and her fear caused by her present situation began to boil to the surface. On impulse, she answered in English. Also on impulse, she decided to lie.

"No flag, no finish, no work now. All done. Sojur take. He gone long time. No see. He no back." Then she added, pointing to the Vietnamese captain, "He no say what you say. He say diffrun'. He say more. He number ten. He lie."

The interpreter jumped to his feet, hooked a foot around a leg of Chi's folding chair and jerked. The chair flew out from under Chi, who fell hard on the concrete floor.

"Hey! Knock that shit off!" yelled the major.

"Sir, this woman is nothing but a communist whore," growled the interpreter, his face contorted by his anger. "She should be taught respect."

"Get him out of here," said the major to the sergeant.

After sergeant had escorted the interpreter from the room, the major helped Chi to her chair.

"I am sorry about what happened. Are you hurt?" he asked kindly.

"No, OK," said Chi, although she knew she would have an ugly bruise on her hip.

"We do not want anything to happen to our loyal civilian employees," said the major, "But we must know if any of our civilian workers lean toward the Viet Cong. Surely you understand that, don't you?"

"Yes, unnerstan'. No communis'. Jus' laun'ry. Jus' wash, sew." said Chi rubbing her hip.

"If you have any flags or any information, please tell me and I will make sure nothing happens to you. The interpreter is a little crazy. I'll keep him away from you. Just tell me."

"No can tell. No flag. No sew. All gone. Sojur take. All gone. He pay, me sew. OK? All gone."

"OK, let me see what I can find out about the soldier. In the mean time, please relax. Would you like a drink of water?" asked the major.

"No, OK," said Chi as she began to relax.

The major left. Chi sat alone for almost an hour. From time to time she could hear muffled voices and footsteps in the hallway outside the door, but no one entered the room. As Chi began to feel drowsy in the heat of the afternoon, the door flew open and the Vietnamese captain burst in.

"You are in for it now, Communist bitch!" he screamed.

Following another long, fruitless day of beating the jungles of War Zone D, C company circled for the night. The routine of bringing in the night kit and settling down for the evening was broken by Lieutenant Colonel McKensie's showing up suddenly in his H-23.

Jace walked to the small helicopter, bowing his head against the blowing dust. Remembering that salutes in the field supposedly showed enemy snipers who the commanders were, he stood respectfully as the colonel climbed out of the small aircraft. Hell, thought Jace, if Charlie was as smart as everyone said, he knew who the commanders were anyway. They were the ones riding helicopters and always sitting or walking in the center of the unit amid a cluster of radio antennas. Still feeling awkward about not saluting the battalion commander, he offered his hand instead.

"I just wanted to come out and make sure you guys are all right. Terrible thing about Nevin," said McKensie.

"Good to see you, sir. How is he?" asked Jace.

"He's going to live, but he's blind. It'll be a long time before he recovers completely. They evacked him straight to Japan. He'll be at Walter Reed in 72 hours. Here's his mom's address if you want to write," said the battalion commander as he fished a slip of paper out of his pocket and handed it to Jace. "How're your boys?"

"Some badly shaken, some scared, some hard to read. A fight is different, I guess. When they're being shot at, they have something to vent their anger towards. A damned booby trap is like getting struck by lightening. Who do you strike back at?" Jace asked as he looked across the perimeter.

"You liked Nevin, didn't you?"

"Yes, sir. He was competent and careful. I'm going to miss him."

"I'm sure you will. Who's taking his place?"

"His platoon sergeant, Munn."

"Oh shit. I didn't realize that. You probably don't know how much you'll miss Nevin. Look, watch that guy—he could be trouble. He's stirred up trouble among the negro troops before."

"Well," said Jace, "That's all I need now."

"I'll get you a replacement officer as quick as I can. Come on, let's walk."

As they had done after Jace's predecessor had been killed, the two commanders walked the perimeter slowly, taking stock and trying to calm nerves. They lingered with the leaders, knowing that the incident with Nevin had again raised old anxieties among them. All of them knew they were probably more likely than the troops to be killed or wounded—after all, hadn't four of the last five casualties in the battalion been officers or senior NCOs?

They walked to the center of the perimeter, to the command post, which was only a poncho held up by poles for shade. McKensie couldn't leave without visiting Five India. The two men shook hands as do friends.

"How're things, young man?"

"Good, sir. If I might, without embarrassing the captain, you wouldn't believe the change in the company. We move through the jungle now like a damned cat. You'd have to see it to believe it."

"We have a new point man, sir," interjected Jace, his face turning red. "He's taught us all some things."

"I'd say a rifle company's performance in combat has a damn-sight more to do with the commander than the point man." said McKensie, his hand on Jace's shoulder.

"We're all learning together, sir. Five India has taught me as much as anybody," said Jace.

They stood awkwardly for a moment, three soldiers with three different ranks, who liked and respected each other immensely.

"Speaking of cats, tell me about this Jupiter thing. C.C. said it had to do with a ceramic cat."

As Jace explained about his father's lecture and the example set by old Jupiter, he rummaged through his rucksack and pulled out the cat figurine.

"I just thought it would be a ploy to make the troops more wary, more watchful, more careful."

McKensie turned the feline form over in his hands. "Well, you can use the devil himself as a mascot if it makes you more successful and keeps your folks alive. From now on, You're Jupiter six."

"Thank you, sir. I guess it is a little unorthodox, but it means something to me—us."

McKensie smiled a fatherly smile as he handed the ceramic cat back to Jace. "You're proud of your dad, aren't you?"

"Yes, sir, I am," answered Jace quietly.

The three men watched silently for a while as the soldiers went about their evening routine.

"Damn, I almost forgot. Five India, go talk to my pilot. He has three cold beers. Keep them out of sight. It's not right to drink when the troops are dry."

"It's all right, sir," said Jace. "The night birds are on their way. Each man will get a coke and a beer with his evening meal."

Five India returned with the beers under his shirt.

"I guess this is as good a time as any to tell you." McKensie said after a long swallow. "I'm leaving."

"What?" said Jace and Five India in unison.

"In two weeks. I'm moving up to be the G-3."

"But, you can't—you've only been in command for—"

"Eight months." replied McKensie. "Two months longer than most battalion commanders. The general wants me to extend my tour for six months so he can have some stability in the G-3 shop. Constant personnel turnover kills us."

"Who?—When?" stammered Jace.

"I don't know who my replacement will be. All I know is that the general will only give us a couple of day's overlap. Hopefully whoever replaces me will be an experienced officer and won't need any more time than that to get his feet on the ground."

Jace shook his head. "I guess I never thought about how long you had been here. I guess I just thought you'd always be around. I reckon you are overdue to leave—but it just won't be the same battalion without you."

"Exactly right." smiled McKensie. "The day after I leave, the battalion will be different. It will have a different feel, a different atmosphere, a different spirit and personality. Notice I didn't say whether it would be better or worse. No one can tell that. The new colonel will color the page differently than I did. You know I didn't always stay within the lines. He may or he may not."

McKensie paused. "We three seem to see eye-to-eye on most things—but you and the new commander might not hit it off. It doesn't matter—the only thing that matters is just to do your job." He waved his hand toward the first platoon, which was busy digging foxholes. "What matters is them—those guys throwing dirt everywhere—leading them and treating them right. Oh yes, and accomplishing the mission. The army might say I had that backwards. The army would say to accomplish the mission first, then take care of the troops—but here, in this place, I don't know. I sometimes feel that keeping them alive is the most important thing we do."

They finished their beers as Five India went back to his radio, answering the hourly communications checks. McKensie patted him on the back as he walked away. Five India looked up and smiled as he talked into the hand set. Jace followed as the battalion commander signaled the pilot to start the engine.

"Sir, we're not doing any good like this. I would like to request your permission to change the way we are operating."

McKensie looked sideways at Jace, squinting his eyes. "What do you have in mind?" he asked.

"I want to cancel the night kits for a while. I believe bringing them in lets the enemy know where we are and what we're doing. They know we can only move so far and so fast from the last place the choppers landed. I believe the daily resupply flights give us away."

"Go on, I'm listening."

"Tomorrow morning, when the birds come to take out the night kit, I'd like three days' supply of rations and some extra ammo. No hot chow, no wire, no extra starlights, no mortar ammo. In fact, we'll send the tubes out on the birds. Besides the food, all we'll need is extra water-purification tablets so we can drink out of the streams."

"You want to go to ground, then?"

"Yes, sir, like a hunting cat. No more camping in the open fields. We'll circle up in the jungle at night. I believe Charlie will lose track of us and we can surprise him."

"How long do you want to operate like that?" asked McKensie.

"Till our food runs out or we need ammo. Probably three-four days."

Lieutenant Colonel McKensie pulled his tactical map from his shirt and unfolded it. With a grease pencil he drew a square around four thousand-meter grid squares. "We'll call this AO Trout. You may operate as you suggested 'til you need resupply. Work the edges of these clearings. Charlie probably stores the rockets in the jungle and moves them to the clearings at night to fire them. If you are going to find rockets, I believe you will find them adjacent to these open fields."

Jace was quiet for a minute as he made his map look exactly like the battalion commander's. "Yes, sir. What I'd like to do is set up company headquarters and weapons platoon in the center of each grid square and send out platoon-sized clover leafs to thoroughly search each one. If a platoon makes contact, the rest of us will be close enough to pile on quick."

"Approved. I'll tell the S-4 to change the supply arrangements."

"Thank you, sir. Tell C.C. I said I miss him."

McKensie grinned. "You two make a lovely couple. Keep your head down, Jace."

"Jupiter's on the prowl, sir."

McKensie ducked under the blades and buckled himself in the bubble. The little helicopter clawed into the hot dusk, then circled the perimeter once. McKensie waved to each and every foxhole before turning south toward Long Binh.

Chi staggered rather than walked through the front door of her house. She had just walked the two miles from the south gate at Bear Cat, where she had been released and told she was free to go—for now. What greeted her was more traumatic than the six hours of interrogation, intimidation, and torture she had just endured. Her house had been ransacked. Jars had been broken, pots and pans scattered, cushions ripped and cut open, food scattered, and walls and floors torn into. It was more than she could take—she swooned to the floor.

She awakened to the screeches and shrieks of her sisters as they hovered over her. The women had huddled in the corner of the back yard since the national police and popular-force soldiers had finished violating their home. Now, they screamed hysterically, both asking questions through their tears at the same time.

What had happened? Why did the soldiers and policemen do this? What had happened to Chi at work? Was she in trouble? Were they in danger? Would they loose their jobs? Would they have to move? Where was Huong? Did his absence have anything to do with the soldiers and police destroying their home?

Chi tried to answer as she lay on the floor, but nothing coherent would come out. How could she explain to her sisters—who, like her before Duc's death, had never had anything bad happen in their lives except the deaths of their husbands—what had happened to her at Bear Cat today? She tried to block the day's horrible experiences from her mind, but she couldn't. They were too fresh, too real, too frightening. She thought of that horrible interpreter who had done unspeakable things to her, and the nice American who tried to soothe her. Why had the American not come into the room and stopped the interpreter from doing what he did. Surely he could have heard her screams.

The area just beneath her ears, both armpits, her forearms, and the base of her nose still hurt from the excruciating pressure the Vietnamese captain had applied to these points with his fingers and knuckles. Her hip ached from the bruise caused by falling on the concrete floor. But more frightening were the threats to her and her family. The violation and destruction of her home was the scariest thing of all. She felt as if there were nowhere to hide, nowhere to feel safe.

She was also worried about her job. She had to work. She simply must keep working at the laundry. How else could she and her family live? Would the Americans fire her for what she had done? Why had she agreed to sew the flags in the first place? And why were the government troops and the Americans so upset over her sewing a few flags, anyway. And why didn't the note the soldier gave her convince them?

In a state of shock, Chi crawled to the corner where a straw sleeping mat seemed to be the only undamaged thing in the house. Ignoring her sister's questions, screams and pleas, she curled into a fetal ball, her eyes wide open in a horrified stare.

She lay unmoving for how long, she couldn't tell, slowly fighting back the fear and the dread. She had done nothing wrong, she told herself. Try as she may to decide what to do, one certainty kept returning to her mind: she would not let them make her quit her job. If they were going to fire her, then they would fire her. If they did, she would have to go on from that point. But, tomorrow she would simply get up and go to work as usual. As she pulled herself together, stubborn determination replaced her trepidation. They would do to her what they would do—but she vowed to herself that they couldn't make her quit her job.

Like almost every other American soldier, sailor, airman or marine in this country, Jace always had a sense of foreboding that never quite left him. The uneasy feeling lay just beneath the surface of his consciousness, most of the time dormant, but sometimes, like on this night, very much alive. Sometimes it was just apprehensiveness, but at other times he could almost smell or taste the fear. At times he had the same feeling he had when he was caught in a thunderstorm and felt as if lightening might strike him at anytime. Some nights in this place were just worse than others—longer, darker, more threatening. Tonight he ecould feel the thunderheads rolling, black and ominous in his mind.

Jace found himself looking at his watch every few minutes, expecting an hour to have passed, but seeing each time he looked that only minutes had gone by. He told himself he would stop checking his watch. After three violations of his vow, he removed his watch and put it in his pocket.

He tried to sleep, but could not. He wanted to walk the perimeter again, but decided against it, lest he make his soldiers uneasy by his own nervousness. Instead of walking, he lifted a starlight scope and pressed the soft rubber eyepiece to his eye socket. The images on the gray-green miniature TV screen inside the eyepiece showed him that everyone was doing what he was supposed to do. Silhouettes of soldiers against the flat background of the jungle were easy to discern. Jace swept the device back and forth, watching as his soldiers sat silently, walked carefully or fumbled in the dark with their equipment. Sleeping soldiers stretched out behind foxholes were cocoons in their poncho liners. Half the troops slept while half were alert. In each platoon, a leader walked quietly back and forth along their assigned sectors. In the mortar platoon, a member of the fire direction center was awake while the gunners snored peacefully. As he swept the second platoon's sector, he saw a soldier looking back at him through a starlight. Jace waved and the soldier waved back.

Jace dropped the night-vision device from his face and squeezed his eyes tight to allow his night vision to return, then looked around the interior of the perimeter. In the darkness, he could barely make out the cook who was rolled in his poncho beside his stove unit and cardboard boxes full of coffee, bread, bacon and eggs. Five India slapped a mosquito, turned over in his poncho liner, fluffed the fatigue shirt he was using for a pillow, and was still again. Tucker was on the radios, absently slapping and scratching.

Jace stood and stretched. A quarter moon stuck one point of its crescent above the jungle, throwing a thin silver sheen across the clearing. A slight breeze carried the odors of sweat, G.I. insect repellent and freshly-dug earth. Breaks in radio squelch, snores and bits of whispered conversation drifted across the clearing in muffled patterns of sound, which blended with the drones of mosquitoes and the calls of night birds.

The night had several different patterns—slower ones of hourly radio checks and sleep-shift changes, and quicker ones of snores, coughs, and footsteps in dewy paddy grass. As the night wore on, Jace noticed that some animal calls dropped off and were replaced by different ones as one species drifted off to sleep or to hunt, and others awakened toward dawn. Some, like the pesky bird that seemed to screech "Re-Up, Re-Up", called all night long.

Jace edged close to Tucker, who nodded at his radios.

"Hey, you sleepy?"

"Yes, sir, a little, but I'm all right".

Jace reached out and tousled the youngster's hair.

"This is one of those nights I just can't sleep, I'll take the radios for a while. Why don't you catch a few Z's"?

"You sure, sir?"

"Yeah, I've got it."

As Tucker rolled in his poncho, Jace took the handset from the radio dialed to his company frequency in his left hand and the one from the radio on the battalion net in his right. He sat cross-legged outside the poncho shelter Tucker had erected. He rubbed his eyes on his shirtsleeves and yawned.

Jupiter, the ceramic cat, had not been put away after the evening meeting, and still sat in the center of what had been the meeting circle. Unmoving in the darkness, it looked strange and ominous. Sightless eyes in a lifeless head silhouetted against the wet grass seemed to stare straight into Jace's soul. Staring groggily at the figurine, he began to wonder if the little black cat were not somehow a bad omen.

He thought about how much his company now resembled a hunting cat. Like huge yellow eyes, his new point team was able to stare, unblinking, to see hidden dangers that others couldn't see. His platoons, like four steel-clawed paws flexed and crept, then waited, poised for a kill. It was what he wanted, wasn't it? Hadn't he purposely transformed this group of young men into a giant, slinking feline? He picked up the starlight scope and looked around again. His hunting cat now lay curled up, dozing, but not all the way asleep, ready to spring at the first sign of danger.

Jace looked at the figurine again. He wanted to move—to get up, walk over, pick Jupiter up and tuck him out of sight into his rucksack. Maybe if he couldn't see the little cat, this sense of foreboding would go away. Maybe he should just throw the figurine away. Hadn't he made his point with it? He wanted to move, but he couldn't—something held him in place. The feeling of impending danger he had felt all night intensified. Was it the chill of the night, anxiety about tomorrow's change in tactics, or was it just being in the jungle, in a war zone, at night? Or was it that damned little cat? As a gray mist settled over the clearing, Jace and the clay cat sat a few feet apart, staring at each other. New bird calls joined nature's screeching racket as the eastern sky grew pink. Men stood and stretched as a new day began.

At eight sharp, when the supply birds landed, Jace was surprised to see First Sergeant Baez running out of the rotor-wash dust. Jace grinned widely as he shook his first sergeant's hand and gripped his arm.

"Good to see you, Top! To what do we owe this pleasure?"

Baez removed his sunglasses and studied Jace carefully.

"Sir, good to see you, too. Damn, when was the last time you slept. You look awful."

"Well, thanks for the compliment," Jace said self-consciously. "I guess I've had a couple of rough nights. Well, who have we here?"

A young African-American soldier peered sheepishly from behind Baez.

"Sir, this is Private Williams. He is a rehab transfer from A company. He got three article fifteens there, and before he is kicked out with a dishonorable, he has to have a second chance. I guess that's us. Which platoon do you want him in?"

Jace studied the youngster. "I know you, don't I?"

"I don't know, suh," replied Williams as he scuffed his boots in the dust.

"Yes, I know you. You were the one that shot the M-79 rounds off accidentally when I observed that so-called ambush that night."

"Yassuh, I guess that 'uz me." answered Williams.

"What did you get the article fifteens for?" asked Jace.

"One for shootin' those rounds. One for sleepin' when I'z s'posed to be awake, one for gettin' lost on patrol."

"Well, the army says you get a second chance. You're starting off clean here. Nobody will know about what happened in A company, except the first sergeant and me. You just do your job and stay alert and you'll be fine."

Jace shook the young man's hand. "Welcome to Charlie company. I'm going to assign you to third platoon. You'll have a good lieutenant down there, and there are some good troops that will watch out for you. You do the same thing for them."

Williams nodded.

Lieutenant Cappaccelli was nearby, supervising the break-down of the supplies. Jace called him over and introduced Williams.

Off to the side, Jace told Cappaccelli, "He's not a bad kid. He just needs close supervision. Take care of him."

As they walked away, Jace turned to Baez. "How're things in the rear?"

"Believe me, I'd rather be out here with you. They're running us ragged. They've attached our tracks to the scout platoon. Our guys have been on convoy escort, road-runners, and every shit detail that comes along. The other night, four of our tracks with some scout platoon guys did a twenty-mile road-runner, clean out of radio and artillery range—supposedly to keep the road open. You know how that is, though. If Charlie wanted to mine or ambush the road, he'd just let them go by and do his dirty work afterward. One of the worst things is convoy escort. We took an engineer convoy to Vung Tau and another to Dong Tam, way down in the delta. Scary as hell. So far, though, no one has been hurt. The XO is running himself ragged gettin' the supplies out to you and handling all the taskings. Too few of us back there, too much stuff to handle. I'll be glad when we're all back together."

"Me too," said Jace. "Me too. Look, are there any problems with the change in the way we're going to resupply?"

"No, sir, actually, it'll be easier. The cooks will appreciate the break. They don't particularly enjoy coming out here every night—oh yes—one more thing. I'm supposed to bring Super Private back with me. He has to go to G-2 to make a statement. Seems that he's been getting the mamasan in the laundry to sew up V.C. flags for him to use as tradin' material. Seems she got in trouble for it and he can clear her."

Jace bit his bottom lip and shook his head without comment, then sent Five India to find Super Private.

"OK, Top, the birds are getting ready to leave. Sure you don't want to stay?"

Baez looked carefully at Jace. "You know, I ought to, just so you could get some sleep. I will if you want."

"No, you need to get the admin and supply done. This mission will be over soon, then I can get some shut-eye."

"Sir, take an old NCO's advice. Make some time to sleep. Your senses will start to dull if you don't," said Baez.

"Don't you worry about me," answered Jace.

"Don't you go tryin' to act like a damned ranger. It's OK to admit you're human and you need some rest."

"I don't know if you're a first sergeant or a nursemaid," laughed Jace.

"A good first sergeant has to be both," answered Baez, motioning for Super Private to join him as the turned toward the choppers.

Super Private couldn't believe his good fortune. He was out of the field! It looked like it would be at least a couple of days before he could get back to the company—and he damned sure wasn't going to go looking for a ride. If they wanted him back out there badly enough, someone would come looking for him. He knew that as long as he stayed in the company area, he couldn't be counted AWOL. He also knew that there was a good chance he would simply fall through the crack for a few days—a few days of sleep, beer and decent food. There weren't many people at battalion rear at Bear Cat, so he knew he could do whatever he wanted—that is after he went to G-2 to make his statement. Before he did anything, however, he decided he would lock up his rifle, have a shower, a change of clothes, and a decent meal.

The S-1 NCO was the only one at battalion headquarters when Super Private went in looking for a ride to division. The sergeant told him to find the duty driver, who would take him to G-2. He was glad he didn't have to walk, since he was dog tired and didn't know exactly where G-2 was. The driver, who was in the mess hall joking with the cooks and eating a ham sandwich, scowled at Super Private when he asked for a ride. It was obvious the driver did not particularly want to go anywhere. He made Super Private wait until he had finished his sandwich, then reluctantly put on his shirt and shuffled to the jeep.

Super Private nervously walked in to the G-2 office, explained who he was, and that he had been told to come here to make a statement. He was led to a captain.

"Oh yes, said the officer, you're the one the laundry woman said that got her to make V.C. flags."

"Yes, sir," said Super Private. "Me and the guys wanted them as souvenirs—and they make great trading material."

"So you did ask her to make the flags?"

"Yes, sir. And she weren't all too happy about it neither—said I'd get her in trouble. Guess I did, didn't I. Didn't mean to though. Am I in trouble too?"

"No, you're not in trouble, but if I were you I'd use a little bit better judgment next time. People around here are mighty touchy about civilian employees being V.C. sympathizers."

"Will this get her off the hook, then?"

"Yeah, let me just get a statement typed up for you to sign."

"Is that all I have to do?"

"Yeah, that's it. I'll only take a minute."

Super Private was already thinking about his cot.

Stony Johnson, the point man, froze. Seeing him go motionless, his two slack men also halted in mid stride. The man at the head of the main body of the company halted when he saw that the point team had stopped, and threw up his right hand in a signal for all behind him to freeze. Charlie company quietly shuffled to a halt.

Johnson turned back toward the company and without moving anything but his left arm placed his index and middle finger in front of his eyes in a signal that meant "enemy in sight." The other members of the point team mimicked the signal back to the first man in the main body who passed it back to the lead platoon leader, then on to the company commander. The whole process took fifteen seconds. Stony slowly turned back toward the enemy and raised his rifle to his shoulder.

Jace signaled the company to one knee, then began to creep forward. As he passed Lieutenant Cappaccelli, he whispered, "What is it?"

The platoon leader shrugged, pointed toward the front, and repeated the "enemy-in-sight" signal. In less than a minute, Jace reached the point team, which had not moved. He motioned the two slack men into kneeling covering positions and edged forward to the point man.

Jace slowly removed his helmet and eased his head up next to Johnson's.

"What do you see?" he asked in a whisper.

"I don't see nothin', but do you smell that?"

Jace raised his nose and sniffed. Sure enough, the faint smell of something— urine? Soy sauce? Rotten fish? All of them together? Something.

"Look," said Stony, pointing at a small rabbit-trail. "And there," he said, pointing at the stumps of saplings.

"They use those little trees for poles to build lean-to's. I'd say they's a base camp within thirty-forty meters."

"You sure?" whispered Jace.

"I can't tell you if it's occupied or not, but there's definitely a V.C. camp right ahead of us," whispered Stony without moving anything but his lips.

Jace peered ahead, but couldn't see anything but foliage. He sniffed again, detecting the faint, foreign odor.

"Stay here," ordered Stony. "I'll send one of the guys back to tell you what's going on."

Feeling slightly out of his element, Jace nodded. Johnson jerked his head at the two slack men, who silently rose and followed him noiselessly into the jungle. Jace signaled for Cappaccelli, who joined him quickly.

"Pass the word back—and do it QUIETLY. Possible enemy base camp ahead. Point's checking it out. Stay down, stay quiet. Platoon leaders forward," whispered Jace.

The lieutenant everyone called Little Caesar nodded curtly and slinked away.

After a seeming eternity, but actually only minutes, Ramos appeared. He nodded at Jace, made the "enemy sighted" signal, and held up four fingers.Jace repeated the signal to the file, then followed with a signal that meant "prepare for action". Jace handed his helmet to the his RTO, dug in his pocket, and pulled out his battered ranger patrol cap. Pulling the cap down over his eyes, he joined Ramos and crept to where Stony Johnson was waiting behind a huge fallen tree trunk, like a dog pointing a covey of quail.

Jace grasped the point man's arm and placed his chin on his shoulder, assuring himself the same field of vision as Johnson's.

There! Through the thick foliage, he could see movement, and could hear singsong, clipped chattering. Jace squeezed Johnson's arm, backed away, and crept away toward the main body of the company. Cappaccelli, together with the rest of the platoon leaders, waited next to the compass man. Jace knelt quietly before them.

"Looks like a base camp with four Charlies," said Jace in a whisper. "Look, this could be dangerous—a trap. Little Caesar, there is a big fallen tree on the ground where Johnson is waiting. Line your platoon up on that log—it's a good firing position and it'll give you some cover. First and second platoons, form a tight perimeter about thirty meters back from here. If we get pinned down, I'll tell you how to maneuver by radio. Weapons, you are reserve. Don't move unless I tell you to. Caesar, move NOW, and quietly."

Jace stood by Johnson, who had not moved. The small noises made by the wary soldiers of third platoon were swallowed by a slight breeze in the trees and the calls of jungle birds and insects. Within two minutes, third platoon was in position.Jace eased back to where Johnson stood.

"You found them, you get to fire the first shot," whispered Jace.

Stony Johnson grinned without taking his eyes off of the whisps of movement he could barely see through the thick jungle. Jace backed away and took a position on the log next to a third platoon soldier. Tucker squatted beside him and took a long, hard look at his company commander. Johnson must have already had his weapon's selector switch on "automatic", because there was no preliminary clicking of the safety, just the ripping chatter of his M-16, followed immediately by a firestorm from third platoon. This time, there was no lull in firing. Lieutenant Cappaccelli had designated certain soldiers to fire automatic and the rest to fire semi. As a result, the soldiers lined up on the log expended and changed magazines at different times, guaranteeing a sustained volume of fire. The "thack-crump" of M-79 grenade launchers and the deep-throated thumping of M-60 machine guns formed a bass behind the tenor of rifle fire. Next, Jace called for artillery blocking fires to seal escape routes. There was no return fire.

Jace stood, yelled at the top of his lungs, and motioned the charge. At first, no one saw or heard him—they were too busy firing and changing magazines. Then, seeing their company commander standing atop the fallen tree, the troops began scrambling over, as Cappaccelli screamed for them to spread out and keep firing. Jace joined the rush as third platoon surged forward, running at the crouch through the dense undergrowth. They swept through the camp, firing as they went. Three enemy bodies were sprawled on the ground. A small fire smoldered under a battered teapot. Where was the fourth man? Or were there more?

"HOLD UP! CEASE FIRE!" shouted Jace above the crackling of M-16's. Slowly the volley slowed to scattered shots.

"I said CEASE FIRE, dammit," roared Jace. "Hold up! Little Caesar, form a half circle around this place. Watch for booby traps! Point team, do a quick search."

In the sudden silence, Jace became aware of the crumps from the artillery blocking fires. He grabbed the hand set, but decided to let them continue to fire for a while, he had more important things to do.

"Jupiter One Six and Two Six, this is Jupiter Six," yelled Jace into the company hand set. They acknowledged.

"Everything seems to be OK. Stay where you are 'til we check everything out," he said quickly.

Then, grabbing the battalion set, he gave a hurried report to C.C. who was panting for information. As he filled his friend in on the contact, the point team quickly searched the small camp.

"Would you look at this!" shouted Cappaccelli.

"What?" asked Jace, jerking his head around. The lieutneant walked up holding a cloth bag, half filled with rice. Printed on the fabric, above the image of two shaking hands, were the words: Donated by the people of the United States of America.

"The bastards are eatin' our rice," said Cappaccelli, shaking his head.

"Sir, here's the other one," yelled Stony.

Jace walked to a small foxhole. Inside, crumpled into a lifeless squatting position, head on his knees, was the fourth guerrilla. His right shoulder was gone—

and so was the top of his head. Jace shuddered as he looked down into the man's gray matter.

Once he was relatively sure there would be no counter-attack or further action, Jace stopped the artillery fire and brought the rest of the company up. Third platoon rounded up the enemy weapons and equipment.

"Sir, check this out," said Stony, as he pitched Jace a cheap plastic wallet.

As he opened the billfold, Jace saw that his hands were shaking. Inside, behind a yellowing acetate pane, was a faded photograph of a woman and two children, who wore plain, peasant clothing, and were posing in front of potted palm trees. Jace stared at the little family for a long moment as he thought of his sister and her kids, safe in Tennessee. Then he looked through the rest of the wallet, which held what looked to be an identification card and a few North-Vietnamese piasters. He quickly removed the card and stuck it in his pocket. As an after thought, he also took the bills, for what purpose, he did not know. For souvenirs, he supposed. He had the feeling he did not want to forget this day. He knew he had things he should be doing, but he stood still, holding the wallet and staring at the photograph. Suddenly, anguish swept over him as he looked at the lifeless bodies on the ground before him. Somehow, they didn't seem like enemies. They hadn't even fired a shot as third platoon cruelly cut them down—and they had families, and homes somewhere. Maybe it would have been different if they had shot back. He didn't know. The pay team he had ambushed in the rubber plantation had not shot back either. But they hadn't carried photos of their families. Now he realized that he had the same feeling of remorse he had had the first time he had shot a rabbit. The small animal had seemed so defenseless and so appealing, as if it should have been in a pet shop somewhere. But it had been dead—by his hand—just as these human beings were.

The voice on the battalion radio screamed for information. Also, the brigade commander was overhead in his chopper, on Charlie company's frequency, demanding that Jace pop a smoke grenade so he could see where the battle had taken place. Gunships circled below the brigade commander, asking for targets. Higher up, another Huey, probably the division commander's, orbited the scene. Everyone was demanding a body count.

Not knowing what else to do, Jace gently placed the tattered billfold next to the dead guerrilla's body. Moving away, he turned his attention to the radios and tried to put the wallet out of his mind.

CHAPTER 9

▼

27 October 1967

"You are lucky," said the training officer of the C-240 Viet Cong Battalion. "You will have only eight days of training. In the north, we had eight weeks of very difficult drills before we were called soldiers."

How arrogant, thought Huong. This man trained for eight weeks, then spent a month walking down from the north in relative safety. Couldn't he see that with only eight days of training Huong and his comrades would go directly into combat against the Americans?

As the seven new recruits listened intently, the training officer explained the week's regimen. They would learn close-order drill, firing positions, how to use the bayonet, and the correct way to throw grenades. Because of ammunition shortages caused by stockpiling for the upcoming general offensive, weapons training would consist mostly of dry firing. The eighth day, Huong learned, would consist of political training. After that, he would be assigned to a company to begin unit training, which would teach the recruits the fine points of ambush, attack, defense, and anti-helicopter tactics, as well as how to lay mines and destroy armored vehicles. Much of this training, Huong found out, would be done on-the-job, during actual combat operations.

After the orientation session, Huong ran to Phun, who was preparing to leave.

"Where will you go?" he asked. "When will you be back?"

Despite his bravado in the face of danger, Huong was still a teenager who clung to the security of being with the older woman.

"I have duties at the regimental headquarters," she answered. "Also, I must try to find out what happened to Comrade Lau. I must go," she said as she started to walk away.

"When will you return?" asked Huong.

She turned and added thoughtfully, "Learn your lessons well, younger brother. Remember, if you had stayed with your mother, you would have been drafted by the government forces—a sure death sentence. Here, you are surrounded by friends who believe in you and in ridding our country of the imperialists. By coming here, you have literally saved your life. Be thankful and be strong. Study hard—not only weapons and tactics, but the rules of secrecy, attention, honor and discipline. Learn how to respect the people and their homes as we live and fight amongst them."

"Can you visit my mother and tell her where I am? I left without a word and I know she is worried," cried Huong, almost giving way to tears.

"I am under orders," answered Phun. "If my duties bring me near Long Thanh I will get word to her. But we have all been seen by the police there. If Lau has been arrested, Long Thanh will be dangerous to us. Remember that if you have occasion to go there. Your mother's house is probably being watched."

"Take my motorbike," said Huong. "I won't need it here. You can make good use of it."

"Your motorbike has been given to the battalion to use as the commander sees fit. I will not have access to it."

"Luck, Older Sister," offered Huong. "Find Uncle Lau, and tell my mother that I am safe and I will return to see her soon. In the meantime, I will be a good soldier."

"I know you will," said Phun, turning away and joining the small party of guerrillas. As she picked up her knapsack, she turned, smiled and waved. Without another word, the small band melted into the jungle. Despite his hatred for the enemy who had killed Duc, Huong felt small and terribly alone. And he missed his mother.

C company was finishing the fourth day of its search of AO Trout. Other than the one small contact, they had seen no enemy and found no rocket-launching sites. The platoon-sized clover-leaf patrols had come back to join the weapons platoon and the command post earlier than expected. When the company was together again and had taken a short rest break, Jace moved them in search of a good night position.

As the jungle thinned out atop a gently rolling hilltop, the point team turned and signaled "what about this place?" Jace raised his hand in the halt signal. Soldiers knelt and faced in opposite directions. Looking around as he pulled his plastic-wrapped map from inside his shirt, Jace instinctively surveyed the small piece of high ground for defensive possibilities. Viability was good here; so were fields of fire. A good stream ran past the base of the hill to the south, so water was available. Vines and undergrowth were sparse on the small hilltop so leaders could make their way noiselessly about the perimeter. It was still early, but this place looked good. Jace nodded to the point team and signaled for the platoon leaders to join him.

After going through the now-familiar routine of assigning platoon sectors, checking, adjusting, then giving the O.K. to dig in, Jace called C.C. to report his company's night position. He decided not to send out ambushes, but to order each platoon to send out a listening post. Then, sitting back against a tree, he took stock. The troops were tired, but they were alert, confident and steady. They had improved greatly from the motley mob he had met at Binh Son in early September.

Tucker plopped heavily beside Jace and removed the PRC-25 radio from his rucksack, changed the battery, and set his gear up for the night.

"Where do you want our hole?" he asked Jace.

"Just scratch us out three prone sleeping trenches. Let's dispense with the deep hole tonight," answered Jace.

"Groovy," smiled Tucker as he unfolded his entrenching tool. Jace watched as the youngster began to scrape at the jungle floor with the shovel. Tucker's hair was matted with insect repellent and perspiration. Dirt and grease streaked his face, and three-day whisker stubble dotted his chin. The knees and seat of his jungle fatigue pants shined with a patina formed by weapon-oil, C-ration grease, grass stain, sweat, insect repellent, and red clay. Huge rings of moisture saturated his shirt beneath his arms. His jungle boots were scuffed to a red-brown suede.

Jace asked himself where Tucker might be if he weren't in this God-forsaken jungle, ten thousand miles from his Ohio home. Maybe he would be trying a semester of college, probably working at a gas station or bagging groceries, or taking his best girl out to a drive-in on Saturday night. Yet here he was, incredibly filthy, exhausted, scared and anxious, yet boyishly happy to be digging shallow slit trenches instead of a five-foot-deep foxhole.

Jace looked down at himself. He was just as filthy as Tucker. He rubbed his own beard stubble wondering what his lieutenant classmates at the jungle school would think if they saw him now.

"Five India, tell the point team to come here. I have a mission for them."

Noiselessly, Five India slid away to find Johnson and his buddies. They appeared in less than a minute.

"Go down to the stream," ordered Jace. "Find a good spot that can be defended. Check up and down stream. Make sure everything's secure. I'm going to let the troops take a bath."

Johnson nodded and jerked his head at the others. They moved off a few feet, checked their map, then quickly disappeared down the hill.

A platoon at a time went to the stream. Twice, Jace had to send Five India to remind them that this was not an afternoon at the old swimming hole; that they had to keep the noise down. A squad guarded while each platoon scrubbed, splashed, swam and shaved. The troops beat their nasty fatigues against rocks to thrash away at least some of the filth. The bath in the leech-infested, tepid stream made Charlie company's morale soar.

After everyone had bathed, Jace, Tucker and Five India took their turns. Jace couldn't remember when his last bath had been. His daily ritual of sponging his feet, arm pits, crotch and crack had at least kept infection at bay. He knew a good bath was healthy, even necessary in this place. But floating in this cool stream was more than bathing, it was heaven. Jace somehow felt a little decadent, even guilty as he lingered, soaking and removing the cigar-sized leeches that continuously tried to attach themselves to his white flesh. There were things to do, but they could wait—he needed this.

The late afternoon seemed a little less hot. Perhaps it was only the cooling effect of drying clothes, but the company seemed more comfortable as afternoon turned to early evening. Jace hated to smear on more insect repellent after his bath, but he reluctantly applied the greasy liquid to his neck, ears and face. Without it, he knew the mosquitoes would eat him alive. He walked the perimeter, talked with C.C. a bit on the radio, made small talk with Five India, and even dozed a little. The bath had made everything seem different, more relaxed.

As soon as the sun dived behind the jungle hills, the moonless dark came on, quick and thick. Jace tried to set all his worries about his responsibilities aside. Tonight he decided he would trust his platoon leaders to do their jobs. He was going to sleep.

As he drifted off, he dreamed about Fort Bragg. He was walking toward an aircraft for a jump, but everyone had a parachute but him. Where had he put it? He looked everywhere, but he couldn't find it. Had he even been issued one? He ran back to the parachute packing shed and darted into a room piled to the ceiling with parachutes. No matter how hard he tugged, none of the parachutes would come free from the stack. He ran outside to find a truck full of parachutes parked near the aircraft. Frantically he pulled one parachute after another off of the truck, but each was defective in some way. The loadmaster was closing the doors of the jump aircraft, but still he couldn't find a serviceable parachute. He ran to the plane and scrambled on, then went down the line of troops sitting in the red canvass jump seats. There was Johnson, Tucker, Five India, and Super Private. He did not know they were jump qualified. He would ask Five India where his parachute was—Five India knew everything. A hand was on his arm. Good. Someone had found his 'chute.

"Cap'n, you asleep?"

"Not now."

It was Doc Roberts. "Got to talk. Something you need to know."

Jace rubbed his eyes. Insect repellent brought tears as he sat up and shook away the sleep. "Yeah, what is it?"

"You may not even know, but you—we—got a problem."

"That you Doc?"

"Yessir. You need to watch second platoon. The colored guys are getting fed up with Sergeant Munn. If somethin's not done pretty soon, one of 'em's liable to kill him."

Jace was awake now. "What do you mean? How do you know?"

"Troop talk, sir. We're close, you know. Don't matter what color anybody is. What platoon. We're tight. We stick together. Munn's driving a wedge, though. The colored guys in second platoon are banding together, separating—and the coloreds in the other platoons are supportin' 'em. Who can blame 'em? Munn's on 'em all the time. They can't do anything right. They're the only ones he puts out on LP. They're the only ones he sends on water detail. They're the ones he makes dig his foxhole. He makes them clean their weapons twice, three times before he says they're clean enough. He gives them every shit detail that comes along. Him and his buddy, Sergeant Breath, they screw with the coloreds all the time. Call them names, pick at them."

Jace sat quietly in the darkness.

"Sir?"

"Yes, I heard you. I was just thinking. Look, I can't tell you how much I appreciate your telling me this."

"Just thought you needed to know. I figured you's smart enough to see it in time, but then it might be too late. I figured you needed to know now."

"Yes, I do need to know now. Thanks."

"If anybody asked, I never talked to you," said Roberts as he slipped away in the dark.

Jace couldn't go back to sleep.

Specialist Fourth Class Dewayne Howell was the squad leader of second squad, second platoon, and Staff Sergeant Ezell Munn did not like that fact one little bit. Howell was a huge, powerful hulk of a black man. Not only was he very large, very strong, and very quick, he was well-liked by his squad members, black and white alike. Howell had been a machine gunner—and a good one—before his promotion. When the previous squad leader had been wounded, Howell, the ranking man left in the squad, had assumed the post.

Although Howell lacked formal education—he had quit school in the tenth grade to support his grandmother and his two sisters—he had common sense, a naturally sharp mind and an easy sense of humor. He cared for his troops and they for him. And he meant to keep them alive.

A quarter moon lit the jungle floor through the trees. Although it was well past midnight, Howell was awake, watching his sector of the platoon line. He had four foxholes in his thirty-yard sector, manned by his eight soldiers, on fifty-percent alert. In the faint moonlight, it was easy for him to sit in the center-rear and watch them all.

Since Munn had become platoon leader, Sergeant Smith, known as Sergeant Breath to the troops, now acted as the platoon sergeant. He was walking the platoon sector. As he passed in front of Howell, just behind the foxhole line, every ten or fifteen minutes, he never said a word or acknowledged the squad leader's presence.

"What the hell?" Angry words split the night from the left side of Howell's line.

"Wake up, you sorry bastard."

"I ain't asleep, Sarge."

"I catch you asleep again, I'll stomp your sorry ass."

Howell was at his far-left foxhole in ten seconds.

Sergeant Smith was standing over the hole, occupied by the young black soldier named Peoples. As Howell arrived, Sergeant Smith, now shaking with rage, kicked the man in the side of the head. The first knowledge Smith had of Howell's presence was the sensation of flying backwards. Howell had grabbed his equipment harness with a ham-sized hand and had simply thrown him five yards to the rear.

"You black sonuvabitch, I'll kill you for sure," screeched Smith, as he scrambled to his feet in the darkness. Howell stood silently between him and Peoples, who was holding the side of his head. Muffled voices and scuffing sounds in the dark were evidence of the company's being shocked into instant alertness. Munn was on the scene in seconds, followed quickly by the company commander.

When Jace arrived, Sergeant Smith, still blind with rage was hissing that he wanted Howell court-martialed for assault and charges brought against Peoples for sleeping on duty. Munn stood shoulder-to-shoulder with Smith, glaring at Howell, who stood like a rock between them and Peoples. Peoples' foxhole buddy, who had been asleep, was sitting up in his bedroll scratching his head in the middle of the confrontation.

"What the hell is going on here?" demanded Jace in a hoarse whisper.

Munn and Smith answered loudly at the same time. Shushed to a loud whisper by Jace, they continued with different versions of the same demand: Peoples and Howell must be court-martialed. Howell still had not said a word, neither had he moved from his protective stance over Peoples, who still rubbed his face. Nobody missed the fact that as he faced his accusers, Howell was holding his M-16 at port arms.

"Five India, have the company come to one-hundred-percent alert. I want a full stand-to!" yelled Jace into the darkness. "You four, come with me."

Nobody moved except Peoples, who began climbing out of the foxhole. Jace walked over and took the M-16 out of Howell's hands, instantly realizing that he had made a serious mistake. Wanting to diffuse a dangerous situation, he had appeared to side with Munn and Smith, who, if what Doc Roberts had said were true, were the probable instigators of this incident. Red lensed flashlights flicked on.

"Come on," said Jace, "we'll sort all of this out.

When Howell still did not move, Jace placed his hand on his arm.

"Come on, Howell," he repeated, "We'll get to the bottom of all this."

Howell violently jerked his arm away from Jace's grip.

"Why're you blamin' him?" came a voice from the darkness. "He ain't done nothin'. Why're you blaming the coloreds?"

"I'm not blaming anyone." answered Jace into the darkness.

"Then why'd you take his weapon?"

More voices chorused agreement.

"Listen, all of you. This is a dangerous situation. We are in enemy territory, in the dark, yelling at each other at the top of our lungs. I am not taking sides. I simply want to diffuse this situation and find out what happened. If you yell out in the dark, you put us all in danger! Now turn off the flashlights!"

Thinking quickly and desperately, Jace sought a device to bring normalcy back to his company.

On impulse he yelled, "We have compromised this location. We must move. Platoon leaders, have your people saddled up in fifteen minutes."

Jace turned and said more quietly, "I am now going to give an order to all four of you. I want you to think over the consequences of refusing a lawful order by your company commander in a dangerous situation in a combat zone. Five India, you are the witness to this order."

Jace paused to let the seriousness of his words sink in.

"Sergeants Munn and Smith, Specialist Howell, and Private Peoples will report to the company command post at this time."

Howell's shoulders sagged a little as he exhaled audibly.

"Yes, sir." he said. "Can I have my rifle back?"

Much to the disgust of the two NCOs, Jace handed Howell his M-16, then turned and walked quickly to the company command post, which was being dismantled by Tucker and Five India.

The fifteen minutes passed with nothing being resolved between Jace, Munn, Smith, Howell, and Peoples. Charge and counter-charge flew as heated voices ripped the night.

Abruptly, in the middle of the angry exchange, Jace stood and thundered into the night, "Order of march will be third platoon, company headquarters, second platoon, weapons platoon, and first platoon. Point team turn on a red flashlight. The company will form a file on that light. Take up an azimuth of 315 degrees. We will move in two minutes."

Turning to the sullen group still standing at the center of the perimeter, Jace said, still loudly enough to be heard by the whole company, "Howell, you and Peoples will remain with the company headquarters. You are not being accused of anything. The only thing I want to do is to keep a further confrontation from breaking out until we are safe and have a chance to get to the bottom of this. You two NCOs return to your platoon. Everyone check and make sure you have all weapons and equipment. From this point on, I want absolute quiet and light discipline enforced."

Jace grabbed the radio handset and reported the move to battalion. Shouldering his rucksack, and picking up his CAR-15, he then made his way to third platoon, where the point team's flashlight shone. He found Lieutenant Cappaccelli.

"Are you ready to move?" he asked.

"Yes, sir," came the answer.

"Kill the light and move out, point team."

Charlie company plunged into the darkness.

After moving a thousand meters, Jace halted the company. He could feel the tension and unease in his soldiers. Since it was only two hours before dawn, there would be no time to dig in. He circled the company into a tight perimeter in the dense jungle, put them on one-third alert, and ordered them to get some sleep. When the sun came up, he allowed his soldiers to continue to rest as he moved out of ear-shot to make a radio call to battalion.

As quickly, but as thoroughly as he could, he briefed Lieutenant Colonel McKensie on the previous night's incident. He promised the battalion commander he would fill him in further once he had done a preliminary investigation.

McKensie ordered Jace to move to Tan Uen, about eight kilometers away, where the company's armored personnel carriers would meet them. From there the company would proceed to Bear Cat for a three-day stand down during which Jace would have time to sort out what had happened in detail. McKensie also told Jace he would assign a new platoon leader to second platoon at Bear Cat.

As the heat of the day awakened even the tirdest troops, Jace called the participants in the previous night's incident together. He read each man his rights, then, in turn, listened to each of their stories. Simply wanting to hear the sequence of events from each man's viewpoint, he interrupted them only when they started to make accusations. The stories took a half-hour to tell.

After listening to each, Jace sat quietly for several minutes. He knew if he made the wrong decision, or appeared to wrongly play favorites, he could have a full-scale riot on his hands. Unspoken amongst all of them was the realization that the race riots that had demolished several cities during the previous summer could materialize here in the jungle, where everyone was armed to the teeth.

Finally, he spoke. "Sergeant Smith, you are relieved from your position as platoon sergeant of second platoon. There is no doubt that you kicked Private Peoples. You will be dealt with when we return to Bear Cat."

"That's bullshi—" began Munn. Jace hushed him with a pointed finger.

"Do not—I say again—do not interrupt me again, any of you! Peoples may have been asleep and he may not have been. I ask you to remember the first night I was in command of this company. All of you were asleep. I could have court-martialed you all. Instead I chose to paint red Xs on the side of your vehicles to make a point. We're all tired. Any of us can doze off at any time—you, me—any of us. That's why I have leaders walking the perimeter—as a positive measure against our troops going to sleep. If they doze, wake them up—don't kick them. None of my troops will ever be kicked or struck while I am in command of this company. Physical violence is not leadership."

"What about Howell? He assaulted me!" blurted Sergeant Smith.

"I told you not to interrupt me. There is no mark on you. There is no evidence you were struck. Plus, there are witnesses who say that all Howell did was pull you off of Peoples. No action will be taken against Howell. I believe that all he was doing was protecting his man from wrongful assault."

"Sergeant Munn, as far as I can tell, you have done nothing punishable under the Uniform Code of Military Justice. But I must inform you that several complaints have been registered with me that you have been mistreating your negro soldiers. I'll remind you that one-half of this company is colored. We cannot—and will not—treat anyone differently because of their skin color or national origin. We're all in this together, no matter where we're from or what we look or talk like. I am informing you now that until we get back to Bear Cat, I'll watch you very carefully to see how you treat your soldiers."

"Sir, you can't—" snapped Munn.

"Yes, I can—and I will!" interrupted Jace. "Last, I am moving Lieutenant Otis from the weapons platoon to be platoon leader of second platoon until a new lieutenant is assigned. He'll have the mission to watch you carefully, too. The weapons platoon sergeant can handle the job of platoon leader until we return to Bear Cat. That's all I have for you four at this time. Peoples and Howell may return to second platoon. Sergeant Smith, you will remain with company headquarters until further notice. Five India, get me the platoon leaders. We have a change in mission."

Huong had endured the week of basic training, appalled at how little he had actually learned. To fight the Americans, he would need to know more than how to throw a hand grenade or fire his weapon. At least he knew how his SKS rifle worked. He had only fired three live rounds from it and had not been sure he had hit what he was shooting at.

Now he was being assigned to a platoon. The training officer who had been so arrogant explained to the recruits that the real meat of their training would take place in actual combat against the foreigners and their puppets. Huong was now a member of the National Liberation Front. Although he was now a guerrilla, a soldier, and a freedom fighter, he felt like a dumb, scared teen-ager who missed his mother. This was not at all how he thought he would feel when he joined the Viet Cong.

It was now evident to Huong just how pampered he had been. His mother's house was large, cool and comfortable. He had never slept a single night in the jungle. In fact, the only place he had ever slept other than his mother's house, had been in Duc's small cottage.

He had been terrified the first three nights in the jungle. The mosquitoes, ground leeches, and ants had feasted on his flesh, the ground was hard and uncomfortable, and the night noises were unnerving. More disconcerting than any of these had been the dreams and images of the huge Americans in their gray-green fatigues, round helmets and black rifles creeping noiselessly into their camp. By the fourth night, exhaustion had taken its toll and Huong had slept soundly.

Now, a new terror faced him. He was to go on an actual mission! He tried to concentrate on what he was being told, but fear caused his mind to wander. Huong had to force himself to listen.

"You will find that the closer they are to their base camp, the more lax the Americans become," the platoon commander was saying. "With that in mind, we will strike right outside of rifle and machinegun range of their base. There, the jungle is closest to the road. We will place a mine in the road, await a single vehicle, and blow it up. Now to the details."

Huong listened as the platoon commander assigned one squad to provide security on each side of the mine site. The other squad would surround the platoon leader, who would command-detonate the mine. That squad would rush into the road to finish off any enemy still alive and to steal weapons, radios and equipment. Huong learned that he would be assigned to this squad. The platoon would rehearse the mining the rest of the day. They would move into position tonight and would strike early in the morning.

"The Americans are slow to react, initially. We will have two to five minutes before anyone comes to help the mined vehicle. But after that, overwhelming firepower will be brought against us. You can expect tanks and infantry carriers to roll to the mine site first. They will be firing everywhere at once. They will fire artillery and mortars at the jungle near the site to try to cut off our escape. Remember, we will be operating near their airfield, so we must be camouflaged so we cannot be seen from the air as well as from the ground. Their helicopter gunships will sweep overhead looking for us. If helicopters are overhead, we will go to the ground and not move. If we are still, they will not be able to see us. If we run, they will cut us down," the platoon commander continued.

"Our escape must be well planned. We cannot stay at the mine site for more than a minute. There are only small bushes and knee-high grass between the road and the jungle. After the mining, we will run as quickly as possible to the safety of the forest. Once there, we will use a small trail to run as far as possible away from the road before the enemy reacts. Speed is everything—if you hesitate, we will leave you. There are bunkers along this jungle trail, about four hundred meters from the road. We must be at these bunkers before the artillery begins to fall. I will not explode the mine if there are helicopters overhead or if there are other vehicles are soldiers nearby. We will strike a lone vehicle, take all we can carry, then make our escape."

It sounded easy. Huong had grown up adjacent to the highway that ran through Long Thanh. He remembered how many lone jeeps and trucks had passed his house. Many of these had only a driver and one passenger. What he had no experience with was how quickly the Americans might react. This worried him. He was young and fast, but he couldn't outrun a bullet. As the platoon moved off to the rehearsal site, Huong began to shake his anxiety and fear. This could be done, he thought. It really could. Tomorrow, he would begin to avenge Duc's death.

Dogs barked somewhere nearby, and there were voices, but he couldn't tell whose they were or what they were saying. Had he been asleep? It was hard to tell—the line between sleep and consciousness had become blurred. Lau couldn't tell what was a dream and what was real.

It was time to try to move again. He had lain for some time in a fetal position, and his legs screamed for relief. He had to straighten them. In the confines of the steel and bamboo so-called "tiger cage" which measured four and a half feet long and three feet wide and high, he could never stretch completely out. When he straightened his legs, he had to sit up or lie on his side, bent at the waist. Lau learned that enduring the heat was easy compared to the torture of never being able to completely stretch out.

The change in positions was painful. The bamboo mat on the floor of the cage did little to insulate the heat emanating from the steel bars underneath. The roof-less cage was in the open, and Lau, wearing only a loin cloth, was viciously sun-burned and suffering from heat cramps. He had been given water only twice in the two days since he had been moved from the police station to the Long Thanh Special Forces camp.

As the afternoon wore on, a tall American wearing camouflaged fatigues and a green beret, and a Vietnamese major walked to the cage. They were speaking English, so Lau did not know that they were discussing whether or not he had gone into heat stroke. The American stuck a finger through the bars and touched Lau's side, which was moist and clammy. The American and the hard-looking major spoke, nodded and seemed to agree. Lau was brought water, and a poncho was stretched across the top of the cage for shade. It seemed that they wanted to keep him alive.

The night brought blessed relief. Still the confines of the cage, the headache and cramping caused by heat exhaustion kept him from deep sleep. Several times he drifted off into tortured dreams of Phun, danger, pain and horror. As the sun came up, the American and the Vietnamese major returned.

The major spoke. "We are going to give you one chance to talk. If you are honest with us, you may live. If you lie, your death is guaranteed."

"I have told the police, and I tell you, I am a sergeant in the government army—the same army of which you are a member. There has been a terrible mistake. We all know of the inefficiency of army record keeping. Why am I being treated like this?"

Without answering, the major removed the lock on the cage and let down one side.

"You may come out," he said.

Lau rolled out of the cage and fell heavily to the ground. He couldn't stand by himself. The major and the American lifted him by his arms and helped him to a low, sandbagged bunker where he was told to sit on the roof. The huge American put one hand on either side of Lau and leaned to within inches of his face. As the American scrutinized him, Lau remembered what had been his burning desire to come face-to-face with the enemy. Well, here he was—but it was not what he had envisioned. After being studied carefully by the foreigner, Lau was given rice, which he could not yet eat, and water, which he sipped slowly.

The Vietnamese major then took his turn eyeing Lau carefully. "You say you are from Vinh Long. Describe the town for us, please."

Lau tried to remember the facts he had been told about the town in the Mekong Delta.

"Vinh Long is on the Mekong River. It is a medium-sized town with no large buildings. The Americans have an airfield there, north of the town."

"Facts you could have gotten out of a book or from someone who has been there. Describe the market place," demanded the major.

Lau described a general market that could be in any Vietnamese town—thatched roofed stalls where merchants offered vegetables, fish, chickens and various implements. What he had not been told was that the market in Vinh Long was adjacent to the river, with mooring places for boats from which fresh fish and wares from other river towns were sold.

The Vietnamese major grinned and nodded at the American green-beret, then quickly walked away. No more questions were asked. Lau was left alone with a shotgun-toting, bare-footed mercenary, probably a Cambodian or Chinese Nung. Unlike the disinterested regional-force troops who had guarded him at the Long Thanh police station, this man seemed to be waiting for a chance to kill him.

After a while, Lau was able to force down a little rice with his water. When the pair of officers failed to return, he began to relax a little, even under the malevolent stare of the guard. Foolishly, he hoped that they had begun to believe him.

Having never flown before, Lau was terrified. Now, sitting on the floor of the banking helicopter, he looked out of the right door straight into the treetops two thousand feet below. With the aircraft sideways in the air, he could not understand why he didn't fall out.

The American in the green beret and the evil-looking Vietnamese major squatted on the floor behind the pilots. Lau sat bound and cross-legged on the floor at the back of the seatless cabin beside another trussed captive. As the American leaned toward the major and yelled something into his ear, the Vietnamese officer grinned and nodded, then slid across the floor towards the prisoners.

"I am going to ask you one question each. If I do not hear the answer I want, something very, very bad is likely to happen," he yelled over the noise of the rotors and the wind.

Turning to Lau's fellow prisoner, the major yelled, "What is the name of your Viet Cong unit?"

The prisoner simply looked at the major with no expression on his face whatsoever.

"I will not repeat the question. You have ten seconds to answer."

The stand-off continued for a moment as the prisoner stared straight ahead and said nothing. Then, suddenly, the officer grabbed the man's shirt and drug him to the gaping door of the Huey. With no prelude or hesitation, the major positioned himself in a sitting position behind the prisoner with his feet on the man's back, and kicked hard. Still expressionless, the prisoner flew into the wind and disappeared. As soon as the man was kicked from the helicopter, the pilot, who had been watching over his shoulder as the scene unfolded, put the aircraft into a violent bank so that the passengers could see the falling body crash into the trees two thousand feet below.

With an evil grin, the major then turned to Lau and yelled over the noise, "I will ask you one question. If I do not hear the answer I expect to hear, you will join your comrade, do you understand?"

Lau's mind raced. If this had happened months ago in the north, he had no doubt what he would have done. But now, after meeting and falling in love with Phun, he hesitated. The rational part of his mind told him to die for his country; his heart told him to live for Phun. His eyes darted to the green-beret American. Again, he thought of how he had often fantasized about coming face-to-face with one of the foreign devils—and here he was again, staring into the round, hateful, ugly eyes of this imperialist dog. It seemed that every time he faced an American, the confrontation was different from the way he imagined it would be.

Lau's attention was jolted back to the Vietnamese major who was yelling, "Who are you and what Viet Cong unit are you from? Like your comrade, you have ten seconds in which to answer."

Lau hesitated only four second before he screamed, "I am Colonel Nguyen van Lau, political officer of the Second Regiment of the Fifth Division, National Liberation Front.

Huong squatted with his carefully-camouflaged platoon in the pre-dawn gray. During the night, the guerrillas had crept to the edge of the south access road to Bear Cat, just off the end of the airfield's runway, where they hid in the flat brush and tall grass. Despite the warmth of the sub-tropical morning, he shivered.

As he raised his head to look about, Huong recognized the roof of his mother's house, a scant two kilometers away. He could stand up and simply walk home, he thought, with no one in Long Thanh the wiser about where he had been. Of course his platoon commander might have something to say about his leaving. Thinking about his mother making tea, boiling rice and preparing for another workday made him terribly homesick. He knew she was probably frantic with worry about him. He might as well be a thousand miles away, he thought as he shivered and shifted positions.

As the morning brightened, activity increased inside the American base where he had once worked. Huong smiled as he remembered how he had been treated as a valuable asset when his commander had learned that he had worked inside Bear Cat. His platoon commander and the commander of the battalion's mortars had picked his brain of everything he could remember about the interior arrangement of the enemy base. The mortar commander had told him that much of what he had remembered would become valuable targeting information for his gunners. Huong had felt very proud.

Now, he felt very scared. Suddenly, just as his commander had predicted, about twenty troops, walking in front of two huge trucks, came out of the south gate and began moving slowly down the road toward them. As they grew nearer, Huong could see two soldiers with mine detectors working their instruments slowly and carefully back and forth in front of the others.

As the enemy engineers came closer, Huong's platoon flattened itself to the ground and disappeared into the scant vegetation. The hairs on his neck stood straight, and gooseflesh appeared on his forearms as the soldiers that were so familiar to him slowly swept past. No one moved.

During the half-hour before the engineer unit returned toward Bear Cat, several helicopters took off from the airfield and flew directly overhead. As the leader had planned, Huong and his platoon hugged the ground and let their camouflage do its job. Lax now after clearing the road, the minesweepers and their security element rode back toward Bear Cat in the backs of the five-ton dump trucks, laughing and joking as they rode past the Viet Cong platoon, heading for breakfast.

As the engineer road-clearing team entered the Bear Cat gate, barely visible in the morning mists, the platoon commander and two sappers darted into the road. Without looking toward the American base, only six hundred meters away, they went to work.

The commander squatted at the edge of the road while one sapper dug a hole in the road with a pick. The other used a small hand tool to scrape an inch-deep trench from the hole to the edge of the road. A flat block of Czech-made Semtex, the ubiquitous communist-block plastic explosive, was placed in the shallow hole by the first sapper. After plunging an electrical blasting cap into a hole he had made in the green explosive, he covered the mine with dirt as the second sapper buried the connecting wires in the shallow trench. After everything was set, the platoon commander ran into the road with a palm branch and swept away the evidence of their digging, then placed an innocuous-looking aiming stake in the ditch adjacent to the mine. The whole operation took two minutes.

Back at his command post, the commander plugged one of the wires that ran from the mine into a discarded American radio battery. He held the other wire, which was wound around a nail, in his right hand. At the right time, all he would have to do was touch the nail to the bare wire he had placed in the opposite pole of the battery.

The sun broke over the antennas and tin roofs of Bear Cat before any movement appeared on the road. As the sun burned the morning mists away, a platoon of armored personnel carriers bristling with machine guns screamed and rattled out of the gate and down the road. The commander looked left and right and shook his head. The negative signal was silently passed down the line. The earth shook as the passing eleven-ton monsters ground the roadbed into a thick cloud of red dust.

When the APCs were out of site, the platoon commander raised his head for a look at the mine site. He had no way of knowing whether the steel treads had broken the connection from his battery to the mine. As he strained to look, he heard another vehicle.

An MP jeep, followed by a cloud of dust, which would hopefully block the vision of the distant gate guards, rolled toward the mine. The commander curtly nodded, then flattened himself. Holding the nail partially wrapped in electrical tape, he concentrated on the aiming stake.

Through the bushes, Huong could see the enemy approaching. There were only two men in the vehicle. They wore shiny black helmets with huge white letters painted on them, MP arm bands, and sunglasses. They were talking calmly as they drove through the morning. Huong was proud that he could read the English words painted at the base of the windshield: MILITARY POLICE. He had learned quite a bit while he worked at the American base.

The jeep was traveling at about 35 MPH as its front bumper drew even with the aiming stake. When the platoon commander touched the nail to the bare wire from the battery, a blinding flash and a deafening crack erupted from the road. Without its left-front wheel, the jeep slid sideways, and when it struck a pothole, began to flip violently, ejecting both Americans from their seats.

Through the gray cloud of smoke from the explosion, and the accompanying pall of red dust, Huong watched the jeep bounce down the road, throwing weapons, radios, helmets and bodies into the air as it went. One MP landed on his head, obviously breaking his neck. The other tumbled head-over-heels like a rag doll. Clods of laterite showered the platoon as it remained concealed in the bushes.

As a new recruit, Huong had been assigned to the squad that had the mission of retrieving radios and weapons from the vehicle and searching the bodies for any items of intelligence value. On the edge of his consciousness, he saw his comrades moving and heard his commander yelling, but he remained motionless, stunned by the blast and the wreck. Suddenly galvanized into action by the fear of being called a coward, Huong darted behind his squad members into the road.

He tried to look toward Bear Cat, but smoke and dust blocked his vision. He was trembling all over when he reached the jeep.

"Everything is smashed. Get their weapons. Bring the radios—we might be able to use them for spare parts," ordered the commander.

Huong picked up a pistol and stuck it in his belt. As he bent to pick up an M-16, he heard his commander yell for him.

"Huong, come here, quickly."

Huong raced to where the commander stood over one of the Americans.

"This one is still alive. As a new recruit, you will have the honor of finishing him off. Use his own pistol!" said the commander, pointing to the .45 in Huong's belt.

As Huong fumbled with the heavy weapon, the commander jerked it from his hand, chambered a round, checked the safety, and handed it back.

"Do it!" ordered the commander.

The American was breathing in rapid, shallow gasps. Huong couldn't tell if he were conscious or not—his eyes stared in glazed shock. Huong looked at the commander, then at the American MP.

"We have no time! Do it NOW!"

Huong pointed the pistol at the American's head. The MP's eyes suddenly focused, looking at Huong with a pleading, horrified look. Huong hesitated, then thought of Duc and pulled the trigger. The pistol kicked upward as blood, brains and red dust flew from the road The commander pounded him on the back, then turned to bark orders. Huong stared at the mess that had been a human being. He wouldn't have lived anyway, he thought. He was horribly injured.

"Prepare to move. We must be gone before they react," yelled the commander.

Huong scooped up the M-16, then, on impulse, reached down and grabbed a shiny pair of handcuffs lying next to the MP's body. Having started toward the safety of the bushes, he suddenly stopped, realizing the handcuffs wouldn't be much good without keys. He ran back to the body and jerked free the key chain that was fastened to one of the dead MP's belt-loops. Standing in the road, Huong took one last look at the roof of his mother's house, then darted off the road to follow his comrades. Only two minutes had elapsed since the explosion. As the Viet Cong platoon sprinted to safety, no one at Bear Cat had even realized something had happened on the access road.

Charlie company emerged from the jungle into a beautiful pastoral scene. Farmers in black pajamas and round conical hats bent to their work in the paddies as children sat on the backs of water buffalo standing shoulder-deep in a stream. Nearby, the village of Tan Uen, with its thatched and red-tiled roofs, stood peacefully in a grove of tall palm trees. Lined up on the road a half-kilometer away were Charlie company's twenty APCs. Lieutenant Colonel McKensie's bubble-nosed H-23 sat in a rice paddy adjacent to the tracks.

Jace's shoulders sagged with relief. Under the guns of his tracks, he relaxed for the first time since the company had landed in War Zone D. As he began to think about a shower and a decent night's sleep, he was startled by the sharp crack of an M-16.

Turning, Jace saw a water buffalo thrashing about in its death throes. Children were screaming and running in all directions. Jace ran to where second platoon stood.

"Who shot that animal?" he demanded.

Soldiers hung their heads and backed away from the company commander's fury.

"I said—WHO SHOT THAT ANIMAL?"

"I did." Sergeant Munn stood haughtily, helmet pushed onto the back of his head. "Damn thing was charging at us."

"Was not, either," said a voice from the platoon. Private Peoples stepped forward. "He just shot it out of meanness," he said.

"Shut the hell up!" shouted Munn. "What the hell do you know, anyway?"

"I was raised around cattle. I know when one's chargin' and when it's not."

"That ain't no cow," screeched Munn. "That's a mean-assed buffalo, and I say it was chargin'"

"I saw it all, Sarge, and I say it was jus' standin' there."

Jace was fuming. He shot a glance at Lieutenant Otis, who shrugged that he had not seen the incident. Jace then looked around at the farmers, who had stopped working and were staring angrily at the Americans.

"I'll tell you what," spat Jace, "If these people were not V.C. this morning, they probably are now—and I'll tell you something else—there are a lot of things you can do to scare off a charging buffalo, like shooting in the air. You just took away a large part of these people's livelihood."

"And I say the damn thing was chargin' at me, and my life was in danger," yelled Sergeant Munn.

"And I say you're going to pay these people for the animal," said Jace, regaining his composure.

"It'll be a cold day in hell 'fore I do." said Munn.

Second platoon was watching closely, and Jace knew it. They all knew his feelings about winning the hearts and minds of the people. They all knew that Sergeant Munn was challenging Jace openly, and they waited to see what was going to happen. Although Munn was not directly involved in last night's incident, Jace knew that he had either instigated it or condoned it. Hadn't he backed Sergeant Smith, who had kicked an American soldier? Something had to be done.

Jace drew up and squared his shoulders as he tried to control his anger.

"Sergeant Munn, you are relieved as second platoon sergeant. You will be reassigned as soon as we get to Bear Cat."

"I'll tell you this, I ain't gonna be relieved over no gook buffalo! I got witnesses!" exploded Munn. "I'll not be treated this a-way! You been favorin' these shit-for-brains troops over us NCOs ever since you been in this company!"

"Right now you have only been relieved. One more word and I'll court-martial you for insubordination. Five India, take Sergeant Munn's weapon," said Jace, just loud enough for second platoon to hear.

"I want to see the battalion commander!" snarled Munn. "We'll see who has the last laugh."

"Permission granted," said Jace. "In fact, we'll both see him together—right now. He's standing over there next to his helicopter."

Lieutenant Colonel McKensie and C.C. stood chatting with First Sergeant Baez as the troops of Charlie company walked tiredly toward their armored personnel carriers. The trio was startled by Jace's agitated state as he made his way toward them.

"Well, Jupiter Six, did you finally decide to emerge into the sunlight?" asked McKensie.

"Yes, sir," answered Jace. "And none too soon. I think if I had to stay another night in the jungle with some of the assholes in this crowd, I swear I'd shoot 'em!"

At first, McKensie thought Jace was joking, then saw that he was deadly serious.

"What was the rifle shot all about?" asked C.C.

"Just one more incident in the proud career of one Staff Sergeant Ezell Munn," answered Jace. "It seems that he decided to disregard my standing orders to treat the Vietnamese people with dignity and respect and at all times to try to win their hearts and minds. It seems that he decided to shoot a water buffalo— just for the hell of it."

"Jace, you need to calm down, you're gonna bust a blood vessel," exclaimed McKensie.

"Sir, I had a racial incident in the jungle last night. While he may not have been one of the main players, Munn was sure in the middle of it. I relieved Sergeant Smith for kicking a private and Munn wanted to back him up. Now today, without any reason, he shoots a water buffalo—in direct violation of a company standing policy. I want that sonuvabitch out of my company right now. I swear, I believe my outfit is coming apart."

"Jace, NCO leadership is getting to a critical level in the battalion. I'm not sure I can justify pulling this many leaders off the line. Are you sure you can't reassign them internally? After all, they're your problem children. If they're as bad as you say, I hate to dump them on someone else."

"Colonel, you told me when I assumed command that if I needed anything, all I needed to do was ask. Up until now, I haven't asked for anything except for some ping pong equipment and a new call sign. Now I'm asking. I want Smith and Munn out of my company before they start a full-scale riot."

"Sir, I can put one of them to work in company supply. I can keep an eye on 'em there," First Sergeant Baez offered.

"Damn, Top, I haven't even said hello to you. Sorry I'm so fired up," exclaimed Jace.

"Understandable, sir," answered Baez, who then turned to McKensie. I'll keep Smith, sir, if it's OK with the company commander. But I do recommend we split those two up. If you could find a place for Munn at battalion or brigade—"

"OK, that sounds like a reasonable compromise," said McKensie. Who are you going to replace Munn with?"

"Spec Four Howell, sir. I'll make him an acting sergeant ASAP. He's not long on book learning, but he's experienced and the guys trust him. I will need a new lieutenant—quick. Otis from the weapons platoon is overseeing second platoon now. He's doing a good job, but he's the only mortar-trained officer I've got."

"OK," said McKensie. I'll put Munn in S-4. Do you think this will put an end to this mess?"

"I hope so, sir. I certainly hope so."

"You not even going to speak to me?" asked C.C. with a sly grin.

Calming, Jace said, "I'm sorry, Major. I guess I'm a little tired and keyed up. Good to see you, sir—excuse me for a second—Top, go get Munn and bring him here. I don't want to waste a minute getting him out of here. Colonel, if I could send him back on your bird, I'd appreciate it."

"Sure," replied McKensie. "I'll send the chopper back out as soon as the S-3 and I get back to the TOC."

They were interrupted by loud whoops as the soldiers of Charlie company arrived at their armored personnel carriers. The gunners tossed cans of beer and soda to the thirsty troops as they clamored aboard their tracks. Even though they were still in a combat zone, being out of the jungle and back on their tracks caused a security lapse in the entire company. Troops were not interested in watching for the enemy. They were too busy telling their track-bound buddies about their experiences during their search of War Zone D. Jace called for the platoon leaders and told them to see to security. Now was as dangerous a time as any.

Returning to the command group, Jace said, "Sir, I'd like to pay for the water buffalo. If we could get someone from G-5 to figure out a fair price. If possible, I'd like to come out with an interpreter when we pay the people."

"I'm sure we can work something out," said McKensie. "Well, I've got to go. Crank up the bird, C.C.—Jace, come by headquarters tonight and we'll all have a beer. And one more thing—"

"Yes, Sir.

"Get some rest, you look like hell."

"Gladly, sir—once I get this mess straightened out."

"See you tonight, Jace," waved C.C.

"You bet, Major."

After the battalion commander and the S-3 lifted off, Jace sent for Sergeant Munn. Angry and sullen, Munn was escorted to Jace by Baez.

"Sergeant Munn, it gives me great pleasure to inform you that when the commander's bird returns, you will fly back to battalion where you will be assigned to S-4. If you still want to see the battalion commander, you can see him at his headquarters.

"Captain, I'll not have my career ruined over a damned water buffalo. I'll go to the I.G.—I'll—"

"You do whatever you feel like you have to do. You just do it somewhere else. Don't say another word to me. Top, get him out of my sight."

"You heard the man, shitbird," said Baez.

"You'll be sorry," said Munn. "Both of you. I swear I'll get even!"

CHAPTER 10

▼

1 November 1967

The mercenary who had been guarding him roughly dragged Lau from his cage. Since the terrifying helicopter ride, he had known this time would come—and he had dreaded it. For some twisted reason his captors had left him alone for three days, during which he had slumped into a dark depression.

How could he have broken so easily? Why couldn't he face death more bravely? What would happen to him now? What would he be forced to tell his captors? How much could he lie about? How much could he hold back? Would he become a traitor to his cause, to his comrades? Would the Americans and government troops use torture, drugs, or both on him? What had happened to Phun? He was convinced he would never see her again.

The guard pushed and kicked him to the camp headquarters building where he was led to a room that held only a small table and a folding chair. The mercenary shoved him to a corner and gestured for him to squat. Again, he waited. He tried not to dwell on the fact that he was starving. Since the helicopter flight, his captors had given him only water, and precious little of that. He thought of asking the guard if he could have a drink, but thought better of it. The evil-looking man looked as if he could kill at the slightest provocation.

Lost in his thoughts and depression, Lau had no idea how long he had squatted in the corner when the government officer who had kicked the prisoner out of the helicopter suddenly burst in. At first the major said nothing—he just laid a small leather case on the field table. Opening the case and spreading the contents, he finally turned to Lau.

"Well, Colonel! Now we shall learn everything you know. You learned from the helicopter ride that I only ask questions one time. If there is not a quick, truthful answer, the consequences will be immediate and final. I do not believe in half-measures. You will have one chance, then—."

Lau said nothing. He did not look at the major or act as if he had heard or understood him. The major motioned to the guard who jerked Lau to his feet and shoved him to a position in front of the table.

"I want you to examine what I have in my hands. This is a thin glass tube— very thin indeed. Here is a jar of petroleum jelly. This is a rubber mallet. Please examine each item carefully."

When Lau refused to look down for only a second, the guard's vice-like grip closed on the back of his neck. Excruciating pain shot through his neck and shoulders as the mercenary pressed a pressure point. Lau's knees buckled as his head snapped downward. There were tears in his eyes, but he could see the items on the table.

"I will explain what I am going to do so you can think about the consequences of your not answering my questions. First, I will coat the glass tube with the petroleum jelly. Then, while my friend here holds you in the required position, I will insert the glass tube into your penis, which I will then stretch out on the table. I will then ask you a question. If I do not have an immediate, truthful answer, I will smash your organ and the glass tube inside, with this hammer. Do you have any questions?"

Lau was terrified. The thought of trying to urinate through broken glass paralyzed him. He had no way of anticipating the excruciating agony of such a torture. And if he ever did get away to rejoin Phun, what kind of marriage could they have if he had a horrible sexual mutilation? No doctor he knew of could ever repair that kind of damage.

The major signaled the guard, who with one quick motion, jerked Lau's loincloth to his knees. The mercenary locked his arms behind his back and shoved him to a standing position in front of the table. The major grinned as he picked up the glass tube and waved it in front of Lau's eyes. He was coating the tube with petroleum jelly when the door opened. The tall American with the green beret spoke rapidly in English to the major, who looked disappointed.

After studying Lau's face for a long moment, he said, "It seems you have a short reprieve. We have been ordered to take you to Saigon."

Even before he had admitted his identity, the American green beret and the Vietnamese major had somehow guessed that Lau was a high-ranking enemy officer. As he shuffled along in the dust, prodded by the muzzle of the guard's shotgun, Lau had no idea that both the helicopter incident and the glass-tube threat were parts of an elaborate preparation for his interrogation in Saigon.

He now had a clear idea of what would be waiting for him during his next interrogation. Almost as bad, he realized that he would probably never see Phun again. He wished he had taken the time to tell her how he felt about her. He had tried to express his feelings to her on several occasions, but words had always failed him. Now he just hoped that she had been able to see through his inability to verbalize how he felt. He hoped he had been able to show her somehow that she was the only woman he had ever truly loved. He desperately regretted not having told her.

The guard literally threw him onto the helicopter. With his hands bound behind him, he had no way of breaking his fall. While the South Vietnamese major and the green-beret American climbed aboard, he struggled to retain some dignity by raising himself to at least a sitting position. As the helicopter lifted off from the special forces camp, Lau tried to think of a strategy to use during his coming ordeal in Saigon. He had witnessed first-hand what these people were capable of, and fully understood it would probably be useless to try to resist.

After several moments of trying to think of logical courses of action, Lau decided he had only two options: tell everything he knew or try to die as bravely as he could. Although he had no idea how he would be treated if he told all, he would certainly never be allowed to return to Phun. He knew that if he were killed in captivity, Phun would never learn what had happened to him or how he had died. But if he met her in the afterlife, he wanted her to know he had been brave. With grim resignation, Lau decided to die with as much dignity as he could muster. Once he came to his decision, he sat back against the bulkhead and relaxed. He dreaded the pain and suffering. He just hoped that they would kill him as quickly as they had the guerrilla they had pushed from the helicopter.

As the helicopter climbed out over Bear Cat, Lau was again amazed at the size of an American base. Tents, trucks, motor parks, buildings, piles of supplies—even an airfield with scores of small airplanes and helicopters—slid by underneath. He remembered the similar feeling he had had when his bus had passed Long Binh. How could the National Liberation Front ever hope to defeat such power?

The chopper was headed west now, passing over the strip of jungle that separated the village of Long Thanh from the grassy tidal flats formed by the merging of the Nha Be, the Dong Nai, and the Saigon rivers. As they crossed the first stream in the maze of waterways southeast of Saigon, they dropped to within feet of the saw grass to avoid the traffic patterns of the Bien Hoa and Tan Son Nhut airbases. The helicopter was chattering along just inches from the swampy ground when the pilots saw the first of the green tracers sailing directly toward their windshield.

"Taking fire!" screamed the pilot into the intercom as he pulled back on the stick and kicked the bird into a violent, climbing right turn. The door gunner on the left side could not see a target for his M-60, so he began to fire at the general area from where the tracers were coming. He had gotten off only one short burst when the helicopter rocked violently beneath him. The gunner was horrified as he cut a quick glance toward the cockpit. The windscreen was shattered and there was blood all over the front of the cabin. The pilot's shattered body slumped forward onto the stick, making it impossible for the co-pilot to right the falling bird. With his free hand, the co-pilot jerked the dead pilot away from the controls as the American green beret lunged toward the cockpit to help.

"Hold him!" screamed the co-pilot. The green beret couldn't hear above the blast of the rotors and the wind, but he instinctively knew what was needed. Wedging himself between the cockpit seats, he held the pilot's body away from the controls. At an altitude of ten feet, the co-pilot pulled the nose up and gained control of the staggering helicopter, just as a 12.7 millimeter machine-gun bullet took his head off.

The flaring caused by the aviator's last action slowed the aircraft just slightly before the tail plowed into the swamp. As the tail boom broke away, the rotors churned into the mud, snapped and flew in all directions. With a sickening thud, the skids smashed into the swampy ground and snapped off.

When the helicopter hit the ground, everything and everyone, including Lau, flew forward. The Vietnamese major's head smashed against the door frame, killing him instantly. The right-side door gunner, who was not wearing a safety belt, broke his gun mount as he flew out and splashed head-over-heels into the swampy ground. The left door gunner was torn apart by rotor-blade fragments as he sat behind his gun. Lau's forward progress was broken by the green beret's body, the top half of which was now entangled in the wreckage of the nose.

After being momentarily unconscious, Lau awakened to the sound of the screaming turbine engine, which incredibly was still running. The cabin of the helicopter was resting on its right side, full of smoke. As his vision cleared, Lau looked from the crew to the green beret, then to the mangled door gunner. As he struggled to a sitting position in the wreckage, he realized that everyone in the helicopter was dead but him. The smell of spilled fuel choked him as he slid his bound wrists behind his buttocks and the backs of his legs. He then quickly freed one foot at a time. Now at least, he had his hands in front of him so he could climb from the wreckage. While he struggled to free himself, the engine died and all was quiet.

As Lau strained to pull himself up and out of the left door, he could see black-clad figures running through the calf-deep mud toward the downed aircraft. He slid over the edge of the door, cutting his side on a jagged rip in the fuselage. Falling heavily onto the swampy ground, he saw now that he was in new danger. Standing unsteadily, he held his bound hands over his head and began yelling, "Don't shoot, comrades! I am one of you!"

The five guerrillas splashing through the muck toward the smashed Huey hesitated when they saw Lau with his bound hands over his head.

"Everyone on the aircraft is dead. Hurry! Other aircraft will be overhead any moment! We must get away from here," he shouted.

The Viet Cong leader slogged up to Lau.

"For someone flying on an enemy aircraft, you seem very bold indeed, shouting orders. I would not be too hasty in assuming we are your friends."

"I am a Colonel, the political officer of the second regiment of the 5th Viet Cong Division. I was captured at a roadblock as I was doing my recruiting duties. They were taking me to Saigon for interrogation."

"So you say!"

"Listen to me," shouted Lau. "Since you are in this area, you must be a member of the C-240 battalion based south of Binh Son. Your battalion commander is Major Doan. I have visited him and your battalion headquarters several times. If you do not believe me, then leave me bound and take me to Major Doan. He will verify who I am. One thing I can tell you for sure—in a very short time, the sky will be full of angry American helicopters. We must get away from this aircraft!"

The guerrilla leader paused for a heartbeat, and then jerked his head toward the Huey. The other four Viet Cong dashed to the helicopter; two clamored aboard. One ripped the M-60 from the dead gunner's mount and tossed it to a comrade standing on the ground. The other man took pistols and rifles from the dead, looked for documents, and then memorized the frequency setting on the chopper's radio. Finding nothing else that could be carried away, he grunted to his friend who was tossing machine-gun ammunition to the ground.

"Please throw me a canteen from one of the dead. I am nearly dying of thirst," shouted Lau.

In a few seconds, one of the guerrillas appeared from the helicopter's interior and tossed a canteen to Lau, who immediately opened it and drank deeply. Without further communication, the two Viet Cong climbed down from the Huey and scooped up their booty.

"We will untie you. We can travel faster that way—but remember, you are unarmed. You will be treated with suspicion until we can verify your story and your identity," said the leader, who whipped out a knife, and with one stroke freed Lau's hands. "We must go now. If enemy aircraft appear, do as we do. Do not walk in a straight line, you must weave back and forth so as not to leave a clear trail through the swamp that can easily be seen from the air."

Lau quickly learned how much his ordeal had taken out of him. After a few meters, the fast pace over the swampy ground sapped his strength. The V.C. leader turned impatiently and scowled at Lau.

"You must keep up. You endanger us all."

"I have been caged like an animal for days. I find I am very weak," answered Lau.

The leader grunted, turned and slogged off. Lau did his best to keep up. They had gone only a short distance when they arrived at the heavy machine-gun position. Without talking, the guerrillas broke the heavy gun into three parts, distributed the load, and then prepared to move out.

With the five men laden with the heavy machine gun and captured weapons and ammunition, Lau found the pace more to his liking. They had gone less than five hundred meters when they firstheard the flapping of rotor blades. Without hesitation, the leader stopped and shrugged off his rucksack and threw down his rifle. He snatched up several clumps of swamp grass with muddy roots attached. Lau looked around to see the others doing the same thing, so he followed suit. The leader reached into his sack and pulled out a bundle of reeds, pulled out two, kept one for himself and tossed the other to Lau.

"Work your body into the mud, then place clumps of grass over yourself. Breathe through the reed if you have to. Do it quickly," ordered the leader.

Lau looked around—the four guerrillas behind him had simply disappeared. He watched as the leader covered the weapons and packs with clumps of grass, then lay down on his back and wriggled into the muck. As he disappeared into the mud, he placed clumps of grass over his legs, crotch and chest. He smeared his face with mud and pushed his head back into the swamp.

Lau shot a quick glance toward Long Thanh. A pair of sleek Cobra gunships escorted by two small observation helicopters appeared a kilometer away over the jungle. He quickly did as the others had done, disappearing into the muck. The only part of him that was above the swamp was his face, which he had smeared with mud. Happily, he learned that his camouflage protected him from flies and mosquitoes as well as from American gunners. After trying a few breaths through the reed, and finding that it caused his breathing to be labored, he removed it from his mouth and placed it in plain view next to his right shoulder. He felt that he would not need it unless the enemy walked right on top of him. The mud was warm and he was extremely exhausted. Even the thrumming of helicopters landing nearby could not keep him awake. Soon, he slept soundly.

The first helicopters on the scene were scouts and gunships, which circled protectively. In a few minutes, four Hueys hovered low over the site. They could not land on the swampy ground, so the platoon of troops jumped from the hovering helicopters into the muck and quickly formed a perimeter around the downed bird. A dust-off hovered while the bodies were loaded, then, with the Hueys following, nosed over and swooped away. About an hour later, a huge Chinook chattered in. Soldiers hooked the wreck onto long steel cables, and signaled to the pilot. Slowly, the giant bird, with the sad crumple of junk that had been a helicopter slowly spinning underneath, strained into the sky. Then the Hueys returned, picked up the soldiers and flew away. In just under two hours after being shot down, the destroyed Huey, the bodies of the crew and passengers, and all evidence that anything had happened here, were gone.

The voice coming from the darkness was muffled and faint.

"What did you say?" called Lau as he strained to recognize anything perceptible in the darkness. "I cannot hear you or see you. Who is there?"

Again the muffled voice came from the darkness.

"Who are you?" choked Lau.

"Do you not recognize the voice of your wife?"

"But you are no longer among the living!"

"You are correct, Husband," she said as she emerged from the shadows. She wore a fresh white tunic, black silk pants, and a large white flower in her hair as she had on their wedding day.

"Are—Are you from the spirit world?"

"Yes, my husband"

Lau suddenly became self-conscious. Did she know of Phun?

His wife stared expressionlessly at him. "Your parents and your children are anxious about you since you have come south—as I am. We wonder if you will ever return to be in our presence at our home.

"When all of you were killed, I volunteered to come south to fight. I intended—intend to return to the spirits of my family and my ancestors when the war is over."

"Will you, my husband? We are all concerned that you might not."

"Everything is so confusing during these times. I might die here. It might not be possible to—"

"Fate will determine when and where you will die. Then your spirit will be with us anyway.

"We have no place to which we may return to commune with you," she said as she began to fade.

"Please do not go," begged Lau. Tell me of the children. Tell me about…"

When someone stepped on him, Lau snapped into a sitting position. The guerrilla leader, who was covered with mud from head to foot stood over him.

"You are either very brave or very tired," he laughed.

Lau wiped as much of the muck off of his face as he could.

"Very tired, very tired," he said as he struggled to his feet.

The party gathered weapons and equipment from the swamp, donned their loads, and without another word, moved off toward the south. Lau again found it hard to keep up, even with the loads the others were carrying. But he found that water and the rest had refreshed him greatly.

After walking for about an hour, during which time they had to go to ground twice because of passing helicopters, they came to a tributary of the Nha Be River. The small party stopped and spread out. The leader walked up and down the bank until he found what he was searching for—a carefully hidden sampan. The twenty-foot craft was so well camouflaged that it looked like an extension of the riverbank. Someone could have stepped on it before realizing it was a boat.

The leader was already pulling back the swamp grass that covered the entrance to the boat's cabin when he signaled for the rest of the party to join him. As the others arrived, they jumped into the water to cleanse the mud from their bodies and equipment. Then they clamored into the boat. The leader pulled the swamp-grass camouflage behind him as he entered and the craft simply disappeared again.

"We must wait here until dark, then we will travel into the Rung Sat."

"What is the Rung Sat?" asked Lau.

"I thought you were familiar with our battalion's area and operations," said the leader.

"Remember, I am a political officer, concerned mostly about the correct attitudes of our fighters. I admit I do not pay as close attention as I should to tactical details."

The leader studied Lau for a moment in the half-light in the cabin. He suddenly wondered if this man were the commissar he said he was, what he might think of his own attitude this day. Since he was no threat to them—he was either who he said he was, or he was their prisoner—the leader decided to treat him as if he were the colonel he claimed to be.

"The Rung Sat is a tidal flat south of here. The tides come and go, leaving either mud or several meters of water. Since the Americans cannot patrol there, all they do is fly over in their machines. Well-camouflaged sampans operate freely there. There are groves of trees under which to hide, and open channels to take us near our bases. We use this method to bring in weapons and food. You will see, soon enough, comrade colonel."

"How soon will we get to battalion headquarters?" asked Lau.

"This group is not going to battalion headquarters, but we will arrange for a guide to take you there."

"You are most kind. And, I might say your operation today was executed flawlessly. I gather that your mission was to shoot down a helicopter," offered Lau.

"You are correct," answered the leader, silently sighing with relief.

"For some reason, the enemy fly their aircraft very low in this area. We sometimes bring an anti-aircraft weapon here to try to ambush one of them. Today we were successful."

"I am certainly glad you were. There is no doubt I would have been tortured to death in Saigon. I am grateful to you and your men. I shall mention your skill and your bravery to Major Doan."

"Thank you, comrade colonel. Now, if you are hungry, we have rice. If you are thirsty there is plenty of water. Then, we have nothing to do but sleep until dark."

Lau had never been so hungry in his life.

Phun had just returned from another liaison mission to Saigon. She had taken the bus from the capitol to Xuan Loc, changed clothes, and slipped across the rice paddies into the jungle. She had carried no documents. She had memorized all of the instructions and information she must pass to the commander of the second regiment.

Now she waited outside the crude above-ground office of the regimental commander. In the small room built at the end of a thatched and camouflaged class room, the commander of the second regiment was meeting with his staff. When he became aware of Phun's presence, he called her in.

"Well, younger sister, what news do you bring from division?"

"Comrade Colonel, all is in readiness for the general offensive. The dates, objectives, and time tables for the attacks remain unchanged. There is only one new order. The division commander orders us to cease all offensive operations on the first of December so we can devote our full energies to planning and preparing for the general offensive and popular uprising. All troops are to remain in base areas. No patrolling, no attacks, no ambushes, and no mining operations are authorized. All troops will be schooled on their objectives and tactics. You are also ordered to take your battalion and company commanders into Bien Hoa to personally reconnoiter your objectives."

The commander nodded thoughtfully. "What about my request for information about resupply points?" he asked.

"The division commander told me to inform you that you must arrange for your own logistical support. Very little in the way of resupply is anticipated since the people will be rising up and rallying to our side. If we run out of ammunition, we are ordered to pick up enemy weapons and continue to fight."

"What? We can expect no supply assistance from division? We're on our own?" What about the cache the enemy took from the C-240 battalion's area? That was nearly everything they had! It is true they are rebuilding their stocks, but how can they have all the ammunition they need by the end of January? Bringing stocks in by sampan takes time."

"That is what the commanding general said, Comrade Colonel," said Phun quietly, unnerved to have upset the regimental commander.

The colonel turned to his supply officer. "Get me the latest figures on ammunition stocks from the battalions. Tell the commanders they must keep me updated daily on their stocks and how much they are short."

"Yes, Comrade Colonel," snapped the supply officer, all too aware of the tremendous effort this mission would take, since the battalions were scattered so widely.

"Phun, get to the battalions with the order to cease all offensive operations on 1 December. Tell the battalion commanders exactly what you have told me. I know you are tired. You may rest tonight, but I want you traveling at first light."

"Yes, Comrade Colonel," Phun answered. She was glad she would have the opportunity to travel again. She was determined to go through Long Thanh to see if she could find out anything about Lau. She also wanted to stop by Huong's mother's home and tell her where her son was. She was tired—exhausted would be a better word—but tomorrow she would try to find out about Lau. For the first time since his capture, her pain and grief became hope. At least she would be doing something positive. As tired as she was, she found it difficult to go to sleep.

After a boring day at the laundry, Chi dejectedly walked through the front door of her house. With few soldiers coming in the shop, she had had hours on end to worry about Huong and to wallow in her sorrows. Hardly acknowledging Duc's young widow or the children, she made tea, then squatted in the doorway, watching the early evening traffic stream past.

As her sisters came home from work, the voices in the house blended into a sing-song prattle of gripes, woes, and small talk. The other members of the family felt Chi's pain and gave her space. Duc's widow occasionally buried her face in her hands and wailed, knowing Chi's sisters would hasten to console her. Chi remained oblivious to the monotonous swirl of evening activity as she rocked on her haunches, sipped her tea, and stared. Her thoughts drifted to the past, to a time of happiness, when her husband was alive and Duc and Huong were young and carefree. When the evening meal was ready, she ate little.

Less than a hundred meters north of Chi's house, Phun daintily climbed from the back of a lambretta, paid the driver, then joined the throng of pedestrians returning from the day's activities. Dressed in ao dia, conical hat, and sandals, she appeared to be just one more young woman heading for home this evening. Stopping short of Chi's house to adjust a sandal, she carefully looked around. Observing only the mass of humanity trying to get to safety before the start of curfew, and no police or soldiers, she made her way quickly to Chi's doorstep.

As Chi saw Phun walking toward her, she covered her mouth with her hand, spilled her tea, and fell backward into the house. The other women were stunned into silence as Chi screeched and pointed toward the door.

"Please, please, do not be threatened or offended by my presence. I seek only to inform you of your son's whereabouts," said Phun sympathetically as she stood in the doorway.

Calming slightly at the mention of Huong, Chi sobbed, "You must leave here. The last time you came, you brought disaster! My son is gone. What have you done with him? Where is he?"

"He is safe. He is doing what he wants to do. He is with friends who will protect him."

"Protect him? He will be killed by the Americans the same way Duc was. How can anyone protect him from them?"

"Please listen, Grandmother," said Phun quietly. "If he remained here, he would be drafted by the government and forced to serve in their corrupt army—a sure death sentence. As it is, he is safe in the jungles, surrounded by freedom fighters, who are committed to drive the killers of your older son from our country. Huong is young, so they will not give him dangerous responsibilities. They will watch over him and protect him."

"Where is he?" demanded Chi.

"That I cannot tell you, because I myself do not know," lied Phun. "All I can tell you is that he is safe. He told me to tell you not to worry—that he will return to you soon."

Chi's entire family was lined up in the front room staring at Phun. None of them spoke.

"It is nearing curfew. I have no place to sleep. May I spend the night with you?"

"Your being here endangers us all," said Chi. "Please go."

"With respect, Grandmother, I have come here near curfew time, after a full day of travel, to bring you news of your son. I have nowhere else to go. It would be more dangerous for us all if I were caught in the street. I am certain I was not observed as I arrived. Please allow me to sleep in your home tonight, and I will be on my way at dawn."

After a long, thoughtful silence, Chi ordered, "Get her something to eat. She can use Huong's sleeping mat since he'll not be here."

Feeling that everything in her life was beyond her control or influence, Chi threw up her hands in resignation and withdrew to her bed. At least, she thought, she knew Huong was alive.

Charlie company rolled through the main gate at Bear Cat in a great cloud of brick-red dust. The same troops who had been scared, homesick boys in the unforgiving jungles of War Zone D, whooped with manly bravado as they swept past the rear-echelon soldiers of the division base camp. Olive-drab cravats worn as bandannas over their noses transformed them into goggled and helmeted bandits. Antennas swished and engines screamed as clattering tracks shook the ground. Jupiter was coming home victorious. They had killed, and, though bloodied, had suffered no dead of their own. They were the Infantry, by God, and they wanted all REMFs to know it.

As Jace's armored personnel carriers rolled past the PX, starched and pressed headquarters troops who were ghosting from their desks looked up to watch them pass. The infantrymen hooted at the military policemen who sternly scouted the parking lot for anyone out of uniform. Some of the tracks slid sideways on the hard-packed road as they took the right turn in front of first brigade headquarters just a little too fast. Inside the clapboard building, staff officers looked up from their maps and memoranda, distracted by the whine and clatter.

A covey of replacements scattered from the road as the steel and aluminum monsters thundered toward their motor pool and their company area—the closest things to home in this country. Passing the snack bar, several troops waved to the tiny woman sitting in the door of the laundry. She did not wave back.

As the battalion motor sergeant screamed at drivers to slow the hell down, the company roared into the motor pool and skillfully lined up in their assigned places. Jubilant soldiers pulled headsets and helmets from their heads, bandannas from their faces, and flak jackets from their bodies as NCOs barked orders that no one was to go anywhere until equipment was stowed and tracks locked down. The fuel tanker had already made its way to the first track to begin the refueling as filthy, sweating teenagers jumped from their mounts.

"Give me a formation," yelled First Sergeant Baez to the platoon sergeants.

"Grab your weapons and fall in behind the tracks. Leave your rucksacks and duffel bags where they are for now," echoed the NCOs.

"FALL IN!" roared Baez over the hubbub and excitement.

Troops milled about, bumping into one another as they sorted themselves into squads and platoons. Soon they stood at attention in the blistering sun.

"AT EASE!" yelled the first sergeant. "All right, listen up. First—clear your weapons! We don't need anybody gettin' shot in base camp. Priority of work is as follows: First, lock down and secure the tracks, particularly the ammo and explosives. Second, move your personal gear to your hooches. Third, clean and turn in your personal weapons. Forth, shower, shave, and get into clean clothes. And put some polish on them scuffed out boots. Anyone without clean fatigues, report to the supply sergeant and he will DX you a set from bulk stocks. Platoon sergeants, release no one to go to the PX who does not pass your inspection. I want no pink slips given any Charlie company infantryman by a REMF M.P. for being out of uniform. Last—LAST! but not least! There is a jeep trailer full of iced-down beer and soda—and the steaks are on the grill! No one eats or drinks anything but Coke 'till the work is done. After that, kick back and raise hell, Charlie company. You deserve it. Cap'n, you have anything to say?

"No—uh—No, first sergeant," answered Jace, who was caught off-guard in an exhausted haze. "I'll have a beer with each platoon this evening and tell 'em how proud I am of 'em. Dismiss the troops."

"Yes, sir. COMPANY, Ah Tench HUT! FALL OUT!"

The scramble, shouting, and laughter began anew as each soldier clamored through the jumble of equipment to find his gear.

"Top, how in hell—where did you—" began Jace.

"Now, sir—ask me no questions and I'll bullshit you not."

"You know, it sure is good not to have to do everything myself. You sure make things look easy."

"It is easy, sir," grinned Baez. "It is easy. You've been doing the hard stuff."

Sergeant Smith skulked past dragging his duffel bag.

"Hey, First Sergeant. I need a bunk. Where'll I sleep?"

"Five India will tell you where to bed down. Oh, yes. One more thing—I want you to stay to hell away from second platoon. Your case will be handled as quickly as possible. In the mean time, I want no more trouble out of you till then. You understand?"

"Yeah, Top, sure," Smith said tiredly.

"He'll cause you no more trouble, sir. I promise you that. If it's one thing I love to handle, it's a bigoted shithead of an NCO that thinks he's better than a colored soldier or a chili-eatin' top-kick."

"I'd not want you on my case," laughed Jace.

Lieutenant Driscol walked up and saluted.

"Compliments of the battalion commander, sir. He wants you to join him for a beer as soon as you've had a shower. Seems he has some news."

"Hello XO," Jace said, extending his hand. "The support you gave us in the bush was outstanding. What's the Old Man's news? Do you know?" asked Jace.

"No, sir. But take it from a not-quite so green anymore lieutenant who's been around a little bit: Any time a commander calls folks together for news, it normally turns out not to be good."

"I think I've heard that before, if I'm not mistaken."

"Did it turn out to be true then?"

"As I remember, it did."

"Come in, Jace, and join us," called Lieutenant Colonel McKensie.

Jace squinted as he came in from the dark, the screen door banging behind him. The battalion XO, the sergeant major, C.C., and Captain Thomaston of B Company sat around McKensie's quarters, drinking beer. Although he had showered, shaved and dressed in fresh jungle fatigues, Jace remained overwhelmed by infantryman's fatigue. He desperately needed sleep, but he knew there would be none until he had paid his respects to McKensie as he had been requested to do.

"Good evening, sirs," Jace said, nodding to the two majors and the colonel. "Sergeant Major, good to see you. John, how's B company?"

"Fine Jace. I hear Chargin' charlie made a kill. Good goin'"

"Thanks—lucky, I guess."

"Sorry to hear about your lieutenant."

"Yeah, that was a tough one."

McKensie spoke as C.C. handed Jace an ice-cold Black Label: "Well, guys, this is it. I'm leaving."

"What?" stammered the XO. "I thought you had another week or so."

"So did I," answered McKensie. "The G-3 got permission from the general to go home early to watch his daughter graduate from high school. The general figured that a week wouldn't matter much one way or the other. Besides, my replacement's here and ready to go to work. The bad news is we'll only have tomorrow as overlap. The general wants me at division day after tomorrow, else I won't have any overlap at all with the G-3."

Jace was stunned. In his head he knew McKensie was leaving soon, but deep in his gut he believed—hoped, really—that the colonel wouldn't really leave.

"Who's your replacement, sir?" asked Jace.

"Lieutenant Colonel Randal Price. West Pointer, coming from the Pentagon. Served his first tour with the 101st," answered McKensie.

A paratrooper, thought Jace.

"When do we get to meet him?" asked C.C.

"First thing tomorrow morning. We'll make the rounds, meet the company commanders and staff. XO, I want a good staff briefing on logistics, personnel, intel. Sergeant Major, you will accompany us on our rounds. You be ready to answer any questions on the enlisted side. C.C. you give him a separate briefing on the AO and our current operations."

"Yes, sir," answered the two majors in unison.

"Well, I might as well give it all to you at one time. The XO is leaving too. He's going to move to assistant G-4. I'm moving Major Churchwell to XO. The A company commander, Captain Cole, will move to S-3. He's slated to be on the next major's list."

Jace was stunned again. The same captain who commanded the company that was so screwed up on the ambush mission he had observed right after he arrived? That guy would be planning operations for the whole battalion? He hoped C.C. would watch him closely. But as XO, C.C. would have to worry about administration and logistics. How could he supervise a screwed-up S-3? Draining his beer, Jace tried to put it all out of his mind. Maybe all these changes wouldn't have much effect on his company anyway. Yeah, right!

"When was the last time you slept?" asked McKensie, looking carefully at Jace.

"Near as I can figure, I caught about three hours night before last, sir."

"Son, go to bed. I give you permission to sleep late. Price and I will visit your company last, late tomorrow evening."

"Anything special I need to have ready? Dog and pony show or anything?" grinned Jace.

"Just the usual song and dance," answered McKensie.

"Then, gentlemen, I bid you goodnight," said Jace, standing.

"One more thing, Jace. Despite the trouble you had with your two NCOs, your company did an outstanding job out there."

"Thank you, sir. I'll pass that along to the troops."

"No need. I'll tell them tomorrow myself."

Jace staggered sleepily out the door and through the dark back to his company. Tomorrow, the whole world might change, but tonight he would sleep. The hollow thunder of outgoing artillery startled him as he jumped over the drainage ditch that marked the boundary of his company area. He stopped to relieve himself in one of the piss tubes that jutted from the ground beside the latrine.

As he buttoned his fly, he noticed a soldier sitting dejectedly on a sandbag wall. Walking toward him, Jace recognized Tucker.

"What're you doing out here all by yourself?" asked Jace.

As Tucker looked up, Jace saw tear streaks highlighted by the ever-present parachute flares.

"It's my girl, sir. She's pregnant, and I guess you can figure out the baby ain't mine."

Jace didn't know what to say, so he just placed his hand on the youngster's shoulder.

Tucker continued, "I wrote and told her it didn't matter to me. I'd keep the baby as my own if she just wouldn't leave me."

"Is that her answer you're reading?" asked Jace.

"Yeah. She says she loves the guy and is gonna marry him."

Jace stood in the dark with his hand on Tucker's shoulder for a long moment. Neither of them spoke.

"Is there anything I can do?" Jace finally asked.

"No, sir, ain't nothin' anybody can do," said Tucker, wiping his eyes.

"At times like this, people like me always tell people like you that there are other fish in the sea. You really loved her, didn't you?"

"Still do. Always will. Ain't no other fish for me?"

"You aren't going to do anything stupid are you?" asked Jace.

"What do you mean?" replied Tucker.

"I mean you aren't going to hurt yourself or anything, are you?"

"Oh. No, sir. Don't worry about me. I'll be all right."

"If you need to talk, you know where I am," said Jace.

"Yes, sir. I think I'll just go to bed. I'm awful tired."

"Me too. Good night, Tucker."

"Good night, sir."

Continuing toward his hootch, Jace caught snatches of murmurs and sharp laughter from his relaxing soldiers.

"If I caught anything, I caught it from yo' damn mama!"

"Man, I'm too short for this shit."

"Look here, man, I so damn short I can't see over the tops o' my boots."

"You think you short, Man? I only got twenny-three days and a wake-up."

"Yeah, man—I can't wait fo' the duffel-bag drag."

"I tell you, I'm looking her up soon 's I get home. All I been thinkin' about the whole time I been over here was the last time I was with her."

The soft strains of a Smokey Robinson tune told him where the blacks had gathered. A Beatles song came from the college boys' area. The rednecks were gathered in another tent listening to Buck Owens. The Puerto Ricans had gathered near the mess hall where they rapped in Spanish and banged out Latin rhythms on empty oil drums.

Jace remembered that he had told his soldiers that he would have a beer with each platoon. He should have realized that they wouldn't be in platoons—that they would drift to the friends they were comfortable with. Although he was bone tired, Jace kept his promise as best he could. He ate a steak with the African-American soldiers. He had a beer with the country boys as they talked rodeo. He watched as a young Puerto Rican did an outrageous dance to a hot Latin tune blasting from a phonograph. He thought he caught a whiff of marijuana smoke at the Beatles gathering. After warning them he had better not catch anyone smoking the weed, he joined them for one last beer. As he dragged himself toward his cot, he ran into First Sergeant Baez, standing sober in the middle of the company street, silently watching everything.

"Go to sleep, sir. Please! Don't worry, I'm watching."

"I know you are, Top. Thanks. Look, the colonel and his replacement are coming by tomorrow afternoon."

"Yeah, I heard," answered Baez.

"You might want to make sure everything is policed up. I have permission to sleep late. Let the troops do the same. There should be plenty of time to clean everything up by the time they get here. Oh, yes. Keep an eye on Tucker. He just got a dear-john from his girl. He's awful down."

"Yes, sir, I will."

"And something else—"

"Captain, if you say another word, I swear on my Spanish-speaking mother's sacred head I will knock you out and carry you to your bunk."

Jace started to answer, then grinned and walked toward his hootch again. This time he made it all the way to his bed.

Jace slept the sleep of the dead. It was well past noon when First Sergeant Baez came to wake him.

"Time, sir. The colonel will be here in a while. Better roll out. You might want to look around the area. Here, I brought you a cup of coffee."

Slowly, Jace came awake.

"OK, Top—OK. I've got to get a briefing ready anyway. Thanks for letting me sleep."

"The rest of the time I'm your first sergeant, me and you are going to fix it so's you get all the rest you need. You can't function in a fire fight if you're asleep on your feet."

"First Sergeant, I swear you're gonna spoil me."

"My momma worked as a nursemaid—I can't help it."

Jace dragged himself out of bed and stopped at the piss tube on the way to the shower. The cold water from the tank over the bath stalls jolted him awake. After shaving and finishing his coffee, he flapped back to his hootch in his shower clogs. He found that his only clean set of jungle fatigues were wrinkled and his jungle boots were scuffed red-brown. He knocked the dust off of his jump boots he had left under his cot and finished dressing.

The sun was bright and hot when he walked to the orderly room. No evidence of last night's party was left. The entire company area was as clean and neat as his company area back at Fort Bragg. Even the troops who had looked like Ali Babba's forty thieves yesterday afternoon were clean-shaven and shined today.

In his small office, Jace began to organize his thoughts for the briefing he would give the new colonel. He guessed that authorized versus actual personnel strength, equipment status, leadership, and recent operations would suffice. He didn't want to sound as if he were bragging, but his company's record since he had taken command was pretty good, he thought.

"Top, give me our latest strength figures, if you would. Five India, put me a map of our operation in War Zone D on the wall. Put our routes, phase lines, and AOs on it. Also, I'll need a pointer. Tucker, get me another cup of coffee—and see if you can round me up a sandwich of some sort."

Lieutenant Colonel McKensie was correct when he said that Charlie company would be the last on the list to visit today. Dusk was gathering when he and the new battalion commander arrived.

"TENCH HUT!" thundered Baez as the two colonels and the battalion sergeant major entered the orderly room. Jace saluted and reported. The tall paratroop colonel towered over McKensie's slightly lumpy frame. Square-jawed, wide shouldered and fit, Price exuded confidence. He wore starched jungle fatigues, spit-shined jungle boots, a camouflaged scarf, and sun glasses. Jace ignored all these accouterments and cut his eyes to Price's chest. A pair of novice parachutist's wings were the only decoration above the U.S. Army patch over his heart—no Combat Infantryman's Badge. A black, yellow and white screaming eagle patch adorned his right shoulder, emblematic of his first-tour combat service with the 101st Airborne Division. The rest of the patches on his fatigues were embroidered with black thread—only the Screaming Eagle was brightly colored. Fleetingly, Jace took in the miniature compass on Price's watch band and the huge Gerber fighting knife on his left hip.

Baez guided the two colonels to folding chairs, handed them cold cokes, then nodded to Jace.

"Sir, I am prepared to brief you on our present company status and our recent operations."

"First," said McKensie, "let me tell you what will happen tomorrow morning. We will have a formal change of command at 0800 in the HHC company street. Since your troops are the only ones here, they will stand to for the ceremony. We don't need a rehearsal—just have them in mass formation in steel pots—no weapons. I'll pass the flag to Colonel Price. The whole thing should take only a few minutes."

"Yes, sir," responded Jace.

Colonel Price nodded imperceptibly, the army-wide signal to begin a briefing. In relaxed, conversational tones, Jace told the new battalion commander everything he should need to know about C company. Besides the company's current situation, Jace briefed anticipated personnel losses and the morale status. When he finished, he asked if there were any questions.

"This is the company that has the racial problem, isn't it?" asked Price.

Jace, Baez, and McKensie all turned to look at him.

"Sir, we don't have a racial problem in this company. We had an incident which was addressed as soon as it happened. Action was taken that I believe will preclude any further incidents."

As if he had heard nothing Jace had said, Price continued, "We cannot afford any racial strife in this battalion. We all know what happened in the states this last summer. We simply cannot have racial problems here."

"I totally agree," said Jace. "As I said, I believe this incident has been taken care of."

"We'll see," sniffed Price.

An awkward silence followed.

Sensing that something needed to be said, Jace asked, "Are there any other questions, sir?"

"I understand you are on a three-day cooling off stand-down after the racial incident. When do you feel you will be combat effective again?"

"Sir, we are combat effective right now. As for why we are having a stand-down—I assume it was to give the troops a much-needed rest after a very arduous operation."

McKensie interrupted, "The purpose of the stand down is for rest and reorganization. Jace had to make some leadership changes and it made sense to sort them out here instead of in the field."

Price nodded slowly as he looked Jace up and down.

"A ranger and a senior parachutist, huh?" he asked.

"Yes, sir," answered Jace.

"Where did you do your jumping?"

"Eighty Second, sir. Fort Bragg."

"Ah, yes. The Almost-Airborne. I happen to believe there is only one airborne division—the One-0-First."

"A fine unit, sir. Where did you serve with them during your first tour?"

"I was assistant G-5."

Baez, standing behind the two colonels, rolled his eyes.

Not knowing what else to do, Jace said, "Sir, this completes my briefing."

"Next time, some charts would be useful when explaining personnel strength," offered Price.

"Yes, sir," answered Jace as he felt himself getting angry.

Seeming to sense Jace's darkening mood, McKensie stood up.

"First Sergeant, would you show us around the company area?"

"Yes, sir," answered Baez as he grabbed his fatigue cap.

"You can continue what you were doing here, Jace," instructed McKensie, who appeared to be establishing the fact that until tomorrow, he still commanded the battalion. "Your first sergeant can guide us."

"Yes, sir." responded Jace stiffly, as he offered his hand to Price. "Welcome aboard, Colonel. Looking forward to serving under you, sir."

As Price shook Jace's hand, he said, "Next time you give a formal briefing, a little press on your fatigues and a little Kiwi on your boots might present a better image."

"Yes, sir, Colonel. I'll work on that," replied Jace.

As the party left the orderly room, Jace grabbed the field phone and cranked the handle forcefully.

"Hello, S-1? Is Major Churchwell there? I need to talk to him!"

CHAPTER 11

▼

2 November 1967

The sergeant major took the battalion's flag from the color bearer, did an about face and handed it to Lieutenant Colonel McKensie. McKensie turned and offered the colors to the brigade commander, who quietly said a few words of congratulations for a job well done. The brigade colonel faced about and presented the flag to Price, who grasped the staff with both hands. Price stood impatiently while the brigade commander congratulated him on his new command, then practically jerked the flag from the colonel's hands, did a half-right face, and gave the flag back to the sergeant major. After the flag was back in its place in the color guard, Jace ordered parade rest as McKensie stepped aside. Price, in a loud, forceful voice, began his first address to the soldiers of the 5-39 Infantry.

"As I assume command of this proud battalion, I can't and I won't guarantee you anything. But I do have a promise for you. We will pursue the Viet Cong guerrilla to hell itself if necessary to be victorious. We will not pause, we will not rest, we will not give up until this country is free of the communist scourge."

Standing in front of his company, Jace kept his eyes on Lieutenant Colonel McKensie. As Price spoke, McKensie bowed his head and quickly swiped at an eye with his thumb.

When the troops were dismissed, many of them surrounded McKensie, wishing him luck, shaking his hand, patting his back. Some just wanted to reach out and touch him. They knew they were losing a friend and an advocate. They ignored Price. Only the officers stepped up to welcome him to the battalion.

Price said, "There will be a command and staff meeting at 1600 at the TOC at Fire Base Cougar. I will send my chopper for you, Captain Spencer. I will have nothing for you until that time." He then hurried after the brigade commander, who was leaving. After saluting, Jace turned and hailed Colonel McKensie.

"Sir, if you are not in a hurry, I would like to ask you to have a cup of coffee."

"Jace, I've got to go straight to division. I tell you what. Meet me at the club later and we'll have a drink instead."

"Yes, sir," replied Jace.

Jace would not see him again for two months.

A parachute flare hung over the jungle beyond Bear Cat's berm, lighting the ground like a candle lights a dark room. Distant crumps of artillery and drones of far-away aircraft kept the night from being still. Jace, First Sergeant Baez, and Five India sat in the dark on the sandbag wall surrounding one of the tents in C company's area. Five India's face briefly turned luminescent red as he took a deep drag on his cigarette. Baez slapped a mosquito.

"What did you think?" asked Jace.

"'Bout what?" asked Baez.

"You know damn well what—the new colonel!"

"Oh, him. You really want me to tell you?"

"Yeah," answered Jace, "that's why I asked."

"Off the record?" countered Baez?

"What record? Hell, it's just us. Tell me what you thought."

Baez grinned and cocked his head. "Hand me another brew and I might."

"Dammit, Top!"

"OK, OK. Looked like a freakin' Saigon cowboy to me. No CIB, starched and shined. Looks good. Too damn good."

"What did he do during the walk-through?" queried Jace.

"Funniest thing, he never said one word to a soldier. Talked to Colonel McKensie, the sergeant major, and me, but never looked at a troop."

They all sat quietly for a time.

"Grass cutter," said Five India.

"Come again," said Jace.

"Grass cutter."

"What d'you mean?" asked Baez.

"Just a local Fort Dix derogatory term, I guess. I was in the admin company there. Had three different captains during my tour. One was good—really cared for the guys. Other two were grass cutters."

"Meaning?"

"All they cared about was what things looked like. You know, if the area was policed, the rocks painted, the grass cut. Troops could be plotting a mutiny and the C.O. wouldn't know it as long as the grass was cut."

"Well," said Jace, "loyalty is the cornerstone of a unit. We owe him a chance. I've been wrong on first impressions before. Maybe he's O.K."

"He was in G-5 his first tour. You know where I heard he worked in the pentagon?" drawled Baez?

"Well, don't keep us in suspense," ordered Jace.

"Public Affairs. Press relations."

"Shit," replied Five India.

"If he went to command and staff at Leavenworth before his first tour, that makes—what—four, five years since he last smelled sweat?" Jace thought aloud.

"If you really think about it, how much impact can he have on us as long as we do our jobs?" asked Baez.

"I'll make a prediction," offered Five India. "An educated prediction from watching grass cutters for two years."

"Go ahead," said Jace.

"You can depend on him to project a good image upward. Remember Captain Wilson?"

Jace shuttered. "Don't talk about the dead."

"Just remember my prediction," said Five India. "Won't matter much to me. I'm short. I go home in a month. But you guys better pay attention."

"Jace turned and looked at Five India as if seeing him for the first time. I didn't realize you were that short. What the hell will I do without you."

"Sir, if you haven't thought about it, it's time you did. We're coming up on a year since the division arrived in country. Over three-fourths of the company will DEROS within the next 45 days." said Five India.

"I know I knew that, but until you said you were leaving, I guess I hadn't put meaning to it."

"That's right, sir," chimed in Baez. "The XO, three platoon leaders, three platoon sergeants, and most of the squad leaders. Your point man, Johnson will be staying, but lots of the old regulars, like Super Private and Tucker will be gone."

"No, Top. Not Tucker," said Five India. "I typed up a 1049 for him today—a request for a six-month extension. He said he's so upset over his girl that there's no way he can go home."

"Put him somewhere safe, out of harm's way, then," said Jace.

"No, sir. He specified that he wanted to stay in his current position."

They sipped quietly for a time.

"It's funny, Colonel McKensie's leaving caught me by surprise, even though I knew it was going to happen. Look, Top, get me a list of everybody who is due to leave in the next couple of months. I need to look at what we will have left in terms of experience and leadership."

"Yes, sir. I'll have it on your desk in the morning."

"I just keep thinking about what Colonel McKensie said when he told me he was leaving the battalion," said Jace.

"What?"

"That the day after he left, everything would be different. I guess I was too dumb to know what he meant."

At the edge of the C-240 battalion headquarters complex, sentries warily peered from bunkers to see who was calling the password from down the trail. After several tense moments, a small party of travelers was escorted to the command bunker.

"Comrade Colonel Lau! We thought you were captured—or dead," shouted the battalion commander.

"I came very close, Major Doan," said Lau. "I would like to tell you the whole story, but first I must rest. Would you allow me to eat and sleep before I am debriefed? My companions are also tired and hungry."

"Of course, colonel. Sergeant! Take the colonel to a bed. Bring him food at once. You men. You know where to find something to eat. Thank you for bringing Colonel Lau to us."

The gaunt guerrillas bowed and left.

"Is there anything important I must know?" asked Lau.

"Yes, Comrade Colonel. A liaison runner came through this morning to tell us that we have been ordered to cease all operations beginning the first day of December—to prepare for the coming operation that you are familiar with. You must recuperate from your ordeal quickly. I would suppose that there is much political work to be done."

Lau wanted desperately to ask if anyone had seen Phun. But knowing that personal relationships were frowned upon in the National Liberation Front, he kept quiet.

"I must return to regimental headquarters as soon as possible," he said.

"We will make arrangements. First, you must regain your strength. If possible, I will send word to regiment that you are alive and well."

"Thank you for your kindness."

After Lau was taken to a stream to wash, a medic dressed his cuts and scratches and gave him a shot of antibiotic. Then he was given a generous bowl of rice and a cup of hot tea and taken to a bed in a deep bunker. He had eaten only two bites of rice when he fell asleep.

When he awoke, he had no idea where he was our how long he had been asleep. Still stiff and groggy, he climbed out of the bunker and relieved himself. Realizing that he was still extremely hungry, he wandered about the camp in search of food.

"Ah, Comrade Colonel Lau," the voice said from behind him.

"I trust you slept well?" It was the battalion commander, Major Doan.

"Yes, thank you. I feel much better today," replied Lau.

"If you are hungry, I will have rice brought to you."

"Yes, I am starving!"

"A good sign. How are your wounds?"

Lau felt the itch around the cut on his side.

"I have the sensation that the largest cut is beginning to heal. The others are not worthy of mention. The shot must be taking effect."

"Good. Now eat. When you feel up to it, you can tell us what happened to you."

"Thank you. I can never repay your kindness. As soon as possible, maybe as early as tomorrow, I would like to go to regimental headquarters. There is much I need to do."

Lau did not mention that the main thing he wanted to do was to find Phun.

"That can be arranged," answered Doan. "I suggest strongly that you travel the jungle trails. Since you were captured on the roadways, you might be recognized. A healthy man could easily walk from here to regiment through the jungles in a day. Given your condition, you might consider a two day trip. We will give you the location of a camp that is about half way," said the battalion commander."

"I will plan to make it in one day. If I feel I must rest, I will take your advice, thank you."

"Guards and guides will be sent with you. I cannot spare many. They will stay at regiment until someone has a need for them to return—and my numbers are low already."

"A couple of guides will suffice," said Lau. "If we encounter the enemy on the way, we do not plan to fight, anyway."

"Very good. You can leave at first light tomorrow. Now, please eat, then we will talk. Then you must get more rest."

After leaving the C-240 battalion headquarters, Phun walked out to Binh Son, where an old man waited to take her to Highway 15 on a motor bike. She planned to take a bus or lambretta to Phouc Le, where she would meet guides to take her to the C-80 battalion.

She stood in the market place in Binh Son. Wearing a fresh *ao dai*, she looked like an innocent school girl or a young wife. The old man was tightening the chain on the motor bike while he talked non-stop. She wasn't listening—mind was far away.

After finding no trace or word of Lau in Long Thanh, she felt tremendously depressed. It was not fair, she thought, to find a true love, then lose him in such a short time. It was probably best to put him out of her mind forever. By concentrating on her work, by requesting more responsibility, and by becoming even more fanatical about the cause, she would try to sweep Lau from her memory. Wartime was no time for romance or marriage, anyway. Perhaps she would arrange for a transfer. Perhaps she would stop being a liaison officer and become a fighter. Danger might serve her well, now.

She wondered how Huong was doing. When she had stopped at C-240, he was out on an operation with his platoon. She left word to give her regards to the boy. She thought about his mother and how the Americans had turned her life upside down. She felt sorry for the woman at one level. At another, more practical level, she wondered if Chi could be turned into an agent to fight the Americans. After having one son killed and another to join the Viet Cong, she might be a prime recruiting candidate. She would be a very useful asset since she worked inside the American base.

The motor bike was ready now. The old man motioned and bowed. After he had started the machine, she climbed on behind him and they were off. She wondered if she would ever see Binh Son again. Fate, she thought. She would turn herself over to whatever fate would bring. She would take one day at a time and make no plans. And she would try not to think of Lau.

The last day of Charlie company's stand-down was chaotic. The troops were allowed to sleep in as the leaders jumped through a variety of hoops. Despite the hub-bub, Jace found time to go to division G-5 and make arrangements for replacing the water buffalo that Munn had shot. He wrote a letter of apology to the village chief explaining that a soldier had wrongfully shot the beast and had been punished for it. The assistant G-5 assured Jace that the letter would be translated and read aloud when the buffalo was delivered to Tan Uen.

Jace and his company were being ordered to Fire Base Cougar. Alpha company would take to the bush this time, searching Base Area 302, east of Highway Two. Bravo company remained at Binh Son. An entire battalion from the 199th Light Infantry Brigade now searched War Zone D for rocket-launch sites.

Jace sat at his desk in his small office adjacent to the orderly room. He reflected on last night's command and staff meeting at Fire Base Cougar. He had had to call C.C. to arrange for the H-23 to pick him and Bravo Six up and fly them to Cougar. It seems that Price had forgotten to send the chopper. The meeting was an hour-long speech from Price about how screwed up the battalion was and how he aimed to fix it.

Before noon, a skinny, scared-looking second lieutenant named Jeffers knocked and reported to Jace. As one of his last acts as battalion commander, Lieutenant Colonel McKensie, who was always true to his word, had arranged for a new officer to replace Lieutenant Nevin in second platoon. Jace moved Lieutenant Otis back to weapons platoon and spent an hour briefing the new man on his duties.

Jace had moved the massive losses and replacements that would happen in December to the front of his priority list. As he poured over the list of leaders and troops that would remain in country after Christmas, he realized that his whole chain of command would soon be different. He hoped the new leaders would be good ones. He also realized that he would have to train the new men. That would be a burden—training while continuing to operate at normal pace.

While Jace mulled over his company status in his office, Staff Sergeant Munn was moving in to S-4. He learned from the S-4 captain that he would be the chief operator in getting supplies to the companies. The S-4 would be at Cougar most of the time, planning the logistical support of the battalion and coordinating with the rest of the staff. Munn was pleased to learn that he and the support platoon would shove the supplies forward from Bear Cat. He may have to work hard all day, but the nights offered time for two of his favorite pastimes—drinking and gambling.

Munn sat in a folding chair in the S-4 shop as Sergeant Breath walked in.

"Let's go to the PX," said Smith.

"I don't need nothin' from the PX. 'Sides, I'll be here full time and I can go any time I want."

"Come on," begged Smith. "I don't want to go by myself."

"What's the matter? You 'fraid you'll run into one of the niggers from second platoon? 'Fraid you'll get yore ass whupped?"

"Ah ain't 'fraid o' none-a them bastards. Just want some company, that's all."

"OK, but I ain't a-walkin'," said Munn.

"How's else we gonna get there?"

"You jus' tag along behind old Sergeant Munn."

The pair walked out of the S-4 shop, crossed one of the roads that criss-crossed Bear Cat, jumped a drainage ditch and entered the motor pool.

"Just pick a jeep," said Munn.

"They's all locked up," answered Smith.

"That's one of the small privileges when you're in S-4," grinned Munn. "I got a master key."

"Then, let's take one of Charlie company's," urged Smith. "They 'bout the only ones here."

"How 'bout the first sergeant's? He don't go nowheres anyhow. Always got his wet-back nose up the captain's ass."

Munn searched his key ring, found the series master key, and unlocked the vehicle. The pair jumped in and roared off in a cloud of dust.

At the PX, they took their time walking the isles, looking at the usual writing paper, tobacco, candy and novelty items.

"Might as well get a couple cartons o' cigarettes," suggested Munn.

"I got plenty," said Smith.

Outside, the M.P.s were roaming the parking lot writing delinquency reports for soldiers who did not have name tags sewn on their uniforms. A soldier from Jace's company was objecting vehemently as he was being written up.

"We just come in from the field. I ain't got no fatigues with name tags on 'em any more. They got tore up. Either that or they rotted off. You tellin' me I can't come in from the field and come to the PX without gettin' wrote up? That'll mean an article 15! Ain't nothing' in the damn PX anyway. All you REMF assholes buy everything up. The damn infantry ain't got no chance."

Munn and Smith pulled their hats down over their eyes and, avoiding the M.P.s, made their way to the jeep. As they walked up to the vehicle, an M.P. appeared.

"This your jeep?" he asked, sternly.

Munn cut his eyes to the padlock swinging freely from the steering wheel. He had forgotten to lock it. He thought fast.

"No, man, this ain't my jeep. I'm in battalion S-4. This vehicle b'longs to C company. I just seen it was unlocked and I thought I'd better lock it," lied Munn.

"Well, whoever left it unlocked is gonna pay."

Just then Private Williams, the rehab transfer from A company, walked out of the PX. Peoples was with him.

"There! That's the two I seen drive this vehicle up here. We wuz walkin' up the road and they damn near run over us!" shouted Munn.

"You two! Get your asses over here," shouted the M.P.

Surprised, the pair of young African-American soldiers cautiously approached the jeep.

"You left this vehicle unlocked. I gotta write you up. Lemme see your driver's license and I.D. cards."

"I wudden drivin' nothin'," said Williams.

"Me neither, said Peoples."

Munn pointed at Williams. He figured he wouldn't run afoul of Peoples again. His buddy Howell was too big and too mean.

"He'uz the one drivin'"

"Yeah, I seen 'um too," agreed Smith. "It'uz that'n a-drivin'."

"Come on, let me see your license and I.D."

"Here's my I.D. card. I ain't got no driver's license."

The M.P. beamed. A double whammy. Driving without a license and misappropriation of a government vehicle. This would be bigger than a D.R. He would formally arrest these two.

"Get in my vehicle. Sarge, would you mind driving this vehicle back to where it belongs?"

"No problem," laughed Munn. "Be glad to."

As before, Jace sent his XO and Five India as an advanced party ahead of the company. They bounced into Fire Base Cougar and drove directly to the TOC, where they found Lieutenant Colonel Price sitting in a folding chair reading a paperback.

"Sir, we are the advanced party for C company. We need to know the sector we will occupy," said Lieutenant Driscol.

"Don't bother me with that crap," said Price. "Go find the headquarters commandant. He'll tell you where to go."

Driscol and Five India walked around the entire perimeter looking for the headquarters company commander. Finally, they found him, asleep in a hammock stretched between two tracks.

"Hey, sir, where do you want Charlie company to fill in on the line?" asked Driscol.

Sitting up and rubbing his eyes, the captain said, "Look, I'm responsible for the TOC and the rest of the headquarters. The perimeter line is the responsibility of the S-3."

Driscol and Five India walked back to the TOC. Finding Captain Cole, the new S-3, they asked where their company should go.

"Nobody told me a damn thing about sectors," said Cole, scratching his head. I better ask the colonel.

Driscol and Five India stood aside as Cole bent and exited the 577.

"Sir, where do you want me to put C company in?" he asked.

Whirling, Price stormed, "Look, I already told you two that the headquarters commandant would place you. Why are you bothering my S-3? Now get the hell out of here."

Having seen all that had transpired, C.C. motioned Five India outside.

"Sir, we just need to find out—"

"I know," said C.C. gently. "The new colonel just hasn't learned how we do things. I'll show you where to pull in. We just need to get the scout platoon to pull off line. They'll be going on a road-runner tonight and they might as well circle up in reserve right now. You guys will have the whole perimeter. I'll go tell Scout Six."

Driscol and Five India looked at each other and shook their heads.

"Somehow you might inform the new commander that the headquarters commandant only has responsibility for the battalion headquarters. That he doesn't have any authority to tell the line companies anything," said Five India.

C.C. removed his steel pot and rubbed his hand through his crew cut.

"I know," he said. "I'll just add that to my list of things to educate him on."

As C.C. hurried off to get the scout platoon to move off line, the first of Jace's tracks pulled off of Highway 1 onto Firebase Cougar's access road. The company had to sit on their tracks in the sun as the scout platoon moved into reserve inside the perimeter.

"What the hell is taking so long?" Jace asked Five India.

"I'll tell you later, if that's OK, sir. It'll take a while to explain."

Lau awoke early. He was anxious to get started to regiment, ostensibly to get back to work, but realistically, to find Phun. He had breakfast, then went to the medic, who changed the bandages on his cuts and gave him another antibiotic shot. He found the battalion commander and thanked him again for his kindness and hospitality.

"I have arranged for five men to guide and protect you," said Major Doan. "Here is a rifle and ammunition for you. As usual, these men will stay at regiment until there is a reason for them to return. Unnecessary travel on the jungle trails is dangerous. They should be joining us at any min—"

"Comrade Lau!" a voice shouted.

Turning, Lau looked into Huong's beaming face.

"What are you doing here, younger brother?"

Huong embraced Lau unashamedly. "After you were detained, Phun and I were caught in a battle at Binh Son. We came here to avoid the fighting. I have joined this battalion."

Now, he had an excuse to ask. "And where is Phun?"

"She left. She had other duties." said Huong.

"She was the liaison runner who brought word about going into hiding on December first," said Major Doan.

Just missed her! thought Lau. How close they had come. Where was she now?

Turning to Major Doan, Lau said, "This is the first fighter I recruited. He helped Phun and me escape from Long Thanh. If it is possible, can I keep him with me? I have much to do and I could use an orderly."

"It might be good for you to take him to regiment with you." said Doan. "We are too close to his mother's home. He might be tempted to run home to her. Yes, please take him. Although we are short-handed, one soldier will not make a great deal of difference. He is brave. I understand he has already made a kill."

Huong beamed. "Do you mean I can stay with you, Comrade Colonel?"

"Yes, it does," said Lau. "Now let us prepare. We have a long way to go."

"May I be excused for one moment?" asked Huong. "I must return to my platoon area—I have forgotten something."

"Yes, but hurry. We must be on our way," said Lau.

Huong jogged back down the narrow foot path to the bunker he had occupied with his mates. From the corner, he scooped up the remainder of his belongings, and most importantly, his handcuffs and key.

Life on the fire base was a mixed blessing for Jace. On one hand, his company was scattered to the four winds, escorting convoys, doing road-runners and squad and platoon-sized patrols, ambushing, and guarding the perimeter. On the other hand, for him personally, life had improved. He was actually catching up on some of the sleep he had missed in War Zone D.

"I've been watching how this outfits operates," Baez had said when the company returned to Cougar. "You monitor the radios, go to meetings or out on operations all day and you walk the perimeter half the night. You never sleep. From now on, I want you in bed at night. I'll walk the perimeter. I can get the morning report and the rest of the admin done in about two hours in the morning, then I can sleep during the day. That way you'll be rested enough to command this company the right way."

Jace hadn't argued. He was exhausted and he knew it. He thanked God for sending Baez his way.

It was a violently hot afternoon as Jace walked the perimeter, making sure the guards behind the .50s were alert. Then he walked to the TOC. Another benefit of fire base duty was that he could visit C.C. any time he wanted.

"How do you like being XO?" asked Jace as he dropped his helmet to the ground.

"Not much change. Now I get to worry about the whole staff, not just the S-3 shop."

Lowering his voice, Jace asked, "How's the new boss?"

C.C. hesitated for a moment, looking around.

"Different. We all just got to learn what's important to him. Damn if I can figure it out, though."

"The TOC looks neater," observed Jace.

"Yeah, that's one thing. He's a stickler for how things look. He's got the sergeant major scurrying around worrying about policing up."

"I haven't heard much out of him in the way of operational guidance," said Jace. "Haven't seen him walk the perimeter or visit the troops the way Colonel McKensie used to do. I haven't even heard his voice on the battalion net."

C.C. nervously lowered his voice.

"Well, we owe him our loyalty," he said. "Things may be different, but he's the commander. Ours is but to do or die."

"I wish you wouldn't say that," chuckled Jace, nervously. "Might be bad luck."

"Then I take it back," said C.C., hoping that it was possible to take something back once it had been said.

Just then, a Huey chattered in for a landing on the helipad. The crew threw off mail bags, boxes of repair parts, and the beat-up brief case used to ferry paperwork to and from battalion rear. Mechanics hurried to the pad to retrieve the repair parts as the mail clerks began to sort through the gray sacks. The S-1 clerk grabbed the brief case and carried it into the TOC.

"Let's see what glad tidings come from Bear Cat," said C.C. as he took the satchel from the clerk. "Looks like the same old crap. Uh-oh! Here's some bad news for Charlie company. Two D.R.s."

"Oh, great," moaned Jace. "Just what I need. What are they for?"

"One for being out of uniform at the PX and one for leaving a vehicle unlocked and driving without a license. This one looks serious," said C.C.

"My policy is for all such violators to receive mandatory Article 15s." It was Lieutenant Colonel Price. Jace and C.C. had no idea he was around, much less listening to their conversation. "We can't have troops going wild at Bear Cat. Makes the whole battalion look bad."

"Yes, sir," answered Jace and C.C. in unison.

Even in the heat of the day, Price looked cool and comfortable in his starched jungle fatigues and spit-shined boots. Jace was suddenly self-conscious in his wrinkled and sweat-stained battle dress and scuffed boots.

"Well, I'd better get back to the company. See you later, sir—afternoon, Colonel." C.C. clapped Jace on the back as he left. Without further word, Price turned and walked away. As he walked across the fire base toward his command post, Jace had the feeling that nothing seemed right—nothing felt familiar.

"Go find me private Williams in third platoon. He's going to get an Article 15. And get this other guy too," said Jace, handing Five India the pink slips. "And make sure the word gets out that the new colonel's policy is for all uniform violations at the PX in Bear Cat to get automatic Article 15s."

Holding his helmet against his chest, Williams cautiously entered Jace's command tent.

"You wanted to see me, Suh?"

"Yes, Private Williams. Looks like I'm going to have to give you another Article 15."

"But Cap'n, I never—"

"Don't say anything until I have read you your rights."

Jace knew the Miranda rights by heart, but he took the card from his wallet and began reading. Williams stood staring straight ahead, sweat beading on his ebony forehead.

"You are charged with driving without a license, misappropriation of a government vehicle, and disobeying a direct order to lock all unattended vehicles. You have 24 hours to think over the charges. You may consult with an attorney during this time if you wish. (Where in hell could he find a lawyer on this fire base, thought Jace.) You may choose to accept or you may refuse punishment under Article 15 of the Uniform Code of Military Justice. If you feel you are not guilty of these charges, you may refuse the Article 15, and choose trial by court-martial. Do you understand?"

"Suh, I don' need no twenny fo' hours. I ain't done nothin'.

All's I did was to walk up to the PX. Me an' Peoples. We got permission 'fore we went. We come out and this M.P. yelled fo' us to come over to him. Sergeant Munn and Smiff wuz standin' there wif th' M.P. Said we had left the vehicle unlocked. Said we had drove it. Ax Peoples. We walked up there."

Jace was quiet for a moment. Munn and Smith. Something was rotten, all right.

"O.K. Tucker, go to second platoon and get Peoples. I need to talk to him."

"Suh, I gits one mo' Article 15, I gits a dishonorable discharge. Never git no job then. I swear, I never done nuthin.'"

Jace looked at the young man differently since Munn's and Smith's names had come up.

"Just don't worry right now. Let me get to the bottom of this. If you are not guilty of anything, you'll not be punished."

Peoples came and verified Williams' story. The other soldier came, had his rights and charges read, then left. Jace walked up the ramp of the track and sat down on the board seat inside. It did not take much intelligence to figure this one out. Munn and Smith had taken the vehicle, left it unlocked, and when caught, blamed it on the first two Charlie company soldiers they saw. The only trouble was that it was Munn and Smith against Williams and Peoples. The word of two NCOs against two privates. Two white NCOs against two black troops. How could he prove Williams was innocent?

At Two Field Force Headquarters at Long Binh, the defector stood rigidly before a map. A recent deserter from the 274th Viet Cong Battalion, he was helping the Army of the Republic of Vietnam and the Americans.

The interpreter asked, "Can you locate your battalion headquarters on this map?"

"No, I cannot," the *hoi chan* answered. I was never at our battalion headquarters. Our platoon camp is where I stayed. But I did travel to regimental headquarters once. I have never seen a map like this."

"Alright, here is Bien Hoa, Here is the American base at Long Binh—here is where we are right now—this is Highway 1, and here is Xuan Loc. Does that help you?"

The former guerrilla again studied the map.

"Can you estimate where your regimental headquarters was?" asked the interpreter.

"That would be easier. Once, members of my platoon and I escorted a dignitary from Xuan Loc to regiment. It took about two hours to walk there through the jungle. I think we traveled more to the south. The sun was to our right front in the afternoon."

"How far could your platoon travel in an hour?"

"I am sorry, but I cannot tell you. As I have said, I simply followed the others. I can tell you this, we did not travel fast—we moved very carefully, so I believe we did not go far."

"Who was the dignitary?" asked the American intelligence officer through the interpreter.

"I did not learn his name, but he was a high-ranking political officer, newly assigned from the north."

"Thank you," said the interpreter, "You have been most helpful."

"Look at this, sir," said the S-2. We have two agent reports, both rated B-1 or better, plus the word of a *hoi chan* defector that puts the second regiment headquarters of the 5th V.C. division somewhere south-west of Xuan Loc.

Lieutenant Colonel Price stood silently, nodding.

"Sir, if I may make a suggestion," offered C.C.. "We have three different indicators that something is there. Let's request an infra-red mission to see if we can pick up camp fires under the trees. Also a people-sniffer mission might pick up ammonia from their urine."

"I heard those people-sniffers are not very reliable," said Price.

"May not be, but if all these indicators coincide, we may have ourselves a regimental headquarters," countered C.C.

"Alright, order the missions," said Price. "A regimental headquarters would be a nice feather in our cap, wouldn't it."

C.C. nodded to the S-2, who turned away to begin his requests.

"Yes, sir," agreed C.C., "A right nice feather."

Lau and his party made it all the way to regimental headquarters in one day. Although he had thought he was not physically up to a twenty-mile march, his desire to find Phun pushed him to the limit.

Lau was not sure how he felt about Huong being a guerrilla. Although his platoon commander was pleased with his performance so far, he seemed too young to be a fighter. Lau had a selfish, almost fatherly pride in his first recruit. Plus, he was pleased at how Huong seemed to be ecstatic at being his orderly. In a way it was like having another son with him. Watching Huong go about straightening up his living area, he realized that he had not thought about his family in quite a while. Memories of his children pained him, so he tried to concentrate on other things.

"Do you know what I have learned to do?" asked Huong as they rested.

"No, little brother, what?"

"I have learned to fire the machine guns, both light and heavy. I even got to fire some live rounds from the 12.7."

Lau was amused at Huong's boyish exuberance.

"You probably won't get much of a chance to fire machine guns while serving as my orderly," laughed Lau.

"That is fine with me. I will do whatever you require of me. But I hope, someday, to be able to fully avenge my brother's death."

"There will be plenty of time for that. You must grow older and more experienced before you become a full-fledged fighter. You will have plenty of time—"

He almost added that the war would go on for years. But the general offensive and popular uprising would end the war in January, would it not? It didn't seem possible.

"Now, I have your first instructions as my orderly. I want you to see if you can find out where Phun is. Ask around the camp, but do not ask any officers. They might think it improper. Do you understand?"

"Yes, Comrade Colonel."

Huong jumped up and darted away.

"Huong, be sure to take your rifle with you at all times."

"Oh, yes, sir." answered Huong ashamedly as he reached back for his SKS.

Perhaps having an orderly would not be such a bad thing after all, thought Lau.

"So you are refusing the Article 15?" asked Jace.

"Yassuh. I shot them '79 rounds. I even admit I was asleep on guard. An' I sure did git loss on that patrol! I prolly deserved them other 'uns, but this time, I ain't done nuffin.'"

"OK, let me talk to the colonel. I'll see if I can let this one slide."

A nervous smile crossed Williams' face.

"Thank you, suh."

"Sure, now get on back down to third platoon."

The field phone buzzed. Tucker answered.

"They want you at the TOC, sir."

"Tell 'em I'm on my way," said Jace.

As he walked across the fire base, Jace wondered how he could raise the issue of Williams and the Article 15 with Price. Until now, the new battalion commander had not shown any sign of compassion toward soldiers. In fact, he had not acted as if his soldiers even existed. Well, he would have to do something. Williams was going to refuse non-judicial punishment and demand trial by court martial as was his right. It would all come out anyway, so he might as well get it over with.

Jace ducked under the tent-frame as he entered the TOC.

"Got a hot one, Jace," said C.C..

"What is it this time?"

"How'd you like to go after a regimental headquarters?"

"No shit?" exclaimed Jace.

"No shit. Look. We got agent reports, we got a defector that's been there, and last night we got hot readings from infra-red and people-sniffer missions."

"You still acting as S-3?" Jace asked under his breath.

"Now, now, give him a chance," whispered C.C..

"Is there a plan?" asked Jace, talking louder.

"The S-3 will brief you. We're not hurrying. We're going to do this one right."

"Where's the old man?" queried Jace, looking around.

"Taking a nap," answered C.C.. "S-3, brief Charlie Six on the scheme of maneuver. We go day after tomorrow."

"OK," said Cole, pointing at the map. "We're flying A company in to block escape to the south. They'll go in to an LZ—here. Scout platoon will screen Highway 2 to make sure they don't escape to the east. We'll fire 155, 8-inch and 175 to the west to seal off escape that way. Your company will air-assault in to an LZ located about a click north of where we think the objective is. We should have them boxed in."

"What size force is there?"

The S-2 answered. "The defector, what do you call them, oh yeah, the *hoi chan*, said that when he was there, only a platoon-sized security force was around the headquarters. May be more now."

"Who's going to secure the fire base while we're gone?"

"We'll have to use clerks, jerks, and bottle washers. Hopefully you won't be out overnight. If need be we can pull the scout platoon back. Questions?" asked Cole.

"A couple," answered Jace. "Will I have an artillery unit firing just for me? You mentioned all the blocking fires. If I get into heavy shit, I want a unit that is responsive to me and not tied up with the blocking-fire missions."

"Yes, you will have the 155 battery here in the fire base, the four-duce mortars and of course your 81s. They will answer only to you," answered C.C.. "The other stuff will fire out of Bear Cat, Long Binh, and Black Horse."

"Also, who will control any gunships? We'll be under heavy canopy. Those bastards get trigger-happy sometimes and I don't want them shooting us up."

"They'll be under battalion control. We'll be sure of targets before we cut them loose."

"If the shooting starts, I want them under my control," said Jace. "And one last thing: air strikes. I want an air strike on call."

"Timing might be questionable here," said C.C.. "We don't know when you might make contact—or even if you will. We'll try to have fast movers overhead, but we might have to settle for strip-alert at Binh Hoa, or an immediate."

"Well, I want a forward air controller up at any rate," demanded Jace.

"FAC will be up," said Cole. "Also, brigade has put the 2-47 on alert in case they have to back us up. If we find anything big, we'll pile on fast."

"OK. Is that all for now?"

"That's it. We'll update you tomorrow. You will have time to plan this one thoroughly," said C.C..

"Well, I'd better get back and issue my warning order. When the Colonel wakes up would you buzz me? I've got something I need to talk to him about."

"I'm awake now." said Price, striding into the TOC. "What is it?"

"It's about one of my troops, sir. The one that got written up at the PX at Bear Cat. He's refusing the Article 15. He's been charged with driving a jeep to the PX without license or permission and leaving it unlocked while he was inside. But he's got a witness that says they walked to the PX. Sir, the two NCOs that claim my troops took the jeep are the same ones who instigated the racial incident in the field. The soldier that is witnessing for Williams is the one that Sergeant

Smith kicked. I believe strongly that the two NCOs were the ones that drove the jeep to the PX and left it unlocked. I believe they blamed the two colored kids when they got caught."

"So what are you asking me to do?" asked Price.

"Since the whole thing appears to be very questionable at the least, I recommend we let this one slide.

"You are aware, are you not, of my policy requiring automatic Article 15s for all offenses of this nature at Bear Cat?"

"Yes, sir. But these were the same two NCOs that instigated the racial incident in the field. I believe this is just a continuation."

"I thought you said you had taken care of the racial incident. Now you say it's back?"

"No, sir. I handled the incident by punishing the NCO who kicked the private and relieving both of them from the platoon. At Bear Cat, I believe they happened upon each other and the NCOs blamed two innocent privates for misappropriating the jeep—the jeep that they took to the PX themselves."

"If you would just follow my established policy, there would be no problem."

"But the circumstances—"

"I don't care about the circumstances. You appear ready to take the word of two privates over the word of two NCOs."

"But sir, these NCOs—"

"Just do what I tell you to do, captain! Give him the Article 15. If he refuses it, court martial him."

"Yes, sir," said Jace, formally. "If that's all, sir, I'll be getting back to my company."

"I expect my company commanders to follow my guidance. Don't question me again!"

"Yes, sir."

Jace picked up his helmet, put it on, saluted, did an about face and flew out of the TOC. He stormed across the firebase in a furious haze. Coming to his command post, he stopped for a moment to clear his head. There was no sense taking his anger out on his troops. He stood in the sun until he had regained composure, then ducked into his tent.

"Tucker, toss me my rucksack. Five India, call for the platoon leaders. I've got a warning order for them."

Tucker rooted around inside the command track, found Jace's rucksack and unceremoniously threw it over the back ramp. When the rucksack plopped at his feet in a cloud of dust, Jace glared at Tucker and started to yell at him. Again, he hesitated. Hadn't he told the boy to toss the rucksack to him? He realized he was still angry at the battalion commander. He had to cool off before his officers arrived.

"Tucker, toss me a coke," said Jace gently. "And try not to knock me down with it this time."

"Yes, sir. Sorry, sir," grinned Tucker sheepishly.

"Thanks," said Jace, regaining his composure.

Jace jotted notes for his warning order. He would not have much information until he received a more detailed order from battalion. At least he could get his platoons started preparing. As his officers came into the tent, Jace opened his rucksack to retrieve the ceramic cat for its ritual place in the center of their circle. He was studying the map on the wall of the tent as he groped for the figurine. Suddenly his full attention shot to his rucksack. He was shocked as his hands ran over the shards in the bottom of the sack. Jupiter, the cat was broken.

CHAPTER 12

▼

3 November 1967

"There's not been one artillery round landed on the LZ," screamed the new A company commander on the battalion net. "Where's the gunships? We're going into an un-prepped LZ."

"This is Cougar Six. Don't get excited. We'll get the arty in."

"This is Alpha Six. Too late we're on final now. Do you want us to commit or not?"

"Cougar Six, this is Mauler Six on your push!" It was the brigade commander intervening. "Execute a go-around. Do not—I say again—do not put any of my troops down on an LZ that has not been prepped."

"This is Cougar Six, Roger. Alpha Six, go around!"

"This is Alpha Six. Wilco!"

Broken into the familiar six-man aircraft loads, Charlie company sat on the same pick-up zone on Highway 1 from which it had lifted into War Zone D. Jace, Five India, and Tucker sat with three other soldiers listening to A company's airmobile insertion on the battalion net.

"Damn, that new captain in A company is pissed!" exclaimed Five India.

"I'd be pissed too if they tried to put me in on an un-prepared LZ. Wonder what happened?"

"I don't know. The S-3 and the arty liaison officer are in the C&C ship with the colonel. I can't see what the problem would be."

"Me neither," said Jace. "We all got the Vietnamese air, ground, district and province clearances at the same time. It took hours to get, but they were approved. All the arty had to do was shoot."

"Clearances?" asked Five India.

"You know, we have to get Vietnamese permission before we fire artillery unless our troops are in direct contact with the enemy."

"I thought I knew about everything that went on in this place, but I have never heard of that. That sounds screwed up to me."

"Just another little lovely detail in a political war," mumbled Jace.

"Will this delay affect us?" asked Five India.

"It'll damn sure affect the time schedule. I hope the S-3 and the new colonel are flexible," replied Jace.

They both looked at each other.

Jace and Five India were unsettled listening to the chaos of Alpha company's uncoordinated flight into its landing zone. The A company commander was furious while Lieutenant Colonel Price was defensive, knowing the brigade commander was listening to the whole thing.

Jace's flight of choppers swept in as he double-checked his map. As the Hueys settled in the dust next to the six-man loads, Charlie company soldiers bent and dashed for their rides. As before, Jace stood apart, insuring that all were loaded, then gave an OK signal to his pilot and dived aboard.

From altitude, Jace could see the smoke that marked Alpha company's LZ. It was cold, thank God. There was the command and control chopper and the forward air controller in his Cessna Bird Dog, orbiting the scene. Higher in the sky was another Huey. Jace guessed it belonged to the brigade commander.

Where were the gunships? Both companies had been briefed that gunships would spray their LZs just before touchdown. Jace could see the gray puffs of artillery fire walking the tree lines adjacent to the open field that would be his company's LZ. He grabbed the battalion radio hand set.

"Cougar Three, this is Jupiter Six, I thought we had gunship support."

"This is Cougar Six, who the hell is Jupiter Six?"

"Sorry. This is Charlie Six," shouted Jace, realizing that Lieutenant Colonel Price had never heard the Jupiter story. "Where are the gunships? Over."

"I expect you to use proper radio procedure. The guns are on their way. OUT!"

Jace flung the handset at Five India as he angrily looked out the gaping door. No gunships. There would be a gap in suppression after the artillery lifted and before the door gunners took over. If there were VC waiting, they would have time to come out of their holes and sight their weapons. While they were still a mile out, Jace saw the smoke round marking the last artillery shot. A whole minute with no ordnance falling on the LZ. A minute could be a lifetime.

They were committed. As the Hueys flared and slowed, door gunners, sensing the danger, opened up early. Holding helmets on their heads, soldiers hit the ground running. Once clear of the rotor blades, they all flopped on their bellies, waiting for the choppers to lift out.

No firing. Thank God Almighty, the LZ is cold, thought Jace. Feeling naked and exposed, He stood and gave the hand signal to advance to the jungle's edge. Just then, out of nowhere, gunships swept over, blasting the treeline with mini-gun fire. Angry and frightened, Charlie company hit the ground again.

"Cougar Three, this is Charlie Six. Cold LZ. Call off the guns, we're almost in the treeline."

"This is Cougar Six. I'm running this operation. The gunships will continue to fire until they are expended."

"This is Charlie Six. If they have fuel to stay for a while we might need them later."

Price's answer came back, aloof and threatening: "Do not argue with me!"

"This is Charlie Six, Roger—"

Jace knew that the safest place for him and his company now was in the treeline, but they would have to wait. After the gunships had finished firing, his troops would still have 75 meters to run to the trees. Viet Cong could still be waiting in bunkers, protected from the gunships, holding their fire. All Jace and his men could do now was wait in the open.

"Cougar Six, this is Charlie Six. Request you tell me when the last pass is made so we can be off and running."

"This is Cougar Six. That was the last pass," radioed Price curtly.

"LET'S GO!" screamed Jace as he jumped up and waved his troops forward.

As they sprinted toward the edge of the jungle, a gunship suddenly appeared and made one last run down the treeline with miniguns blazing. Cursing as they glared skyward, Charlie company hit the ground once more.

Helicopters swept over the jungle canopy directly above them. The sky seemed to be filled with enemy machines.

"To the tunnels. Take everything that is above ground. Leave nothing," shouted the regimental commander.

Guerrillas kicked dirt onto their small cooking fires, gathered weapons and belongings and dashed up the narrow trail to the underground bunker complex. Officers hurried about, looking for anything left behind. The regimental commander calmly stacked his paperwork, stowed it in his knapsack, looked around his thatched-roofed office, then walked up the trail to the invisible bunkers.

One by one, the guerrillas dropped into their spider holes. When they were safely underground, comrades placed the carefully camouflaged lids in place. The holes simply disappeared. The commander placed the lid on the last spider hole, then, with difficulty caused by the thick vegetation, slowly walked around his defensive position. He pointed out a few flaws in the camouflage, which guerrillas corrected immediately. Once everything was to his satisfaction, he crawled into a tunnel entrance hidden under a large bush. The small, flat hilltop looked like any other patch of jungle.

Lau and Huong huddled deep in the main vault connected to fighting positions and escape hatches by small tunnels.

"Will we get to fight?" asked Huong.

"We probably will not have to fight," answered Lau, hopefully. "We are camouflaged so well, they will probably never find us."

"If the fighting starts, may I join the heavy machine-gun team? I know where they are located," pled Huong.

"They will probably not need you. You might just get in their way." Lau felt as if he were talking to an anxious child instead of a trained guerrilla. The feeling again made him miss his children.

"I can hand up ammunition from below, and if one of the crew is wounded, I can replace him."

"Let's see what fate brings us. We both might have to fight, or none of us may have to fight. Let's wait and see," smiled Lau in the darkness. May the spirits of my ancestors protect Phun, he prayed. Let her be far away from here.

This time there was no searching as they went. Charlie company moved from the LZ, straight toward the suspected enemy headquarters. As before, the point team crafted a tunnel through the jungle through which their buddies noiselessly followed. After they had moved only a few hundred meters, Lieutenant Colonel Price's voice crackled over the radio.

"Charlie Six, this is Cougar Six."

"This is Charlie Six, over."

"Pop smoke, over."

"This is Charlie Six. I'd rather not. We're getting close to the objective and we might give ourselves away."

"This is Cougar Six. Maybe you did not understand the order. I say again—pop smoke over."

Jace jerked a smoke grenade from Tucker's harness, pulled the pin and tossed it into the jungle. It took a few moments for the cloud to work its way to the tree-tops.

"I identify purple," radioed Price. You are moving entirely too slow. If you don't get moving you'll disrupt the timetable for the entire operation."

"This is Charlie Six. I'm not concerned with how fast we're moving. I'm concerned about moving quietly. We're getting near the objective. I don't want to blunder onto it, over."

"This is Cougar Six. You do as you're told. Get a move-on. Out!"

Jace angrily threw the hand set at Five India. "If he calls again, tell him he's broken and distorted. I don't want to talk to him till we're on the objective."

"Yes, sir!" grinned Five India.

After they had gone about seven hundred meters, Jace signaled a halt and motioned for the point team to join him.

"We should be about three hundred meters from the objective. I want you three to scout ahead. Look, we are here," said Jace, pointing to his map with a twig. "We think the objective is on this small hill top—Hill 108. Be careful, for God's sake. Take no chances. Just take a look-see and come back and report. Check your radio. Make sure it's working OK—and turn the volume down. You don't want the damn thing squawking at the wrong time."

Johnson and his two buddies nodded sternly, stood and moved away.

"Cougar Six, this is Charlie Six. Pontiac, I say again, Pontiac, over." Jace sent the code word meaning they were beginning the search for the objective, then he sat down against a tree, expecting another chewing from Price, which did not come. There was nothing to do now but pick leeches, slap mosquitoes, and wait.

"Cougar Six, this is Alpha Six. Chevrolet, over." Alpha company was in its blocking position.

"Cougar Six, this is Romeo Six. Ford, over." The scout platoon was in its screening position on Highway 2.

Despite the uncoordinated airmobile insertion, the operation was smoothing out. Distant rattling and swishing followed by loud CrrrUMPs told Jace that the blocking artillery fires had commenced.

Jace started as Stony Johnson tapped him on the shoulder. He must have dozed.

"We've found it, sir. Not on the hill, though—it's in a small draw on the side of the hill. Looks deserted. Just three thatched shacks. One looks like a classroom or mess hall. Other two are smaller."

"How far?"

"I make it 150 meters. I left Ramos and Nolton to watch. If they see anything, they'll break squelch twice."

"OK," whispered Jace. "Good work. I'll get everyone up and you can lead us up there."

Jace signaled for the platoon leaders to join him. He briefed quickly, then stood the company to and moved out.

When Stony Johnson signed "objective in sight", Jace placed second platoon in reserve, first platoon off to the right as a base of fire, and left third platoon poised to move forward to search the objective. Then he crept forward to join the point team. Seeing nothing but the thatched shacks, he decided not to have his troops open fire. Carefully, he moved forward with third platoon.

"Look here, Cap'n." Super Private motioned Jace over. "Fires has been put out, but they're still warm. No sign of anything else."

"OK, keep looking."

To Cappaccelli, Jace whispered in hoarse voice: "Don't touch anything, just look. The place might be booby-trapped."

He was joined by Stony Johnson.

"Sir, there's one of them little narrow foot trails leading away up the hill. The hilltop is still a hundred or so meters up yonder-way. Somethin' still may be there."

Jace nodded.

"They don't live here." Johnson said after a pause.

"What do you mean?" asked Jace.

"No smell. No piss, fish, soy sauce, sweat-smell. You get that smell where they live."

"What do you make of this?"

"Looks like a mess hall or classroom. Them small hootches got no sleeping mats or smoothed-down places like where they sleep. They ain't barracks. More like offices or sumpthin'."

"Did you guys go up on the hill top?" asked Jace.

"No, sir. Just got far enough up to look. Didn't see nothin'."

Jace put third platoon in a tight perimeter around the camouflaged shacks, then called the platoon leaders together.

"Look, I don't believe this is the objective. I want to search that hilltop. There may be a bunker system up there, so we're going in carefully. I'm going to leave second platoon here in reserve. I want first and third platoons on line—first on the right; third is the base. We'll have to go about 150 meters through thick jungle to get there. You all know that a line abreast is a hard thing to control in thick bush, but we need to be configured so we can assault if something's there. Take it slow and easy. Second platoon, be ready to maneuver; stay on the radio in case we need you. I'm going to call mortars in on the hilltop before we go up. FO, crank up the fire mission. You guys take this time to brief your troops and line 'em up. We'll move up as close as we can under the mortars. As soon as they start falling, we'll move out."

Deep underground, Lau and Huong felt the thuds of the mortars as dust fell from the ceiling of their underground hideout.

"They have found us. We will have to fight for sure, now.

Please, Comrade Lau, please allow me to go help fight. I know the heavy machine-gun team will need help with ammunition. Please!"

"Yes, you are probably right. I too must find a place where I can help. Go along, now, but be careful." Lau realized he had a real affection for this boy. He prayed he would be safe.

Huong grabbed his rifle and his pack and scrambled off up a narrow tunnel, knowing exactly where he was going. Fascinated by the big 12.7 millimeter gun, he had visited the position several times. Lau sadly watched him go, then moved away to join the regimental commander. As a senior officer, he would have duties other than shooting.

Huong found the gunners huddled in small holes dug on each side of the gun. Thick logs stacked three deep and covered with dirt formed the roof of the bunker, which was built in the middle of a dense thicket. The gunners had even planted greenery on top of the roof for more camouflage. The heavy gun covered what the guerrillas thought to be the most dangerous avenue of approach onto their hilltop. Two light machine guns covered other approaches.

With eyes tightly shut, the gunners squatted with their hands clasped over their ears. Dirt from the bunker roof streamed down as each mortar round exploded. Huong tugged at a trouser leg.

"I am here to help you with the ammunition," he said grandly.

"You had better keep your head away from that aperture, or you won't be helping us with anything."

Chastened, Huong moved back down the tunnel a ways. At least they hadn't told him to go away. He would get to fight—in a real battle—to avenge Duc. He realized he was shaking all over.

"Cease fire, end of mission," said the forward observer into his handset as Jace loudly urged the company forward. After the mortar barrage, there was no need to be quiet. With vines and undergrowth slowing their advance and hampering their vision, soldiers picked and stumbled toward the hill. Despite all the leaders could do, the line began to show gaps after moving only a short distance. Jace waded back and forth through the dense foliage, adjusting the formation, shoving his troops forward, and shouting encouragement. Finally, in a long ragged line, Charlie company advanced on to the top of Hill 108.

"There's nothing here!" said Lieutenant Cappaccelli, thankfully.

"Don't let your guard down," said Jace. "Have your guys spread out and search."

Jace moved to the center of the hilltop as his platoons fanned out. For a long, terrible moment, all was quiet.

Suddenly, Stony Johnson, wearing an expression no one had ever seen on his face before, ran in a tight crouch, straight to Jace.

"They're here. They're here, I tell you."

"What? How can you tell?"

"I smell 'em! I smell piss! I tell you they're here! We're right on top of 'em."

"Everybody hold up!" roared Jace. Come back the way we came. Quick." The tone of the company commander's voice shook the young soldiers of Charlie company who began working their way back toward where they had mounted the hill.

As he watched his soldiers withdrawing, Jace suddenly sensed violent movement to his left. Stony Johnson had disappeared up to his waist into the ground and was thrashing and kicking wildly. He had stepped on top of, and fallen into, a spider hole—right on top of a Viet Cong. As he struggled in panic, he placed the muzzle of his M-16 between his feet and fired, killing the enemy soldier beneath him. With that one shot, Hill 108 erupted. From ten meters away, the Viet Cong heavy machine gun cut Stony Johnson in half as guerrillas popped from spider holes and fired point-blank into Jace's soldiers. Super Private, seeing Johnson go down, flopped to the ground, jerked a grenade from his harness, pulled the pin, and threw it into the thicket. The blast was too close and too loud, but the heavy gun stopped firing.

Jace hit the jungle floor and pulled Tucker to him. Grabbing the company hand set, he yelled for his platoons to continue to move back in the direction from which they had come. Bull-whip cracks from supersonic bullets, thumps of muzzle blasts, grenade blasts, screams of the wounded, and leaders yelling orders seemed to be all around him at once.

Sudden movement again startled Jace. He pointed his assault rifle at the blur as Doc Roberts crawled by on his knees, pulling a wounded soldier behind him.

"That way, Doc—down the hill!" yelled Jace. More soldiers came by, some crawling, some turning to fire as they went, some running wild-eyed, the fight gone from them. Gray-brown smoke-dust and the smell of cordite covered the hill. Doc Roberts crawled back toward the battle as Lieutenant Cappaccelli scrambled by on all fours. Jace grabbed him and pulled him down beside him.

"I saw two of my men killed. We knocked out three spider holes and a bunker, but you can't see 'em," heaved the lieutenant.

"Round your guys up. Get down over the side of the hill out of the grazing fire!"

Jace grabbed the lieutenant by the harness and threw him back into the battle. Then, jumping up, he ran towards where he thought first platoon was. There, he found more chaos. A group of wounded soldiers huddled together in a pile while others fired in all directions at once.

"Try to get your guys down over the lip of the hill. You'll have some protection from the fire there. Take everybody with you. Don't leave anyone behind!"

Once he saw them beginning to inch backward, he ran back to Tucker as bullets chopped trees and kicked dirt all around him.

"Have you seen Five India? I need the battalion radio!"

"No, sir, yelled Tucker above the din. I haven't seen him since—"

"Over here, sir!"

Jace crawled toward the voice. Five India lay in a small depression, out of the fire.

"Give me the battalion radio," ordered Jace as he threw himself down next to Five India."

Five India offered the hand set to Jace.

"Not the hand set! Take the radio off and give it to me!"

"What do you mean, sir?"

"I mean you've got a month left in this place. I want you to go back to the LZ and organize everyone as they come off this hill. Tell Little Caesar to be ready to counter-attack if I need him."

"Are you sure, sir? You might need me."

"Yes, dammit, I'm sure! That's an order! Now move!"

Yes, sir—good luck, and keep your head down!" shouted Five India as he rolled out of the depression and scampered away.

Dragging the PRC-25 behind him, Jace crawled back to Tucker. The firing seemed even more intense. Finally finding the time to notify battalion of their situation, Jace radioed, "Cougar Six, this is Charlie Six. Heavy enemy contact, over."

"This is Cougar Six. That's great. What's the enemy body count? Over."

"No way of knowing. They were camouflaged so well that we were amongst them when they opened up on us. I've got several wounded and two KIA that I know of. My three-six element said he had knocked out three spider holes and a bunker."

"This is Cougar Six, Roger. Update the body count when you can."

"Roger. Look, I'm going to leave this freq for a few minutes. I'm changing to the fire support net. I've got to get some arty in here. If you need me, change to my internal freq."

"Roger, I'll be overhead in two minutes. Hold on. I'll get help."

As Jace changed to the artillery frequency, he wondered what Price meant by "I'll get help." What the hell could he do?

After only two or three bursts had been fired by the heavy machine gun, there had been a tremendous blast and both crewmen had fallen back into the tunnel, the gunner dead and the assistant wounded. Huong had leapt through the dust and smoke to the gun, which had been covered with dirt from the roof of the bunker. Hurriedly, he had brushed the soil from the weapon and tried to charge it. It had jammed. After a while, the wounded assistant gunner had climbed to join him. Huong had bandaged the man's head and then they had gotten to work. Now, as the battle raged around them, they tried to clear the gun.

"Here, we've got to get the dirt out of the breach", said the wounded Viet Cong.

Huong removed the ammunition belt and together the two guerrillas lifted the gun from the tripod, turned it upside-down and banged it vigorously to knock the dirt free. With an oily cloth, Huong cleaned out the innards of the gun and checked to see that there was no dirt in the barrel. Then they lifted the gun back onto the tripod and locked it in place. Huong inserted the belt of ammunition and, with all his might, pulled back the charging handle. Holding his breath, he snapped the trigger. Nothing happened. The gun was still jammed.

Like water flowing down hill, the soldiers of Charlie company sought out the low places in the ground, where inches made the difference between living and dying. Jace crawled back and forth making sure his troops were pulling back. Since there were still several troops unaccounted for, He now faced a terrible decision. To save the majority of his men, he had to get some supporting fire onto the hill top. But he knew there might be several of his wounded or dead still lying among the spider holes and bunkers. First platoon, after beginning to make its way to safety, was again pinned flat where it was. Although some of third platoon had been able to back down off of the hill to relative safety, several were unable to move from where they were.

Now, Jace called second platoon, with its untried platoon leader, to move from its reserve position, through third platoon, which had been hardest hit, up on line with first. If this fresh platoon could take some pressure off, first platoon and the remainder of the third might be able to break contact.

As badly as he hated it, Jace made his decision. None of his pre-planned targets would get artillery fire on the ground as quickly as he needed it, so he called a fresh mission to the 155 battery on Fire Base Cougar.

"Automatic 33, this is Cougar Charlie Six, fire mission, troops in contact, danger close, will adjust. Grid 065982, direction: 185. Over."

"Roger," came the reply from the artillery. There was a pause as the mission was plotted and the battery aimed. Then: "Shot, over."

"Shot, out," answered Jace.

With all the firing, he couldn't hear the rattle of the incoming projectiles. But the CrrrUMPs of the explosions off to the south were unmistakable.

"Drop 100, left five zero." Jace made bold adjustments to get the rounds on the target as quickly as possible. Wide-eyed and out of breath, Lieutenant Jeffers of second platoon ran up to Jace, who reached up and jerked him into the prone position.

"Here is your line. Bring up your troops, then crawl over there and see if you can find first platoon. Tie in with them and get up a volume of fire, then we'll start to back out of here."

Without answering, the lieutenant clamored away on knees and elbows.

Jace walked the heavy artillery closer and closer. As he did, first and second platoons formed a solid line. Although they remained pinned down, they were at least intact, and outside of the nest of holes and bunkers. Third platoon slid away down the hill, out of the effective fire, licking their wounds. Finally leaders counted heads. Jace received the report: six dead, eighteen wounded, one missing.

The regimental commander climbed up the tunnel to the bunker where Huong and his wounded comrade were working feverishly on the gun.

"Is the gun damaged?" shouted the commander.

"I believe it is only jammed. We should have it firing in minutes," answered Huong.

"We must have it operational. The enemy is beginning to fire heavy artillery and we might have to evacuate. That gun must cover us if we do. Get it firing!"

"Yes, Comrade Colonel," shouted Huong down the tunnel.

Looking hopefully at his wounded friend, Huong loaded and charged the gun one more time, then pressed the trigger. Dust flew and expended cartridges banged into the bunker wall as the big gun blasted into action once more. Huong looked out of the aperture, along the field of fire the crew had carefully cut along the jungle floor, a few inches from the ground. Yards away, he saw movement—tops of helmets, elbows, and rifle muzzles. He swung the gun in that direction and fired a long burst.

"Dammit!" yelled Jace as he dived into a depression behind a tree root. "I thought that gun was knocked out!" The tree trunk above his head splintered as branches and bark fell on him. "Where is it? Can anyone see it?"

"No, sir," came several voices in unison.

Jace tried to raise his head. More bark flew from the tree.

"Can you tell where it is from the sound?"

"I think it's right in front of me in that pile of bushes!" someone yelled.

"Get a grenade out there—you might get lucky."

The blast was too close.

"Bounced off a tree!"

"Anyone hurt?"

"I dont thank so!"

"Try again."

Another grenade exploded, followed by another.

"Keep firing. I'm going to call the artillery in closer!"

Jace knew they had had it now. The 12.7 was protected by riflemen in holes and bunkers so there was no way to approach it from the side. And no one could get up to begin an assault—they would instantly be cut down. With their heads down, troops held their M-16s above them and sprayed the jungle to their front. Cuddling the radio, Jace walked the heavy artillery closer and closer until the last volley sent huge jagged steel fragments ripping through the jungle just over his head. That was as close as he was going to get it.

"Fire for effect," he yelled into the handset. "Keep it coming till your barrels melt!"

When his elbow got a little high as he changed the frequency back to the battalion net, he was rewarded by a thunderous 12.7 burst that tore at the roots around him.

"Cougar Six, this is Charlie Six."

"This is Cougar Six, how're you doing down there, son?" Price asked expansively.

"The artillery is hitting yards away and it's not doing anything to help us. Get me an immediate air strike. That's the only thing that'll get us off this hill." It was not a request. It was an order from the man on the ground.

"Roger, I'll have a strike on the way to you in nothing flat. Hang on. Do you have an enemy body count yet?"

Jace did not answer.

"Keep the fire up, guys! Keep shooting!" he shouted.

"Gittin' low on ammo over here, Cap'n"

"Me too!"

"Leaders, can you hear me? Redistribute the ammo. Throw it along the line if you can. I can't hear a '60 firing. Get the machine guns up if you can! Tucker, call third platoon and tell them to get back to the LZ and set up a perimeter. When the air strike gets here, we'll fall back to them."

"Charlie Six, this is Cougar Six, fast-movers are on the way. Hold on, son."

Lau climbed up the tunnel to where Huong sat hunched behind the 12.7, blasting away. The wounded assistant gunner fed the ammo from the piles of belts all around the gun.

"Huong, we are leaving. The artillery is starting to cave in some of the tunnels. We must flee while we can!"

"You go, Comrade Colonel. I will stay and hold them off until you escape."

"No! The order has been given. Come—now!"

"No. I cannot. I will not. I will hold them back while you escape. Now, you go, Uncle Lau."

The wounded guerrilla hesitated, looking from Lau to Huong, then through the aperture to the enemy. As Lau struggled upward to grab Huong by the ankle, a grenade burst just outside the bunker.

The wounded assistant gunner, finally having had enough, dived past Lau down the tunnel. Huong kicked his leg free from Lau's grip.

"I will not leave! I finally have a chance to avenge my brother. I do not know if I have killed any of them yet and I will not go until I do!"

"It is an order," pled Lau. "We all must go."

"I must stay," said Huong, more quietly.

Lau had a glimmer of hope as he saw Huong reach for his knapsack, but was shocked when he saw what the boy was doing. In one swift motion, Huong removed a pair of handcuffs from his pack and locked one end on his left ankle.

"No!" screamed Lau as Huong locked the other cuff onto the heavy tripod of the gun. Digging again in his knapsack, he found the key and threw it out of the aperture. Then he looked calmly down into Lau's face.

"Say goodby to my mother for me."

Without another word, Huong turned, aimed the gun and loosed a long burst. Lau hesitated one more second, then slid into the darkness of the tunnel.

"Charlie Six, this is Cougar Six. The FAC has got a flight on the way. I'll put the strike in for you. You just hold on."

"This is Charlie Six," Jace shouted into the handset. "There's no way you can control the strike. Us and the VC are not ten yards apart. All you can see from up there is smoke. I'll have to put the air strike in."

Lieutenant Colonel Price's voice became cold again. "I am in an advantageous spot where I can see the whole battlefield. I am in control of this battle and I will put in the air strike."

"This is Charlie Six," growled Jace. "Now listen, the minimum safe distance between troops and a normal-sized bomb is 300 meters. I am ten yards from a machine-gun bunker. If you put bombs in here you'll kill us all!"

"This is Cougar Six. At some point you will have to admit to yourself that I know what I am doing."

Locked in a desperate situation that he did not expect to live through, Jace lost control.

"Our insertion sure didn't indicate that you knew what the hell you were doing!" he screamed. "The damn gunships nearly shot us up once we were on the ground—and now you want me to trust you to put bombs and napalm ten meters from me? I and I alone am responsible for these troops on the ground with me. I demand that you allow me to call in the strike!"

"Charlie Six, this is Cougar Six. If you continue in this vein, I will be forced to relieve you."

"This is Charlie Six. It is your prerogative to relieve me any time you wish. But you will have to wait until we are off this hill. I am in charge here and I will stay in charge until we escape or until you kill us with your damned air strike!"

"Cougar Six, Charlie Six, this is Mauler Six on your freq."

The brigade commander's voice was like cold water on the hot exchange. "Both of you are getting out of control. Charlie Six, do you feel you are in a position to control the air strike?"

"This is Charlie Six. That's affirmative, over."

"All right. Cougar Six, let the man on the ground do the job," the brigade commander ordered in the same tone a father might use to settle an argument between two children over a bicycle.

There was no mistaking the ice in Price's voice when he answered: "This is Cougar Six, Wilco, over."

"Mauler Six, meet me on my push—out!"

Jace yelled to Tucker to ask if third platoon was withdrawing. Tucker answered yes. Seeing that he was out of rifle ammunition, Jace checked his pistol. He had one magazine left in his .45. Finally realizing there was nothing further he could do, he forced himself to relax and wait for the air strike while the heavy machine gun chopped timber inches above him and fragments from the artillery shredded the nearby trees.

Finally: "Cougar Charlie Six this is Earache 77 on your frequency, over." The welcome voice of the forward air controller squawked from Jace's hand set.

"This is Charlie Six."

"Roger, I've got a flight of six fast-movers out of Bien Hoa. The only problem is that they are being diverted from a strike up north. I'm afraid they've got wall-to-wall 750 Snake-eyes, over."

"Look, I'm ten meters from the enemy bunker line. My troops are pinned down. A 750-pound bomb won't do on the first pass. Do your birds have cannons or miniguns?"

"That's affirm," answered the FAC.

"OK, here's what we'll do. My troops are in a fairly straight line running east and west. I will mark my line with smoke. The bad guys are to the south of us. If you have your pilots make their run from the west, down the smoke line, have them fire just to the south, or the right of the smoke. Do you understand?"

"This is Earache 77. Your line runs east to west. Understand there are no friendlies south of that line. First pass will be west to east with twenty-millimeter. You need to be up and running when the first rounds hit. Next pass will be 750 high-drags."

"That's it. Wish us luck. If you're in contact with Automatic 33, you can stop the artillery when the fast-movers arrive. Tell me when to pop smoke."

"Roger, I'll call off the arty. Luck and God speed," said Earache 77 almost reverently.

With a gravely, failing voice, Jace screamed the instructions to his soldiers.

"When I say to, throw smoke to your front. When the first cannon rounds hit the ground, be up and running. Take everyone with you—dead or alive. We'll only have one chance!"

He listened as leaders relayed the order down the line.

"Charlie Six," radioed the FAC, "Pop smoke now."

"OK, guys, THROW YOUR SMOKE!"

Again, leaders echoed the order.

"This is Earache 77, I've got your smoke line. I'm clearing in the first pass. Good luck."

For the first time in two hours, Jace rolled over and looked up. The jungle canopy, once lush, thick and green, was gone, blasted away by the mortars and the artillery. The trees left standing looked like winter maples, with not a leaf left on them. Some trees had fallen, their trunks and limbs slashed and splintered by bullets and fragments. The air near the ground had a pale brownish-green hue from pulverized leaves, smoke and dust. In the bright purple sky above, he could see Earache 77 circling lazily in his Cessna. He took his last white smoke grenade from his harness, pulled the pin and tossed it toward the thicket where the heavy machine gun still thumped away. Then rolling onto his back, he watched death approach.

The F-100 Super Saber was upside-down in its attack run. Jace guessed that all the pilot had to do was look up through his canopy to see the target. Lying behind his tree root, he watched the jet roll over and noiselessly trail a stream of dotted white smoke behind it. A split second later, shells from the high-speed cannon ripped into the ground twenty yards away like the teeth of a giant weed eater. All too near to Jace and his troops, the shredded jungle erupted into yellow flashes, gray smoke, and flying splinters. In rapid succession, the other members of the flight followed their leader down the smoke line, unleashing their torrents of fire and steel.

"GO NOW!" screamed Jace.

Through the flying fragments and debris, Charlie company soldiers, responding to the frantic shouts of its leaders, got to their feet and ran for their lives. Carrying wounded and dead, plowing through undergrowth, and tripping over vines and roots, bleeding and sweating teen-agers dashed from the hill. As Jace led Tucker toward safety at the end of the radio mike cord, He radioed the FAC to put a bomb on the white smoke in the middle of the line.

There was a strange quiet after the jets made their cannon passes. While Charlie company was withdrawing, Viet Cong firing had been reduced to random crackles as enemy soldiers also sought escape from certain death. Half deaf now, Jace tried to listen for movement around him as his troops thrashed to safety. Worried that stragglers might be killed by the air strike, he lagged behind to make sure everyone was off the hill. Though he hesitated only a couple of seconds, it was long enough for him to lose sight of Tucker. Back under the jungle canopy now, he couldn't see the F-100s, but knew they would be climbing and turning, setting up for their bomb runs. As he paused once more to make sure that all of his troops were off the hill and moving toward the LZ, one mind-numbing fact prodded him into motion again: The minimum safe distance for a 750-pound bomb is 300 meters. He guessed he had gone only about 150. As he turned to take one last look toward the hill, his mind could not comprehend what he saw. Approaching at the speed of sound, the shock wave from the first bomb was pushing the humidity in the air into an opaque-white blast wall—straight toward him.

Lau's only thought now was survival. Slithering down the tunnel from Huong's gun position, he tumbled into the main underground vault as a tremendous explosion outside caused one entire wall to cave in. He tried to remember which tunnel led to the escape hatch at the stream. Trying one exit and running into a wall of dirt, he backed out and tried another. All seemed to be dead ends, blocked by collapses caused by the continuing blasts which were many times more violent than the heavy artillery.

"Who is that?" shouted the voice of the regimental commander from the darkness.

"It is Colonel Lau. Where are you?"

"Here, come quickly—I will show you the way out!"

Lau lunged toward the sound, savagely banging his head on some unseen object. The commander had hold of him now, pulling him through a dark passageway. Lau gave over to his fear and became a child being led by the hand to safety by an adult. Twice they took forks that led to dead ends and had to turn and try other routes. Blood dripping into Lau's eyes from the wound on his head dimmed his vision, but finally he made out a faint smudge of light in the distance. Duck-walking and dragging his knapsack, the commander led Lau to the exit. Outside, hell itself waited. Without a pause, the regimental commander stepped into the open only to be swept away by the shock wave from a 750-pound bomb, as the roof of the tunnel collapsed onto Lau.

When Jace came to, he had no idea where he was. All he knew was that he had a tremendous headache and there was a ringing in his ears. Looking around, he remembered he was in the jungle. But where were his troops? He sat up and looked around for his weapon, which was no where to be seen. He grabbed for his holster, but his pistol was also gone. And so was the battalion radio. Now he recalled the battle and the air strike. Adrenaline surged through him as he realized he was alone and unarmed. He jumped up and began running wildly down the hill. After stumbling and falling flat, he forced himself to lie still.

"Get hold of yourself, Jace, old boy," he told himself aloud, though he couldn't hear his voice. Calming, he examined himself by feeling his head, chest, limbs and back. The only thing he found was that his nose was bleeding. Forcing himself to breathe deeply, he felt control returning. He got to one knee, paused for a second, then began to stand.

As he did so, he saw movement. Easing back into the prone position, Jace watched as the blurs and moving foliage took form. Three Viet Cong carrying Kalishnakovs hurried past him away from the hill, looking as if they too were in shock from the bombs. Jace lay breathless, gripping the handle of his father's K-Bar. He waited and watched, but saw no more enemy soldiers. Then, pulling his compass from his harness, he oriented himself, and stood up. He vowed that he would walk calmly back to the LZ.

As he took his first step, a movement in is peripheral vision jerked his head to the left. He found himself looking into the face of a tattered guerrilla, not ten feet away. The small man, who looked as battle-weary as Jace felt, first stood motionless, then raised his AK-47, only to realize that there was no magazine in the weapon. Jace stood stunned for a half second before he ripped the K-Bar from its scabbard. As he did so, the guerrilla reached to the muzzle of his assault rifle and clicked the folding bayonet into place. In a crouch, the Viet Cong approached Jace with the bayonet held throat-high. Jace, also in a fighter's stance, waved his left hand in front of his face and held the knife blade-down against his right thigh. The two men stared into each other's eyes as they circled and bluffed. The VC made two feints, then lunged. Jace was surprised by the tremendous advantage his size and strength gave him as he seized the barrel of the Kalishnakov and wrenched the weapon from the small man's hands. As he did so, he drove the K-Bar up into the guts of his foe. Now Jace learned the shocking reality of killing with a blade—it took a long time and it was very, very ugly. The guerrilla, feeling death upon him, kicked at Jace's knees, scratched at his face, and bit his arms. Jace stabbed and sliced until the bowel-stink blubbered from the V.C.'s sliced throat. The little man did not go down easily—he fought to his end. After a seeming eternity, Jace pushed his enemy to the ground and pried the man's dying fingers from his wrists.

Lieutenant Cappaccelli had taken command of the mad scene at the LZ. Five India helped him grab the dazed and bloody soldiers as they drifted in and shove them into an ever-expanding perimeter. Doc Roberts, the other medics, and several volunteers worked frantically on the large number of wounded. In the center of the perimeter, eight bodies were lined up in a poncho-draped row.

The lieutenant desperately screamed into his radio handset only to find that there was no answer on the company net. Why hadn't he memorized the battalion frequency, he asked himself. He needed a medevac and didn't even know how to call it. Why had he relied so totally on the company commander? As he pounded the ground in frustration, Five India walked over and calmly changed the dial to the battalion frequency.

"Cougar Charlie Six, this is Dust-Off 047, over," came the immediate call.

Cappaccelli screamed with relief as he answered, "This is Charlie Three Six, please hurry!"

"OK, your higher gave us your location. What's your sitrep? Over."

"We—We're at the LZ," stammered Cappaccelli. "Get here quick, we got a heap o' wounded."

"Roger, I'm about zero-two out. What's the enemy situation?"

"No fire, now. All's quiet. LZ is secure."

"Roger, pop smoke, were inbound."

Cappaccelli threw a yellow smoke grenade into the center of the perimeter.

"Smoke's out," he radioed.

"Roger, I see yellow, I say again, yellow."

"That's affirm, that's us."

As the medical evacuation helicopter hovered in through the swirling smoke, Cappaccelli shaded his eyes from the late afternoon sun to be sure he was seeing what he thought he saw. A lone figure, covered with blood and carrying an AK-47, calmly walked out of the treeline toward the perimeter.

As Lieutenant Colonel Price and the sergeant major touched down in the H-23, Jace lay on his back in the center of the perimeter, staring at the early-evening sky. He stood as Price stalked toward him, starched and shined.

"Did you ever get a body count?" demanded Price.

Standing, Jace answered, "No, sir, but I can report one."

"One? What the hell do you mean? A rifle company is in contact with the enemy for four hours and all you report is one body?"

"He's the only dead one I saw. I saw three live ones and a dead one."

"Did anybody else see dead V.C.?" asked Price looking around.

Troops stared dumbly. No one answered.

Then Jace said quietly and shakily, "I've got a body count for you, sir. Eight killed, one missing, and 27 wounded."

"Where are the wounded?"

"Gone on the dust-off birds. It took four of them to get them out."

"You mean to tell me that you put all 27 on dust offs?"

"Yes, sir." replied Jace.

"I know good and well that some of them could not have been that seriously wounded. Our battalion medics could have patched them up and they could have been back to duty in two or three days. Once you put them into the medevac system, we won't see them for three weeks. That cuts into my foxhole strength."

"I don't give a damn if we never see them again," Jace said tiredly as he pulled himself up to his full height. "Most of those kids had less than a month to go in this place. I hope they get patched up and get sent straight home."

"Regardless of what you think or hope, from now on, screen your wounded and evac only the more seriously wounded."

Suddenly, Jace's tension, anxiety, and anger let go like a broken dam. Totally out of control now, he shot back, "I'll guarantee you this, Colonel: If I've got wounded with holes in them, I will put them on the dust off—period. I'm no doctor."

Price stood silently, feet wide apart, brows furrowed, his eyes hidden behind sunglasses, considering what to do next. Realizing that the whole perimeter was facing inward now, watching the exchange, he blinked, and for the first time, really looked at his C company commander. Smeared with blood, scratched and cut, Jace wore the teary-eyed scowl of someone who had just been slapped. He trembled as if it took all his strength to keep from swinging at the battalion commander.

The sergeant major broke the stand-off.

"Captain Spencer, those are bite-marks on your arms. You've been in a hand-to-hand fight! Is that what you meant when you said you could report one body?"

Jace said nothing; he simply glared at Price.

The sergeant major continued, gently, "Sir, you really should get a shot of antibiotics. Human bites can be nasty."

After a long pause, Jace said in a very even, very controlled voice, "Colonel, we're going to stay here tonight. I've got a missing boy up there on that hill and at first light tomorrow, I'm going back up there to find him. These men here have been in a nasty fight and I'm sure they would appreciate some words of encouragement from their battalion commander."

Price looked long at Jace, nodded, then walked away. He circulated a bit, shook hands with a few men, then stalked to his chopper and flew away. Just before dark, the battalion surgeon and the chaplain flew in. The doctor treated Jace's wounds, checked his ears, and gave him a shot while the chaplain made his rounds, talking, asking, calming, touching. When the chopper left, the troops dug in and went on one-third alert, but no one slept.

The small boy scampered on all fours through the dark of the caved-in tunnel. He paused before the half-buried figure just inside the tunnel entrance.

"Father, you must wake up. It is dark now. The Americans will be coming back at dawn. You must get away!"

"Is that you, my son?" Lau asked through half-consciousness.

The small boy did not answer. He just looked at Lau for a long moment, then retreated into the darkness of the shattered tunnel. Blinking his eyes to clear his vision, Lau called again for his son, but got no answer. From his position just inside the exit tunnel, he had been protected from the fire and fragments of the bombs, but not from the concussion. The tunnel roof had collapsed, burying him to his shoulders. He lay still for a long while trying to shake off the dizzy cloud that covered his thoughts. Finally, he remembered where he was. He even remembered seeing the regimental commander die. Painfully and slowly, he worked his arms free from the cave-in. They were scratched and swollen, but not broken. Slowly, with his fingers, he began to dig himself out.

As he freed his legs, he found they too were sore, but relatively uninjured. He gingerly touched his forehead, and found that it ached fiercely. He vaguely remembered bumping it on something while he was trying to escape. Slowly, he crawled from the tunnel exit into ghostly moonlight. He was surprised that the jungle canopy that had hidden the regimental headquarters so effectively, was completely gone. He wondered if the Americans were still around, but decided that no one, friend or foe could have survived the bombing. He tried to walk a little way up the hill to survey the damage, but tripped and slid into a huge bomb crater that was thick with the odor of death. Roots, twisted metal, branches, shredded tree trunks and pulverized flesh hampered his movement as he frantically clamored from the hole. As he climbed, he wondered to himself if he were the only one to live through the battle. He knew there was no use looking for Huong after he had chained himself to the gun. He was surely dead.

He stood for a long while in the moonlight, thinking of his son and trying to orient himself. He figured that the nearest, safest place to go was the 274th Battalion. He had walked to it from regimental headquarters several times, but he had always been guided. Could he find it on his own? Were the Americans still nearby? If he ran into them in the jungle, alone and unarmed, he would surely be killed—or captured again.

He looked at the quarter moon, low in the heavens. He could think of nothing else to do but watch it for a while to see where its arc across the sky was taking it. He sat on the edge of a crater, silently watching the moon fall to the west, which would be the direction he would have to travel to find the 274th. Not being able to think of anything else to do, he followed the track of the moon into the jungle. The Americans would probably be back here tomorrow to count the dead and pick through the remnants of the battle, so he needed to get as far away from here as he could. He would find a trail and walk and maybe he would run into friends. Maybe somehow he would be able to find the 274th. Or maybe somehow he would be able to find Phun.

In the morning, Charlie company warily returned to Hill 108, where initially they found only jagged craters and splintered trees. After a while, they found the body of the missing soldier. He was horribly disfigured from the bombs, but he had fallen with his head toward the hill top. His friends all agreed that he had died facing the enemy and seemed to be glad for it. Continuing their search, they found rifles, packs, radios, helmets, bodies and parts of bodies.

"See if you can get the colonel his damned body count," Jace told the platoon leaders. Then he wandered quietly around the hill, lost in his memories of the day before. He tried to find the tree root he had spent the afternoon behind, but it was gone.

"Sir, look at this," yelled a soldier.

As Jace joined him, he pointed to the berm of dirt thrown up around a bomb crater where a 12.7-millimeter heavy machine gun lay half buried. Handcuffed to the tripod was a leg.

"How can they expect to win this war if they have to chain their men to their guns?" asked Lieutenant Cappaccelli.

No one answered, but they all considered the implications.

"Did you hear what he kept yelling?" asked Cappaccelli.

"No, what?" responded Jace.

"He kept yelling 'Duke' or 'Duck' or something like that. Hell, he didn't have to tell me to duck!"

CHAPTER 13

▼

5 November 1967

Everyone treated Charlie company like a teenager who had lost a best friend in a car wreck. The staff, other commanders, chaplains, and friends all came around like country neighbors, checking to make sure everyone was all right. But Jace could see that they were really just curious and that they whispered to each other as they left.

In the hours following the battle, Jace forgot all but his most important tactical responsibilities; the rest he left to First Sergeant Baez. He spent his time watching and ministering to his soldiers, some of whom grieved, some of whom appeared to be in shock and some of whom acted as if the whole thing had not bothered them at all. He was worried most about these. The more healthy appeared to be the ones who were simply glad they had survived. In the meantime, Lieutenant Colonel Price kept his distance from the company, while Jace stayed away from the TOC.

C.C. came in the balmy evening and sat with Jace on sand bags and talked for awhile about everything but the battle.

"I've always considered myself a loyal soldier," said C.C. "Loyalty to the boss has always been a given with me. But now I have some real conflicts. You're my friend, Jace, and I'm loyal to my friends, too. I feel like you're someone that comes along only once in a lifetime. I'd like to think that when we get out of this mess that you and I will always be friends."

Jace didn't know how to respond, so he nodded and waited. Finally, C.C. said, "The colonel is livid about your taking the air strike out of his hands and talking to him the way you did after the fight. Watch him, Jace. If I know him, he'll try to get even."

"Why doesn't he just fire me? Hell, it's no big deal. Just because I've always planned on an army career doesn't mean that's the way it has to be. I'll just get out when I get home and go to grad school. There's a lot I can do besides the damned army."

"He can't fire you. The brigade commander was listening to the whole thing on the radio. By the way, he thought you did a hell of a job with the air strike and getting your guys off that hill, and he told the colonel so. And, besides, he's put you in for an impact Silver Star, so I don't think the old man could fire you too easily. Plus, and I don't know this for sure, but I believe someone from division was monitoring, either Colonel McKensie or the general himself. The word is that they feel you did a great job too. Colonel Price blew it bad and he has no one he can blame it on. He has to keep you—for the time being—but he doesn't want to is my guess. Watch him Jace. He may not be able to relieve you right away, but he's going to be looking for his chance. You made him look bad—and I don't get the feeling he likes to look bad—ever."

"He made himself look bad," answered Jace.

"Jace, just don't cross him."

"Look, I've decided I'm going to command this company to the best of my ability. I'll do what I can do to accomplish the mission, but I'm going to take care of my troops. And if he or General Westmoreland himself doesn't like it, they can fire me and send me back to Tennessee."

"Let me ask you something. How are you?"

"Me—don't worry about me. When the general goes AWOL, I'll still be hanging on." They both laughed, but didn't feel happiness.

Jace had Private Williams in to sign the papers refusing non-judicial punishment and requesting a trial by court martial. He took the packet of papers to the adjutant, who would process it and coordinate with the brigade legal section, which would set the date for the trial. Technically, Jace was out of the picture now, but somehow he just couldn't leave it alone.

Walking the perimeter, he came to Howell, now the acting platoon sergeant of second platoon. He was filling sandbags, his huge black muscles rippling in the sun.

"Since when does the platoon sergeant fill sand bags?" smiled Jace.

"Oh, hey, sir. I do this for exercise. Ain't nothin' on this fire base to do, so I do this."

"Listen, I've meant to ask you. How did Williams do in the fight?"

"He was scared like we all was, but he hung. He stuck with us. He never run," answered Howell.

"Is there anything we're missing? Do you think anybody else saw what happened? I'm talking about the incident back at Bear Cat."

Howell put down the shovel and wiped his brow on an army-green towel. "B'lieve me, sir, we all been thinking' on the case. We axed everbody we know if they seen or heard anything that can he'p the boy. Nobody know nothin."

"Well, I'll tell you one thing. Munn and Smith are not gonna win this thing without a fight. Let me know if anything comes up."

"Yes, sir," answered Howell as he picked up his shovel again. "I tell you what, Cap'n. Them two crackers do this to Williams, and this new colonel lets 'em git by with it, they be hell to pay."

Back in his command track, Jace watched Baez toss and turn, trying to sleep in the heat of the day.

"Tucker, did you drive top's jeep the day we got to Bear Cat?"

"Yes, sir. Top sent me to battalion to pick up distribution and to get some ice."

"Where did you leave the jeep when you got back?"

"Top told me we didn't need it no more and to take it back to the motor pool."

"Now Tucker, this is very important. Try to remember exactly. Did you lock the chain around the steering wheel when you parked?"

"No need for special rememberin', sir. I always lock vehicles up. It's kind of a thing with me. I don't ever leave anything unlocked."

"Who had the key to the vehicle?"

"Top gave it to me when I drove and I gave it back to him when I got back."

"And you're sure the jeep was locked up?"

"Absolutely, sir."

Jace sat in thought for a long while.

"OK, thanks, Tucker."

He sat quietly for a while longer, then picked up the field phone and cranked it. "Let me have S-1," he said to the switchboard operator.

"Hello, Mr. Adjutant, you old paperwork dog, you. Listen, put on your morale-and-welfare hat for a minute. I need a set of horseshoes, a volleyball and a net and if possible some badminton racquets and birdies. If you can think of any other games that might fit on a firebase throw those in too."

Later, Jace was out briefing the leaders for the evening's ambush patrols when Baez woke up. Despite the heat, the first sergeant made himself a steaming cup of

C-ration instant coffee. When Jace came in, he brought the first sergeant up to date on the day's activities. During the day he had written letters to the next-of-kin of the eight soldiers killed on Hill 108. The water trailer needed filling, the 2-1 track wouldn't start, and the paperwork needed to drop from the property book all the equipment and weapons lost during the battle was complete. He had also written recommendations for two Silver Stars and eight Bronze Stars for the action on Hill 108.

After a break, Jace asked, "Top, do you remember giving Tucker the key to the jeep to go get ice the day we came in from the field?"

"Yes, sir. He went to S-1, then to the ice plant, and right back. He gave me the key when he finished."

"Is that the only key to the jeep?"

"No, sir. There's a spare in the motor pool and S-4's got a master—"

"You see what I'm driving at, don't you?"

"Sir, even Ray Charles could see who's behind this."

"Top, give me your best shot at what will happen around here if Williams is convicted."

"Well, I'll tell you, sir, the mood amongst certain segments of the society is bad. The colored kids feel like when something bad happens, they always get blamed for it."

"Yeah," answered Jace thoughtfully. "Look, you know how these cases go. Just because Williams refused an article fifteen doesn't mean that the appointed prosecutor will spend any time investigating anything. He'll just bring in the M.P.s and Munn and Smith. Let's assume the prosecution will be lazy."

"You got me there, sir. I've charged a bunch for court-martial, but I ain't been to many."

"Here's what I want you to do. Go back to Bear Cat and dig up anything you can to help Williams. Find out who the defense counsel will be. Tell him Howell, Doc and Tucker can testify. It'll be good to have some friendly faces at the trial. Get the S-4 to show that Munn had access to the master key. Tucker will say the jeep was locked, and you can tell about who had the only key to the vehicle."

"What about Doc and Howell—what do they have to do with this?"

"If you can get it slipped in, they can testify about the incident in the field— you know, how Munn and Smith have established a pattern of discrimination against the colored kids. I plan to be there the day of the trial."

"Yes, sir, and I don't want you to think or say another word about this. I would not want the case affected by undue command influence. You just let old

Hector Baez, better known as the Mexican Perry Mason, handle this. I'll tell you what you need to know, but don't ask."

"OK," replied Jace.

"I'll need to get back and forth to Bear Cat a few times. I might mess up our day-night routine for a while."

"You take the mail chopper in when you need to. I'm rested now. I'll watch the perimeter at night. You do what you can to help Williams."

"Now, sir, you are the one that preferred charges—even if you were ordered to. You can't order me to help him. I didn't hear a word you said. The noise around here is awful." Tucker grinned, already looking forward to a couple of days at Bear Cat.

Baez rubbed his hands together. "The only thing I always wanted to be other than an Airborne Ranger, Infantry First Sergeant, was a lawyer," he laughed.

The sports equipment Jace ordered was on the next afternoon's mail chopper, which Baez joyfully boarded and flew away to begin his legal career. Besides horseshoes, volleyball and net, and a badminton set, there were two footballs, a basketball and a hoop, and three new chess sets. Young troops forgot about evening chow as they scraped away space for a volleyball court and tried to figure out how to erect the basketball goal. The country boys had the horse shoes clinking minutes after their arrival. Jace had to make sure proper guard was posted, because everyone wanted to play; no one wanted to sit behind the machine guns in the sun.

Even battle-shocked youngsters responded when the basketball goal finally went up on the boom of the tracked wrecker. As Baez lifted off from the helipad, he could see skinny black, white and brown youngsters, stripped to the waist and jumping, dribbling and shouting joyfully at play. He prayed that these kids, as they slowly recovered from the horror of Hill 108, wouldn't have to face another trauma—the ugliness of injustice.

The crew threw the mail from the chopper before it even touched down. Ducking low, the headquarters company mail clerk and Tucker darted under the whirling blades to retrieve the bags. There were other miscellaneous items to be unloaded, but the mail was what everyone was after. Tucker lugged the bags back to the company CP, where the troops gathered before mail call was even announced, forcing him to shoo them away until be broke out a pile for each platoon.

"Sir, here is something from the first sergeant," he yelled above the noise of the departing Huey.

Jace opened the envelope. The note read:

Cpt Spencer,

I'm going up-country to Pleiku. Catching a C-130 at 1400. I'll brief you later. Be back tomorrow or next day. The defense council will be Lieutenant Brown, the brigade headquarters company XO. I've already talked to him. The case will be tried next Thur. Please send Doc, Howell, and Tucker in on Tue. or Wed. to get ready.

Baez

The rest of the week was routine. Patrols and ambushes went out and came in. Road runner platoons clanked out to the highway to thunder meaninglessly up and down the road. Tracks left to escort convoys. Artillery boomed, mortars thumped, helicopters came and went, cooks cooked, mechanics fixed, medics nursed and the chaplain prayed. Officers went to meetings, sergeants inspected and troops bitched. Men drank coffee, beer, cokes, even water, by the gallon. They read mail, threw knives, cleaned weapons, pitched horseshoes, spiked volleyballs, pulled guard, and wrote letters. Between all this, they told stories about home, women, and cars. As the lazy, busy rhythm of firebase life droned on in the sun, Charlie company slowly recovered from the trauma of Hill 108. But when Jace listened to the talk, he could tell that a new wound was festering: the court martial of Private Williams.

Doc Roberts entered the CP tent as Jace cursed. Cement glue in hand, he was trying to piece the ceramic cat back together. Doc stood silent and watched for a moment.

"Somehow symbolic, huh, sir?" he asked at length.

Jace looked up, surprised. "Yeah, I guess that's one way of looking at it. It'll never go back together, the clay wasn't fired right and it crumbles. Oh the hell with it anyway!" he said, scooping up the pieces and tossing them into the trash bag. "What can I do for you, Doc?"

"I want to look at those bite wounds again. One looked like it was getting infected."

"Oh, they're all right," replied Jace.

"Then you won't mind me takin' a look, then will you?"

Jace submitted. Doc hummed as he removed the bandages and cleaned the wounds.

"Bet you never thought you'd get a purple heart for gettin' bit. Well, they're not too bad, but I want you to get over to the battalion aid station and get another shot. That's an order, captain."

"Yes, Doc, I will."

"Today, captain."

"Yes, Doc, I will," Jace repeated, grinning.

Doc smiled and put his gauze and scissors back in his bag. At the tent flap, he paused. "Sir, do you think top will be able to get Williams off?"

"I don't know, Doc. I hope so. How did you know he was trying?"

"You know there ain't no secrets in this place," grinned Doc.

"I smell Tucker in this somewhere," laughed Jace.

"Sir, you need to know that all the brothers in the company—headquarters company, too—are watching this close—maybe even too close."

"What do you mean, Doc?"

"I mean there are some bad feelings brewing. In some ways worse than before you got here."

"OK, Doc, spill it."

"Things were pretty much hopeless before you took over. We all knew we never had a chance. No matter what we did, somebody was gonna end up gettin' screwed. You changed all that. You've made things better. You really have. Now—"

"Go on, Doc."

"Now, the guys are starting to feel that the system will grind them off at the nub, even if we've got a C.O. and a first sergeant that try to do what's right. They—we feel like the green machine is against the black man."

"What do you think will happen if Williams is convicted?"

"I can't say for sure, but I think some of the hot-heads will try to get back at the system somehow."

"Doc, do you know something I need to know?" asked Jace carefully.

"No, sir. I swear. It's just a feeling. I hear talk, you know. The guys need to know somebody gives a shit."

"Doc, I give a shit. Don't they know that?"

"They think you don't matter. You can't stop the shit from rolling down hill. If the system gets on your case, that's it. You're dead meat."

Jace sat, stroking his chin, looking at the ground.

"Sir, you asked me what might happen if Williams is convicted."

"Yeah?"

"I think this whole battalion is gonna blow wide open."

Lau's journey to the 274th was a nightmare. Staggering from Hill 108, he fought his way through the dense jungle foliage until daylight. Head pounding, needing sleep, but somehow realizing that he shouldn't give in to fatigue, he pushed on. Finally he came to a small foot path, but it ran north and south instead of west. Giving in to the human tendency to follow the path of least resistance, he took the trail to the north. As the day wore on, his pain and dizziness increased. He felt hunger, but no desire to actually eat. As the sun sank and the jungle floor grew darker, he saw movement on the trail ahead. Creeping forward, he ran into the back of a file of shot-up guerrillas who had also escaped from the regimental headquarters.

The group had no leader. As senior officer Lau took charge, only to realize that they were as lost as he was. They slept in the leech and ant-infested jungle that night. The moans of the wounded and the pain and itch of insect bites combined with hunger and thirst to make the night interminable.

Dawn brought little hope. The group continued northward until they neared Highway 1, where by accident they stumbled upon a trail leading west. Stopping only to bury one of the wounded who had died and to drink from streams, they continued marching into the heat of the day. Near exhaustion and nearly crippled by a severe headache, Lau took his turns carrying the makeshift litters. Finally, near dark, one of the guerrillas excitedly recognized a trail junction he knew to be but a short distance from the 274th. Lau hardly remembered staggering into camp and being put to bed. Early the next morning, an orderly awakened him and asked him if he felt well enough to see the battalion commander.

"Comrade Colonel Lau," said the 274th commander cordially, "We are extremely glad that you survived and found your way here. How are you feeling? Would you like tea?"

"Yes, thank you. I am doing much better," lied Lau as he wondered why he had been summoned so early. After some required small talk, he learned.

"Your comrades told me of the battle and of your escape. Comrade Lau, Do you know if the regimental commander survived?"

"No," answered Lau sadly, "Unfortunately, I saw him die."

After a long pause, the commander continued, "I am senior to the other battalion commanders. Until I hear something contrary from division, I feel I must assume command of the regiment. As the only other senior officer available, you must take command of the 274th Battalion."

"But I am a political officer. I have not been trained to fight," argued Lau.

"The task before us is more of a political operation than a military one," replied the commander. "You will be perfectly suited to manage the popular uprising following the general offensive. The attacks have been planned, the company commanders and platoon leaders have been briefed, and they will do their duties. When the population rallies to our side, there will be many political duties to accomplish that I am not qualified for. Your extensive training will serve us well in the first critical hours of the offensive. As far as tactics, none of us have experience in attacking populated areas. We are jungle fighters. So, you see, you have as much experience as we in planning a battle in a major city. Besides, you might be able to give us a political slant on our tactics as we plan and train."

Lau tried to think of something else to say, but could not come up with anything that did not sound cowardly. So he said nothing. The new regimental commander continued, "I will command the regiment from this location, where I will be able to help you learn your duties. I can coordinate the defense of this base while you concentrate on planning the general offensive and popular uprising."

"When do I start?" asked Lau.

"Right now," said the commander. "Your first duty will be to personally reconnoiter your battalion objectives for the offensive. I would like you to leave as soon as you feel you are able. When do you think you will feel like traveling?"

"The journey from the scene of the battle hurt quite a bit." Lau almost laughed at the understatement. "But I am recovering quickly. I should be able to travel in a few days."

"Good. I will have the company commander who is responsible for the defense of this site take you on a tour of our positions. He will also give you the tactical training you will need."

Lau's thoughts were jumbled as he returned to his sleeping mat. His head still ached and he was exhausted. He supposed his main concern should be learning what he should know to command. Instead, his main thought was that somehow, maybe all of this would offer him an opportunity to find Phun.

Except for meetings, Jace had not been to the TOC since the battle. He dreaded going this day, but he felt he had to. He bent under the tent flaps and found the battalion commander sitting in a folding chair reading the *Stars and Stripes*.

"Sir, I would like to ask your permission to return to Bear Cat tomorrow," said Jace.

"What for?" asked Lieutenant Colonel Price, curtly.

"One of my troops is being court-martialed and I would like to be there."

"Is this the guy that stole the jeep?" asked Price, annoyed.

"He is the one charged with that offense, yes, sir."

"What role do you have in this? Are you going to testify?"

"No, sir," replied Jace patiently. "I just feel he is getting a bum rap and I think it's important for me to be there. My troops feel the same way," he added.

"Bum rap, huh? If you remember, I cautioned you about supporting my policies."

"Sir, I will support and comply with all of your directives and policies. I will also tell you what I think. I owe it to you to tell you the truth—and the truth as I see it is that Private Williams is an innocent victim. If you would allow me to explain the circumstances perhaps—."

"We've been through this, before. The bottom line is that I told you to punish this man for an offense and you feel that he's getting a bum rap. It looks to me that you are purposely defying me."

"Sir, this is not personal. I just know the background and the circumstances. This young man has had three article fifteens. One more and he will be out of the army with a less-than-honorable discharge. I feel that I am supporting my soldier, not defying you."

"What's so great about this private? If he's already gotten three article fifteens, he's already shown that he's a bum. What's so special about him that you would leave your rifle company in the field for a full day?"

"There's nothing special about him, sir. He's just a soldier. A soldier that stood with me on Hill 108."

"That's what this is all about, then, isn't it? Who was with you and who was against you on that damned hill."

"No, sir," Jace said tiredly. "My only point was that he fought. Some others did not, but he did. And for that, I owe him."

"Well, you may not go, so forget it."

Jace had already thought this possibility through.

"Sir, I am up for R and R soon. I request permission to spend three days in Bear Cat in lieu of a week on R and R out of country."

Price put down his paper and looked thoughtfully at Jace.

"This guy is important enough for you to give up a week in Australia or Hong Kong?"

"Not only this guy, but all of my soldiers—any one of my soldiers."

"Denied. You need your R and R. I need you in the field commanding your company. You stay here."

"Yes, sir. Thank you for your time, sir."

Jace saluted, spun on his heel and left the TOC.

The two groups stood apart outside the jungle school classroom, where the trial was to take place. Inside, the president of the court-martial, a division staff major, reviewed procedure with the five other members of the court. Smith and Munn, confident that they would have their way, laughed a little too loudly at the jokes told by the prosecutor, a transportation corps captain. The small group of Charlie company soldiers talked quietly near the door. Williams stood apart and stared at nothing. Finally, all were summoned inside and the ritual began with the reading of convening orders, the instructing of the court, and the arraignment of the accused.

"Private Williams please stand. I will now read the charges, "said the president of the court. "You have been charged with violating Article 92, failure to obey a lawful order. In that Private Clyde W. Williams, having knowledge of a lawful order issued by the commanding officer, Fifth Battalion (Mechanized), 39th Infantry to lock all unattended vehicles, an order which it was his duty to obey, did, on or about 4 November 1967, fail to obey the same by willfully leaving an M-151 quarter-ton truck, bumper number C-07, unlocked and unsecured at the Bear Cat post exchange parking lot."

The president went on to read the charges of violating Article 121, wrongful appropriation of government property, and Article 134, driving without proper military operator's license."

After a pause, he asked, "How do you plead?"

"Not guilty," responded Williams.

"Will the prosecution make an opening statement?"

"Yes, sir, a very brief one. This is an open-and-shut case, sir. Two NCOs were nearly run down by this man driving a jeep that he wrongfully appropriated and was driving without a license. The M.P.s found the jeep unsecured at the PX just as Private Williams here and his buddy were coming out of the building. Sir, this man is not a good soldier. He received three article fifteens in his previous company before receiving a rehabilitation transfer to C company. His record speaks for itself. As soon as he arrived in C company, he started the same stuff he was doing previously. He is guilty and I will prove he is guilty."

"Thank you," said the president of the board. "Defense counsel, do you have an opening statement?"

"After the prosecution rests, sir."

"All right, the prosecution may call its first witness."

"Sir, I call Staff Sergeant Ezell Munn."

"State your name, rank and assignment for the record."

"Ezell R. Munn, Staff Sergeant, battalion S-4 sergeant, fifth of the 39th Infantry."

Munn took the oath, sullen and smug.

"On the fourth of November, what were you doing right after noon chow?"

"Me and Sergeant Smith decided we'd walk up to the PX and get some cigarettes."

"Did you have occasion to see Private Williams as—"

"Objection! Leading."

"Sustained, rephrase the question."

"Yes, sir. On the way to the PX, did anything unusual happen to you?"

"Yes, sir. We wuz nearly runned over by a jeep."

"Did you happen to see who was driving that jeep?"

"Yes, sir."

"Is he in this room right now?"

"Yes, sir, he is rat thar."

"Let the record show that the witness pointed to Private Williams. Now, did you see this same jeep—let's see, bumper number C-07—at any other time during the day?"

"Yes, sir, at the PX."

"And what happened there?"

"Some M.P.s asked us if we knowed who'uz drivin' that jeep. Just then these two—Williams and Peoples came out of the PX and I recognized them and pointed them out. I said Williams wuz drivin'. The MPs arrested him."

"No further questions, sir."

Lieutenant Brown, the defense counsel approached.

"Sergeant Munn. Which direction were you walking when the jeep nearly ran you down?"

"Torge the PX, why?"

"The same direction the jeep was traveling?"

"Yes, sir."

"If the jeep was approaching you from behind, how did you know it was about to run you down?"

"We looked back just in time."

"So, you were dodging?"

"Yeah, we wuz jumpin' out of the way."

"After it passed, could you see who was driving?"

"Yes, sir, he wuz lookin' back and laughin'."

"Isn't the road kind of dusty this time of year at Bear Cat?"

"Yes, sir, I reckon so."

"So, while you were dodging and the jeep was driving away from you in a cloud of dust, you were able to identify the driver?"

"Yes, sir. It 'uz Williams thar."

"In the confusion and dust, couldn't you have misidentified the driver?"

"No, sir, It 'uz him, alright."

"That's all I have—no, I have one more question for Sergeant Munn. Was the lock cut?"

"Sir?"

"You drove the vehicle back to the motor pool didn't you?"

"Objection—leading the witness."

"Sustained."

"Who drove the vehicle back to the motor pool after Williams was arrested?"

"I did."

"Had the lock been broken or cut?"

"No, sir."

"Did you secure the vehicle once you arrived at the motor pool?"

"Yes, sir, I locked it up."

"Doesn't a series 200 padlock require a key to lock it as well as unlock it?"

"Yes, sir."

"How did you lock it then?"

"I went inside the motor pool shed and got the master key and locked it up."

"No further questions, sir."

"Sergeant Munn, you are excused, subject to recall," said the president of the court.

Munn's grin was a sneer as he swaggered past Williams. Neither Baez, Doc Roberts, nor Tucker looked at him as he left.

Sergeant Smith was called next. He repeated Munn's story almost verbatim, but became subdued when defense asked about the kicking incident in the jungle. The M.P. then testified about finding the jeep unlocked and how Munn had pointed out Williams as the driver. Under cross-examination, however, he admitted that he had not seen Williams actually driving.

"Sir, prosecution rests."

"Defense, you may make an opening statement."

"Thank you, sir," replied Lieutenant Brown, expansively.

"Gentlemen of the court, I intend to prove that Private Williams did not, in fact could not have been driving that jeep that day. He did not have a key to unlock the vehicle, which was locked in Charlie company's motor pool. In fact, if the truth were known, somebody else—someone with access to a master key—unlocked the vehicle, drove it to the PX, and left it unlocked as they went inside. Then, as the actual driver came out and was confronted by the M.P.s, he blamed the crime on the first Charlie company soldier he saw—Private Williams."

Lieutenant Brown then called Tucker, who testified that he had left the jeep locked after he had made his rounds. He did not bend under cross-examination. The motor sergeant testified that a master key was not kept in the motor shack, as Munn had said. He swore that a set of duplicate keys were kept locked in a desk in the shack and that only he had the key to the desk. The S-4 captain was called to state that the only master key to the lock set was kept on a key ring in the S-4 shop. He admitted that anyone who worked in S-4 had access to the master key. Peoples testified that he had indeed walked with Williams to the PX and that they had not driven a jeep at any time. He also told the story about being kicked by Smith. Doc Roberts, over vehement objections by the prosecutor, was allowed to testify about the two sergeants' roles in the racial incident in the jungle.

Then the defense counsel called First Sergeant Baez to the stand.

"First Sergeant, have you reviewed Private Williams' 201 file?"

"Yes, sir," answered Baez, confidently.

"Does Private Williams' record show that he has ever had any type of driver's training?"

"No, sir."

"What are Private Williams' assignments to date?"

"He went to basic training at Fort Jackson, and advanced individual training at Fort Benning. Then he came straight to Vietnam."

"Is there driver training in basic or infantry AIT?"

"No, sir."

"How do you know that?"

"Because I served a tour as a drill sergeant at Benning. I know about the curriculum of basic and advanced individual training both.

"Then, as far as his record is concerned, Private Williams has never received training in the army on how to drive a vehicle?"

"That's right, sir."

Brown went on to ask Baez about how he had had control of his key to the vehicle except when Tucker drove it to S-1 and the ice plant. Then, again over prosecution objections, Baez told of the racially charged atmosphere in the company and the incident with the water buffalo. He claimed that Sergeant Munn and Smith seemed to be at the center of every bad thing that had taken place in the company since he had been assigned there.

During a short recess, Baez, Roberts, Tucker, and Peoples gathered outside for small talk. Munn and Smith stayed to themselves, scowling, mumbling, smoking and spitting.

When the court reconvened, the president of the court-martial asked, "Defense counsel, do you have any more witnesses?"

"Just one, sir. At this time I would like to call Specialist Fourth Class Raymond Davis."

The back door of the classroom opened and a tall African-American soldier with the huge First Cavalry Division patch sewn on his left shoulder walked in. As he walked to the witness chair with long, lanky strides, Williams beamed and raised his left forefinger in a small wave. Davis grinned and nodded, then turned to face the president of the court.

"Do you swear or affirm that the testimony you are about to give will be the truth, the whole truth, and nothing but the truth, so help you, God?"

"I do."

"Be seated."

"State your name, rank and unit for the record."

"Raymond A. Davis, Spec Four, A comp'ny, First of the Seventh Cav, First Cavalry Division—Garryowen."

"Objection, sir. This man has no knowledge of the incident. I understand he was flown here from Pleiku yesterday. Any testimony he may bring in this case is bound to be irrelevant!" yelled the prosecutor.

"Sir, I will show his connection to this case right up front," said Lieutenant Brown.

"Proceed," said the president. "But the link better be made quickly."

"Yes, sir," said Brown. "Specialist Davis, do you know Private Williams, the accused in this case?"

"Yes, suh, tha's him rat there," grinned Davis.

"How do you know him?"

"He my cousin. We'uz raised together, me'n him. Our granny raised us like we'uz brothers. Since we'uz jus' little."

"You grew up together?"

"Yes, suh."

"You did everything together?"

"Yes, suh."

"Objection, no connection to this case!"

"Counselor—" warned the president of the court.

"Yes, sir. Right now, sir," said Brown.

"You two lived together until you joined the army?"

"Yes, suh, we jined together. Same time."

"Do you believe Williams drove that jeep he is charged with taking and leaving unsecured?"

"No, suh."

"Why not?"

"He caint drive, suh. Me neither. We never had nothin' but mules to plow wif on the farm. My uncle's mules. We he'ped him, but we never drove. We'nt have no car, no truck, no tractor. Nobody never let us try to drive nothin. We never did have no chance to learn."

"No further questions," said Lieutenant Brown.

Phun walked past the two innocuous-looking, but alert body guards into the small Saigon restaurant. Getting the appointment with the commanding general of the 5th Viet Cong Division had been difficult—and intimidating. Several times, she had almost convinced herself to cancel the appointment, though it would mean a tremendous loss of face to do so. Finally, she had screwed up her courage and pushed ahead.

The general, a young, and pleasant-looking man, politely offered Phun a seat at his table. Two other men, whom Phun assumed were staff officers, commissars, or commanders, abruptly stood and left as Phun sat down. The general placed a plate in front of Phun and offered *nem rau*, the delicate vegetable spring rolls popular in the Mekong Delta. He poured tea and asked about her family, her home town of Xuan Loc, and how the weather had affected the last rice crop.

After twenty minutes of small talk, the general finally asked, "How may I serve you, younger sister?"

"Comrade General, I request another assignment," said Phun.

"Young woman, you have been one of the best liaison couriers we have ever had. I can always count on you to get messages from headquarters to headquarters in a timely, accurate manner. You are needed where you are. What is the reason for this request?" asked the major general.

"Comrade General, I can only state that I have personal reasons. I wish to fight. I feel that I can serve the cause better as a fighter than a messenger."

"We do have women fighters. I do not wish to seem too forward, but for the most part, they are not as frail and feminine as you. Do you believe you can carry the burden of living in the jungle, marching with heavy loads and killing?"

"General, I have been in fighting. I have been shot at. I have cared for the wounded. I have marched through the jungle. I would like the chance to show what I can do."

"Your bravery is a matter of record. But today, your demeanor is very sad. I hope you are not acting impulsively. Is there a problem I should know about? Have you suffered loss? What is it that suddenly makes you want to be a fighter?"

Phun suddenly burst into tears. "Yes, there is something. But as I said, it is personal. I respectfully ask that you respect my wishes and my privacy. I have been a good soldier. Can I not make a request without explaining the reason?"

"All right, I grant your request—reluctantly. I will make arrangements for your training, which will begin soon."

"Thank you, Comrade General. There is but one more small favor I would like to request."

"And that is?"

"That I be transferred from the second regiment."

"But you know the area, the people, the officers, and the fighters," said the general.

"Yes, sir, I do. But if you would allow me. The problem that I humbly ask to keep to myself, that I wish to escape from, is in the second regiment. I request that I be allowed to serve in another unit, far from Long Binh, Binh Hoa, or Xuan Loc."

"If anyone else had asked me, especially at this critical time, I would be forced to say no. But your service has been exemplary. For me to deny such a heart-felt request from one who has been so loyal would be unthinkable. I will assign you to first regiment, north of Saigon. But I warn you—the objectives for first regiment during the general offensive are in the heart of Saigon, and are very, very dangerous. They include the American Embassy."

"At this stage of my life," replied Phun, "danger is of no consequence. In fact I welcome the challenge."

"I will make the arrangements. Can you leave at once?"

"Yes, Comrade General. I simply ask that I be allowed to go home to Xuan Loc to gather a few belongings and to say goodby to my family. If I could report to first regiment in a week, I would greatly appreciate it."

"May I venture an observation?"

"Certainly, Comrade General."

"From all outward appearances, I would say that you are in love. Is that it?"

Phun sobbed anew. "Any other time, I would be very happy. But now, during this historic time, I am afraid the feelings that I have for this man might interfere with his duties and mine. I feel that it would be better for all concerned if we stay apart."

"Then I understand and concur. Good luck, little sister," said the general.

"You have been most kind," answered Phun. I will not let you or the National Liberation Front down."

As the court-martial board deliberated, Tucker, Howell, Doc, and Davis sat on sand bags in the shade of the mess hall across the road, talking and waiting nervously. Baez hovered near the door, awaiting word.

"How long do you think they'll take?" asked Tucker.

"There's no way of knowing. I'll bet—" began Doc.

"Don't be lookin' over here at us like you want to do somthin'", interrupted Baez as he yelled at Munn across the street.

"First Sergeant, I'll look anywhere I want. I 'ont work for you no more, so you might 'uz well leave me alone."

The two NCOs stared malevolently at each other across the short distance, then Munn spat and turned away.

"Ain't no secret what he thinks of me, is it?" Baez asked.

"They've got a verdict!" shouted Tucker as he returned from checking things out.

"Come on!" shouted Baez. "Let's see what shakes out."

The small gallery and the court filed back into the classroom. Williams took his place with his counsel at the defense table.

"We have reached a verdict," announced the president of the court-martial. "Private Williams, please stand."

Williams cut a quick look at Baez, who gave him a thumbs-up.

"The members of this court-martial board, unanimously by secret vote, find you not guilty. You are free to go."

Lieutenant Brown shook Williams' hand as the Charlie company contingent went wild. Doc and Howell hugged each other as Baez pounded them on the back.

Munn scowled first at Williams, then at Baez, then back at Williams. As they all spilled out into the street, he approached Baez and shouted, "Don't you even think about sticking me with this. There ain't no proof of nothin'. Don't think because you got a bunch of lying——"

"Go ahead and say it. Go ahead and call them niggers and I'll knock your rotten teeth down your throat," hissed Baez.

"I'll tell you what. This ain't finished. I'll get even, by God. I'll get even."

"Just exactly who are you gonna get even with?—and how?" asked Baez.

"Anybody that crosses me. Any way I can. You'll see, by God."

"Are you threatening me, Sergeant Munn?" asked Baez, quietly and evenly.

"Naw, that ain't no threat," sputtered Munn.

"I don't know where you got that high-and-mighty attitude," said Baez, "but if I was you, I'd watch my mouth. Insubordination is a court-martial offense, too, you know."

For a long moment Munn stared at Baez, then spun on his heel and slouched away. Baez watched him go, then turned toward his troops. Williams and his cousin, surrounded by Doc Roberts, Howell and Tucker were talking at the same time, at the top of their lungs.

"Top, do we have to go back to the fire base tonight?" asked Tucker.

"I don't see how we can. We got no transportation till tomorrow. Tonight I declare a party. Williams is guest of honor. We'll go to the NCO club, by damn. You are all my guests—and I'll whip anybody that tries to throw us out."

They all walked to the snack bar where they gorged on Buddha's burgers and beer. After showers, shaves and shines, they all walked to the division NCO club. Despite Baez's bravado, he explained to the manager what had happened in the afternoon and told him that the soldiers were his guests. He made sure no one would hassle them.

That night, Howell got very drunk very quickly. After each beer he finished, he roared, "Eight months on the line and I'm still alive!" before crushing the can on his forehead. Doc waxed philosophical, wanting to discuss the crusade of Martin Luther King Jr. Williams and Davis, reverting to their boyhood habits, sipped and talked about times gone by. Tucker just wanted to play the pin-ball machine. Baez watched over them like a mother hen, drinking and saying little.

After midnight, as parachute flares hung silently over the dark horizon, the six thoroughly drunk soldiers tumbled loudly from the club. Far in the distance, a stream of tracers noiselessly stitched the night sky. They walked for a while, stopped to urinate in the road, and then continued weaving toward their bunks. Outside their tents, they stood quietly with arms on each other's shoulders. Davis broke the silence.

"I wanna thank y'all fo' he'pin' my cousin," he said, seriously.

"Shee-it!" yelled Howell.

They all laughed at nothing until their sides ached.

Mid-morning, Baez saw to it that Davis, feeling sick and shaky, flew back up-country on a Caribou from Long Thanh airfield. Then he arranged for the others to fly back to the field on the mail bird. As the Huey approached Fire Base Cougar, the five hung-over soldiers lay atop mail bags and parcels.

From across the fire base, Jace read the body language as soon as his soldiers stepped out of the bird.

"Don't look good for the home team."

"What do you mean, sir?" asked Five India, looking up from the book he was reading.

"If I've ever seen a picture of defeat, there's one," answered Jace. "We've lost for sure."

Baez led the woozy contingent to the CP tent affixed to the rear of Jace's command track. Tucker crawled in next to Five India and lay down on the board seat. Doc sat heavily on a folding chair. Howell grabbed on to the tent pole as Williams hung back sheepishly.

"Is no one going to tell me what the hell happened?" screamed Jace.

"Williams is a free man. We won," answered Baez. "Just please don't yell, sir. We're a bunch of hurtin' puppy dogs."

Also mistaking hang-overs for the body language of defeat, angry-looking soldiers began to gather outside the CP. Cautiously, they approached Williams, who was as self-conscious as he was hung over.

"You don't look so good, man. What happened? How'd it go?" asked a black soldier.

"I got off," said Williams quietly.

An excited yelp rose from the group, was joined by others, then grew into a loud, traveling murmur. It bounced from bunker to bunker, track to track until it almost reached the level of a cheer.

"Well, Perry Mason, you did it. What happened?" asked Jace.

"Sir, we kicked their ass. Now, with all due respect and all that shit, I've got a hangover like a vodka-drinkin' Russian jumpmaster. Can I take a nap and tell you later?"

"Top, you can do any damn thing you want to," laughed Jace.

He walked outside and approached Williams. "How 'bout you, young man? You hurtin' too?"

"Yassah, perty bad."

"I didn't have a chance to tell you how proud I was of you in the fire fight. Howell said you hung with us. He said you fought good. I'm glad you're one of my soldiers."

"Suh, can I go get me some sleep? I feel real bad."

"Sure, Williams, sure. Sleep the rest of the night. We'll worry about puttin' you back on guard tomorrow—and congratulations."

A short distance away, Lieutenant Colonel Price heard the commotion erupt around the perimeter. "XO, go find out what the hell is going on out there. I won't have a bunch of rowdiness on my fire base."

"Yes, sir," replied C.C., who knew exactly what the excitement meant. "I'll go check it out."

CHAPTER 14

▼

11 November 1967

It took almost a week for Lau to feel like he could travel. During that time, he slept all he could, ate as much rice as he could hold and drank green tea continuously. His strength returned quickly and his headaches eventually began to subside.

As Lau and his party walked the familiar foot-wide path toward Highway 1 where he would catch the bus into Bien Hoa, his body guards were more wary than ever. Since the battle at regiment, they stopped often to listen to the sounds of the jungle. Suddenly a guard dropped to one knee and held up his hand.

"What is it?" asked Lau in a whisper.

"Americans. Listen."

Lau cocked his head, at first hearing nothing. Then a clink of metal and a cough filtered through the jungle.

"I smelled them before I heard them," said the guard.

"What do you mean?" asked Lau.

"I smelled their cigarette smoke and their insect repellent. If you get close enough, you can smell their bodies. They have a strong, foul odor—from eating so much meat."

"What do we do?"

"We will back off down the trail and wait. They are probably a patrol from their camp near the highway. It is too early in the day for them to be in an ambush position so they should be moving on soon."

In a few minutes, Lau could hear the rustle in the jungle and the soft scuffling of feet on the forest floor. At one point, he could see foliage moving as it was being bumped and pushed aside by the enemy. Slowly the sounds diminished, then disappeared completely. Carefully, the lead guard crept ahead along the trail. In a moment he returned to nod that the way was clear. They moved on, even more carefully than before.

They came to the highway near a small village where Lau could wait for the bus. He thanked the guards, looked about, then stepped into the open and walked calmly and normally to the road. The villagers who saw him emerge from the jungle ignored him. The less they saw of the comings and goings of both sides in this war, the better off they were.

Lau watched for a moment to see if there were any signs of government soldiers, and then asked an old woman when the bus was due.

"It comes in the early afternoon," answered the betelnut-chewing crone. "My nephew has a tea stand near the road if you would like refreshment while you wait."

Lau thanked the woman and walked to the stand. Ordering tea, he looked off down the highway toward Xuan Loc. Fear rose in his chest as he saw an American convoy approaching in a cloud of black diesel smoke. Still feeling the trauma of battle, his first impulse was to run, but with great effort, he forced himself to be calm. To the enemy, he told himself, he would be just another villager drinking tea. As the trucks and armored vehicles rumbled past, the children of the village ran to the roadside to wave and beg. Some extended their middle fingers in the same greeting the Americans often gave them. Others mimicked the peace sign the foreigners flashed continuously. When the troops tossed candy and canned rations to the children, a mad scramble erupted, causing the Americans to laugh and point. It sickened Lau to see Vietnamese acting this way, even if they were only children.

He had finished his second cup of tea and was feeling drowsy in the heat when someone yelled that the bus was coming. He got to his feet, stretched, and picked up his knapsack. Walking to the roadside, he raised his hand and watched the old Mercedes bus brake to a squealing stop. Relieved, he saw that there was no one riding on top of the vehicle. He thought to himself that he might actually get a seat this time.

The door opened and Lau climbed the two steps and paid the driver. As he turned down the isle to find a seat, he was startled by a scream as someone slammed into him and grabbed him around the waist. Adrenaline surged as he balled his fists and prepared to fight for his life.

Jace was timing one of his mortar crews as they went through a practice mission when Lieutenant Colonel Price found him.

"Good afternoon, sir," Jace said as pleasantly as he could manage.

"I see you are still defying me," said Price.

"What do you mean, sir?"

"You know exactly what I mean. I told you to punish that man for stealing a jeep, and you work as hard as you can to get him off."

"Sir, you told me to give him an article fifteen, which I did, and which he refused as was his right. You told me to court-martial him, which I did. He was found not guilty. I don't see how that can be construed as defying you."

"Do you deny that you sent your first sergeant to Bear Cat to find witnesses? Do you deny that your first sergeant even flew to Pleiku to bring back someone to testify?"

"No, sir, I don't deny that at all. I felt that if Williams was going to be court-martialed, he deserved the right to call any and all witnesses that could prove his innocence."

"That's what I'm talking about. I told you to punish him and you continued to try to prove he was innocent."

"Sir, he is innocent. He was found not guilty in a court-martial. I did everything you told me to do, but the man is still innocent."

"Undue command influence in a court-martial case is not something I will condone," hissed Price, his face turning red.

"Sir, I did not interfere. I sent my first sergeant to help find witnesses, that's all. The man had a right to his witnesses, one of whom happened to be up-country. Someone had to see that he had a fair defense."

"That's why he had a defense counsel. You had no right or business to—."

"To what?" exploded Jace, violently angry now, and not caring about the consequences. "To make sure he got a fair trial? To make sure he wasn't railroaded?"

"Railroaded? Are you accusing me of railroading a soldier?"

"No, sir, I am not. But I thought you only ordered me to bring charges against him. I had no idea you were ordering me to make sure he was found guilty. That's command interference for sure."

"Now you're accusing me of command influence on a court-martial?"

"Sir this isn't getting us anywhere. Obviously, you aren't pleased with my performance as company commander. No matter what I do, it seems to piss you off."

"Captain, I can see by your attitude that you think for some reason I won't relieve you."

"Sir, as I told you before, it is your prerogative to relieve me any time you wish. In the meantime, it is my responsibility to take care of my troops—which I will do to the best of my ability as long as I am standing."

Red-faced and furious, Price stared at Jace, then turned away to stalk back toward the TOC. The mortar crew, having witnessed the whole conversation, stood dumbfounded.

Believing himself to be under attack, Lau struggled to stay on his feet as he grappled with his assailant on the crowded bus. As he drew back his fist and prepared to strike, he looked with disbelief into the face of the woman he loved. Both of them stunned, Phun and Lau fell into a seat, clutching each other furiously. The other passengers stared at them, curious and offended at the same time by this unbelievable public display of emotion and affection.

With their hands gripped tightly, Phun and Lau both wept unashamedly.

"I thought you were dead—or in prison," sobbed Phun. "I thought I would never see you again."

Realizing the scene they had made, Phun announced to the other passengers, "My husband is a soldier. I thought he had been killed. We are sorry for the disturbance."

The men acted offended or uninterested, but some of the women smiled as they returned to their own conversations. Some people continued to stare.

"We cannot talk here," said Lau quietly. We will get off in Bien Hoa and I will tell you all that has happened."

They left the bus in the middle of the city and went straight to a hotel, where Phun waited demurely as Lau rented a room. They walked up to the second floor to a room with large open windows that overlooked the street. A large fan whirled above them as they embraced in the steamy heat of the late afternoon. Without talking, they threw their clothes aside and for a few precious hours, forgot their fears and anxieties. Both knew they had fearsome news for the other, but that could wait. Everything could wait as they clung to each other desperately.

That night, they ate in the small restaurant next door to the hotel. Still reluctant to share the dangers that lay ahead for each of them, they simply stared into each other's eyes and held hands. Later, when they returned to the room, they both understood it was time to talk, though neither wanted it.

Lau began by telling her about everything that had happened to him since they had been separated on the road to Binh Son. Finally, he told her about Huong's death and about being assigned as the commander of the 274th battalion. He didn't have to say more. With the coming general offensive, they both knew what being a commander of a Viet Cong battalion meant.

"I too have something I must tell you," Phun said reluctantly. "When you failed to return after your capture, I lost hope. I could not continue to travel the roads and trails and go to the villages we had gone to together. The sadness, the pain and the sense of loss overwhelmed me. I had nothing to live for, so I decided that fighting would be a better course for me than being a messenger."

"No, I won't—" began Lau.

"Please, let me finish. I went to the general and asked to be assigned to another regiment and that I be allowed to fight. At first, he was reluctant, but in the end, he agreed. I have been assigned to the C-10 battalion north of Saigon in the Michelin rubber plantation where I will be an ordinary squad member."

"No—I will have you reassigned to my battalion where—"

"You and I both know that would not work. You would be more concerned about my safety than you would be about doing your duty. Everyone in the unit would know we are in love and there would be accusations of favoritism and inappropriate behavior. Also, I would be so anxious over your safety that I would be worthless as a soldier. No, you must command the 274th and I must go to the C-10 battalion."

"Then please, ask the general if you can resume your duties as liaison courier." begged Lau. "You would be safer carrying messages than fighting the Americans. That way we could see each other from time to time."

"You know I cannot do that. After asking for another assignment, it would be a tremendous loss of face to go back and ask that the orders be canceled simply because I found you. No, I must do as I requested. The task ahead is vital and dangerous and should be foremost in both our minds. We can never have a life together as long as the enemy occupies our land. I could not stand the shame if we did not do our part to win final victory. If we both live through the general offensive, and if the people rally to our side as predicted, then, and only then might we have a chance for a life together."

"Right now, I care about nothing about final victory," said Lau. "I care about nothing but your love and your safety. I do not want to command the battalion. When I left the north, all I wanted to do was come face to face with an American so I could avenge my family. I miss my children still, but my love for you has replaced my desire for revenge. I want us both to live. I want you to marry me."

"Your love means more to me than my life," whispered Phun as she cradled his face in her hands. "But we are in the midst of a war. Think of all you have been through and what we all must go through still. You should not say you do not want to command the battalion. Of course you must—I would have it no other way. If we die, then we will be together in the spirit world. If one of us dies, we will simply wait for the other on the other side. If we both live, then we can marry when the country is united and free."

Lau suddenly realized how weak and afraid he must sound. Desperately afraid he might lose face in front of Phun, he sobered quickly.

"When must you report to your battalion?" he asked, anxious to change the subject.

"In three days. What are your duties?"

"I must reconnoiter my battalion's objective here in Bien Hoa. I have no time limit."

"So," said Phun authoritatively, "I will accompany you. A couple will be less suspicious than a lone man. And that means we have two more nights together."

Everyone on the fire base looked up as the shiny new Huey circled and lined up for landing. Lieutenant Colonel Price and the sergeant major stood near the helipad, watching as the helicopter landed. Something different was happening and the troops whispered and pointed as they strained to see whom the visitor might be.

"It's the CG. The general is here." The word spread quickly.

Price and the sergeant major saluted then led the way into the TOC. Quietly, sergeants directed soldiers to pick up their trash and straightened up their uniforms. Although they all continued their duties, they kept a wary eye on the headquarters.

After a tedious half-hour, Jace's field phone rang. Tucker answered and said quickly, "Sir, they want you at the TOC."

As he stooped under the canvas flap, Jace saw Lieutenant Colonel Price standing nervously beside the general.

"Young man," said the two-star, "I hear you fought a hell of a fight the other day. I just wanted to swing down here and tell you myself what a great job you did."

The general nodded to his aide, who said, "Attention to orders." Everyone in the TOC braced as the captain read:

"Special order number 104, dated 24 November 1967: Headquarters, 9th Infantry Division, Republic of Vietnam. The Silver Star, for gallantry in action, is awarded to Captain Jason W. Spencer, Commander, Company C, Fifth Battalion (Mechanized) 39th Infantry. Citation: When his company came under intense enemy fire while attacking an enemy bunker system, Captain Spencer repeatedly exposed himself to danger as he organized his troops for the assault. When his company became pinned down, Captain Spencer called artillery and air strikes on top of his position. At one point, Captain Spencer resorted to hand-to-hand combat to repel an enemy counter attack. His actions are in keeping with the finest traditions of the 9th Infantry Division and the United States Army."

As the general stepped forward, the aide handed him the medal which he pinned on Jace's pocket flap. Next to it, the general attached the Purple Heart.

"I listened in on your frequency to part of the battle. I want you to know that I think you did a tremendous job getting your boys off that hill."

"Thank you, sir, but my men deserve the credit. They fought a helluva fight," said Jace as the staff lined up to shake his hand.

"I hear they did. Let's go visit them. We have some medals for some of them, too, don't we Bob?"

"Yes, sir," answered the aide as the general put on his helmet and swept from the TOC with Jace, C.C., the sergeant major and Price in tow. Enjoying himself immensely, the general took his time at each track and bunker, asking soldiers about the battle, their families, and where they were from. Price followed behind, from time to time offering a comment. C.C. hung back, a faint smile on his lips.

As they were leaving the third platoon, a voice yelled, "Hey General, wait a minute." Super Private bounded over a bunker, handed his camera to Lieutenant Colonel Price, and ran to the general's side. Grinning broadly, the general put his arm around Super Private's shoulder as Price focused and snapped.

"Thank you, sir," beamed the scruffy soldier. "Nobody back home will believe this!"

"My pleasure," said the general.

Before he left, the division commander pinned Silver Stars on Doc Roberts and Lieutenant Cappaccelli, and Bronze Stars on eight of Jace's riflemen, including Williams. Jace stood beside C.C. and Price at the edge of the helipad as the general and his aide strapped themselves into the helicopter. The three officers saluted as the general lifted and sped away, already on the radio dealing with new situations. When the dust settled, Price walked back to the TOC without saying a word.

"Did you have anything to do with this?" Jace asked C.C.

"Me? Naw—not a thing." grinned the major. "But it will be hard to fire you now, won't it?"

"Comrade Lau," said the regimental commander. "Come in."

"Thank you, Comrade Colonel," Lau said as he bowed.

"Would you like tea?"

"Yes, thank you."

"I have been reading your report on your battalion objective. You seem to think that it will offer no particular challenge. Is that correct?"

"Yes, Comrade Colonel. There were only gate guards and a few troops guarding the headquarters. Even if there were twice as many troops there, I am confident we could be successful."

"As you remember, I chose you to command the 274th because of your political expertise. There are tactical issues you still need to consider before the general offensive. Things you have not experienced."

"I have been in battle several times," said Lau, his pride pricked.

"From all reports, you have done very well in combat. You have even escaped from captivity. But you have not experienced the full weight of the enemy's power."

"I do not wish to experience any more weight than that of heavy artillery and aerial bombs."

"That is true. Those are powerful weapons indeed. But they are supporting weapons. You have not experienced the raw strength of the enemy's organic weaponry. Correct me if I am wrong, but you have only fought dismounted infantry, is that correct?"

"Yes, Comrade," answered Lau, somewhat sheepishly.

"And you were underground during the shelling and the bombing?"

"Yes, Comrade." Lau was becoming uncomfortable under the close questioning of his superior.

"I mean you no disrespect. You have served well. But, if you are to throw your battalion against the puppet division headquarters, you can expect a rapid response from the Americans. I agree with you. Taking your objective will be relatively easy. Holding on to it will be extremely difficult. That is why you must get the citizenry to rally to our side immediately. With them in the streets, the Americans cannot get to you. Remember, you will be above ground this time, vulnerable to the same artillery and bombs you experienced underground. Also, allow me one more question."

"Yes, Comrade Colonel."

"How many heavy machine guns were in the battle at regimental headquarters?"

"Only one, Comrade. Ours. The enemy carried only their M-60s."

"Comrade Lau. Think about this when you are making your plans: an American armored infantry company will have 20 heavy and numerous light machine guns, plus recoilless rifles, rocket and grenade launchers, mortars, and more hand grenades than you can count."

Lau was stunned to silence. He had not considered this before.

"While you are planning the political side of the battle, have your company commanders work on plans to stop the American reinforcements. In the narrow streets, if you can knock out the lead vehicle, you will stop all the others behind it."

As Lau left the regimental commander's office, his confidence was shattered. How could he even think he could command in combat when he had no idea about the firepower he would be up against? He was out of his element and he knew it. His mind went back to the times he had seen American convoys on the highways. He had never even thought about counting the heavy machine guns. Now, however, he remembered that every vehicle larger than a jeep had carried a heavy gun. He had seen them with his own eyes and had not understood what they had meant in terms of battle ratios. He had witnessed the awesome firepower of Huong's heavy gun during the battle. What would twenty enemy heavies firing at the same time—at him—be like? What would the artillery and bombs be like above ground? Even if they could take their objective, how could they hold on against such power? What was he going to do?

Chi wearily shuffled home from the road junction where the truck had dropped her after work. Depression had overtaken her since Huong had run away to join the Viet Cong. As she approached her house, all she could think of was going to bed. Sleep was her only escape from the worry, torment and grief that now were her main emotions.

Duc's widow met her at the front gate with a barrage of complaints about things Chi cared nothing about. She shoved her way through the young children who were jumping about, wanting her to settle a dispute over a shirt. Looking around the house, she was appalled at the dirt and the clutter. What had gone on here today that was so important that they couldn't at least clean the house? When she saw there was no evening meal prepared, she lost her temper. Children scattered as she tore into the young widow.

"I cannot believe that you did not have the courtesy and the thoughtfulness to cook some rice for those of us who have been working. What did you do all day? Were you—"

"Mama Chi," shouted a youngster. "Someone is here."

Still fuming, Chi went to the door. As she saw the young man wearing a sun helmet sitting astride a motor bike, ice water replaced the blood in her veins.

"Greetings, Madame," bowed the stranger. "I regret that I must be the bearer of bad news. My colleague, Mr. Lau, whom you no doubt remember, asked me to come and bring you news about your son."

"Where is he? Is he hurt? Can he come home?" Chi screeched.

Dismounting from the bike, the young man held his helmet in front of him with both hands and bowed.

"Madame, your son has been killed fighting for our country. Mr. Lau asked me to inform you that he was doing exactly as he wished—he would have had it no other way. He said to inform you that Huong died avenging the death of his brother. His last request was for us to tell you goodby for him. He died bravely— you can be very proud of him."

Chi let out a wail as she ran to the messenger and pounded on his shoulders with her fists. The young man stood quietly and respectfully, stoically absorbing the blows. Her strength quickly spent, Chi slumped to the ground, still howling incoherently. Duc's widow and the children ran from the house to surround her and to scowl at the stranger, who bowed, pushed his bike into the road, and rode away.

Lau and three of his officers crept to the edge of the jungle near Fire Base Cougar. While discussing the Americans' firepower, one of his company commanders had recommended a way for Lau to witness the enemy's strength without endangering any of their soldiers. Now, they were ready to put the plan into action.

For a long moment, Lau watched through his binoculars as the Americans calmly went about their business. The senior company commander pointed out the important parts of the enemy's defenses.

"Each armored vehicle mounts a heavy gun. There are 20 such vehicles in a company. Notice that between each vehicle is a bunker. Each of those bunkers holds a light machine gun. Comrade Colonel, please observe the wires running from the infantry carriers and the bunkers. Each wire leads to an anti-personnel mine. There are at least four in front of each position. I think you can see the metal stakes in the concertina wire. There are trip flares on each of those stakes. I ask you to keep in mind that they are in defensive positions. On the move, the light machine guns that are now in the bunkers fire from the sides of the armored vehicles. In the attack, of course they will not have the anti-personnel mines, but all of their other weapons can be brought against us. Inside this base, they have both heavy and light mortars and six heavy howitzers. The artillery in the base is too close to fire on us. Of course they can lower their tubes and fire direct fire, but they would not do that unless we brought an overwhelming attack against them. They will bring artillery fire on us from far-away bases. When we open fire, all of these weapons will be brought to bear on us. It might be helpful to time their response to see how quickly they can call for the artillery. I ask you to keep in mind that only about a third of their weapons will fire—only those on this side of the perimeter. Are you ready?"

"Yes, I am ready," answered Lau.

"Then I would ask you to get into your hole. We will run away between the time they stop firing and when they will send a patrol to look for us."

The company commander selected a soldier sitting on a bunker. He did not want to kill a heavy machine gunner since he wanted Lau to experience fire from all the weapons on one whole side of the perimeter. He braced his scoped bolt-action rifle on the side of a tree and took careful aim. When he squeezed the trigger, the young GI's head disappeared in a pink spray. At the same time, the two other V.C. officers fired a magazine each into the perimeter. They barely had time to dive into their camouflaged spider holes before the firestorm from the perimeter erupted.

Forty seconds after they had fired the first bullet, mortars began to thud into the jungle's edge. Two minutes later, heavy artillery joined the barrage. The volume of machine-gun and rifle fire coming from the enemy was unbelievable. Small trees splintered and fell as wood splinters flew in all directions. Leaves, branches and undergrowth shredded into a green mist. Gray-brown smoke covered the tree line, dust choked the guerrilla commanders in their holes, and dirt clods fell like hail as the crescendo continued unabated.

For five full minutes the firing tore the jungle to bits. Then, slowly, as enemy leaders shouted orders, the volume of fire diminished, then stopped. Anxious to run, Lau raised his head from his hole.

The senior company commander hissed, "Not yet, Comrade Colonel. Let them gain confidence that there will be no more firing from us, then they will return to what they were doing and we can escape."

Several minutes had elapsed when the Viet Cong leaders heard the sound of rotor blades approaching. Fearing gunships, they hunkered lower in their holes. When no rockets or miniguns were fired, Lau ventured a peep from his hole. A helicopter with huge red crosses pained on the nose and sides hovered into the enemy camp. As he watched, he saw enemy soldiers standing and walking around again.

"Now!" cried the senior company commander. The four guerrilla leaders climbed from their holes and dashed into the jungle. Despite the fact that the foliage around them had been blasted away, no one on the fire base saw them leave.

At Thanksgiving, missions changed again. The 5-39 gave up the Binh Son rubber plantation to another battalion. Bravo company relieved Charlie on Fire Base Cougar. Alpha began a sweep south of Cougar to follow up the battle for Hill 108. Jace's new mission was to guard engineers who were repairing bridges and clearing Highway 1 east of Xuan Loc.

Feeling as if a ton had been lifted from his shoulders, Jace happily waved goodbye to the gate guard at Fire Base Cougar. No matter what Highway 1 might bring, he wouldn't be under Price's thumb for a while. The day was bright and hot. Tropical cotton-ball puffs of clouds dotted the clear blue sky as Charlie company's tracks, jeeps, and trucks bounced eastward along the pitted pavement.

In the late afternoon, Jace circled his vehicles, half on either side of the highway, three miles east of Xuan Loc. A hot Thanksgiving meal of turkey, rolls, dressing, vegetables, pumpkin pie and eggnog were flown in to the hungry troops.

First Sergeant Baez invited the chopper crew to shut down and join the company for dinner. He supervised the chow line, laughing and joking with his soldiers, making sure everyone got all he wanted. Troops lingered long over their food, taking second and third helpings, savoring every last morsel. Jace sat quietly in front of the CP tent, talking with any and all who stopped by, paper plates in hand, to chat—particularly the friends of the first-platoon soldier killed by the sniper. When the empty chow containers and out-going mail were flown out, Baez returned to the CP.

"Just heard some bad news," said Baez.

"What?" answered Jace.

"There was a big battle up in the central highlands—place called Dak Tho. Damn near the whole second battalion of the 173rd Airborne was wiped out."

"What? Who told you?"

"Chopper pilots. Said the Herd got surrounded on top of a mountain. When they ran out of ammo, they got over-run."

"That was one of the units I wanted to go to," said Jace. "The second battalion was the one that made the combat jump back in February during Operation Junction City."

"Damn lucky you didn't go. The pilots said nearly every officer in the battalion was killed or wounded. You want to know the scary part?"

"I'm not sure I do," answered Jace.

"While they were surrounded, the air force put a five-hundred-pound bomb right in the middle of their perimeter."

Jace couldn't even answer.

At dawn, the lone communist guerrilla crept out of the jungle and into the outskirts of Long Thanh. As the village began to come to life, he crept between two houses to a refuse heap that gave him concealment plus a clear view of the highway. There, he squatted down to wait.

Several small convoys drove past but he ignored them—he was waiting for something particular. Finally, as the rim of the sun peeked over the jungle, a platoon of APCs rattled down the highway, heading south. While they were still a hundred meters away, the guerrilla clicked the safety of his AK-47, and without aiming, sprayed the vehicles with a full magazine. As soon as his weapon was empty, he sped back the way he had come. As he disappeared into a small hut, which had a safe underground bunker, the APCs on the highway opened up with everything they had. The thin walls of Chi's house did not even slow the huge .50-caliber bullets as they passed through. Neither did the thin body of Chi's sister.

"XO, have we ever received replacements for the weapons and radios we lost on Hill 108," asked Jace, thoughtfully.

"No, sir," answered Lieutenant Driscol.

"How about checking with the S-4. That stuff should have been here already."

"Will do, sir," Driscol said as he left.

"Sir, we haven't been getting a lot of things we've requested. We're even short of toilet paper," said Baez. "The cooks are complaining that the stuff they use for scrubbing the pots is running out."

"You thinking what I'm thinking?" asked Jace.

"You smell Munn in this somehow?" responded Baez.

"I'll talk to the S-4 myself. I want a resupply ASAP. Make a list of everything we're short. If there's anything we need airlifted out from Bear Cat, make a separate list of that. With Munn in S-4 and Smith in our supply operation, we need to keep an eye on things."

Driscol ducked back into the tent. "Sir, I just talked to the S-4. He said he had no record of a request for the combat-loss stuff."

"Look on my clip-board, XO. I kept a carbon copy. Make it out again and get it to the S-4 personally. In the mean time, radio it to him so he can get on it. It might not be a bad idea to tell him that it looks like several of our requisitions have been lost."

"Yes, sir," said Driscol as he left again.

M.P.s, local police, government soldiers, medics and civil affairs officers from division G-5 descended on Long Thanh after the shooting incident. Chi's sister was the only human casualty, but a house had burned down, torched by tracer bullets. Many other homes were shattered and punctured by bullets. The population of Long Thanh kept its distance from the Americans as they tried to smooth the fabric of fear and distrust.

Chi was in such severe shock that the American medics took her to the Bear Cat hospital for observation. They kept her overnight, allowing her to leave just in time for her sister's funeral. This time, when the Americans released her, they drove her home instead of releasing her at the gate. When she arrived at her house, the young widow met her at the door, crying. It was obvious at first glance that no one had done anything to clean the house during the day. Seeing her sister's blood still covering the floor where she had fallen, Chi's anger again took over. As she began to rail over the condition of the house, a fresh look at Duc's widow calmed her. It was clear that the young woman was immobilized by a deep depression. After greeting Chi, she returned to the filthy little nest she had made for herself in a corner. Squatting down, she stared expressionless into the wall as hungry children whined around her.

"Top, there is no plan that can be dreamed up that will get us through what we're about to go through. The way I see it, when all the guys leave in December when their year is up, we'll have 37 troops left. That includes, you, me one platoon leader and one platoon sergeant. We'll simply become a platoon manning a company's equipment and wait for replacements."

"Yes, sir," answered Baez. "And I'll tell you something else. I'll bet battalion ain't got no plan to get over a hundred soldiers out of the field back to Bear Cat in time to out-process."

"There's where I bet you're wrong," said Jace. "Major Churchwell supervises admin operations. I know he'll have a plan."

"We'll see," sniffed Baez.

"Sir, there's something you've got to see," interrupted Lieutenant Driscol as he burst into the CP.

"What the hell is it now?" asked Jace.

"The resupply just came in. It's the water trailer. It's contaminated with what smells like diesel fuel."

Jace grabbed his helmet and pistol belt and followed the XO into the sun. He opened the nozzle on the trailer and caught some water in his hand. Sure enough, the strong smell of diesel filled his nostrils.

Driscol continued, "Also, we didn't get all of the ammo we requested, we're four cases of C-rations short, and the cooks still didn't get all of the cleaning materials they asked for."

"Five India, tell third platoon to crank up. I'm going to run back to the fire base to see Major Churchwell and the S-4. I'll get a fresh water trailer out here to replace this one. Top, check to see how many water cans are full. We may have to get an emergency airlift of water. That asshole Munn is behind this and I'm gonna nail his ass."

There was quite a large crowd at the funeral of Chi's sister. The small community of Long Thanh had come to stand by Chi and her family during their time of grief. Clustered in the sun at the cemetery, some neighbors mourned loudly, some offered food and assistance, and some simply bowed their respect and best wishes before leaving. No one paid any mind to the three strangers at the funeral. When the ceremony was over and the crowd started to break up, one of the strangers spoke in a loud, clear voice.

"I wonder how long we will have to take this kind of insult to our families, our villages and our country. How long can this kind of indiscriminate killing continue before we rise up to say it is enough? How long will babies cry for their mothers? How long will mothers have to cry for their sons before we rise up valiantly and strike back? Oh, I know you are not fighters. I know you know nothing of waging war. But soon, the entire population will spread its anger like the hood of the mighty cobra to throw off the oppressive regime in Saigon and their benefactors, the hateful Americans.

"You do not have to fight—there are a thousand other ways you can help. Many of you work inside the base. There are hundreds of things you can do there to help us. For those of you who do not work for the Americans—grandmothers can cook meals for our travelers, heads of households may offer your homes for those of us who need temporary shelter, mothers may nurse one of us who has been wounded. You may give money or rice to help feed our fighters. Or—you brave few who wish revenge—you brave few who do not want to wait for liberation—you may join us in our struggle to rid our land of the vile Americans and their puppets in Saigon. You do not have to make up your mind right now. Just give us your name and we will contact you later to help you decide what is appropriate for you to do. Remember, there will be a time when your deeds, or lack of them, will be remembered. After unification, those who have helped will be rewarded. Those who did nothing, and those who helped the Americans and their lackeys will have a bad time of it. You will want to be on the correct side when the end comes—and it is coming very soon."

Some of the crowd walked hurriedly away, afraid to be anywhere near Viet Cong recruiters. Some lingered, trying to decide what, if anything to do. A few people gave their names to the strangers, although they knew it to be a dangerous thing to do.

As the crowd slowly departed, Chi remained kneeling at her sister's graveside. Finally, she stood, bowed one more time with her hands held together, prayer-like under her chin, then walked directly toward the three young strangers.

"I am ready to do what I can to help," she said simply.

With Jace sitting behind the .50 caliber of the second track, third platoon rolled into the entrance at Fire base Cougar. Dust swirled as he jumped down and walked confidently to the TOC. He had decided that he would be polite to the battalion commander, but would not be chastised any further, even if it meant his being fired.

"Jace," cried C.C. as his friend entered the TOC. "What are you doing here?"

"Sir, I need to talk to you. It seems we have a problem in supply." answered Jace, relieved to see that Lieutenant Colonel Price was nowhere around.

"What's wrong?"

"Well, besides lost paperwork on our combat-loss equipment, a contaminated water trailer, short rations, no cleaning material for the mess equipment and a total lack of toilet paper, nothing."

"Have you talked to the S-4?"

"My XO has. The reason I wanted to talk to you is that I believe Sergeant Munn is behind this. My first sergeant said that at the court-martial, Munn swore he would get even. This sure looks like he's trying to get back at the whole company," said Jace.

"I'll check on it myself. Other than that how are things going?"

"By 15 December my personnel strength will be 37 bodies, including officers. What about replacements?"

"With nearly every soldier in the division going home at the same time, every maneuver battalion will be in the same boat. We're assured by the G-1 that MAC-V is turning the replacement hose on the division and we'll be back near a hundred percent by the new year."

"What are we supposed to do in the mean time?" asked Jace.

"Pray the V.C. don't realize how many people are leaving. The plan is to lay low with just local patrolling until we're full again. No major operations are planned."

"What about getting the men out of the field en masse?"

"Chinooks will lift them out in batches. The plan has already been made—in fact, here's the schedule."

Jace scanned the paper then lowered his voice. "Where's the colonel?" he asked.

"He flew back to Bear Cat to a meeting at brigade on this very subject." answered C.C. "It's funny—he's been different lately. Since the general came down, he's been keeping a low profile. Stays in his tent a lot. Almost never leaves the TOC. By the way, for a while, your supposedly bad attitude was all he talked about. Now, he never mentions you at all. It's really been strange."

"Oh, well! Look, it's chow time, are you eating?" asked Jace.

"Sure," answered C.C.. "Let's go over to the mess tent and see what they've dreamed up. Make sure your troops get chow too."

Paper plates in hand, Jace and C.C. walked back to a G.P.-small tent set up beside the TOC. As they ducked into the tent, Jace couldn't believe his eyes.

Inside was a large table with a camouflaged parachute table cloth, silver coffee service, crystal salt and pepper shakers, and fancy paper napkins.

"Officers' mess," grinned C.C. "The colonel says the fact that we're in Vietnam in the middle of nowhere is no reason we can't eat like gentlemen."

"Does he know how the troops eat?" asked Jace.

"Jace, except for over-flying your battle, he hasn't been out of this TOC—how does he know anything about the troops?"

Once she had made her decision to avenge the deaths of her sister and her two sons, Chi's mental outlook changed dramatically for the better. Taking charge of her household once more, she gave orders like a drill sergeant as her family labored to clean and repair the damage. Chi would allow no one else to clean up her sister's blood—that she did herself. Realizing that Duc's widow was incapacitated by depression, she left the young woman alone, treating her as an invalid. She was more cheerful at work as well, where she returned to her practices of joking with Buddha and eating with the cooks. Forcing herself not to think about her boys or her sister, she allowed the familiar routine of each day comfort to her.

As Catholics, Chi and her family made a practice of celebrating Christmas. After work, she supervised as the children decorated the house with greenery and red ribbons. Despite her tragedies, she would at least have enough money to buy gifts for the surviving members of her family. As she placed ribbons over the front door, a stranger entered the yard.

"I bring you greetings from the National Liberation Front," the neatly-dressed visitor said, bowing.

No longer afraid, Chi returned the bow and offered tea. As was the custom, the stranger did not come to the point of his visit immediately. He played with the children, commented on the decorations, and complemented Chi on the delicious jasmine tea. Finally, Chi led him into the yard, away from the squeals and squabbles of the children.

"I have come to ask you what you may feel like doing to help our cause," said the stranger, politely.

"When I told you I would help, I had nothing exact in mind. I work at the laundry at the base. I come in contact with soldiers every day, but I do not know what I can do. I do not understand their language well, so gathering information would be hard for me."

"It would be a great help if you could map key locations inside the base. Their headquarters are normally bristling with antennae making them easy to identify.

If we have accurate maps of their facilities, their heavy gun sites, vehicle parks and airfields, our mortar gunners can be more effective."

"It is dangerous to try to carry anything like a map in or out. The guards search us sometimes."

"No need to draw maps. Just memorize the locations. If you can determine distances from known points such as the corners of the base, it would be of great help."

"How could I determine distance?" asked Chi.

"Pace the distance off if you can. Remember the number of steps. We can measure the length of your stride later and determine the exact distance."

"I don't know," said Chi. I normally stay at the laundry. I do not walk around much. If I were to suddenly start pacing distances, I might arouse suspicion."

"That is true," said the visitor. "You said you are searched when entering or leaving. What do you carry with you?"

"In the morning, I bring a ball of rice for the noon meal. In the evening, sometimes I bring home some food from the snack bar."

Chi's reference to the snack bar caught the stranger's attention. "Where is this snack bar," he asked.

"It is adjacent to the laundry. It is a large building with a kitchen, many tables and games the soldiers play."

"How many soldiers come to this snack bar?"

"Most of the time, not too many, but on some occasions, such as pay day, it is full—sixty or seventy then," answered Chi.

"Do you have access to batteries?" asked the visitor.

"What kind of batteries?" asked Chi.

"Any kind—flashlight batteries are most common."

"Yes, the manager has a flashlight for when the generator goes out at night. He keeps a box of batteries under the counter. I have seen it."

"How about wire—you know the black wire the Americans use for their telephones?"

"That black wire is everywhere inside the base. It is on the ground and on poles strung from building to building. In fact, there is some inside the snack bar, running from the wall to the telephone."

The visitor was silent for a moment, then: "A plan is coming to mind. If you have no objections, I will return soon and tell you about it. In the mean time, thank you for your kind hospitality and the tea."

"Charlie Six, this is Cougar Four on your push, over."

"This is Charlie Five India, wait and we'll get Charlie Six, over. Hey Tucker, go get the old man. Tell him the S-4 is on the horn."

Jace was walking the perimeter when the call came. He jogged back to the command track.

"This is Charlie Six, go."

"Cougar Four. I checked into the situation we were talking about. I drug the man in question over the coals. Of course he denied messing with requisitions or the water trailer. There's no proof—no paper trail I can get him with either. I'll watch him close from now on."

"Roger, what about the stuff I'm short?"

"Everything I can get aboard will be on tomorrow's mail bird. The rest will come out on the next refueling run. We had to wash the water buffalo out with detergent five times to get the diesel smell out. It'll be back to you tomorrow. If you need anything else, call me."

"Thanks, buddy. I know you probably think I'm paranoid and making all this up," laughed Jace.

"No, there is something definitely rotten here. But if the man in question did it, he's smart enough to cover his tracks. Sorry for the inconvenience."

"No problem. Come out and have a beer with us sometime."

"Will do. Cougar Four, out.

The engineers' rome plows, huge bulldozers with slanting blades designed to cut brush and small trees, slashed at the jungle lining Highway 1. Their aim was to push the green wall back from the road to make it more difficult for the V.C. to hide their ambushes and mining teams. Meanwhile, engineer crews rebuilt and repaired bridges the enemy had destroyed or damaged. Like watchdogs, Jace's troops sat on their tracks with ponchos stretched above the .50 calibers for shade. Each day, Jace sent dismounted patrols into the jungle on either side of the road, looking for the enemy. Each night, squads of soldiers, who were becoming more and more apprehensive as the end of their tours approached, filed into the jungle to set ambushes. The only break in the routine had come when first platoon had been airlifted to the top of Gia Rai mountain to guard the signal installation for a week.

"Good morning, Cap'n," said Super Private, shaking Jace awake. It was 0550 on the tenth of December, 1967.

"This better be good, I only hit the sack two hours ago," said Jace. He had been awake half the night because one of the ambushes kept reporting noises around them.

"Request permission to fire my weapon, sir."

"Soop, what's—oh yes, today's the day, isn't it?"

"Yes, sir. Last day in the bush. Flying back to Bear Cat today. I've put my time in the weeds, Cap'n. Alls I want to do is shoot my weapon one last time."

Jace was awake now. Tucker handed him a cup of coffee.

"Well, I don't guess I could say no to that, now could I?"

"Thank you, sir."

"How can I tell you how much I appreciate you, you little shit." asked Jace.

"What do you mean, sir?"

"You've backed me, you've taught me, and you've told me what I needed to know, often just in time."

"Shit, sir, I just have this habit of saying what I think."

Jace took a sip of his coffee, then reached for his jungle boots.

"I reckon I just want to tell you that I've seen what you do. You've kept the morale up. You've kept the guys laughing when they needed to laugh most. I know for sure that you've kept a lot of them alive. You're a better leader than most of the sergeants I know. I just couldn't promote you because of all the damned article fifteens in your record. What are you going to do when you get out?"

"Damned if I know, sir."

"Look, use the G.I. bill and go to college. As smart as you are, you can make it big doing anything you want to do."

"Have to finish high school first," laughed Super Private.

Jace offered his hand. "Then do it. I'm going to miss you. If I don't get to see you before you take off, good luck. I couldn't have done this without you."

"Bullshit, sir. You could command anything anywhere. You don't need no help from me or nobody else. Now, with all due respect, I don't want to miss my queue. You can watch if you want to."

Jace finished lacing up his boots and reached for his helmet.

"I've got a feeling I shouldn't miss this," he said.

Super Private had an audience waiting for him. Almost all of third platoon was gathered around as he walked to the edge of the perimeter, turned his transistor radio up as loud as it would go, then carefully placed it on the ground. At exactly six a.m., as the Armed Forces Network announcer cried, "GOOOOOOOOOOOOOOOOOOOOOD MORNING, VIETNAM!", Super Private's M-16 cracked one last time. The radio flew into a hundred pieces. Third platoon cheered.

It was three days before the Viet Cong recruiter returned to Chi's home. With him was a small, bent, older man.

"This is Mr. Trung," said the recruiter. "He is a specialist of sorts."

After tea and small talk, the recruiter got down to business."We have an idea. It is potentially very dangerous. It will take a person with very steady nerves to accomplish this. If you do not feel you can do it, we will find something else for you to do."

"Please tell me what you have in mind," said Chi, who was nervous, but intrigued.

"Do you know what this is?" asked Mr. Trung as he handed Chi a small white ball.

"No, I do not, sir," Chi answered as she fingered the soft clay-like substance.

"It is a very powerful explosive," he laughed as Chi gingerly handed it back to him. "It is very stable. It will not explode if you drop it. It will not even explode if you hold a flame to it. It takes a blasting cap which causes shock and flame at the same time to set it off. It is very safe to handle." He demonstrated by throwing the ball to the floor, hard.

"I don't know about such things," said Chi, cringing. "What do you want me to do with this?"

"Is there a place near the snack bar where you can hide this and a lot more like it?"

"Yes, there is a loose board in the wall between the laundry and the snack bar. I hide things behind it sometimes. No one knows about it but me."

"Good, said the recruiter," cutting a glance at Mr. Trung. "What we have in mind is for you to hide a small piece of this explosive in your rice ball each day. When you arrive at work, you can place each piece behind your loose board until you have a substantial amount. Then we will tell you how to rig a trigger. That is why I asked you about flashlight batteries. They will be the power source for our bomb. You can prepare it just before you leave at the end of the day. When you return home, you will have to go with us, because you will be a prime suspect after the explosion. The bomb will not go off until the trigger is activated by one of their soldiers the next day, when you are not there."

"I have thought about helping, but I never considered leaving my loved ones and my home. The spirits of my husband and my family are here. I could never leave them."

"No matter how you help us, you must realize that your coming under suspicion is always a possibility—in which case you would have to leave anyway. Also, keep in mind that when our cause is victorious, you may return here as soon as you wish."

"This is much to consider. Please allow me to think about it."

"That is certainly not much to ask. We will take our leave, now. We will return the day after tomorrow. Thank you for your hospitality," said the recruiter who bowed deeply as he and Mr. Trung left.

Chi's mind swirled. She desperately wanted to get back at those who had killed her family members, but leaving her home was almost unthinkable. She did not think she was afraid of dying. But if she did, she knew she wanted to die here, where she had spent her entire life—not in the jungles somewhere. She knew that was something she would not even think of negotiating. But she also had to consider her remaining family members. If she ran away, they would probably be blamed. If the authorities came to get her after the bomb exploded, she could take full responsibility and absolve them. Couldn't she? By midnight, she had made her decision. She would make the bomb. But when she returned home, she would not run away. She would simply wait for them to come for her.

The hurricane caused by the landing of the twin-rotored Chinook blasted trash and dust in all directions and tore at tents and ponchos as the huge machine touched down right outside Charlie company's perimeter on Highway 1. Carrying all their belongings, 16 soldiers from the third platoon ran through the artificial storm toward the back ramp. Jace had said his goodbyes. Although he hated to see them go, he knew no one in his right mind would be unhappy to see them return home in one piece. Super Private and Lieutenant Cappaccelli were the last ones to board. Cappaccelli did not look back. But as Super Private stepped onto the ramp, he turned to see Jace standing, watching. As their eyes locked, Jace realized he would probably never see this odd little man who had done so much for him again. Perhaps a salute would have been appropriate, but Jace would always remember the wave he got instead.

Walking away, Jace surveyed his perimeter. Things looked about the same as they always had, but they felt different. Without the men who had shared with him every event, whether good or bad, everything would seem different. As Lieutenant Colonel McKensie had tried to explain before he left the battalion, when someone leaves, everything changes. Jace realized it was as true for the troops as it was for colonels. No matter what, from this point on, Charlie company was going to be different.

Soldiers from the weapons platoon were beginning to line up for the last Chinook. Among them, Five India.

"Look, I hope you understand, I'm not going to say goodbye to you, I'm just going to wish you luck and walk away," choked Jace.

"I understand," said Five India. "So why don't you go now before we both say or do something stupid."

"Good luck," said Jace as he shook the young man's hand.

Excitement mounted as distant blade-chatter could be heard. Jace went down the line, saying goodbye to his mortar men. When the Chinook landed in a swirl of debris and purple smoke, the troops shouldered their gear and headed for the ramp. As their buddies yelled and waved from tracks around the perimeter, they disappeared into the darkness inside the fuselage. Five India started toward the helicopter, then turned, ran to Jace and hugged him. Feeling it was more than he could take this time, Jace hurried away.

Chi awoke much earlier than usual. Today was to be far different from any other day of work. Although she was frightened, her senses were alert. Her fear, her anger, and her hatred for those who had killed her family members made her feel more alive than she had felt in a long time. After she put the rice on the fire and made tea, she walked to the front gate. In a small hole behind one of the posts, she saw what the visitor had told her would be there. After looking around and seeing no one, she plucked the wad of paper out of the hole and unwrapped it. Inside was a golf-ball-sized wad of the explosive.

After finishing her routine, she carefully wrapped rice around the explosive forming the familiar ball she carried to work each day. She tidied up, woke the rest of the family, then walked to the junction.

At the Bear Cat gate, her breathing came in short gasps as she realized she was sweating, despite the relatively cool morning temperature. As she joined the inspection line, she felt as if everyone were looking at her. As the line got shorter and shorter, the urge to run came strong upon her, but she forced herself to stand still. As her turn came, the guard smiled at her and asked to see what she was carrying. Nervously, she handed him the paper containing the rice ball. The M.P. did not even unwrap it.

"Rice?" he asked.

Chi nodded once as she looked at the ground.

"OK, Mamasan. Who's next?"

Chi could hardly believe it. She had walked right in with no problem. During the day a dilemma did present itself, however. What about the Vietnamese cooks and Buddha? Killing the Americans who had destroyed her family was one thing. But Buddha had always been good to her. And the cooks, who were just trying to make a living as she was, certainly did not deserve to die. She had already committed to making the bomb and did not want to back down. But she vowed to find a way not to harm her fellow workers.

At first, replacements came in a few at a time on the mail bird. After a while, Huey loads came two or three times a day. As Christmas neared, Chinooks roared in to disgorge scores of young soldiers with fresh faces, wide eyes, and crisp, new jungle fatigues.

Baez tried sizing up the replacements, assigning them to squads and platoons where he thought they would find their niche. Soon, he gave up, realizing there was no way to look at a rookie and tell how he would perform in combat or even get along in a squad. If they didn't work out where he put them, he could move them later.

"Sir, I swear, this is a sorry-looking crowd," said Baez, throwing down his helmet in disgust.

"Now, Top, the guys who just left probably looked just as green when they got here."

"No, sir, I mean it. I swear one of our new cooks is mongoloid."

"What do you mean? Downs syndrome?"

"I swear to God, sir. You look at him."

"Must be one of MacNamara's hundred thousand," thought Jace, aloud.

"What's that?" asked Baez.

"Read it in Army Times. MacNamara is bringing in a hundred thousand of the lowest mental category—supposedly to be assigned to non-combat jobs. I guess our cook is one of them. Watch him close. You don't think he'll wander off somewhere do you?"

"Don't know, sir. I'll get the mess sergeant to keep a close eye on him. Speaking of Army Times, here's the latest copy."

"Thanks, Top," said Jace.

Jace took the paper and sat down as Baez leaned against the tent pole, watching the day's routine. Tasks that were accomplished automatically by the old hands had to be explained in detail to the replacements, making everything take longer. Jace read the front page in detail, then skipped to the casualty pages.

Although he hated to do it, morbid curiosity compelled him to search the names of the dead for someone he knew.

"Top, did you see this?" asked Jace. "Must be from the 173rd's big fight last month. Here's my next-door neighbor at Bragg—and Rusty Doyle! I saw him at the 90th Replacement Company when I first arrived in country. Went to ranger school with him. And—"

"What is it sir?" asked Baez.

"All seven of the officers from our brigade's hail-and-farewell party at Bragg. We spent an evening together in San Francisco the night before we flew over. All dead. All dead!"

Having realized how much he did not know about leading in combat, and having witnessed first hand the awesome fire power of the American army, Lau elevated his senior company commander to the role of deputy commander for tactical operations. To him, Lau delegated all of the planning for movement, staging, rehearsing, and the attack itself. The tactical plan for assaulting the divisional headquarters in Bien Hoa had already begun to take shape. It would be straight-forward and simple. One company would storm the compound while the other two companies would ambush the roads on which relief columns were expected to roll to the rescue.

With someone else worrying about tactical planning, Lau was free to work on the political side of the operation. From the assault companies, he organized a cadre to teach the civilian population how to fire American weapons, since he expected a windfall of captured arms during the battle. He chose officers to organize and lead platoons of civilians who would be willing to fight, and assigned them key road-block objectives in the city of Bien Hoa. Critical to his plan was a shock cadre of fanatical young guerrillas who would race from house to house encouraging the populace to take to the streets, and kill any government officials, policemen or soldiers they found at home during the holidays.

The only aspect of the plan that worried Lau was that he could get little or no information about supplying his battalion. His soldiers would carry no packs, and very little ammunition. They would carry rice balls and eat at food stands and restaurants as any other pilgrim on the roads during Tet would do. What bothered Lau was that no information was forthcoming about how to resupply the fighters with ammunition after the battle had started. The party line continued to be that no resupply was needed since the population would rise up and overthrow the government and the Americans. But what if the civilians did not respond before his guerrillas ran out of ammunition?

"I thought the battalion was in bad shape when I got here," said Jace. "Those guys at least had intensive unit training with the division before they left the states. These kids have been to basic and AIT—and that's it. I agree with you, Top. They are so green it's scary."

"We'll just have to train them, that's all," said Baez. "We got no other choice."

"We had a training stand-down when I first got here," Jace responded. "Colonel McKensie gave us the time and the assets to train right. But now most of our experienced leaders are gone. With the whole division turned upside-down, we can't expect any slack this time. We'll have to train as we operate."

"It'll be hard to train while we're guarding these damned engineers. They take up too much of the company just sitting on their tracks."

"Let me think," said Jace. "This might be a better situation than we think. Ramos is the only remaining point man—he can train new point men. I want each platoon to have its own trained point team. We can do hand-and-arm signals, immediate-action drills, and formations right in the middle of Highway 1. The same tracks that guard the engineers can protect us as we train. Actual patrolling will be the hard thing to do. I can't leave the majority of the company to go out on a squad ambush. If the company gets hit while I'm out there, there's no way I can command."

"Sir, what the hell am I—chopped liver? This ranger tab on my shoulder is just like yours," said Baez. "I'll be glad to take 'em out and teach 'em how to ambush."

"I appreciate it Top. I didn't volunteer you because it's not in your job description," grinned Jace. "I'll make a training schedule. The sooner we start, the better off we'll be. I just pray nobody gets killed before we teach them how to stay alive."

Later, Jace brought in Howell, Doc Roberts, Ramos, and Lieutenant Jeffers to explain the training concept. Although they were not necessarily the ranking men in the company, they were the only experienced leaders he had left. He wanted to fill them in and get their input before he called the new leaders in. Although Jeffers was new, at least he had survived the battle on Hill 108, which made him a veteran. The fact that Jeffers and Howell were together as platoon leader and platoon sergeant made second platoon the logical choice from which to form a training cadre.

During the week before Christmas, Charlie company's small base on Highway 1 was alive with soldiers practicing hand-and-arm signals, battle drills, mock ambushes, and dry-run patrols. As rome plows chugged and groaned and trees crashed to the ground, the company danced, parried and charged like martial artists in kata. Together, the hard-working engineers and the practicing infantrymen slowly carved into the jungle. Ahead of them stood green walls of forest, behind them, bare swaths on either side of the highway.

As the Christmas-new year's truce went into effect, Lieutenant Colonel Price radioed that all combat operations were to cease immediately. Jace asked if this included local security patrolling. When Price gave permission for close-in patrolling only, Jace realized that this was a perfect opportunity to train the whole company in movement techniques.

Leaving veteran gunners on the tracks, Jace led the newcomers of the company into the jungle. He had planned a rectangular route that took the company around its base, never more than 800 meters from the perimeter. Jace stopped often to make corrections and patiently teach the new leaders. Ramos, having been Stony Johnson's protégé, was the expert on point now, instructing a new company point team and two point men from each platoon. Jace saw to it that new soldiers were trained as compass and pace men as well. He made sure that each platoon had its chance on point. At the end of the day, Charlie company was moving through the jungle almost as efficiently as before the veterans left. All that was left to teach them now was how to change formations in the thick jungle using only hand-and-arm signals.

On the day before Christmas, Jace led his troops into the jungle once more to teach formations and reaction drills. In the early afternoon, he brought them in and ordered the platoons to go one at a time down to a nearby stream for baths. As the evening approached, the troops were tired, but clean.

With the sun going down behind the jungle, Baez gathered the platoon sergeants for a meeting. As they split up, Jace could see something was up. In the gathering dusk, the NCOs brought bags of goodies into the center of the perimeter. All the troops had donated something from their own private caches of snacks and goodies sent from the states for the holidays. On poncho liners, the sergeants laid out candy bars, fruit cakes, canned delicacies, and even some fancy cheeses. Although no ice had been delivered, cans of coke and beer had been cooled as much as possible in the stream.

The guards on the tracks were brought in for first grabs at the goodies. Once they had chosen, they made their way back to their .50 calibers, munching contentedly as they went. Then the remainder of the soldiers were brought in for the impromptu party. Like the children many of them still were, they bartered, bargained, and laughed as they traded their treats. Darkness had fallen when they returned to their platoons. Suddenly, from the engineers' area, a hand-held rocket shot into the sky. As the parachute flare lit the perimeter with a pale, erie light, strains of "Silent Night" were lifted, off-key and wavering, over the dusty camp.

As Christmas day dawned bright, clear and hot, Baez arranged for the track guards to be changed every hour so that no one spent too much time on security. Charlie company had the day off. Soon horseshoes clanked and radios blared rock music. Plywood targets for knife-throwing contests were erected and the volleyball net was set up.

At noon, the chow chopper landed with a turkey dinner with all the trimmings. The troops whooped when they saw the five-gallon container of vanilla ice cream and the extra rations of coke and beer. Mid afternoon, the headquarters company first sergeant, dressed in a Santa suit, landed with a "doughnut dolly" to hand out Red Cross gift bags. Extraverts among the troops strutted and bragged in front of the only American woman they had seen in a long while. Most of the newly-arrived soldiers shyly took their gifts, not knowing what to say to the pretty young female.

Jace spent the afternoon walking among the soldiers, wishing them Merry Christmas and sampling their goodies sent from home. He took advantage of this free day to learn the names of his new soldiers and get to know the new leaders. After the food containers and the visitors were flown away, the troops straggled back to their platoon areas. Jace walked back to the CP tent, where on his cot he found a small package wrapped in newspaper and tied with a red ribbon.

"What's this?" he asked Baez.

"Don't know, sir. Didn't see who left it."

"Well, let's see what it is," said Jace.

Inside the paper was a cardboard box. Jace carefully lifted the lid. Wrapped in tissue was a small, carved wooden figurine of a cat. A note inside said, "This one won't break."

"Well, well," he said. "Looks like Jupiter's back in business."

In Saigon, two men pulled the rented truck loaded with firewood into the auto-repair shop on Phan Thanh Gian street, five blocks from the U.S. embassy. While one guarded, the other quickly moved the wood aside so he could get to a satchel containing fifteen pounds of plastique explosive. A middle-aged woman took the satchel from him and carried it through the door into the adjoining house. The men hurriedly pulled the truck back into the street and drove away. Nearby, two national policemen lounged against a telephone pole, smoking and talking. Neither one of them had seen anything unusual.

Charlie company continued to train hard during the Christmas-new year's truce. Each night, First Sergeant Baez took a squad into the jungle to teach ambushing. During the day, Jace worked his soldiers relentlessly on visual signals, tactics, and movement techniques. The engineers used the time for maintenance on their rome plows and dozers.

Both Jace and the engineer commander worried about their soldiers becoming lax during the stand-down. They both increased their security activities, having officers check the perimeter almost on the hour, all night long. Jace pushed small patrols each day and listening posts at night into the jungle to insure the enemy could not sneak up on the base undetected. The duty was long, dirty, hard and tiring.

New Year's Eve was on them before they knew it. Jace had made no plans for any type of celebration. The troops had enjoyed their party during Christmas—that would have to be enough. Having a gnawing fear of losing the edge he had honed them to during the truce, Jace continued to train his new troops hard into the darkness of 1967's last night.

Despite his plans to the contrary, an impromptu celebration began on its own. As midnight approached, first one, then another, then a volley of hand-held flares arched into the night. The radios erupted with unauthorized chatter as excited troops wished each other luck during the coming year. Soon, trip flares were thrown blazing into the dark void beyond the perimeter. Then the firing started. Several soldiers, having loaded magazines with all tracer rounds, fired red streams into the air. Troops howled and hooted as pyrotechnics popped and sizzled above and around them. Red and green star clusters and streams of red tracers laced the sky. Like floating, smoking light bulbs, parachute flares hung in the darkness above the perimeter.

Angry at first, Jace climbed to the top of the command track and considered how to stop the madness. As he watched closely, he saw that no one was doing anything really dangerous. They were just using pyrotechnic signaling devises as fireworks. Morale was high and the company was letting off steam. Calming, Jace decided to let them have their fun for a while. Besides, with all the chatter on the radio, he would have a tough time breaking into the net to order the company to do anything. He thought he might look a little foolish charging around the perimeter shouting for them to stop. Also, if the V.C. attacked—which was doubtful with all the noise and light being generated—the company would get serious quickly enough.

"What do you think?" asked Baez, standing in front of the command track.

"Let them raise a little hell," said Jace. "Watch them close, Top. If they start anything stupid, cut it off."

The commander of the engineers approached. "Some show, huh?" he asked, feeling out Jace for his reaction to the breach of discipline.

"Yeah," answered Jace. "Let's let them go on for a few more minutes, then we'll shut it down."

The engineer lieutenant nodded his agreement.

The new weapons platoon leader ran up. "Sir, can we fire some illumination rounds? Might be good practice," he asked excitedly.

"You may fire five illumination rounds," shouted Jace over the din.

The mortars banged and bright new lights filled the sky. The large flares hung high in the dark under their parachutes, painting bright patterns on the ground. Shadows danced and swayed as the flares rocked in the wind.

"What the hell is going on out there?" asked C.C. on the battalion net.

"This is Charlie Six. Just a little new year's celebration," answered Jace.

"Little, hell! Somebody could hear you guys in Saigon."

"There's no problem, is there?" asked Jace, suddenly concerned about Lieutenant Colonel Price's reaction.

"Naw, just be careful, that's all."

"Where's Cougar Six?" asked Jace on an impulse.

"He's in bed," laughed C.C..

"Well, then, happy new year," offered Jace.

"Same to you pal. See you soon. This is Cougar Five—Out."

Hiding in the nearby jungle, two Viet Cong guerrillas tried to make sense of the light show they were watching.

Chi did not have to go to work on New Year's Day since it was an American holiday. She would celebrate the new year during Tet, with all other Vietnamese. Still, she appreciated the day off which she spent cooking a huge meal for her family. After dinner, as she and the children stood in the yard trying to launch a red-and-black paper kite, she glanced quickly at the hole behind the gate post. There, she caught a glimpse of balled-up paper.

Seeing the hidden ball of explosive shocked her from the fun she was having with the youngsters. Sharing the rare day off with her family, she had temporarily forgotten the seriousness of what she was undertaking. Now, she realized anew that in a few days, a week, or a month, she would be in custody of the government soldiers or the Americans. Her surviving sister would have to become the head of the family. Chi hoped that her sister's job as a cleaning woman at the American base would earn enough to feed the children and Duc's widow. She felt sadness at the thought of leaving the family. She hoped that her actions would not bring trouble to her loved ones. But, above all else, she felt the gnawing need to avenge the deaths of her sons and her sister. She felt as if she were being pushed by the unseen hand of fate toward a point of no return—a point she knew would come all too soon.

On the tenth of January, the mail bird circled the Charlie company's perimeter, hovered in, and touched down. As the mail sacks were thrown out, a familiar figure jumped from the helicopter.

"I'll be damned," cried Jace. "It's Five India!"

Dressed in brand-new jungle fatigues and black, shiny jungle boots, Five India jogged to the command post.

"What in hell are you doing back here?" asked Jace, gripping Five India's hand.

"Hell, Captain, this crowd's more of a family to me than my own flesh and blood. Besides, I was in this company when things were shitty. You've started something here and I guess I wanted to see how it would all turn out."

"You've been promoted—you're a staff sergeant!"

"Yeah, reenlisted and changed my MOS too. I'm now a proud member of the infantry—no longer an admin puke."

"Well, well, well. So you're back," said Baez, joining them."Just couldn't stay away from me, huh?"

"Howdy, Top. Did you miss me?"

"Like a damn tooth ache," laughed Baez. "Where you been for the last month?"

"Back home in the states on reenlistment leave. Do you know my mom and dad didn't even know where Vietnam is? Dad kept wanting to know what all the fuss was about over some little island in the middle of the ocean."

"In the infantry, now, huh?" asked Jace. "Well, don't think I'm going to put you in a squad or platoon. You're gonna run my CP, just like you did before."

"Sir, that's all right with me. But before this tour is over, I want a chance as squad leader or platoon sergeant."

"You've got it," grinned Jace. "Now, get the hell to work."

"Yes, sir. Hey Tucker. Get the track straightened up. It's a damn mess."

Tucker beamed as he shook Five India's hand. Within five minutes, it was as if he had never left.

After carefully checking to see that there was no one around, Chi removed the loose board behind the counter in the laundry. Quickly, she scraped away the rice covering the ball of white clay-like explosive and mashed it into the mass inside the wall. Before she replaced the board, she examined the explosive she had pressed between the studs during the past month. It formed a mass a foot high and sixteen inches wide, the thickness of a two-by-four.

After replacing the board, she picked up her tea pot and walked into the snack bar. Behind the counter, she stood patiently while one of the cooks heated water for her tea. As she waited, Chi looked under the counter to the place where Buddha kept his flashlight and batteries. Seeing that the snack bar was empty, Buddha was in his office, and the cooks were busy, Chi bent and quickly retrieved a battery from the box. After the cook turned and handed her the pot of hot water, Chi shuffled back to the laundry to make her tea and hide this battery with the ten others she had stolen. She only needed one more. Mr. Trung had said that twelve would do.

CHAPTER 15

▼

25 January 1968

Jace enjoyed the feeling of freedom he had rolling down the road on his APC. Fire bases, even one as large as Cougar, and the jungle could be claustrophobic at times. Despite the danger of enemy ambush, the open road, the sunshine, and the relatively cool breeze seemed to breathe life into him and the company. Also, commanding the long column of armored vehicles made him feel powerful. Jace thought he knew what Patton must have felt like driving Third Army across France.

Charlie company was rolling now, down Highway 2, to link up with the 11th Armored Cavalry Regiment. Intelligence claimed to have found a large enemy buildup and Jupiter was part of the forces that were "piling on".

"Hey, FO! Do you know where we are?" Jace yelled to the young artillery lieutenant attached to his company as liaison officer and forward observer. Jace had been watching him as he joked with Five India and knew the lieutenant was not doing his job.

"You mean right now? Uh—not exactly, sir."

"If we got ambushed right this second, what're the coordinates you would use to call a fire mission?"

"I get your point, sir," said the lieutenant as he unfolded his map. "I'll get on it."

"Good man. Right now we're coming up on this road junction right here," said Jace, pointing with a pencil.

"Yes, sir, Thank you, sir. I'll watch my map from now on."

Jace's company had an easy part of this operation. As part of the blocking forces, Charlie company would outpost a dirt trail to keep the enemy from escaping. As with the previous weeks' engineer-guarding duties, all the soldiers would have to do would be to sit on their vehicles and watch for V.C. crossing the road. Jupiter would be the anvil—the 11th ACR would be the hammer, searching a broad, sparsely-vegetated flat south-west of Xuan Loc.

Jace knew in his gut there would be no contact during this operation. Everyone felt too light-hearted. No one seemed to feel threatened since during the past month the Viet Cong had practically disappeared. The sniper incident, which had killed a first platoon soldier two weeks before he was to go home, was the last enemy contact anyone in the battalion had had. In any event, Jace made sure his soldiers remained watchful and alert, in case they were all wrong.

The afternoon wore on, hot and humid. In his jeep, Jace drove back and forth along the length of his mile-long blocking position on the dirt trail, keeping an eye on his troops. He had placed the company so the soldiers on each vehicle could see the tracks on either side of them to preclude the enemy from crossing the road unseen. Soldiers who were not on alert dozed in the sun, read paperbacks, or listened to their transistor radios. By dark, the 11th ACR had searched every inch of their area of operations without finding any sign of the enemy. At 1800 hours, when Charlie company's attachment to the cav expired, Jace checked in with battalion for orders. The S-3 directed him to circle his vehicles in an abandoned rice paddy and dig in for the night.

Maybe it was the recent holiday season, the new year, or the approaching Tet cease-fire. Jace didn't know. But he did know that the apprehensive, uneasy feeling he had had in War Zone D and at times on Fire Base Cougar was gone.

"Top, I want you to watch the perimeter like a hawk tonight. The guys seem to think the war is over. I'm afraid they'll let their guard down. That's when we'll get hit for sure."

"Don't you worry none, Captain," replied Baez. "They ain't gonna go to sleep on the old first sergeant. Do you know something I need to know?" he asked.

"No," answered Jace. It's just a feeling. Today, everyone seemed to act like we are on vacation or something. Just make sure they are extra alert tonight."

As a full moon rose over the paddy, Jace sent patrols, ambushes, and listening posts into the jungle to give depth to his defenses. The night was warm and bright and morale was high. Several times, he had to make a net call to tell platoon leaders to keep the volume of talking and laughing down. As the moon tracked across the black sky, night birds and insects raised a loud, continuous racket, which added to the company's secure feelings. After all, when the VC were creeping around, the birds didn't chirp—at least that was what they had been told. Jace laughed to himself, knowing that didn't make sense, because he had patrols moving in the jungle and the birds and insects ignored them, didn't they? An odd night, he thought. His sixth sense told him the enemy was a thousand miles away. But at the same time, his brain told him that this just might be the time when the enemy would strike, when he and his soldiers least expected it.

When the eastern sky warmed to a gray-pink, Jace was still awake. Nothing at all had happened during the night and he was angry with himself for missing badly-needed sleep for nothing. After breakfast, battalion made a net call, ordering all units back to Bear Cat, where the 5-39 would revert to division reserve during the up-coming Tet cease-fire. If morale had been high before, it soared now. Reserve duty meant soldiers could sleep, read, listen to music, take showers—do anything, as long as they could grab their weapons and get to their tracks within minutes if an enemy attack occurred.

Black smoke belched from exhausts as drivers fired up their vehicles. Jace was amazed at the speed at which his troops rolled concertina, broke down aiming stakes, picked up claymores and filled in bunkers. They were going home again.

Mr. Trung bowed low as he entered Chi's front gate. After the tea was made and poured, Chi led him to the front room where she offered him a seat on a cushion. Mr. Trung, uncharacteristically for a civilized person, went directly to the point.

"I have come to show you how to trigger your bomb. This will not be the only time I will teach it to you. I will show you several times, then I will watch you construct the device many more times. Only when you can do it automatically will I give you the materials to take to the base."

Chi's eyes blazed with interest as Trung pulled a small roll of cloth from his shirt. From the packet, he took an inert electrical blasting cap, a small roll of tape, and a two-meter-long piece of the American telephone wire. Then he asked one of the children to go into the yard and bring back a stick of any length. The youngsters squealed as they argued over who would have the honor of bringing in the piece of bamboo left over from Christmas decorations. Chi complemented them on their manners when they all lined up, bowed and handed the bamboo to Mr. Trung.

"We will pretend the piece of bamboo is the row of batteries. I will show you how to prepare them later."

First, Trung separated the doubled wire into single strands, and cut one of the strands in two. Then, using his small pocket knife, he stripped two centimeters of insulation from each end of the three wires.

"The long wire will go from one battery terminal directly to one of the wires on the blasting cap. The wire I have cut in two will become the trigger. The bomb will explode when an electrical circuit is closed so that electricity can run from the batteries through the wires to each of the leads on the blasting cap."

Trung was quiet for a moment as he taped one end of the long wire to the simulated row of batteries and twisted the other end to one of the wires extending from the blasting cap. He then fashioned small loops out of the bare wire on one end of each of the two short pieces of wire that he had cut. Next, he threaded each of the short wires through the loop in the other so that when the ends were pulled, the two un-insulated loops would slide together and interlock.

Then he carefully explained to Chi, "Notice that the wire I have cut in two now is joined together in the middle by these two interconnecting loops, which freely slide back and forth. When you are assembling your bomb, do not, under any circumstances, allow the two bare loops to touch. They must be slid well up on the insulation to keep them apart. Once you are sure that no bare wires are touching, the last thing is to make the final connection to the blasting cap and the other battery terminal."

Chi watched intently, but still could not understand the concept.

"Now, the way the bomb will be triggered. Tie one end of a piece of string around a movable object—let's say a chair leg—and the other to one of the wires joined by the loops. When an American pulls out the chair, the bare loops will be pulled together, and the circuit closed. The bomb will then explode. Do you understand?"

As Asian custom dictated, Chi said she understood. To do otherwise would cause the teacher to lose face at not being able to explain his subject to the student. At the same time, Chi used body language to convey that she didn't really grasp the idea.

Trung, realizing that she didn't understand, asked, "Do you have a flashlight?"

Chi nodded, then rose from her cushion and went to the kitchen. From a cabinet drawer, she took a small pen light she had found outside the laundry and brought home. She took it to Trung, who flipped it on to insure that it worked. Moving quickly, he cut the wires making a miniature version of the circuit. He disassembled the flashlight and taped the wires to the batteries and the bulb.

"Now, we have made a small version of our trigger. Let's use the light bulb for the blasting cap. As you can see, the bulb is not lit. When I pull this wire causing the loops to slide together—like this—the light comes on. Imagine now that instead of a light bulb, this is a bomb. Boom!"

Chi laughed and clapped her hands. Trung knew she understood.

As Charlie company rolled into Bear Cat, the troops learned that this time there would be no party. This was not a stand-down—they would remain on alert. Jace met with his leaders to order the tracks refueled and to establish a priority of work. He directed that only truckloads of troops supervised by an officer with radio communications be allowed to go to the PX or the laundry. Other than these controlled shopping trips, the troops were restricted to the company area.

Jace sat in his office, glad for once that he had no article fifteens to administer—the new soldiers had not been in country long enough to get into trouble. In the company street, Baez stood in a wide-legged stance, arms folded, watching the company's maintenance activities. Jace looked out through the screen window as Doc Roberts and Tucker agitatedly ran up to the first sergeant.

"All our stuff's gone, Top. Khakis, civies, duffle bags—everything we left in the hootches. Gone," cried Tucker. "Who'd steal a damn khaki uniform?"

Almost at the same time, the new third platoon sergeant approached Baez. "We got hit too, Top. One of my troops got his stuff stole."

"Whose stuff?" asked Baez.

Jace watched and listened through the screened window, knowing the answer to the first sergeant's question.

"Williams," answered the platoon sergeant.

Phun rode in the cab of a Japanese-made truck, loaded to overflowing with baskets of tomatoes, sacks of rice and barrels of cooking oil. The driver was the hard-muscled leader of a sapper platoon assigned to the C-10 battalion. He said little as the truck crept along in the sweltering heat and traffic of the dry-season afternoon. Constantly watching the mirrors for danger, he took a circuitous route through the city, arriving at the auto-repair shop on Phan Thanh Gian Street as the sun went down. He curbed the truck near the repair shop, raised the hood and pretended to tinker with the engine. As he did so, Phun scanned the streets for danger, then went to the door of the garage to pretend to ask for help. Seeing no danger, she signaled her comrade, who dropped the hood, climbed into he cab and quickly pulled the truck into the garage.

Working fast, the driver closed the garage door, then began to unload the cargo. The tomato baskets hid dozens of Chinese-made potato-masher hand grenades. Inside each large sack of rice were three RPG-7 rockets. Ten assault rifles and a light machine gun were packed inside the barrels of cooking oil. The pleasant middle-aged matron who owned the adjoining house showed Phun and her companion where to hide the weapons, and then invited them inside for the evening meal. Because of the curfew, they would remain overnight as the woman's guests. Tomorrow, they would travel back to the Michelin rubber plantation to pick up a load of ammunition.

In the darkness, Doc Roberts flapped along in his shower clogs toward the bath house. As he opened the screen door, a voice called from the shadows.

"No need to scrub yo' black ass, nigger. Hit'll be jes' as nasty soon's yore done."

"Who's there?" yelled Doc.

"Don't matter who's here. You jes' keep yore nasty mouth shet or you'll never make it outa hyar alive. No matter what that damn cap'n asks you 'bout who stole yore stuff, you don't say nuthin' to nobody. We watchin' you nigger. You shoulda never testified in that court martial—that was your big mistake. Now you'll keep your mouth shut or you'll pay. You understand?"

Unable to see anything, and feeling defenseless wearing nothing but a towel and shower clogs, Doc did not know what to do. The voice said "we". That meant there were more than one of them. He could run, but something—probably pride—kept him from it. He just stood there with his hand on the shower-stall door and said nothing.

"I axed you if you understan', nigger!"

Doc eased the screen door shut and turned to face the voice in the dark. Still, he did not answer.

"You gonna learn to answer when I ask you a question, boy."

Too late, Doc heard a slight noise behind him. You really do see stars, he thought as he sagged to the ground. I thought that was just a figure of speech.

Chi stood behind the counter in the laundry. Soldiers crowded the small room and stood outside waiting with their dirty clothes. The snack bar and laundry had not been this busy in weeks. She guessed that there must have been a major change in what the Americans were doing. She would tell Mr. Trung, who had told her that even the smallest bit of information might be the key to unlocking a major secret.

In the late afternoon, as the flow of customers slowed, Chi found herself very tired from lifting and tying bundles of laundry and standing on her feet all day. Knowing it was near time for the truck to come to take her home, she turned her attention to the bomb she was constructing. She did not yet know how the batteries would be arranged, so she contented herself in looking for a way to run the string from the chair leg through the wall to the wire with the interconnecting loops. The first part of the puzzle solved itself easily. The board floor of the snack bar was roughly constructed. She saw that a stout string could easily be laid out-of-sight in one of the cracks between the boards. Running the string through the wall proved to be a more difficult challenge. The plywood wall on the snack-bar side had no seams or cracks. She couldn't put the string underneath the wall, since she had filled the bottom of the space behind the loose board on the laundry side with explosives.

As the five-ton truck pulled up outside, she eliminated the possibility of boring a hole in the plywood above the mass of plastique. The string running half a meter up the wall to a hole would be too obvious. Besides, she couldn't drill a hole in clear view of everyone in the snack bar—someone would surely ask what she was doing. That left only one possibility. She saw that she would have to move the mass of explosives and pack it against one side of the space behind the loose board. Then she would have working room to gouge out a space underneath the plywood large enough to push the string through. An important benefit of this plan would be that she could do all of the required labor behind the loose board in the laundry, out of sight from the snack bar. With the numbers of soldiers now coming to the laundry every day, however, finding the time to accomplish this task might prove difficult, she thought.

"I tell you there's no proof, Top. The S-4 said there was no paper trail that could prove Munn screwed with our requisitions or messed with our water trailer. There's no proof who stole the guys' stuff. There's no witnesses to the assault on Doc. We all know who's doing all this, but we have no case."

"Well, I guess our hands are just tied, then," said Baez, smiling.

"I don't like the look on your face or the tone of your voice," said Jace. "What have you got in mind?"

"Sir, I don't have nothin' in mind. I'm just agreeing with you that Sergeant Munn has tied our hands in this matter and there is nothing any of us can do."

"You and I both know you're up to something. Whatever it is, just don't get caught doing something I can't defend you on."

"Sir, I don't have any idea what you're talking about," grinned Baez as he stood, putting on his cap and pulling the bill down over his nose. "I just hope that mean old Sergeant Munn don't bother none of our boys again."

Sergeant Smith was alone in the supply tent. With the troops in Bear Cat, there was more to do than usual. He moved boxes, looking for the one that held division patches that the new troops had to have sewn on their uniforms before they could go to the PX. As the screen door slammed, Smith turned to face the form of Dewain Howell that filled the entire doorway.

"What chew want?" asked Smith.

Howell said nothing. He just walked toward Smith.

"I said—what do you want?"

Howell felt the word "nigger" had been reluctantly omitted from the end of Smith's question as he pretended to look past Smith to the stacked boxes.

"If you're lookin' for patches, you'll have to wait till I find 'em,' said Smith.

"I've found what I'm lookin' for," said Howell as his huge fist slammed into Smith's solar plexus. Smith, caught off guard by the blow, doubled over, his breath gone. Howell leaned over, his lips an inch from Smith's ear.

"You listen to me, you white-trash honky. I know you'uz the one hit Doc Roberts from behind. I know that other shit head Munn wuz with you. I want you to listen real good. I want you to think of the worse thing that could ever happen to a man. Are you thinkin'? If you so much as get near a colored soldier again, that's what'll happen to you. And I'll be the one holding you—hell I might even take a turn—and I guarantee you don't want that to happen. You understand me shit-breath?"

Smith, still bent and clutching his stomach looked desperately toward the door, groaning, but saying nothing. Howell slapped his face.

"I axed if you understan'—answer me!"

When Smith failed to respond again, Howell slapped him once more, hard, but not hard enough to leave a mark.

"I'm gonna ax you onest mo' then I'm gonna tear yo' adam's apple out through yo' nose. You unnerstan' that, don't you?"

Smith nodded.

"Say it!"

"I understand."

"One mo' thing," said Howell, standing. "You even think of doin' anything to get back at us—I got six coloreds ready to kill you at the drop of a hat. All I have to do is get hurt or give them the word. Think hard 'fo' you try somethin' else."

Smith, clutching a box for support, began to straighten up as Howell turned to leave. Then, with a move surprisingly fast for a big man, Howell spun and slammed Smith in the stomach a second time.

The truck loaded with vegetables slowed as it approached the roadblock on the outskirts of Saigon. The driver looked at Phun and said nothing. Remembering the experience when Lau had been detained, Phun had insisted that they rehearse every contingency they could think of. The plan they had agreed to use if they encountered a road block was for the driver to pretend he was deaf—a disability that would have kept such a strong young man out of the government army. Therefore, the police should not wonder why he was not a member of either the army or the Viet Cong. This plan would also allow Phun, who was not only disarmingly pretty, but faster-thinking than most of her male comrades, to do the talking.

The road block consisted of a wide board with long spiked nails protruding vertically from it. If the driver tried to run the obstacle, he would have four flat tires. There was no place to turn around and the traffic behind the truck ruled out backing up.

The policeman sauntered up to the open window. "What are you hauling?" he asked.

The driver looked at him, then at Phun, who leaned across to yell to the policeman, "My brother cannot hear. I will be glad to answer your questions."

The policeman repeated the question.

"We are carrying vegetables from our farm to several restaurants, the proprietors of which are our regular customers."

The policeman eyed the driver, who pointed to his ear and shrugged.

"Would you like to see what we are hauling?" asked Phun.

The policeman nodded and walked to the back of the truck. As he did so, the driver pulled a nine-millimeter automatic pistol from beneath the seat.

"I cannot get up on the bed of the truck by myself. Can you help me?" Phun smiled prettily.

The policeman grinned as he placed his hands on her tiny waist and lifted her onto the back of the truck where baskets of tomatoes, squash, onions, peppers, and cabbage were piled high. The officer swung up beside her, moved some of the vegetables aside, and probed deep into a basket of squash. As he did so, he glanced to the street behind the truck where traffic was backed up for two blocks.

Jumping down, the policeman offered Phun his hand to help her off the truck. As he walked back to the front of the cab, he looked the driver over once more. After glancing again at the backed-up traffic and taking one more long look at the pretty young woman, the policeman nodded to his colleague who pulled the spiked board aside. The driver slid the pistol back under the seat, put the truck in gear, and waited as Phun climbed into the cab. He then nodded to the officer as he drove away. Beneath the false bed of the truck were thousands of rounds of rifle and machine-gun ammunition bound for the auto-repair shop.

"Well, well, if it ain't my old buddy Sergeant Munn," said Baez as he and Five India walked into the battalion S-4 shop.

"I came to check that no more Charlie company requisitions got lost."

As Baez walked to where Munn was standing, Five India placed himself at the door, watching the outside.

"I done tole everybody—and I'll tell you the same—I ain't got no idea what happent to them requests."

"Well, then, maybe you can tell me what happened to Tucker's, Doc's and Williams' B-bags."

"How the hell should I know?" answered Munn, nervous now.

"OK. I have one more question. Why did you and Smith attack Doc Roberts?"

"Look, First Sergeant, I—"

Baez's palms slammed into Munn's collar bones, breaking his balance to the rear. At the same time, Baez shot his right foot around behind Munn's heels. Munn went down hard. Before he could move, Baez placed his left boot on Munn's right biceps.

"That was a cross-hoc take-down—one of the fascinating techniques I learned in ranger school. Now that we're in a better position to understand each other, I'm gonna talk and you're gonna listen. Either that, or I'll show you some other fascinating things I learned with the rangers. Are you with me?"

Munn nodded.

"My army and my company ain't no place for any of your klan bullshit. It stops here! Now, I've got some things for you to understand. First, by evening chow, I want the stolen B-bags here in this office. Don't worry about us bring charges against you—we just want the bags back. I'll come down in my jeep and get them. If you've thrown them away, you've got just a couple of hours to replace everything that was in them. If they are not here, I'll give you a sample of what will happen to you."

Still standing on Munn's biceps with his left foot, Baez stomped hard on Munn's abdomen with his right. Munn cried out in agony.

"Second: You'll personally come to my orderly room at 0900 every morning while we're here at Bear Cat to pick up any supply requisitions we may have. Now get up."

Munn struggled to his feet, clutching his stomach.

"Five India, come over here and tell the good sarge the third thing he needs to understand."

Five India walked to Munn while Baez took up watch at the door.

"I've spent five years in admin," said Five India. "I know every way in the world to screw up your records. I can make sure you don't get promoted or get credit for this combat tour. I can add article fifteens, change efficiency reports, or make your records disappear altogether. I know all the clerks at division and many of them, including a couple of finance clerks, owe me favors. You may think you know how to mess with paperwork. I can assure you that you have no idea. If you screw with any soldier in our company again, you'll not get paid the whole time you're in this country. Oh, yes, and your medical records will indicate you've had every disease from syphilis to crotch-rot."

Five India stared into Munn's eyes for a long moment, then turned and nodded to Baez. The first sergeant walked back toward Munn who was now sweating profusely and gasping for air.

"One thing more," he said. "Give me one indication you want to try to do something funny again and I'll arrange for you to spend a whole night with Sergeant Howell and the black soldiers of second platoon. Have a real nice rest of the afternoon!"

When Mr. Trung returned, Chi quickly and proudly assembled the trigger for him. She had practiced the procedure many times and was absolutely confident in her abilities.

Mr. Trung was very pleased. "Now, I want you to look at this," he said as he held out a piece of intricately carved and hollowed-out bamboo almost a meter long. Chi turned the artistically carved bamboo tube over in her hands. "It has holes in it like a flute, but it does not look like it would make a sound."

"It is not a flute, but it has been fashioned to look similar to a musical instrument. Hopefully the holes will convince anyone searching you that this is some sort of musical instrument and not anything to fear. Do you think you would have any trouble getting this into the enemy's base?"

"I do not think it would be difficult. I could tell them it is something a soldier asked me to carve for him. I often bring embroidery and sewing home to work on, so the guards are accustomed to seeing me carry things in and out. Besides, this does not look dangerous. What is it for?"

"This bamboo tube has been fashioned to tightly hold exactly twelve flashlight batteries. As short as are the wires that will run from the batteries to the explosive, the bomb would probably explode using fewer than twelve, but we want to use that number to make sure, in case some of the batteries are weak. All you have to do is place the batteries, with like poles all in the same direction, in the tube. Notice you can put the batteries in from only one end. The other end is carved so they will not fall out. If you tape the open end when you attach the wires, the batteries will be held securely together. Will this fit behind your loose board?"

"Yes, easily," answered Chi.

Mr. Trung pulled a small roll of cloth from his trousers pocket. As he unfolded it, Chi saw that it held an electrical blasting cap.

"Unlike the one we used for training, this one is real—you must handle it very carefully. Please take this in your rice ball tomorrow. All you have to do is to make a hole in the explosive with a pencil or a small stick. Gently push the cap into the hole and press the plastique around it. You now have everything you need to assemble the bomb except the wire. It might be dangerous for you to carry wire into the base. Do you think you can find it there?"

"As I told you, it is everywhere. Finding a length that is not connected to anything will be difficult, but I will try."

"If you cannot find wire on the base, you will have to carry it in, although I would rather not take the chance. Also I must know when you plan to finish rigging the bomb so that we can make arrangements to transport you safely away from Long Thanh."

Chi did not tell him she had decided not to go. She did not know how Mr. Trung would react.

"Good," said Trung. "Now, please show me how large the space behind the loose board is and where the explosive is located in it. Then we will practice assembling the bomb inside the space you will actually be working in."

At exactly 9 a.m., Sergeant Munn walked into the Charlie company orderly room.

"Yes, Sergeant Munn," said Baez. "What can we do for you?"

"Uh—I jes' come down to see if ya'll had any supply requisitions."

"Well, now, I don't know," said Baez. "Let's us just walk down and see Sergeant Smith and find out."

Jace watched carefully as the first sergeant donned his cap and escorted Munn to the door. As he passed Jace's office, he looked in and winked. Jace rose and walked to the screen door, watching them leave.

"Wonder what the hell is going on?" he asked no one in particular.

"I don't know, but Top got our stuff back. He brought it to us after chow last night," said Tucker.

"Five India, do you know what's up with Munn and the first sergeant?"

"Sir, I will admit that I am privy to some small bits of information regarding the matter at hand. Of course if you insist, I'll tell you what little I know, but I would request that you talk to First Sergeant Baez about it. I would not want to say something inappropriate, or preempt the prerogative of a senior non-commissioned officer—if you know what I mean, sir." answered Five India, seriously.

"I know a ration of shit when I hear one," answered Jace shaking his head. "This is one of those times when a commander can tear the place apart and get to the bottom of what's going on—or just forget it and go with the flow."

"Captain, I respectfully recommend you go with the flow," said Five India.

The setting sun painted the company's weathered tents a liquid orange as Jace sat on his cot writing letters. As badly as he wanted to tell his father about the battle for Hill 108 and how the old K-Bar had been the only weapon he had had at the end, and how he had killed with it, he just couldn't. He understood even more fully his father's silence about Guadalcanal. How could anyone describe something that was as horrible, as irrational, and yet so defining as battle?

What had he learned that he could tell his father—that his father didn't know already? That combat was extremely personal on the one hand and totally random on the other? That when the enemy was shooting at you—when you knew it and he knew it—war was extremely personal? But the vast majority of bullets and shells fired by both sides were simply sent in the enemy's general direction, mostly only tearing up the jungle or blowing craters in rice paddies. But sometimes these random rounds, by whatever fate, karma, will of God, luck, or lack of it, found the flesh and blood of a human being. Some of these randomly-fired projectiles killed while others maimed, with only fractions of inches making the difference between someone living or dying. Some bullets creased skulls without penetrating while some blew humans into pulp—and there was no rhyme or reason to it. A soldier could do all he could to keep himself covered, camouflaged, hidden, or protected, and that one blindly-fired round could kill him dead simply because he was crawling, walking, running, standing, sitting, or lying at the wrong place at the right time. Jace knew that his dad had understood these truths on Guadalcanal, so there was no need to describe battle to him. Instead, he wrote about the operations, the politics, the country, the people, the weather, and his men. He knew his dad could read between the lines. He knew he would understand.

To his sister, he wrote light-hearted anecdotes about soldiers having scorpion races and catching lizards. He told stories of Vietnamese children, water buffalos, and flocks of wild parakeets that were noisy, nervous specs of color in the trees. He wrote of the beauty of the country, the terrible predictability of the weather, and how the Vietnamese people and American soldiers continued to live their lives in spite of the war. He told of catching glimpses of real live elephants, tigers, and fifteen-foot pythons. He wrote about Charlie Chicken, a huge red rooster that had been liberated from a VC base camp, who now strutted and clucked around the company area.

He found that his girlfriend was the only one to whom he could open up. She became his pressure-relief valve—the one person to whom he could be absolutely honest. To her he wrote of the incessant demands and responsibilities of command. He wrote of the heartbreak of losing a soldier to the enemy. He also wrote of loneliness, hopes, dreams and memories—and became closer to her with each exchange of letters. This evening, he was asking her to meet him in Hawaii when he got his R and R.

As the dusk darkened the inside of the screened-in tent, Jace went to sleep with paper and pen on his chest. Suddenly, a gunshot jolted him from his sleep. He ran out the door into the company street to find several men running toward a first-platoon tent. Pushing soldiers aside, Jace made his way to a cot where a young soldier writhed in pain, holding his leg.

"Walker? What the hell happened?" asked Jace.

"Jarnigan was cleaning his rifle. It went off and hit me in the leg."

Doc Roberts was on the spot in less than a minute, despite the bandage on his head and a slight concussion.

"It's not too serious," said Doc. "I suggest we put him in a jeep and take him to the clearing station at division. They can send him on to the 93rd Evac if they need to."

"OK. Somebody get Tucker to bring my jeep. Five India, make the rounds and tell all the platoon leaders I want all weapons cleared—even if they've been cleared before. I don't want anyone killed inside the damn division base camp."

The next morning, the command and staff meeting began at 0800, sharp. As executive officer, C.C. supervised the staff and therefore their presentations at the meeting. Lieutenant Colonel Price sat in a folding chair at the front of the large S-3 shop/TOC that was part of the 5-39 headquarters building.

The S-1 brought the assemblage up to date on the personnel strength. The battalion was back to 96% strength only a month after the wholesale departures of veteran troops in December. The S-2 gave a detailed briefing on the enemy situation, stating that there were some indications that the V.C. and the North Vietnamese were planning to break the Tet cease-fire and that everyone should remain alert. The S-3 gave an operational summary and a forecast of anticipated tactical deployments. After Tet, the battalion was scheduled to resume working with the engineers clearing Highway 1, possibly all the way to Phan Thiet. The S-4 briefed the supply status, then stated that he had a report to complete by mid-February on the number of times M-16s jammed during fire fights. He asked for company commanders' assistance in submitting the data to him.

C.C. rose to admonish the commanders to submit timely reports and to let him know of any problems that could be handled by the staff. There was a question and answer session, during which Jace said nothing, then Lieutenant Colonel Price stood and spoke.

"We had an accidental discharge of a weapon last night in Charlie company. Everyone check their weapons. We cannot afford to lose foxhole strength because of non-battle casualties. There are continuing instances of soldiers going to the PX without patches sewn on their uniforms. This will stop. We cannot have the battalion look bad in base camp. Have your troops make maximum use of the barber shops and laundry while we're here. And make sure they don't walk around in their scuffed-up boots. Make your soldiers smear on some Kiwi to at least make their boots look black, even if they are past shining. Also, I want all of you to tighten up military courtesy around here. Five soldiers this morning alone passed me without saluting."

C.C. had the last word. "If what the S-2 says about the enemy breaking the Tet cease-fire is true, we may have to react quickly. Have your men where you can get your hands on them in a moment's notice in case we have to respond. Sir, do you have anything else?"

Price shook his head.

C.C. said, "Thank you, gentlemen. You are dismissed."

As he stood and saluted, Jace thought it odd that the X.O. was giving operational guidance while the commander was worried only about what the troops looked like at the PX. This meeting confirmed the feeling that had been in the pit of Jace's stomach for weeks: that Lieutenant Colonel Price had relinquished actual command of the battalion to C.C.

As the sun rose high enough in the sky to begin its daily baking of the paddies, jungles and hot, dusty roads, Chi rode in the back of the five-ton truck toward the south gate at Bear Cat. Despite her growing anxiety, she sat stoically as the truck waited in line to be admitted into the base. When their turn came, she dismounted with the others to be searched. Despite the fact that she had carried over ten pounds of plastic explosive through the gate, her fear now almost overwhelmed her. Perhaps it was because the blasting cap in her rice ball was so different and dangerous. The bamboo tube also unsettled her. She felt like running away.

For some reason, the soldiers were taking more time looking through the belongings of the workers this morning. When Chi got to the front of the line, the M.P. took her cloth bag from her.

"Whatcha got here, Mamasan? Rice?"

Desperately afraid that her facial expression might betray her, she looked at the ground as she nodded.

"And what the hell is this?" asked the M.P. as he examined the bamboo "flute". "Hey sarge, come and look at this."

The tall, stern-looking sergeant approached, took the tube and examined it. "What's this for, Mamasan?"

"No bic," said Chi pretending not to understand.

"What is it?" asked the sergeant, more forcefully.

With a look of abject horror on her face, Chi shook her head, her fear immobilizing her.

"OK, you stand over there until we get an interpreter down here to check it out," said the NCO as he gripped Chi's shoulder and guided her to the side of the road. An M.P. walked to the parked jeep and made a radio call.

"You can go ahead and take off if you want," he said to the truck driver. "It'll be a few minutes."

"Naw, I take Mamasan to the laundry every morning. I'll just wait," said the driver.

Twenty minutes later, a jeep came down the road in a cloud of dust from the interior of the base. As it slid to a stop, Chi almost screamed. The Vietnamese officer who had tortured her for sewing the V.C. flag stepped from the vehicle.

"Well, we meet again," said the man in Vietnamese. "What are you up to this time?"

"She's got this piece of bamboo. Strange-looking thing if you ask me. I asked her what it's for and she didn't understand—at least that's what she said," said the M.P.

"So, what is this used for?" asked the interpreter in Vietnamese as he turned his attention to Chi.

"Sir, I do not know. A soldier drew a picture of what he wanted and I agreed to carve it for him."

"It has the appearance of a flute, but you and I know that is not what it is."

"He told me he wanted it for a decoration in his home in America. You know how strange these people are. I have no idea what this is or what he wants it for. All I know is that he paid me well to carve it."

"Well, I am going to hold on to it until I have time to investigate this matter more fully," said the interpreter.

"Sir, I ask you not to keep the carving. The soldier has already paid me. I promised that I would have it finished for him today. He said he is leaving this base soon and wants to mail it home." Then as an afterthought, Chi added, "He is an officer and I am afraid I will get in a great deal of trouble if I don't have it for him today."

"An officer, huh?" asked the interpreter, who became suddenly quiet. If an officer had ordered the carving and the woman told him who had taken it away from her, he could have some explaining to do. He turned the tube over in his hands, carefully examining it. It was obviously not a weapon. Nor was it any kind of art that could be embarrassing to the government. If the American officer thought that this ridiculous-looking object was Vietnamese art, that was his problem.

"Very well, then. This does not look like anything we should be concerned with," said the interpreter as he nodded to the M.P.s.

"Thanks for your trouble, sir," said the M.P. as he saluted. Handing the bamboo tube back to Chi, he said, "On your way, then, Mamasan."

After the frightening search at the gate, Chi rode with the cooks across Bear Cat on the truck's board seat, her feet barely touching the hot metal floor. She fought desperately to regain her composure. Today was not the day to act suspicious in any way.

As the truck neared the laundry and geared down in a cloud of black diesel smoke, she was electrified by what she saw. By sheer chance, she found herself looking directly at what she desperately needed, but as yet had found no way of getting her hands on. At the base of a telephone pole on the side of the road, not a hundred meters from where she worked, was a small wad of the black military telephone wire. It appeared to be the excess an installer had carelessly left near the pole after stringing a connection. It did not even appear to be attached to anything.

In the laundry, she waited on an endless succession of young soldiers turning in soiled fatigues and picking up clean bundles.Her mind never left the small wad of wire. Somehow, she knew she must find a way to retrieve it, but no matter what she came up with, fear drove the plan from her mind.

Late in the afternoon, the steady flow of customers slackened to a drip. Finding herself alone at last, she walked outside and went to the corner of the building. Looking down the red dusty road, she could see the telephone pole—not so far, but too far away.

Picking their way through the traffic jams caused by people trying to get home before the Tet holiday began, Phun and the platoon leader made one last trip from the Michelin rubber plantation to the auto-repair shop in Saigon. Beneath the false truck bed, they carried loaded AK-47 magazines and RPG rockets. In the baskets of fruits and vegetables were more grenades. Even though she and her driver/commander were tense with fear and sweating profusely, their journey into the capital was uninterrupted. The police, faced with the flood of holiday travelers, had ceased searching entirely and now stood aside only interested in traffic control.

In other trucks, busses, cars and on bicycles and motor bikes, the rest of the C-10 battalion filtered into Saigon. They would stay in safe houses, hostels, rented rooms in private homes or they would simply mill about in the holiday crowds until it was time to report to their assembly areas. Several of their objectives were in Cholon, the Chinese quarter of the capital. The main objective of the battalion during the attack would be the U.S. embassy.

One by one, the members of Phun's platoon drifted into the repair shop. As they reported, the squad leader handed them their assigned weapons and gave instructions for preparing for battle. Phun knew the mission and the plan by heart. She also knew the danger. She had traveled around the country and the city enough to know the importance of the American embassy. By watching the other members of her team, she realized that they had never heard of and did not understand the significance of the target they would strike during the offensive.

As the leader gave his platoon their final briefing on the attack, he did not mention an escape plan, reinforcements, or resupply. Phun knew that when their embassy was attacked, the Americans would react with ferocity, strength, and speed. With growing horror, she realized that she was part of a suicide mission.

In the jungles southwest of Xuan Loc, Colonel Lau gave final orders to the officers of the 274th Viet Cong Battalion. The soldiers of the battalion had already begun infiltrating into Bien Hoa. In their innocuous-looking suitcases, knapsacks, and holiday packages, they carried their disassembled weapons.

As in the biblical story of Christ's birth, the Vietnamese took to the roads to return to the place of their birth—not to be counted for tax purposes as in Jesus' time, but to be in the presence of the spirits of their ancestors during the new-year's celebration.

Tet Nguyen Dan, or simply Tet, is the most joyously celebrated holiday in Vietnam. Combining a secular observation of crop-planting time with Buddhist religious celebrations and ancestor worship, Tet is the equivalent of western Christmas, New Years, Easter and Halloween all rolled into one.

As the holiday approached, people donned their finest clothes and gathered at temples for prayers inviting the spirits of ancestors to return to the family hearth for feasts, parties, and visits. City streets were filled with the aroma of traditional *banh chung* cakes made from meat, beans and sticky rice. *Cay neu* poles made of bamboo and decorated with betel nut swayed over homes to frighten away evil spirits. And through it all, youngsters stood in doorways or zipped about on motorbikes lighting one string of firecrackers after another to chase away evil. Among the throngs of holiday revelers, Viet Cong guerrillas made their way to their assembly positions in the cities, some even test-firing their weapons in the racket of exploding fireworks.

"We got word down from G-2 that something is definitely up," said C.C. "The Tet cease-fire has been cancelled. The battalion has been ordered to positions from where we can react to any enemy attacks more quickly. Alpha company, you'll be near the south gate of Long Binh. Bravo company, you'll be inside Long Binh, near II Field Force Headquarters. Jace, Charlie company will circle up just outside of Long Binh on the eastern access road. Battalion headquarters along with the 4.2 mortars and the scout platoon will be inside the wire near 90th Replacement Company. The exact locations are on the situation map—get them before you leave. We remain in reserve. We don't think anything much will happen, but with all the headquarters, installations and ammo dumps at Long Binh—and of course the Bien Hoa airbase—division thinks it prudent that we move closer to where the action is liable to be if something does happen. Questions?"

"When do we move?" asked the A company commander.

"I guess that would be helpful information," laughed C.C. "We move ASAP—as soon as you guys can get saddled up."

"Where's the colonel?" asked Bravo six. "I've got some stuff he needs to sign."

"He's at a meeting at brigade. He asked me to brief you."

"Do we move as a battalion or separate companies?" asked Jace.

"Good question. You will move as separate companies. Jace, you have further to go, so you move first, then Bravo, then Alpha. Headquarters company will bring up the rear. Don't move your units until you're sure the outfit in front of you has cleared. The last thing we need is a traffic jam. If there is nothing else, get moving."

Lau, dressed in black slacks and open-collared white shirt, bowed at the door of his assigned safe house. The owner of the house and his wife, a prosperous middle-aged couple, bowed in return and invited him inside.

"The things you asked for are here—the government army uniform and, of course, an assault rifle, your pistol and canteen. Please relax and have something to eat. It will be a while before dark, so there is nothing you can do. You might even enjoy a nap. If you need anything, all you have to do is ask."

Lau joined the couple for a hearty meal of barbecued fish fillets, *nuoc mam*, rice, *kho pho* soup, and beer. After lunch, his host and hostess, assuming that Lau had much to think about, made themselves scarce. Realizing he had nothing to do until he was scheduled to meet his battalion in their assembly area just after dark, He tried to rest, but sleep would not come. As they did every time he had idle time on his hands, his thoughts turned to Phun. He prayed that she would survive the offensive unhurt. Surely the C-10 battalion commander would have seen her abilities and her intelligence and would have assigned her duties out of harm's way. She was much too valuable to waste as a common rifleman. Lau prayed she was on the battalion staff or was again a liaison runner.

Jace led his company out of the eastern access gate of the Long Binh base. In the open area that had been cleared adjacent to the perimeter of the sprawling installation, he circled his tracks and ordered the company to dig in. As the troops labored at their holes through the afternoon, the continuous cracking of fireworks drifted to them from the villages on the other side of the base. As the warm, humid dusk settled over them, they watched as roman candles, star clusters and streams of tracer bullets dotted the horizon.

Three kilometers away, Lau shoved his way through the crowded streets to the back alley where his battalion had gathered. In back yards, empty buildings, vacant lots, and a cemetery, his civilian-clad guerrillas pulled their weapons from their bags and assembled them. Quickly and quietly they donned black pajamas or olive-drab fatigues over their holiday clothes. As Lau loaded his AK-47, he prayed the populace would respond quickly when the attack began. His guerrillas had only two or three magazines apiece for their assault rifles. Despite his repeated requests, he had never been told anything about resupply.

"All Cougar stations, this is Cougar Six. I want all element leaders at my location by 1900 hours for a meeting. Acknowledge in turn, over."

Jace waited his turn and radioed his "wilco", then picked up his situation map and plotted his route to battalion headquarters. He decided not to take a track, since he could make the whole trip inside the Long Binh base.

"Tucker, fire up the jeep. We got just enough time to get there," yelled Jace. "Top, keep a close eye on everything. If something happens, I'll radio where I'll meet the company."

"Hell, sir, ain't nothin' gonna happen tonight. All the dinks is celebratin' too hard."

"May be. I've just got a different feeling tonight. Not good, not bad, just different. I'll be back quick as I can."

At the battalion TOC, Lieutenant Colonel Price passed on the information he had received at brigade. From MAC-V on down, the chain of command was afraid that the enemy might violate its self-imposed cease-fire. It took only fifteen minutes for him to pass on his guidance. Then, he dismissed his company commanders without a further word and disappeared into his tent. C.C. motioned Jace outside.

"Look, keep a sharp eye out tonight. I don't like the feeling."

"Me neither," responded Jace.

"I survived Tet during my first tour," said C.C. "All it was was a bunch of eating and drinking and partying. The cease-fire held and everyone had a hell of a good time. Maybe it was because I was with the Vietnamese my first tour. Maybe it just feels different in an American unit."

"That's what I told my first sergeant before I came here tonight—that this whole thing just feels different," said Jace.

"Anyhow, happy new year. The year of the monkey. And keep your head down."

"Yeah, you do the same. Good night, sir."

Jace jumped into his jeep and picked up the company hand set.

"Charlie Five India, this is Charlie Six, over."

Five India responded.

"This is Charlie Six. While I'm out, I'm gonna swing by the 93rd Evac and see our man in the hospital. I'll be back in about an hour, over."

"Five India. Everything is groovy here. Take your time."

Jace walked around to the front of the jeep and studied his map in the gleam of the headlights.

"OK, Tucker. Let's go.

"Where's the hospital, sir?"

"'Bout a mile from here. C'mon, I'll show you."

In the early evening, Phun, along with the other members of her platoon, had been given last minute instructions. She was to be the assistant gunner in a light machine-gun team that would cover the attack on the American Embassy. The assault team would drive to the objective in a stolen taxi and a small Peugeot truck. Phun, the gunner, and the ammunition bearer would infiltrate the five blocks through the back streets to the corner of *Mac Dinh Chi* Street and *Thong Nhut* Boulevard. From a position in the mouth of an alley, they could fire on anyone responding to the attack down either of the wide streets that paralleled two of the embassy walls.

The platoon ate together, and then checked their equipment and weapons. No one asked any questions about escape plans, resupply or what they were supposed to do if the attack failed. If they realized that they were headed into a suicide mission, none of them showed any concern.

Jace and Tucker pulled into a parking space outside the red-cross-emblazoned Quonset huts that made up the 93rd Evacuation Hospital.

"Wait here," he said to Tucker. I'll just be a couple of minutes."

Inside the hospital, bone-tired doctors and frazzled nurses went about the business of keeping American soldiers alive. Jace asked where he could find Walker. As he walked through the wards looking for his man, he looked closely at a tough-looking nurse in jungle fatigues. He realized that as a company commander, he was able to see the country, interact with his soldiers, even enjoy some good times. The medical personnel here did nothing but deal with the maimed, dead and dying. Jace could not imagine how depressing that must be day in and day out. Infantry soldiers often joked about how the doctors had it made—walking around with white jackets and clip boards all day and chasing nurses all night. From the atmosphere in this place, Jace guessed that all the doctors and nurses did when they got off shift—if they ever did—was sleep.

He found Walker propped up, writing a letter.

"Hey, sir. You come all the way here just to see me?" asked the soldier.

"I didn't have to come far. We're camped just outside the Long Binh gate. How're they treating you?"

"Fine. Chow's good. I wuddent hit too bad. They said I'll be back to the company in 'bout a week. Believe it or not, I'll be glad to get out o' here. This place 'll getcha down."

Jace pulled back the sheet and examined the boy's leg. "Does it hurt much?"

"Naw, it don't bother me much at all. They keep me full of pain pills. They say I'm healin' good."

"Anything I can get you or do for you?"

"Naw, I 'preciate it, though."

"Well, I gotta run. Take care of yourself. Enjoy laying on your ass. You'll be back to work soon enough."

Jace shook the boy's hand and tousled his hair. On the way out someone called to him. Turning, he saw a young man lying naked on a table with tubes running into his body from every direction. Large fans droned like C-130s behind him.

"Hey, son. You from the 5-39?"

"Yes, sir. You command C company, don't you."

"Sure do. What company you in?"

"Alpha. Got hit down south of Xuan Loc. Hit me in the back."

"Anything I can do for you?" Jace asked.

"No, sir. If you see Alpha, say hi to the guys for me."

"Sure," said Jace as he turned to leave. "Get better quick."

"Are you from his unit?" asked a doctor as Jace left the ward.

"Same battalion, different companies. How's he doing?"

The doctor shook his head. "His liver's shot up. He won't live till morning."

"What's the matter, sir?" asked Tucker as Jace slid into the passenger's seat. "You look like you just seen a ghost."

"I probably just did, Tucker. Let's go."

CHAPTER 16

▼

30 January 1968

"Damn! They've locked the gate," said Jace in frustration. "Pull over to that bunker and let's see if somebody's got the key."

"Hey, sir," said the bunker guard. "Can I help you?"

"I certainly hope so. I command the mech company that's camped right out there. Do you have the gate key?"

"No, sir. A lieutenant come and locked it. He gots the key."

"Do you have radio contact with him?" asked Jace.

"No, sir. Hell, I don't even know who he was. Must be new. I can call the TOC and see if they can run him down."

"Shit! Naw—that could take half the night. Tucker—turn around and let's see if we can find another way home. Thanks anyway, son."

Every road they tried inside the base ended in a dead end against the fence. Jace got out and checked his map once more in the jeep's lights.

"As much as I hate to, we're going to have to go out the main gate and drive all the way around Long Binh on the highway."

Tucker said nothing for a moment. He just looked at Jace apprehensively.

"Sir, we could leave the jeep and climb over the fence. Top could meet us at the gate."

"If we did that, someone would steal the radios. And tomorrow morning my jeep would have different bumper markings and would be parked in some Long Binh REMF's driveway. No, we're gonna have to make it back on the highway."

The M.P. at the main gate held up his hand in a signal to stop. Jace got out and returned the man's salute.

"I can't let you go out tonight, Captain."

"Look, I'm not on a joy ride. I was called inside Long Binh to a meeting. I command a mech company that's outside the back gate. Now it's locked. Do you know who's got the key?"

"No, sir. But I've been ordered not to let anyone out this gate. It's just too dangerous out there. There's millions of people and a lot of shooting and fireworks."

"Well, you're going to let me out. I'm going to get back to my company."

"Well, sir, my orders are—."

"I know what your orders are. My orders are to get back to my company— which I am going to do! Crank it up, Tucker."

The M.P. stepped in front of the jeep. "Sir, I'll have to—"

"What are you going to do?" asked Jace, aggravated now. "Arrest me? Shoot me? Drive on, Tucker."

The M.P. jumped out of the way and ran to his field phone. Jace told Tucker to turn northeast on Highway 316 that paralleled Long Binh's fence line. As they passed II Field Force Headquarters, they ran into a mele as American M.P.s and white-shirted national policemen tried to move holiday revelers away from Long Binh's fence line. Inside the wire, nervous bunker guards watched the near-riot.

"Turn around. We'll have to go through Binh Hoa," said Jace.

Tucker audibly exhaled as he shook his head.

"I don't like it either, but maybe that road will be open. Take a right at the 90th Replacement."

"Yes, sir, you're the boss," said Tucker, unhappily.

At first the way was clear. They drove the two miles to the road junction in the city unimpeded. As they turned east on Highway 1, however, they found themselves in the middle of an enormous street party. Jace, thinking that the trip to battalion would be entirely inside the Long Binh Base, had only brought his .45 pistol, which he drew from his holster and chambered a round, while Tucker nervously laid his M-16 across his lap. They crept along at 5 m.p.h., waving drunk and noisy people from their path.

"We're going to have to find another way. Let's see if we can find a side street that parallels the highway."

"Damn, sir. I don't like this one little bit," said Tucker. "I'm scared shitless!"

"Me too," said Jace, beginning to understand that he had made several bad decisions in a row. He should have listened to Tucker. "We'll try this. If we can't get through, we'll go back and shoot the lock off of the back gate or climb over as you suggested. Turn left here."

Lau stood at the edge of a grown-up a vacant lot surrounded by the guerrillas of his battalion. Out on the main highway, Tet celebrations were in full swing. People packed every nook and cranny along the main highway, but avoided the back streets, as if they instinctively knew that danger lurked there.

Suddenly, vehicle lights appeared in the narrow back street. Lau dove for cover as his guerrillas ducked into the deep grass and behind houses. He crawled behind a fence, stood, and then cautiously peeked out to see an American army jeep approach. It was too late to yell to his men not to fire. Although he had told them not to initiate action until his signal, he knew his fighters were extremely nervous. If his soldiers fired on this vehicle, they would spring the offensive in Bien Hoa five hours too soon. As he quickly considered his options, he ventured another look to be sure that no convoy followed the jeep. What could he do? All it would take to initiate a catastrophe would be for one of his men to fire. He knew that one shot could cause the rest of the battalion to open up also. If the enemy in this vehicle got off a radio call before they died, or if they turned up missing, other Americans would come looking for them. Either way, the 274th would have a choice: fight or flee. And Lau knew that whether they fought or ran, they would probably not be able to accomplish their objective. Lau was soaked with sweat as the gears of his mind ground to a stop. Watching the enemy vehicle drawing closer and closer, and not knowing what else to do, he hid his pack and his assault rifle in the tall grass and stripped off his fatigue jacket. Hiding his 9-millimeter in his belt under his under shirt, he stepped into the street.

"Stop, Tucker!" Jace yelled as the small man appeared in the headlights.

Gripping his pistol tightly, Jace stepped out of the vehicle.

"What do you want?" he asked. "Do you speak English?"

Lau walked up to Jace, who towered above him. After a six-hundred-mile journey and almost a year of bombings, torture, capture, escape, and battle, his wish had again been granted. He stood face to face with an American—only to find that he had to save his life.

Lau knew few English words. He would have to improvise. Looking at the tall American's pistol, he waved his hand back and forth in front of his face.

"No good, No good. Beaucoup VC! Beaucoup V.C.!"

"What? Where?" stammered Jace.

"Go! No good," shouted Lau as he pointed down the dark side street. "You go!"

As the small man motioned for Tucker to turn around, Jace's eyes darted around the buildings and the vacant lot which were illuminated by the jeep's lights. Why were there no people here? Who was this man? If he knew there were VC nearby, why hadn't he told the police or the ARVN? If he were a Viet Cong, why hadn't he merely ambushed them on the dark street? Amid all the fireworks, no one would have even heard. Jace stared hard into the small man's dark eyes shining intently in the headlights.

"Tucker! Turn around, we're going back the way we came."

Jace extended his hand to the man. "*Cam Ong,*" he said, thanking him. The man took Jace's hand with a weak, almost feminine grasp.

"*Xin Toi, tam biet,*" said the man, bowing.

"Thanks again," said Jace in English. "You probably just saved our lives."

The man bowed again as Jace climbed into the jeep which was still in the process of turning around. As Tucker let out the clutch and roared away, Jace waved. He felt very foolish and very lucky as he and Tucker turned back onto the highway and crept through the crowds back toward Long Binh. To battalion, he radioed the man's contention that many VC were in Binh Hoa city. Then he radioed Baez and told him to take a track to the east gate and break it open.

At 2:45 a.m. the small truck and the taxi sped down Mac Dinh Chi street with their lights off. The Vietnamese policeman in the kiosk built into the eight-foot-high wall around the American embassy saw them coming and melted into the shadows. With tires squealing, the two vehicles turned right onto *Thong Nhut* Boulevard and slid to a stop just short of the main gate. From inside the vehicles, Viet Cong opened fire at the two M.P.s guarding the gate. The M.P.s fired back, slammed the huge iron gate, then shut and locked it with a large padlock. As the gate clanged shut, two guerrillas jumped from the taxi and took up guard positions as their comrades began to unload satchels of explosives and RPG rockets from the truck.

In the dark, Phun could make out little of what was happening. She saw the truck and the taxi make the turn toward the main gate, and saw them skid to a halt. Since then, however, she had heard firing but had seen nothing. As she and her two comrades on the machine gun dropped back into the shadows and waited for the enemy reinforcements that were sure to come, a Viet Cong sapper placed a satchel containing fifteen pounds of Semtex against the embassy wall. After motioning to his comrades to scatter and take cover, he ignited the fuse and ran to safety himself. Seconds later, Phun winced as a shattering explosion tore a three-foot hole in the wall. As soon as the dust and smoke began to clear, the platoon leader motioned his men to follow him as he dived through the hole. Immediately, a fierce firefight broke out between the assaulting guerrillas and the M.P.s guarding the front gate. Within seconds, two Viet Cong, including the platoon leader, and the two M.P.s on the gate were dead.

For the next hour, a battle raged all through the embassy compound. The swish-boom of RPG rockets slamming into the front of the chancery building and the sharp crack of exploding hand grenades punctuated the shooting and shouting inside. To Phun's great surprise and relief, no organized reinforcements responded to the attack. A few figures running toward the wall in the dark, and the whining of over-reved jeep engines were all she could see or hear outside the compound. Her machine-gun team still had not had a clear target on which to fire, so they remained silent.

"All Cougar stations, all Cougar stations, this is Cougar Three. Bien Hoa air base, the Long Binh complex and all ARVN compounds are under heavy mortar and rocket attack. All units be prepared to move, over."

Jace acknowledged then made his own net call alerting his troops, who needed no prompting since they could clearly hear the explosions of the enemy projectiles landing nearby.

"Saddle up," he yelled as he jogged around the perimeter. "Don't worry about filling in your holes. Pick up your claymores. We'll leave the trip flares and the concertina if we have to. Just get moving. Saddle up!"

Within minutes, the company was picked up, packed and ready to roll. All they needed were orders.

Baez ran to the front of the command track. "What do we do with the cooks and the wheeled vehicles?"

"Have them pull inside Long Binh. You go with them. Park near some unit that has some firepower. Keep our stuff and our guys together no matter what. We'll come back and get you when this is over."

"I'll be damned if I will! I'm coming with the company. I'll have the mess sergeant take charge of the trains."

"Top, dammit—" began Jace.

"Sir, you know my place is with you and the men," interrupted Baez. "I'm coming with you!"

"OK," said Jace, shaking his head. "Just go get them moving."

"Yes, sir," yelled Baez, as he disappeared into the dark.

"What do we do now?" asked Lieutenant Jeffers.

"We wait," said Jace.

With his assault company, Lau crept through the back yards and alleys of Bien Hoa toward the ARVN division headquarters that was his objective. Behind him, his mortar teams were firing as fast as they could hang and release their shells. The steady CrrRUMPs of the impacting rounds guided his troops toward their target. On either side of the objective, his other two companies slid into their ambush sites to await the inevitable American relief columns. As the battalion moved into its battle positions, the elite shock troops spread out to rally the populace.

As they reached Highway 1, which separated the enemy headquarters from the adjacent residential area, Lau nodded to a sergeant who cocked his flare pistol and fired into the sky. The streaking red fireball was the signal for the mortars to cease firing and for the assault to begin.

All around him, automatic rifle fire erupted as guerrillas shouted and charged across the road. From the corners of the enemy compound, machine guns opened up, criss-crossing the street with deadly bands of hot lead and tracers. Hand grenades bounced onto the pavement and exploded amongst the Viet Cong as they hurled themselves at the wall. Although the defenders were few, they had the advantage of fighting from covered positions, they had plenty of ammunition and they had nowhere to run. As Lau's men surged at their objective, the enemy defenders began to cut them to pieces.

"Charlie Six, this is Cougar Five." Jace recognized C.C.'s voice even before he heard his call sign. He felt oddly comforted knowing his friend was in real control of the battalion.

"This is Jupiter Six," answered Jace, instinctively conjuring the company's totem for the upcoming battle. With certain danger and possible death lying ahead for him and his soldiers, he suddenly didn't care what Lieutenant Colonel Price might say or do. He and his men needed their talisman now more than ever.

"This is Cougar Five. The airbase, Long Binh complex, and all ARVN compounds are under heavy ground attack. Get to the ARVN Third Division headquarters ASAP. It is in danger of being over-run. Do you know where it is?"

"This is Jupiter Six, that's affirm. We're rolling, out!"

"Two Six, lead the way. Let's roll!" yelled Jace into his hand set. The idling tracks exploded into life, lurching forward toward the east gate of Long Binh.

As they thundered wide open though the Long Binh base, Jace radioed, "Two Six, go out the main gate and take a left, then a right at the 90th Replacement."

"Roger," came the acknowledgement from Lieutenant Jeffers. Jace had decided to lead with his most experienced platoon.As they charged out of the main Long Binh gate, the tracks accelerated to their top speed of thirty-five miles per hour. Worn-out rubber track pads allowed the steel treads to strike the asphalt, causing sparks to fly as tracks chewed up the thin pavement. Jace ordered the headlights doused—there was enough light from fires and flares to illuminate their way. As he passed the 90th Replacement Company, he looked down into the compound. Soldiers in khaki uniforms, with boarding passes in the folds of their garrison caps, milled around weaponless and vulnerable in the dark. They would not be going home today.

Jupiter company turned right onto Highway 15 and streaked toward the city at top speed. As Jace's track made the turn at the top of a slight rise, a horrible panorama opened before him. The city of Binh Hoa was afire. Columns of black smoke towered against an orange sky. The red tracers of the Americans and their allies and the green ones of their communist foes streaked and ricocheted above burning buildings. Parachute flares and the navigation lights of helicopters punctuated the sky. Here and there, flashes of explosions popped like flash bulbs among the houses. Rockets with exhausts like blue diamonds streaked from a helicopter gunship to explode in the city.

"OK, Jupiter," Jace yelled into the handset, "Watch out for an ambush. If we get hit, blast away and keep moving. Don't stop for nothing."

Gunners who had not already done so jerked back on their charging handles, chambering rounds. Troops riding on top of the tracks hunkered down to a lower profile. Engines screamed and treads clattered as Jupiter roared toward its objective.

At 5 a.m. a helicopter moved in low over the chancery building and tried to land on the rooftop helipad. The guerrillas in the compound, as well as Phun's machine-gun team, opened up with all they had at the rotor blades flashing red in the glow of the helicopter's navigation lights. The machine hung in the intense fire for two long seconds, then veered off and dived away.

Phun was surprised when no one returned fire at her and her team. When the relative quiet returned, she and her comrades backed further into the darkness and listened to the scattered firing across the street. Despite the fact that no organized enemy reinforcements had come, the continuing battle inside the embassy compound caused Phun and her team to have serious doubts about the success of the attack. Soon it would be daylight and they would be in the open and vulnerable, whether the attack had succeeded or failed. They had been given no instructions as to what to do next. All they had been told was that the population would soon come to their aid. So far, the streets were empty.

"Ambush!" yelled Lieutenant Jeffers over the radio. As he did so, four RPG rockets slammed into his lead track, setting it ablaze. As wounded and burned soldiers jumped to the ground and took cover, every .50 caliber in the column opened up on the houses closely lining the road. Despite Jace's orders to keep moving, the burning track now blocked the road. RPGs flew amongst the stationary vehicles as Jupiter's heavy guns took the shoddy buildings apart.

Suddenly Dewain Howell appeared at the rear of the blazing APC, pulling the end of a tow cable. Shielding his face from the flames, and braving the deadly volume of enemy fire, he attached the cable loop to the trailer hitch of the stricken vehicle. The cable, which he had already attached to the lifting shackle on the track behind it, tightened as that vehicle started to back up. Slowly, the burning infantry carrier was pulled to the rear and off to the side, leaving just enough room for one track to squeeze by. Howell ran back to the burning APC and disconnected the cable, burning his hands as he did so. As he sprinted back to the safety of his track, he was cut down.

Doc Roberts was at Howell's side in seconds. Grabbing the large man by the armpits, he dragged him to the rear of Lieutenant Jeffers' track. Roberts pounded on the escape door built into the back ramp until someone opened it.

As strong hands hauled him inside, Howell yelled to Roberts, "Doc, tell the cap'n I didn't mean what I said I'd do to Sergeant Smith. I was just tryin' to scare him."

"I don't know what you're talking about," Doc shouted back over the din of battle."

"Just tell him! I don't want him to think bad of me!" shouted Howell.

"I will!" Roberts nodded and gripped Howell's hand. As Doc backed out and turned to find other wounded, someone slammed the hatch.

"Go! GO!" screamed Jace into the radio. "Don't leave any wounded!" The volume of enemy fire had slackened, overwhelmed by Jupiter's firestorm. Now was the time to get out. The paint on Lieutenant Jeffer's track blistered and soldiers shielded themselves as best as they could from the flames as the second vehicle in the column squeezed by the burning hulk. As soon as it was clear, it leapt off down the road, leaving room for the next track to follow through the gauntlet of fire. One by one, Jupiter's APCs, firing as they went, escaped past the charred hulk to freedom.

At 6:15, another helicopter hovered in over the embassy. This time there was little firing from inside the compound. Feeling alone and exposed, Phun's gunner decided not to fire. The aircraft landed on the roof and discharged three cases of ammunition while three wounded soldiers were loaded aboard by men on the roof. The helicopter lifted, nosed over and sped away. The three cases of ammunition were for M-16 rifles. The marines and M.P.s inside the embassy were armed with submachine guns, pistols and shotguns. The crew of the helicopter had braved enemy fire to deliver ammunition that was useless.

"Where are the people? They are not taking to the streets!" screamed Lau as he pounded his fists on the ground. Two blocks away, his assault company was pinned down in the houses and gardens across the highway from the division headquarters. The pavement was littered with the corpses of his guerrillas. Now they were running low on ammunition.

The leader of the shock troops found Lau. "Comrade Colonel, the people have all fled to the churches. There is no one in their homes to rally to our side. We entered the grounds of a large cathedral to find the courtyard was packed with thousands of people. They all ignored our demands and our pleas to take to the streets. They turned their backs on us."

"Then bring in your shock cadres. If the people will not come to our side, you will join the assault. We must try once more to take our objective."

The young fanatics with their red head and arm bands crawled up beside their beleaguered comrades across from the ARVN division headquarters. Lau watched as his troops pulled away their wounded, redistributed their ammunition and gathered their last remaining RPG rockets.

"RPG gunners must take out the machine guns that have pinned us down," ordered Lau. "Go and begin firing now. When the guns have been knocked out, we will attack."

The swoosh-bang of the RPGs soon rose above the noise of enemy rifles and machine guns, which stopped firing as the communist rockets slammed into their positions.

"NOW!" cried Lau. "Up and in. For your party and your country! GO! GO! GO!"

As one, the men of the 274th battalion rose from hiding and dashed across the highway, shooting as they went. ARVN riflemen inside the compound fired from loop-holes in the wall as guerrillas boosted each other to the top of the barbed-wire draped barrier. With the machine guns silent, RPG gunners turned their attention to the main gate, which disappeared in a cloud of gray-brown smoke.

"We're going to do it!" yelled Lau to himself as his soldiers began clamoring over the wall and through the front gate. Suddenly huge geysers of red dust flew into the air, accompanied by thunderous cracks. Large chunks of the masonry wall flew as bullets and red tracers struck sparks on the pavement. As one of his fighters spun to the ground with his left leg hanging by a shred of skin, Lau turned to see American armored personnel carriers roaring toward them with all guns blazing.

No order had to be given. No one had to call off the attack. The 274th simply broke and scattered in all directions. Lau desperately hoped that his men could remember the rally point where they were supposed to assemble if they were split up. As he ran through the deserted back alleys, heavy machine-gun bullets tore through the flimsy walls of houses and sheds all around him. Tracers started fires in thatched roofing as poorly-made brick walls shattered and fell.

Jace's command track and his mortar platoon pulled through the main gate into the division headquarters compound as his three line platoons chased the retreating VC. A frazzled American Lieutenant Colonel and a scared-looking Vietnamese one-star general climbed out of a bunker adjacent to the main building.

"Man, are we glad to see you, said the colonel. I thought we were gonners."

"Glad to help, sir." said Jace. "Where can we set up our mortars? The platoons will be calling in fire missions soon."

"Sorry, you can't fire mortars," said the colonel.

"What? Why not?" Jace shot back.

"Bien Hoa is a friendly city. No indirect fire of any sort can be fired by any of our troops."

"That sure didn't stop the VC from firing mortars, did it?" .

"Look, captain, I don't make the rules."

"Yes, sir, I'm sorry, sir. Things have been a bit stressful this morning."

"No sweat. We appreciate your getting here. Did you have any problems?"

"Got ambushed. We lost a track and took eleven wounded but we fought our way through it. Is there any place we can land a dust-off chopper?"

"We have a helipad out back," answered the colonel. "But we can't land the bird while the shooting's still going on."

"I'll send a platoon to clear around the pad. Most of my wounded are not too serious, but we need to get four of them out as soon as we can," said Jace, thinking mainly of Dewain Howell.

"I'll have my RTO call for the dust-off," said the colonel. "Look, what are your orders now? Are you going to stay here?"

"I don't know, sir. I was told to get here to relieve you. I guess I need to call battalion for instructions."

"When you do, tell them I have only twelve ARVN troops still walking, and two of them are slightly wounded. If you leave, we'll be in deep shit."

"Where are the rest of your troops? Don't you have a security force?"

"General Thanh pulled them away to guard his mansion. I guess he figured that was more important than his division headquarters."

"Captain Spencer! The battalion commander wants you on the horn," yelled Five India from the command track.

"Excuse me, sir," Jace said as he ran to the vehicle and answered the radio. "Cougar Six, this is Jupiter Six, over."

"This is Cougar Six, what is your sitrep, over."

Price ignored the Jupiter call sign.

"Objective secure. We have eleven WIA, four serious. We fought our way through an ambush to get here. There are seventeen enemy bodies in the street in front of this position, over."

"Good going. As soon as you put your boys on the dust off, I have a new mission for you."

"Roger, be advised the senior American at this location says he is thin on friendlies to secure the objective if we pull out."

"Understand. Can you leave a sub-unit there to help them out."

"My indirect-fire element can stay. I understand they can't fire anyway."

"Approved. Attach them to the unit at your objective. Now, I'm over you at this time." Jace looked up. He could barely see the H-23 high above the city. "Romeo Six is working his way from east to west toward you. I want you to clear the built-up area along the highway eastward to meet him." Romeo Six was the call sign for the reconnaissance or scout platoon.

"This is Charlie Six, wilco, over."

"This is Cougar Six, do you need anything?"

"This is Charlie Six, affirmative. I need an ammunition resupply ASAP. All calibers."

"Cougar Four will be in touch shortly. Keep up the good work and get me a more complete body count as soon as you can. Out."

In the growing dawn, Phun and her comrades watched as a helicopter loaded with heavily-armed soldiers landed on the roof of the chancery building. Only sporadic fire from the ground met them as they jumped from the aircraft and ran down the stairway. At the same time, an M.P. jeep crashed open the main gate. Soldiers and camera men dashed in behind the vehicle and took cover behind large concrete planters. As the relief force began to spread out, one final explosion rocked the compound. A wounded Viet Cong had pulled the pin from a hand grenade, but had been too weak to throw it. Through all of this, Phun's gunner again had decided not to fire. It was getting daylight and it was obvious that the attack had failed and the battle was over. The mission of shooting at the embassy or at reinforcements was replaced by a new, self imposed objective for Phun's team—escape.

"What do we do now?" asked the ammunition bearer. "The people have not taken to the streets as we were told they would—plus, we have been given no instructions.

"It appears that we are on our own," said the gunner, his eyes showing defeat. "What should we do with our weapons? If we walk through the streets armed, we will be shot down."

Although Phun had no rank, she had vastly more experience traveling through cities and towns than these two ex-farmers. She was well aware of the dangers they now faced, but she also knew some useful tricks. She took charge.

"Leave the weapons here. Adjust your clothing to look as much like civilians as possible. Travel the back streets. When you find a crowd of people, join them. Make your way back to the battalion when you can," she said as she stripped off the black pajama shirt she was wearing. Reaching into her knapsack, she pulled out her *ao dia* tunic, slipped it on and buttoned it. "We should also split up. I wish you luck, comrades—Now GO!"

Phun watched the men run into the alley and disappear. When they had gone, she stood for a moment, collecting herself. Knowing exactly what she was going to do, she stepped into the street.

Leaving the mortar platoon to secure the ARVN headquarters, Jace led the rest of Jupiter company eastward along Highway 1. As the lead platoon drew adjacent to the second enemy ambush position on the other side of the headquarters, the Viet Cong knew at once that the battle had been lost. They understood that if the Americans were approaching from the west, they were coming from the ARVN compound. That meant that the attack on their main objective must have failed. Also, it was clear that the civilians had not joined the battle as they were supposed to do. Not knowing what else to do, the remaining company of the 274th battalion opened fire from its ambush position.

Jace was able to extract the platoon caught in the kill zone by covering them with withering fire from his other tracks. He then dismounted a platoon on each side of the road and kept one platoon aboard the tracks as a reserve. Unable to fire mortars or artillery, he had Jupiter use their .50 calibers, M-60s, recoilless rifles, light anti-tank rockets, and M-79 grenades for support as they tore into the remnants of the 274th battalion. Infantrymen trained as jungle fighters now fought as many of their fathers had in World War II, dashing from house to house, throwing grenades and firing point-blank through windows and doors. When they were held up, they marked targets for the heavy machine guns with smoke grenades. Through it all, the Viet Cong guerrillas fought like cornered animals.

"Sir," shouted a soldier who had run up to Jace's track. "The L.T. told me to tell you we're gettin' short on ammo."

"O.K." yelled Jace. "Tell him to hang on, I'll get us some as quick as I can." Then he yelled into the interior of the track, "Put me on the log net, quick."

Getting a thumbs up from Five India, he radioed, "Cougar Four, this is Jupiter Six, over."

Static. Then, "Cougar Four, go."

"This is Jupiter Six. Where the hell is our ammo resupply? We're gettin' desperate."

"This is Cougar Four. The ammo truck should be getting to your position any time now. Watch for him, over."

"Roger, thanks, out."

Jace assumed the truck would be coming from their rear along the same route his company had traveled. He was shocked when he looked ahead and saw the five-ton speeding westward, head-on toward the front of his column—straight toward the enemy ambush. How the hell had the truck gotten past the scout platoon, thought Jace. Having no radio communications with the vehicle, he stood and waved for the driver to turn back. Helplessly, he watched as the truck's tires were shot flat and the canvas bed-cover was shredded by enemy fire. As the truck flapped to a stop, Sergeant Munn dived out of the passenger's seat and took cover at the edge of the road. The driver never moved. Jace assumed that he was dead.

Recognizing the predicament the supply truck was in, Jupiter's .50 gunners blazed away anew. Sergeant Munn, seeing the suppression of the enemy's fire, saw his chance, jumped up and sprinted toward the company's lead track. He had gone ten meters when his legs were shot from under him. As he went down, he began screaming "MEDIC!"

Doc Roberts, protected by the lead second-platoon track, was treating a soldier when he saw Munn go down.

"Here, hold pressure on this," he told a nearby soldier. "I'll be right back."

Running to the front of the vehicle, he paused and looked into the kill zone. Then he looked back and locked eyes with Jace for a half second. Jace tried to scream for him to stay where he was—that it was suicide to run into the kill zone of an enemy ambush. But before a single word could form on the company commander's lips, Doc turned and dashed into the open. As he hit the ground and rolled to a stop next to Munn, Jupiter company let loose with every weapon it had. Covered by the heavy fire, Doc got to his knees and struggled to drape Munn over his shoulders in a fireman's carry. As he stood and began a wobbling run to safety, an enemy machine gun tore both of them apart.

Lau ran into the rally point in a bamboo grove adjacent to a clearing on the north side of the highway. He collapsed on the ground, struggling to breathe. One of his company commanders was already there guiding the straggling guerrillas in and forming a perimeter. Nearby, Lau heard the battle raging between the enemy mechanized column and his eastern ambush force. As in the demonstration his company commander had arranged for him, the volume of heavy machine-gun fire coming from the Americans was simply unbelievable. Already, he could see men running from the fight toward the assembly area. As houses began to burn, the volume of fire slackened and more of his soldiers dashed away from the battle. Regaining his breath, Lau realized he had to find a new escape route. The one he had reconnoitered through the village was ablaze and under enemy fire. Nearby was a small stream with tall grassy banks running past the bamboo grove from a culvert under the highway. Following the grassy ditch with his eyes, Lau saw that it flowed through the clearing to a row of houses about two hundred meters to the north. Beyond the houses stood the green wall of the jungle, and safety.

Finally, the firing stopped and no more of his men ran from the battle. Lau then knew that the fifty-odd guerrillas with him at the rally point were all that was left of his three-hundred-man battalion.

"Quick, follow me," shouted Lau to the senior company commander.

In a crouch, he sprinted the short distance to the ditch and splashed headlong into the grassy stream. With his remaining soldiers following him, he waded north, away from the highway, toward safe.

Four hundred meters away, Jace received a casualty report from the platoons. The ambush had cost five dead, including Munn, the truck driver Doc Roberts. In addition, Jupiter had taken seven more wounded. Jace dispatched Baez in his track to carry the casualties back to the ARVN compound for evacuation. Although the ammunition truck had been severely shot up, miraculously it had not exploded. Jace found that much of the ammunition aboard was still serviceable. The company remained stationary while it reloaded depleted stocks.

Crawling through the shallow stream, the survivors of the 274th neared the row of houses some distance north of the highway.

"Keep the men down," said Lau. "I will try to find an escape route."

The company commander nodded as Lau splashed away downstream. Warily he emerged from the ditch and crept between two of the houses. On the other side of the dirt path that connected the buildings was a patch of open ground that served as a vegetable garden. Beyond, and slightly down hill, stood the green haven of the jungle.

Lau went to the first house. Inside were an old man and a small girl. When they saw Lau, they bowed so low, their faces were on the dirt floor. Lau ignored them and ran to the second house.

Freshly loaded with ammunition, Jupiter company crept slowly along the highway across the clearing. Having been ambushed twice, soldiers were frantically careful now. The second platoon, still leading, rattled over the culvert through which the small creek ran. Jace's command track was immediately behind second platoon. A hundred-meter gap separated Jace's track from the first platoon, which was next in the column. Jace radioed for them to close up as the last platoon, the third, was just entering the clearing.

Farther to the rear, First Sergeant Baez's track was returning from taking the casualties back to the ARVN compound. As he hurried to catch up, he saw that the company had left the ambush site and was crossing an open field. Scanning for danger as he went, Baez ordered the driver to full speed as they entered the clearing. Nearing the culvert, he thought he saw movement in the streambed off to the left.

"Driver, stop!" shouted Baez into the intercom. "Wheel left!" he ordered. Right on top of the culvert, the track driver pulled back on the left lateral lever and pushed hard to the front with the right as he gunned the engine. The APC spun ninety degrees to the left and lurched to a halt. Baez scanned the streambed. There! A small bush moved as if someone or something had bumped against it.

"Jupiter Six, this is Jupiter Seven. I'm half way 'cross the clearing. I've got movement in the streambed to the north. Send help, I'm engaging."

Baez trained his .50 caliber at the bush and cut loose a long burst. As he did, the tracks of the third platoon spun about in the road and rumbled back to help the first sergeant. Enemy fire cracked from the stream as soldiers on Baez's track jumped to the ground and opened fire with their M-16s.

Lau was looking in the window of the second house when the firing erupted. Disregarding what danger might be inside, he dived through the window into the front room of the shack. Finding it deserted, he took what cover he could and tried to think of what to do next.

The guerrillas in the stream found themselves faced with a dilemma. They could remain hunkered in the creek bed to be cut to shreds by Baez's .50 caliber, or they could try to escape. Suddenly, the five Viet Cong nearest the row of houses jumped up and ran for it. Two were downed by rifle and machine-gun fire as the other three ran between the houses toward the freedom of the jungle. With the firepower of the third platoon joining the fight, there was little hope for the remaining Viet Cong.

When the shooting started, Jace turned his track around and weaved through the first platoon, heading back toward the gunfire. When he entered the clearing, he found Baez's track and the four APCs of third platoon sitting on the highway blazing away at the stream. He quickly ordered the first platoon to turn and come back into the battle, but left the second up the road in reserve. When the first platoon arrived, Jace lined them up for an attack. Using the tracks on the road as a base of fire, he led the first platoon in an assault against the stream bed. Faced with overwhelming odds, some of the VC tried to run, but were slaughtered. Several others stood where they were with their hands in the air. As the battle wound down, Jace leap-frogged third platoon to the row of houses at the far end of the clearing to seal the only escape route, and then brought second platoon back to help in the mopping up.

Lau lay on the floor of the empty house listening to the dying battle. When three of his soldiers had run past him, headed for the jungle, his impulse had been to follow them. Stubbornness, pride and sense of duty had kept him where he was. How could he run away, leaving the few survivors from his battalion to be killed or captured? Now, with enemy armored vehicles surrounding his hideout, he realized he had forfeited his only chance for escape.

Several of Jace's men herded prisoners to the highway as others pulled bodies and threw weapons from the stream. Jace radioed Lieutenant Colonel Price to ask what he should do with the prisoners.

"What's your sitrep at present?" asked Price.

"We're still at the clearing, east of our original objective, mopping up. No new friendly casualties, thirty-five enemy bodies and twelve enemy POWs, over."

"Roger, I'll be at your location in zero five. Is there any enemy fire at present?

"That's a negative. Everything's secure here." responded Jace.

"Understand. I'll get a bird for your POWs. Stay put."

Phun walked along Thong Nhut Boulevard, away from the embassy. Repeating to herself that naked is the best disguise, she believed a frightened young woman in plain view, hurrying away from the scene of a battle on a main street, would look less suspicious than one sneaking through the back alleys. As she walked, she heard firing off in the distance. That was surely other units of the C-10 battalion fighting for their objectives. She prayed they would be more successful than her platoon had been. Hurrying along, she approached a corner where a Catholic church stood. If she had wondered what had happened to the populace that was supposed to rise up and help fight the Americans, she now learned the bitter truth. The churchyard was packed with hundreds of people seeking sanctuary. Making an instant decision, she turned the corner, ran to the main gate and squeezed inside. She decided that she would stay at the church until things cooled down, then she would go to Bien Hoa to find Lau.

Lieutenant Colonel Price's H-23 landed in the road between two of Jace's tracks. Price jumped out, starched and shined as always, and strode to where Jace was standing. He offered his hand. It was only the third time Jace had talked to the battalion commander since the battle began.

"Great work, Jupiter Six." Jace noted Price's use of the nickname. "The ARVNs counted 72 bodies at the place you were first ambushed this morning. Those, plus the ones here and around the ARVN headquarters comes to 142. Have you counted the ones at the second ambush site?"

"No, sir, we haven't had time."

"You might send somebody back there and get a count. How about your boys?"

"Sir, I've had three killed and eighteen wounded. Also, a driver and a sergeant from the support platoon were killed trying to bring us ammo. One of my tracks was destroyed and three have been hit by RPGs. Two are still running. We're towing the other one." Jace paused tiredly. " My senior company medic was one of the ones killed."

"That's too bad. Hello, first sergeant," said Price as Baez walked up.

"This is the hero of this fight," said Jace as he removed his helmet and mopped his forehead with his arm. He was coming back from evacuating the wounded and spotted the VC in this ditchline. He was the first to engage them."

"Good going, Top," said Price as he gripped Baez's hand.

At that moment, their attention was diverted by the tracks of the scout platoon entering the clearing from the east. The link-up marked the end of this phase of the battle. Jace looked at his watch and couldn't believe it. It was two o'clock in the afternoon. His company had been fighting since 4:30 in the morning.

"Sir, Three Six wants you on the horn," yelled Five India.

"Excuse me, sir," said Jace as he turned to jog to his track."This is Jupiter Six, go."

"This is Three Six. We've got an ARVN sergeant here. He just walked out of a house next to us. Guess he was home on holiday leave or something and got caught up in the fire fight. What do you want me to do with him?"

"You can come on back and join us now. Bring your friend back with you."

"Three Six, roger, out."

Price congratulated Jace again, visited the scout platoon for a moment, then strapped into his helicopter and flew away. As he left, a Huey landed to take away the prisoners.

In a few moments, the third platoon bounced across the field in a dust cloud. Sitting next to the platoon leader on top of his track was a small man in a government army uniform. After the third platoon had rumbled to a halt, Jace motioned for the platoon leader and his guest to join him. As the Vietnamese man followed the lieutenant climbing down from the APC, Jace studied him closely, thinking that something looked very familiar about him.

"I'll be damned," exclaimed Jace. "This man saved my life last night."

The small man bowed and smiled shyly as Jace grasped his hand to feel the same weak grip he had felt the previous night.

"So what you told me was true, huh? There were beaucoup VC in town."

With a pained look in his eyes, the man caught the gist of what Jace said, smiled nervously and nodded.

"Keep him with you on your track, Three Six. When we get to a secure area, you can let him go."

Jace walked a short distance away and stood alone for a moment. After the constant din of the day-long battle, the silence overwhelmed him. He stood, looking off down the road in the direction of Bien Hoa city, which was still smoldering in the distance. He rubbed the back of his neck, forcing his knotted muscles to relax. He took a deep breath. Then, like demons from the deep, his emotions surfaced. The anxiety, the fear, the concern for his live soldiers, the sense of loss for his dead ones, and his relief—and guilt—at still being alive, rose from his guts and consumed him. Jace carefully placed his helmet in the middle of the road, sat down on it, and cried like a baby.

Standing in the road with the third platoon leader, Lau watched the enemy commander as he sat and sobbed. Remembering Huong and his other dead guerrillas, many of whom had become friends, Lau knew exactly how the American captain felt.

CHAPTER 17

▼

31 January 1968

Chi huddled fearfully in her home with her family. She had not had to go to work during Tet and had planned to enjoy a relaxing day with her loved ones. Now, the food she had bought for the holiday meal lay untouched on the sideboard. She and her surviving sister tried to keep Duc's widow and the young ones quiet and in one place. Before dawn, the screaming of armored vehicle engines and the bup-pup-pup of distant machine-gun fire had awakened her. Although she had heard the bumps of explosions and the rattle of small-arms fire all morning, the only thing she had seen of the battle had been the frenzied scurrying of American vehicles on the highway.

Even though the battle sounds were frightening, she was more afraid that communist fighters would appear at her door demanding sanctuary. She was also terrified that government soldiers, Americans or national policemen might come to search her home or accuse her of aiding the enemy. Having had National Liberation Front personnel in her home and having been interrogated and tortured by the government officer, she felt extremely vulnerable.

As she lay on the floor, she thought about the small wad of wire she had so far been unable to get to. Every time she had thought she had a chance, some American would enter the laundry and spoil her plans.

She wondered if this was the battle the National Liberation Front recruiter was referring at her sister's funeral. What had he said? "You will want to be on the correct side when the end comes, and it is coming soon." If this were the final battle for liberation, maybe she wouldn't have to set off her bomb. Maybe she would be able to leave the little wad of wire where it lay. She hoped the freedom fighters would expel the killers of her family members without her having to become involved further. She hated the thought of having to leave her family and being hauled off to prison. But, as she lay shivering with fear, somehow she knew that if it came to it, she would risk anything to avenge the deaths of Duc, Huong, and her sister.

Following the slaughter of the guerrillas in the streambed, Jace was ordered to sweep a burned-out section of town south of the highway to mop up any remaining pockets of resistance. Jupiter company suffered three more soldiers wounded as it rooted out more prisoners, killed more guerrillas, and counted more bodies. Soldiers who had learned to live, move and fight in the jungle hesitated at first, then became ruthlessly efficient at house-to-house fighting. Taking advantage of being supported by large numbers of heavy machine guns, rocket launchers, and recoilless rifles, the troops gained confidence and momentum all through the afternoon's combat. The fact that the Viet Cong had nearly run out of ammunition and were trying to escape was an advantage just becoming apparent to the Americans.

At dark, when the shooting throughout Bien Hoa had ceased, Jace was ordered to outpost Highway 316 to give depth to the defenses in front of II Field Force Headquarters. In the dark, his nervous troops sat on their tracks, hugging their weapons and scanning the few still-standing buildings under the yellow light of parachute flares.

Three times during the afternoon Lau had motioned to the third platoon leader that he wanted to leave the track. All three times the lieutenant had shaken his head no, believing they were still in too much danger to let an allied soldier go off alone. Horrified, Lau had been forced to watch as soldiers from his regiment were shot down or captured. The sight of so many of his comrades lying bloody and smoldering on the ground or being led away in captivity agonized him. Riding on the enemy vehicle had shown him just how futile his battalion's attack had been. This one machine that he was riding on carried more ammunition and grenades than his whole battalion had during their attack. Sitting among foreign soldiers, even eating their food and drinking their water, Lau felt like an abject failure, a traitor, a coward. It would have been so much better to have died fighting with his battalion, he thought. But that had not been his fate.

Then Phun, who was always at the back of his mind, floated to the front of his consciousness. He wondered if she were alive or dead, safe or in danger, well or hurt. He looked off to the southwest where fires illuminated the scattered clouds over Saigon. If the offensive had been such a miserable failure here, could he expect her battalion to have fared much better in the capital? The agony of not knowing was almost too much to endure.

An hour before midnight, Jace's growling stomach reminded him that he had not eaten all day. With a flashlight, he scrounged through the debris on the floor of his track, finding a bag of PX peanuts and a warm Falstaff beer. With his booty, he climbed up behind the .50 caliber and sat quietly in the dim flare-light, fighting back the tears that once more welled in his eyes. As he finished the peanuts, he lifted the beer in a final salute to his dead troops—particularly Doc Roberts. What had Martin Luther King said about judging a man by the content of his character rather than the color of his skin? He marveled at the content of Doc Rodgers' character. Would he ever be able to truly fathom the irony of Doc's dying while trying to save the life of a man who hated him? For a long while, he sat watching the shadows cast by flares slowly sinking to the horizon. Then, draining the can and tossing the peanut bag to the wind, he vowed to do his best to put the ghosts of his men out of his mind. He still had living soldiers to worry about.

Throughout the night, C.C. called often for situation reports, and just to talk. He told everyone on the net about enemy body counts and the successes of other units in the brigade, and asked for requests for anything his battalion staff might do to help. While the battalion commander slept, C.C.'s calm, businesslike voice assured the battalion's leaders that despite the surprise of the enemy's attacks, the trauma of combat, and the losses of the day, everything was, and was going to be, all right.

At dawn, a supply column brought fuel, rations, water, and ammunition. While the company took on supplies, Baez went from track to track, gauging the morale and feeling the pulse of the company. Like a doctor screening patients, he looked deep into each soldier's eyes, watching for signs of combat-induced neurosis. He listened carefully, searching for any soldier whose loss of a friend might trigger a bad incident, such as a suicide or a revenge-motivated killing spree. Later, the battalion maintenance section came to haul away the shot-up track the company had towed through much of the battle. As his men went through the familiar routines of eating, cleaning, reporting, and straightening up, Jace stayed apart, not yet ready to talk to anyone.

At noon, Jupiter Company was ordered back to the position outside the east gate where they had been the night before. Rolling to the southwest on Highway 316, they passed a section of Bien Hoa that had been untouched by the fighting.

"Jupiter Six, this is Three Six, over."

"Jupiter Six, go," answered Jace.

"Our ally keeps wanting to leave us. Should I let him off? It doesn't look too bad along here?"

"Sure," agreed Jace. "He's probably worried about his family. Tell him thanks again, for me."

The company rolled to a stop. Ahead, Jace watched as the small man nimbly climbed down off of the armored vehicle. Carrying a C-ration meal the troops had given him, he walked a few steps away, then turned and bowed. All the troops on the track waved to him as they drove away.

As Jace passed the smashed back gate, the ordeal of the previous evening seemed as if it were a year ago. The company did not have to dig new foxholes and bunkers; the ones they had left the previous night were still serviceable. Exhausted troops simply pulled their tracks back into their positions and began straightening up the concertina, setting out claymores, and rigging trip flares.

"Top, I want a hot meal fed to the guys tonight." said Jace.

"Sir, we don't have no rations to cook. C's is all we got, answered Baez."

"Well, First Sergeant, we just drove through one of the largest American bases in this country. In fact, the gate we destroyed is not two hundred meters from where we are standing. If you are half the scrounger you claim to be, you should be back with hot chow in less than an hour."

"Well, sir. Now I understand the mission."

Jace laughed. "It's funny. I took off on my ill-advised soiree through Bien Hoa last night because I didn't want to leave my jeep inside Long Binh. Then, when we moved out, we left it inside the wire anyhow. Damnedest thing huh? I hope the cooks kept an eye on it. While you're looking for something to eat, see if you can find our wayward chefs and bring them and our wheels back to us."

"I'm sure they didn't go far. They're probably scared shitless. And don't worry, I'll find us some chow," said Baez.

"Once I told you to go get it, I stopped worrying about it," grinned Jace.

At dark, the men of Jupiter company ate roast beef, mashed potatoes with gravy, and green beans, courtesy of an M.P. battalion. They also had bread and chocolate sheet cake from a bakery that served all of the REMFs on Long Binh. There were seconds for everyone. They washed it all down with a double ration of Malaysian Tiger Lager beer, courtesy of whomever had left the connex container in which it had been stored unguarded.

"You, sergeant. Why are you walking around here? You need to be with your unit. Where are you going?" asked the ARVN lieutenant.

"Excuse me, sir," said Lau. "I was home with my family on pass for Tet. When the fighting started, my family fled to a churchyard. They have all returned home except my father. He is old and forgetful. I, along with the rest of my family members, am looking for him."

"Well, your pass has obviously been cancelled. Get back to your unit—now!"

"Yes, sir," responded Lau as he saluted and hurried away. He knew he had to get out of the government uniform. Bien Hoa was crawling with government soldiers, all of whom would be demanding that he return to his unit.

Desperate now, Lau turned into a narrow side street. The houses that lined the alley, like nearly every structure in the city, showed signs of the recent battle. He walked slowly, keeping his head straight, but cutting his eyes right and left, looking for a deserted house. It was clear that the people had returned from the churchyards and were trying to put their homes in order. The alley was alive with people dumping trash, beating straw sleeping mats, and hanging wash. Here and there, someone was on a rooftop trying to patch shell holes or replacing burned thatching.

As he neared a cross street, Lau noticed laundry hanging on a front fence. On impulse, he grabbed a plaid cotton shirt and stuffed it inside his uniform blouse.

"Hey, soldier," screamed a woman. "Come back here with that! Help! Stop thief!"

Alone, unarmed and vulnerable, Lau could do nothing but run. He sprinted to the corner and turned right, down the cross street. Looking back, he saw a small crowd of angry people chasing him. Running hard, but tiring fast, he turned left into another alley. Seeing what appeared to be an empty dwelling, he darted into the yard and through the open door. Gasping for air, he sat down under a window with his back to the wall. The small crowd of vigilantes milled around outside, then, finding nothing, turned and left.

"I knew someone would come eventually," said a raspy voice.

Squinting to adjust his vision to the dark interior of the small shack, Lau saw a skeletal old man, dressed in rags, lying on a mat against the opposite wall.

"Please get me some water, then tell me what has been going on outside. It sounds as if the war has come to the city," said the man.

"You are right, Grandfather," said Lau respectfully. "The war has come to Bien Hoa. Have you been here through it all?"

"Yes. I live here by myself. I am too weak to move. When the fighting started, everyone went to the churches and left me here alone. The woman who lives next door feeds me, brings me water, and empties my waste. When the people came back from the churchyards, she was not with them. I have not had anything to eat or drink since the fighting started. Please, get me some water. I am very dry."

"Yes, grandfather," said Lau, as he stripped off his battle jacket and donned the sport shirt. He took the ladle lying next to the old man's bed and went into the yard. Feeling safer in the civilian shirt, Lau walked through adjacent yards looking for water.

"What do you want? What are you looking for?" asked a voice from behind.

"The old man who lives down the street needs water. May I have some please?" he said as he turned to face a toothless, wrinkled woman of indeterminate age.

"Of course you may have some water. The barrel is around at the side of the house. Be sure to put the cover back on."

"Thank you, older sister," bowed Lau, deciding not to say anymore than was absolutely necessary.

As he dipped water from the barrel, the woman asked, "You are not a relative, are you?"

"No, older sister. I am simply a traveler who is seeking sanctuary."

"I see. Why are you taking him water? Where is the woman who looks after him?"

"I do not know."

"Well, my guess is that you went into his house looking for a place to hide and he surprised you."

Saying nothing, Lau stood staring at the ground.

"I will not ask you which side you are on. I do not care—as long as you leave me out of the war and harm no one, you can do whatever you wish. If you and old Mr. An are hungry, I will give you some of my rice."

"Thank you, older sister," bowed Lau. "First I must take him the water. I will return later for the rice if that is all right with you."

The woman nodded. Lau walked back to the old man's house, carefully balancing the ladle.

"Ah, thank you, my son," said Mr. An. After he had drunk deeply, he leaned back on his elbows, squinted one eye, and looked hard at Lau.

"You are one of two things," said An.

"And what is that, sir?"

"You came in to my house on the run. You were wearing a government army uniform, then you changed into a civilian shirt, which appears to be stolen. You look outside a lot, as if you are hiding from something. That means you are either a deserter from the government army or you are one of the communist guerrillas. I would guess that you are a member of the National Liberation Front."

"And why would you guess that?" asked Lau.

"Your hair is too long, you need a shave, and you don't know how to lace up your boots. See, the laces are hanging out. Soldiers tuck them into their boot tops."

"And if I fit into either of those categories, will you turn me in?"

"Me?" An cackled. "I cannot even sit up. Whom would I tell?"

"Oh you could send anyone for the police, even a child."

"If you have not noticed, there are no children in this section of the city. We are old here. We are the parents and widows of soldiers who have died fighting for the government. We receive a small hut and some rice as a pension from Saigon. It is very little, but we survive. Besides, even if I did send someone to the police, they would pay no attention. They mostly ignore us. We are no threat and we are too poor to pay their bribes."

"So your son is dead?" asked Lau.

"Yes," answered An. "He died two years ago fighting the Viet Cong. He was a member of a ranger battalion. All I have left of him is that red beret there on the shelf."

"I see," said Lau. "So if I were a member of the Viet Cong, I would be your natural enemy?"

"I have had many enemies, but now I have none."

"Who were your enemies?" asked Lau.

I hated the French. I thought they were cruel and oppressive—until the Japanese came. They were unbelievably harsh. They raped and killed my wife and beheaded my oldest son who was trying to protect her. After that, I joined the forces that fought them. At the end of the war, the French came back and I joined the Viet Minh to fight them. When the French were defeated, my enemy became the Catholic monster Diem, who hated all Buddhists. But when my son was drafted into the government army and joined the *Biet Dam Quan*, I decided to stay out of the fighting, not wanting to put him in a dangerous position. Now the Americans are here and I am too old and feeble to do any fighting on either side. What do foreigners want in this poor, wretched country anyway?"

"They are part of an international reactionary conspiracy that are trampling the rights of the proletariat," said Lau, mouthing, but no longer enthusiastic about the party line.

"Ah, so you are Viet Cong."

"Yes," said Lau, feeling relieved at the old man's admission that he had fought with the Viet Minh. With irony in his voice, Lau continued, "I suppose I am part of the valiant struggle to rid the world of imperialism."

"I remember when I used to spout such nonsense," said the old man. "If there is a world-wide struggle, it means little to us here. The struggle in Vietnam is for survival. The people do not care who sits in a Saigon palace, they simply want to be left alone. I can assure you that no matter who wins, life in the villages will go on as it always has. No, my young friend, the struggle in Vietnam is not for anything national—it is for the next village, the next rice paddy, the next treeline. And I have found that whoever wins each little struggle, whether they be government, communist, Japanese, French, or American, can be equally as cruel as the others whom they blame for the war. In short, it matters little who fights or who wins."

"But you fought with Uncle Ho. You were with the Viet Minh! You should feel like a hero."

"At one time in my life, I was an angry man. Everything and everyone was my enemy. I don't think I was a hero, but I fought, and I fought hard. Now my son, I have only one enemy—time."

Lau was silent for a moment, then said, "A woman who lives down the street offered us some rice. I will go and bring it back,"

"Then take those boots off—you look ridiculous wearing them with that civilian shirt. Take my sandals in the corner. I have no need for them anymore," said An as he lay back on his mat, wiping the spittle from the corner of his mouth with a filthy rag.

Chi had gone to the corner in the morning, but no trucks had come to take any of the workers to Bear Cat. She had no idea what was happening. All she knew was that there had been a large battle night before last and she was extremely anxious.

Everything she needed to complete the bomb, except the wire, was now behind the loose board in the laundry. She fought back the fear that the trucks had not come because someone had found the bomb. But if it had been discovered, she argued with herself, the police would have already come to arrest her. She made more tea and tried to be calm. She had nothing to do but try to salvage some of the food left from the Tet meal she had not been able to cook—and wait.

Walking through the violently hot afternoon, Phun made her way through the outskirts of Saigon. With savage fighting still going on in Cholon, the Chinese quarter of the city, citizens were watchful as they tried to put their lives back in order. Keeping their ears cocked toward the distant gunfire, merchants and residents nervously swept the streets and hauled away the debris of battle. As Phun searched for transportation to Bien Hoa, it dawned on her that a private in a Viet Cong battalion did not make as much money as a liaison runner for a regiment. She rummaged through her cloth bag searching for coins, trying to come up with enough for bus or lambretta fare. Unfortunately, she learned that fares had skyrocketed with the demands of thousands of battle-shocked holiday travelers trying to get back to their homes. Hungry and discouraged, she decided to spend what little money she had on rice and soup. Looking northeast through the mirage-shimmers dancing over Highway 1, she knew that Binh Hoa was thirty kilometers away.

As the sun set over the tin roofs and antenna poles of Long Binh, Jupiter company sat in the sun-scorched clearing outside the demolished east gate. Having been baked in the tropical heat all day, armored personnel carriers were still hot to the touch. On the trim-vanes of the tracks, troops had painted large cats in all sorts of poses, each as different as the artists who painted them. No longer ostentatious enough to represent the company's ego, the six-inch feline forms Jace had ordered had been painted over. Jupiter company now proudly displayed its totem for all to see.

As a platoon slowly pulled away from the perimeter for a mounted sweep around the outside of the base, two dismounted squads shuffled away on diverging azimuths, bound for jungle ambush sites. In the maintenance area, mechanics labored to replace a radiator in a second platoon track that had been holed by an RPG. After a hot evening meal, soldiers threw their empty paper plates into a burn pile and ducked back inside the ovens that were their tracks. Near the command post, naked-to-the-waist youngsters tossed a football while Jace readjusted the perimeter to fill in the space left by the departing platoon.

The next morning, Chi had again gone to the road junction, ready for work, but not knowing whether the Americans would ever come to pick her up again. But the trucks had come as if nothing at all had happened.

As she bounced along on the back of the five-ton, she smiled inwardly. It was ironic that this morning, when she was carrying nothing but her lunchtime rice ball, the gate guards waved them through without a search. Now, as the truck neared the laundry, she watched anxiously for the telephone pole that marked the spot where the small wad of wire lay. The morning was cool and bright, with puffy tropical clouds dotting the sky. Everything at Bear Cat looked normal. There was not the slightest hint on the huge base that the Tet offensive had happened at all.

As the truck geared down, Chi stood to get a better view of the place where she had spotted the wire. It was still there! After the truck had squealed to a stop in front of the laundry, the giant man who drove the vehicle smiled as he lowered the tailgate and offered his hand to Chi.

"C'mon, Mamasan. Time to get yore ass to work," he said as he swung her to the ground.

As the cooks clamored from the five-ton, Chi placed her conical straw hat on her head and glanced the short distance down the road to the telephone pole. Without any reasoning at all, she decided to do it now. She waited until the cooks entered the snack bar, then pointed down the road and began to chatter in Vietnamese. By hand motions and broken English, she tried to tell the driver that something that belonged to her had blown out of the truck.

"You go now! Mamasan go look. You go!"

"What is it, Mamasan? What did you lose?" asked the driver, removing his hat and scratching his head.

Chi put her hands on the big man's waist and shoved him toward the snack bar.

"Go—eat. Go now!"

The driver held up his hands and said, "OK, Mom. Don't get your drawers in a wad. I'm going. What's with you anyway?"

As the driver walked up the steps into the snack bar, Chi ran to the corner of the building, crossed the drainage ditch, turned up the road, and started toward the wire. With her hands balled into tight fists at her breast, she waddled along in a swinging, jogging gate, her eyes glued to the base of the pole. Close enough now to actually see the wad of wire, and breathing hard, she increased her pace as she looked around for danger. Fifty meters to go!

In the distance, a jeep approached in a cloud of dust. Thirty meters. As the jeep came closer, she hesitated. If the jeep carried the hateful American policemen, they would surely stop and ask what she was doing so far from where she worked. She turned and took a step back toward the laundry. But she was almost at the pole—only fifteen meters from the ball of wire—and she might never get another chance like this. As the jeep bore down on her, she tried to think what she would say if it stopped.

It was too late now. The vehicle was almost on her. She was too far from the laundry to even think about getting back safely. She turned back toward the pole, but realized she couldn't reach for the wire now. If she did, the men in the vehicle could see what she was doing. She would have to wait. As the jeep drew even with her, Chi looked up and waved. The driver was a young boy, the passenger an older man. The boy returned her wave; the man scowled. In the cloud of dust swirling behind the jeep, Chi darted to the base of the pole, grabbed the wire, and placed it under her straw hat. Before the dust cleared, she was back on the road again, walking more slowly back toward the laundry. Now she had everything she needed.

"What's the Akron area?" asked Jace.

Its about seventy-five square kilometers of jungle between Bear Cat and Phuoc Le." answered C.C. "Everyone calls it the Akron area because Operation Akron took place there in 1966. It's bad country, Jace. Lots of booby traps and tunnels. Intel says that the C-80 V.C. battalion was not badly hurt during Tet and they've got a base somewhere in there."

"When do we go?"

"Tomorrow we head back to Bear Cat for a two-day maintenance stand down—then we hit the weeds. It'll be similar to your operation in War Zone D. The jungle's too thick to operate tracks, so we'll be setting up two fire bases about five clicks apart. We'll keep the tracks with minimal security at the bases while the rest of the battalion beats the bushes."

"After the house-to-house stuff in Bien Hoa, I think I'll actually be glad to get back in the jungle."

"I think we all will," said C.C.

"Buy you a beer tomorrow night?" asked Jace.

"I'll let you buy the first one."

"Where's the old man? He's been keeping a low profile, hasn't he?"

"Sure has. I'm sure this'll make you happy. Somebody put him in for a Silver Star for the Tet battle."

"What?" shouted Jace. "The only time he came below three thousand feet was when he landed on the road. We had everything secure by then. He never heard a shot fired in anger!"

"Maybe not," replied C.C.. "But his chopper took a stray round. Made him look like he was in the thick of it. He's wearing a CIB now, too."

Jace shook his head. "Who wrote up the recommendation?" he asked.

C.C. shrugged. "For all I know, he wrote it himself."

"Hey. Where's that legendary loyalty you were touting when he got here?"

"I've still got it. I wouldn't say what I just said to anyone but you. How's he been treating you, anyway?"

"Sugar wouldn't have melted in his mouth when he landed during Tet. He actually complemented us. Hell, he even called me Jupiter Six."

The major laughed, and then asked, "Jace, how're you holding up? You look beat. Are you all right?"

"Yeah, but I'll admit I'm a little tired. I try not to think about my men—especially Doc Roberts."

C.C. put his hand on Jace's shoulder.

"You'll get a new medic when we swing through Bear Cat. Oh yeah, while we're there, we'll have a memorial service for our dead. You up to that?"

"Sir, I'm fine. Honest."

"OK, Jace," said C.C. as he walked back to his jeep. "We're having a command and staff meeting at 1800. See you then."

"Thanks for coming down. Good to see you."

"Jace, I'm glad you came through it in one piece."

"Thank you, sir. I'll see you tonight."

Jace watched as his friend drove back through the east gate. Then he turned and walked back to his command post, dug Jupiter the cat out of his rucksack, placed him in the middle of the circle of folding chairs, and called his leaders together for a warning order.

In his sport shirt, uniform pants and Mr. An's sandals, Lau walked along Highway 1 through Binh Hoa. As he went through the area where his company had ambushed the relief force, he was appalled at the devastation. The enemy heavy machine guns had simply annihilated the buildings adjacent to the road. His men had been forced to fight that firepower with a few RPGs and two or three magazines each for their rifles. How could brave men have been thrown away like that? How could he have believed that the population was going to rally to the communist side? Looking back, it all seemed so foolish. Seemingly intelligent men with high rank had assumed the people would do what they wanted them to do simply because they wished it—and he had bought into it. Why had the leadership not been able to see what was going to happen? He had certainly had reservations. Had he not witnessed first-hand the awesome power of the American mechanized infantry? Why had he done nothing to stop the madness of the offensive? Why had he simply gone along?

Turning a corner, Lau walked toward the hotel where he and Phun had agreed to meet. As he neared the place, nothing looked familiar. He stopped and tried to gain his bearings. Then, with a shock, he realized why nothing looked right. The hotel where he and Phun had spent their three precious days and nights had burned to the ground.

The traffic in the laundry was light. Chi knew that if she were going to assemble the bomb, this was probably the best time to do it. She had the time and she knew how to put it together. Somehow, though, she could not bring herself to actually start work on the device. She looked into the snack bar where Buddha and the cooks were bantering while two soldiers, the only customers, took their time with their burgers and sipped cokes. Now that the actual task was at hand, the seriousness of it intimidated her. While she shrank from actually starting to assemble the bomb, she kept telling herself that she had to get to it. She had come too far to turn back now. Checking outside, and seeing no one, she forced herself to move.

She walked behind the counter in the laundry and moved the loose board aside. The batteries, the tape, the wire, the bamboo tube and the blasting cap all sat atop the moldy-looking mass of plastic explosive. Quickly, she pulled a length of string from a ball she kept on a shelf in the counter. With a chopstick, she pushed the end of the twine through the crack at the bottom of the plywood that formed the wall between the snack bar and the laundry. She replaced the board and walked into the snack bar. One of the cooks was scraping the grill. The other was stacking cans of coke into the cooler, both ignoring her. Buddha smiled at her, picked up the cash box and walked into the office. Now was her chance.

Chi walked quickly along the wall and without hesitation, bent and grasped the end of the string. Looking again to see that she was not being observed, she pulled the string through the hole and laid it along a crack in the board floor to a folding chair. She started to tie the string to the chair, but decided against it. She tied a knot in the end of the string and wedged it into a tight portion of the crack where she could retrieve it later.

Back in the laundry, she checked for danger, and once more removed the board. She then slid the batteries one at a time into the tube, stripped and cut the wire into the required lengths with a pair of scissors, and assembled the interlocking loops. Looking up often to make sure she was alone, she worked quickly, taping a bare end of wire to each end of the battery tube. To be safe, she put a piece of tape on the bare loops, temporarily securing each to the insulated portion of the opposite wire. Finally, she twisted the other ends of the wires to the leads on the blasting cap. Then, with a chopstick, she gouged a hole in the explosive, pushed the cap in, and pinched the white putty-like material around it. The bomb was complete. When she decided it was time, all she had to do was tie one end of the string to the chair and the other to the wire with the sliding loops. As she replaced the loose board, a tremendous feeling of relief came over her. It was done.

"You must not leave yet, child," said the old woman. You look much too weak. Eat some more rice and drink more water. Stay and rest. It is much too hot for you to be walking on the highway."

"You are most kind," said Phun. "I do not know what I would have done if you had not taken me in. But I must go to find my family."

She was in the small home of the old woman, her husband and her grand-daughter. The house was a short distance off of Highway 1 in the village of Thu Duc, half-way between Saigon and Bien Hoa.

As the previous night had had approached, Phun had shuffled along with the swarms of refugees up the highway. Fields and vacant lots had been full of people who had stopped to sleep where they could. Some had even lain where they dropped from exhaustion on the highway shoulder. Away from home, and with no place to stay, many had simply kept moving until the police and the army had forced them off the roads to observe the curfew.

Exhausted, dehydrated, and well into her second night without sleep, Phun had stumbled into the old couple's yard and cried for help. The old woman had helped her inside and had given her water, rice, and a place to sleep.

"I know it is hot, but I must go. Perhaps I will be able to find a ride—who knows?"

"Then take some rice and some water. All I have is an empty beer bottle, but it is better than nothing. I will fill it for you. You must promise me you will stop and ask for help if you need it."

"Yes, of course I will," said Phun. "You have been most kind. I can never repay you for what you have done for me."

"You can repay us by finding your family, child. Protect them. Keep them safe until this terrible war is over. Then be prosperous and happy—and have many children."

Without knowing why, Phun placed her hand on her belly for an instant. Then she bowed and walked out the door. When she reached the edge of the highway, she turned and bowed again to the old couple and waved to their grand daughter. Then she took to the road, joining the throngs heading toward Bien Hoa.

The men of the 5-39 were more subdued than the last time they had rolled into Bear Cat. Even though they had killed or captured over 500 of the enemy in a single day, their own losses made the victory seem hollow. Twelve soldiers lay in the division morgue; 32 were in aid stations, evacuation hospitals or were on their way to more sophisticated medical facilities in Japan or the states. Even looking forward to a two-day stand down did not cheer them. They were tired and sick of the shooting and dying.

As they took their places in the motor-pool line up, the troops wearily tossed equipment to the ground and climbed down from their mounts. Sergeants counted, pointed, fussed and ordered. Officers stood in groups and talked quietly.

Jace threw his rucksack and weapon in the back of his jeep. On impulse he ordered Tucker to drive him by division headquarters. Tired, dirty and depressed, he walked into the G-3 shop and asked a duty officer if the G-3 was in.

Lieutenant Colonel McKensie sat behind his desk proof reading a document. He looked up, saw Jace and held up one finger as he continued to read. He called for a sergeant, pointed out the mistakes he wanted corrected, then stood to offer Jace his hand.

"Son, you look like shit. But I hear the battalion did one hell of a job in Bien Hoa."

"We kicked ass, sir. But we lost some damn fine men in the process."

"I know," said McKensie. "In a way I want to know who, and in a way I don't."

"I'll tell you if you want me to," said Jace.

"No, that's all right. I hear there's going to be a memorial service. I intend to come to that. I guess I'll find out soon enough. How's the boss doing?"

"The only thing I'll say is that a lot of people in the 5-39 miss you a lot—me included."

McKensie nodded slightly, then stared for a second.

"I hear Five India extended," he said at length.

"Yes, sir. Him and Tucker both. Sure makes the CP run like a clock."

"Sir, the general wants you," said a major looking around the door.

"On my way," said McKensie. "I'll see you at the memorial service. By the way, Jace, after you've served your time in the trenches, I'll make room for you in the G-3 shop. Just let me know."

"Yes, sir. I appreciate that. I'll take you up on it."

"Jace, you're one of my boys. Whether I retire as a light colonel or make four stars, I'll take care of you every chance I get. Keep your head down, son."

"Yes, sir," answered Jace. "You do the same."

McKensie grabbed his notebook and a pen and started for the commanding general's office. He stopped at the door.

"Who, Jace? Go on and tell me."

"Doc Roberts, sir. He died trying to save Sergeant Munn. Them plus some new kids that you didn't know. Also, Sergeant Howell was wounded pretty bad."

"Damn," said McKensie as he hurried to the general's office.

The snack bar was full of 5-39 soldiers bolting down burgers and swigging beer. Business was brisk in the laundry, too. Carrying bundles of dirty fatigues to the back room and bringing out clean ones, Chi didn't have a second to herself. The bomb behind the loose board was constantly on her mind as she went about her job. If she could find a spare second to rig it, this would be the day. When troops came in from the field, they tended to remain in Bear Cat for a day or two. Tomorrow would likely be as busy as today. If she could rig the bomb, she would go home, listen for the explosion, and wait for them to come to get her.

Lau stood by the fire-flattened hotel. Although he was nervous standing in the open with all the police and government soldiers around, he had to remain visible in case Phun showed up. This was the third day since the battle. If she had survived, she would have been here by now. Lau now told himself he had to come to grips with reality. His own battalion had been obliterated. Observing how quickly things had returned to normal here in Bien Hoa, he assumed that the offensive was over everywhere. No doubt the battalions that had attacked Saigon had suffered the same fate as the 274th. Although things looked bad, he fought coming to the inescapable conclusion that Phun was dead.

Backing into the shade of a building, Lau considered his options. He could go back to Xuan Loc to the battalion's base in the jungle. Some of his men would surely show up and they could start rebuilding the battalion. But what if no one had survived? He would be in the jungles alone, with no food and no hope. Besides, without guides, he was not sure he could find his way through the maze of trails to the hideout. He could stay here in Binh Hoa with Mr. An and try to find a local cell of the party that could guide him to a new unit. Or he could set off to the Michelin plantation in search of the C-10 battalion in hopes of finding Phun. Perhaps she was under orders and simply not able to leave her unit to come to Binh Hoa. That certainly made sense. If her unit had escaped, they would have gone back to their base to refit. He smiled to himself. Why even consider options? If she had not been able to come to him, he would go to her. He would leave tomorrow.

The course on which Chi had set herself seemed to take on a life of its own. Before, she had been careful to the point of being obsessive; now she became daring to the point of being reckless. It was unusual to have this many soldiers coming to the laundry and the snack bar at the same time. Plus, she felt that every day the bomb sat hidden behind the loose board, she became more vulnerable. She knew she could not pass up the opportunity to kill this many Americans.

There was no lull in the traffic in and out of the building all day. If she thought there would be a time when the laundry was empty so she move the loose board and tie the string to the wire with the loops, she was wrong. It seemed that many soldiers had no business in the laundry at all, but since it was one of the few places away from their units for them to go to, they swarmed in anyway.

Then she came up with a new plan. Instead of waiting for a lull in the traffic, she decided to watch the ages and ranks of the soldiers, and to act when only young, inexperienced ones were around. When older men with stripes or bars were in the laundry, she played dumb and acted subserviently. She knew the young ones, while talking loudly and looking at the jackets and trinkets she had for sale, were not observant.

Late in the day, a group of fresh-faced youths entered the laundry. As they milled about, Chi made her way through them to the door. Looking outside to make sure no one who looked like a leader was coming, she walked directly behind the counter, removed the board, and shielded the open space from observation with her body. While the young soldiers laughed, horse-played, and looked at the trinkets and jackets, she tied the string running under the plywood wall to the wire with the loops. Then she quickly removed the pieces of tape holding the loops in place and replaced the board. Turning back to the counter, she was relieved to see that none of the youngsters had noticed anything.

As she finished taking dirty laundry from the last group of soldiers of the day, she heard the horn of the truck that would take her home for what she assumed would be the last time. She placed the closed sign on the outside of the laundry door, shut it and locked it from the inside. Then she walked into the snack bar and headed straight to the folding chair she had selected. Without even looking to see if anyone was watching, she bent and tied the end of the string to the chair leg. Then, feeling as if lightening might strike any time, she walked straight out the door and joined the other workers climbing on the truck. While the laundry closed at 6 p.m., the snack bar stayed open until 9 o'clock. During those three hours, some soldier would surely move the chair. As the truck pulled away, she waved to Buddha who was standing in the snack-bar door smoking a cigarette. She hoped he would survive.

Jace and C.C. sat on the patio at the division officers' club, sipping cold beer and discussing everything except the recent fighting. They talked about the world situation, the war in general, the battalion, the training, the leaders, and the men. They talked all around the dangers of the pending Akron mission. In the last week, there had been too much pain, and anticipating more of the same was just too taxing, so they left it alone. They switched instead to past and hoped-for assignments, families, and dreams for the future.

"Where do you think you'll go when you leave here?" asked C.C.

"I'm sure I'll go to the advanced course. Most of my contemporaries have already been. I guess I'll only be at Benning a year, then I'll come right back over here, probably as a MAC-V advisor—if the war's still going on a year from now."

"I've been thinking about going to Benning," thought C.C. aloud. "It'd be great if we were there at the same time. I'd like to teach in the Battalion/Brigade Operations Department. It'd give me a chance to grade your papers—see how smart you really are."

"Speaking of the war going on a year from now, what do you think? It seems like the VC shot their wad during Tet," said Jace. "We might get the upper hand and win this thing."

"I don't know. Have you read the papers or heard the news?"

"Now how in the hell could I have heard the news out in the bushes? The only thing we get out there is Stars and Stripes and the armed-forces radio network—and the news on that is sterile, to say the least."

"Well, smart-ass," replied C.C., "I thought you might have a short wave. I picked up some state-side stations on mine. The commentators are playing the Tet offensive as a big loss for our side."

"What?" shouted Jace.

"It's true," said C.C. "They quote Johnson and Westmoreland as saying we're winning, we're winning, there's a light at the end of the tunnel, then they talk about how the commies almost took over the whole country. They keep using words like shock, setback, and surprise. Evidently the attack on the embassy in Saigon shook those sniveling bastards to the core. Westmoreland is calling it a piddling little platoon action, but nobody in the news business is buying it."

"But they didn't take over anything," said Jace. "I know the Marines are still fighting up in Khe Sanh and Hue, but it's over everywhere else. We kicked their asses."

C.C. tiredly rubbed his eyes. "That may be, but the news hounds aren't mentioning that. They just talk about the surprise, the embarrassment, and the casualties we suffered. And they keep comparing Khe Sanh to Dinh Binh Phu. Hell if the people start believing that noise, they'll be convinced there's no winning this thing. Then what?"

Jace drained his beer and ordered another. "Remember when I said I could whip Muhammed Ali? All I had to do was get him to fight under the same rules we are under here? He'd eventually get pissed and just go home. If the folks back home get pissed enough, that's what they might make us do—just quit and go home."

"That'd be too bad wouldn't it?"

"What do you mean?" asked Jace.

C.C. emptied his glass and stretched. "You'd miss the fun of living in the field for a year with an ARVN battalion.

At dawn, Lau left Mr. An still asleep and crept to the charred hotel once more. He felt compelled to check again for any sign of Phun. As the curfew lifted, few people were about. To appear less suspicious, he ordered tea at a nearby street stand so that he could remain stationary as he surveyed the scene. It was the fourth day following the battle, and there was still no sign of her. As dangerous as it would no doubt be, he knew for sure now that he must go to the Michelin plantation to search for her.

He finished the cup and ordered another. As he sipped, he scrutinized every young female that joined the growing morning crowds in the hope that fate might bring her to him as it had once before. The sun shone on the rooftops as the streets became crowded with people heading to work and repairing battle damage. Depressed and disillusioned, Lau bowed to the tea merchant and joined the milling throngs. He walked once more to the place where the main entrance to the hotel had been. After making one final visual sweep of the area, he turned to go—and couldn't believe his eyes. Tacked to a telephone pole was a small piece of cardboard. Penciled on the box fragment was: Phun—2-4-68.

Chi rose from her bed, tired and anxious. Anticipating the explosion that she was sure she would be able to hear, she had not slept at all. But there had been no blast other than the routine booms of the out-going artillery. Now she was in a quandary. If the Americans had found the bomb and she did not go to work, she would surely be arrested—and she would have accomplished nothing. If she did go to work, the bomb might be set off as she walked through the door. Not that she was afraid of dying—her death in the explosion would free her family of suspicion. If there was something technically wrong with the device, she was not sure she could fix it. And the thought of having to try worried her. As her decision firmed in her mind, she stood and began to get ready. To make sure the bomb went off, to try and save Buddha and the cooks, and to insure her family remained above suspicion, she must go to work.

Lau said goodbye to Mr. An and went to the burned hotel as soon as the curfew lifted. His anxiety over Phun forced him to violate the cardinal rule that a guerrilla must never set an identifiable pattern. He returned to the tea stall across the street, ordered a cup, and sat down to watch the street. Feeling more anxious than he had during the entire trip down the Ho Chi Minh trail, he forced himself to remain calm and still.

As he nodded sleepily in the morning sun, A man approached him from the side.

"Comrade Lau, the regimental commander wants to see you. Now!"

His fate sealed, Lau stood and looked about once more, then turned to accompany the messenger. As they walked away, he couldn't resist the urge to turn and look one more time. And there stood Phun.

With enormous trepidation, Chi walked from the truck to the door of the snack bar. She told herself to keep to her normal routine as she climbed the steps. Imagining all sorts of frightening possibilities, she was totally surprised that everything was as it usually was. Buddha came out of his office to begin the day's banter with the cooks as soon as they hit the door. Already there were several soldiers drinking coffee and awaiting breakfast. As she made an effort to fuss with Buddha as she normally did, Chi glanced at the folding chair near the back of the dining room. It had been moved. But instead of pulling the chair away from the wall, which would have tightened the string and pulled the loops together, someone had moved it toward the wall.

Since there was no one in the back of the room near the chair, Chi waited patiently for the hot water for her tea. The cooks put the pot on the flame, then chattered noisily as they fired up the grill and pulled bacon and eggs from the cooler. After she had poured her hot water and added the tea, she walked back to the folding chair and sat down, waiting for a chance to untie the string from the leg.

"What's a matter, Mamasan? Why you all by yourself? You no like talk to Buddha no more?"

The big man walked back to where Chi was sitting. She did not feel like joking and playing today.

"Go way! Buddha numba ten. Mamasan no feel good!"

"Aw now, Mamasan, don't be that way. Ole Buddha's just wantin' to know what's wrong. Here let me help you. I'll take you to the laundry. You can sit on yore ass there as good as you can out here."

Buddha walked around behind the folding chair, and with Chi sitting in it, picked it up and started toward the laundry. When she realized what was happening, she screamed hysterically and slapped at the big man, who was stunned by her reaction. In all the time they had worked together, she had never done anything like this.

"I'm sorry, Mamasan. I'z just playin'. I didn't mean to scare you."

Chi's eyes, normally just slits in her face, were wide with fear as Buddha placed the chair gently back onto the floor. Although she didn't want to call attention to the string by looking at it, she couldn't help herself. She was horrified to see that the strand was stretched tight between the leg of the chair and the hole at the bottom of the wall.

"I'm sorry, Mamasan, honest," Buddha was saying.

"OK, you. You go. Mamasan go work. OK, OK, OK you."

Shaking his head, Buddha headed toward the office. The cooks and the soldiers were staring at her as she moved the chair back to slacken the string. When everyone had returned to their business, she bent and quickly untied the string and tucked it back into the crack in the floor. Then, sweating profusely, she walked into the laundry and removed the loose board. The wire loops had been pulled to within an eighth of an inch of each other.

Jace and his troops slept late. Over coffee and powdered eggs in the mess hall, he, Baez and Five India planned the next day's load-out and departure for the Akron area. Just before noon, he called his leaders together in the mess hall and gave them a detailed, formal operations order. Then he left the company to the first sergeant as he coordinated artillery and heavy mortar fires and visited battalion headquarters several times to clear up minor problems. In the motor pool, he checked to see that his damaged tracks had been repaired. Then he went to his office to proof-read and sign the combat-loss report for the track and equipment lost and destroyed in the Tet battle. After a short break, he penned letters to the families of his soldiers who had been killed. Finally, he wrote recommendations for the Distinguished Service Cross for Sergeant Howell and the Medal of Honor for Doc Roberts.

Lau numbly motioned to Phun and followed the man down the street. Extremely agitated and anxious, he squeezed her hand and stole a quick look at her face.

"It will be all right," he said, not meaning it.

"I know," she answered. "I have found you."

"How did your unit fare during the attack?" Lau asked.

"I do not know for sure. I assume all nineteen were killed attacking the American embassy. Only three of us escaped," answered Phun. "And your battalion? How did it do?"

"We were annihilated," Lau answered.

"What are you going to do now?" asked Phun.

"All I know for sure is that I will never allow you to leave me again, unless you want to."

"Then we will be together always," she said.

They were silent for the rest of the walk.

The regimental commander was sitting in a restaurant four blocks from the destroyed hotel. Lau was ushered straight in and told to sit, while a body guard directed Phun to another table.

"Comrade Colonel! What a surprise. Will you have tea? Breakfast?"

"Only tea, please," answered Lau.

The regimental commander poured and remained silent while Lau sipped.

"Where is your battalion, comrade?" he asked at length.

"They are dead—or captured," answered Lau.

"But you are alive. How can an entire battalion cease to exist and only the commander survive?"

"I'm sure you know by now that our attack failed. An American motorized infantry unit smashed us as we were on the brink of victory. After the attack on our objective was interrupted, and both ambush companies were destroyed by heavy machine-gun fire, I led the survivors away along a stream. While I was separated from them, searching for an escape route, the American armor attacked and destroyed them. I escaped by donning a government uniform and pretending to be a government soldier. As you know, the people did not rally to our side as they were predicted to do."

"We have been watching you," said the regimental commander as if Lau had said nothing. "You have not tried to return to our base or find a friendly unit. You have stayed with that old man in the government village and you have been waiting and watching for something or someone at the burned hotel. At first we could not understand what you were doing. We thought perhaps you had turned against us. But I see now why you were waiting," said the commander, motioning at Phun.

"What do you want of me?" Lau asked, suddenly angry.

"I want to know why you have not returned to your duties."

"I have no duties. I have no battalion. I am a political officer who had no tactical training. Even so, I agreed to lead the battalion during the offensive. After we were annihilated I believed I had failed because I was an inexperienced commander. Now I can see more clearly why we lost—and I do not believe I was to blame any more than any other commander—including you."

"Go on, comrade," said the commander, shifting in his seat. "I am interested in your reasoning."

"We failed the men, you and I. And so did the general, the Central Office of South Vietnam, General Giap, the politburo, the Central Committee and yes, even Uncle Ho."

"You had better explain yourself, comrade," said the commander. "And you had better be careful!"

"I will be glad to explain myself. As I said, I am a political officer. This was supposed to be a political battle in which the people were an integral part of the plan. The only thing was that no one told the people what part they were supposed to play. There was no political preparation of the populace. We conducted a major offensive based on nothing but wishful thinking. You and I came down from the north thinking we had all the answers. We told our men that we knew what was going to happen once the battle started, and they believed us. Those good men followed us to their deaths. And we could not even tell them where to get ammunition when they ran out."

"As you know, I tried to find out about resupply," interrupted the commander.

Lau ignored him and continued. "One of my responsibilities as a political officer was recruiting. I have a large burden of guilt having seen men I helped to recruit thrown away for nothing—sacrificed to a plan that was doomed to fail from the start. You knew it. I knew it. But we said nothing. We let it happen. These losses will not be easily replaced. I believe this foolhardy offensive has probably set our war effort back ten years."

"Your criticism is harsh, comrade colonel. Particularly coming from one who has lost his entire command."

"Where is your command, colonel? hissed Lau. "I suspect the rest of the regiment is as dead as my battalion. After the battle, I was on the highway in front of the American headquarters that was one of your objectives. The enemy was continuing as if nothing had happened. So, you see, I know at least one of your other attacks also failed. I might ask you the same question that you asked me: How have you survived when your regiment is gone?"

Nervously, the commander tried to change the subject. "How many of your men do you think survived?"

"I saw only three, but I am sure there were more. They will turn up eventually. If you doubt my description of the battle, I am sure they will tell you the same story. The truth will come out. And the truth is that the 274th battalion fought bravely to the death even though it was betrayed by the commanders the men trusted to lead them. Blame me if you will. I will admit that I was not the best combat leader. Before the battle I tried to tell you that I am a political officer and not a line officer—but I will not have you insinuate that I am a coward or that I left my battalion to die so that I could live. I was with them until the end. Fate alone spared me."

"It is not your bravery I question. I have spoken to some of the survivors and they tell the same story as you."

"If you knew what happened, why are you questioning me like some sort of criminal? Remember I am skilled in political interrogation. Your technique needs improvement, comrade."

"Then forgive me. All I really want to know is why you have not returned to duty."

"Then why did you not simply ask. I will be glad to tell you. I am now and will always be a part of the movement to unify our country under the communist flag. But when I realized that our men had been sent on a suicide mission and sacrificed like pigs, I decided I could no longer be a part of an organization that betrayed everything I believed and told my men. I am leaving the National Liberation Front. I will continue to support the communist cause politically whenever and however I can, but I will not be a part of throwing away our countrymen as we did in this battle."

This conversation was not turning out the way the regimental commander had intended it. Realizing that Lau, an officer of equal rank and a commissar to boot, was using him as his reason for leaving the organization, he backed away from his accusatory tone.

"But Uncle Ho has said the war might last a hundred years. He has said if the Americans kill a hundred of us for every one of them we kill, we will still win in the end."

"I would agree with that concept if those hundred men die for something. But if they are killed in the service of inept commanders trying to implement unreasonable and unworkable plans, then their deaths cannot be justified."

"Your leaving certainly has something to do with that woman, doesn't it?" asked the regimental commander, again trying to change the subject.

"It does. She is coming with me."

"You do not think I will allow you to simply walk away, do you?"

"Then what will you do, comrade colonel? Shoot us? I have been a member of the party for ten years—and I will remain a member. I have served faithfully and I will continue to serve in accordance with my abilities and my training. I hate the Americans and I wish as much as anyone for them to be thrown out of our country. I lost my wife and children to their bombs. I have fought and now I choose to fight no more. If you are going to shoot us, then shoot us."

The commander's expression was a mixture of disbelief, anger and fear. High-ranking members of the party did not like criticism. As Lau stood and motioned for Phun to join him, body guards tensed and leaned forward. As he took her hand and led her from the restaurant, the regimental commander gestured a negative signal to the guards, who reluctantly sat back.

At 1550 hours, Jace saluted and shook hands with Lieutenant Colonel McKensie, then joined his troops whom Baez had marched to the front of the battalion headquarters for the memorial service. M-16 rifles with bayonets attached were stuck between the toes of twelve pairs of spit-shined jungle boots that were in a line facing the battalion formation. Helmets with new camouflage covers sat on the butts of the rifles. One helmet, Doc Roberts', was adorned with a white circle with a red cross. The chaplain read scripture, led a prayer and said appropriate words. Lieutenant Colonel Price, subdued and hesitant, called the names of the dead soldiers and spoke sincerely about honor, sacrifice and duty. Having cried all the tears he could cry for his men, Jace stood solemnly at attention as the volleys were fired. Following the ceremony, he turned the company over to Baez and joined C.C. for evening chow.

"What did you think about the old man's remarks," asked C.C.

"I'll tell you the truth," replied Jace. "I thought he seemed real for the first time since he took the battalion. I think he honestly felt something for those guys."

"That's the same feeling I had. I think he's changed. Maybe we ought to start giving him a break."

"Well, anybody that could stand there facing those helmets, rifles and boots and not feel something is a cold-hearted bastard as far as I'm concerned. I'm glad to see him coming around."

"Oh, by the way," said C.C.. "I don't know if you've heard, but he put you in for another Silver Star for Tet. Maybe he does really see you differently now."

"Yeah, thanks mostly to you," grinned Jace. "But I don't feel like I did anything special during Tet. Controlling my company under fire is my job. A man shouldn't get a medal for just doing his job."

"There are a lot of people in this country who don't do their jobs and get medals, so don't knock it," said C.C. standing. "What are you going to do right now?" asked C.C..

"I'm caught up. I'm just going to walk around and check on the guys and turn in early. Why do you ask?"

"I need to go to the laundry and I don't know where my jeep is. Why don't you run me down there.

The traffic in the snack bar had not slackened as troops from the 5-39 made their last visits to enjoy something other than mess-hall food before leaving for the jungles of the Akron area. Having already picked up the last of their clean clothes, very few of them came into the laundry. As the soldiers in the snack bar ordered burgers, fries and beer, Chi actually had time to sit and consider what she was going to do with the bomb. The incident with Buddha picking her up in the chair had shaken her confidence badly. Now, sadly, she realized she had no plan.

Customers entered. Two officers, one even able to speak Vietnamese, came to politely ask for their laundry. Doubt and confusion continued to plague her as she went into the back room to rummage for their bundles. After a moment, she found their odd, foreign-sounding names scrawled on the laundry slips—Spencer and Churchwell. Although the two men were tall and ugly, they were extremely polite. Chi thought if all Americans were like these two, she might not hate them so badly.

As the two officers left, another jeep pulled into the parking space just outside. Dust billowed through the door as a man in uniform mounted the steps. As he paused on the stoop to remove his sunglasses, Chi recognized him. It was the Vietnamese officer who had interrogated and tortured her.

"Well, communist whore, I see you are still working here. I assumed that by now you would have been sent packing."

Anger flashed as Chi answered. "Do not call me names!"

"Oh, do you think I cannot call you any name I wish?" asked the cruel-mouthed man.

"I am not a whore and you have no right to call me such a name."

"Ah, I noticed that you did not deny being a communist!"

Something other than logic took over in Chi's mind. All of her sadness, hate, anxiety and sense of loss combined and rolled into a knot in the pit of her stomach. Violently angry, she threw away her caution.

"Since you mention it, I am a communist," she spat. "I was not a communist before, but after you tortured me and after the Americans killed my two sons and my sister, I decided to become one and fight all of you."

"Well, now, you old whore! You have just signed your death warrant," snarled the officer. "But what can an old hag like you do fight the Americans?"

Chi shrieked at the top of her lungs to the cooks: "Run outside. Quickly! Take Buddha with you! Something terrible is going to happen!"

The cooks, having lived for years in the fear and turmoil of a war-torn country, did not have to be told twice. Without hesitation, they bolted toward the door, grabbing Buddha by the arms as they went. At first, Buddha started to object, then seeing the abject terror in their faces, followed them out the door. As they tumbled into the street, they were nearly run down by a jeep pulling out of a parking space. As the cooks ran between the buildings on the other side of the road, Buddha stopped to explain to the officers in the vehicle that he had no idea what was happening.

Inside, the Vietnamese officer looked on with a mixture of hate, curiosity and smugness. "The only terrible thing that is going to happen here is that you are going to be arrested!"

"Do you think so?" screeched Chi as she ripped the loose board away from the wall and threw it aside. "Do you remember the 'flute'? Well, here it is!"

It took only one quick glance at the jumble of wires, bamboo, tape and plastic explosive behind the wall for the officer to know exactly what he was looking at. As he slapped at his holster, Chi laughed hysterically and grabbed one of the wires connected by the two loops. It was funny—almost a game. Holding the wire, she watched while the officer fumbled desperately for his pistol. She waited as he pulled open the flap, grasped the hand grip, pulled the weapon free, placed his finger on the trigger, and finally raised it toward her face. Their eyes met for an instant, and then the officer pulled the trigger as Chi pulled the wire.

Startled by the proprietor and the cooks dashing from the snack bar, Jace and C.C. had stopped to see what was happening. Getting nothing coherent from the NCO, they had shrugged and gotten back into the jeep. As Jace hit the starter, a crack louder than a nearby lightening bolt stunned him. A white-hot flash, hundreds of times larger and brighter than a strobe light, blew the snack bar in all directions at once. Jace instinctively dove to the ground and covered his head as pieces of board, shards of metal roofing, nails, wooden splinters and pieces of furniture crashed all about him.

As he regained his senses, Jace wondered why there was no fire. What had been the snack bar and laundry was now just a pile of unrecognizable junk. Here and there men walked or crawled from the wreckage. Jace looked at Buddha who was sitting in the road, blubbering and wiping blood from his face. Getting unsteadily to his feet, Jace turned to look for C.C., but couldn't see him. He pulled an unidentifiable piece of debris from the driver's seat of the vehicle and scrambled on his knees to the passenger's side. On the ground on the other side of the jeep, C.C. lay on his back in a widening pool of blood, the head of a large nail protruding from his left temple.

The old Mercedes bus bounced to a halt at the edge of the Xuan Loc market place. Lau and Phun, dressed in civilian clothes and carrying all their worldly belongings, climbed down from the top of the vehicle. The driver cursed and gestured for them to hurry as they pushed into the interior of the crowded bus. A few people helped, but most frowned and turned aside as the couple struggled to carry the frail old man down the steps and into the sunlight. After carefully placing him in the shade of a palm tree at the edge of the market, Lau patiently held his canteen to the old man's lips while he drank.

"Wait here," said Phun. "I'll hire a lambretta. We're only minutes from my father's home."

Mr. An raised himself on one elbow and grinned a toothless grin. "No hurry, child. I have all the time in the world."

After waiting for a while in silence, Lau asked, "What do you think our ancestors will think of our new lives so far away from them?"

"I have made peace with those in the spirit world long ago. What are you feeling, my son?"

"I still feel guilt for abandoning them."

"Then answer this," said An. "Have they again appeared to you in dreams?"

"Not since the last time I told you about."

"Then I believe they know your plight. They understand the circumstances brought about by the war. I believe they understand that you love this young woman."

"Do you really think so?" asked Lau.

"I do. I also believe that you are about to marry into a family with their own traditions and spirits. Perhaps your family and your ancestors are communing with the spirits here in Xuan Loc and know you will be taken care of. At any rate, I think it is time for you to stop worrying and get on with your life."

"Thank you Grandfather," said Lau, gripping the old man's hand. "Look, here comes Phun with the lambretta."

Like a hunting cat, Jupiter company crept noiselessly through the dense jungles of the Akron area. As Ramos had taught them, the new point men cut a tunnel through the foliage for their buddies following them. At halts, Jace sent the platoons out like steel-clawed paws to feel out wide swaths of his assigned area of operations. At night he sent squads slinking away to nearby trails to sit staring into the darkness, silently awaiting the enemy. Each dawn, the troops ate chopped ham and eggs, pecan cake roll, and fruit cocktail, and drank canteen cups of instant coffee. They toweled off their armpits and crotches and changed their socks. After picking off the previous night's leeches, they applied new coats of insect repellent, brushed off their weapons, and swung their rucksacks to their backs to begin a new day.

Two weeks into the mission, Lieutenant Colonel Price's H-23 circled and landed in the clearing where Jupiter had circled for the night. He walked the perimeter with Jace, then stood and talked quietly for a while. As the bubble-nosed chopper lifted out, Baez walked over.

"What did he want?" asked the first sergeant.

"He offered me a job—two jobs really. Cole is leaving and a new major is coming in to replace Major Churchwell. The colonel wants me to be the S-3."

"What was the other choice?" asked Baez.

"Colonel McKensie wants me in G-3."

"You really gonna leave us, huh?"

"Yeah. I have no choice. A new captain's already on the way to take over the company."

"Do you know what you're gonna do?"

"As much as I'd like to work for Colonel McKensie, I can't leave this battalion. Colonel Price is coming around—slowly. If we all pull together, we might make a decent commander out of him yet. But the main thing is that I'd feel like I was being disloyal to Major Churchwell if I left. He and I both invested a lot in the 5-39."

"I'd say he invested more than a lot," Baez said quietly.

Jace nodded, then thought for a minute. "Top, I'd like to take Five India and Tucker with me. If you want, I'll find you a job too. I'm sure Colonel McKensie will help me find something for all of you. Get the hell out of these woods while you can."

"No, sir. I know it's time for you to go—You're overdue. Take Tucker with you—he's paid his dues and I'm sure he'd appreciate a nice safe job in the TOC. But I doubt if Five India will go. He keeps asking about a job as a squad leader or platoon sergeant, and I'll have to give him a shot—he's earned it. As for me, somebody has to stay here and make sure the new C.O. treats these guys right and that's a first sergeant's job. When are you due to leave?"

"Day after tomorrow. I'll have a day and a night of overlap with the new commander."

"Shit. I knew this would come one day."

"That's how I felt when Colonel McKensie left. I take it as a complement, Top."

"Well, don't get the big head. Oh yeah, one more thing, sir."

"What's that?"

"Williams wants to be a cook."

"What?"

"Yes, sir. Says he'll be the best damn cook in the army—if we'll just let him out of the weeds."

"What do you think?"

"If you approve, I'll make room for him in the mess section."

"Sure, go ahead. What about you, Top? You gonna be all right?"

"Sir, I'll just be drivin' on!"

CHAPTER 18

▼

27 June 1968

Rotor blades blasted rain drops into a stinging mist as the helicopter touched down on one of the Long Binh helipads. Needing a shave and wearing wrinkled jungle fatigues, no underwear or socks, scuffed boots and his old ranger patrol cap, Jace threw his duffle bag from the helicopter. One of the .45-caliber pistols that had been dropped from the property books as lost in combat was tucked into his belt at the small of his back. His father's K-bar knife hung from his belt under his shirt-tail. Shouldering his bag, he walked to the muddy road adjacent to the landing pad and stuck up his thumb. A two-and-a-half ton truck screeched to a stop in a large mud puddle. Jace waded to the passenger's side and climbed in.

"Where you goin', sir?" asked the driver.

"To the 90th Replacement Company. Gotta catch a plane." grinned Jace.

When the truck dropped him off outside the gate, Jace couldn't resist walking across the road and pausing to look down into Binh Hoa. The last time he had been at this spot, it was dark and his company was turning off the highway to fight its way into the burning city. Now, one could scarcely tell anything had happened there at all.

Stalking down the hill and through the gate, Jace returned the guard's salute and headed to the orderly room. Glancing at the telephone, he remembered the surly clerk and the aborted call to the First Cav. It had been a year ago, but it seemed like yesterday. The new clerk was helpful and polite as he took Jace's orders and directed him to the officers' barracks building.

Jace threw his bag on a cot and thought about taking a shower, but decided to go to the officers' club for a beer instead. The rainy season was back with a vengeance. The skies dumped sheets of warm rain onto the steaming earth as he dashed the short distance down the street to the club. Ducking inside, he removed his patrol cap and slapped it against his leg. As his eyes adjusted to the dim light inside, someone hailed him.

"Jace! Jason Spencer!"

Squinting into the murk of the lounge, Jace recognized an acquaintance from Benning. "I know your face, but I can't remember your name," he apologized.

"Jerrod Keifer. We went to jump school together."

"Yeah, I remember now. You were with us the night we took on Phenix City. Remember?"

"Do I?" laughed Keifer as he signaled for beers and motioned Jace to a chair. "I thought we were all gonna end up in jail. As I recall, it was your cool head that got us home in one piece, So, what're you doin' here?"

"Finished my tour. I'm goin' home."

"No shit. You lucky sonuvabitch.! I'm just gettin' here. This is my third day sittin' here waitin' for orders. What do you think the chances are of gettin' in an airborne unit or one of the LRRP companies?"

"I wouldn't get my hopes up, but if you're unassigned, you might as well ask. Back last September, they almost put me in a LRRP unit against my will. The LRRPs are part of II Field Force, about a mile from here. If you're serious, you might walk over there and ask. You don't happen to have a sponsor do you?"

"What do you mean? Do they assign sponsors to new officers like they do in the states?"

"No, that's not what I mean. It's one of the first lessons I learned when I got here. Do you have a general or a congressman that will help you get the assignment you want?"

"Hell no. I'm just an ROTC weenie like you. Nobody knows or cares where I go. What do you think I should do?"

"It's not for me to say. I guess it depends on what you want. The only thing I know for sure is no matter where you go, there will be troops there waiting for you. It doesn't matter if they're airborne, ranger, or leg. An AK-47 bullet will punch a hole in one set of jungle fatigues just like another, whether parachute wings or ranger tabs are sewed on them or not."

"May be, but I heard the leadership in an airborne unit is head and shoulders above what you'll find in a leg unit."

Thinking of McKensie, Baez, Five India, and especially C.C., Jace felt his anger flash. He sat quietly for a second, biting back a sharp answer.

"My advice is to go where they send you. There will be American soldiers there, and you'll learn quick that your highest calling is to simply keep them alive."

As his friend stared quietly at him, Jace reached behind his jungle tunic, pulled out the .45, and slid it across the table.

"I can't take this on the plane. Hold on to it—you might need it."

In his wrinkled khakis, Jace rode the bus through the city of Binh Hoa where his men had fought during Tet. Several burned-out structures remained along the road, and bullet holes pocked the walls of others. Other than that, there was little evidence that a battle had ever taken place here. Incredibly, he could not recognize the place where he and his men had first been ambushed on that January morning. He pressed his face against the window as the bus passed the ARVN division headquarters his troops had saved during the battle. He wondered if the Lieutenant Colonel he had met that day still worked there. As he scanned the highway and the buildings looking for places he remembered, the bus turned onto the airbase access road.

Jace and the soldiers from the line of busses dismounted and walked in the rain toward the sheds beside the ramp. The DC-8 that would take them home sat in the puddles on the tarmac. As mortar shells crumped in the distance, soldiers in travel-rumpled khakis appeared in the door of the plane, and, holding their noses, started down the movable stairs to begin their tours in Vietnam. As they streamed toward the busses, a howl rose from the veterans who greeted their replacements with cat-calls and insults similar to the ones that had greeted Jace a year before. As the long line of jet-lagged replacements passed the jeering veterans, Jace did not even notice the paratroopers among them.

EPILOGUE

▼

Night had fallen, but as in every large city, it was not completely dark. The angry low clouds reflected light from the millions of bulbs below, giving the national park rangers sufficient illumination to accomplish their nightly task.

They used cardboard boxes—trash bags would have conveyed the wrong message to many of those whose wounds had never healed. The rangers worked quickly in the cold, but their haste did not cause them to treat the items callously. The flowers would not keep and would of course be discarded later. But each note, letter, photograph, and item of memorabilia would be carefully collected, catalogued and stored. To do otherwise would dishonor the feelings that motivated people to leave these gifts at the base of the wall.

Over the years there had been unusual, even strange, items left at the memorial. Pieces of C-ration boxes, P-38 can openers, dog tags, hand-grenade pins, baby rattles, clothing, shoes, boots, maps, and hundreds of other things had been placed at the wall. Most of these gifts meant nothing to anyone except the two people involved—one alive, the other a name on a black granite slab. Normally the rangers did not speak while collecting the offerings. Sometimes, however, they found things so unusual that they called to each other to share their find. This item was so small and it blended so well with its background that the ranger missed it at first. But as she moved the letter next to it, she bumped it, causing it to fall over.

"Claude, come and look at this," the ranger called to her co-worker.

"What is it?" he asked with a mixture of mild curiosity and disinterested politeness.

"This is the oddest thing I've found in a long time," she said as she showed him the small, carved figurine of a cat.

978-0-595-35132-9
0-595-35132-8

Made in the USA
Middletown, DE
11 September 2015